All That Compels the Heart

ACKNOWLEDGEMENTS

I would like to take this time to thank everyone who has helped to make this novel a reality. I would like to begin by thanking my friends for all of your unwavering support of me throughout this crazy journey. Your belief in me has outmatched my belief in myself at times, and without all your patience, love, and support, I am not entirely certain I would have made it through this process. I truly could not have done it without you.

A huge thanks to Kit and Robert from Kit Foster Designs, who created the wonderful cover design you see on the front of this novel. It was great working with the both of you throughout the whole process of choosing the right design and look for the novel.

An equally huge thanks to Jeremy for sharing his knowledge and experience of the self-publishing world with me. You've been so patient with all of my questions and I want to thank you for taking the time to guide me through this process.

I'd like to give a big thank you to Ian for all of the Irish-language help he provided. I really appreciate you taking the time to share your knowledge of your beautiful country with me.

A special thank you to my editor, Elyse, for being patient with me throughout the editing process. I know that it was not always an easy process (for you more so than for me), but we made it through to the end!

Any resemblance to persons living or dead is purely coincidental.

2nd Edition

First published in 2018.
Copyright © 2020. All rights reserved.

Table of Contents

Chapter One 1
Chapter Two 18
Chapter Three 39
Chapter Four 45
Chapter Five 55
Chapter Six 67
Chapter Seven 73
Chapter Eight 80
Chapter Nine 91
Chapter Ten 101
Chapter Eleven 104
Chapter Twelve 113
Chapter Thirteen 127
Chapter Fourteen 141
Chapter Fifteen 147
Chapter Sixteen 163
Chapter Seventeen 176
Chapter Eighteen 181
Chapter Nineteen 185
Chapter Twenty 198
Chapter Twenty-One 216
Chapter Twenty-Two 229
Chapter Twenty-Three 243
Chapter Twenty-Four 255
Chapter Twenty-Five 276
Chapter Twenty-Six 283
Chapter Twenty-Seven 288
Chapter Twenty-Eight 295
Chapter Twenty-Nine 305
Chapter Thirty 312
Chapter Thirty-One 324

Table of Contents (Cont.)

Chapter Thirty-Two 328
Chapter Thirty-Three 348
Chapter Thirty-Four 356
Chapter Thirty-Five 363
Chapter Thirty-Six 372
Chapter Thirty-Seven 389
Chapter Thirty-Eight 396
Chapter Thirty-Nine 406
Chapter Forty 422
Chapter Forty-One 438
Chapter Forty-Two 448
Chapter Forty-Three 468
Chapter Forty-Four 476
Chapter Forty-Five 487
Chapter Forty-Six 496
Chapter Forty-Seven 507
Chapter Forty-Eight 514
Chapter Forty-Nine 531
Chapter Fifty 543
Chapter Fifty-One 550
Chapter Fifty-Two 561
Chapter Fifty-Three 568
Chapter Fifty-Four 583
Chapter Fifty-Five 590
Chapter Fifty-Six 604
Chapter Fifty-Seven 613
Chapter Fifty-Eight 624
Chapter Fifty-Nine 632
Chapter Sixty 643
Chapter Sixty-One 647

Chapter One

It is an indisputable fact that when one part of your life is going incredibly well, some other part of your life will fall spectacularly apart. This was the thought running through Aoife O'Reilly's mind like it was on some unending loop.

Numbness consumed her. The noise generated by the bus and that of the other passengers reduced to mere background noise, as if her head was being held underwater. Her vision blurred at the edges as she gazed out at Dublin city, not truly seeing it as it streamed past. She only knew where she was on her bus route home because her body had memorized every bump and turn in the road, her mind operating solely on the mechanics of motor memory.

The light weight of the small cardboard box in her lap was the only physical reminder that she hadn't completely drifted into the numbness. She looked down at the box, seeing how few items it contained. Most of them were things she had pilfered from her workstation: some nice-looking pens, some Post-Its from the supply room, a bottle of lotion, and a box of tissues. She hadn't been the type of employee to keep many personal items at her desk; the only non-work related item in the box was a framed photo of her with Bex and Millie, her two best friends, when they were on holiday in Malta last summer. She wasn't exactly sure why she'd taken the stationary items from her desk. She supposed – if she really had to think about it – that she'd done it out of spite.

And why not? Am I not allowed to be at least a little *spiteful in this situation?* She shifted the box on her lap a little, agitated at the very recent memory of having just been fired.

Suddenly and without warning, she'd found herself a victim of the global economic collapse. No longer did the financial crisis that had befallen America – and now Europe – affect nameless and faceless people she passed on the street, or read about briefly in the newspapers. It now stared up at her like a chasm in the earth when one dug a grave, and she was now another victim to its cruel, unfeeling, cold shoulder.

Still, she knew she was lucky that she didn't have to worry about being evicted from her flat any time soon, like some of her coworkers. She could always go back to her family for help, and that's what bothered her the most about being fired: her loss of independence. Aoife had an uneasy relationship with her family at the best of times; she hated to think what they'd say about her at Sunday dinner now. Ever since the age of eighteen, she'd tried to strike out on her own, turn her back on her family's money and find her own path. Now that she'd lost her job, she'd be tied to them financially once more, a thought that filled her with dread.

As she mulled over this particularly unpleasant thought, the bus stopped in front of her flat in Ranelagh. Exhausted, she slowly shuffled her way to the front door, awkwardly trying to open it while at the same time trying not to spill the contents of her box. The faint smell of chlorine from the ground floor swimming pool wafted its way to her nose. While the other residents in the building complained about the odour, Aoife found it oddly comforting. Her mother had spent most of Aoife's childhood and adult life working wherever she was sent by their family's pub chain business, and Aoife had become used to the smell of chlorine from all her summers and holidays spent in hotels while her mother worked. Between boarding school and hotels, Aoife could count on two hands the number of times she'd actually spent in her mother's home in Ballsbridge, southeast of Dublin city centre. And so, having become so often acquainted with the scent of chlorine, somewhere along the way Aoife had begun to associate it with a quasi-sense of home, just as someone might do with the scent of baked goods in the oven. It had been a nomadic childhood, and she couldn't exactly say it had been all that happy, but it was the only one she'd known. Being settled in one place felt more foreign to her now than living out of a suitcase did.

The heels of her boots made a clicking noise as she crossed the criss-crossed the nut-brown floor tiles, past the overstuffed tan leather furniture with matching lightwood side tables. As she came to a halt in front of the lift, she noticed caution tape placed across it in a big yellow X with a handwritten sign from her landlord stating, "Out of Order."

"You've got to be joking," she muttered to herself, balancing the cardboard box on her hip. *Can this day get any worse?* She mentally chastised herself for asking the question lest it tempt the Fates to throw anything else unexpected her way and headed for the stairs.

The place she called home could be viewed by most as little more than a functional living space. The clang of the metal as the keys jangled against the yellow ceramic bowl by the door echoed throughout the empty flat. Placing the box on the floor and abandoning it there, she headed straight for her refrigerator, the contents of which would probably put a frown on the face of most health experts. Rummaging past the bottles whose contents were now rather dubious, and the mouldy cheese, she found that it contained nothing even remotely edible. Crossing the room to the cupboard where she hid her alcohol, she found the bottle of rum she'd stashed there weeks ago. Aoife considered herself more of a "social drinker," never much interested in drinking at home by herself. However, after the day she'd just had, she felt that this may warrant a temporary change in habit. She took a long, deep swig, letting the alcohol leave a warming sensation in her throat as she gazed out the floor-to-ceiling windows that lined her open concept kitchen/sitting room.

Normally, she would be astounded by the fantastic view of downtown Dublin before her, but today her grey-blue eyes gazed out dispassionately.

Everything will be grand, she reminded herself. She looked over at the photo of herself, Bex, and Millie from their Harvard days she had on the mantle of her living room fireplace. It was no accident Aoife had chosen to put an entire ocean between herself and her mother's family when it came time to go to university. Her grandmother and head of the family, Grainne O'Reilly, had wanted her to go to Trinity College Dublin, to keep her "close by." Aoife had seen it for what it really was: yet another attempt to control her.

"Well, if you won't attend Trinity, couldn't you at least attend Oxford or Cambridge?" Grainne had asked petulantly when Aoife had told her of her plans.

"No Granny. Harvard's given me a full scholarship and I've accepted."

"Well, at least they have a reputable business program," Grainne had sighed.

"Oh, I won't be studying business, Granny." Aoife remembered the surprised look not just from her grandmother at this revelation, but from the rest of her assembled family as well.

"Then what *do* you plan to study?"

"English Literature."

Aoife's grandfather, Paddy O'Reilly had nearly choked on his drink at seeing how his wife and daughter's faces had clouded over and coughed loudly to clear his throat. Aoife was grateful for the small distraction as she was certain that, despite her advanced years, Grainne was planning in that very moment to fling herself at her youngest granddaughter and choke some sense into her. Aoife had snuck a glance at Maureen but didn't find any safe harbour with her mother. Not that she'd expected to; when it came down to it, Maureen would always choose Grainne's side of any situation. Her number one priority was always her own self-preservation, and her entire income depended on remaining in Grainne's good graces.

Grainne had refused to speak to Aoife for a full two months after that. This suited Aoife just fine, but it was the disappointment in her grandfather's face she couldn't bear. The only person neither Aoife nor Grainne could ever stand falling out with was Paddy, and so it was that the two women had reluctantly found themselves on speaking terms again before Aoife had left for America.

Harvard had been everything Aoife had hoped it would be for her: a fresh start. In America, virtually no one knew who she was. Despite her family owning several *O'Reilly's* pubs all across the country, no one thought to associate her with the famous name.

Not only had Harvard given her the new life she'd been looking for, but it had also given her the two best friends she could ask for: Rebecca "Bex" Martin, a Greek-American from New York City who became a home-away-home for both Aoife and Millie, a British exchange student who formed the third part of their friendship triangle. Camilla Johnson – who had never once been called "Camilla" except for the day her mother had named her for the birth certificate – was a quick-as-a-whip Londoner, savvy in the field of "life studies," insomuch as she was still trying to figure out what exactly it was that she wanted from it. Having grown up the proverbial boring suburbanite, Millie was never one to pass up the opportunity to try anything at least once, and was often the catalyst for all of their best stories.

Bex, on the other hand, was more serious, an overachieving self-described bookworm studying History. Like Aoife, Bex had decided to carve a path separate from her parents' fashion business, where her mother – a former Greek national who emigrated to America when she was a girl – created the designs, while her father did the day-to-day managing of the business. This shared experience provided an instant amiability between Aoife and her "Mediterranean goddess" of a roommate, as Aoife liked to call her.

There was no denying Bex was the most attractive of the three friends with her long, wavy light blonde hair, highly intelligent teal-coloured eyes, a seemingly unblemished olive-skinned complexion over high cheekbones and a rounded chin, and a natural hour-glass figure that was the envy of every woman around her. The only person who seemed *not* to notice her beauty was Bex herself, for as drop-dead gorgeous as she was, she was a modest woman whose one major splurge was on shoes, of which she had dozens, each one characterizing a different facet of her personality.

"And where exactly do you think we're going to fit all these?" Aoife remembered asking Bex on their first day of dorm life, marvelling as she had held up a beautiful pair of rainbow patterned wedges. Fate had thrown the two of them together, putting them in the same dorm room, with Millie in the room just across the hall from them.

"Hmm... I'm beginning to think I may have brought a pair or two too many," Bex had said, looking at each pair lovingly packed in her luggage like each one was a child she couldn't bear to be parted from.

"You think?" Aoife had replied, but seeing the worried expression on Bex's face, she had softened her tone. "I'm sure we'll find somewhere for them all."

Not being particularly interested in shoes – or fashion in general, for that matter – Aoife herself hadn't brought many things with her and so she'd happily relinquished most of her half of the closet to Bex.

Being less concerned about her appearance than most young women her age, Aoife kept her style simple, classy, and chic, although this was more of a coincidence than out of any effort of her own. Her auburn curls were often hastily and haphazardly pulled back from her face and stuffed into a clip, with only a little make-up over her pale, Irish skin. She was less curvy than Bex, but not quite as skinny as Millie's pole-like figure.

Aoife had met Millie on her first day of class. The English department had hosted an introductory lecture and small reception for its new students and the both of them had ended up sitting beside each other. Having arrived nearly late – as Aoife was prone to do – there had been few places left in the auditorium. Two open seats on either side of a stern-looking young woman caught her attention. Everyone else around her seemed slightly intimidated by the young woman, trying to avoid her at all costs. Not put off by the numerous ear and nose piercings, heavy make-up, and all-black clothes, Aoife promptly sat down next to her as everyone else in the auditorium shot her sympathetic looks. Looking past the spiky dog collar and henna tattoos, she was completely unfazed by Millie's obvious attempt to persuade everyone that she was some sort of unapproachable badass. Aoife reached across the small, foldable desk separating them and had held out her hand to her, smiling.

"I'm Aoife. How do you do?"

Millie had looked at the proffered hand for a good long second, her face drawing down even further. Just as Aoife's heart began to sink in her chest and she was beginning to think she'd made a big mistake in trying to be friendly with the other woman, Millie must have determined that she was being sincere and stuck out her own hand to shake Aoife's firmly.

"Ee-fa... that's an interesting name," Millie had replied, feeling out the simplicity of the pronunciation. It was something Aoife had become used to, people mispronouncing and/or misspelling her name. She and her older cousin Connor had made a game of it when they were children, trying to see just how off the mark people could get. It had produced some rather amusing moments.

"It's Irish for Eva," she'd explained.

"Ahhh." She could see comprehension coming over Millie's face. "I'm Millie. Millie Johnson."

"What brings you all the way over to America, Millie?" she'd asked, noticing Millie's soft London accent.

"Escaping the mundanity of normal life."

"I hear you on that one," Aoife had echoed her sentiment as she'd settled into her seat.

"You know what? I'm beginning to like you," Millie had told her, a smile on her face. "Most people are terrified of me because of how I look but you, you don't seem afraid of all that."

"Well, my Grandad always did tell me not to judge a book by its cover."

It had been a simple start, but it proved the catalyst to one of the best and longest friendships. As the two of them got to talking, they'd discovered that Millie was living across from Aoife and Bex with a girl named Dominica, as if fate had meant the three of them to meet. For once, Aoife felt that fate may have gotten things right.

In their second year, Bex and Aoife moved out of their dorm and rented a two-story, three-bedroom house near campus with Millie. The place suited them well, and the three of them settled into a happy routine. For the first time in her life Aoife felt like she had a home, somewhere to be grounded.

Graduation had come too soon for all of them. Aoife had been offered an internship at Broadstone Publishing, an up-and-coming publishing company in New York City. Bex had decided to stay on at Harvard for the summer to get a jump on completing her master's degree, which had left Millie – who'd never actually managed to complete her degree, having been unable to decide what exactly she'd wanted to major in – to return to London and work a minimum wage job in her parents' chemist shop.

While the three of them separately loved what they were doing over the summer, each of them felt the strain of being parted for the first time. Aoife did her best to throw herself into her work, thoroughly enjoying the friendly atmosphere of her coworkers. Broadstone had that "new business" feel, run by a couple of millennials bent on changing the publishing world, which created an infectious energy that made her excited to wake up every morning and go to the office. She was even given the opportunity to take a couple of publishing and writing classes while there, with Broadstone encouraging a great mentor program for new writers.

Despite the friendly warmth of her coworkers and bosses, Aoife had still felt the loss of her friends. Staying with Bex's parents – who'd been kind enough to let her live with them while she was completing her internship – had helped, but by mid-autumn, even she couldn't deny how much she missed Ireland. It had been four years since she'd seen any of her family, with Connor being deployed most of the time she was away, and although she'd tried her best to stay in touch with her grandfather, their daily calls had become weekly calls, which had turned into once-a-month calls here and there. She'd not even attempted to talk to her mother or grandmother beyond the obligatory call at Christmas and birthdays.

Feeling the first true wave of homesickness since leaving home, and with her internship coming to an end soon, she had packed up her things and headed back to Dublin. Thanks to a great reference from her supervisor at Broadstone, she easily found herself a job working for Arbour Hill Publishing and settled herself back into life in Dublin. Although it didn't salve the wound of missing her friends, it did help being back around her familiar surroundings. It also helped that her new boyfriend Danny, whom she'd met at Harvard, had just relocated to Dublin and Aoife would have been lying if she'd said that Danny hadn't been a large factor in her choosing to come back home.

While Danny and Aoife settled into their life in Dublin, it wasn't long before fate threw Aoife and her friends together again. An opportunity to do a year abroad at Trinity College Dublin presented itself to Bex, which she promptly accepted. Hearing that her friends were both now going to be living in Dublin, it didn't take Millie long before she'd told her parents that she was quitting her job and going to Dublin to finish her degree.

"I think they're just happy that I'm going to finish something," she'd told Bex and Aoife when they'd asked how her parents had reacted to her just upping and leaving them in the lurch like that.

Bex and Aoife had smiled knowingly at each other; they too would've liked to see Millie finish something she started, but they knew that was about as realistic as hoping to see a unicorn. It just wasn't in Millie's nature to settle into one thing when new opportunities might present themselves later.

Thinking of her friends, Aoife put down the bottle of rum on her coffee table and rummaged around in her purse for her mobile. Her best friends were exactly what she needed right now.

"Hello?" Bex picked up the phone after three rings.

"Bex! It's Aoife."

"Hi!" Bex's voice – raspy from the occasional smoking habit – sounded surprised to hear from her. She supposed it would be kind of unusual considering it was the middle of the afternoon and she'd be expecting her to still be at work. "What's up?"

"Oh I'm grand," she replied a bit hesitantly. Now she was faced with having to tell everyone she no longer had a job, she suddenly became terribly embarrassed and self-conscious.

She wasn't sure why; it wasn't like it was her fault, after all. She hadn't been let go because of anything she'd done.

Ever the observant one, Bex picked up on her uncertainty. "Are you sure? Because you sound like someone killed your dog."

"Who killed whose dog?" Aoife heard Millie's voice in the background.

"Aoife," Bex shouted back over her shoulder at her flatmate.

"But she doesn't have a dog!?" Aoife heard Millie shout back. "Did she get one recently?"

"No," Bex replied exasperatedly. "It's a turn of phrase. I didn't mean that someone *literally* killed a dog. She just sounds out of sorts, ya know?"

"Why?"

"That's what I'm trying to find out if you would stop yelling at me and let me talk to her!" Bex snapped back.

"What happened?!" Millie asked again.

"I just said that I don't know. You never listen to me!"

"You didn't say you didn't know; you just said you were trying to talk to her," Millie corrected her.

"Well, I *don't* know and I'm *trying* to find out. Satisfied?"

Aoife couldn't stop herself from laughing out loud at her friends' bickering. After living together for so long, they'd begun to sound like an old married couple. But once she started laughing, the emotions she'd been keeping under lock and key throughout her exit interview and the bus ride home began to bubble to the surface. Her laughter turned to sobs and somewhere through her tears she heard a foggy voice yelling in her ear.

Jesus, Joseph, and Mary, what's wrong with me?

She could count on one hand the number of times she'd cried like this in her life and it came well short of the number five. It wasn't that she was an unfeeling or uncaring person; quite the opposite, really. It was just that she'd become so used to being the person everyone depended on in a crisis that she'd learned to cocoon herself behind a wall and keep her emotions firmly on the other side so she could function. And yet, here she was blubbering like a fool on the floor.

"Aoife? Are you there? What's wrong sweetie?"

"What's happening?"

"I don't *know*! That's what I'm trying to find out!" she heard Bex say again through gritted teeth.

"Here, give me the phone." There was a pause as a heated argument over who was best at trying to calm her down ensued and finally she heard Millie's voice loud and clear on the other end of the line asking her what was wrong. She wanted to answer, to let them know that she was fine, but she couldn't get the words out between the sobs.

"Alright, that's it. We're coming over straight away," she heard Millie say in a firm "I'm-not-taking-no-for-an-answer" way.

"Shit," she mumbled to herself and wiped at her eyes and nose with the back of her hand like she was five years old again. She hadn't wanted to scare them, but she couldn't help it. She couldn't manage to bring herself to not feel some worry about her future right now and to not feel some sadness over losing a job that, by all accounts, she'd mostly enjoyed, despite the management team running the place.

She sighed and walked laboriously over to the sofa in her sitting room and collapsed dramatically onto it. She knew Bex and Millie would be over soon to grill her endlessly about what happened and the thought exhausted her. She closed her eyes and hoped that when she opened them that this would all be just a bad dream.

Sometime later – she wasn't exactly sure when – she heard the buzzer of her doorbell. Struggling to open her eyes, Aoife tried to remember where exactly she was. The whine of her buzzer, more persistent this time, pierced her brain like the whine of a mosquito. Clumsily, she raised a forearm and made sweeping motions around her head as if to shoo it away.

"Shit!" she exclaimed as she jumped up from the sofa, remembering her friends. Grumpy and annoyed at being woken from her impromptu nap, she trudged her way to the front door where her buzzer had gone from long whines to short, punctuated buzzes meant to emphasize Millie's annoyance at being kept waiting outside. She pressed the button on her keypad to let her friends in and trudged her way back down the corridor when her front door crashed open and she was accosted by Millie, who threw her arms around her into a hug so tight it was difficult for her to breathe.

"Oh love! What's happened?"

"Millie!" she said in a strangled tone. "Gerroff me!"

"C'mon Millie, let the poor girl breathe! You'll kill her before we even get in the door." Bex's voice dripped with dry humour.

Millie suddenly let her go, and a rush of air returned to Aoife's lungs. She rubbed her breastbone lightly, the sharp spikes of Millie's heavy chain necklace having left red marks on her skin. Although her words may have been sharp, the big grin on her face let Millie know she hadn't meant it to be. She felt a great sense of relief sink into her bones at the sight of the two of them.

"Well don't you look a fright!" Millie gave her a once-over, examining her tear-stained cheeks and the smell of rum emanating from her damp shirt. "Did you drink an entire pub's worth of alcohol already?"

"Thank you," she replied, her tone snarky. "And no, I did not. I just had a wee tipple when I came home."

"Oh, don't mind her," Bex said placing two large paper bags full of groceries on Aoife's counter and coming over to hug her. "She just says whatever pops into her head without thinking." Her kind eyes smiled behind the trendy cat-like frames of her glasses.

"Well she *does* look a fright," Millie said to them defending herself, hands on her hips. "You poor thing; it looks like you've been crying for hours. Your mascara's all over your face and you're all puffy and red."

"Wonderful." She wiped at her eyes in the hopes of making herself look somewhat presentable again but the black smears on the backs of her hands made her think she was not achieving her goal.

"On that note, we have come bearing moral support and booze in whichever order you prefer," Bex said, producing several large bottles of alcohol from her Dior bag. "Don't worry, we're not proposing an entirely liquid diet," she said, noticing Aoife's look, "though I admit that we did focus a little too much on buying out the liquor section at the corner store. But we did think to get a few things to keep us going for the night."

She reached into one of the bags and began pulling out the ingredients for making nachos. Bex had introduced her and Millie to the Mexican dish during their university years and it had quickly become the house favourite party food. Aoife peeked in the last bag, which contained a large chocolate cake and a tub of ice cream.

"And what's wrong with getting completely drunk?" Millie asked.

"Well, I'm not saying we *can't* get entirely shit-faced by the end of the night, but as Aoife looks to have gotten a head start on us, why don't we start with some food and then we'll all be on more of an even playing field."

Bex slipped out of her sharp, black stilettos and carried the nacho ingredients over towards Aoife's oven, moving around the kitchen with a familiarity even Aoife didn't have with the place. Millie tried to follow suit, struggling to remove her black, lace-up, knee-length Doc Martens.

"You know you don't have to worry about taking off your boots, Mill. I honestly don't care."

"No... I'm fine..." Millie said, struggling with a lace. Aoife left her to it, knowing it was futile to argue with her. Instead, she walked around to the other side of the counter to help with the food, though how much help she was, was kind of in doubt. Aoife had never really enjoyed cooking or baking or doing anything in the kitchen, if she was being honest. It would come as a surprise only to anyone who didn't know her well that her friends knew their way around her kitchen better than she did.

Bex located the apron Aoife kept in one of her drawers and tied it around her waist to protect the grey tweed dress she was wearing just as Millie came over to join them, having freed herself from her boots. It hadn't failed to escape her notice that both of her friends expertly grabbed all of the ingredients that involved using sharp, pointy objects, leaving her with grating the cheese. It was probably for the best, given that she found it hard enough to use the grater without scraping her knuckles. Seeing her struggling with the cheese, Bex gently took the grater from her hands.

"Why don't you go and have a seat and leave the cooking to us. You've clearly had a hard day."

Content with being shuffled to one of the stools on the other side of the kitchen island, she watched as her friends prepared dinner. As Bex popped the nachos into the oven, Millie rifled around in the kitchen drawers until she located Aoife's corkscrew and opened one of the bottles of white wine she'd brought, pouring a glass for each of them. Not protesting as Millie placed one of the glasses into her hand, despite the fact she didn't really like to drink wine. Right now, though, the only thing going through her mind was how lovely it was to just sit around the kitchen, the aroma of food wafting throughout the kitchen, sitting in comfortable silence with her friends. The only thing to break the silence was the sound of the buzzer ten minutes later, indicating the nachos were ready. Bex jumped up before the rest of them could make a move, pulling the pan out of the oven and placing it on the wooden cutting board in front of the other two. Not caring that they were still too hot to eat, the tantalizing scent of the food before her being too much for her to resist, and she grabbed at one of the nacho chips, her fingertips and tongue smarting from the heat. As the three of them devoured their meal, Aoife could feel Millie's eyes on her, wanting to ask her what the hell was going on but trying to decide if it was the right time or not. Clearly deciding she didn't care either way, she finally spoke up.

"Ok, Aoife; time to spill. What the hell is going on?"

Aoife looked down at the crumbs in the pan and pretended like they were the most interesting thing she'd seen in her life. Her last bite of nachos seemed to lodge itself firmly in her throat and she felt like an eejit again. Bex silently and deliberately dragged the pan across the counter away from Aoife's grasp so she no longer had anything to hide behind.

"You know if you don't answer her then she'll just torture it out of you anyway."

She knew it was true. Taking a deep breath, she blurted the news out all in a rush. "Arbour Hill fired me. They hauled me into the office just after lunch and handed me my notice."

All That Compels the Heart

Bex reached across and took her hand in empathy while Millie exclaimed, "Those bloody bastards! They don't know what they're doing! You're the best thing to happen to them!"

She smiled at her friends' different reactions, comforted by both in equal measure.

"You two are the best." Bex squeezed her hand in solidarity.

"Of course we are," Millie piped up.

"I don't know why I'm so upset about it. I know you're both right, but it just threw me for a loop, you know? I know it doesn't take a genius to realize the economy across the continent is in tatters. We knew there were going to be job cuts coming; I guess I just didn't think it would happen to me. And despite it all, I *did* like working there. Well, I liked the work anyways."

She shrugged.

"I guess I just have to move on and see where life will take me."

"And where exactly do you see life leading you at the moment? Or dare I ask?" Bex looked at her like she didn't really expect an answer.

"I have no sweet clue. I really don't." She hadn't had time to think about it since this afternoon and now she realized she really didn't have a plan for the future.

"Maybe it's a good thing, then, that you will have some time to think about it. And who knows? This time in a year, maybe you'll have everything you ever dreamed of and this will all seem like just a tiny bump in the road," Millie told her, ever the positive thinker.

"If only I knew what that was." It suddenly bothered her that she didn't have a back-up plan. Arbour Hill had never seemed like the sort of place she'd wanted to stay at permanently, but she'd been content enough there that she'd stopped making plans for the future career-wise.

Or any-wise.

Not only did she not have a job plan, she had no future plans at all. She and Danny were at a comfortable stage in their relationship where they had their own places, their own careers, and hadn't given much thought to taking things to the next level. This comfortability with the way things were had meant that she'd stopped dreaming of what she wanted ten years, five years, even *one* year down the line, not just from her career, but from her personal life. It suddenly all made her feel adrift and terribly naïve for not always having a future plan.

"Well, if nothing else happens in the next year, at least you know one thing will still be there for you."

"You're going to say "you" aren't you, Millie?" she asked with a smile.

"You know me too well," she winked at her.

"You're such a sap," Aoife teased her and hopped off her stool to come around and hug her.

"Well, for tonight, you don't need to think ahead or make any rash decisions," Bex assured her. "Tonight, you only need to think of one thing."

Aoife raised a curious eyebrow in response.

"Which movie we're going to watch," Bex smiled at her.

"I vote a chick flick!" Mille said excitedly, hopping off her stool and heading for the freezer where she'd earlier stashed the ice cream.

Aoife and Bex both threw her disapproving looks. Millie was the only one of their little trio who liked chick flicks.

"Fine," Millie said, exasperated. "Let's compromise. I'll watch *Bridget Jones' Diary* with you *again* for the millionth time because it's the only bloody chick flick you *will* watch."

"Deal," Aoife said with a big grin.

Millie and Aoife began carrying in the bottles of booze to the sitting room, along with the cake and ice cream and flopped onto the sofa as Bex popped the DVD into the player.

A couple of hours, and several empty bottles of liquor later, Millie began yawning.

"Aoife, I love you but if I don't go home soon, I'm going to be sleeping on this couch."

"I'm alright with this." As if to emphasize her point, she snuggled further under one of the large afghans she kept on her sofa.

"Yeah, except some of us have an early morning study group in… six hours." Bex's face fell as she realized how late it was.

"We should help clean up the mess," Millie said sighing, as she looked blearily around at the mess they had created.

"Oh leave it; it's not like I've got anything to do tomorrow anyways. I'll clean it up then."

"You sure? We can stay a bit. It won't take more than a few minutes."

"Nah, it's fine. I'll get it in the morning. You guys get on home now." She pulled herself up from the comfort of the sofa, afghan still wrapped around her and walked her friends to the front door. "Thank you for coming over tonight and be safe getting back home."

"Just remember: you'll get through this," Bex reassured her, placing a hand on either side of Aoife's face, much like a mother would do to a daughter. "We're here for you any time you need us."

"I love you two," she said, kissing each of them on the cheek. "Be safe!"

She closed the door behind them and, deciding that she was far too tired and drunk to care about the mess they'd made of her living room and kitchen. She collapsed back onto her couch again, turning the DVD back on, falling asleep to Renee Zelleweger miming to Celine Dion's "All By Myself."

Chapter Two

Aoife woke the next morning to the sound of the alarm on her mobile buzzing loudly against the glass top of the coffee table beside her. She flailed aimlessly towards the direction of the noise without opening her eyes until she managed to grasp the cursed thing and turn it off. She could tell from the light on the back of her eyes that it was well into morning already. The scent of chocolate cake and alcohol filled her nostrils and her stomach flip-flopped slightly. Braving the inevitable hangover, she cautiously opened one eye and looked at the time.

Crap!

It wasn't morning, as she'd thought. Rather, it was early afternoon and she had overslept to the point where she was now going to be late for dinner at her grandmother's. Normally, this weekly dinner appointment would have been held on Sunday, but her grandmother had notified the whole family only yesterday that family dinner had to be moved up a day early for some unknown reason.

Aoife hated Sunday dinner. For any other family it would be a quaint, but beloved tradition, a time for the whole family

All That Compels the Heart

to get together and talk about the week's events, cocooned in the safety of their family's love. But the O'Reillys were not a normal family. For them, Sunday dinner was, at best, the detestable chore no one wanted to do, and at worst, it was paramount to torture.

According to Aoife, her grandmother, Grainne O'Reilly was a determined, self-centred woman who valued business over family but who exuded an air that she was a loving grandmother determined only to do what was best for her children and grandchildren. No one who met Grainne would dream that she'd come from the same poor Henrietta Street tenement as her husband, Paddy; so tirelessly had she worked to eliminate all traces of her past that no one knew a thing about her before she took what had once been a small local pub started by her husband, and turned it into a global business. Not even her own children or grandchildren knew where their grandmother had come from, so rarely did she talk about it. Grainne preferred to live in the present, and the present included hosting a dinner that Aoife was now very late for.

Grumbling to herself, she stumbled over to the bathroom and hopped quickly into the shower. The blast of cold water hit her skin and made her curse loudly. Not waiting for the water to warm up, she squirted a big dollop of shampoo into her hand, letting the lilac scent wake her up as she worked it quickly through her auburn tangles. After the world's shortest shower, she quickly towelled off, catching a glimpse of herself in the mirror and sighed. It would take hours to make herself somewhat passable under grandmother's scrutiny, but her little pity party last night afforded her a mere fifteen minutes.

Ten minutes later, her mostly dry hair was pulled back into a messy ponytail and some light make-up applied to distract from the dark circles under her eyes. Locating the least wrinkled dress on her bedroom floor, Aoife threw it on and slipped on a pair of nude heels before racing out of her flat at breakneck speed. Managing not to kill herself running down the stairs, she called for a taxi as she headed to the lobby. Lucky for her, one showed up within a few minutes and she hopped in.

"Malahide. Fast as you can." The driver looked at her, a little surprised by her abruptness but she didn't have time to worry about it just now.

It was a gloriously sunny Saturday afternoon, but Aoife barely noticed it as she hid her still light-sensitive eyes behind large, Audrey Hepburn-esque sunglasses, doing her best to prepare herself for what lay ahead of her. All too quickly, the taxi drove up the circular stone driveway, stopping in front of the neo-classical mansion, its pale red brick façade and white pillars gleaming so brightly in the sunlight as to look almost pink. She thanked the taxi driver and gave him a large tip as she exited the car. A tiny part of her worried about spending so much money at a time when she should be saving, but she figured the driver probably needed it more than she did right now. Self-consciously, she smoothed her hair and dress and with more confidence than she felt, she strode quickly up the stone steps to the house. Right on cue, Moore – her grandmother's butler – opened the door for her, frowning slightly at her tardiness and her appearance.

"Good afternoon Miss Aoife," he greeted her with a fake smile. "The others are already in the library."

It didn't escape her notice the way in which he emphasized the word "already," intentionally drawing attention to her tardiness. She let the snide comment slide, instead nodding politely in Moore's direction and went directly to the library, her heels echoing down the cream-coloured hallway. As she walked down its hardwood floors, the eyes of various historical figures stared down at her from seventeenth and eighteenth-century frames, their soulless, beady eyes judging her from behind their canvas prisons. Few people beyond the immediate family knew that none of the people portrayed in the paintings had any relation to her family at all, which was exactly the way Grainne O'Reilly wanted to keep it.

On such a sunny day, light filtered in from the skylight above the main staircase, filling the ground floor with light and warmth. If she were not still suffering slightly from her hangover, she may have felt comforted by it, but as it was, she wished she could put her sunglasses back on and pretend the rest of the world didn't exist.

All That Compels the Heart

The library was located at the far end of the main hallway. The high arched windows along one wall provided a magnificent view of the back garden with its lush plants and flowers, enclosed by a tall, vine-covered stone wall, affording the family privacy from their neighbours.

The library was one of the largest rooms in the house, second only to the drawing room where her grandmother liked to entertain her particularly wealthy guests. The library served a dual function: as well as being the library, it was also her grandfather's study. An avid reader like him, this had been Aoife's favourite room in her grandparents' house, the one she escaped to as often as she could.

Standing in the doorway, she could see her whole family was indeed assembled, just as Moore had said. A fire burned in the great, grey marble fireplace making her feel uncomfortably stifled and hot. The scent of the leather couches on either side of the fireplace and her grandfather's secret stash of cigars lingered in the air. No matter how often he tried to air the place out so Grainne wouldn't bother him about smoking, the scent stubbornly refused to budge. For Aoife, it was a comforting scent, one that reminded her instantly of her beloved Grandda.

"Ah, here she is! So you finally decided to join us then, Aoife?" Grainne's voice rang out across the large room, dripping with a fake pleasantry at the arrival of her youngest granddaughter.

Aoife grumbled to herself that dinner wouldn't be served for another thirty minutes or so anyways so it wasn't like she'd missed anything important, but she held her tongue.

"Yes, Granny, I'm here. Sorry I'm late." She hoped no one would notice the effort it took to keep the edge out of her voice as she dutifully crossed the room to kiss her grandmother on the cheek in greeting. Despite her years, Grainne looked at least a decade younger than she should. Aoife suspected it was down to some cosmetic enhancements, although her grandmother would vehemently have denied such allegations.

Aoife didn't bother to provide an excuse for her tardiness; none would be accepted anyways.

"You're not planning to wear *that* to dinner, are you love?" Her grandmother's words nicked her as sharp as any blade. It was not a deep cut; after all, she was used to her grandmother's criticisms of her wardrobe, no matter how nicely she was dressed. It did not, however, mean the cut didn't sting all the same.

Self-consciously, she glanced quickly down at her dress looking for some flaw with it. She had to admit that she could have quickly run an iron over it before putting it on, but in an attempt to not be any later than she needed to be, she'd forgone the iron and just slipped on the sleeveless royal purple, V-necked satin dress with the white floral design stitched along the bodice. The knee-length dress had been a present from Bex for her birthday last year, an attempt on Bex's part to spruce up her friend's wardrobe. She knew it was beautiful and it looked good on her, but her grandmother's comment niggled at her self-confidence like a termite burrows its way through wood. She tried to remind herself that it wouldn't have mattered what she wore, that Grainne would still have found some fault with it, but she had to admit it was a struggle.

Aoife forced a small smile onto her lips, reminding herself that this was how her family was: outwardly perfect to the rest of the world, but behind these walls, any one of them would happily stick a dagger in your back.

Ladies and gentlemen! Aoife thought, *For tonight's dinner entertainment the O'Reillys present to you their favourite game called: "Who can tear down another family member the fastest?"* She snickered ruefully under her breath. She wished it wasn't an accurate description of how this dinner would actually go, but she'd survived enough of them to know it was the truth. Her family were worse than a pack of wild animals toying with a poor, helpless creature they intended to slaughter.

"Of course it is, Granny," she replied, her own fake smile still pasted on her face as she left her grandmother's side to kiss her grandfather in greeting, ignoring the look of shock that crossed Grainne's face.

"Hello, Grandda."

"Hello, love." Paddy's face beamed up at her and Aoife's small smile turned into a larger one. The sting from her grandmother's words melted away as she basked in the light of her grandfather's love.

A quiet, unassuming man, Paddy was universally beloved by all members of his family. He was one of those people who had that rare ability to make everyone around him feel special, a trait that made everyone around him adore him.

Taking a seat beside her older cousin, Connor, Aoife ignored the way Grainne's lips flattened, her calm attitude antagonizing her grandmother. No doubt she'd hoped to get a rise out of her.

Only twenty-nine more minutes to go and I can ply myself with enough alcohol to not care what she says to me.

Aoife figured she could just about live with that. Her family was the only exception to her "drinking only on social occasions" rule. Five minutes with the O'Reillys was enough to make even the most sober person in the world a drunk.

Like sharks who smell the scent of fresh blood, everyone in the room was suddenly incredibly interested in the scene playing out before them. She noted the faintest flickers of approval from both Paddy and Connor – her only allies in the family – pleased at her gumption for standing up for herself. Her other cousin, Caitlin, her aunt and uncle, and her mother, however, looked eagerly at Grainne to see how she would choose to torture Aoife for her perceived lack of deference. The only ones not interested in seeing Aoife raked over the coals were her grandfather, cousin, and her stepfather, Anton, who looked impassively around the room like he would much rather be anywhere but where he was right now. There could be no doubt that Aoife's response to her grandmother's snide comment would be seen as "talking back," something she knew she would pay for later. However, those who'd been hoping for an immediate retaliation were sorely disappointed when Grainne turned her attention instead to the topic of Connor's return.

"I was just saying to your grandfather, Aoife, how wonderful it is to have Connor back with us."

Aoife merely smiled at her cousin, happy to see him again. He was almost more like an older brother to her in many ways, and she missed him terribly when he was gone.

"I do hope your time in Afghanistan served its purpose to let out whatever pent-up, boyhood dreams you had about being a hero, and now you've come to your senses and will take up a sensible career."

There was no doubt about what "sensible career" Connor should be entering into. Grainne had been trying to get Connor to join the rest of the family at *O'Reilly's* practically since he'd been old enough to know what the business was.

"Thank you, Granny. It's nice to be home, and it's comforting to know you were all thinking of me while I was away. And no, I have no intentions of leaving the military any time soon." His words were kind but firm.

An exasperated sigh escaped Grainne's lips and her body sagged, as if she had the whole weight of the world on her shoulders but said nothing more. As the only male grandchild, Connor was able to get away with far more than either his sister or younger cousin could hope to in the same situation. Blonde-haired and blue-eyed, he'd successfully made the transition from a cherubic and precocious young boy into a handsome young man, affable, charming, and kind to others. He'd inherited his good looks from his mother and grandmother before him. He'd also inherited Grainne's drive and ambition to succeed, although he chose to use it differently. The innate charm he'd inherited from Paddy, combined with his good looks, made him a fine catch for any young woman looking to marry. While it may seem an archaic thought to anyone of Connor's age, it was at the forefront of his parents' and grandparents' minds to see him settled down with a girl from a "good" family.

"You should listen to your grandmother, Connor. You can't stay in the military forever. And don't you think it's about time you went for a more practical career choice? Don't you want to work for the company your grandparents worked so hard to build? Da isn't getting any younger, you know. Don't you think you should do your part to help him out while he's still here to guide you? This is your legacy, Connor. John, talk some sense into your son." Connor's mother, Siobhan, spoke up from her perch on the arm of the sofa across from where her son sat.

All That Compels the Heart

Connor's father, John, looked awkwardly at both his wife and his son, looking like he distinctly wished he hadn't been placed in the middle of this argument.

"I... well, I mean, there's nothing wrong with letting Connor stay in the military for the time being. It's not like there's any rush for him to start up with the business..." John's voice trailed off at the glowering look his wife was giving him.

Growing up the son of the British ambassador to Ireland, John Brady, came from a long line of men who'd served in some sort of public service going back generations. He'd had a rather distinguished career of his own in the military, until a mission in the Falklands had gone wrong and left his leg injured, effectively consigning him to a life of working in the financial sector. It was no secret how proud he was that Connor had chosen to follow in his footsteps and join the military after finishing secondary school, and he had no wish to see his son's career cut short like his own. He'd conceded most of his life to his wife and her family – including letting his children take the O'Reilly surname, at Grainne's insistence, since she'd had no son of her own to carry it on – so it was his way of holding onto the one thing that made his son – in his eyes – a Brady.

Connor gave a small sigh of his own and shared a knowing look with Aoife. The two of them had promised long ago as children that they would never bow down to the expectations of their family. As the spare to Caitlin's "heiress" position, it was easier for Aoife. She was expendable, and therefore had to endure less meddling in her life and career than either Caitlin or Connor faced. No matter how much Connor might attempt to resist his mother and grandmother, they all knew it was inevitable that he would end up running Paddy's company one day. He just kept trying to put that day off for as long as possible.

"If Connor wants to be a soldier, then leave the boy alone. He's well able to make his own decisions."

Connor looked over at his grandfather appreciatively, grateful for the support.

"I'm proud of you, son. You've done well for yourself."

Caitlin snorted derisively at this comment, crinkling her perfect, surgically altered nose. It wasn't that she necessarily disagreed with her grandfather. She snorted more to draw attention to herself than anything else, not able to stand when the focus of everyone in the room was not on her for longer than a few minutes.

Caitlin was, down to the perfect blonde hair and slate-grey eyes, every bit the younger version of her grandmother and, consequently, Grainne's favourite. It would have been understandable for both Connor and Aoife to be jealous of the lavish amounts of attention their family heaped on Caitlin – and there was no denying that both of them *had*, at times, succumbed to fits of jealousy over it – but as they came to realize the burden and responsibility that came with being the favourite, they'd both taken up their place standing just outside of the spotlight that shone permanently on Caitlin.

"Done well for himself? Have you all suddenly forgotten that I'm currently the only grandchild who has a real job? I'm the only one who's even remotely taken an interest in Grandda's business, or have you forgotten that I'm the one who manages the business while Connor's off gallivanting in the desert and playing at being a soldier, and Aoife, well, she's always got her nose in a book." The note of petulance in Caitlin's voice rang out loud and clear.

"No one's discounting your contribution to the business, love," Grainne reassured Caitlin in said in what Aoife supposed she'd meant to be a reassuring tone, but it was difficult not to hear the ring of patronization hidden beneath the consolation. Perhaps Caitlin had heard it too, but needing the validation too much, chose to ignore it.

"It's just that it would be even better if both you *and* your brother worked for the company, don't you think? After all, it's meant to be a *family* business. Isn't that right?"

This last question was directed towards her husband.

"Hmmm? Oh yes, yes."

Aoife noted the distraction in his voice, and she realized that he'd been quieter than normal. There was something about the way he'd answered that left Aoife with an inexplicably unsettling feeling.

All That Compels the Heart

"There, you see? Of course we value your contribution to the company. Often, I wonder how you take on so many duties all by yourself! Wouldn't it be nice if your brother was there to help you out?"

Aoife coughed politely behind her hand at the notion that Caitlin had "too much work" to do. It was a well-known secret in the company that she'd been made the head of marketing in name only, with most of the decisions being made by a trusted team around her that kept her far from any real decision-making opportunities.

She felt Caitlin's steel-grey eyes search out the person who dared contradict this statement. While Siobhan and Grainne might constantly be crowing about Caitlin's "accomplishments," the only thing she'd really managed to do in her life so far amounted to using her good looks to get herself married to Nathaniel Donovan, the son of a wealthy banker and one of the investors in O'Reillys. It was then she realized that Nate wasn't present.

Must be away on a business trip with Danny… Shit! Danny!

It was the first time she'd really thought of her boyfriend since yesterday. She probably should have tried to call him to let him know about losing her job at Arbour Hill. She made a mental note to call him when she got home.

Caitlin's husband, Nate, worked in the same investment firm as Aoife's boyfriend, Danny Fitzgerald. She only now remembered that Danny had mentioned something about needing to travel to Asia for some conference. To her shame, she had to admit that she hadn't been paying attention to what he'd told her, *if* he'd told her. He was away so often for business that they rarely seemed to see one another these days. One conference turned into another, with new business opportunities coming up all the time, all of which required his personal attention. She knew she should be proud by the fact that his superiors felt enough confidence in him to send him away to deal with clients face-to-face so often.

She was interrupted from worrying about Danny and what she was going to say to him about her losing her job, by Caitlin taking her argument to the next level.

"Are you saying that I don't know how to do my job, now? That I need my younger brother there to supervise me?

Is that what you're saying?" Her eyes welled up with crocodile tears, threatening to spill over her high cheekbones.

If her face wasn't constantly drawn up like there was as perpetual nasty smell around her, Caitlin might be what some people considered beautiful. Like her twin brother, she'd inherited her mother and grandmother's pale blonde hair. While Connor had rakish good looks, Caitlin looked more like her father with high cheekbones, a delicate chin and a bit of a snub nose. She'd convinced her mother to let her have rhinoplasty when she was sixteen and now she had a rather more dainty nose, if still a little short for her face.

Everyone in the room – including Connor who, despite his sister's insecurities and shortcomings, couldn't bear to see Caitlin upset – were muttering platitudes to calm her down. Everyone except for Aoife, that was. She recognized Caitlin's attempt to bring herself to the brink of tears for what it was – pure manipulation – and she wasn't going to dignify her sulky behaviour. Right now, she desperately wanted to smack them all for playing right into her hands and perpetuating her bad behaviour. But that would leave a mark on her forehead and what would Grainne say to that?

She began giggling to herself at the thought.

I must still be somewhat tipsy...

She hadn't immediately realized how the room had gone quiet while she had been contemplating exactly how tipsy she still was until she heard her grandfather cough politely to draw her attention to the situation at hand. When she looked up she realized everyone's eyes were on her.

"And what exactly do you think is so funny, Aoife?" Caitlin's sharp tone cut across the room. "Is my contribution to our family such a joke to you? And who are *you* to judge me? It's not like you've even made an attempt to work for the business."

She'd been doing so well at keeping her family from choosing her to be the one to pick on today, minus the incident when she'd first arrived, but now, everyone's attention was firmly back on her. Aoife wracked her brain to find a way to distract her family from her again, but she wasn't fast enough.

"And how is your work at the publishing house, Aoife?"

All That Compels the Heart

It was the first thing Aoife's mother had said to her since she'd arrived. While this may have seemed odd to most people, Aoife had become used to it. She was, in fact, surprised that her mother actually knew that she had a job at all, since she'd barely seemed interested any time Aoife had tried to tell her about Arbour Hill.

Aoife now had a dilemma on her hands. She could lie and hope that news of her being fired had not yet reached either Grainne, Maureen, Siobhan, or Caitlin's circle of society friends who always seemed to know every bit of gossip before the rest of the town; or, she could tell the truth. Past experience had taught her that one was usually just as bad as the other, which wasn't particularly helpful right now. Anything she'd ever done in the past that was remotely humiliating had always been discovered, one way or another, and stored in her family's collective memory to be brought out at every family occasion so they could laugh openly and torment her until the wounds that once had just smarted, deepened and bruised beneath the skin. There was no doubt about it: she was stuck squarely between a rock and a hard place.

"I believe that dinner is ready to be served," Paddy cut off his eldest granddaughter's attempt to torment her younger cousin. Aoife followed Paddy's gaze and noticed Moore lurking outside the doorway, no doubt hanging back on purpose to watch Aoife's interrogation.

Her shoulders dropped slightly in relief at her grandfather's intervention. Everyone in the room, excluding Paddy and Connor, looked disappointed to have the interrogation interrupted before it got started. Even Moore, still hovering around the doorway looked disappointed not to have seen the show. However, still respecting Paddy's nominal position as head of the family, they dutifully obeyed the intended command and shuffled out of the library to the dining room.

Aoife held back and let the others leave the room, noticing that her grandfather had done the same.

"I didn't tell you earlier but I think you look lovely, my dear," he told her, kissing her on the cheek.

"Thanks, Grandda."

"And I just wanted to let you know that there's always a place for you in the company. You know, seeing that you may have a bit more free time on your hands now."

She looked up at him, surprised. "So, everyone knows I got fired, don't they?"

Her grandfather nodded. She smiled at him, grateful for the advanced warning on how to play this out when the topic came up again.

"Gossip spreads like wildfire in this city," her grandfather told her ruefully. A dark, reflective look crossed his face, and the same inexplicable anxiety she'd felt before returned. There was something about the way his face drew down that seemed more than just his disappointment in his family's desire to poke the fresh wound of Aoife's job loss.

As they walked towards the dining room, she thought that her grandfather seemed less himself than normal. He seemed somehow shrunken, his posture more frail and stooped. Somehow, he'd changed right before her eyes without her realizing it until just this minute.

Perhaps I'm just imagining things. That had to be it, right? The alarming thought that something may be wrong with her beloved grandfather was almost too much to bear. She pushed the thought down as she followed him into the dining room.

Everyone was already seated, ready to begin their meal. The dining room was quite large, able to easily seat all ten of them around the long, cherry-wood table in its centre. A large marble fireplace along the nearest wall warmed the room. Aoife noted how strange it seemed now that every room in the house had a fire burning despite the warmth of the late summer's day.

She wasn't the only one. She noticed how Connor, his father John, and her stepfather, Anton, had all loosened their ties around their necks as much as they could get away with while still being respectable in front of Grainne, as well as taking off their suit jackets. She noticed a slight sheen of sweat on Caitlin's forehead; dressed in a black satin peplum dress as she was, she had to be feeling the heat of the room. Her mother, aunt and grandmother also seemed to be feeling the warmth; she noticed how each of them had hastily begun to consume the water in their glasses as soon as they'd sat around the table. The only person who didn't seem affected by the heat was Paddy, who had on a thick dress shirt under his dinner jacket and his tie firmly around his neck.

She was distracted from her musings by the arrival of one of the maids through one of double archways on either side of the fireplace, one of which led to the kitchen and the other to the butler's pantry. She took a sip of water to calm her nerves, the light from the chandeliers above her head glittering off the crystal goblet and casting shadows across the pale, cornflower blue of the walls and the crown moulding. Today, as always, the dining table was perfectly arranged, not a single utensil or napkin out of place on its deep red surface.

One of the servants placed a bowl of tomato bisque in front of her. Unusually for the O'Reillys, they began to eat the first course in silence. Perhaps Paddy's earlier unspoken warning about bothering Aoife still fresh in their minds.

Or just looking for their next target…

She knew her family too well to think they'd forget about the interruption to their earlier interrogation. They were just biding their time, waiting for the right moment to strike. Perhaps after Paddy had excused himself to his library and left them alone with Aoife and he wasn't there to protect her anymore.

When they were halfway through the soup, Grainne broke the silence with a delicate clearing of her throat. Everyone in the room held their breath, waiting to see who would become her next target. Completely aware of the power she held over them, Grainne turned her attention to the female servant who'd brought their meal into them. Aoife noticed the poor girl trying to blend into the wall behind her as much as she could. She didn't recognize her from previous visits to her grandmother's; she must be new. Her grandmother had a difficult time keeping servants for the long-term; only Moore had been around since before Aoife was born.

Crooking her index finger in the girl's direction, Grainne beckoned for her to step forward. "Come here, my dear."

From the petrified look the poor thing gave Aoife, she didn't expect the girl would be around much longer than her predecessor, who'd lasted all of three months.

"Yes, ma'am?"

"It's a lovely bisque," Grainne finally pronounced after a moment of watching the girl squirm. "Do be a dear and tell chef."

"Y-yes ma'am," she stammered, clearly not expecting such a casual-sounding request.

When she didn't move, Grainne continued to stare at her until she realized that she wanted the command carried out right away.

"Yes ma'am. Sorry ma'am."

Curtseying her way out of the room, the young girl – Aoife figured she couldn't be much older than eighteen or nineteen – accidentally bumped into the archway, which prompted one raised eyebrow from Grainne.

"Poor girl; she's not bad but needs more training."

Murmurs of assent rippled around the table, everyone glad that they'd all dodged a bullet for the moment.

"I think she's doing rather well for having only started at the beginning of the week," Paddy spoke up and everyone around the table looked at him, surprised. This was the second time he'd dared contradict his headstrong wife, something that was extremely out of character for him.

She'd always marveled at exactly how her grandparents had managed to stay together for as long as they did. Unlike his wife, Paddy had never tried to hide his working-class background from the world. He wasn't ashamed of having grown up in a tenement; in fact, it was having had this experience that often made him kinder to those of a similar background. Aoife still marveled at how Paddy and Grainne could grow up in the very same place, and yet, come out so differently from one another, how her grandfather could be someone so kind and generous, while her grandmother was simply *not*.

"And where is Nathaniel today, Caitlin?" Grainne quickly changed the subject in order to cover up her husband's defiance.

All That Compels the Heart

It was an innocent enough sounding question, but everyone present knew it was laced with disapproval. There were very few legitimate excuses for missing Sunday dinner, and they were exclusive to grave illness, maiming, or death, and even then, Aoife believed Grainne O'Reilly would find a way to consider it a personal insult.

"He had to be away on a business trip, Granny. With Danny. He sends his love, and his regrets." Caitlin was quick to come to her husband's defense, not for any display of affection for a man she barely knew or cared to be married to, but to erase any implication that she, by extension, was at fault for her husband's preference to be at work than to be with her family. Aoife couldn't help but notice how she'd thrown in the dig about Danny also being absent today, most likely to ensure that if she were going to catch any flack about Nathaniel being absent, that Aoife would also get in trouble for Danny's absence as well.

If the marriage hadn't been practically arranged by their parents, it likely wouldn't have come to fruition. Nate, like Danny, had little desire to be saddled with an incessantly needy wife and so he often took any excuse to leave Dublin – and his wife – behind him.

"That's the third family dinner he's missed in as many weeks. Is there anything the matter in your marriage?"

The look that crossed Caitlin's face showed that Grainne was picking at a festering wound.

"Of course not, Granny," Caitlin replied, a little too quickly, subconsciously fiddling with the massive diamond ring on the ring finger of her left hand. "Everything is grand. Nate will be here next week, I promise."

For once, wanting to deflect attention from herself, she asked, "Why don't you ever bother Connor or Aoife about their relationships? At least I've gotten married."

Grainne *did* in fact bother Aoife and Connor about their relationships, at great length, and everyone knew it.

"It's not like we're old, Caitlin," Aoife snapped defensively. "I'm only twenty-five, and Connor's only twenty-six. There's no reason for either of us to rush into a loveless marriage."

She made sure the jab about Caitlin's marriage hit its mark and she saw the flush it brought to her cousin's face. Selfishly, it gave her a feeling of smug satisfaction. While she may disdain her family's habit of purposely antagonizing one another for sport, she knew she wasn't above playing the game from time to time herself.

Caitlin wasn't the only person in the room to feel uncomfortable by the comment. It was well-known that both Aoife's mother and aunt had both married out of convenience rather than love. Maureen had been young when she'd married Aoife's father. It had been an intense relationship from the start, but not one that could sustain itself. Not wanting to be tied to a clingy wife, Aoife's father had walked away one day, leaving his wife with divorce paper, not long after Aoife was born. She'd never met the man, but having experienced how self-absorbed Maureen was the last twenty-five years, Aoife often found herself empathizing with her absentee father instead of judging him for not staying. Far too childish to be a proper mother, Maureen had been too wrapped up in herself to love another person, something that plagued every one of her relationships going forward.

Where Siobhan might have inherited their mother's looks, it was Maureen who'd inherited their mother's shrewdness. Not one to be underestimated, she'd just as much business acumen as her mother, and as such, held a permanent position on the Board of Directors. But for all her success, Maureen was plagued by insecurity, stemming from a lack of love from a distant mother and a string of failed marriages. Her latest marriage was to Anton Dabrovic, a Ukrainian national who immigrated to Ireland ten years ago. He was older than his wife by about ten years, his dark brown hair already showing signs of greying at the temples. Aoife was ambivalent towards her latest stepfather; sure, he treated her and her mother quite well, but talking to him was about as interesting as watching paint dry on a wall.

He was about as interesting to look at as he was to talk to. He had a sizeable paunch on him, accented by the colourful buttoned up shirts he favoured, but this didn't bother Maureen; Anton's whole world revolved around accounting, which was why she'd married him. It never hurt when her husbands brought a sizeable fortune with them into the marriage. This was a philosophy both Maureen and her twin sister had inherited from their mother, and had let it influence the men they'd married.

"And, if you haven't forgotten, you're not the only one in a relationship. Just because Danny and I aren't married now doesn't mean that we won't be one day."

She surprised herself with her comment. She and Danny hadn't, in any way, discussed getting married or settling down. She mentally chastised herself for even opening herself up to this line of questioning because she knew it was like throwing a bone to a pack of ravenous hyenas. Her grandmother was especially taken with Danny, and Aoife knew she was keen for her youngest granddaughter to marry him. He was the only boyfriend of hers that the family had really taken a liking to, something which probably should have raised alarm bells in her head.

"And are you and Danny thinking of settling down together, love?"

The question came not from her grandmother or mother as she would have expected, but from her grandfather. Inexplicably, his face looked concerned at the thought, his dark blue eyes clouded with worry.

"No, not at all. I'm just saying that it's the next logical step, right?" She looked around at the others assembled before her, suddenly unsure of herself. "I mean, I'm sure it's not going to happen for a long time yet, but one day."

Just as she was mulling over the prospect of being married to Danny, Connor spoke up to defend the both of them.

"Aoife's right, Gran. We're too young to settle down just yet. Caitlin was obviously ready when she married Nate." Connor smiled at his sister, trying to look supportive. "Aoife and I just aren't there yet."

"Lord only knows why. It's not like you've been without plenty of prospects," Siobhan complained. "Whatever happened to that girl you brought home at Christmas? Sadie, I think her name was? Or Jean? We liked her. And before that there was… Mary? I think that was her name?"

"You liked her, and yet you can't remember her name," Aoife muttered into her glass of water.

Connor never seemed to have the problem of being without a girlfriend for any special occasion or holiday; his problem was always keeping them around for longer than a few months.

"What can I say? It's not exactly like many women are eager to sign up to be a soldier's wife, Mam."

"This is *exactly* the point I've been trying to make all day long! Isn't it Maureen?" Siobhan was about to begin another litany about how Connor should give up his career as a soldier when Paddy's voice cut across the chatter that had arose.

"That's enough, now. Siobhan, you've made your point."

"Yes, Da," Siobhan replied quietly, her near-permanently frozen face looking as contrite as the Botox would allow.

"And Caitlin, you need to stop trying to get the better of your brother and your cousin. Yes, you are loved, and you are a valued member of this family, but so are Connor and Aoife. Can we all not just get through a meal together as a family without trying to kill one another? Lord knows what will happen to you all when I'm gone."

Her grandfather's last words were like a knife in Aoife's heart. She never liked to think about what life without Paddy would look like, and she abhorred any talk that alluded to it. Clearly she wasn't the only one to pick up on the mood which had descended upon the room.

"What does that mean, Da? Is something wrong?" Maureen asked him, an unusually concerned look crossing her face. The only person in the room she possibly cared for other than herself was her father.

The tired look Aoife had seen in his eyes earlier had returned, and his face seemed even more drawn than before. There was something about the fragility of his appearance that made her stomach drop and the tomato bisque churn uncomfortably. The undercurrent of anxious dread she'd felt all afternoon arrived again in full force. She noted the look of support Grainne gave to her husband, encouraging him to go on, and she knew before he even said anything that her whole world was about to change.

All That Compels the Heart

Paddy cleared his throat. "There's no easy way to say this, so I'm going to just come straight out and say it. On my last visit to the doctor he found a spot on my liver. They did a whole bunch of tests and the long and short of it is that I've got cancer. Stage four. There's no curing it; doc says I've not got much time left."

It was said simply, as if he were discussing nothing more serious than the weather but for everyone else in the room, it was like a bomb had gone off and destroyed everything in their world. A chorus of gasps and choked sobs arose from each member of the O'Reilly clan, disbelief and numbness settling in. Aoife noticed tears welling up in her mother's and Caitlin's eyes, the kind of tears that were not being faked. For her part, she was too stunned by the news to feel anything for the moment, her body going into shock. So many questions spun through her mind: Why? Why was this happening to the kindest, gentlest person in the world? How could she fix this?

There was a small pause while everyone reeled from the shock, and then the questions running through Aoife's mind came flooding out of everyone else's mouths. Grainne held her hand up silently against the flurry of concerned questions and tears, everyone falling silent at her unspoken command.

"I know that everyone is concerned right now." There was only the slightest catch in her voice as she spoke. "But let's let him breathe for a moment."

Everyone took a breath of their own and watched their patriarch carefully, in case every breath he took might be his last.

"I know you all want to know what will happen now," he began. "Well, what comes next is that I will be using what little time I have to live as best as I can."

"You'll have plenty of time to live yet, Da," Maureen spoke up, wiping at the tears on her cheeks, for once not concerned with smearing her make-up. "There are plenty of new drugs and treatments these days, even for patients with stage four cancer. We'll find you the best oncologist and begin you on a course of treatment right away."

Paddy shook his head slowly. "No."

His tone was firm, decided. It nearly broke Aoife's heart, as she knew that no matter how much anyone in the family would try to cajole Paddy into treatment, there was no forcing him to do anything he didn't want to do.

"What do you mean, 'no'?"

"I mean what I've said. I mean to live out whatever days are left to me on my own terms and not be hooked up to a bunch of tubes and machines. I want to live, and die, with dignity and on my own terms."

While Paddy may have had time to come to terms with his illness and come to this decision on his own, it did not sit well with his family. Another outburst of questions and fury at his words erupted but once again quietened down when he held up a tired hand.

"I'm feeling quite tired all of a sudden. I think I will retire to the library."

"Well, I think I have quite lost my appetite, and I think everyone else has too." Grainne indicated for the servants to remove the dishes from the table.

Everyone rose from the table and headed towards the drawing room while Paddy shuffled slowly along the hallway to the sanctity and quiet of his library. Aoife watched his frail form and tried to hold back the tears that threatened to escape her.

Chapter Three

"Aoife, go home. I'm not going anywhere, anytime soon. I promise."

Her grandfather's words still rang in her head as she wandered Dublin's streets in a haze. While everyone else had gone into the drawing room with her grandmother, Aoife knew she'd find no comfort in its clinically white walls and matching furniture; the place reminded her too much of a hospital right now and that was the last thing she wanted to think about. Instead, she'd followed her grandfather into his library, wanting to be near to him. The two of them had just sat there quietly, her listening to him breathe, reassured every time he inhaled and terrified every time he exhaled, worried it would be the last breath he'd ever take. Feeling her nervous agitation, he'd gently hugged her and called her a taxi. The image of his frail form standing in the stone drive waving to her as she exited the tall, wrought-iron gates, sunlight glinting off his white hair and a big smile on his face, would forever be imprinted on her mind.

The long drive back to the city seemed even longer to her, the car feeling confining and restrictive.

"Could you pull over here, please?" she'd asked the driver.

"But, Miss, this isn't where you wanted to get off."

"I know. I'd just rather walk from here, thanks."

She'd handed him a couple of large bills and hurried out of the car before he tried to give her back her change. She could have chastised herself for spending money so frivolously when she had no job, but she didn't really care right now. She didn't really care much about anything at all right now. Her mind was too full of questions she couldn't answer: How could this be happening? When did everything start falling apart? Why hadn't she noticed that something was wrong? Had she always known and just ignored the signs?

She'd noticed her grandfather had been more tired lately, maybe a bit thinner, but she'd just attributed this to stress, and thought that her grandparents' recent trip away to the Caribbean would help him bounce back to his normal self. Paddy had recently stepped back completely from the business, allowing his wife and daughters complete control; was this why he'd stepped down? Because he'd known he was ill? Because he knew he would…?

Aoife couldn't even finish the thought, the large lump in her throat making her eyes water, tears threatening to spill over. Once again she had the sensation of not being able to breathe, that the world was closing in around her. Unable to walk any farther, she sat down on the pavement, not caring if it made her dress dirty, and leaned her head back against the grey stone wall of the building she'd been walking past. Its solid immovability gave her some comfort, reminding her that not everything was crashing down around her.

Allowing the cool, dusk air to clear her mind, she realized she'd been wandering aimlessly around the city and she no longer knew exactly where she was. She wiped at the tears that had fallen onto her cheeks, stood up, and looked around for a street sign to help get her bearings again. Turning around, she found herself standing in front of the *O'Reilly's* in Temple Bar. This was *the* O'Reilly's; the original pub her grandfather had taken over when it had originally been known as *Murphy's*. Somewhere in the fog of everything that had happened to her in the last twenty-four hours, her

All That Compels the Heart

subconscious had brought her somewhere safe, somewhere she'd feel at home. Suddenly feeling the need to be close to her grandfather once more, she headed inside, the scent of leather, beer, and smoke clinging to the air around her like a blanket enfolding a child. Even though smoking was no longer permitted in pubs, decades of regular patrons smoking inside these walls could not be erased entirely. The scent reminded her of her grandfather, whose clothes were infused with this particular bouquet no matter how many times her grandmother washed them with scented products.

Booths lined the periphery of the pub, each one a solid, carved walnut frame with forest-green leather seats. Despite being over a century old, the leather seats had been kept in excellent shape, having been built during an era when things were made to last. The only sign of wear on them was the occasional imprint from the bottom of a regular patron. Stained glass partitions with Celtic designs provided privacy between booths. Against the back wall stood the bar. Large mirrors hung behind it, catching the light from the green and gold stained glass light fixtures hanging from the ceiling, the light fragmenting and glittering off all the bottles of alcohol proudly on display behind the bar. The central mirror featured the O'Reilly name in pride of place. Instantly, she felt the homey atmosphere her grandfather had always striven for in his pub, before his wife had taken the business to the next level and launched it onto the global scene with fancy menus and celebrity patrons, robbing it of any feelings or personal touches. This was the only *O'Reilly's* in the world that still looked as Paddy O'Reilly had envisioned it.

Aoife had spent many a time as a child sitting at the bar, drinking a Shirley Temple, while her grandfather talked to punters and his staff. Just as she used to do when she was five, she headed straight for the bar, sat on one of the stools, and politely waited her turn to be served. Paddy had ingrained in her that just because she was his granddaughter did not mean she was above anyone else who walked through the pub's doors and she was expected to treat everyone the same.

"Hey Aoife! Haven't seen you in here for awhile. The usual?" Gerry asked her after serving a couple of pints. Gerry had been the bartender at this particular *O'Reilly's* since before she was born; she didn't have a single memory of this place that didn't include the portly man. Somewhere in his mid-fifties, if she had to guess, he looked as timeless as he always did. That is to say that he looked as ancient as ever; the lines on his face from hard labour and long hours would not look unusual on a man much older than him.

"No, Gerry. Something a little stronger, please. And by a little, I mean a lot."

His eyebrows raised in surprise at the request, but he didn't ask her to explain. You weren't judged when you came into *O'Reilly's*; it was one of the reasons people felt so safe here, which was exactly what Paddy had wanted when he'd taken over the place.

Placing a shot glass in front of her, he filled it with one of the most expensive whiskeys and she downed it in one gulp, the amber liquid burning her throat. She indicated for him to pour another.

"One of those kinds of days?" Concern crept into his voice.

"Something like that."

She trusted Gerry like an uncle, and she wanted to blurt everything out, confide in him, but this was not her secret to share. Even though her grandfather hadn't told her to not tell anyone, she knew him too well; he would want to tell everyone he knew in his own way and on his own time, and he wouldn't have told Gerry – no matter how much he considered him like family – before telling his immediate family.

She downed the second shot as quickly as she did the first and indicated for another.

"You want to talk about it?"

"Nope."

Gerry shrugged and poured another. He knew she'd open up to him when she was ready to. Their little silent ritual continued for drink after drink until she began to feel the alcohol running through her veins. She'd begun to lose track of how much she'd had to drink, but somewhere in the fog of alcoholic bliss she heard Gerry ringing the bell for last call. She caught his attention and called for another shot and brought out her wallet to settle her bill.

"You, young lady, are cut off. And you know you get the family rate, so put your wallet away," he admonished her.

"I severely disagree with the first of those statements," she replied, her words only slightly slurring. "And my Granddad taught me to always pay my bills, so you're not going to stop me. Now shut up and take my money."

Gerry smirked at her offense at being called a drunk but did as he was told.

"Yes ma'am," he said to her, taking the wad of bills she handed him and put it in the Community Fund jar, the same old milk jug that Mr. Murphy had placed there a million years ago. When her grandfather had taken over the pub from him and made it his own, he'd kept the tradition of raising funds to support the community.

"The local parish priest thanks ye kindly for your donation," he told her with a smile.

"What are we raising money for this time?"

"A new roof for the church. It's in a bad state of repair."

She nodded and made a move to get off her barstool, but somehow she couldn't seem to make her legs work properly and ended up almost tripping over herself.

"There now, love. You'll want to watch yourself." An elderly man caught her arm as she stumbled forward, his grip surprisingly strong as he helped her right herself.

"You hold on there, Aoife. I'll drive you home," Gerry told her.

"Nah, I'm grand. I'm only a few blocks away."

"I'm still driving you home." His tone was firm and the look on his face warned her not to argue with him.

In an act of complete drunken petulance, she expelled a frustrated sigh and sat down heavily at one of the nearby tables while she waited for him to wipe down the bar and settle the bills with the other customers.

"Nicky, I'm driving Miss O'Reilly home. Close the bar up for me?"

Nicky caught the keys his father tossed to him and nodded to him before continuing to sweep up.

"Come on. Let's get you home," he said to Aoife. She managed to struggle to her own two feet and walk out of the pub on her own, the cool air sobering her up a bit. Gerry held out a protective hand to her at all times, there to catch her in case she stumbled again but she got to the car fine and buckled herself in. By the time he'd driven to her building, she was sober enough to walk mostly in a straight line.

"Need any help?" he asked her as she unbuckled herself and opened the door.

"Nah. I'll be grand. Thanks for the lift, and sorry for telling you to shut up earlier. I was just being a brat."

"No problem at all," he reassured her. "If you want to talk about what it is that's bothering you, you know where to find me."

"Thanks Gerry."

She closed the car door firmly and headed inside her building. Even though he knew she'd be fine, she knew that he'd still wait there outside until he was sure she was inside.

Making it up the stairs to her flat, she walked through the darkened space – she didn't want to deal with the resounding headache she knew she'd get from the fluorescent glare of the overhead lights – and flopped face-first onto her bed, sinking into blissful unconsciousness.

Chapter Four

In the three weeks since her grandfather had revealed his diagnosis, his condition had deteriorated faster than expected. Despite his stubborn refusal, he'd been transferred to the hospital, but Grainne had conceded that if he didn't want treatment then she wouldn't force him to have it. They all knew it was just a matter of time now and the hospital was only making him comfortable until the inevitable occurred.

Aoife hated hospitals. She knew everyone did on at least some level, but this was more than just a general dislike for doctors, needles, or disapproving and judgemental nurses. She hated the drab colours on its drab walls, the sound of machines substituting normal body functions, the smell of disinfectant and death that haunted its corridors. She hated their sterile unfriendliness, which always left her uncomfortably on edge.

Her grandfather dozed peacefully as she entered his room. He'd insisted he didn't want to be put in a private room, that he could be in a general wing just like everyone else, but Grainne had quietly seen to it that he'd had his own room anyways. Even with all the sleeping he'd been doing lately, he still looked tired, and her heart sank a little in her chest. She hated seeing him look so frail and small where once he'd been the biggest, strongest male figure in her life.

Choking back tears, she moved quietly around the room, trying not to disturb him. She noticed the little window ledge and the bedside table were full of flowers, their scent not quite strong enough to combat the smell of the hospital. There were the obvious ones from the family, some from the head office, a few from workers at the pub who were close friends, but many were from people she'd never heard of before, people her grandfather had helped over the years. She supposed she should have brought him some flowers herself so she was represented in the fray but, knowing him well enough to know he had no use for them, she'd instead brought him an iPod filled with his favourite songs; everything from Elton John to Beethoven to the traditional Celtic music he enjoyed so much. She'd also brought him a copy of Bram Stoker's *Dracula*, his favourite novel. While she knew she wouldn't have been able to bring his dog-eared copy, which was quite literally falling apart at the seams, from his library, she'd bought him a new one from the little gift shop downstairs. She'd asked him, once, why he was so fascinated by this particular story. He'd told her that no matter how many times he'd read it, he still couldn't comprehend the concept of immortality. He just didn't understand why someone would want to live forever.

She perched herself on the taupe-coloured, worn out chair beside his bed and settled in while she waited for him to wake up. To keep her mind busy, she picked up the day's newspaper that had been tossed carelessly onto the little moveable table beside his bed. Paddy had already begun the crossword, his favourite part of the paper. He'd finished all but one of the words, she noticed.

Three down: a synonym for farce that was eight letters and began with the letter T…

"Travesty."

Her grandfather stirred in the bed and she was startled by his voice.

"What?"

"An eight-letter synonym for farce that begins with the letter T. Travesty." He pointed to the paper she was holding in her hands. "Be a dear and fill it in for me, would you?"

She fumbled around in her purse and pulled out a pen.

"I've only got a pen, Granddad. You sure you want me to fill it in? What if you're wrong?"

"And since when have you ever known me to be wrong Aoife Maeve O'Reilly?" he asked her with a pointed look.

"All I'm saying is that you're not as sharp as you used to be, you know," she teased him. Her grandfather's lips widened into a grin as big as her own.

"You always were the troublesome one of the family, ye know. You've got too much of my humour in you for your own good."

"Why thank you." It was the best compliment she could receive. "So does this mean I'm your favourite granddaughter?"

"You know I don't have favourites," he admonished. "I love all of my children and grandchildren just the same."

Aoife did as she was told and completed the crossword puzzle.

"There," she said, returning it to her bedside table, avoiding the subject of Caitlin or anything else they may end up arguing about. She didn't want to spend her last few days or weeks with her grandfather arguing about things that couldn't be changed.

The last few days or weeks.

The thought brought tears to the corners of her eyes and she quickly wiped them away. "Eyelash," she said in response to her grandfather's unasked question.

Paddy nodded, accepting the answer even if he knew it wasn't true. "I know you and Caitlin aren't the best of friends, and I don't expect you to be, but she's not as bad as ye think, ye know."

"I don't think she's a bad person, Granddad," she replied, her tone defensive. "She's just a lot like Gran, is all."

"And is that such a very bad thing? I love your grandmother very much, Aoife, and I don't regret a single moment of this life, especially marrying your grandmother. Without her, I wouldn't have you."

She gave him a watery smile.

"I'm a blessed man, Aoife. I've had a successful business, two beautiful daughters, and three wonderful grandchildren. What more could a man ask for? This spot of illness is well worth everything I got to have before it."

He reached out and took her hand, giving it a gentle squeeze. She sniffed and wiped delicately at her nose, trying to put on her best brave face. She didn't know how he could be so optimistic in the face of death, but she knew she needed to step up and try to be as brave as him. He'd been her hero since she was born, the centre of her whole world. She needed to start carrying her own weight now.

"So how is the job hunt going?" he asked, changing the topic of conversation.

"Not as well as I'd hoped," she admitted. She'd spent the last few weeks sending out applications to other publishing houses but no one seemed to be hiring at the moment. She'd begun to wonder if maybe she shouldn't try another approach by going back to school and getting her master's degree or changing careers completely. She just couldn't seem to settle on something.

"Have you thought about writing your own stories instead of editing others'?"

"No," she replied immediately. "I mean, yes, I have but it's difficult to get published and besides, I'm not sure I have a story interesting enough to tell."

"Oh I'm not so sure about that. Maybe you should give it a try."

"You're just saying that because you're my grandfather," she teased.

"No, I mean it. I want to see you happy, Aoife, and if writing makes you happy, then I want to see you doing something that is going to help you make the most of life."

"I think you have this whole advising thing wrong," she continued to tease him. "You're supposed to tell me to do something sensible with my life and get a practical degree or something."

"Life is too short to be practical, love." Paddy's face became quite serious and it made her raise her head to meet his eyes. "You need to live a little, do something that will make you happy. You don't want to get to my age and have regrets that you can't change."

"What am I going to do without you," Aoife asked suddenly, not just for some kind of response from him, but because she honestly couldn't imagine what life without him was going to be like. Her grandfather had always been the guiding light in her life, reminding her of where her safe harbour was and without him, she feared she would be set adrift forever.

Aoife gave his hand another little squeeze just before they were interrupted by the night nurse coming in to check on him. She was a short woman, with steel grey hair that was gelled up into short spikes. Aoife imagined she might be a pleasant woman, if it wasn't for the no-nonsense look currently on her face.

"Visiting hours are over now, miss, and Mr. O'Reilly needs his rest." She checked Paddy's vitals, clearly annoyed with Aoife's presence.

"This is my youngest granddaughter, and she only just got here. Surely we can bend the rules a little and let her stay a bit longer? You wouldn't deny a dying man his last request, would you?" Her grandfather was clearly turning up his best charms for the nurse's benefit despite the outright look of disapproval on her face.

"That line might work with the younger nurses, Mr. O'Reilly, but you won't get me into trouble by breaking hospital rules. Visiting hours are over now and I'm going to have to ask your granddaughter to leave." She looked pointedly towards Aoife, expecting her to take her cue. Not wanting to cause a fuss, Aoife rose from the chair and began to gather up her purse.

"It's fine, Grandad; I need to head back into the city anyways."

"Surely you can give us a few more minutes together, nurse?" Paddy O'Reilly asked the nurse again, clearly upset at having his visit cut short. The nurse pursed her lips together tightly but reluctantly acquiesced.

"Say your goodbyes quickly." Her unsaid implication that she would be back to make sure Aoife left promptly hung between them as she turned on her heel and walked briskly out of the room.

"I've been sleeping all day. It's the curse of old age," her grandfather apologized.

Aoife walked around the bed to where the nurse had just been standing and planted a big kiss on top of his head. "It's grand, Granddad. I'll come back tomorrow and visit again, this time a bit earlier so we can have more time, alright?

"Now, I have to get out of here, otherwise Nurse Stick-Up-Her-Arse over there is going to come back, and next time she's going to bring security with her to throw me out. But I *will* be back tomorrow, I promise."

"Be a dear and bring me some caramels with ye, eh?" Her grandfather looked up hopefully at her.

"First you try to get me kicked out of this place by security and now you want me to sneak you in sweets? If you're trying to get me into trouble, you're doing an excellent job of it."

"Oh never mind that old fusspot. She won't be working tomorrow; it's her day off." His face had the sweet hopefulness of a five-year old and Aoife found she couldn't resist.

"Alright. I'll do my best."

"I love you, dear."

"I love you too, Grandad. I'll see you tomorrow."

She turned to go from the room, briefly pausing in the doorway for one last look before heading out. Her grandfather smiled at her and gave her a small wave. She waved back, trying not to wonder how many more of these moments she would have with him.

As she walked down the corridor to the elevators, she noticed the nurse from earlier glaring at her as she passed by. Aoife had a childish impulse to stick out her tongue at her but decided she should be a grown up and instead hit the button for the elevator and rode it back down to the lobby.

As she headed out into the night, she noticed the various shopkeepers and vendors who worked in the lobby were closing up for the night. The lobby was crowded with people, the families and loved ones of those being treated in the hospital who'd held on as long as they could before being kicked out for the night by the hospital staff. The crowd separated into two groups: those heading towards the car park and those waiting for the last bus. She moved over to the right with those waiting for the bus and put in the earbuds to her iPod, not wanting to be disturbed.

She was about halfway through the playlist when the bus dropped her off in front her building and she walked up to her flat.

Feeling a bit restless and yet tired at the same time, she wasn't sure what she wanted to do: stay up and do something or go to bed. She wandered aimlessly around her kitchen, tired of staring at its tidy white walls and stainless-steel surfaces. In all the time she'd lived here, she still hadn't managed to make the place feel like her own. Like her former workspace at Arbour Hill Publishing, she'd incorporated few personal touches about the place, most of her personal effects still boxed up in the storage room. The only signs she lived here at all was the pile of dirty dishes around the sink.

Having nothing better to do, she decided to tackle the dishes, hoping the routine of the chore would calm her, but she still felt inexplicably anxious and unsettled. Drying her hands, she went back into the sitting room and turned on the television, flicking through the channels over and over, the images passing before her eyes in an unrecognizable blur. Giving up, she switched the television off and decided to go to bed, despite the relatively early hour, and headed towards the bedroom, pulling the covers up around her chin despite the warmth of the room. As she switched off the light on the bedside table, she couldn't seem to shake the inexplicable sense of impending dread hanging over her.

ಬಿಐ

After what seemed like hours, she'd finally managed to fall into a deep, exhausted sleep, which made it all the more startling for her when she jolted awake for no apparent reason. She lay there a moment, her breathing laboured and panicked, trying to re-orientate herself in her transition from sleep to wakefulness.

The screen on her mobile phone suddenly brightened, nearly blinding her in the darkened room. It vibrated angrily against the solid wood of her bedside table, the name "Maureen" flashing across the screen. Instantly, the sense that something was wrong came crashing down on her. Maureen wasn't the type of mother to just call and check in on her every now and again, especially not at three in the morning. If she was calling her daughter, it was because she wanted something, or something was wrong.

"Hello?" Aoife flipped the switch on her bedside table and blinked, coloured spots floating in front of her eyes from its piercing light. Panic gripped her throat and her voice was tense.

"Aoife? It's Maureen."

Aoife had never called her mother some affectionate, maternal name; she'd always simply been "Maureen" or "Mother" to her.

"Grandad has passed away. The hospital just called Granny to notify her."

Her mother's words rang in her head like a bell falling through a tower, clanging off every surface, lonely and echoing. She'd known, of course, why her mother had been calling long before she picked up the phone; it had been the logical response. But knowing the punch to the gut was coming didn't make her stomach recoil from the pain any less. She was breathless, immobile, unable to speak. She held the phone to her ear for a few seconds, her mouth agape until she heard her mother's shrill voice screaming at her.

"Well, aren't you going to say anything?!"

Her mind raced through a million different things to say and rejected each one, finding that none of them could begin to describe how she felt right now. She was stunned, completely at a loss for words.

"Well I would've thought you'd have been a bit more upset at the death of your grandfather," her mother snapped at her and hung up the phone, leaving only the sound of the dial tone buzzing in Aoife's ear.

Eventually, she hung up the phone, unsure of what to do. She didn't cry; she was still in too much shock yet to do that. She knew she should probably call her mother back, apologize to her and try to offer her some comfort, but she thought that might only make things worse right now. She would leave Anton to look after Maureen as she lashed out at the world.

Her first thought was to call Bex and Millie, but she also didn't want to wake them up in the middle of the night. She knew they'd come rushing to her side without her even having to ask them, but she didn't want to disrupt their sleep right now. She would call them later, talk to them when everything had sunk in a little more.

One person she knew would still be up at this hour was Danny. He was still away on business, so he'd be up working to all hours of the day and night. Without hesitation, she dialled his number. It rang several times before she heard his voice.

"Hello?"

There was a lot of noise in the background, like he was in some sort of dance club.

"Hiya. It's Aoife."

"Aoife? What's going on? It's like, four in the morning."

His tone was annoyed, but also somewhat concerned. She rarely called him when he was away on business, not wanting to disturb his work. She waited for him to call her when he could find the time.

"I just wanted to hear your voice. I miss you." Her voice was high and thin, needy. She knew she was being ridiculous, that he wouldn't appreciate the early morning phone call, or the neediness. She wasn't bothered that he was at a bar; deals with clients were rarely sealed in the office. "You've been gone for weeks now, and I just wanted to talk to you."

It was a feeble excuse, but it was all she could think of in that moment. She hated that she was acting like one of *those* girlfriends; the ones who clung to their boyfriend for dear life, lest they ever leave their side and decide that they'd rather be with someone less needy. She knew Danny hated that quality in his girlfriends.

"I miss you too, babe, but let's talk some other time, alright?" The tone in his voice was clear that he was in the middle of something and wanted to get this conversation over and done with so he could get back to whatever it was that she'd interrupted.

You just caught him at a bad time. He's not really annoyed with you, she reminded herself. Still not quite ready to let him go, she blurted the first thing that came to her mind to make him stay on the line.

"Grandad died."

Tears filled her eyes. She hadn't exactly wanted to tell him just now, and certainly not like this, but she'd had to get it off her chest before the weight of it crushed her completely.

She wasn't sure he'd heard her but, a few torturous seconds later she heard him inhale sharply.

"Ah babe I'm so sorry."

To his credit, Danny *did* say sorry, and she instantly forgave him for being annoyed with her earlier. "When's the funeral?"

"I… I don't know." She hadn't asked her mother, not that she'd likely have known this soon. Arrangements would have to be made.

"Well listen, leave a message for me at the office with Chloe and she'll make sure I get it. If I can be there, I will, ok?"

An awkward silence hung between the two of them as it was left unspoken that he was only trying to mollify her and he wouldn't come to the funeral. His social anxiety flared up in these situations and they both knew he wouldn't show.

The silence was broken by the sound of a woman on the other end of the line and she heard Danny cover the receiver with his hand, their voices muffled. Aoife thought she recognized the tone of the voice, but she couldn't tell over the steady beat of the club music.

"Look, babe, I need to go but I will call you later, alright?" He didn't wait for her response before hanging up the phone.

She nodded, even though she knew he couldn't see her, and wiped at the silent tears that had fallen onto her cheeks, the dial tone from her phone ringing in her ears once more. Hanging up the phone and placing it on the bedside table, she turned off the light and lay there in the dark silence.

Chapter Five

It was a cool and rainy day, the rain pouring down from the heavens as if they couldn't contain all the sadness they felt at Paddy O'Reilly's passing. As was typical for Ireland, the weather was the number one topic of conversation at the funeral home while everyone tried to think, and talk, about anything other than what was really on their minds.

Aoife hated it all: the endless prattle about unimportant topics, the constant flow of people who wanted to shake her hand and look at her with pity. She didn't want their pity; she wanted them all to go away and leave her alone to be miserable and sad and lonely. But she wasn't allowed to be any of those things right now. Right now, she had to be the one person in the family who could keep calm and cool under pressure, someone who could keep it together long enough to make decisions regarding the wake and the funeral, from flower arrangements to headstones, and it was clear from the rest of her family that none of them were going to step into that role for her. And so, she pushed her emotions to one side, locking them away in a box to be dealt with at another time.

It was this unemotional state that allowed her to function. She didn't mind being the one to make the arrangements or deal with all the inane details. In truth, they helped take her mind off things.

She arrived early to the funeral home where her grandfather's wake was being held, her grandmother insisting it would not be held in the original *O'Reilly's* as Paddy had wanted. Aoife knew she could've fought her grandmother on this point, but the last thing she wanted right now was to antagonize her further, so she'd conceded to have the wake at the funeral home. She figured her grandfather would forgive her this minor change of plans.

She knew everyone in the family – with the exception of Connor, of course – hated her for the way she pushed her emotions to one side to help them deal with their own grief. They didn't understand why she couldn't just break down and cry, sob her heart out in front of everyone else like them. What they didn't realize was that she was barely keeping it together, and her so-called "strength and endurance" was pure numbness, her mind's way of protecting her. They didn't forgive her for being the rock they depended on, the reason they were able to vent their own emotions. They saw only their own pain and grief. She didn't really mind the way they lashed out at her; the numbness protected her from their barbed insults. What they didn't see was that her emotions were simmering right below the surface. Aoife was afraid that if she *did* cry, those floodgates would burst open wide and never close again, so great and deep was her pain.

She was interrupted from her thoughts by one of the funeral home staff bringing in another bouquet of flowers.

"Where would you like this, Miss?"

"Over there to the right of that little table, please," she told him quietly and kindly. She wanted everything in place and "just so" by the time her grandmother arrived.

As if she intuited that her youngest granddaughter was thinking of her, Grainne sauntered through the door. Aoife met her halfway across the room, kissing her gently on the cheek.

"Hello, Granny."

"Where's Caitlin?" Grainne asked, not acknowledging Aoife's presence. "She should be here. People are going to begin to arrive soon. What are they going to think if she isn't here?" A note of alarm and slight hysteria crept into her grandmother's voice.

"I'll go and find her, Granny."

"Why weren't you keeping an eye on her? Why didn't you make sure she was nearby? The wake is about to begin and she needs to be here. People will expect to see her."

"Sorry, Granny," Aoife apologized, though she didn't know what for exactly. It wasn't like Caitlin was a small child who needed a minder all the time.

She's just grieving; she doesn't mean what she says.

Aoife knew it wasn't true no matter how many times she told it to herself. People used the thin guise of civility grief provided for them as a license to say exactly what they'd been meaning to say to others all along. And, because of the delicacy of the situation, no one could complain about the abuse without seeming to be selfish or impertinent.

Her grandmother didn't even bother to respond to her, instead walking in the opposite direction, fussing about the floral arrangement Aoife had just been dealing with. She left Grainne to her fussing and set off to find her eldest cousin. If she knew Caitlin, she'd be hiding somewhere where she thought no one would find her.

She silently cursed Caitlin for choosing this particular moment to have one of her little meltdowns. She supposed she should be grateful that her older cousin had chosen to hide herself away while she sorted herself out, but now she'd made herself Aoife's problem.

She felt a little stab of guilt at her unkindness. It wasn't like Caitlin didn't deserve it; she'd tormented her plenty when they were growing up and if karma had chosen to pay her back for her cruelty, Aoife wouldn't stand in its way, but it also wasn't like she couldn't empathize with how Caitlin was feeling right now. She knew all too well the weight of the grief that was crushing the both of them.

Just one more day, she reminded herself. Just one more day of compartmentalizing her feelings, of having to deal with her family and she could be on her own and deal with her grief in her own way. She could get through today and tomorrow. She had to.

She walked through the funeral home without any sort of plan, trying to think of a spot Caitlin would think she wouldn't find her in, as if they were playing a grown-up version of hide and seek. She passed by several empty viewing rooms, not finding her in any of them. At the end of the hallway was a small staff kitchen. Figuring that Caitlin might think Aoife wouldn't go in there, she opened the door and looked around. The place was empty.

"Where the feck are you?" she asked the empty room. She was just about to return to the hallway when she noticed that a door on the opposite end of the kitchen was slightly ajar, propped open with the handle of a broomstick.

As she opened the door, she felt the humidity of the recent rain on her face. It took a few seconds for her eyes to adjust to the blinding light of the sun that poked through the clouds. She was surprised to find not Caitlin, but Connor, sitting on the steps by the back door. Although his back was turned to her, his shoulders hunched and shaking slightly, she could tell it was him. Carefully arranging her black silk dress beneath her, she sat on the step beside him.

Neither of them spoke; she simply placed her hand in his, giving it a little reassuring squeeze and placed her head on his shoulder, offering what little comfort she could while he sobbed. The rough wool of his military uniform chafed beneath her cheek and it smelled of dampness but she didn't move, not caring about the minor discomfort.

A few minutes later, he laid his head briefly on hers in a grateful gesture of affection and lightly kissed her hair.

"I just miss him so much, you know?" he said.

"Yeah. Me too."

The lump that had been firmly stuck in her throat over the last few weeks threatened to make her cry again.

"Granny was looking for Caitlin inside, but I couldn't find her anywhere. Do you know where she is?" she finally asked, breaking the silence.

He lifted his head, tilting it to one side, giving the question some serious thought. "No, but if I had to guess, I'd say she was in the car park sneaking in a smoke before she gets caught."

"Well, let's go and see if we can find your sister, shall we?" She patted his knee gently to indicate they should get up.

Sure enough, as they rounded the corner of the building a moment later, she saw Caitlin leaning against the side of the building, smoking a cigarette just beside the car park, just as Connor said she would be.

"So, this is where you're hiding."

Caitlin looked up at the sound of Connor's voice. She made a move to put out her cigarette against the stone wall behind her, but seeing it was just them, she stopped and continued smoking. She'd always been a closet smoker, a habit she'd no doubt picked up from their grandfather.

"I'm not hiding." Her tone was defensive, but her shoulders were slumped in acknowledgement of the accusation. "I just couldn't deal with it, you know? I walked up the front steps and this wave of… panic just hit me."

Caitlin struggled to find the right words to describe how she was feeling.

"I just couldn't take the thought of all those people in there wanting to shake my hand and hug me, telling me all about Grandad, pretending they were as close to him as we were. They've no idea who he was to us. How can they stand there telling us what he was like?"

Her voice rose with every word, practically into the stratosphere by the end of it. She drew a long drag from her cigarette.

"I'm not feckin' going in there again. You can't make me."

She was right: once Caitlin was being obstinate, there was practically nothing that could budge her from whatever stance she'd taken.

Aoife looked to Connor for help; this was a task that was going to need both of them.

"I'm not here to make you go back inside."

"Don't lie to me, Aoife; I know Granny sent you out here to look for me."

"I didn't say Gran didn't send me to look for you; I just said I wasn't going to make you go back inside."

Connor, taking Aoife's cue, came and stood on the other side of her. "Can I bum a smoke from you?"

Caitlin looked at him with surprise but reached inside her Balenciaga and handed him one along with her lighter. In an unusually generous gesture, she handed one to Aoife as well. Normally she didn't smoke, but today she made an exception.

The three of them stood there, leaning against the funeral home wall, smoking their contraband cigarettes, watching the reflection of the clouds in the puddles as they drifted lazily by. It was the first time in as long as any of them could remember, that they'd ever spent time together, just the three of them. It felt strange to her, foreign.

"Do you ever wish we were a normal family?" Caitlin asked, to no one in particular.

"I don't think we'd know what 'normal' looked like if it came up and slapped us in the face." Aoife looked over at Caitlin and gave her a small smile. The three of them chuckled in agreement.

"I suppose we've Gran to thank for that."

"Don't say that, Connor," Caitlin admonished her twin. "She isn't all that bad."

"That's exactly what Grandad said to me the day before he died," Aoife revealed to her cousins, a lump forming in her throat again.

"Really?"

She nodded. "He said that she couldn't be all that bad because he'd fallen in love with her."

"Did he tell you anything else?" Her cousins looked at her with hope and expectation, clinging onto the last words of the grandfather they'd all adored.

"Just that he wouldn't have done anything in his life differently because everything he did gave him a family he loved and adored. Even if we are all feckin' out of our minds."

Caitlin and Connor both laughed at this.

"Alright, so those might not have been his exact words, but I'm sure the sentiment was the same."

The three of them continued to stand there, smoking their cigarettes, silence descending upon them once more.

"God, he would have hated all of this, wouldn't he? The people fussing and wailing over him, the spectacle of it all."

"Wakes and funerals are for the living, not for the dead." Aoife shifted against the wall, her heels beginning to make her feet ache.

"Is that why you gave in to Granny and had the wake here instead of *O'Reillys*?" Caitlin asked her. "I know that's what he wanted."

"Gran needs this. She needs the spectacle of it all, as you say. I did it for her. Granddad won't know the difference anyway."

"That's mighty generous of you," Caitlin said as Connor said, "That's awfully bleak, Aoife."

"Since when did you become religious?" she asked him, ignoring Caitlin's astonishment.

"I'm not saying I'm religious, but it's still a bit bleak to think there's nothing out there after we die, isn't it? I mean, don't you wonder where we go? Our spirits and all?"

"No," she lied.

Of *course* she thought about it; to her knowledge, everyone did at least once in their lives. She supposed, though, that someone in Connor's position had to contemplate the cold hand of Death and what came after more than the rest of them.

"Do you Connor?"

"What?"

"Think about death?"

He shifted uncomfortably against the wall, his sister's questions slightly unnerving him.

"Yeah of course."

"Are you ever afraid?"

Connor's shoulders stiffened as her questions became more probing.

"Loads of times."

"Are you ever afraid you won't come back home?" None of them liked to bring up his military service lest it jinx his chances of returning home safe and sound, as if they could prevent fate from intervening and sending him down a darker path just by avoiding the subject.

"Of course."

"So why do you do it then?"

None of them had asked him why he'd signed up for the military when he'd first joined. They'd known he'd had his reasons and they all just filled in the blanks with their own versions of what that could be: he was doing it to spite his Grainne, he was doing it out of some sense of duty to country, etc. It was easier that way; if they just believed what they needed to, it might make the times he was away facing death and danger a bit easier.

"Because I'm helping people, people just like us, ordinary people. People who are just trying to make the best of whatever shitty situation the world has thrown them into. There's so many people who need our help; you can't even imagine."

"I wouldn't exactly call us ordinary. I thought we'd previously established that," Aoife deflected with humour, her scapegoat when a conversation got too serious or real.

Sensing her reluctance to talk about it anymore, Connor shrugged. "Maybe you're right, Aoife. Life's for the living; not focusing on dying. That's how Grandda would want us to remember him: for how he lived, not for how he died."

The three of them mulled over his words, each of them pondering why the hell they were on this earth to begin with, and what the hell was going to happen to them after they died. How would history remember them?

"We have to go inside, don't we?" Caitlin asked, finally breaking the silence.

"Yeah," Connor confirmed for her. "But not right yet; not if you don't want to."

"No, let's get this over and done with. Then we can all just move on with our lives. Focus on the living." Finishing her cigarette, she stamped it out on the pavement with the toe of her Jimmy Choo heel. "Shall we?"

The three of them walked around the corner to the front of the building and entered into the fray. The humidity had seeped inside the building, enhancing the perfume of all the flowers around them. The place was full of mourners come to say their goodbyes to Paddy and to pass on their condolences to his family. Everyone spoke in hushed, reverent tones as she, Connor, and Caitlin gently made their way through the crowd and into the viewing room.

All That Compels the Heart

"Ah, there you are," Maureen greeted her daughter, niece, and nephew. "Your grandmother has been looking for all of you. I thought we may need to send for a search party."

Aoife noted her mother's tone was more one of annoyance than that of actual concern.

"No need. We're here now," she replied nonchalantly, taking her place in the line of immediate family members.

"Ah Caitlin, love, I was so worried about you," Grainne said, exasperated, coming over to hug her eldest granddaughter.

"I'm here Granny. No need to worry."

"Is that cigarette smoke I smell?"

"There were some smokers outside as we came in. It must be clinging to our clothes," Connor quickly jumped to his sister's defense.

"Come, come. Stand over here with me," her grandmother told her, taking her hand and forcing her over to the head of the line of mourners.

Although she wasn't sure exactly how, Aoife managed to get through the next few hours of handshaking and condolences, forcing a small smile onto her face so that those who were trying to offer her comfort would feel that their mission had been accomplished. When the last mourner had left, Connor came over to her.

"Well, I'm glad that's over with."

"Me too."

"Come on then, let me drive you home."

"Nah, you're alright. I can get a taxi."

"I know you can, but I'm not quite ready yet to be alone so you're going to let me do something nice for you."

She was too tired to argue with him; she'd have enough battles to fight before tomorrow was over.

"Alright then."

The sun was beginning to set over the horizon when they headed back out to the car park and got into Connor's Bentley. They sat in comfortable silence as they drove through Dublin's streets towards Aoife's building. When they finally pulled up in front of her flat, Connor took her hand in his and gave it a comforting squeeze.

"Thank you for earlier."

"I didn't do anything," she protested.

"You were there for me when I needed someone and that means a whole lot to me."

She smiled at him and put her hand on the door to get out when he spoke up again.

"And I want to thank you for helping with Caitlin back there. I know the two of you don't get along very well, but it was nice to see the two of you working together instead of trying to claw each other's eyes out."

"Yeah, well, she doesn't make it easy, but I didn't think the family could handle another death so close to Grandad's."

Connor chuckled. "Well, I know none of them will thank you for it, so let me be the one to say 'thank you' for all the work you've done with the wake and the funeral. You put in a lot of effort and I know that Grandad would be proud."

Her eyes began to water and her throat tightened.

"Thanks," she said, kissing him on the cheek.

"So, I'll pick you up tomorrow, o' eight hundred?" he asked her, changing the subject. "That's eight o'clock in the morning for you civilians."

"I know military time," she said with mock offense. "And that sounds grand."

"See you then," he smiled at her as she got out of the car and he sped off into the night.

☙❧

Sure enough, just like the trained soldier he was, Connor was waiting outside her building at eight o'clock sharp. He was dressed immaculately in his uniform, and she couldn't help but think how much his smile reminded her of their grandfather. Smiling slightly back at him, she got into the car, careful not to wrinkle the black velvet of her dress.

Both of them were solemn and quiet on the drive to the cathedral. It was a cloudy day again, still humid from the rain the day before. Thunder and lightning loomed on the edges of the clouds and it was clear a storm was going to break loose; it was only a matter of when.

All That Compels the Heart

The church was packed and everyone was using their programs to fan themselves in the close, damp air. Aoife and Connor took their places at the front of the church with the rest of their family. As they walked up the central aisle, she recognized some of the faces from the wake the day before, but most of them passed by her vision in a blur. Two faces that stood out from the crowd were Bex and Millie, sitting in the pew directly behind her. Bex was dressed in a simple little black dress like Aoife, while Millie was dressed in her typical gothic fashion, complete with black fascinator and veil. She smiled thinly at them, appreciative they had come to support her.

The funeral passed by her in a blur. Her body somehow managed to remember from the few times she'd been to church, when to stand and when to sit, when to sing, and what to say. Connor had given the eulogy, Caitlin having passed on the opportunity, saying she'd only end up crying the whole time. Grainne hadn't even bothered to ask Aoife if she'd like to do it. She hadn't been upset; much like Caitlin, she didn't think she'd have been able to say anything without breaking down and crying anyways. But she knew Connor would do their grandfather justice, give him the proper send-off he deserved.

When all the words had been spoken, and everything had finished, those assembled in the church went to the little graveyard behind the church. As they stepped outside, she noticed the clouds had become darker, the thunder and lightning coming closer. She could tell the priest and those assembled were anxious to have the burial over and done with before the rain broke.

With the coffin placed on its bier, the priest said his prayers quickly and made the sign of the cross, just as a loud crack of thunder broke close to them, making them all jump. The priest indicated to the pallbearers to begin lowering the coffin into the ground. With it lowered into its final resting place, each member of the family took a step forward, tossing the white lilies they held in their hands – Paddy's favourite – into the grave.

When it came time for her turn, Aoife stood there immobile. She could feel the eyes of her family on her, wishing she would just hurry up and finish it all before the rain broke. After a few long seconds, Connor stepped over to her side.

"Aoife?"

She looked up at him, only seemingly just realizing that he was there.

"Do you want some help?"

She stared at him blankly for a moment. He didn't look like Paddy, but there was something about him so familiar to her grandfather that it snapped her out of her dazed state. She had to remember her duty to her grandfather.

"No. I'm grand."

She cleared her throat and stepped forward, letting the white lily fall from her hand into the deep, cold grave. As it landed softly on top of the coffin, the clouds above her broke, the cold rain drenching her through.

Chapter Six

Frank McNally walked up the long, cobblestone pathway to the front door of the O'Reilly mansion. The paving stones were still wet from the earlier downpour, which had cleared up as suddenly as it had come. The puddles glistened from the sun as it peeked behind the parting clouds. He wished mightily that he could be down in *O'Reilly's* right now instead of here to read Paddy's will to his family. Paddy's man, Gerry, had arranged for the proper wake Grainne had denied her husband and Frank was missing out on it.

He was a small man, Frank, almost gaunt-looking despite the fact he was as robustly healthy as any man half his age. He was also a nervous man with an agitated disposition and, although he might only be in his early fifties, his colleagues often joked that they weren't sure he'd make it to his retirement, given that he looked as if he might keel over any day now. Seeing as how he now had to face Grainne O'Reilly, he wasn't entirely sure he *wouldn't* keel over from fright of the austere woman.

In his estimable experience, there were a few ways that these kinds of situations could go. The best outcome, of course, was that the recently deceased had discussed at great length exactly what it was they were putting in their will and all the beneficiaries of said will were pleased with the result. In all his years as a lawyer, Frank had rarely seen this happen. The more likely scenario was that at least some of the beneficiaries, or expected beneficiaries, did not get exactly what it was they'd been hoping for and feelings of resentment and anger could boil to the surface. In the latter situation… well, that did not bear thinking about. It would just be best for him to get this reading over with and get back out of the house alive and in one piece.

As he stood in front of the great black door at the front entrance of the house, he took out his handkerchief from his breast pocket and wiped at the sweat that was forming profusely on his forehead, dampening his thinning hair. There'd been few times in his life that he'd wished he'd gone on and become a policeman like his four older brothers and father before him – at least as a lawyer he wouldn't need to deal with bloodshed or having people try to shoot at him had been his thinking at the time – but Grainne O'Reilly was certainly making him question his career choice now.

Like most people who knew the O'Reillys, he'd never quite figured out what it was that kept the two of them married. Sure, Paddy was a fine man and a good friend, but the same couldn't exactly be said for his wife. If he was being honest, Grainne constantly made him feel like he was under a microscope. It was an uncomfortable, uneasy feeling that had never gone away in all the time he'd known her.

He hesitated before ringing the doorbell, making sure one last time that he had his briefcase with everything inside it. Squaring his thin shoulders, he took a deep breath and rang the doorbell.

It was a classic doorbell ring, he noticed. Not one of those chiming ones that played a particular song or theme. He liked those kinds of doorbells; there was something charming and quaint about them, but Grainne O'Reilly would never have such a thing; she'd think them tacky, and there was no room for tackiness in Grainne O'Reilly's home. Within seconds, Moore, the family butler, arrived and opened the door to admit him. He looked McNally up and down, like he was some sort of beggar sitting on the front stoop even though Frank had been to the many times in the decades he'd known Paddy and Grainne.

"Mr. Frank McNally to see Mrs. Grainne O'Reilly," he said, hoping he didn't sound too nervous.

"Right this way," Moore responded in his usual monotone, ushering him through the entrance and through the house to the library.

When they drew up in front of the closed, carved doors, Moore indicated he should let himself in and left McNally to his own devices. His briefcase nearly slipped out of his sweating palm, and he pulled out his damp kerchief to wipe his forehead again. It was a useless gesture he knew; once the nervousness set in, he wouldn't be able to stop sweating until whatever was agitating him was done. His hand slipped on the metal doorknob as he opened it, causing him to slightly stumble into the room instead of float in confidently, as he'd been striving for.

"Good… Good afternoon everyone," he greeted them, trying to clear his throat and sound official.

"Mr. McNally," Grainne greeted him formally, not rising from her place in the green leather armchair across the room. No one from the family rose to greet him, though he did notice that all but two of them seemed to be greedily eyeing his briefcase, like a pack of hyenas eyeing a fresh kill. He supposed they were as anxious for him to get this over and done with as he was, though most certainly for other reasons.

Not knowing where exactly he should sit, his eyes settled on Paddy's large, oak desk and decided it was as good a place as any. Setting the briefcase on the desk, he opened it, the metal clasps making a loud *click!* in the silent room. He took out a series of sealed envelopes and placed them on the edge of the desk for all to see. Each one was addressed to a member of the family, their names written clearly in Paddy O'Reilly's own hand. He kept back the larger of the envelopes, which contained the will itself. He'd thought about sitting in the large oak chair behind him, but Grainne's piercing gaze made him think otherwise.

"Shall we get started then?" she asked, although Frank knew it wasn't really a request.

"Y... yes," he stammered slightly. He cleared his throat again, tugging slightly at his tie, which continued to feel too tight around his neck.

"Well, there is not much about the estate of Mr. Patrick O'Reilly which hasn't been taken care of in this will. Mr. O'Reilly left everything in good, clear order." He smiled at them all reassuringly, but only continued to receive blank stares. Deciding to continue, he took the will out of its envelope and began reading aloud.

"I, Patrick James O'Reilly, presently of Dublin, Ireland, declare that this is my Last Will and Testament..."

ඡා

A deafening quiet filled the room, broken only by the sound of the logs burning in the fireplace.

"But that would mean that, eventually, Aoife and Connor will have a controlling interest in the company."

Caitlin's voice cut through the silence like a sharp knife. "Why would Grandad leave *you* a controlling interest in the company?" she asked accusingly of Aoife. "Connor, I understand, but *you*? You don't know the first thing about running *O'Reilly's*!"

Frank noticed that Paddy's youngest granddaughter didn't seem to know how to respond to the question, her face bewildered and confused. It had been a question he'd wondered himself. When he'd been helping Paddy write his will, he'd broken his one rule: not to ask the clients why they were leaving certain possessions to some family members and not to others. It was none of his business why his clients did what they did; it was simply his job to record it and make it legal. However, it had seemed too unusual a decision for Paddy to leave his beloved company to his youngest granddaughter who, for all intents and purposes, seemed not to have the slightest interest in running it.

"Frank," Paddy had smiled at him, "That's *exactly* why I'm leaving it to her. Aoife has no desire to make *O'Reilly's* into anything other than what I originally dreamed it would be: a family pub. Sure, my wife and daughters have done a wonderful job in turning it into a successful restaurant chain, but they haven't made it into a family pub, a safe space for those in the neighbourhood. Aoife knows how to fix that, and that's why I'm leaving it to her and Connor. They'll do right by it."

As if a bomb had exploded in the room, the place filled with noise, everyone talking – more like shouting – at each other all at once. While everyone around her hurled insults, Aoife remained immobile, quiet, as if she stood in the eye of the storm. This type of explosive behaviour was exactly what Frank had wanted to avoid, and he saw his opportunity to make his getaway before things worsened. Before he had the chance to leave, he was cornered by both Caitlin and Grainne, who looked like they had a bone to pick with him. Trying desperately to sidle himself towards the door he tried to calmly explain to them that he had no control over the will and its contents, that everything was legal and above board. Just as Caitlin was about to turn around and make some other snide remark at her cousin's expense, she asked, "Where's Aoife?"

Everyone in the room stopped for a moment and looked around them: she was nowhere to be found. Frank glanced at the desk and noticed that the envelope with her name on it had disappeared, along with its owner, in the fracas. He noticed that in its place was one of the agreements he'd drawn up. Aoife had to sign the agreement in order to receive her portion of the will. Sidling back towards the desk while the others were busy arguing about who should have been watching Aoife to make sure she didn't leave, he quietly picked up the signed document and placed it in his briefcase. Wanting to give the girl a head start before her family descended upon her like the angry mob they were, he cleared his throat and tried to speak as confidently above the fray as he could.

"If you could all just sign these agreements for me, I can just leave you all to the rest of your day."

No one listened to him.

"Moore!" Grainne roared.

Seemingly out of nowhere, her ever-faithful butler appeared at the library doors. No doubt he'd been standing there eavesdropping on the whole conversation.

"Yes ma'am."

"Did Aoife leave?"

"Yes ma'am. She left a few minutes ago and seemed to be in a bit of a hurry. I would have stopped her, but she was far too quick for me," he was quick to reassure his mistress lest anyone think that Aoife's escape was any fault of his.

"Would you like me to call Miss Aoife and have her return?"

"No Moore, that it will be all for now. We will deal with Miss Aoife another time. Now, Mr. McNally. Shall we conclude this business?"

McNally wilted under her direct gaze and gulped. His tie was feeling very tight around his throat again. Very tight indeed.

Chapter Seven

Aoife woke to the distant sound of sirens, a few blocks away. Her bedroom was dark, the air stale and close around her. She had no idea how many days she'd just been lying here in the dark with the curtains pulled across her window to block out any signs of the outside world. The days since her grandfather's funeral had been a haze of booze and half-sleep. She knew she should probably be worried about the state she was in, but she didn't have the capacity to care about anything right now. The only thing she cared about was staying asleep, because in the nothingness of sleep she could forget her grandfather had died, like it was all just an awful dream.

Those were the worst moments: when she would wake up realizing that the nightmare was a reality that just wouldn't stop. When she hit that level of consciousness, she'd shut her eyes tight against the tears welling up inside of her, willing herself back to sleep and into the inviting arms of depression.

But today was somehow different. She couldn't exactly explain what had changed; it wasn't like today was any different in how it began than any other day that week, but something about it felt different to her. When she was awoken by the sirens, she still felt the realization that the most important person in her life was gone and it was still every bit as painful as before. However, something inside of her would not let her go back into the haze of numbness. Maybe it was that the stale air finally chafed at her lungs or the sound of the sirens had been too loud in her ears, but something would not let her sleep anymore, urging her out of bed. Angrily, she listened to the voice telling her to get out of bed, all the while cursing it for its insistence.

She pulled back the duvet she'd been hiding under and swung her legs around to the edge of the bed. The action made her head swim with dizziness and she sat there for several minutes, gripping the edge of her bedside table, waiting for the feeling to pass. She knew she shouldn't be surprised; she hadn't eaten anything in days and now her body was starved of energy. A small part of her told her to give up then and there. This was further than she'd come in the last few days, so why should she push herself to do more when she could just sink back into the comfort of her bed? But it was the other voice in her head, the one that had insisted she get herself together and get up that pushed the other one down, telling it to run back and hide in the dark depths from which it had come.

Managing to get her feet under her, she stumbled her way to the bathroom. As she flicked on the switch, the light above her mirror blinded her, spots purple and green spots floating before her eyes.

"Jaysus, Mary, and Joseph!"

Blinking several times in a row, her eyes finally adjusted to the blinding light in the darkened gloom of her flat and she almost wished she hadn't bothered with the light. To say she looked like shit would have been an understatement: she looked downright awful.

She'd always been pale, but after being sequestered in her room for the last who-knew-how-many-days, it seemed she'd become almost translucent. Her face was gaunt and thin where once it had been fuller, her eyes dwarfed by the dark circles underneath them as big as inky thumbprints. Her skin had become dry and flaky. Her auburn hair was greasy, stringy, and dull. In a word, she was falling apart.

All That Compels the Heart

Deciding she was long overdue for a shower, she stripped out of her pyjamas placed them in her clothes bin, idly wondering if she should just burn them instead of clean them. She'd been wearing them for so long they could probably get up and walk away on their own.

She turned the water on full force, the steam quickly filling the room. She gasped as the scalding hot water touched her skin, forming a rosy red hue like a sunburn as it sluiced off the grime. She lathered shampoo and conditioner in her hair, washed it all out, and then repeated the same steps two more times until she was satisfied that her hair and scalp were somewhat resembling cleanliness again. A full twenty minutes later with her hot water running out, her skin had been rubbed raw, her hair had been scrubbed until every bit of grime disappeared. Beginning to feel more like a human being again, she towelled off and walked back into her bedroom. Her mobile was flashing.

Tapping the screen, she saw she had several missed messages. Not entirely sure if she wanted to listen to them, she dialled the number for her voicemail anyways and turned it on speaker phone so she could listen to them while she stripped and re-made her bed.

Beep!

"Hi Aoife, it's Bex. We just wanted to check in with you and see how you're doing. We know it's a tough time, but we just want you to know that we're here for you if you need us. Give us a call."

Beep!

"Hi Aoife, it's Connor. I have to head back to the barracks in a few days and I was wondering if you had time for a visit before I do? No one's seen or heard from you since the will was read, and I just want to make sure you're doing ok. Call me."

Beep!

"Hello Miss Aoife. This is Moore. I am calling on behalf of your grandmother. Mrs. O'Reilly would like very much to speak to you about what you would like done about these books and the other possessions Mr. O'Reilly left you. Please give her a call back at your earliest convenience."

Beep!

"Aoife, this is Maureen. Honestly dear, these histrionics are becoming ridiculous. No one has heard or seen from you in days and your grandmother is waiting on you to decide what you would like done with the things your grandfather left you. Give her a call back right away."

Beep!

"Hiya love, it's Millie. Bex and I are getting really worried about you. Connor called the other day and said he hasn't heard from you since your grandfather's funeral and that was ages ago. He's really worried about you and so are we. *Please* give one of us a call, at least to let us know you're still alive. We love you honey, and we just want to make sure you're alright."

Beep!

"Hi, it's Danny. Bex called me. Anyways, she was looking for you, saying she was worried about you. I'm not sure why she called me about it, but could you just give her a call so she and Millie will stop texting me, please?"

Beep!

"Hi, it's Bex again. We're *really* worried about you. Millie says she's giving you an ultimatum and you know she's being serious. She says that either you give one of us a call back to let us know you're still alive, or we're coming over to your place tomorrow afternoon and dragging you out of bed. We care about you. Just please call us."

"Tell her I'm serious about coming over there!" she heard Millie shout in the background before the message ended.

"End of messages. To save your messages please press…"

She smiled to herself at Millie's threats as she picked up the phone and deleted the messages. She glanced at the time and noticed that it was eleven o'clock in the morning. Millie and Bex's latest message had been from the day before.

"Shit!"

Her flat was in no shape for company, especially for whatever intervention Millie had planned for her. She dialled Millie's number quickly but it went straight to voicemail.

"Hi Millie, it's me. Sorry to worry you and Bex; I just needed some time on my own. Anyways, this is me letting you know I'm alive and there's no need to come over. I'm fine. I promise. Love you!"

She hoped Millie would hear it in time to put the kibosh to whatever intervention she'd planned to get Aoife out of her depression. But just in case, she thought, she'd better clean the place up.

Feeling like the air was going to close in around her, she opened up all of the windows in both the kitchen and the sitting room, letting the breeze sweep in some fresh air. Half an hour later, everything in the flat had been cleaned, dusted and wiped down. As she put the last of the cleaning cloths in the bin, she noticed the purse she'd taken with her to the reading of her grandfather's will sitting on her kitchen counter, the letter he'd written her sticking out of it. She didn't know if she would ever be ready to read it, but she supposed today would have to be the day.

You've come this far already. Might as well get everything over and done with.

With trembling hands, she carefully opened the envelope.

It wasn't a long letter, no more than a couple of pages. She felt the tears beginning to well up in her eyes at seeing her grandfather's writing, a familiar, cheerful sight for her sore eyes. Wiping away the tears, she began to read:

Dear Aoife,

> *Let me just say that I am so proud of you, love. You've grown into a wonderful young woman, and I love you so much. I hate being so melodramatic as to begin this letter with the statement "If you are reading this letter then I am no longer for this world," but there it is. I am gone, and you my sweet girl, are hopefully alive and thriving. However, if I know you (and I do pride myself on knowing you quite well) your first instinct was to go and hide away from the world for as long as you could.*

"You *do* know me too well, Grandad," she spoke to the empty room around her.

> *While I understand this instinct, let me just say that I hope you don't do this. You are such a wonderful young woman, with so*

much to offer that it would be a shame for you to hide away out of grief. I know you grieve for me dearly, but I'm gone now and nothing is going to bring me back. I've lived a long and good life. I'm content and at peace with how my life turned out, so don't mourn for whatever few years you feel I was robbed of. I don't feel as if Death has cheated me of anything.

Once the shock has worn off, I'm sure you'll have some questions or, rather, one question: why did I leave you so many shares in O'Reilly's? Frank McNally asked me that very same question when I was writing up the will, and I'm going to tell you the same thing I told him: you are the one person in this family who knows best how I want the business to run.

Oh, your grandmother, aunt, mother, and Caitlin have done a wonderful job bringing O'Reilly's to the public around the world, but you and I both know it was never about making the company a global success for me. That was always their dream.

I want you to know that I will understand if the pub is not your dream. While I'd like to hope one of my grandchildren will carry on my legacy, I understand that it was my dream, and you need to go and find your own. I will be at peace with whatever decision you make, my love.

Now then, dry your eyes (yes, I know you've finally allowed yourself to cry now).

She smiled as she wiped at the tears that fell over her cheeks, acknowledging her grandfather's words.

The time for tears is over. It is time for you to go out and find your way in this world.

If you're looking for a little inspiration to get you started, I recommend visiting a little place called Glendalough. I know you've heard of it before, but I don't think I've ever taken you there. It's a dear place for me; it's the last place my family and I went to before my father passed. He had a love for the place and wanted me to see it, and now I want to share it with you. I hope it helps you find the path you're meant to take.

I wish you all the best in the world, love. Promise me you will make the best of this world, because to my knowledge, you only get one try at it.

Love always,

Grandad

P.S. – If I found out that we do in fact get one more shot at life than just this once, I'll be sure to come back and let you know.

And suddenly, seeing her grandfather's words on the paper before her, Aoife broke down and sobbed on the floor of her kitchen, letting all of the grief she'd been bottling up for so long finally flow out of her.

Chapter Eight

As the city started slowly fading in her rear-view mirror, Aoife began to feel more and more relaxed. It was a gorgeous day to drive in the country with no itinerary and no agenda. She wasn't sure where she was headed but she felt she just needed to get out of the confines of her flat.

Heading down the M11 towards Wicklow, admiring the coastal views of the Irish Sea, she came upon a sign for the exit for Glendalough. She remembered her grandfather's letter. Signalling for the exit, she headed in the direction of the monastic ruins.

She'd heard of Glendalough before, of course. She remembered the place had something to do with St. Kevin, something about birds and hermits, but that was about it. Following the signs through the wooded landscape, and soon reached the car park for the Visitor Centre. She decided to skip the centre itself; she was sure it had a lovely display, but she was more interested now in seeing the place up close.

She passed through The Gateway, watching her steps on the paving stones that had been worn smooth from thousands of visitors to the site over the last fifteen hundred years. The ruins of various buildings stood just to the front and left of her, but it was to the right that she decided to walk, drawn by the sight of a large tower. The Round Tower was visible from all around the site, drawing the eye to it like a beacon on a dark night. Surrounding its base were dozens of gravestones, all weather-beaten and aged by wind and rain and time. Some had intricate Celtic crosses; some were mere rock headstones with barely legible names carved into them. She felt a sadness for the people buried here whose names would soon be worn smooth from the stone, their names erased forever. There was no one left from their time to remember them, nothing left of them other than their bones. She wondered in that moment who would remember her grandfather now that he was gone? Sure there was herself and her immediate family, but what about all the future generations who'd never know what a wonderful man he'd been? At what point in time would he just become a name in the family bible, a distant memory with no personal recollection?

The thought made her very sad. Quietly pulling herself together, she continued down the path towards the next building on the site, a little stone church enclosed with a low, stone wall with a perfect view of the Lower Lake. The Wicklow Mountains rose on either side of her peripheral view, a landscape that had withstood the years of weather and human activity. A light breeze picked up from the lake and brushed against her skin, cool to the touch. Standing in this sacred place she felt a peace and calm settling over her, a feeling she hadn't had in quite some time. It didn't matter that she was stuck in a moment right now; the feeling would pass, and she'd be able to move on. Like the hills surrounding her, she would endure.

She moved through the rest of the site, the feeling of contented aimlessness taking her over again. Not really sure what she wanted to do, but knowing she wasn't ready to go back to Dublin just yet, she got back into her convertible and headed out of the car park. The fresh air had done her wonders, but it had also made her suddenly realize she'd not eaten in quite some time. Remembering that she'd passed a sign for a village not too far from here on her way down, she turned back in its direction.

The road before her rose with the hills, offering views of a village below. The area was heavily wooded, the tree-line giving way slowly to the occasional cottage or field. It was a rugged sort of place – unlike the usual pastoral scenes one was used to seeing in films – but still looked almost too beautiful to be real, as if it were a painting.

She'd only gone a few minutes down the road, when she came upon a sign with an arrow that read, simply: "For Sale." Not sure why she'd done it exactly, she turned down its narrow, stony lane barely big enough for her convertible to fit down. The left side was bordered by a low, stone wall, as long as the lane itself, overgrown with vines and low-lying shrubs, while the right side had a wooden fence separating the lane from the sheep pasture beside it. After a slight bend in the lane towards the left, the shrubs thinned out and the lane opened into a wider gravel area for parking. On the other side of the parking area the lane continued, bending and twisting down towards the village, a little stone church being the only other structure along the path. On her left, was an old, three-storey stone house with another sign on the front reading "For Sale."

Putting the car in park, Aoife got out and stood before the house. The place was quiet, empty, except for the soft braying of the distant sheep and cattle in the pasture across the lane. It was a bit rundown, but still beautiful, like an unpolished stone. It looked mid-seventeenth or eighteenth century, made from a reddish-brown stone with a pale grey stone roof. On the front of the house, there were four large windows complete with window boxes on the ground floor, two on either side of a white door whose paint was badly peeling. There were five large windows on the second floor, all in white frames. The third floor was more of a half-story, shortened by the peak of the roof. There were three windows on this floor, each of them jutting out from the roof in little peaks.

She walked up to the door, but when she tried to open it, she found it locked. Undeterred, Aoife walked over to the nearest window and peered in. She saw a large front room

All That Compels the Heart

with wooden floors, and through the doorway on the left, she could just see a bit of the main staircase with its carved banister. The room was spacious and open, with lots of light from the windows at the front and side of the house. The paint looked in need of a fresh coat, but otherwise, it was a grand room. It would make a great drawing room for entertaining. Another door off the end of the room seemed to lead to the kitchen. Deciding to walk around the grounds, she tried to see what she could of the house from the outside. On right side of the house, she saw a glassed-in enclosure. It looked like it had once been a solarium, but now it was just an empty space with the remnants of a few dead plants. Aoife found it too was locked when she tried to open the door, so she decided to move on.

The house was very large: big enough for a family of five or more she guessed. As she continued down the path, she noticed a carriage house, made from the same stone as the house. Someone had been using it for storage once for she saw old furniture stacked inside it. Aoife found herself thinking about how it would make a nice garage once she took out the furniture and made some room.

The thought surprised her. She hadn't realized she'd been walking around the house with the intent to buy it, but that's exactly what she'd been doing this whole time: sizing it up, thinking about what she'd have to do in order to spruce the place up. There was something calming about making such a profound decision.

"Well if I'm going to buy the place, I might as well see the rest of it," Aoife said to herself.

Continuing towards the back of the house, her breath was taken away by the beauty of the sight before her eyes. The landscaped lawn before her sloped gently towards the village nestled between the mountains. The only thing breaking the sea of green was the gravel drive running through it towards a small parish church off to the right-hand side, and then onwards towards the village. It looked so tiny and quaint, like a pearl in a great rolling green ocean of trees and hills. Beyond the village was an astounding view of the Upper and Lower Lakes near Glendalough. If she hadn't already been sold on the idea of getting the house, this view alone made her sure. She felt she could sit here all day, could see herself sitting here every morning on the porch, looking at this view while she sipped her tea in the morning.

Continuing her tour through the grounds, she came upon a high stone wall with a metal gate for an entrance. While the gate was locked, she could see through the bars that inside was what used to be a private garden. Heavy vines covered all the walls, giving the place a rustic feel and reminded her of *The Secret Garden*, one of her favourite novels. Inside were the remains of flowerbeds, overgrown now with weeds, interspersed with birdbaths and replica Roman statues. A bay window jutted out from the side of the house on the ground floor, looking out from what she presumed to be a sitting room.

Satisfied with what she'd seen of the place, she walked back around the way she'd come, down the front path and through the little gate to her parked car. She felt such a sense of home looking at the house, something she'd so rarely felt before. It made her all the more determined to buy the place. There'd been no number on the "For Sale" sign, so she decided to go into the village and see if she could find out more about it.

It was a small place; only a couple of hundred people at the very most. On the far side of the village, a stone bridge spanned the little creek that formed a natural border around Ballyclara. At its heart was a little square with a large, stone cross and a fountain, relics from another time. Across the square was a post office and corner store, a bakery owned by the O'Sullivan family, a chip shop, Drummond & Drummond – which appeared to be some sort of solicitor's office – and Byrne's hardware shop. On the opposite side of the square from the post office, there was a pub, the name *O'Leary's* emblazoned in gold lettering on a black background.

It was a rustic place, a two-storey, red-brick building, mid-eighteenth century. It was well-kept; the paint job around the front door and the framed windows looked fresh, as if painted in just the last year or so. A window box hung below each one on the front of the building, filled with brightly coloured flowers, giving the place a quintessential homey feel, picture perfect, as if it could be featured on the front of a magazine. A small, paved car park stood to the side of the building, mostly empty. She pulled the convertible into spot near the entrance and headed inside.

The inside was dark, especially in contrast to the bright sunshine outside, and it took a moment for her eyes to adjust. She could see that, like the car park, the pub wasn't especially full. A couple of tourists sat in one corner, their rucksacks beside them, but everyone else in the pub looked to be locals: a group of middle-aged women sat at a table gossiping and sipping their tea while an equal number of middle-aged men – most likely their husbands – sat at the bar, drinking their pints. Everyone, except for the tourists, looked up at her as she stepped inside. Feeling slightly awkward, she quietly chose a booth along the side wall, close to the bar.

"Hello!"

The friendly bartender came over to her after she'd settled herself and placed a menu and cutlery in front of her. "The name's Brendan. Brendan McCaffrey. Can I get ye anything to start?"

He was a youngish man, early thirties, of medium height and build. He kept his light brown hair short and his eyes – almost the same shade as his hair – were kind, with faint laugh lines surrounding them. His nose was slightly crooked and looked like it had been broken once, possibly twice, but it didn't diminish his handsomeness.

"I'll have a Coke, please," she smiled at him, and then began examining the menu.

"And anything to eat, Miss?"

"Ah yes. I'll have the seafood chowder to start, the chicken sandwich and fries, and a Caesar salad, please. Also, can I have a slice of apple pie for dessert?"

"No problem at all. I'll be right out with ye're order, Miss."

"Aoife," she supplied her name, though she wasn't sure why. She supposed his affability wearing off on her.

"Aoife," he repeated her name. "You're not from these parts are you, Aoife? I think I'd have recognized ye, if you were."

"No, I'm not. Just down here from Dublin for a bit of a visit to the ruins."

"Ah, I see then."

He headed back towards the kitchen and disappeared behind its swinging doors. She was pleased to see him return only a moment or two later with her chowder and her drink, and tucked into both quickly, nodding her thanks to him. He returned a few minutes later with the rest of her food. Picking up her bowl, he was clearly surprised to see the chowder completely devoured and the bowl practically licked clean.

"Can I get you anything else, love?" he asked, looking her up and down, clearly wondering where she'd put anything else.

"Actually, yes, there is. I was wondering if you knew anything about the house that's for sale? The one on top of the hill looking down on the village?"

"Ye mean the Old Rectory? Aldridge Manor?" he asked, clearly curious why she was asking about it, but too polite for the moment to ask her why.

"I suppose," she replied uncertainly. "I didn't see a sign on the place, giving it a name."

"It sounds like ye're talking about the Old Rectory. Sure, ye'll be wantin' to talk to Dermot and Sinead Flanagan then. They looked after the place for the old parish priest, God rest his soul." Brendan genuflected out of respect for the passing of the old man. "Father Patrick said he didn't want the place when he came here; said it was too grand for him, so the Church has been trying to sell it ever since. But so far we've not had many interested in it."

Aoife's face must have looked a bit drawn for he rushed to allay any fears.

"That's not to say the place is that badly off. It's grand, really. If you're thinkin' o' puttin' in an offer on the place, Dermot and Sinead are the ones to talk to."

"Great. And where can I find them?" she asked him.

"Well, they'd be just up the road, back towards the Old Rectory. They've a little cottage there down the lane from it. If ye're going from this direction, it would be the last one on the right. If they're not in, ye could always try their son's place, Michael Flanagan. Or better yet, ye could wait here for him. He'll be on shift in a bit."

"Thanks," she said to him, grateful for the information.

"I can leave a message with him if ye'd like," Brendan told her. "Have you a number you can be reached at?"

"Yeah, sure," she told him, taking out one of the business cards Millie had made for her online as part of a project she'd had to do for a design class. He took the card from her, reading it over.

"So, you're a writer, then?"

"Well, trying to be," she admitted.

"Anything I might've read? Or do you work for one of those fancy magazines or newspapers in the city?"

"I was working for a place called Arbour Hill Publishing in Dublin but I'm taking a wee break from it now to focus on my own work."

"Well, best of luck with that, and hopefully I'll get the chance to read something of yours one day."

She could see he was sincere.

"And cheers for the card. If you need anything else, just give us a holler."

She smiled at his retreating form and tucked into her meal. It was absolutely delicious, the best in pub food she'd had in a very long time. It was definitely something to rival even Gerry's cooking, which was saying something. Once every crumb had been eaten, she sat back, her stomach groaning at having so much food in it after so many days of being starved. She knew she'd end up regretting it later, but right now she didn't particularly care.

As she sat there digesting, she looked up at the sound of the little bell above the front door ringing as a young man entered. She barely got a look at him, only a flurry of dark hair and a coat being taken off and flung behind the bar as he strode quickly towards it. She could tell he was tall, a good head or so taller than Brendan, and about the same age. She noticed how the friendly bartender looked up and smiled, offering a half-wave at the other man who didn't return the welcoming gesture.

"Hello Michael, and how's yourself?" one of the men sat at the bar asked him.

"Grand," Michael responded, not bothering to ask the other man how he was.

As he settled himself behind the bar, Brendan came over to him, holding out her business card and nodding in her direction as he quietly relayed her interest in the house. Or, that's what it looked like anyways as she tried to watch what was happening without appearing to stare.

She noticed how Michael looked at the card like it was something offensive and he wouldn't take it from Brendan, who continued to hold it out to him.

"And what's this?" he asked his friend, loud enough for her to hear clearly from across the room.

"It's from herself over there. She's interested in maybe buying the Old Rectory and wanted to know who she should be talkin' to about it," Brendan replied in a quieter tone.

"So why are you tellin' me then? If she's interested in it, then she should talk to Andrew Drummond about it."

"Well, I figured, seeing as how your parents have looked after the place, that you or them could talk to her about it. You all know more about the place than most everyone in Ballyclara."

Michael didn't seem pleased at the idea.

"Why don't you just go and talk to her, alright? Find out how serious she is about buying it? Maybe she'll be like the others you managed to scare away from the place."

The two of them looked up at her at that moment and she dropped her head, pretending to be very interested in her mobile. She was studiously trying not to look like she was one bit interested in one what they were saying about her that she was genuinely startled when Brendan appeared beside her a moment later.

"Will that be all then, Aoife? Ye've certainly got a good appetite on ye, that's for sure."

She might have been offended by his cheekiness if it weren't for his grin. She couldn't help but think how his warmth and friendliness contrasted sharply with that of his colleague.

"That'll be all, thank you, Brendan. It was quite lovely, and definitely one of the best meals I've had in quite some time. You certainly know how to cook."

"Ah, 'twas nothing. Besides, I'm not the real cook of the place; that'd be my wife, Molly."

All That Compels the Heart

"How long have you been married?"

"Going on nine years now. Soon to be ten."

"Well, tell your Molly that she has my compliments. Have the two of you been running this place for long?"

"About five years now. Michael, Molly, and I bought it when the previous owner died and we've been running it ever since."

"So Michael's your business partner, then?" she asked, wondering exactly how someone so open and friendly could work with someone who seemed as cantankerous as Michael.

"And best mate."

"You're still best friends after running a pub together? That's some friendship," Aoife told him, incredulous.

"Well, that's not to say it doesn't have its ups and downs, but at the end of the day, there's no two people in this world I'd rather be working with than me wife and best friend."

He looked back towards the door leading to the pub's kitchen where Michael had retreated to after their discussion.

"Well, you two have done a fantastic job with the place." She figured he deserved a compliment after having to put up with Michael for the rest of the day, best friend or not.

"I should get that bill for ye so you can be on your way. I'm sure you're in a hurry to get back to the city."

"Oh, no rush on the bill. I'm not in a hurry."

He shrugged and headed back to the till all the same.

She went back to checking her messages on her phone. She noticed a message had just come in from Danny; he would be going straight from his conference in London to another one in Munich. She was just texting back to him to wish him a safe flight when a deep, serious voice mumbled beside her, "I believe this is for you."

"Thank you, Bre…" she began to say, only just noticing the voice who'd spoken had not been Brendan's. "Oh, I'm sorry. I thought you were someone else."

"Clearly."

Finally able to get a good look at him, she saw that Michael was a handsome man, early thirties like Brendan, with dark, earthy-brown hair, hanging about his face in short layers. Most of his hair was slicked back with product, but some of the shorter strands fell into his eyes and he pushed them out of the way of his clear, midnight blue eyes. Unlike Brendan, his face did not contain a hint of a smile for her; in fact, his features seemed to be drawn down into a look of slight scorn.

He had strong features: his nose was long and wide, but not obtrusive on his face. His cheekbones were high, but not sharp, and his jaw was strong, shadowed with afternoon stubble. If she wasn't so distracted by the look of disdain on his face, she may have found him attractive.

"I'm sorry. It seems we've got off on the wrong foot. My name is Aoife O'Reilly."

He looked down at her outstretched hand but didn't take it.

"Michael Flanagan," he replied curtly. Combined with his behaviour from before, she was starting to get the distinct impression that Michael was not fond of her. She wasn't exactly sure why; she hadn't even met him until just now.

God, I hope his parents are friendlier than their son.

"Well, Michael, it's nice to meet you, and I do appreciate you bringing me my cheque. If you wouldn't mind, I'll just go and settle that now for you and be on my way."

She nodded to the register, indicating she'd like him to move of her way so she could get out. He lingered there in front of her for a second before moving aside and holding out a hand to her in a gallant gesture. She slid out of the booth, grabbed her purse and walked over to the till.

"Got everything ye need then, Aoife?" Brendan asked her, a smile still on his face, though it faded slightly as he looked over and saw Michael clearing her plates away.

"Yes, thank you, Brendan." She handed over cash to pay her bill, making sure a generous tip for his kindness was included. "You mentioned earlier that the Flanagans lived just up the road, back towards the Old Rectory, I think you called it?"

"Yes, last cottage on the right." His smile was smug and she couldn't help but have the feeling this was more for Michael's benefit than her own.

"Great, thanks. See you!"

She wanted out of there as quickly as possible, away from Michael whose uncomfortably sharp stare followed her out.

Chapter Nine

"What the hell was that?"

Brendan looked expectantly at Michael, waiting for an answer.

"What?"

He threw his hands up exasperated. He and Michael had been best friends for as long as either of them could remember but there were some days when Brendan mightily wanted to just clout his friend on the head. The two of them had met on their first day of school when they were sat next to each other and had been fast friends ever since. They'd gone through all their schooling together, got houses that were no more than five minutes' drive from one another – which wasn't exactly a difficult thing to accomplish in a place as small as Ballyclara; they'd even gone into business together after secondary school and started up their own contracting business. And when Brendan had decided to marry the love of his life, his dear Molly, Michael had been there by his side. And when old Mr. O'Leary had passed and left his wife the pub, the two of them had decided to buy this place from her and turn it into another one of their business enterprises.

They'd done everything together, those two; separable only by death or calamity. And yet, there was no doubt in Brendan's mind that Michael was the most stubborn, pig-headed person in the whole village.

"What?!" he repeated Michael's question right back at him. "She was interested in buying the Old Rectory. She's gone up to your parents now to speak to them about it. I thought it might be nice if she was able to speak to someone friendly who knew the place well and could give her a good insight as to the state of it."

Clearly, he'd been barking up the wrong tree there.

Michael didn't respond, just stood there polishing a glass he'd picked up which really didn't need it. Brendan snatched it from him.

"Give me that," he grumbled. "Look, I know ye had your heart set on buying the place yourself, Michael, but the price is too dear for the likes of you or me. Even if we combined our two incomes, we still couldn't afford it. Isn't it better it goes to someone who'll have the money to look after the place?"

"'Tis true, Michael," one of the patrons sitting closest to them agreed.

"Mick, you stay out o' this," Michael warned, his face serious. Poor Mick, well into his third Guinness drank silently, doing as ordered.

"Ye can't just do that," Brendan told him, becoming even more exasperated with him.

"What?" Michael asked him again, oblivious to what he'd done, or choosing to be, more like.

"Bullying others because the truth is inconvenient for you. You and I both know that the Old Rectory needs to be sold. The place will start fallin' in on itself if someone doesn't take care of it. Besides, could be a tidy profit in it in for your parents, or even us, if things go well."

"And how do ye figure that?" Michael asked, and Brendan could see him mentally going through the list of bills that were due for both him and his parents.

Despite working two jobs, Michael wasn't exactly rolling in cash. While the pub business was steady during the tourist season, it slowed down during the winter months. And the village was only so big; even though they'd expanded their reach to a few of the other villages closest to them, their contracting business was barely staying afloat.

"Well, your parents have been looking after the place their whole lives, right? Makes sense someone like Aoife would want to hire on some people who know the house well and who'd know how to take care of it for her, especially if she's going to be travelling back and forth between here and Dublin. And, what's more, that place is in need of a good repair. If your parents maybe put in a good word for us and you keep a civil tongue in your head, we could be looking at some contracting work to get us through autumn."

He could see Michael giving the idea some thought.

"And sure with your mother only having Father Patrick's place to mind, and it being only the small place, it's not like they're exactly making a whole lot, and them so close to retirement age."

"I don't need you to remind me of my parents' financials, and I'd appreciate you keeping that information to yourself."

It was a sore point for Michael, he knew, not in a position to let his parents retire and enjoy themselves. He knew Michael would love nothing more than to be well-off enough to provide for his family, but it just wasn't in the cards right now.

"I just hate seeing the place go to some Dubliner who's just going to turn it into a weekend getaway for her and her rich friends."

"Ye don't know what she's got planned for the place," Brendan reminded him. He knew it wasn't what Aoife planned to do with the house that bothered Michael so much as the fact that *he* wouldn't have it.

"Besides, it's all talk at this point. And you don't know that she's rich."

"If she can afford to drive a car like the one she had in the car park, and she can afford to buy Aldridge Manor; she's rich."

Brendan knew he was right.

"Just promise me one thing. If she does come through and buys the place, please try and make her feel welcome here."

"No promises."

At least he's being honest, Brendan supposed as he rubbed his hand over his face out of frustration.

༄

"Hello?" Aoife called out from the gate.

She couldn't see anyone in the front of the cottage, so she unlatched the white picket gate, careful to re-latch it after she was through. She walked around to the side of the cottage, her boots crunching on the stone path. Wondering if maybe she'd heard Brendan wrong and gotten the wrong place, or if maybe the Flanagans were out, she was relieved when she rounded the corner and saw a man in his late sixties/early seventies hunched over a small, postage stamp-sized garden, pulling out weeds.

"Hello!" she called out in greeting again.

The man looked up from his task, a look of bewilderment passing over his face. She knew him immediately for Michael's father; he had the same exact looks as his son: the same clear, midnight blue eyes, the wavy hair hanging about his face; the same long, wide nose and square jaw. Unlike his son, his hair had now turned a brilliant snowy white. Some of his fringe fell into his eyes and he pushed it back out of his face in the same manner as she'd seen Michael do back at the pub. Also, unlike his son, Dermot Flanagan's face was open, kind; not filled with scorn. He looked Aoife up and down, and she noticed that he looked like he was thinking that he should know her but couldn't quite place who she was.

"Are you Mr. Flanagan?"

"Aye, that's me."

He took the weeds he'd been pulling and tossed them onto the small pile at the edge of the garden.

"My name is Aoife O'Reilly. I was just passing through the village when I noticed the house that was for sale. Brendan McCaffrey, back at the pub, told me I should speak to you and your wife if I was thinking of purchasing it."

All That Compels the Heart

"The Old Rectory, ye say?" Dermot stopped what he was doing and came over to the wooden fence that separated the garden from the rest of the yard.

"Yes."

"Well then. Ye better come inside for a cup o' tea," Dermot told her with a smile and gestured with his arm for her to follow him inside.

The inside of the two-storey cottage was cramped. That was the best way she could describe it; every nook and cranny was filled with knick-knacks and homemade gifts. The front door opened directly into the small sitting room. Off to her right was the kitchen, where a middle-aged woman about Dermot's age stood, preparing some dinner.

"Sinead. We have company," he called around the corner to his wife.

"Oh really? Who is it, dear?"

"Aoife O'Reilly, Mrs. Flanagan," she called over from the entrance and Sinead came out from the kitchen, wiping her hands on a tea towel.

"Oh hello, love," Sinead greeted her politely and extended a clean hand towards her.

"Nice to meet you, Mrs. Flanagan."

"Ach, Mrs. Flanagan was my mother-in-law. Please, call me Sinead."

"Sinead," Aoife repeated with a smile as she gave the older woman's hand a final shake and let go.

"As I was telling your husband, I was driving through the village and noticed that there's a house for sale just up the road. Brendan McCaffrey down at the pub said I should speak with you and your husband if I'm interested in buying the place."

"And are you? Interested in buying the place, I mean?" Sinead looked her up and down, sizing up her interest in the place.

"Yes, I am. Very much so."

"Well, please do sit down. I'll get us some tea," Sinead clapped her hands together, a broad smile on her face. There was very little of her in her son, from what Aoife could tell. The slight slant of the eyes, the faint dimples in their cheeks, but otherwise, it was quite clear whose son Michael was.

"Oh, I don't want to trouble you…"

She was still feeling over-full from her large lunch earlier, and didn't know where she'd find the room to put anything more.

"Oh it's no trouble at all," Sinead reassured her. "Now, Dermot go and set the two of ye down at the table and I'll bring the tea over. Milk or sugar?" she asked Aoife.

"Neither for me, please."

"Alright then. Go and sit yourself down," she encouraged her again.

Dermot held his hand, gesturing for her to enter the sitting room and sit where she liked. She chose a rocker by the small fireplace, looking up at the photos arranged on its mantle. There was a lovely older, black and white photo of whom she supposed were Sinead and Dermot on their wedding day. There were some coloured photographs from when she presumed Michael was a child, and there was a girl in some of them as well. More recent photographs showed a younger woman with a child, and some showed what looked like the whole family together. Dermot must have caught her staring at the photos for he stood up and took one of the more recent photos down. It showed the five of them on a rocky beach somewhere.

"This is our family," he told her proudly, handing her the photo. "This is our daughter, Mara, and her little boy, Rory. He's our pride and joy."

He pointed proudly to the photo where a young boy of about nine or ten sat on a large rock in front of his uncle, pulling a silly face. "And this is our son, Michael."

"Ah yes. I met him earlier, at the pub." Aoife did her best to keep her voice neutral. She was thankfully saved from saying more about him by the arrival of Sinead with the tray of tea.

"Here we go," she said, placing the tray on the little coffee table before Aoife, and poured her a cup. Aoife held the small, bone china teacup in her hands, examining its beautiful blue and white floral pattern, enjoying the warmth it radiated into her hands.

"So, Aoife, tell us a bit about yourself. May I call you Aoife?"

"Oh yes. Please do."

"Where are ye from? I take it, then, that you're not from around here?"

The questions were fired at her rapidly, but only out of curiosity. The intense curiosity reminded her of what everyone in the city made fun of the country villages for; the intense scrutiny one faced from everyone knowing your business from the moment you got up in the morning, until you went to bed at night.

"Well, I was born in Dublin, but I've sort of lived all over. I found myself, very recently, in a position to take some time off from the publishing house I was working at in the city and focus on my own work. I was thinking that some time down in the country might be a good place to start working on my own writing."

"You're a writer ye say? Well now, that sounds very interesting!" While Sinead's voice did clearly show an interest in her work, the look she gave Aoife made it clear she was wondering how she was going to afford a place like Aldridge Manor on a writer's wage.

"Yes. Well, I'm trying to be one. My grandfather recently passed away, leaving me some money, and I decided to take some time to myself and pursue my dreams."

Her voice trembled at the mention of her grandfather, and she carefully placed the small teacup back on its saucer, lest she drop it.

"Oh, love. I'm sorry to hear that."

Sinead's voice was kind and sincere. Aoife cleared her throat and smiled, fighting back the tears at the corners of her eyes.

"Well, there, that's me."

She wasn't sure what else to tell them about her. She didn't really want to get into too much about who her family was. After all, she was coming down here to escape all that.

Seemingly satisfied that Aoife had the money to back up her interest in the house, Sinead decided to change the subject back to the matter at hand.

"So, ye say ye were having a look around the Old Rectory, did ye?"

"Yes. I saw the sign from the road when I was driving through, and I stopped by to have a look at the place. I hope you don't mind," she said quickly, it beginning to dawn on her that she should've asked permission before touring the grounds.

"Ach, it's alright. There's not much to see though from the outside. We should go up and let you see the inside before you make the final decision."

"That's alright. I'm quite sure I want to buy it."

Both Sinead and Dermot looked a little surprised at this. After all, who buys a house without looking at the place thoroughly?

Apparently I'm *that kind of person.*

"I noticed there was no price listed with the sign on the house."

"Well, there are a few things to go over first before the place is sold, that's why no price is listed."

"What kind of conditions are we talking about?"

"Well, first of all, the building is a registered heritage site. That means it will be harder to get approval to make any radical changes to the site itself. It's one of the oldest buildings in Ballyclara, and the people here are rather partial to it remaining relatively as it is. Preserving the historical significance of the place, if ye will."

"No problem at all. From what I saw of the outside, most of what needs to be done is cosmetic."

She noticed the way both Dermot and Sinead seemed relieved at this statement.

"Besides, if you don't mind me being so bold as to say so, but it would be great if the two of you could help me with that part, make sure I don't change anything that would be out of character with the place. Only, I heard Brendan mention to your son how the two of you used to look after the place and know it so well. There's only myself, and I know I would need an extra set of hands around the place, possibly more."

The couple looked surprised to hear this. "You mean you would be offering us a job?"

"If you wouldn't mind," Aoife replied hastily, not wanting to offend them. "I wouldn't want you to feel obligated to, just because I asked. I just thought that with you two knowing so much about it that you'd be the best fit."

"Well, that we do," Dermot replied after a second's pause to let the information sink in. "You see, my family's been working up at Aldridge Manor for generations now. It used to be the country home for the lord and lady of the time, but when the last living heir of the family died, a priest ye see, well, he left it to the Church in his will. And ever since, it's belonged to the parish priest. Our current priest, Father Patrick, well, he thought the place too grand for himself and so he took up the little priest's house over in the churchyard. It's a drain on the Church to have it sitting empty, so they decided to sell and let us act as agents for them, but we've had a hard time trying to find someone willing to take it on. I won't lie to you; it's in dire need of a fix up, but with some love and care, it should be good as new."

"And if you need the name of a good contractor to help with the repairs, we can certainly help there. Our Michael has a contracting business with Brendan; they'd be more than happy to help you out, I'm sure. Michael so loves that house."

Aoife nodded at the suggestion; she was beginning to see why Michael might resent her interest in buying the place if he'd been eyeing it himself.

"And our daughter, Mara; she's one of them landscape artists, I think ye call them these days. She could help with any gardening or anything on the grounds, if ye like."

"Well, that's all well and good for me."

"It's settled then."

Sinead took out a piece of paper and pen from her floral apron pocket and wrote something on it, handing it over to Aoife. "This is the price of the house."

She unfolded the piece of paper and was surprised by how reasonable it was. Well, given her newfound income, that was. She nodded to Dermot and Sinead, agreeing with the price.

"Wonderful! I'll have Andrew Drummond draw up the papers for us and clear everything with the archbishop, and then we can have them sent to you in Dublin, if you'll just give us your address."

"Sure thing," she told them, writing down her address on a piece of paper for them and handing it over. "Do you know how long it will take him to draw them up?"

"Oh, I shouldn't think it would be more than a few days or so. Maybe a little longer if the Church has any questions or needs to speak to you about anything. They took the liberty of having most of the paperwork prepared ahead of time, in case a buyer was found, so most of it should just be a formality at this point. I'd say you'd have them mailed to ye by week's end or sometime next week, and then ye can move in."

"I can come back down and sign the papers, if that makes things quicker. Also, saves you the trouble of sending them up to me."

"Are you sure ye don't mind? It's a fair drive between here and Dublin. And Andrew really doesn't mind having them sent up to ye, I'm sure."

"No, I don't mind at all. Might as well get used to the drive, right? Besides, it'll give me a better opportunity to get acquainted with Ballyclara."

"Well, I will have him call ye when they're ready, then. And I'll have a word with Michael and Brendan about the contracting. I'm sure they can do up a proposal for ye in the meantime, give ye an idea of what needs to be done."

"That'd be great."

She smiled at the kind couple in front of her, satisfied with her decision. Something about it just felt right.

"Well, it was a pleasure to meet the both you."

She rose from her chair to shake hands with Sinead and Dermot, sealing the deal.

"I should really be heading back to the city…"

"Of course, of course. Don't let us keep you now. Sure and we'll have plenty of time to talk in future. It was wonderful to meet ye, Aoife."

"And it was a pleasure to meet you as well."

She turned for the door and headed back to her car, noticing that Dermot and Sinead stood outside their cottage, waving her off on her journey back to Dublin.

Chapter Ten

True to their word, Sinead and Dermot had spoken to the local lawyer, Andrew Drummond, and had all the appropriate papers drawn up. They'd even called a few days after she'd been to Ballyclara to say that Michael, Brendan, and Mara would be delighted to help her with any repairs or landscaping that needed to be done around the place. It was all starting to come together.

For her part, Aoife had begun packing some of her things, though there wasn't all that much to do. Most of her things were still in their boxes in her storage closet. Mostly it was her going through what she had and marking which ones she'd like to bring down with her.

She knew it was risky getting so invested in the place before the deal even went through. After all, the Church could turn down her offer, or think she wasn't a good enough candidate. What if they wanted it to go to someone who was actually religious?

Maybe I'll need to start going back to church again.

She'd do it too, if she needed to in order to secure the house.

Despite a couple of questions nagging at her, she really didn't feel nervous that the deal wouldn't go through. No, the only thing that worried her now was how she was going to tell her friends and family.

She'd debated about whether or not to tell Bex and Millie straight away when she got back to Dublin after meeting with the Flanagans, but she'd decided it was best to hold off until everything went through and was approved. After all, she didn't want to get them all worried that she'd be moving away only to have the deal fall through.

Of course, the deal hadn't fallen through, and Mr. Drummond had called her to set up a time to sign all the documents. The only left for her to do was to tell Bex and Millie.

"Are you out of your godforsaken mind?" Bex asked, at the same time Millie exclaimed, "That's wonderful!" when she'd told them the news.

She wasn't sure how to react to either of those questions; at least not right away.

"No. Or at least I don't think so," she said, choosing to answer Bex's question first. "Would I even know if I was out of my godforsaken mind if I really was?" She wasn't trying to avoid the question, but an interesting philosophical conundrum had suddenly just presented itself in the middle of this debacle.

"I think it all sounds romantic." Millie's voice was dreamy.

God bless Millie.

She smiled at her friend's show of support for her decision. She knew Bex supported her as well, in her own way. She wasn't really questioning Aoife's decision; she was just making sure she'd thought everything through.

"You're the biggest romantic amongst us, so of course you'd think it was a great idea," Bex retorted tartly, but she was all bluster and no bite.

"And what's wrong with that?" Millie was only slightly offended. She knew Bex didn't mean it.

"Come on, Bex. This isn't Millie's fault. You're upset with me, so talk to me."

Bex exhaled, a long, deep breath from the depths of her lungs. She didn't speak at once, trying to gather her thoughts. Aoife knew she was carefully trying to find the words, hoping not to say something she'd regret later on.

"I'm not angry or upset," she began. "It's just… it's just a big change. A sudden change. I'm worried about you. Your grandfather just died, and then we didn't hear from you for days after the funeral, then you just upped and left to go to this Ballyclara or wherever without even telling us.

"And then you just decide to buy a house at the drop of a hat? It's just a lot to take in at once. I just want to make sure you're making the right decision for you."

She smiled and reached over to give Bex a big hug. Taken aback a bit at the gesture, Bex awkwardly hugged her friend back.

"I know it's a big change, believe me. I had no idea when I was going down to Ballyclara that I was going to find the house, let alone buy it. But when I first saw it, I just had this sense that I belonged there, like it was home. I haven't felt like that for a long time. It just feels right."

Seeing that Aoife was serious and that she also looked like she was at peace with her decision, Bex's shoulders began to relax. Deep down, she really did just want what was best for Aoife.

"So you're not mad with me?"

"Of course not. Now come on and tell us more about this house you've decided to buy."

Chapter Eleven

Three days later, Aoife looked around her flat, overwhelmed. Who would have thought there'd be so much stuff crammed into such a small space? Her flat wasn't exactly tiny, but it was nothing compared to the enormity of Aldridge Manor.

Lord help me if I ever have to pack it up and move again.

She realized in that moment that she didn't have any intentions of moving out of Aldridge Manor at all, and the thought kind of surprised her.

"Having second thoughts?" Bex asked her from the doorway of her bedroom, seeing the overwhelmed look on her face.

"No," she replied honestly. "Just the opposite, in fact. I was thinking how much work it would be to pack up Aldridge Manor, if I ever left it. It's ten times the size of this place."

"Maybe you'll never move from there."

"I was thinking the same thing," she said, pleased she and Bex were once again on the same wavelength. "I guess the whole point is that I'm not going to move out of it."

"You're really doing this, aren't you?"

"Yes. I am."

All That Compels the Heart

She smiled confidently. It was easy to be confident when she knew she was doing what was right for her.

"Then I'm happy for you."

Bex crossed the room, her arms outstretched and pulled Aoife into a hug.

"Thanks."

She rubbed Bex's arm, feeling the thin cloth of her blouse beneath her hand.

"Alright, let's get the rest of these boxes packed and loaded up so we can go down and finally see that new house of yours!"

They each grabbed a box, cellotaped it, safe and secure, and headed out towards Aoife's car. Millie was already sitting in the backseat, surrounded by cardboard boxes filled with Aoife's things. She had on some Audrey Hepburn shades and a pink floral headscarf wrapped around her hair.

"*Another* one?! Where are you planning to fit this one? I'm already surrounded by boxes as it is."

"These ones are going in the boot," Aoife reassured her.

"Good. Last thing I need on my tombstone is that I was crushed by your boxes."

"You're not going to die," Bex reassured her in a tone that clearly stated how dramatic Millie was being.

"Is there anything else to be brought down, Miss?" one of the movers from the company she'd hired asked her.

"No, I think that's about everything."

She fumbled around in her purse, checking that she had her keys to her flat and to her car. She'd decided on keeping her flat for the time being instead of subletting it. She figured she'd be back and forth between Dublin and Ballyclara quite a bit in the beginning while she got everyone adjusted to her living further away, so it made sense for her to keep the place for now. In truth, she didn't really want to be bothered looking for an appropriate person to sublet it from her.

"Let's get this show on the road!" Bex shouted, jumping into the passenger seat of the car excitedly.

It was a cloudy day, but no threat of rain. Even still, they couldn't put the top down on the convertible, lest one of the boxes fly out. When they finally turned off the highway towards Glendalough, she smiled to see the reaction on her friends' faces. She knew they didn't quite understand why she wanted to move here and she was hoping that the view alone might help explain the need for a literal change of scenery.

She raced her convertible through the narrow lanes of the village, only keeping her speed moderate so that the moving van behind her wouldn't lose her around a twist or a bend. Turning into the lane for Aldridge Manor, a feeling of coming home washed over her. As they drove around to the gravel drive in front of the house, she noticed Sinead and Dermot were standing there, waiting for her. She gave them a friendly wave in greeting as she stopped the car and put it in park, turning the engine off.

"Well, what d'ye think of it?" she asked Bex and Millie, as they sat there in the car, taking it all in.

"It's huge," Millie exclaimed staring up in awe at the front of the house, her neck craning to see more of it from her ensconced position in the backseat. "It's gorgeous!"

"Welcome back!" Sinead greeted them as they got out of the car.

Aoife pressed the button to bring the top down on her car, allowing Millie to climb out over the boxes.

"I hope the drive down was fine."

"Oh yes. It's a gorgeous day for a drive down here.

"Sinead, these are my best friends: Camille Johnson and Rebecca Martin. Bex, Millie, this is Sinead and Dermot Flanagan. They're the couple I told you about, the ones who look after Aldridge."

There was a chorus of "nice to meet yous" and a flurry of handshaking as the four of them introduced themselves.

"Well, shall I give you young ladies the grand tour?" Sinead asked them when the introductions were over.

"Yes please!" Millie replied enthusiastically and bounded after the older woman. Bex and Aoife hung back a second shaking their heads at their friend's boundless energy and childlike enthusiasm, but all with huge grins on their faces.

"Do you want us to wait while you open up the house, Miss?" the driver of the moving van called out to her as they began to approach the house.

"Yes please. We're just going to go in and check things out and then we'll be ready to move the stuff in."

He nodded to her.

As Sinead took them through the house, she heard her friends gasp. She couldn't blame them; the house was even more gorgeous on the inside than it was on the outside, even empty of furniture. Of course, she'd have to put some effort into fixing things up; most of the rooms desperately needed a paint job and there was a mountain of cleaning to be done. There were a few other things to fix as well, but nothing she didn't think she Michael and Brendan couldn't handle.

The foyer was grand, a main staircase stood in front of them leading to the upper floors. A long hallway, its floor dusty and dark, ran the length of the house. There was a large front room to the right when you walked in the door. To the left was a large sitting room with a fireplace. Glass patio doors led into the solarium and garden she'd seen on her first inspection of the house.

They turned to the right first, walking through the front room, which connected to the dining room. Through the dining room, she could see a connecting door to the kitchen. She marvelled at the sight of the kitchen; it took up half the back of the house and was at least twice the size of her kitchen back in her flat.

"Well, you're finally going to have to learn how to cook," Bex teased her as they stood in the big, open space. "It'd be a shame to let all this go to waste."

"Good thing I have you two to help me with that."

"It is a wonderful kitchen, isn't it?" Sinead agreed with them. "Back when my mother and father worked here, this was where I spent most of my time. I used to sit right over there," she pointed to the far wall, looking out onto the back of the house near a small, wooden staircase that must have led upstairs to the former servants' quarters.

"There used to be a table there where the staff used to eat their meals. Over there was where my mother used to prepare meals with the head chef," she pointed to the long, granite countertop that still remained. "I used to watch her chopping and dicing away all day."

Her face looked content, lost in her memories.

"It'd be nice to restore as much of it to its original state as possible. I'm glad you're around Sinead; you can help me with that."

"I'd be glad to!" the older woman replied enthusiastically. "Now, would you like to see the rest of the house?"

They stepped out into the hallway again, and saw a smaller room across from the kitchen, connected to the sitting room. They moved back through to the front of the house and headed upstairs. There were several rooms on the second floor, most of them former bedrooms or guest rooms, all complete with ensuite bathrooms of various size. She could have Danny, Millie, and Bex down to visit her at the same time and still have plenty of room to have others over as well. At the far end of the hallway, the master bedroom had a view over the back of the house and down towards the village.

When they'd completed the tour of the house, she turned to her friends and asked, "Well then, shall we start unloading those boxes?"

For the next few hours, through a few stubbed toes and more than a few muttered curse words, the eight of them unloaded the boxes and furniture Aoife had brought with her from Dublin. Although she'd brought a considerable number of things with her, the large house seemed to dwarf them and swallow them up. She'd need to look at purchasing new appliances, furniture, and decorations in order to make the place look more lived in.

"Is that everything, then?" Millie asked her, looking like she'd really rather do anything other than carry one more box into the house.

"I think that's everything," she replied to a rush of grateful sighs from everyone.

"Thank you all for the help," she told them sincerely.

"Well, if there's nothing more you'll be needing from us, miss, we'll head back up to Dublin," the eldest of the movers, a man in his mid-forties, said to her.

"Thank you," she repeated, turning towards the kindly man and held out her hand for him to shake it. "Have a safe drive back."

All That Compels the Heart

He gave her hand a quick, firm shake and tipped his cap towards her as he and the two younger men headed down the front steps to the moving van. Aoife gave them a short, friendly wave off as they turned the van around the circular drive, the crunch of dirt and gravel under the tires announcing their departure.

"Well, I think we should be heading back home, don't you, love?" Dermot asked Sinead. "These young ladies probably want to get settled and spend some time together rather than have us under foot."

"If ye need anything at all, you just come right down to the cottage and we'll would be more than happy to help ye out," Sinead told her. "Our daughter, Mara, just lives in the one next to us, and Michael in the one just after that. I've left you our number on a notepad in the kitchen, should you need anything at all. Don't hesitate to give us a ring.

"Michael or Brendan will be around tomorrow morning to go over with you what you'd like to do about renovations to the place, and Mara said she'd stop by later tomorrow as well after she drops young Rory off to school."

"Thank you for arranging everything for me."

"No problem at all," Sinead reassured her. "Oh, and if ye need any help with any heavy-lifting of furniture or anything, just give Michael a call. I'm sure he would be happy to help."

"Oh, I'm sure that won't be necessary," Aoife replied, remembering her first encounter with Michael and how he seemed like the sort of person who'd rather do anything other than help *her* with anything. "If I need anything moved, I'm sure my cousin Connor, or my boyfriend, Danny, will be down soon to help."

Millie gave a derisive snort at the mention of Danny doing any heavy-lifting, for which she received an elbow to the side from Bex. She stifled a quiet "ow!" but didn't offer any other sarcastic remarks.

"Well, we'll be off then."

"Thank you," Aoife said for what felt like the millionth time that day. They were such small words, but she didn't know how else to express the gratitude she felt for all the support everyone had given her. She walked them across the foyer and to the front door, watching them as they walked down the front steps and into the driveway.

"Remember, if you need anything –," Sinead turned around and began to say again.

"I'll be sure to let you know," Aoife replied with a wave as she watched them walk down the path to their homes.

When they were out of sight, Aoife turned to come inside and heard Millie say, "Jeez, an insistent bunch, aren't they? I didn't think they'd ever leave!"

"Millie!" Bex exclaimed.

"I thought they were being rather sweet," Aoife replied.

"Well there's a change," Millie replied, her voice sounding more than a little stunned. "You don't even know your neighbours' names in Dublin, people you've lived beside for the last couple of years and yet these people have been in your house and helped you unload your boxes, and you know all of their names and numbers, and you met them only a week ago. Country life really is changing you."

"Oh stop giving her a hard time. It's not like it's a *bad* thing that she's getting to know her neighbours," Bex chastised Millie.

Somewhere in the past few days, Millie and Bex had changed positions on Aoife moving to Ballyclara. Where Bex had initially been reticent about the idea, she'd now come around to the notion that if it made Aoife happy, it was good enough for her. Millie, on the other hand, had quickly gone from thinking it was a good idea to being downright petulant about the whole thing, the idea that she wouldn't be seeing Aoife every day finally having sunk in. And she didn't seem to like it one bit.

Millie pouted at having been chastised, but didn't debate any further on the topic. "Well, I suppose we better get some of these boxes unpacked, or else Aoife won't have anywhere to sleep tonight."

"No, you're alright. I can do it later." The thought of unpacking after bringing all those boxes into the house was the last thing she wanted to do right now.

"So, what should we do then?" Millie asked her, looking around the house.

"Why don't we go down into the village and get Aoife some groceries so she won't starve. If I'm driving your car back to the city tonight, I want to make sure you don't have to carry heavy groceries all the way up from the village by yourself."

"You see? This is why you should stay in the city! You won't have a car to do all the errands you need to do," Millie pointed out one more thing on her long list she'd been compiling of reasons why Aoife shouldn't leave the city and move so far away from her.

"You two are bringing my car back in two days, I think I'll survive without it until then. Besides, I have these things called 'legs' and I can walk where I need to in the meantime."

"And fine legs they are too," Millie said appreciatively.

"Come on, the two of you. Let's check out Ballyclara and see what it has to offer." Bex picked up Aoife's car keys and began heading outside.

ಬಿಂಬ

Aoife was both excited and slightly apprehensive of showing her friends around her new home. She knew how they saw it: a small village in the middle of nowhere with none of the hustle and bustle they were used to in Dublin. Sure, it was in a pretty part of the country, but it wasn't the same as living only a few blocks from her friends and having the option to just walk over to their place whenever she wanted to.

Sure enough, as they drove into the village and parked the car near the Celtic cross at the heart of the village, she saw her friends' faces take in everything around them. Even Bex, for all her support before, looked surprised that this was all there was to the place. Trying not to feel disappointed, Aoife exited the car and began crossing the road to the shops, expecting her friends to follow her. When she noticed they weren't following her, she turned around, looking at where they were looking.

"Who's that man staring at us?" Bex asked, nodding slightly in the direction of the pub.

Aoife looked up and followed her gaze. Michael stood outside of the pub, arms folded across his chest, staring at Aoife and her friends. Despite the relative coolness of the day, and him standing in the shade of the pub's eaves, he was dressed casually in a thin, dark t-shirt and jeans. As if his intense stare willed the cool breeze to blow at precisely that moment, she felt a shiver run down her spine and she reflexively pulled her cardigan tighter around her shoulders, wishing she'd worn more than just the thin silk top underneath and capris.

"Michael Flanagan," she muttered under her breath, just loud enough for Bex and Millie to hear.

"Who's Michael Flanagan? An axe murderer? Because he certainly doesn't look friendly," Millie said, mirroring her own feelings.

"He's… it's complicated," Aoife started.

"Ooooh! What kind of complicated?"

Both her friends were suddenly intrigued.

"Not *that* kind of complicated," she chastised them for thinking Michael might be a potential suitor. That was the last thing she needed. She knew neither of her friends were particularly fond of Danny, and she didn't need them thinking of playing matchmaker for her with the local humbug.

"Wait, Michael Flanagan, you said? Is that the same Michael that's Sinead and Dermot's son?" Bex asked.

"The very same. He's abso-fuckin-lutely the most frustrating man I've ever met."

"Well, I can see you two have become fast friends," Bex told her, heavy sarcasm in her voice.

"What did you do to him to make him so upset?" Millie asked, staring back at him.

"*I* didn't do anything to him!" Aoife retorted angrily. "He's upset with me because I bought Aldridge Manor. I think he had his eye on the place before I bought it.

"C'mon, let's get out of her before we drop dead from the glares he's giving us."

Aoife indicated they should follow her into the shop.

Chapter Twelve

All too quickly, the sun began to set in the sky, the clouds from earlier making it feel darker outside than it really was.

"Well, we should probably head home," Bex said, looking at the sky, trying to gauge whether or not the heavens were about to burst open and rain down on them.

"You could always stay here for the night, if you want. You could leave first thing in the morning."

"And where exactly do you plan to put us? You don't have any furniture in this place."

"True," Aoife replied, looking around at the pile of boxes around her. She didn't even know where *she* was going to sleep tonight, let alone where she'd put her friends.

Millie yawned widely and loudly, her eyes bleary.

"I need sleep," she announced, as if it wasn't already obvious.

Bex smiled and said, "Right, let's get you home to bed then."

Aoife groaned as she stood up from the box she'd been sitting on and hugged both her friends tightly. "Thank you for everything."

"You're welcome," Millie responded, laying her sleepy head on her shoulder.

"Safe drive!" Aoife handed Bex her keys.

"We'll see you on Wednesday, and we'll bring down the rest of those boxes we couldn't fit in on this trip down."

"See you then."

She stood in the darkened driveway and waved her friends off, pulling her cardigan around her in the cool night air. She waited until she could no longer see the headlights as they faded into the distance before heading back inside.

The place had gotten much darker and quieter now that it was just herself, seeming both too quiet and loud at the same time. Without the sounds of people coming and going, Aoife could hear the birds tweeting at her in the trees, as well as the distant lowing of cattle from the farm next to her. It wasn't until just that moment that the tiniest pang of homesickness for the city set in, making her miss the sounds of the cars and buses rushing below her flat.

Doing her best to firmly push the homesickness aside, she closed the front door and seemed swallowed up by the darkness. The power hadn't been turned on yet; the electric company was supposed to be sending someone tomorrow to set it up for her. Turning on the torchlight app on her phone, she moved around the cavernous hallways, looking for a box of sheets and blankets. She was bone-tired, but she knew it was better to unpack some bedding now before she could no longer stand on her own two feet. Willing her aching limbs to move, she located the box she was looking for and pulled out a blanket and some sheets. Throwing the sheets over the sofa and pulling the blanket over her, she settled into the first night in her new place.

☙◊❧

Aoife woke to the bright sunlight through curtain-less windows and the sound of a car driving up her lane, parking just outside of the house. Not sure who exactly it could be, she swung her legs around, her feet touching the cool wooden floorboards beneath. Just as she was arranging herself to look like she *hadn't* just woken up from sleeping in her clothes on the couch all night, her front doorbell rang, loud and sonorous throughout the empty house.

"Hello," she greeted the middle-aged man standing on her front step.

He was a portly man, and the dull grey and taupe uniform of the electric company looked ill-fitting on him.

"Good morning, Miss..." he glanced down at his clipboard. "...O'Reilly. I'm here to hook your power back up again."

She held the door open to him and ushered him inside. She stood there a bit awkwardly, not sure what to do.

"If you could just show me to where your electric box is, I can get you set up," the man told her, seeing her uncertainty.

"Oh. Right through here," she said, heading towards the kitchen.

Thankfully, Dermot had pointed it out to her yesterday when they'd been unpacking.

"I'd offer you some tea, but I've no way of boiling the water," she said, apologetically.

"No problem at all. I'll just have a look here and then we can sort that out for you."

She moved aside, letting him go about his business. Still not sure what she should be doing, she went over to one of the counters and began unpacking some of the groceries she'd gotten earlier. Sorting through the dry goods she'd kept with her, she rummaged around trying to look busy.

Several minutes later, the man from the electric company had finished with his assessments and had the power up and running again.

"There! That should have everything up and running now. I'll just go through and make sure that all the rooms are working."

Aoife nodded and followed him throughout the house, watching as he checked every room. Satisfied that everything seemed to be in working order he turned to her and got her to sign some forms.

"Well, that seems like everything. If ye have any trouble, just give us a call. You have a great day, miss."

"Thanks," she said to him, waving him off.

Silence once more descended upon the house once more. Beginning to feel hungry, she headed back to the kitchen and grabbed her mobile phone to put on some music, filling the void the lack of city noise had created.

"Alright," she said aloud to herself. "Let's figure out how to make some food in this place."

Although she didn't want to admit it, she knew very little about living on her own. She'd always had someone else to look after her meals, her clothes, her entire schedule and routine when she was growing up. When she'd moved away to America for university, she'd taken her cue from Bex and Millie and learned how to do some of the simpler chores like laundry, but cooking was still one of those elusive skills she'd never acquired. She was excited now by the idea of self-sufficiency, *true* self-sufficiency. She soon came to realize that this would not be an easy journey.

Everything in the kitchen was wildly out of date, from the décor to the appliances. The last time anything had been updated in the place seemed to be somewhere firmly in the 1906's or 1970's. The whole colour scheme seemed to be this odd olive green/chestnut brown combination, which was going to be the first thing on her list to talk about with Brendan when he came over this morning to discuss the renovations. At least, she hoped it would be Brendan; she dreaded the idea of talking to Michael.

The next thing to go had to be the gas stove. She approached said appliance with an air of caution and reverence. She knew she wasn't going to be able to avoid using the damnable thing if she wanted to eat, and so she decided to muster up her courage and began looking for something to cook. After all, the village only had one bakery, one café, and the pub; it wasn't like she had many options for eating out, and people would catch on rather quickly if she was never eating at home.

Somehow, a note from Bex placed near the stove had gone unnoticed by her earlier. She picked it up, instantly recognizing her friend's handwriting:

Dear Aoife,

All That Compels the Heart

Welcome to your kitchen! Ok, I admit that it's not really anything to look at right now, but I'm sure you'll have it whipped into shape in no time (and for the love of God, please pick a better colour scheme than whatever the hell you call the current colour. It's putrid and it looks awful).

I know you're probably a bit nervous to try cooking on your own, but too proud to say so, which is why I am writing this note to you. On the counter in front of you, you should find a couple of different types of pasta (Millie said we should give you a choice). I'd recommend beginning with the spaghetti.

Pasta seemed like an unusual choice for breakfast, but not seeing many other options – she'd forgotten about breakfast when they'd been doing her shopping yesterday – she decided to forge ahead.

You should see a pot on the counter beside the pasta; turn on the tap and put some water in it.

"I know how to bloody well boil a pot of water, Bex," Aoife grumbled at the piece of paper but did what it instructed her to do.

When she'd finished filling the pot about three-quarters full, she put it on one of the burners and picked up the piece of paper to keep reading. This was where she was having some anxiety about cooking; she'd never worked with a gas stove before, and she wasn't entirely sure she wouldn't end up burning the whole place down.

Now, slowly turn the knob on the stove to begin the gas.

Aoife reached over and did as she was told, slowly turning the knob to release the gas. Releasing a breath she didn't know she'd been holding when she heard a hissing noise from the burner and managed not to blow the stove up, she went about reading the rest of the instructions.

Now, light a match and place it in one of the holes where the gas comes out of and wait for it to ignite. Quickly remove the match when it has ignited so you don't burn your fingers off!

This was the part Aoife was most concerned about. Nevertheless, she picked up the box of matches Bex had left for her, all the while repeating the mantra, "Please don't blow me up, please don't blow me up."

She scraped the match across the rough edge of the matchbox and place it close to the gas, carefully watching the flame as it ignited with a little *whoosh!* and a little flicker of blue light appeared. As soon as the gas was lit, she pulled her hand – and the match – back out of fright, waving it furiously to put it out. Pleased that she hadn't burned the place down, she set about gathering the rest of the contents for her meal. Just as she was about to put the spaghetti noodles in the pot, red flames shot up around the sides of the pot. Frightened by the sudden turn of events, Aoife stepped back instinctively, self-preservation kicking in.

And that's when she froze. Her brain panicked, knowing it should try to put out the fire, but unwilling to communicate that message to her limbs and she stood there frozen like a block of ice. She was only jolted out of this state by the feeling of rough hands forcibly shoving her out of the way and a man standing in front of her, trying to smother the flames. He successfully turned off the gas and extinguished the flames with the one tea towel she'd brought down with her from Dublin.

"Jesus, Joseph and Mary woman, what're you trying to do? Burn the feckin' place down?" he roared at her.

Aoife looked at him stunned. It wasn't until he'd yelled at her that she finally looked at the intruder and saw that it was Michael Flanagan, Sinead and Dermot's Colin-Firth-levels-of-handsome, and Mr.-Darcy-levels-of-rude, son. She hadn't had time to look at him as he'd come barreling in through her back door, but now she realized she was gawking at him while he was looked at her, clearly expecting an answer to his question.

How *dare* he come in here and begin accusing *her* of being reckless? What the feckin' hell was *he* doing stalking around her place and just bursting inside without asking permission? Who the hell did he think he was, exactly?

She didn't have any time to answer his questions or find out the answers to her own before another flame shot up out of the burner and he roared unintelligibly and patted it out with the tea towel, reaching over once again to ensure that the gas was fully turned off.

"Yes, that's exactly what I was trying to do!"

Somewhere she'd finally found her voice, and her nerve. Perhaps it was just the shock of nearly burning the place down, or perhaps it was all the pent up annoyance she had for him because of his clear dislike of her, but she finally found the nerve to shout at him.

Her voice reverberated back to her in the cavernous room, suddenly sounding unnecessarily loud in the quiet that had descended on the house, the gas from the stove no longer whirring quietly, her heartbeat no longer pounding in her ears, and Michael no longer shouting at her.

"I'm fine by the way. Thanks for asking!"

"I can see you're fine," Michael snapped, looking her up and down, and she found herself unconsciously pulling her cardigan around her – the very same one he'd seen her in yesterday – feeling exposed under his stare. She felt distinctly awkward having him here in her kitchen, standing so close to her. For the lack of anything better to do, she was about to stomp out of the kitchen as gracefully as she could when she heard him mutter something about her being "reckless, fool-headed, and stubborn," as he carefully moved the pot from the stove to the counter to let it cool without the chance of it catching fire again. She felt selfishly pleased when the handle of the pot burned his fingertips and he cursed again.

"Excuse me?" Aoife asked him, rounding on him, her tone accusatory.

"I said -"

But Michael didn't have time to explain what exactly he'd been saying before Aoife stepped right up to him so that she was looking him square in the chest. He was a good half a foot taller than she was and she barely came level with his collarbone, which forced her to look up at him to make her point, only making her further enraged with him.

"I am *not* 'reckless, fool-headed, and stubborn'!" she retorted stubbornly, proving at least one of his points. She knew it sounded as petulant to him as it did to her but she was committed to having this argument now and couldn't – or maybe, wouldn't – back down.

"Oh really?" he replied, his voice dripping with sarcasm. "So what would ye call trying to burn down the feckin' house around your ears, then?"

She was trying to come up with a reasonable response to his question. Knowing that no matter what she said he'd probably try to find a way to poke holes in her argument, she decided to try and save face.

"I do *not* need to explain myself to *you*, Michael Flanagan. You are neither my father, my husband, nor my boyfriend, and even if you *were* – and let me just tell you that you would be the *last* person on this earth I would marry – that it would *still* be none of your business!"

Perhaps he'd been expecting her to thank him, but she could see she'd angered him with her words from the quick flash in his eyes and the way his face clouded over like a dark thundercloud.

"Well, don't ask me to come save your life the next time you decide to do something foolish!"

"Don't worry! I won't!" she yelled back at his retreating back. "And you can just shag right off and get stuffed, Michael Flanagan!"

Much to her surprise, and the surprise of the elderly ladies who'd somehow appeared on the back porch during this argument, Michael took her advice and stormed off the way he'd come, frightening the two women who retreated slightly in the wake of his violent temper.

"Hello?" one of the women said with more than a little shock, clutching what looked like a casserole dish to her stomach, worried that someone else might come stomping out of the house.

"We tried knocking on the front door, but no one answered. We thought we'd come 'round to the back to see if you were in, love," the other woman, dressed in a sunny-coloured dress and green jacket with matching hat, called out to her through the open doorway.

All That Compels the Heart

Wonderful.

The last thing she wanted right now was visitors. However, not wanting to get a reputation as being a bad hostess – a lifetime of guilt from Grainne had taught her how to properly receive guests – she pasted on a smile and said, "Please, come in."

The women looked her over curiously and she realized she was still in the clothes she'd worn from yesterday, which were probably more than a little grimy and wrinkled from all the moving, unpacking, and having been slept in. While she'd attempted to smooth down her hair when the man from the electric company had shown up, she was very aware of the fact that it was still a tangled mess.

Well, if they'd told me they were coming, I would have made myself more presentable, she thought, grumbling to herself.

"I'd offer you a cup of tea, but –"

"Oh no, no. No need to bother," the woman in the yellow dress said a little too quickly, grimacing as she placed her casserole dish next to the burned-out pot still smoking on the granite countertop. "We're fine, Maud, aren't we?"

"Well…" Maud replied, looking like perhaps a cup of tea would be nice, if someone else was offering to make it.

"We're fine," her friend replied assertively. "But 'tis kind of ye to offer."

"It would seem that I'm not used to working a gas stove, just yet," Aoife apologized, trying to make light of the argument they'd witnessed. Seeing the women agree with her, she said, "Why don't we go to the sitting room? I've a bit of furniture in there; it would be more comfortable than standing in here."

They smiled politely at her as she took them through the house, the both of them eyeing the place critically to see if she'd made any changes that they could report back to the rest of the village, even though she'd only moved in the day before. She hurried into the sitting room, quickly removing the bedding she'd thrown on the sofa earlier and gestured for them to sit. "Please, have a seat.

"And excuse the mess; I've only just moved in yesterday. Everything is still in boxes, as you can see."

"Oh yes, we're terribly sorry for visiting so early, only we weren't sure if you'd had any time to make yourself something to eat, what with getting settled in and all. We thought we would just stop by with some casseroles and sweets for you, to welcome you to the village, so to speak."

The woman in the yellow dress gave her a kind smile that brightened her pretty face and Aoife instantly felt bad for not wanting them to visit her. The woman nudged her friend, Maud, and silently gestured for her to show Aoife the tin of baked goods she had in her hands. Bewildered a bit, Maud caught on to her friend's gesture and handed the dish to Aoife.

"Thank you; that's so kind of you. Here, let me take these to the kitchen."

Aoife took the biscuit tin and another casserole dish Maud had been holding onto.

"Make yourselves at home. I'm just going to pop upstairs and change. I'm all dirty from unpacking."

She left the two women to their own devices to snoop about as they pleased, while she put the casseroles in the kitchen and dashed up the back stairs to the master bedroom. She quickly unpacked one of the boxes and grabbed the first thing she could find: a navy jumper and her black skinny jeans. They'd be fine for receiving guests. Quickly changing, she threw yesterday's clothes into a pile on the floor and located her hairbrush and make-up bag, trying to untangle as much of her hair as possible before throwing it up into a clip and putting on some light foundation to cover up the dark circles under her eyes.

She'd been gone for maybe five minutes, ten tops, when she dashed back down the main staircase. She could hear the two women roaming around the hallway, looking at a watercolour of the Colosseum she'd painted on a trip to Italy when she was thirteen.

"Well now, isn't this beautiful," she heard Maud say.

"Oh yes, quite lovely," her friend agreed. "I wonder who the artist is?"

"That would be me," Aoife replied proudly from the stairs. They looked around, startled that they hadn't heard her return.

"Well you've quite a talent there," the woman whose name she didn't know, told her, impressed.

"Thank you, but I'm not so sure about that."

She wasn't being modest; she really *wasn't* sure she was all that good. After that trip, Grainne had made her give up art, saying she'd never amount to anything as an artist. She'd never really taken it up again after that.

"No, you are," Maud insisted. "And now that you're down here with all this beautiful scenery around you, maybe you'll find some inspiration."

"Perhaps," Aoife smiled at them. "Shall we go back into the sitting room?"

She pointed back the way they'd come. Maud and Millie nodded, following her through the other room. They settled themselves back on the sofa where she'd originally left them, while she pulled a white sheet off a matching chair and sat down to talk to her guests properly. After an awkward pause, Aoife realized she had no idea who these people were.

"I'm sorry, I didn't introduce myself earlier. I'm Aoife O'Reilly." She rose from her chair to shake both women's hands in greeting.

"Oh dear, how rude of us not to introduce ourselves. My name is Anna McCaffrey and this is Maud Drummond," the woman in yellow introduced herself, while her friend sat back down on the sofa, adjusting her dress which was in various shades of royal purple, mauve, and white. "We are with the church women's group at the parish. We just wanted to come over and welcome you to Ballyclara."

"Drummond and McCaffrey? As in Andrew Drummond and Brendan McCaffrey?"

"The very ones," Maud replied.

"Andrew is Maud's son, and Brendan's my grandson. Such a lovely, sweet thing he is," Anna said.

Aoife nodded in agreement.

"Brendan was saying to me after you two had met that you seemed like a wonderful young woman," Anna said. "So, my love. Tell us a little more about yourself. It's not often we get to welcome someone new to Ballyclara, unless you're born here, of course."

While the two women seemed pleasant enough, Aoife had been around enough women of their age and social status to know that they were likely the queen bees of their social circles, and likely to pass on whatever information she told them to the whole village.

"Well, let's see. I'm originally from Dublin, but I've kind of lived all over... my family did a lot of travelling around while I was growing up. But Ireland's always been home."

She could see that their interest had been piqued.

"I moved to America for university and then moved back to Dublin after graduation, where I began to work for Arbour Hill Publishing; that's a publishing house. You may have heard of them?"

Maud nodded, looking like she thought she'd heard the name before.

"I heard you left your job recently, is that right?" Anna pressed her for further details.

"Yes." She knew it wasn't strictly true, but it wasn't like anyone down here was going to know she'd been let go from her job and then be able to call her out on it. "I decided it was time for me to focus on my own work instead of just reading others' work all the time."

"Ah yes, that's right. Sinead said you wanted to be a writer. How romantic," Maud told her a little wistfully. "I always liked to think when I was a girl your age that *I* could have been a writer, if only things had been different for women back then."

"You? A writer?" Anna asked her friend, her voice incredulous. "Sure, and what would you have to write about? How best to cook a chicken?"

"And what exactly is wrong with the way I cook my chicken? It was good enough for you last week when you came 'round for dinner!" Maud's nose rose a good half inch in the air, defying her friend to say something inappropriate in front of Aoife.

Seeing that an argument was about to break out, she was quick to try and stamp it out. "And how exactly is it that you cook your chicken, Mrs. Drummond? I've been looking for a good recipe for chicken for quite some time now."

"Well," Maud started, looking pleased as pie to be asked. "The thing is to..."

Aoife could have almost wished she hadn't asked. A half an hour later, and several instances of bickering between Anna and Maud later, Aoife had a plethora of chicken recipes she'd never end up using. However, she *had* managed to avoid an all-out argument between the two women.

"Sure, and your own mam probably has loads of recipes like these that she's taught you over the years," Maud said to her.

Aoife held back the snort she was about to make and remained as dignified as she could. "Um, well, I'm sure she does. We don't tend to cook together."

"Oh, gets a bit crowded in the kitchen, does it, with the two of you?"

"You could say that," Aoife replied, trying to be polite as possible. Before either of the women could press her for more information as to what exactly she meant by that statement, she glanced at her watch.

"Oh, look at the time! I'm supposed to be speaking to someone back in Dublin about moving the rest of my things down here. I hate to rush your visit…"

"It's no bother at all," Maud reassured her. "I'm sure there's plenty of things for ye to be on with. We'll leave you to it. Here's our numbers, in case there's anything you need help with. Don't be afraid to call."

She patted Aoife's hand in a motherly fashion.

"Thank you, that's so kind of you." She meant the words sincerely, even though she was ushering them to the door. "If there's anything I need, I'll be sure to call."

"Anything at all, love," Anna repeated the sentiment as she walked through the front door and down the steps.

"Thank you Mrs. Drummond, Mrs. McCaffrey," she called out to them as they began to make their way back to their homes.

She shut the door behind her quickly, heaving a huge sigh of relief at finally having got rid of them and having the rest of her morning to herself in peace.

⁂

Brendan was propped up at the bar, glancing at the morning's newspaper when he heard the front door crash open and Michael came storming through it.

"What are you doing back so early?" he asked, glancing at his watch. Michael had only left for the Old Rectory about fifteen minutes before; hardly enough time for a proper consultation on the place, even if he did know it like the back of his hand. "Did you find out all that needs fixin' up at the Old Rectory?"

"*You* feckin' talk to the bloody woman if you want to know! And make sure you have the number for the fire department handy!" Michael strode angrily through the pub and into the kitchen, the connecting doors swinging furiously in his wake.

Brendan could hear the clanging of pots and pans and sent a silent prayer above that they'd decided on all stainless-steel equipment; at least Michael wouldn't be able to break anything valuable that way.

"What was that about?" Molly asked, coming through the swinging doors and looking at her husband curiously.

"Fucked if I know," Brendan replied honestly. "But it looks like I've got to go to the Old Rectory now and do that consultation with Aoife."

Chapter Thirteen

"I'm not going to lie to you, Aoife; there's a fair amount of work to be done here and it's going to cost a pretty penny," Brendan told her, taking her through the initial assessment of the house .

"No problem at all. And don't worry about the cost of things. I've got that covered."

"Alright then. I'll have Michael and Jimmy down here first thing in the morning and we'll get things started."

She must have had a dark look on her face at the mention of Michael's name, for Brendan cleared his throat and said, "I don't think you've met Jimmy, have you?"

"No, I don't think I have," she responded, mentally flicking through the list of names and faces she'd become acquainted with in the short time since she'd moved in.

Jimmy Connelly, as it turned out, was a young lad of about eighteen or nineteen and Brendan's apprentice. A tall, gangly lad who looked like he still had yet to grow into his long limbs. He wasn't exactly what Aoife would call handsome, but his infectious smile and the easy way he had with people lent a kindness to him that mattered far more than looks, Aoife thought.

Just look at Michael. All those handsome features couldn't make up for that temper!

She was surprised to find that she thought of Michael as handsome. She pushed the thought firmly from her mind.

It was easy enough to do; she had plenty of people coming and going from her place to distract her. It practically felt that the entire village came with the house when she moved in. She'd had a constant stream of visitors through her door in the first few days; more women from the parish coming to drop off casseroles to her and other goodies they thought she might need. It had certainly saved on a trip to the grocer's in town, for which she was grateful, considering she had to wait for Bex to drive her car back down to her. She'd also met the rest of the extended Connolly, McCaffrey, and Flanagan families, with Brendan's wife, Molly, and Jimmy's wife, Karen, showing up to help, along with Dermot and Sinead's daughter, Mara.

She liked working with Mara over the designs for the gardens. There was no doubt she and Michael were siblings: they had the same so-dark-as-to-be-almost-black hair colour and the same midnight blue eyes. She was tall like her brother as well – standing several inches taller than Aoife – and had the same muscular frame that had been built up from a lifetime of walking around the village and doing physical labour for a living.

The similarities between them didn't just end at the physical; Aoife could tell Mara had the same sharp temper as her brother, though perhaps being a year older had given her just that extra little bit of experience in how to keep it in check. Instead of venting her temper at complete strangers, she fueled it into being a natural leader, barking out orders to both her brother and his friend any time she thought they were falling behind on the renovations. She wasn't afraid to remind Michael which of them was the eldest and that she could just as easily set him on his arse if he tried to argue with her. Aoife believed she'd do it too. And so, under the watchful eye of Mara, they all set about their tasks.

Even the smallest members of the Flanagan and McCaffrey families pitched in. She'd met Desmond, Brendan and Molly's ten year old son, when he'd come up with his mother and father to help with some of the easier tasks, but she hadn't met Mara's son, Rory, until a few days later.

She'd been upstairs in the master bedroom making an attempt to unpack some of the linen she'd ordered online and pack it into the closet across the hallway while she thought the rest of the Flanagans had gone home for a tea break. She'd come downstairs to the kitchen, intending to prepare herself something quick and easy before returning to one of the many tasks on her list to accomplish that day when she noticed someone out of the corner of her eye. Startled, she jumped.

"Jesus, Joseph, and Mary!" she'd exclaimed. Clutching at her chest out of fright, she noticed that the intruder was a small boy.

"Well hello there," she said a little more calmly, once her heart had stopped racing and her breathing had slowed.

"Hello."

He'd barely looked up from the book he was reading as he sat at the table, kicking his short legs idly, bored.

"And who might you be?" His hair and eye colour should have been a clue, looking so much like his mother and uncle, but the comparison didn't immediately register for her.

"Rory," the little boy offered as introduction.

"Rory," she'd said, mulling over the name, knowing she'd heard it somewhere but couldn't remember where. "And where are your parents, Rory?"

"Well, Mam is out back in the garden, and I don't know where my Da is exactly. Ma says she thinks he's in London; that's in England." The little boy – who looked to be around nine or ten years old – said, proud to show off the information he'd learned.

"I've never met him before, so I'm not really sure where he is. But my Grandad says that's ok because, well, he said a bunch of words he told me not to repeat, but mostly he just said that it was enough for me that I have him, and my Granny, my Uncle Michael to look after me, which is better than just having one da around."

"Your Uncle Michael?" Aoife had seen it then, the resemblance to Michael Flanagan. It was all in the eyes, the same clear blue as his uncle's. Immediately recognizing those unmistakeable Flanagan features, she had relaxed, content the boy wasn't just some stranger who'd wandered into her home.

"Mmmhmm," Rory responded distractedly. He'd already gone back to his book now that the pleasantries were out of the way.

"I know your Uncle Michael," she supplied, trying to make a connection with the boy. Now that she knew where he belonged, she wasn't quite sure what to do with him. Should she call out back for Mara? But then again, she would probably be finishing up soon, so should she just keep him entertained until then?

The thought kind of terrified her; she'd had very little experience with children growing up. She wasn't sure she'd know the first thing about looking after one of them. Was he at an age where he could be left unattended and not get into trouble? Her own childhood did not provide much assistance to her questions; she'd not had a typical upbringing and neither had she been a typical child, so she couldn't really base what she should do over what her own mother would have done in the same circumstances.

"I also know your Granny and Grandad, and your mam. They've been helping me with this house."

She was fairly certain she needn't watch him all the time – after all, Mara had left him in here unattended while she worked out back – but Aoife knew the one thing about looking after children was that you did not leave them alone for too long or God knew what they'd get up to.

Glancing around the kitchen to make sure no sharp, pointy objects were lying around the place, she crossed the kitchen and sat down at the table across from Rory, hoping that Mara would be coming back for him soon and would provide some direction as to what to do.

"My name is Aoife, by the way."

She held out a hand to him. He took it and shook it lightly. She figured that if they were going to be sat there in the kitchen while they waited for his mother that they might as well get to know one another.

"I know; Uncle Michael says you're the 'bossy, stuck-up, know-it-all' from the city who tried to burn this 'feckin' place down.'"

Oh he did, did he?

"Aoife," Rory asked, his voice curious, "Why would you try to burn down the Old Rectory? Do you not like living here?" His sweet, little face was full of pure confusion. "I really like this house, and so does Uncle Michael. He was going to buy it before you did. Did you know that?"

"I had an idea of it," Aoife said between gritted teeth, silently cursing Michael for having mentioned the incident with the old gas stove to his nephew. "And it was an accident. I don't want to burn this place down; I love it just as much as you and your uncle do."

Rory nodded, taking in this information. "Well, that's a relief!"

"You see, I'm not used to the old gas stoves, so even though I thought I was doing it right, one of the pots I was using caught fire and your uncle showed up just in time to save it from getting worse."

"Uncle Michael said if he hadn't saved you, that the whole place could have gone up in flame!"

"Well, I don't know about that… What else did your uncle say about me, exactly?"

"Well…" the little boy pondered over what he'd been told. "I don't know that I should repeat it. Mam says I shouldn't repeat gossip; it's rude."

Aoife was about to press him further when he changed topics. "Do ye not have gas stoves in the city, then?"

His face looked like this was an incomprehensible thought.

"Oh I'm sure some people do; I just don't have one in my flat back in Dublin. Truth be told though, I don't really know how to cook on an electric stove, let alone a gas stove, so I think I was kind of doomed from the beginning." She hoped the explanation might dispel any preconceptions he might have had about her from his uncle's account of things.

"You should ask my Granny to help you learn how to cook; she's *really* good!" Rory piped up, the incident between

Michael and Aoife forgotten. "I can ask her for you, if you want."

"That's very sweet of you to offer," Aoife told him, smiling at him. "And I may just have to take you up on it someday . Once I get this kitchen renovated."

She swept her hand around to indicate the mess of carpentry tools and torn out countertops around them.

"Are you really going to change everything in here?" Rory asked, his face suddenly a bit sad. "Only, I heard some o' the boys at school saying their grannies had told 'em that you were planning to completely change *everything*."

Aoife realized then how dear the place really was to him. It was probably the reason he felt so at home sitting at her kitchen table without having met her before; he'd probably been in this place a million times with his mother and uncle, looking the place over, helping with its up-keep until someone could buy it.

"No," she replied, pleased to see the look of relief on his face. "I just want to update things a few things, but mostly, I want to keep it the way it originally was. Just with a few new coats of paint and some other repairs."

"I'm glad," Rory announced, a big smile on his round face. Aoife couldn't help but smile back at him and the two of them giggled for no other reason than that they were happy, just like old school chums did. She realized how pleased it made her feel that she'd made her first friend in the village, even if that friend happened to be only ten years old.

Their little giggle fit subsiding, she asked, "What's this you've got here?" and pointed to the book in front of him.

"Maths homework," Rory replied, his face suddenly turning dark at the thought of his unfinished homework. "Mrs. Byrne assigned us *loads* of it for tonight. She's *so* mean. Mam says she's just angry because her daughter, Karen, is having a baby with Jimmy, but I think she's just mean at heart."

"Oh now. I'm not sure she's mean at heart…" Aoife began to say, trying to be fair to Mrs. Byrne, whom she hadn't yet met. She was about to point out Mara's rule about not gossiping about others because it was rude, but seeing the boy's raised eyebrow, she decided to get off the topic of Mrs. Byrne altogether.

"Would you like a biscuit? You must be hungry doing all that homework of yours."

Rory's face flashed from eager excitement to a frown of concern, looking at the offending gas stove which had yet to be replaced. Following his gaze, she was quick to reassure him. "Don't worry; I didn't make them myself. They're some of the ones Mrs. Drummond brought over for me."

Rory heaved a sigh of relief, and nodded quickly. She smiled at his child-like honesty and went to fetch the biscuits Maud had brought over the other day, placing the tin in front of him. "Help yourself."

He didn't need to be told twice. He'd opened the lid to the metal cookie tin and popped one whole in his mouth quicker than she could get the words out. "Yummmm…"

She couldn't help but smile at him. Crossing the kitchen, she pulled down the only two glasses she had and poured them each a glass of milk, placing one of them in front of Rory who gulped it down appreciatively.

"Mam never lets me have biscuits before tea," he said, wiping the milk stains off his upper lip with the back of his hand.

"Well, we'll just keep it our little secret, shall we?" Aoife winked at him conspiratorially as Rory nodded his assent.

As if the very mention of her summoned her presence, Mara showed up at the back door of the kitchen. "Rory, love, pack up your homework; it's almost time to head home."

The boy looked up at his mother with the most comical look of surprise and guilt on his face. He was clearly wondering how far he could run without his mother finding out he'd broken the cardinal rule of "no biscuits before tea" when Aoife snorted, unable to contain her laughter, and drawing Mara's attention to her.

"Oh! Aoife! You startled me." She clutched her hand to her chest, much in the same manner as Aoife herself had done a few minutes before. Before Aoife could respond, Mara had turned her attention to her son.

"Rory Dermot Flanagan! Are you eating biscuits before your tea?"

Rory looked up at his mother, mouth open, the biscuit he'd picked up before his mother had called out to him still perched precariously between his forefinger and thumb. He dropped it like it was a hot potato, shaking his head and using the back of his hand to wipe the crumbs from his face.

"That was my fault," Aoife spoke up, and Rory looked up at her with a look of gratitude. "I said he could have them while he waited for you to finish in the garden. He's been working so hard on his homework, I figured he deserved a reward."

Mara raised an eyebrow at her son, trying to suss out if this was in fact the truth. Rory beamed up at her with one of his best smiles, the kind that was so full of charm that it could melt an iceberg.

"I'm sorry if he's being a bother to you. He normally goes to Molly's after school, but wee Desmond has caught the flu and so she didn't want to risk Rory getting sick as well."

"I'm not being a bother!" Rory piped up confidently. "Am I, Aoife?"

Aoife smiled at his bold confidence, so like his uncle's. "Of course not."

"See Mam," Rory exclaimed, as if it was the most absurd thing he'd heard of in his life.

"Rory here was just catching me up on all that's happening in the village, including what his uncle thinks of me."

"Yes, I was telling her how Uncle Michael said she's a – ," Rory's words were cut off into unintelligible mumbling by his mother's swift hand covering his mouth. It was evident from the apologetic look she gave Aoife that she knew *exactly* what Michael had been saying about her.

"Yes, well, what have we said about repeating things Uncle Michael says?" she asked her son, looking down at him sternly. The little boy looked a bit sheepish and mumbled something against her hand.

"Now, let's leave Aoife alone, eh? We don't want to bother her anymore, now do we?"

"But she *already* said I wasn't being a bother!" Rory corrected his mother and Aoife smiled at him.

"If Desmond is still ill tomorrow, I'm perfectly fine with Rory here spending some time with us until he's all better."

"Can I Mam?" the boy asked eagerly, probably enticed by the idea of getting to sneak in more biscuits while his mother wasn't looking.

"We'll see. Now, let's get you back to your Granny and Grandad's. And don't think I'm not going to tell your Granny about those biscuits you've had, young man."

"Please, Mam; you *know* what Granny will say!" Rory pleaded with his mother.

"Aye, I do. Now run along. If you're *really* helpful tonight with the dishes, then maybe we'll just forget about this and not have to tell Granny about it."

Rory nodded eagerly and climbed down from his chair, coming around to give Aoife a quick hug before he left. "I'm going to tell Uncle Michael that he was wrong and tell him what you're *really* like!" he told her before racing down the main hallway and out the front door. Aoife and Mara both laughed at the boisterous young boy as he hurried along to do as he was told.

"Come. I'll walk you out," Aoife said to Mara. As they approached the front door, Mara paused a moment.

"Look, I know my brother can be a bit of a jerk sometimes… ok, he can *really* be a jerk sometimes, but he's got a kind heart under all that gruffness, I promise. I'm sure he didn't really mean anything by what he said earlier. He's just got a lot on the go right now; it's not the easiest of times for us financially, and he's just stressed is all."

"I'm sure that's…" She'd meant to say that she was sure that was not what Michael had meant, even though they both knew he'd meant *exactly* what he'd said, but was distracted by her convertible speeding down the lane towards her. As it parked in front of her, she was surprised to find her boyfriend driving it.

"Danny?"

"Hey baby," he called out to her as he exited the car.

He was dressed in his usual dark aviators, a crisp, white dress shirt, a neutral-toned tie, and light brown slacks. She could see his matching suit jacket flung over the passenger seat. He looked like he'd just come down after leaving the office.

"What are you doing here?"

She was completely floored that he'd shown up; she'd been expecting to have to drive up to Dublin and practically kidnap him to get him to come down and visit. Danny had a well-known scorn for anywhere that wasn't within a five-minute drive from the hustle and bustle of a city.

"I thought I'd come and surprise you. Surprise!"

He flashed his near perfect teeth at her in one of those winning smiles, the kind that made her feel like she was the only person in the world.

"I asked Bex for your new address, and she said she and Millie had to drive your car down to you, so I volunteered to do it instead. I figured that since they've already seen the place and I haven't, it made more sense for me to come."

She was suddenly aware again of Mara standing beside her. "Danny, this is Mara Flanagan; she lives just down the lane a bit and is going to be helping to do the landscaping here."

"Nice to meet you," Mara said, extending her hand to him. Danny extended his own hand, shaking hers lightly.

"Mara, this is my boyfriend, Danny Fitzgerald."

"Well, I'll leave you two alone; I'm sure you have some touring around to do.

"Rory! Wait for me," she called out to her son who was well ahead of her on the road to home.

"Well, consider it a mission accomplished," she told Danny, kissing him lightly.

"Hmm?" he asked, watching Mara's retreating backside.

"You said you wanted to surprise me. Consider me surprised."

"Oh," he replied, turning his attention back to her again. "So this is the place then, is it?"

His critical eye took in all the scaffolding and tools around the place.

"This is it: Aldridge Manor." Pride rang out in her voice as she swept a hand around to show off her new home. She took his hand and brought him inside.

All That Compels the Heart

"Bit small, isn't it?" he said, poking his head into the front drawing room and taking off his sunglasses, his hazel-green eyes taking in everything around him.

"It's hardly *that* small. It's five bedrooms, and that's not counting the old servants' quarters on the third floor, which could easily be converted into larger bedrooms."

Danny sniffed, still not seeming to be too impressed. "I was expecting something more on the scale of your grandmother's place the way you were talking it up."

He seemed completely oblivious to the crestfallen look on her face, or perhaps he just ignored it.

"And what would I need a place as big as Granny's for?" she asked him, trying to keep any edge out of her voice. He ignored the question.

"You know, there's a gorgeous seven bedroom place that just went on the market a couple of blocks away from your grandmother's; I saw the listing and I thought: this would be the *perfect* place for us to live in."

"You mean you're thinking of moving in together?"

She was surprised by the suggestion; they both liked to have their own space, their own flats. She'd never really given much thought to moving in with him.

He moved in closer to her, putting his hands on her upper arms.

"Come on, don't you think it would be a great idea? A place for the two of us so we could start thinking of settling down?"

This was another surprise to add to the list since he'd arrived. He spent so much time away on business that there'd only been a few occasions where they were in the same city together at the same time. Lately, it seemed they spent most of their time dating over the internet or the phone.

"And by 'settle down' you mean what exactly? Move in together, get married, and start a family?"

Danny's hands tightened briefly on her upper arms at the mention of getting married and having kids, but then he relaxed them and shrugged. "Well, I'm not saying we need to rush into anything, but why not? I mean, it's the next logical step, isn't it?"

She supposed it was. The two of them had been dating for the last couple of years now; it made sense that the two of them would move in together and get a place of their own.

"I guess I hadn't thought of it until just now," she told him honestly.

"Well, take some time to think about it. I can tell the real estate agent to consider a serious offer from us, and I can maybe buy us a week or two."

He kissed her on the forehead gently.

"Well, if you really want to move in together, why not move in here with me? I mean, I already have the place. Sure, it's not much to look at right now, but once it's fully renovated it'll be great. There's plenty of room in it, it has great views, a wonderful property; it has everything that place in Malahide you mentioned has."

"You're being serious about this?" Danny gave her an incredulous look.

"Yes. Why not?"

He sighed and ran a hand over his tired face.

"Do you really see us living here?" he asked her honestly.

"Well, I'd *hoped* it would be a possibility. I mean, I'm putting enough effort into the place; it would be nice to have us both live here, eventually."

"I didn't ask you to come down here and buy a place, and then put all this effort and money into fixing it up, Aoife. You made that decision all on your own."

"I'm not saying you did." She was taken aback by the accusation in his tone.

Perhaps realizing how he'd sounded, he relaxed his face and changed his tone. "Look, let's just give it some time, huh? Let's just think about the place in Malahide and once you're done renovating this place, maybe we can flip it, or use it as a weekend home, or something. Yeah?"

He placed his index finger under her chin to force her to look up at him and rested his forehead against hers. She nodded silently; there was no point arguing it out with him. He'd decided he didn't like Aldridge Manor and there was no changing his mind about it.

Seemingly pleased that she was mollified, he said, "Now, I'm starving. Where can one eat in this place?"

She almost didn't want to respond, knowing he'd be disappointed by the answer, but she went ahead anyways. "Well, you're spoiled for choice. There's the café – which closed about an hour ago – or the chip shop, or there's the pub."

As she expected, he looked to see if she was being serious that there were only three places for them to eat at. In Dublin, they rarely ate at the same place twice.

"Well, I guess, the pub it is, then."

"Ok, give me five minutes; I just have to change."

"Aoife…" Danny groaned, knowing full well that 'just five minutes' meant more like twenty minutes waiting for her to get ready. "I'm so hungry I could eat *you* at this point."

"I'll be five minutes. I promise," she replied as she headed up the stairs to her bedroom.

"You look fine as you are," he said to her in a feeble attempt to prevent her from changing but followed her up the stairs anyways, knowing it had been a futile attempt.

"Bless you." Their earlier argument forgotten for the moment, she stopped in the middle of the hallway and kissed him quickly. "Now, come help me find something to wear."

"I'd much rather be finding ways to get you *out* of your clothes than into new ones." He smiled at her devilishly, a gleam in his eye that she knew all too well.

"I thought you were starving and wanted to have a bite to eat?" she asked, squirming out of his arms and heading directly for the pile of clothes she kept in a box on the floor.

"Can't I be hungry for more than one thing?" he asked, raising a suggestive eyebrow.

"You naughty boy," she teased before addressing her clothing situation.

She began sifting through some of the boxes.

"What do you think about this?" She held up a pencil skirt and white blouse she'd often wear to work up for him to inspect.

"Sure, that looks fine."

"C'mon, Danny. The sooner you help me find something to wear, the sooner we can go down and eat, and then the sooner you can have your dessert back here."

She saw that she'd finally gotten his attention.

"Well, definitely not that outfit. Not unless you're trying to look like a secretary."

She tossed them to one side with the others.

"What about this one?" He held up a red silk, strappy dress she'd worn to some charity event for Danny's work a couple of months ago.

"Not unless you want me to be branded the village harlot," she teased.

"Can't blame a man for trying," Danny shrugged

Spotting her pair of ocean-blue jeans in amongst one of the boxes, she grabbed them and threw them in Danny's general direction for him to catch. Rifling through the box further, she found her favourite leather jacket, also throwing it over towards the bed. In another box, she found a pair of black pumps that made her legs look great in her jeans, and tossed them lightly across the floor. Making her way over to the bed, she began stripping out of the ratty shirt and jeans she'd been wearing to unpack, pulled on the skinny jeans and slipped her feet into her pumps.

"Unless you're planning to go down to the pub in your jeans and bra – not that I'm complaining about this look at all – I think you'd better find a shirt to go with it."

Danny looked at her admiringly, appreciating what was right in front of him.

"I'm working on that," she smiled at him.

She walked back over to the boxes and began searching them again for the right top to go with the rest of her outfit. After throwing at least ten of them into the "no" pile and with Danny getting fidgety, she threw on her leather jacket, zipping it up and said, "Fuck it."

"Bold choice. I like it," Danny replied, coming over to wrap his arms around her. "Now, come on. I wasn't kidding when I said I could eat *you* if we don't get down to that pub soon."

She giggled as he crossed the room to come nibble on her ear, and lightly pushed him off, following Danny out of the house and down to the pub.

Chapter Fourteen

"Hey Brendan; can I get a bit of help over here?" Michael gestured to the queue of waiting customers standing before him. There were really only about four or five people, most of them locals who wouldn't have minded waiting for Michael to process them.

It wasn't like it was a busy night; just a few of the village gossips and their long-suffering husbands, and a small group of barely legal kids who were giggling in the booth in the back corner, clearly in the throes of too much alcohol consumption and not enough years behind them to have a tolerance for it, but it was the principle of the matter that counted. There was no reason for Brendan to be standing over there, chatting away with Aoife and her boyfriend while there was work to be done.

They'd been given fair warning that Aoife's boyfriend, Danny or something, had arrived in Ballyclara; Mara had made a beeline for the pub as soon as she could and had relayed the latest news about the city girl.

He didn't see what was so special about him that warranted all this fuss from Brendan and Mara; even Molly had come out to gawk at him while Michael feigned disinterest. It wasn't difficult to do; everything from the flashy car, the expensive clothes, and the permanent sneer as he scrutinized every inch of the pub irked him.

Brendan ignored him, continuing to talk to Danny and Aoife. While Aoife and Brendan laughed at some joke he'd made, Danny sat there, offering a slight grimace, looking like no matter how friendly Brendan was, no matter how great a quality the pub was, it wouldn't be good enough for him.

"Pretentious city bastard," Michael muttered under his breath in the general direction of Aoife's boyfriend.

"What, son?"

"That'll be two pounds, twenty, Mark," Michael said a little louder for the elderly patron standing in front of him.

He was deafer than a post most of the time, even with his hearing aid, so he likely hadn't heard Michael's comment. However, he mentally checked himself for letting the pretentious city bastard get under his skin.

Taking his sweet time with his conversation, Brendan lingered a second or two longer before finally sauntering over to give Michael a hand.

"What can I get you, Mrs. Murphy?" he asked the next person in the queue.

Michael continued to be irked, but focused instead on working silently, serving the rest of the patrons. When the queue had thinned out, Brendan turned to him and asked, "So what do you think of Danny, over there?"

He nodded in Aoife and Danny's direction.

"I don't have an opinion," Michael lied, sorting some change into the till. "I haven't met him."

"Well I tell you, I know he's the new girl's young fella and I wouldn't want to speak ill of someone before properly meeting them, but he nearly gave me the fright of my life earlier. He was racing that expensive red convertible around the village like he was in the Grand Prix or something. My poor Daisy has been agitated something fierce since he went roaring up the lane to the Old Rectory." Mrs. Murphy patted her perfectly coiffed perm, as if still agitated on behalf of her herd of milk cows.

"Is that so?" Michael asked her, giving Brendan a pointed look.

All That Compels the Heart

"Yes," she said, taking a sip of her sherry. "And Maud Drummond was only after tellin' me earlier how he raced past her on the main road and she practically had to jump out of the way of him, or else be run over."

"There, there, Mrs. Murphy; I'm sure he didn't mean anything by it," Brendan replied, patting the elderly woman's hand.

Mrs. Murphy, pleased to be the center of attention for a moment, looked mollified after recounting her tale. As she thanked Brendan for the kind words and the pint, she went and sat down with all the other old gossips, probably to recount more tales about Danny.

"Well, there now. I think I've heard all I need to know," Michael said to Brendan.

"Oh come now; give him a chance. After all, Aoife *is* our boss now; might do a world of good for you to go over there and introduce yourself to him, be nice to him. Might repair some of the damage you caused earlier."

"*I* caused?" Michael's tone was incredulous.

"Why don't you take this opportunity to go over there and clear their plates and you can introduce yourself? After all, it's important to keep the customer happy. And at the rate Aoife's paying us, we want to keep her very happy indeed."

"Why don't *you* clear them? You seem to be so enamoured with Aoife and her boyfriend; why don't *you* go and talk to them again for another half hour while I'm busy over here working?"

He picked up a tray of dirty glasses and hauled them off into the kitchen, leaving Brendan at the bar to deal with the place on his own for a few minutes.

Not only did Michael have zero interest in meeting Danny, he had zero interest in talking to Aoife; that is, until she was ready to admit she'd been in the wrong regarding the "stove incident." For there was no doubt in his mind that *she* was the one in the wrong. She should never have been using that stove if she didn't know how to. Reckless, infuriating…

If he'd been hoping to avoid Aoife and Danny altogether, it was a major disappointment to him when he went through the swinging doors to find the very man himself standing at the cash register, waiting to pay his bill. Brendan looked over at Michael with a wink, a convenient queue of punters waiting to be served, preventing him from helping Danny.

At Michael's entrance, Danny looked over at him, clearly bored and looking to get out of here. He held up the bill to him with his credit card in his hand, as if Michael didn't already know why he was standing there. Putting aside the fact the man grated on his nerves, Michael approached the bar.

"Ready to settle up?" he asked him as pleasantly as he could through his clenched jaw.

"Mmm," Danny replied, handing over his credit card.

He rang up the bill and punched in the total into the debit machine – taking it upon himself to add a thirty percent tip to the total, figuring someone like Danny hadn't even bothered to look at the total on his cheque from earlier – and handed the machine over to complete the payment.

"You just stopping in on your way through, then?"

He wasn't sure why he was making small-talk with the man. He wasn't the least bit interested in him, or his girlfriend for that matter, and he never usually bothered with making small-talk with the customers. That was Brendan's role. Michael ran the pub efficiently; Brendan was the friendly face who kept bringing people back.

"Yeah. My girlfriend just bought a place down here. Alton Manor or something."

"Aldridge," Michael corrected him.

"Hmm?" Danny was distracted, putting his PIN code into the debit machine.

"It's called Aldridge Manor."

That's the one. Anyways, yeah. It's just a temporary thing, you know," Danny looked at him like this should be the most obvious thing in the world to someone like Michael. "It's just until she sorts through some things in her personal life. Her grandfather just died. This is just a phase she's going through, on account of the grief. The two of them were really close.

"I think she just needs a project right now, you know?" Danny continued. "Once the house is fixed up, we're getting a place in Malahide. That's just outside of Dublin." Danny said it with the tone of someone who was explaining Ireland's geography to a foreigner.

Michael seethed silently, but continued to keep his face implacable.

"Aoife's a dreamer; like her grandfather was. It's best just to let her run with her crazy ideas, and then when she gets bored with it, she'll be back to normal again."

Michael wasn't sure who Danny was trying to convince more: him, or himself. One thing he *was* fairly certain about was that Danny had it all wrong about his girlfriend. From what he'd heard from his friends and family, she didn't seem like the kind of person who was not committed to living here. It may pain him to admit it, but Aoife seemed like she was planning on staying in Ballyclara for the foreseeable future. She'd put in a lot of interest and effort into restoring Aldridge Manor and went about overseeing every detail of the restoration process. If she'd been more hands off with the project, he might believe she'd just end up selling it and moving back to the city as soon as it was done, but Aoife seemed like she was planning to stay. He couldn't see her abandoning it on a whim.

Michael felt an unusual sympathy for the city girl; not only because of her recent loss, but also for the sorry excuse she had for a boyfriend. It had to be lonely not to have someone who is supposed to love not understand who you were.

Oh sure, Danny was saying all the right words about how he just needed to give Aoife time to work through her grief and be supportive of her, but his tone indicated that the last thing he wanted to do was wait for her to do exactly that. He seemed like the kind of guy who just wanted life to always be uncomplicated. Sure, Michael couldn't exactly blame him for it; it wasn't exactly like he and his fiancée, Eliza, dealt well with "complicated" themselves, but at least they worked through it. After all, if something was worth having, it was worth putting in some effort into keeping it.

"You all done?" Aoife asked Danny, approaching the bar.

"Yep," he replied, kissing her on the nose, looking like he was trying to gauge how much she'd heard.

"Thanks, Michael." He was a bit surprised to see her acknowledge his presence. He didn't realize the two of them were back on speaking terms.

He nodded at her silently, indicating he accepted her defeat in their unspoken staring contest. After all, he didn't need to rub it in her face that she'd been the first to cave in and talk to him. However, he couldn't help himself from muttering, "pretentious bastard," under his breath at Danny's retreating back, watching the two of them walk out of the pub, their arms around each other's waists.

Chapter Fifteen

The visit with Danny had been all too short for Aoife's liking.

While she could have wished he'd been a bit more supportive of Ballyclara, she knew she wouldn't change his mind overnight and accepted that it would take some time for him to adjust. It still stung just a little, was all.

He'll see it in time. When I've fully settled in here and he can see how great the place will be, he'll come around.

She didn't like arguing with Danny; they saw each other so seldom that it just took away from what little time they could be spending together doing better things. And one of those "better things" did not include being stared at by Michael Flanagan.

Of course, she'd known there was a strong possibility that he'd be working tonight. But even knowing that did not prepare her for the intense stare he gave her and Danny as they ate through their meal. She tried to push away the feeling of Michael's eyes on her and just enjoy being with Danny, but it was like an itch right between the shoulder blades that you couldn't quite ignore, but you couldn't quite reach in order to do something about it.

By the time they'd finished their meal and had had a friendly chat with Brendan and Molly, Aoife was more than ready to get away from Michael's negative energy.

"Come on. Let's test out that new bed I just bought," she'd whispered in Danny's ear as they exited the pub. Suddenly perking up, a genuine smile crept across his face, the first smile she'd seen from him since he'd arrived. Putting his arm around her waist, he practically rushed them out of the pub and back up to the house.

But with the arrival of the sun's rays through the open curtains she'd finally gotten around to hanging above her bedroom windows, came the end of their little sojourn. Danny's mobile had gone off, rudely waking the both of them from their slumber; another call from the office. And just like that, he'd gone back to Dublin as suddenly as he'd arrived, leaving her standing there in her tank top and boy shorts as the town car his company had sent down for him sped down her lane. She'd tried to ignore how quickly he'd dashed back off to the city.

"If I hurry, I can be back in the office for when it opens and I can deal with this. And the sooner it's dealt with, the sooner I can come back to you," he'd told her, kissing her on the top of her head. She made the choice to believe him.

Trying to push aside her disappointment, she set about finding herself some breakfast and writing out a list of things she wanted to accomplish today. Mara had told her about a greenhouse and nursery nearby where they could find some flowers and bushes for the garden; she thought today might be a good time for the two of them and Karen to take a trip out there to have a look and see what they could find.

Dermot had advised her that the fence surrounding most of the property should be mended and painted by the end of today or the next; she would leave him, Michael, and Jimmy to the task. Today was Brendan's day to open the pub, so he and Molly would be down there for day, so she set aside those tasks they'd agreed to take on until they returned at the end of the week. There were still several rooms that needed a good scrub down and a good sweep; Sinead had volunteered to work on those before she headed down to help with a bake sale for the parish. Just as she was finishing up her list of tasks, she heard footsteps coming through the front door.

"Aoife?" Mara's voice rang out down the main hallway.

"In the kitchen!" she called back.

"Looks like someone's getting a late start to the morning." Mara nodded at Aoife, still sitting there in her pajamas.

"Oh. Sorry." She'd forgotten she was still in her tank top and boy shorts from earlier. "Danny had to leave early this morning and go back to work, and then I started on the list of things to get done this week; I didn't have time to change. I should go on up and do that right now before anyone else comes over."

Mara shrugged, not overly concerned about her appearance. Aoife was the boss and she could do whatever she liked. The comment hadn't been meant to be a judgement; merely an observation.

"Just give me two seconds and I'll be right ba –,"

She'd had her back turned to the kitchen's entrance as she'd talked, walking backwards towards the main hallway, and hadn't noticed that Michael had been walking towards her.

"Aoife, is there anything you'd like us to start with before –," Michael had begun to ask her as he approached her. At the sound of her name, she'd turned around and, with her usual impeccably awkward timing, she collided with him just as he was coming into the kitchen.

"Woah there," he said, catching her around the waist, steadying her as she nearly toppled over him.

"Sorry," she mumbled, her face going bright red at the sight of him.

His hands felt warm on the exposed flesh of her midriff, making her astutely aware that – as Mara had just pointed out – she was not appropriately dressed to have people who were still largely strangers to her, in her house, no matter how comfortable she might feel around them. Finding herself quite literally face-to-face with Michael, and in such close proximity, she found herself becoming distinctly embarrassed.

As if he too were aware that they were just a little bit too close to one another, or perhaps he was just reassured she would not topple over on him, he pulled back from her, his back stiffening.

"I'll just let you —," he began at the same time as she said, "I'm just going to go upstairs and get dressed."

"Well, don't let me stop you," he said, moving out of her way and gesturing for her to pass.

Awkwardly, she skirted around him. Even though he'd stepped out of her way, the entrance between the kitchen and the hallway was narrow, and he still took up a considerable amount of it. She brushed against him, feeling the roughness of his plaid shirt tug against the cotton fabric of her tank top and she hurried up the hallway as quickly as she could, trying desperately not to focus on the fact she was still, embarrassingly, blushing. Taking a deep breath, she steadied herself, and headed for the master bedroom to get herself ready.

Emerging ten minutes later, her hair brushed and tucked up into a clip, some light make-up on her face to hide any traces of the earlier blushing, and now appropriately attired in a pair of jeans, boots, and a faded blue t-shirt, Aoife quietly went down the stairs, ears alert for any signs of Michael or Mara. Not hearing anything from below, she walked quickly down the main hallway to the kitchen to find it empty, except for Sinead, who looked up at her entrance as she took out a broom and mop from the small closet near the back entrance.

"Good morning, love," she greeted her.

"Good morning," Aoife replied. "I was just looking for Mara."

"She's gone out front, love. Said she was waiting for you to come down as she wanted to talk to you about going over to the greenhouse today with Karen to pick out some plants and bushes for the garden. Said it was on your list of things to do today."

She nodded to the piece of paper where Aoife had scribbled down some ideas earlier.

"Thanks."

Walking back out towards the front of the house, she could hear Jimmy and Dermot in the distance, chatting away as they worked on the fence. She didn't immediately see Mara or Karen, so she rounded the corner of the house, to see if they'd gone to the garden while they waited for her. As she rounded the corner, she noticed Michael up on a ladder, cleaning out the rain gutters of the vines that had been growing around the house. Brendan had warned her that while the vines might look nice on the outside of the house, over time they could cause a lot of problems, and so they should be kept trimmed up as much as possible.

"Michael, have you seen your sister?" she called up to him, shielding her eyes with one hand in the wake of the bright sunlight.

"She's over in the garden with Jimmy's wife, Karen," he replied, tossing down the pile of vines he'd been cutting, dropping them right in front of her. She tried not to scream as she noticed a rather large spider scurry out of the pile right towards her, and jumped back a bit, well out of its way while it made a run for it. She glared up at Michael in response, annoyed he hadn't taken more care with where he'd been throwing the vines. They could have landed right on top of her if he'd tossed them any further. She shivered at the thought.

"Sorry," he called down to her, but the small tug at the side of his mouth indicated he wasn't really sorry at all. Aoife made an unintelligibly exasperated noise at the back of her throat and stalked off in the direction of the garden. She found the two women examining the remnants of the secret garden, conceptually visualizing where everything would eventually go.

"Ah, Aoife! There you are. Aoife, I'd like you to meet Karen Connolly, my assistant," Mara said, introducing the young girl in front of her.

Karen was about eighteen years old and a good five to six months pregnant. She was tall and thin, a small wisp of a thing except for her enormous baby bump, which was barely being covered by her pink and white-striped t-shirt. Being so naturally thin, her stomach looked disproportionately large, making her look more like nine months pregnant than five months.

"It's so nice to finally meet you, Miss O'Reilly," Karen said, her green eyes brightening at the sight of Aoife, and her freckled cheeks widening into a smile.

"Oh, please, call me Aoife. Miss O'Reilly's too formal."

"I thought Karen could join us today. Even though she's the assistant, I swear I'm learning more from her than she is from me, sometimes. She has some great ideas about what could work in the garden."

"Great! Well, should we head out then?"

She pointed to Mara's car, which was parked in the drive. Aoife would have offered her own but she was afraid Karen might not fit in the smaller interior of the convertible.

"Sure thing. Aoife, would you go and ask Michael if he'll come along with us? We're going to need some help getting everything into the car and back out again when get home."

Mara nodded in the direction of her brother who was still on the ladder, pulling down more vines, the pile beneath him growing in size.

"Karen and I just need to move some things out of the car and we can be on our way."

Aoife looked gloomily in Michael's direction. As Karen and Mara walked over to the car, she heard Karen say, "Aren't those two not talking to one another?"

Straightening her shoulders, she walked over to the ladder once more, careful to stand well back from the pile of vines, lest he decide to throw more on top of her.

"Michael?"

He didn't seem to hear her, for there was no response from him except a pile of vines falling from the sky, landing on top of the pile.

"Michael!" she shouted a little louder.

"What woman?" he shouted back at her, clearly displeased with her interrupting his work. She clenched her teeth together, trying not to chafe at being called "woman" in that tone.

"Excuse me?" It slipped out despite her best efforts.

"What is it you want?" he asked her, emphasizing his point.

"Mara wanted to know if you could come to the nursery with us to help with the flowers? She said we could probably use another pair of hands to help with carrying them to and from the car."

"Did she now?" he asked, descending the ladder and coming to stand before her.

"Yes. So, let's go; we're heading out now."

She made to turn and head towards the car when he said, "So you don't need me to come, then?"

She paused, confused. "Yes. I thought I just said that?"

"You may have *said* it," he pointed out, "but I didn't hear you ask me if I'd help out or not. I don't know how you do things up in the city, but down here, we like to be polite and ask people if they will help us."

He folded his arms across his white tank top-clad chest, emphasizing the muscles of his bare biceps, leaning lightly against the ladder. His face turned into a smug smirk, waiting expectantly.

She didn't think her jaw could become more clenched, but somehow it did. Clearing her throat and giving him a pointed look, she swallowed her pride and asked, "Will you come to the nursery with us and help?"

"Sure," he replied simply.

Relieved that that was over, she turned towards the car again.

"If you say the magic word."

She stopped up short, annoyance clearly written over her face as she turned back towards him.

"Maybe they don't say 'please' and 'thank you' up in the city, but down here we do." His face became more smug with every word and Aoife had no greater desire than to punch the look right off him.

Her voice tense and with her temper barely reigned in, she asked, "Will you 'please' help us at the nursery, Michael?"

"Sure," he replied, standing up straight again. He removed his gloves and tossed them aside. "I don't know why you didn't just ask in the first place."

Aoife was about to share with him a few choice words about manners herself, but was interrupted by Mara who shouted over for them to hurry up. Aoife followed him to the car silently, all the while shooting daggers at his back. If looks could kill, he'd have dropped dead on the spot.

She noticed Karen and Mara looked distinctly uncomfortable about the exchange that had just occurred as she and Michael approached the car. As she climbed inside, Mara quietly asked over the hood of the car, "Was that entirely necessary?" to her brother.

Michael's only response was a wide grin.

※

And that was how she found herself in the backseat of Mara's car with Michael for the entire journey to the nursery and for the entire way back. With Karen being so pregnant, it had been logically unspoken that she would take the front passenger seat, there being no other viable option to get her in the vehicle. Mara, being the owner of the car, had logically taken the driver's seat, which left only the backseat for Michael and Aoife.

It had been a tense ride to the nursery, the argument between the two of them still fresh in all of their minds, not helped by the fact that they were forced to sit close together in the cramped interior of Mara's car, their upper arms and legs touching, no matter how often they tried to shift positions to get as far away from one another as possible. Mara tried to relieve the tension by talking about the designs for the gardens, while Karen idly twirled her strawberry-blonde hair around her fingers, picking up on the nervous energy from the backseat. When they finally arrived at the nursery, an audible sigh of relief could be heard from all as they exited the car.

"Aoife, why don't you and I begin with the roses? I've got some ideas on how to spruce up the back garden with some new rose bushes and lilacs..." Karen took her by the arm and led her through the greenhouses, looking for the plants she'd been eyeing a few days earlier when they'd begun drawing up plans for the garden.

And so, Mara and Karen kept themselves firmly planted between Michael and Aoife, allowing the two of them some time apart without making the situation more awkward. As Karen took her through the warm, humid greenhouses, pointing out this flower and that, Aoife began to become truly excited about how the gardens would look. Aoife loved a well-planned garden; she just had no idea how to create one herself, so she was grateful for the expert eyes of Mara and Karen.

By the end of two hours, they had everything they needed to begin with and Michael silently, but willingly, carried everything out to the car for them and loaded them into the little trailer Mara had hitched to the back. He secured each one of the planters and seedlings with care, satisfied they wouldn't fly out the back on them, the four of them began to get back into the car.

"Michael, why don't you drive back? I'm a bit sore from bringing one of those planters out here; I could use a chance to relax my legs a bit." She rubbed her upper thigh for emphasis.

"You seemed fine a minute ago," Michael said, echoing Aoife's thought.

"Would you just drive back for me, aye?" his sister demanded, getting into the cramped backseat with Aoife. Shaking his head, Michael did as he was asked, getting into the driver's seat and reaching back to his sister for the car keys.

It was a remarkably smoother ride back to the Old Rectory compared to the drive down. Aoife suspected Mara's legs had nothing to do with why she'd asked Michael to drive, and all to do with the fact she couldn't bear to put up with another tense, silent drive. She chatted amiably to Karen and Aoife, discussing some of the plans for the gardens, going over with Michael all that they'd need for help. It seemed like no time at all had passed when they were driving back up the lane to the house, Jimmy and Dermot waving to them as they drove past. Dermot was holding a post in place while Jimmy hammered it into the ground, ensuring it was properly secure in its hole. As Michael navigated Mara's car as close to the entrance of the secret garden as he could, the two men stopped what they were doing and came over to greet the returned shoppers.

"How'd it go?" Dermot asked Mara as they emerged from the car, rubbing a gloved hand across his grime-covered forehead, beads of sweat making rivulets through the grime down his cheeks.

"Well, we managed to keep Aoife and Michael at arm's length and not have them kill one another, so I would say it's been a success," she said. Her father smiled at her.

"Well, you know your brother. He knows exactly how to push all the wrong buttons, sometimes."

Meanwhile, Karen had bounded out of the car towards Jimmy, practically jumping into his arms, planting an almost embarrassingly deep kiss on his lips, completely ignoring the fact he was sweaty and covered in dirt from working in the warm sun all day. One would think the two had been parted for years, not a mere couple of hours.

"Ah young love," Aoife said to Michael. She hadn't exactly intended to speak to him, but Dermot and Mara had seemingly headed off towards the garden and it was just the two of them left. She leaned against the car, the feel of the sun-baked metal warm on her back, permeating her t-shirt. "They're such a cute couple."

"Mmmm," he mostly grunted, beginning to lift out some of the heavier plants from the back of the trailer.

"Jimmy, can you come grab some of these and bring them into the garden?" he asked, seemingly ignoring Aoife again. Reluctant to have their moment broken up, Jimmy pulled himself away from his young wife with another kiss and came over to pick up the planters Michael had pointed out.

"Karen; you go and show him where Mara wants them."

"Sure," she said, grabbing some of the seedlings in the black plastic containers and followed where Mara and Dermot had gone, her young husband in tow. Aoife was just about to grab a tray of seedlings and follow them into the garden as well when Michael finally spoke to her.

"They've had a hard road to get to where they are, those two."

He nodded in the direction of Jimmy and Karen's retreating backs. She was so shocked to have him speak to her that she nearly dropped the tray of seedlings. He reached over and put a hand under the tray, helping to keep them upright.

"Oh?" she asked, carefully balancing the tray in her hands with his help.

"Jimmy was all set to go to university in Dublin last term – that was a pretty amazing thing for him, you see – when Karen found out she was pregnant. The two of them were scared out of their minds. They didn't know what to do, or who they should tell, or even if they *should* tell anyone.

In the end, it was Molly who got it out of them. Karen began skipping school and Molly caught her at it one day. Thankfully, it was her and not her parents who found her then; I think she was in a pretty bad place what with the pressure just getting to be too much for her. She finally ended up just needing to tell somebody everything about it."

Much like you're doing now with me, Aoife noted. It was the longest conversation the two of them had had – where neither one of them was shouting at each other – since she'd arrived in Ballyclara.

"Molly eventually talked Karen into telling her parents. It was the right thing to do, but…" Michael's voice trailed off, his face darkening, and she could see how much he really cared about the young couple. It was an odd sensation for her; she wasn't used to him displaying any sort of affection to anyone. So far, she'd only ever seen him angered or agitated, and most of that had been directed at her.

"They were furious with her, her parents. Ye see, Jimmy's parents died in a car crash when he was a baby and his aunt was forced to take him in, being his only living relative. It's been hard enough keeping a roof over their heads, let alone adding another mouth to feed. The Byrnes on the other hand – that's Karen's family – they own the café down in the village and have a sort of respectability around here. Not that it's deserved, given the way their son –"

His voice trailed off and he went silent. They stood there in the quiet, listening to the birds in the trees and the faint chatter from the garden and Aoife wasn't sure he was going to speak again.

"Anyways," he finally said, apparently reconciling whatever wrong the Byrnes' son had done him in the past and putting it aside for now. "They don't approve of Jimmy, nor of their daughter being married to him, and needless to say, Karen's folks kicked her out.

"They insisted she get an abortion, so it wouldn't ruin her chances of getting into university next year, even though Karen and Jimmy insisted that they wanted to get married and focus on having the baby. But, they would have none of it. In the end, the two of them ran off to Scotland and got married there. They didn't want to have it here, ye see. Didn't want to ruffle any more feathers with her folks."

"That must have been difficult for them," Aoife said. "Especially coming back and knowing they didn't have a home to come back to."

"Oh, Molly and Brendan took care of that, though Ma and Da would have taken them in if they hadn't."

She smiled; it sounded exactly like something that both the McCaffreys and the Flanagans would do.

"Before they went to Scotland, Molly went 'round to see them at Jimmy's aunt's – she'd taken them in straight after the Byrnes kicked Karen out, even though she hardly had the space to spare – and Molly told them that when they came back, they'd have a place with her and Brendan to come home to. They've been living there ever since."

Her smile widened.

"What are you smiling at?" he asked her, honest curiosity on his face.

"I was just thinking how it's great that even though they found themselves in an impossible situation, they have such a great support network what with you and Brendan giving Jimmy a job, Karen working with Mara, and Brendan and Molly taking them in and making sure there was a roof over their heads. It's comforting to know there's still decent folk in this world and that you always have someone you can depend on to help you out in a crisis."

"That's small-town life for ye; there's always someone you can depend on. Even when you're not from here."

She looked up at him then and noticed his face was halfway between his usual grimace and something almost softer, gentler. It was an odd thing to say. Was it his way of telling her that this support network suddenly included her and that she was welcome here too? Before she had any time to ask him what he'd meant by it, Jimmy had returned.

"Come on old man; Mara's anxious to get what we can of the flowers into the garden today before those clouds rain on us."

Aoife looked up at the sky and noticed that while she and Michael had been talking, the lazy clouds that had been in the sky earlier had turned darker, threatening rain.

"I thought you and Aoife were supposed to be coming right along, and here you two are, gabbin' away like you've not a care in the world. Get yourself in gear, man," Jimmy teased as he unloaded one of the rosebushes from the back of the trailer.

"Who are you calling an old man, eh?" Michael teased him back. "You gonna let that little girl o' yours talk to ye like that when she's your age?"

"You already know you're having a girl?" Aoife asked as she followed Jimmy and Michael into the garden, carrying the tray of seedlings.

"Yeah, we had a scan not too long ago. We weren't sure if we wanted to know or not, you know, keep it a surprise until the birth and all. But, when we were there in the clinic we just both had to know."

"Congratulations!"

"Thanks," he replied, a happy flush coming to his homely face.

"There you all are!" Mara exclaimed when they walked into the garden. She looked at Michael and Aoife, anxiously scanning them over for any signs of physical injuries or any sign that the two of them had been arguing. Her shoulders visibly dropped with relief when she noticed that everything seemed to be fine with them, but almost immediately raised an eyebrow, suspicion and curiosity written all over her face.

Perhaps instinctively expecting an interrogation, Michael asked her, "Where do you want these?"

With a look that told him she would not be dropping this, and he would have to answer to her later, she said, "Jimmy, put those roses over there. Michael, you can put that planter down over there," she pointed in the opposite direction. "And start planting those rosebushes over there, aye?"

"Yes ma'am," Michael replied, carrying the planter to where his sister had directed him.

All of them worked under the careful guidance of Mara and Karen for the next couple of hours, planting and potting, until the sun began to fade in the sky and great, fat raindrops plopped from the sky.

"How we doing out here?" Sinead appeared at the solarium entrance to the garden, peering in at the work they'd accomplished. "It's nearly going on time for tea and it looks like those clouds are going to break any second."

They all looked at the dark clouds looming above them.

"Well, I think we've got enough done for today. Let's get everything else inside the solarium for now, and we can finish with it tomorrow." Mara stood in the middle of the garden, dark soiled hands on hips, proudly admiring her vision.

"Are you going to need us to help tomorrow, Mara? Only, I was hoping Da and I could finish with the rest of the fence," Michael asked.

"No, we should be grand, so long as we can borrow Jimmy here for the rest of the heavy-lifting. If we get the rest of the big things in tomorrow, Karen and I should be able to manage the rest on our own."

"I'm happy to help wherever I'm needed," the ever-affable Jimmy replied, seemingly pleased just to be needed.

"Great, well ye better get that planter in here before it really comes down on you," Sinead told him gesturing for him to come inside.

No sooner had she finished speaking than the heavens opened and the rain poured down, beating loud as a drum against the glass panes of the solarium walls.

"That was good timing," Dermot said, craning his head towards the glass roof, trying to see if he could see the sky through the rivers running down the roof and walls.

"I'll go around and bring the car up to the front door," Mara said, heading back into the house. "Jimmy, Karen, I'll give you a drive home, and Ma, Da, and Michael; I'll come back for ye after I pick Rory up from school."

"You take the four of them," Michael said, pointing to his parents, Jimmy, and Karen. "I can walk down. A bit of rain doesn't bother me."

"You'll soak through in seconds out there," his mother admonished his idea.

"I can drive you home, Michael. My car's still out front. It's no bother."

Everyone turned and looked at her, surprised at her offer.

"Well, alright then." Michael's look was just as surprised as everyone else's, but curiously, he also looked like he was secretly pleased she'd offered.

"Well then, I'll just go and bring the car 'round."

A few minutes later, Mara had her parents, Karen, and Jimmy bundled into her small car, mostly unscathed by the rain. Michael and Aoife stood in the front doorway, waving them off.

"Should we make a break for it?" he asked, looking up at the skies.

"Might as well."

The rain looked like it was firmly not going anywhere, anytime soon. She picked up her keys from the little stand in the main hallway and thanked God that Danny had thought to put the roof up on her convertible when he drove it down yesterday. Closing the door behind them, she ran through the pouring rain to the car getting inside as quickly as possible.

It hadn't mattered; she was soaked through in the three seconds it had taken her to get from the front door to the car, great splotches of clean skin on her arms and legs showing through the patches and rivulets from the potting soil she'd been working with.

"I'm going to get your car all muddy," Michael said, half-apologetically as he looked down at his own grimy, mud and rain-soaked clothes.

"It's no problem at all. It's better than making you walk home in this." She gestured to the rain pounding down around them.

Starting the car, she turned the heat and the windshield wipers on full blast, hoping to keep the windows from fogging up . She and Michael drove in silence, though a rather more comfortable one than earlier in the day. Only the driving rain and the sound of the car pinging at them to let them know their seatbelts were not fastened broke the empty noise. As she pulled the car up to his front door, she turned to him.

"Thanks for all your help today." She actually meant it.

Perhaps uncomfortable by her sincerity, Michael nodded to her and headed out into the driving room.

"See you tomorrow," he said before closing the door firmly behind him and ran inside.

With a cautious optimism that perhaps she was making some headway with him, she drove back home, a satisfied smile on her face.

Chapter Sixteen

No sooner had Aoife and the rest settled into a routine with the renovations and unpacking of her new furniture than she had a new visitor, though this one from out of town. As she and Sinead were opening some boxes of new tableware she'd had delivered, she heard the crunch of tires approaching the house. Not expecting any further deliveries for the day, she curiously approached the front door to see who it was. Recognizing the Porsche and its driver, her heart leapt with joy.

"Connor!"

Before he'd even put the car in park, she'd bounded down the front steps, pulling him into a tight hug as he exited the car. The cotton fabric of his light blue shirt felt soft against her cheek. She giggled loudly as he swung her around. Putting her back on the ground, he planted a quick kiss on top of her head.

"Well hello, love. And how's my favourite pint-sized person in the whole wide world?"

"I'm not pint-sized," she retorted, punching him playfully in the arm. "You're just ridiculously *over*-sized. And I'm loads better now you're here."

"What? Trouble in paradise already? You've barely lived here a week yet. Don't tell me you're getting homesick already?"

"No, not exactly trouble." She didn't want to get into the whole situation with Michael just at the moment. "I *do* like it down here. There's just a lot to adjust to, is all."

"That's because you're always setting the bar too high for yourself and taking on the whole world all at once instead of just taking it one step at a time."

Connor smirked knowingly at her, resting his hands on top of her shoulders. "Take it easy. Everything will come into place if you give it time."

"I know you're right," she admitted. "It's just that this is the first time I've had a place of my own. I've never settled anywhere before, you know?"

"All too well." Connor's face was pensive. "Our nomadic upbringing didn't exactly foster a sense of belonging to one place, did it? I think it's the reason I joined the military: the regimen, the consistency, and support. Whatever happens, I know there's always someone there to come home to.

"Well, them and you. You're like coming home, too," he told her with a smile on his face.

"Aww. I think that's about the nicest thing you've ever said to me." She beamed back up at him.

"Alright. I want to see this place you're going to call home. Give me the grand tour."

He opened one arm to take in the view before him and hooked his other arm lazily about her neck, pulling her in close as they walked towards the house.

"And who is this?"

Aoife followed his gaze and caught a glimpse of Mara walking around to the front of the house pushing a wheelbarrow full of dead plants and vines, heading for the mulch pile she'd hoped to create to help revitalize the gardens.

"That would be a friend, and you can forget any ideas about flirting with her, young man."

"You do know that I'm older than you by an entire eleven months, right?"

"How can I not when you're so fond of reminding me?"

All That Compels the Heart

"So, you can't boss me around."

"*You* were taught to respect the fact that you come from a matriarchal family, buddy. Sorry, but I take rank over you and you are keeping your eyes firmly *off* Mara Flanagan."

She'd heard him use that tone when looking at a beautiful woman before and it never ended well for the poor women. Connor may have one of the biggest, kindest hearts of anyone she knew, but when it came to women, but he just couldn't focus it on one particular woman for very long.

"Mara? That's a pretty name." Connor's voice drifted, along with his eyes. "She looks nice. Introduce us."

"You're pathetic." She didn't even try to hide the fact that she was judging him just a little.

"I know, but I'm not above begging in order to be introduced to a beautiful woman."

"Ok you really *are* being pathetic now," she teased.

While Aoife might have been hesitant to have Mara and Connor meet, the situation was taken out of her hands when Mara pulled up in front of them. She noticed the way Mara hastily removed her soil-stained gloves and pushed the few strands of dark hair that had escaped her ponytail, away from her face. Predictably, she saw the familiar gleam of interest in her midnight blue eyes as she took in Connor's handsome features.

Oh boy.

It was going to be more difficult than ever to protect Mara from becoming just another name on Connor's long list of girlfriends.

"Hi Aoife." Mara smiled at her. "I see you have a new visitor. Down from the city are ye?"

"Mara, meet my cousin, Connor. Connor, this is Mara Flanagan, my landscape artist, neighbour, and friend." She emphasized this last word, as a further reminder to her cousin to take things slowly and not get himself into trouble.

She could see what they saw in each other. Although Mara might be a few years older than Connor, she was certainly a beautiful young woman with her dark hair and blue eyes. Even dressed in her work jeans and a red tank top, she looked as glamourous as if she were in a party dress. Although she was a few inches taller than Aoife, Connor still fairly towered over the both of them. And with his blonde hair and blue-eyed good looks, she knew exactly what Mara found attractive about him.

"Nice to meet ye," Mara said, taking Connor's hand and shaking it.

Aoife could tell that she was self-conscious about the dirt under her fingernails and the roughness of her calloused hands, but Connor didn't seem to care.

"It's wonderful to meet you too, Mara." Connor turned on all the charm in his flirty tone. Aoife quickly elbowed him in the ribs, trying, but failing to be subtle. In an attempt to put a bit of distance between the two, she turned to Mara and said, "Look, it's almost the end of the day. If you don't want to stick around, you don't have to. It's such a nice day; I'm sure you want to spend the rest of it with your son."

Mara looked a bit surprised by the offer.

"Thanks Aoife, that's really thoughtful of you. I'll just grab my things and head out for the day. See ye tomorrow?"

A look passed between her and Connor that Aoife didn't quite understand.

"It was nice to meet ye, Connor."

"It was great to meet you too, Mara."

"See you tomorrow," Aoife said hastily, trying to move Mara along before Connor decided to jump her bones right then and there. She wouldn't put it past him trying either.

"She's nice," Connor said, watching Mara's retreating backside as she went inside to get her purse.

"*She* has a ten-year old son," Aoife said in a warning tone. "She isn't just one of your girlfriends you can break up with in three months' time and not have there be any major consequences."

"I love kids. You know that." For once, Connor's tone sounded like he was peeved with her. "And it wasn't exactly kind of you to just out the fact she has a kid like that. You were raised better than that."

"Wait, what?" She was genuinely astonished by his sudden change in attitude.

"If she wanted to wait to tell me she has a son, then she has a right to do that."

Connor looked at her, his face drawn into a frown and she realized he really *was* annoyed with her. It wasn't a feeling she was used to.

"And seriously, the fact that you think I would just jump into bed with the first pretty girl I see, or the fact I would run from said pretty girl at the first mention of her having some baggage with her, quite frankly says more about you Aoife, than it does about me."

He put his hands in the pockets of his faded jeans and looked down at his trainers, clearly just as uncomfortable about arguing with her as she was about arguing with him.

She made a shocked noise in the back of her throat, not exactly sure how to respond. "Look, all I'm saying is that you have a bit of history with women."

"Who the hell doesn't this day and age?" Connor asked, still annoyed with her.

"I just think you and Mara should be careful is all; you're both attractive people, yes, but there's more than just yourselves to consider. Rory's a great kid and the last thing I want is to see any of you get hurt, least of all him."

"I'm going to choose to ignore the fact that you clearly have a lower opinion of me than I thought you did and instead, I'm going to let you take me on a tour of your new house, and then you're going to take me out to lunch to apologize."

"I'm sorry, Connor."

He looked up at the sincerity in her voice, her face revealing how devastated she was that he thought she thought so little of him, especially when it wasn't true. Connor was now the single most important person in her life, now that their grandfather was gone. She'd do anything for him. She'd just been trying to protect the people she cared about.

"I know you are." He kissed her quickly on the forehead to let her know he forgave her. "Now, come show me this new house of yours."

Wrapping her arm around his waist companionably, she walked with him inside and took him on the grand tour of the – largely still under renovation – house. When she'd finished the tour and they'd ended up in her kitchen, she said, "Why don't we have lunch here? Wouldn't a lunch apology be better if it were homemade?"

"Under normal circumstances, I would say 'yes' but I've tasted your cooking before, and I count myself lucky that I'm still alive to tell the tale," he teased.

"Touché."

"So, where are you taking me?"

"Well, your options are the pub, or there's the pub." She looked at him half-apologetically, half-teasingly. "There *is* a café and chip shop if you'd prefer either of those options, but knowing you, you'd rather go to the pub."

"You know me so well. C'mon, let's go."

He took her hands, pulling her back to the front of the house and to his car.

"*O'Leary's*," Connor read from the gold lettering above the door of the pub a few minutes later as they walked up to the pub. "So is this a family pub, then?"

"You could sort of say that. It's owned by Brendan McCaffrey and Michael Flanagan, the two guys who are working on the restoration of the house for me. Apparently, they've been best friends since primary school and when the opportunity came up to purchase this place, they did. So, it's only in its first generation so far. I guess time will tell if it becomes a true family pub down the ages."

"Wait, so they own the contracting business as well as the local pub? Is there anything they don't do around here? Maybe you should see if one of them is single; clearly they've got some things going for them."

She and Connor pushed open the door and stepped into the dimly lit pub. As usual, the place was about a quarter full, mostly with locals and a few tourists stopping in on their way either to or from Glendalough.

"Well, I happen to know for sure that Brendan's taken by his lovely wife, Molly, and they have a beautiful son named Desmond, so that won't be happening."

She grabbed the same booth she'd sat in when she first came to Ballyclara, situating herself across from her cousin.

"And what about this Michael, then?"

Connor was like a dog with a bone.

"You do realize that I have got a boyfriend already, right? You've met him several times now?"

She was starting to get a tad annoyed with him trying to set her up with someone one new.

"Are you two still dating?" Connor tried to be coy, pretending he didn't already know the answer.

"You know damn well that we are."

His face contorted somewhere between a grimace and acceptance. She was well aware of his feelings on Danny; they mirrored those held by Bex and Millie.

"And actually, Danny is thinking that he and I should move in together."

She paused to see Connor's reaction to this bit of news. His grimace drew into a frown.

"And are you? Going to move in together?" He looked around the small pub, taking it all in and sizing it up much the same way Danny had when she'd brought him in here, but Connor's gaze indicated much more the reaction she'd been hoping for from her boyfriend.

"I don't know yet," she replied honestly. Even though she'd told Danny she would give it some thought, she hadn't really kept up her end of the bargain.

"So, he'd be willing to move down here with you, then?" Connor's face indicated he didn't think this was a very likely scenario.

"We haven't decided anything just yet," she said, truthfully. "He saw a place in Malahide he thought might be right for us but we haven't made any decisions on it yet."

"Malahide? I thought the point of coming down here was to get away from everything up in Dublin? And what would you be needing with another new place anyways when you've only just gone and bought this one?"

It was roughly the same argument she'd presented to Danny.

"I know; this is why we haven't decided on anything final yet. He's had to go away again on business anyways, so it's not like we're going to be able to make any decisions until he's back."

"When is he ever feckin' *not* away on business?" she heard Connor mutter under his breath, but the two of them were saved getting into another argument by the arrival of Mara.

"Sorry about the wait," she greeted them, placing menus on the table in front of them.

"Well, look who we have here," Connor said, eyeing Mara up and down. "I thought you were going home after we last saw you?"

"Oh well, me da and me son were having such a fun time together that he didn't want to come home just yet, so I thought I'd pick up a shift in the pub."

"Does everyone in this place have more than one job?"

Connor hadn't meant it offensively; he was just shocked at the number of people so far who seemed to be both employed by Aoife and elsewhere.

"Oh well, you w how it is. Gotta make ends meet."

"Mara, Mark over there's been looking for the pint he ordered five minutes ago." Michael had come up silently behind his sister, barking out the order.

"I was just making sure Aoife and Connor here had their menus, Michael. No one seemed to be looking after them."

Her look was pointed, making sure her brother knew whose fault she thought that was. Despite the fact that Mark kept trying to silently get her attention from across the room, Mara lingered, reluctant to leave.

"I'll look after Aoife and her friend," Michael told her. Mara continued to linger a half second longer before finally giving way to her brother and letting him take over.

"Now then, Aoife, is there anything I can get ye?"

She was surprised by his continued pleasant behaviour towards her. Since that day he'd opened up to her about Jimmy and Karen, the two of them had come to some sort of unspoken agreement that they were now on speaking terms again. While neither of them had exactly gone out of their way to talk to the other, she'd noticed a markedly contrasting attitude towards her from their first few encounters. It still took a bit of getting used to.

"I'll have a water and your lamb stew, Michael. Thanks." She handed him back the menu and looked over to Connor to give his order.

"I'll have the same," he declared, handing back his menu to Michael as well. "You say your name is Michael, is it? As in Michael Flanagan?"

"The one and the same," Michael responded, clearly wanting to know why Connor was asking but, for once, seeming too polite to ask him directly.

Maybe he really is *trying to change.*

"Any relation to Mara Flanagan?" Connor nodded once more, this time in the direction of Mara as she stood at the bar filling an order for a customer.

"She's my sister. Why?"

"Oh no reason," Connor hastily reassured him, realizing his probing questions may have come across as offensive. "It's just I met her up at Aoife's place earlier. Just trying to become familiar with all the people in Ballyclara now my cousin is going to be living here. I'm Connor O'Reilly, by the way."

He extended his right hand to Michael, giving it a shake. It was Connor's way of sizing a person up. He always said there was no better way to judge a person's character than by taking them by the hand and looking them in the eye. He must have seen something about Michael he liked, for he nodded to the other man with approval.

"Nice to meet ye. I'll be right back with those orders."

Michael disappeared back into the kitchen, leaving her and Connor alone once more.

"I like it here." Connor's gaze swept around the pub but noticeably lingered longer on Mara. "It's a charming place."

"Yeah, I kind of like it."

She knew what he was referring to, or rather *whom*, but she let it slide for now. She would just try to keep a tight rein on him so he didn't end up making any mistakes that she'd end up regretting later. The last thing she needed was him going and breaking half the hearts in Ballyclara and then she'd have to deal with the fall out when he was gone.

"Michael seems like a nice guy. I noticed you didn't happen to mention that he was married. Don't think I didn't notice how you deflected the question, earlier."

Connor's gaze rested on her until she looked up at him.

"What's there to say? It's not like I'm single and can freely date whomever I like." There was an edge to her voice, indicating her desire to stop talking about Michael Flanagan.

"But if you *were* single, would you date him?"

"Connor! Stop trying to fix me up with every single guy you see!"

"So he is single then? I thought you didn't know?" he teased her.

"I *don't* know," she retorted. "I haven't asked him."

"Well, I like him."

"That makes one of us," she muttered.

"And what does that mean? Has he been causing trouble for you? Because if so, I will be having more than a few stern words with him." Connor's tone had gone from lightly teasing her to deadly serious.

"No, no. Nothing like that, exactly. We just got off on the wrong foot," she hastily reassured him. The last thing she needed was Connor going all protective-older-cousin on her. Much as she might have initially liked the idea of Connor giving Michael a good "what for," she knew it would only cause more trouble between them. "Let's just stop talking about Michael Flanagan, alright?"

Embarrassingly, that was of course when the very man himself decided to show up with their orders. She held her breath, hoping beyond all hope he hadn't heard any of their conversation, but at the same time knowing that her luck was not that good.

"And here ye go." He lifted their bowls of soup and their glasses of water off his tray and placed them before them. "Can I get you anything else?"

She silently shook her head, too embarrassed to ask for anything else she may have wanted, desperately hoping he would just go away quickly.

"No thanks," Connor replied, noting Aoife's embarrassment.

Michael nodded to the both of them, walking away without a further word, either ignoring the fact they'd obviously been talking about him, or he really hadn't heard them. She desperately hoped beyond hope it was the latter.

Aoife and Connor ate their meal in silence, the two of them trying to avoid any further potentially awkward situations. When they'd finished, Mara returned to take their dishes from them, bringing a new sort of tension.

"Let me just get those for you," she said, placing them on her tray. "And will it be two separate bills tonight?"

"Just the one, please," Aoife smiled at her. Mara returned a minute or two later with the cheque and handed it to her.

"Aoife, why don't you go and pay for this and I'll meet you over there?" Connor made eye contact with her, indicating he wanted the chance to talk to Mara alone.

She glared back at him, giving her best "keep-it-in-your-pants" look. Connor looked away, knowing full well what the look meant. She smiled again at Mara as she headed for the cash register to pay for her bill. She'd been hoping her luck might have turned around and she would get Brendan to serve her, but he was at the far end of the bar talking with a customer. Michael, noticing her standing there, came straight over to her and took the cheque from her to ring it through.

She stood before him in awkward silence, not sure if she should bring up the fact that she and Connor hadn't really been talking *about* him earlier, so much as discussing his viability as a potential suitor for her. Which, of course, she would never be interested in whatsoever. However, every scenario she quickly ran through in her mind always ended with her coming across as a huge eejit.

Desperately willing Michael's hands to ring up her bill faster, it felt like every move he made was happening in slow motion. She silently handed him her credit card, for once grateful that Michael didn't like to make small talk. That would have just made everything worse right now.

"Everything to your satisfaction?"

She sighed mentally. She didn't *want* to be forced to talk to him.

"Oh yes, everything was fine."

She punched in her PIN code, got it wrong in her haste to be out of there as quickly as possible, and the machine beeped loudly at her.

"Sorry, I think I put in the wrong password," she mumbled, handing him back the machine so he could re-enter the information.

"No problem at all," he told her, dutifully putting in the numbers again and handing her back the machine.

Ok, focus now.

She carefully re-entered her PIN code again and gave him a generous tip to make up for the prior misunderstanding, and gave a little sigh of relief when the machine whirred to life, accepting the code this time. She handed it back to him, about to wave off needing the receipt, when Connor came up behind her.

"Mara said there's a waterfall nearby she thought I might like to see. We're going to hike up there. I'll see you up at the house later, alright?"

He kissed the top of her head quickly, eager to head out with the beautiful Mara.

"But what about…?" She was going to say "But what about our plans?" only realizing now that they hadn't made any. No good, plausible excuses came to mind as to why he should stay with her and not go with Mara, as he so obviously wanted.

"You be careful out in those woods, Mara. It's getting towards dusk and you know how rocky that path can be." Michael's voice was full of concern and not just for the fact that the terrain out to the waterfall was rough. A look of brotherly concern came across his face that indicated he might be as worried as Aoife was about the potentially budding romance between his sister and Connor.

"Sure, and we'll be fine." Mara brushed off the comment. "I know that path just as well as you do."

"Just remember that Rory goes to bed soon and he'll be looking for his mam to read to him," Michael muttered, pointedly bringing up her son in front of Connor much in the same way Aoife had, to see if it would make him flinch. He held his ground.

"My son is staying with his grandparents tonight and he's having a great time," Mara retorted, clearly annoyed at both Aoife and Michael's attempts to thwart whatever she and

Connor were trying to do. "Why don't you keep Aoife here company until we get back, aye?"

She nodded at Aoife standing there in front of him.

"Oh, I should be getting back to the house," Aoife replied at the same time Michael said, "I think Mr. O'Sullivan's looking for a refill of that pint."

Mara smirked at them and turned to Connor and said, "Shall we?"

He put his hand in hers and the two of them headed out in the late afternoon light, off on some adventure.

"God help us all," Aoife muttered to herself. She thought she saw Michael nod in agreement before she too headed out.

Chapter Seventeen

Connor didn't come back to the house until well after dark. She had to remind herself that he was a grown man and it was none of her business what he got up to in his love life. Except when that love life impacted someone she considered to be a friend and was someone she not only had to live in the same village as, but also had to work with on a daily basis. That's what irked her.

When night had fallen and he still hadn't come home, she'd gone upstairs and made up the bed in one of the spare rooms that had just been recently re-done, the only one with a proper bed in it. After bringing his suitcase up the stairs and placing it at the foot of the bed for him, she was left with the decision of whether to wait up for him or go to bed herself. Her body ached slightly from moving around some of the furniture the day before, and she was still trying to catch up on sleep. She decided to leave Connor to make whatever mistakes and problems for her he was going to do. It wasn't like there was anything she could do about it by waiting up for him, anyways.

Even though she lay there tired, she couldn't sleep. She tossed and turned, like a mother waiting up for her errant son.

"This is ridiculous!"

All That Compels the Heart

Frustrated with herself, she turned on the bedside lamp and reached over for her laptop. She'd been trying to work on a story the last couple of days, but she'd been struggling with trying to get the right words down on the page.

She stared at the bright white blank page in front of her, willing the words to come out. Struggling for the better part of an hour to fight her drooping eyelids, knowing she'd feel wide awake the moment she laid down again, she typed out whatever came to mind, the keys of her keyboard clacking loudly in the emptiness of her large bedroom. Hating everything she'd just written down, she was about to give up when she heard the crunch of tires coming up her lane.

Instantly alert, she listened to see if they'd pass by the house and head out to the main road, but they stopped firmly outside of the house. She quickly turned off the bedside lamp and closed the cover of her laptop, hoping Connor wouldn't have seen the light on from outside the house and think that she'd been waiting up for him.

Because of course you're not waiting up for him. You were trying to do some writing.

It even sounded like a hollow excuse to herself. She placed the laptop on the bedside table once more and pulled the covers up around her, willing herself to go to sleep by the time he came inside.

He lingered outside for several minutes and just as she was beginning to think that maybe it wasn't Mara driving Connor home at all, she heard his boots on the front step and he entered the house. Although she could tell that he was trying to be quiet, every move he made rang out through the cavernous foyer as he took off his boots and navigated his way up the main staircase in the dark. She heard him creep through to the end of the hall, stopping at her door, knocking softly. In a fit of childishness, she ignored his attempt to see if she were still awake.

If he wanted to spend time with me, he wouldn't have gone out and spent all of his time with Mara.

She knew it was petulant of her but right now she felt an inexplicable anger towards him, upset that he'd chosen to spend time with someone else over her. She pulled the covers around her neck more, burrowing under them and closed her eyes, listening to Connor retreat to the spare bedroom and fell fast asleep.

※ ※ ※

When she woke the next morning, the light around her was gray and she could hear rain dripping heavily from the freshly cleaned eaves. Rolling over to look at the clock on her bedside table, she realized she'd slept in well past when she wanted to. Knowing Connor's army discipline, he'd already been up for hours. She'd wanted to get up, make him breakfast or something to make up for her behaviour last night.

Although she felt she could have slept at least another two hours, she pulled the covers back and went about her morning routine. Beginning to feel hungry, she headed downstairs.

"Connor?" she called out as she walked down the stairs, not hearing him anywhere in the house. He hadn't been in the spare room when she'd walked by, his suitcase gone.

"In here." His voice had come from the sitting room.

Something about the way he'd said those two, simple words set alarm bells off in her head. He sat on the sofa across the room from her, her painting of the Colosseum that Maud and Anna had been admiring hanging on the wall behind him. The way he sat there, shoulders slumped and elbows resting on his faded jeans, she knew he was leaving for deployment again.

She got straight to the point. "When are you leaving, and for how long this time?"

He raised his blonde head, looking at her with surprise. "How do you always do that? Do you have some secret line to my commanding officer's private documents or something?"

"Oh you know me; I have connections everywhere," she teased, though the words came out rather more hollow than she'd intended. It was difficult for her to hide not only her disappointment that they'd had such a short time together, but that time had been marred by them arguing. She hated that part most of all.

"I don't know," she confessed, getting real this time. "Maybe it's just because I know you so well." They sat in silence a moment before she asked, "So when *are* you heading out?"

She glanced at his suitcase on the floor beside him, everything neatly squared away and ready to leave at a moment's notice. A lifetime of shuffling from location to location had taught him well how to pack lightly and be ready to leave at any time.

He glanced at his watch. "Right now."

She wanted to ask, "But can't you just stay awhile? Just stay for breakfast with me?" but she knew it would make it worse for him, so she kept her thoughts to herself.

"Do you know how long you'll be gone this time?" She mentally prepared herself for the agonizing months ahead, worrying every day if that was the day she was going to get the call that said he'd been gravely injured, or worse, that he wasn't coming home at all.

"At least six months, maybe more."

"Well, I guess I better give you a hug and send you on your way, then."

She opened her arms to him, crossing the distance of the large room and met him halfway, pulling him into a tight hug. She felt safe in that instance, like the rest of the world didn't matter because Connor would keep it at bay for her. She held onto the feeling, using it to get through the next six months.

"If I write Mara letters, will you make sure she gets them?" he asked her, his voice muffled as her ear pressed against his chest. She burrowed her nose a little against his cotton t-shirt, breathing in the smell of his aftershave, pretending she hadn't heard him.

Knowing it wasn't fair of her to hold onto this resentment and not wanting to spoil these last moments with him, she sighed. Try as she might to keep the two of them apart, fate had decided it should be otherwise.

"Yes, alright. I will." She knew he'd send them to her anyways, even if she didn't agree to it and then they'd just sit there, judging her, and she would feel guilty for not giving them to Mara. He knew her just as well as she knew him and he played it to his advantage.

"Thanks," he gave her a quick kiss on top of her forehead with brotherly affection, and then he was gone, leaving her standing there, the scent of his aftershave still lingering in the air and the sound of his car driving away ringing in her ears.

Chapter Eighteen

In the weeks since Connor had been deployed, Aoife had thrown herself into the renovations of Aldridge Manor whole-heartedly. The work helped to take her mind off the darker thoughts and the worry. With the majority of her new furniture moved in and the interior restorations complete, she declared the place fit for company. She'd been largely staying at Aldridge Manor during most of the renovations, only returning to Dublin a handful of times to see Bex and Millie, and to go up for the occasional Sunday dinner. Although, without both her grandfather and Connor around, they seemed even more of a trial for her than normal. She did her best to muddle through them on her own, but the more times she could use the renovations as an excuse to stay away, the better.

As she sat at home on a Thursday night after all the Flanagans and McCaffreys had left for the day, she decided to call Bex and Millie. She missed seeing them every day. Even though they called or texted each other at least once or twice a day, it still wasn't the same. The phone had barely rung once when it was picked up.

"Hello?" Bex's American accent echoed down the line.

"Hi Bex, it's me." Bex must have mouthed Aoife's name for Millie's benefit to let her know who she was talking to, for Aoife heard Millie shout, "Give me the phone!" in the background.

She could hear Bex speaking in an annoyed tone despite her best attempts to put a hand over the receiver and block out what she and Millie were saying. There must have been a tussle for the phone, for a few seconds later, Millie's breathless voice said, "Aoife, you still there? We got you on speaker phone."

"Yes, I'm still here."

"How is the house coming along? Have you managed to get things unpacked?" Bex asked.

"Well, as much as I can. You know me; it takes me forever to unpack."

It was true. After a lifetime living in and out of a suitcase, she loved to pack, but she hated the reverse.

"We've been loving the photos you've posted so far. It looks great. We're so excited to see the place when it's done. Aren't we, Millie?"

There was a long pause before a muffled "Ouch!" and then, "Yes, we are," in a reluctant tone. Aoife smiled. She knew Millie was still a bit sore about her having moved away from Dublin.

"Well, that's partially why I'm calling. I thought you both might like to come down and be the first to see how it looks now that it's mostly all finished? Well, at least the interior is mostly finished. The grounds still need a fair amount of work, but we're getting to that soon."

"We could have a party!" Millie exclaimed, excitedly.

"No, no. Abso-fuckin-lutely not."

She knew what Millie's "parties" were like. They usually ended up with all three of them completely drunk and hungover for days, and half the city of Dublin invited. She was embarrassed to admit that the police may have been called more than once to break up one of Millie's parties, her neighbours not exactly fond of the loud music and crowds taking over their building. Since living with Bex, she'd become a bit more tame, but now she seemingly had a great excuse to throw a big bash. Aoife began to cringe internally;

this wasn't exactly the way to endear herself with the rest of the village.

"Great! It's all set then. We'll be down tomorrow after class. Love you! Bye!" Millie hung up right before Aoife had the chance to disagree with her one more time.

"Good Lord. What have I gotten myself into?" she asked the empty bedroom.

⊗)⊂⊗

The sounds of revelry pierced the night. The steady *thump thump thump* of a bass and drum echoed around the night air, seeming as loud as thunder to Michael. He wasn't sure if he was just imagining it or now, but everything in his cottage seemed to shake just a little from the noise up at the Old Rectory. Considering how the sound traveled easily across the distance between here and Aoife's, the party was on in full force.

He tried to drown out the incessant pounding of the bass drum by smothering his ear with his pillow, but his brain was too awake now for him to fall back asleep. He lay there on his back, shutting his eyes tightly, willing himself to go back to sleep, but it was no use; the sounds of the party were just loud enough to keep him awake and annoy him for the rest of the night.

Aoife and her friends had been at it since earlier that day. He and Brendan had been standing out on the front step of the pub, sneaking in a quick cigarette break when they'd seen the first car race through the main street towards the Old Rectory. It had begun with just the one car, and then another, and another, until there was a whole string of fancy cars – Mustangs, Bentleys, Jaguars – all racing down the narrow lanes of Ballyclara.

"Looks like the new girl's got a céilí on the go," Brendan had said, ogling a silver Jaguar enviably as it had zoomed past them.

"She must've invited the whole damned city of Dublin down here," Michael had grumbled.

He hadn't liked the way the city folk seemed to think Ballyclara had become an unofficial racetrack. There were children playing in these streets, for Christ's sake, one of them happening to be his young nephew, and one of them happening to be Brendan's son Desmond, Michael's godson.

"Oh well, look at the upside."

"And what's that?" He had glanced sideways at Brendan, wondering what could possibly be considered an upside in this situation.

"That lot is going to be hungover like hell in the morning, and they're all going to be lookin' for a greasy breakfast to cure them."

He'd thrown down the butt of his cigarette, stamping it out with the toe of his boot and had given Michael a firm pat on the shoulder in what he'd supposed his friend had meant to be comforting. Or commiserating.

He'd pushed the city girl firmly out of his mind for the rest of the night; it was Friday night, the busiest night in the pub, and he had priorities, and Aoife O'Reilly wasn't one of them.

It had been well after midnight, after he and Brendan had closed the pub for the night and cleaned the place up, that he'd gone home and heard the noise from the Old Rectory. He'd been annoyed, of course, but it *was* Friday night, after all. How long could they party for? Eventually they'd tire themselves out. He'd resolved to get ready for bed and not let it bother him.

He'd been sorely mistaken to find out that the city girl and her city friends were like Energizer bunnies; they just kept going and going. When two o'clock in the morning rolled around, the party still showed no sign of abating. And that's when he finally made a decision. *Enough is enough.*

Throwing back the duvet, he swung his feet over the side of the bed, put on some jeans and a t-shirt, he went downstairs and put on his boots and coat. By the time he'd gone out into the cool night air and began walking briskly towards the Old Rectory, he'd planned to give Aoife a fair piece of his mind.

Chapter Nineteen

The day had started out wonderfully. It had been a beautiful morning and so Aoife had decided to take her laptop out to the back porch, hoping to find some inspiration for her novel in the beautiful view of the village nestled between the sweeping hills before her. Just as she was settling into a rhythm with a particularly good scene, her doorbell rang. Annoyed at having been disturbed, she'd gotten up from her wicker chair and walked through the house to the front door, peeking through the peephole, lest it be a villager she wasn't particularly interested in seeing. She immediately flung the door open and gave Millie and Bex a big grin, her annoyance replaced with joy.

"Welcome to my humble abode."

She bowed dramatically, inviting them in with a sweep of her arm. As she sauntered through the doorway, Millie couldn't help but sweep Aoife into a big hug.

"I *missed* you!"

"I missed you too. Now, stop trying to choke me, or you won't be seeing me alive again."

"Sorry," Millie had mumbled apologetically but with a smile that indicated she wasn't the least bit sorry at all.

"Wow, nice place!" Bex had clearly been impressed with what Aoife had done with the place so far, and Aoife had felt a thrill of satisfaction at her friend's approval.

"Come on in. You haven't even seen the best parts yet."

She'd taken them on a full tour of the house, showing them which parts she'd already unpacked and furnished, and what she planned for the few rooms she hadn't gotten to yet.

"I'm planning on converting the old root cellar into a wine cellar, and see: the kitchen looks gorgeous, doesn't it?"

"Wow, I wouldn't have thought you could modernize this place so much in just a few weeks. It's completely different than it was the last time we were here."

Millie had stood in the centre of the newly renovated kitchen, taking in the classic stone walls, the newly added appliances, and the all new hardwood floors. Sinead had managed to find some old photographs of the way it had looked before, and they'd been using them to guide the choices they made in restoring the place to its former glory. Finally gone were the green and brown hues that had been painted on to the wooden frames meant to cover the original stonework beneath. Now the place looked, and felt, more like a proper kitchen.

"Yeah, they did an amazing job, didn't they?"

"I should say so," Millie had said, appreciating the beauty of the room.

"Come on into the sitting room. We just finished renovating it a couple of days ago."

She'd gestured for her friends to follow her down the hallway and into the airy sitting room. She'd chosen to paint it white, restored the crown moulding, and used her own paintings and furniture to decorate the bare walls. Changing the paint colour back to white again allowed for the dark wood fireplace to once again become the focal point of the room. On its mantelpiece, she'd placed photographs of the three of them from various trips and their university days, as well as an old one of her and her grandfather from when she was a little girl.

"It's looking really great!" Bex had admired the photographs, smiling at the memories. "I love what you've done with it."

All That Compels the Heart

"Oh, and here is something I think you're really going to enjoy adding to one of these rooms." Millie had handed her a package wrapped in silver paper with a white bow.

"You didn't need to get me something," she gushed, wondering what could be in the box. It was expertly wrapped in Bex's neat and tidy style. It was large and deep, and felt heavy in her hands.

"Oh just open it already," Bex had told her, excited to see her face when she saw what it was. Aoife had given Bex a curious look, lifting the top off to reveal some leather-bound books, which, although in extremely good condition, looked to be quite aged. She'd lifted the first one out of the box and turned it over in her hands, looking at the spine.

"Oh my God!" she had exclaimed in excitement. "This is a first edition copy of *Great Expectations*! It's only my second favourite book in the world!" She was astounded by the gift.

"Oh I remember," Bex had replied, a smile on her face, clearly pleased with her choice of gift. "I remember you always talking about how much you loved Dickens. And, after all those hours you used to spend in that little, old used bookstore downtown, I decided I'd go down there and ask the owner to put me on his list of contacts in case any special copie of *The Secret Garden* came up because that's your actual favourite, but he said they didn't know of any that were for sale, but he did have a complete set of all of Dickens' works, and so I rushed down to the shop to get there before anyone else snatched them up. I was going to save them for your birthday, but I figured now is as good a time as any to give them to you. Besides, I couldn't wait to see the happy look on your face when you saw them."

"Thank you both so much. You two are the best friends a gal can have."

"You might not think that when you find out Millie still had plans to have a party tonight," Bex warned.

"Millie!"

"Oh come on; it's just going to be a small party this time, I promise. Nowhere near the scale of my previous ones, which I'll admit, may have gotten out of hand once or twice.

"Or every time," Aoife contradicted her. Resigning herself to the inevitable, she said, "Well, if we're going to have a party, then we'll need some supplies because I've got nothing."

Bex and Aoife headed out to do the shopping, leaving Millie to put away anything that could be stained or broken in the likely event the part got out of hand. Thirty minutes later, they'd returned to find the furniture pushed out of the way in the sitting room to create a dance floor, and the whole place as clean as a whistle. After putting away the food and booze she and Bex had bought, Aoife suggested the three of the retire to the back porch for a bit of calm before the storm. That's when she'd heard the sound of a car in the gravel driveway out front and the ring of her doorbell.

Both she and Bex had looked at Millie, one eyebrow raised, knowing this was her doing.

"What? It's just a few people," Millie had grumbled. Just as she'd finished her sentence, they heard a couple more cars arrive. Aoife had given her an exasperated look and turned to walk back into the house to greet the guests that she'd not invited.

"And who exactly are these 'few people'?" she'd asked Millie as they walked towards the front door.

"I know you said you didn't want a big to-do, so I only invited a few of our friends from the city. You know, Justin, Ashleigh, Dominica, and Mark. Don't worry, it won't be anything big and fancy."

She knew what would happen now Millie had invited a "few friends." Those few friends would invite a few friends of their own, who'd invite more friends, who'd put it on social media and would invite whomever responded, and a "small gathering" would turn into a large house party with a bunch of people she didn't know, and a mess she'd have to clean up in the morning. This is what had happened when Millie had decided to throw her a housewarming party when she'd returned to Dublin and the night had ended with the gardai coming over to write her up for disturbing the peace. The tabloids had had fun with that one: "Granddaughter of prominent city businessman is cited for disturbing the peace with society friends" they'd all read. Her grandmother had practically strung her up by her ankles when she'd found out.

She was interrupted from her worst-case scenario daydream by a familiar voice.

"Hello! Well there you are. I was beginning to think no one was in. You've left your front door unlocked, by the way; you really shouldn't do that; you never know who might wander in."

Aoife spun around to find Danny standing in front of her.

"Danny!" she yelled and leapt into her boyfriend's arms, excitement at his arrival making her a little over ecstatic. "I thought you wouldn't be back from Dubai for at least another week!"

The two of them hadn't seen each other since the last time he'd come down to Ballyclara to see the house. By the time she'd gone back to Dublin for a quick visit, he'd gone to Dubai on another business trip.

"Whoa there," he said, patting her shoulder gently. "Careful love, or we'll end up on the ground."

"I'm so glad you're here!"

"I'm glad to see you too," he hugged her back, patting her shoulder gently. It felt good to have him back again, their previous row over her moving here seemingly forgotten.

"I decided to cut things a bit short. The firm had enough reps at the conference, so I figured they wouldn't miss little ol' me. Besides, we already spend too much time apart; it's time we both made some effort to be together more often."

She was surprised by his mention of wanting to spend less time on business trips; it wasn't something he'd previously been willing to do.

Maybe he really is willing to make a change so that the two of us can live together.

The doorbell rang again just then but Aoife didn't want to let Danny go.

"Come on. Let's not leave your guests waiting," he told her, gently prying her hands from around his waist. He and Aoife walked briskly through the house to the front door. As she opened it, there stood before her were a small group of, mostly, Danny's friends: Dominica and her husband, Justin; and Ashleigh and Mark, a brother/sister duo from Belfast who were both reps for the same company as Danny and Justin.

They all shouted "Hooray!" as she opened the door for them.

"This is for you, darling," Ashleigh told her, handing her a bottle of champagne and kissing her on the cheek, the strong scent of rosewater emanating from her. Ashleigh's long, white-blonde hair hung in loose curls about her face, perfectly suited to her bohemian chic style with her flowing, flower-patterned maxi dress. One of the curls tickled Aoife's cheek as she had leaned in close to greet her.

"Thanks! You didn't have to get me anything."

"I'm sure we'll put this to very good use," Danny said, taking the bottle out of her hands and checking the label. It was important to him and his friends to always drink the best.

"I love what you've done with the place!" Dominica said, stepping in, her brightly-coloured ruffled dress a pop of colour in the otherwise simple foyer.

"Wait until you see the rest of the house," Aoife said with a smile as she accepted hugs and more housewarming gifts from her friends, which seemed to mostly be other bottles of alcohol. "Come on in! Is anyone hungry? We haven't begun dinner yet, but we could get something started."

"No, don't worry about us. We ate on the way down," Dominica replied in her thick Madrid accent. The instigator of many a social event, Millie's old roommate, Dominica, was always dragging Bex, Aoife, and Millie out to clubs and parties. It was, in fact, at one of these parties where Dom had introduced her to Danny.

She'd invited her new friends out with her then husband/now husband, Justin, and some of his work friends. Ashleigh had been a guest DJ at the club, providing them all with a great excuse to go. When Dom had found out Danny and Aoife were both single, she'd devoted the entire night to trying to get the pair together because she thought they'd make a great couple. They'd been dating ever since.

"Come on through to the back and I can show you around the rest of the house."

Aoife spent the next half hour showing the others around the house. Everyone was impressed; everyone that is, except for Danny. Clearly, their time apart had not changed his mind about Ballyclara or her moving down here.

"I thought you said that the two of you were planning to flip this place, Danny? It looks more like Aoife has plans to stay."

Justin, who'd remained quiet up to this point, finally spoke up at the end of the house tour. Like Danny, he didn't seem impressed with Aoife's new place. "I thought you said the two of you were planning to move into that place in Malahide?"

"I didn't know you were planning on moving back to the city," Millie interjected, curiosity piqued. She may not like either Danny or Justin, but she was eager for Aoife to be closer to home again.

"Well… it was just one idea we'd been discussing…"

Aoife wasn't sure how to respond. She wished Danny hadn't gone and started talking about their decisions for the future before the two of them had actually made them yet.

"I just said we were thinking about it." Danny's defensive tone was directed towards her.

"Well, whatever you decide, I'm sure the two of you have a lot to talk about before anything is finalized." Bex, ever the calm, sensible one, tried to smooth everything over before an argument broke out.

"Let's break out that champagne and put on some music." Dom picked up on the tension in the room and, like Bex, tried to dispel it. "Danny, Mark, Justin; why don't you all go into the kitchen and open some of those champagne bottles for us? We'll take care of the rest."

She kissed her husband quickly, lightly patting the sleeve of his navy jumper and indicating he should take the other two guys into the kitchen while she smoothed things over with Aoife. Taking the hint, the guys went to the kitchen, while Dom turned to Aoife and asked, "Have you set up your sound system yet?"

"Yeah, Bex and I set it up earlier. It's in the sitting room."

"Fantastic! Let's crank up the music and get this party started."

She grabbed Aoife's hand and practically dragged her into the sitting room, enlisting her help connect her iPod to the sound system as the sounds of The Script's "Hail Rain or Sunshine" began pumping through the surround sound.

Mark, Justin, and Danny returned with the champagne just as the music began playing. Danny crossed the room toward her, champagne flutes in both hands and handed her one of them. In a move of reconciliation, she accepted and took a sip. Clearly encouraged that their little tiff had blown over, he grabbed her around the waist with his free hand, making her giggle, and the two of them began dancing. Their small group continued on like this for the better part of an hour until the champagne had well set into her veins and sloshed around her stomach. Unexpectedly, the doorbell rang. Immediately, she looked at Millie.

"Ok, who invited people over *this* time?" Aoife, her tone exasperated.

"Don't look at me." Millie raised her hands in self-defense. "I promise I did not invite anyone else except the people standing here in this room."

"Guilty as charged."

Danny put his hand up, dancing his way across the room towards her, with one of those charming grins on his face which he knew would get him anything he wanted. She'd seen him use it plenty of times on other women, young and old, and it never failed to get him whatever he'd set his eye on, no matter how inaccessible.

"Oh come on, baby," he said, grabbing her by the waist and twirling her around, dipping her back in a classic dance move from the films in the wake of her slight pout. "It's just a few friends from work. It's only a little bit of fun. We haven't done anything fun together in weeks now, and I wanted to make sure that you had a good time breaking in the new place."

More like breaking down the place, she thought grumpily, however, she acquiesced to his charm.

"Put me back on my feet," she said, play-punching his chest.

He smiled at her, ignoring the punch and quickly stole a kiss. She frowned and punched his chest a bit harder this time, but smiled as she said, "Well go on then. Invite your guests in before they beat down my door. You don't want to keep them standing around outside all night, now do you?"

There were shouts of "Welcome!" and laughter as he invited them all in. Aoife noticed there was quite a large crowd of them, only some of which she recognized from Danny's office. She had no idea who the others were.

Danny acted the perfect host, as comfortable in Aldridge Manor as if it were his place too. He beckoned them all to come inside, took their coats and hung them up, inviting them to all come into the sitting room and join the party.

As they entered the room, Danny came over and put his arm around her waist, introducing her. She could see how his face brightened around his colleagues; he spent a great deal of time with them on business trips and conferences, and when they weren't working, they were usually hanging out at other social events. It was important for him to make a good impression. He was always reminding her how important it was to maintain his brand, and part of that brand included her as his dutiful partner.

She was used to the role. Being the youngest granddaughter of one of Dublin's wealthiest men meant she had to attend galas and parties from time to time to represent *O'Reilly's*. Much as she may hate being made to dress up and smile in front of the public, she knew it came with the territory. It was the same in her relationship with Danny. She just had to keep reminding herself how much it was helping his career. She could schmooze and pretend for awhile if it was helping him. So, she smiled dutifully and shook hands. Most of them were pleasant enough but unremarkable, except for one, a blonde named Alice.

She was absolutely gorgeous, the kind of woman with legs up to there, perfect hair, skin, and teeth; everything about her completely flawless. She was that kind of perfect goddess that made every other woman in the room instantly feel insignificant.

"Ah! Alice!" Danny said with a big grin on his face.

"Danny," Alice replied with a voice that practically purred, kissing Danny on each cheek. "And this must be Aoife. I've heard so much about you; Danny can't stop talking about his wonderful girlfriend. It's a pleasure to meet you."

Alice took her hand in a limp handshake, a fake smile plastered on her face. Her tone had been just the right pitch of disinterest in Aoife but trying to be polite about it.

It's not a pleasure at all to meet you, you gorgeous cow, Aoife thought. She offered her own best fake smile.

Two could play at this game.

"When Danny said you were planning to leave Dublin and live in the country, I must confess, I thought you quite mad. I mean, who does that? But after seeing the beauty of this house, I can quite see how you came to fall in love with this place. It has quite a," Alice paused deliberately, trying to find the right and socially appropriate word, "*rustic* charm to it."

The way she emphasized the word "rustic" betrayed her real thoughts on the house. Her insult landing exactly where she wanted, Alice proceeded to ignore Aoife and began talking about work with Danny, effectively cutting Aoife out of the conversation.

Aoife had very little knowledge of what it was exactly Danny did at the investment firm. If she was being honest, she didn't really care. They had completely different interests when it came to their careers, and while she tried to support him as much as she could, she just couldn't bring herself to find anything interesting about his day-to-day work.

Watching him and Alice talk, Aoife couldn't help but notice the way she stood a little too close to Danny, the way she put her hand lightly on his forearm, always establishing some sort of physical contact with him at all points during the conversation. Her entire body language, from the way she smiled to the way she flipped her long blonde hair over her shoulder, always drew his attention to her and away from Aoife. And like an eejit, he was completely enthralled by her. Aoife couldn't stop the pang of jealousy settling in the pit of her stomach. To drown it out, she drank down her glass of champagne, pretending to listen to the conversation; not that it mattered, because neither Alice nor Danny seemed to notice she was there anymore. Finding she'd reached the bottom of her glass, but unwilling to relinquish her place by Danny's side, she focused on how much she'd really like to knock those perfect teeth right out of that perfect face. Aoife was concentrating on this idea so much that she didn't realize Alice had suddenly addressed her.

"Oh love! Look at us prattling on about work. We must be boring you to death. And here we are supposed to be partying and celebrating your new home."

It was at this particular moment that Bex and Dom swooped in on either side of Aoife.

"We just need to borrow Aoife for a bit," Dominica said with a polite smile while Bex tugged on her arm and practically pulled her away.

"What do you need me for?" Aoife asked, annoyed at having been thwarted from her plan to choke the life out of the gorgeous Alice.

When Dominica had successfully moved her out of earshot she said, "You looked like you were about to pounce on Alice and rip her face off, so we thought it best to intervene."

The smile on Dom's face indicated that while she might like to see Aoife try and kill Alice, she didn't think it was the best of plans.

"I was *this* close from ripping that perfectly engineered face right off her, and *you* two stopped me from it," Aoife muttered sullenly.

"Here, have another glass of champagne." Bex filled her empty champagne flute, which Aoife proceeded to down in one gulp.

"Well, I didn't mean for you to do it all at once." Bex's tone was admonishing but also contained a hint of approval. Aoife just glared at her, and she didn't say anything else, just refilled the glass.

"Oh don't get all hot and bothered about *her*," Dom told Aoife gently. "Alice is like that with all the boys in the office. I remember when Justin first met her. She couldn't stop flirting with him no matter how many times he pointed out he had a girlfriend."

"How did he finally get her to stop?" Aoife asked.

"When I find out, I'll let you know," Dom replied, ruefully.

"You mean she still flirts with him even though he's married to you?" Bex asked, her tone incredulous. "That's pathetic."

"A perfectly perfect pathetic creature," Aoife grumbled, not sure who she meant: Alice or Danny.

It was difficult not to see the way he was completely fascinated with her, observing her every move. Aoife didn't want to admit it to herself, but she'd never seen him take such an interest in *her* before. They never talked about work, unless it was about Danny's work. Danny would pretend to listen to her when she talked about her dreams of being a writer, but she could tell whenever she talked about it that his eyes would get that glazed look, and so she'd just change the subject back to something he was more comfortable with. But with Alice, she could tell that Danny was *truly* paying attention, and that thought made her want to drink more.

"Come on," Dom said, taking her glass and putting it down on the table and pulling her out into the middle of the room, which had become a boisterous dancefloor. "Forget about her. She's pathetic, but harmless. Danny's smart enough to know what a good thing he's got in you. Just forget about them and let's party!"

A cheer went up from the people on the dance floor and someone turned up the music. Feeling the alcohol hit her blood stream, she swayed to the music, losing sense of time and space, just letting the stress of the last few weeks melt away. But Aoife could only maintain this level of drunkenness for so long.

All of a sudden, the inside of the house was beginning to feel claustrophobic, the music ringing in her ears competing with the loud buzz of conversation all around her. Feeling the distinct urge to get away from everyone, she tried to push her way through the throng of people. She wasn't quite sure how, but there seemed to be more people in her house than she remembered seeing the last time she'd checked. She had no idea how they all had gotten here. Weaving her way through the crush of warm, sweaty bodies, she somehow managed to make it to the front door. Pushing it open, she stumbled out into the cool darkness.

All That Compels the Heart

The sudden change in temperature hit her with full force and she shivered involuntarily. She realized only then that she was wearing only a sleeveless, thin, silk shift top, her leggings, and a pair of sandals. It had been fine for the warmth of the house, but outside in the cool air she was woefully underdressed.

Even outside, her front lawn was packed with people. Small groups stood in the drive and more were in the garden, drinking and dancing to the music blaring from some speakers someone had brought with them set up outside so that those who couldn't fit inside would be able to party. Just wanting to be alone right now, she pushed through the people blocking her path and walked away from the house.

She made it a few steps down the front path when she was forced to stop abruptly for a group of revellers who ran past her, plastic cups in hand, screaming like banshees. She let them brush past her before continuing down the lane a bit, the blaring sounds of rock 'n roll revelry fading behind her. Her head was beginning to clear enough to let her know that the rest of her body was not entirely happy with the amount of alcohol she'd consumed this evening, so she stopped and leaned against a fence post, the soft lowing of her neighbours' sheep competing with the noise from her house. She bent over, hands on her knees, and took a deep breath.

She was just starting to feel a bit better when she heard the sound of someone to her right muttering to themselves as they walked up the lane towards her house. In the gleam of the moonlight, she saw it was Michael Flanagan and immediately a feeling of annoyance settled over her skin. The last thing she wanted to deal with was him tonight. Any other neighbour coming to yell at her would be preferable right now.

Sighing, she stepped into the lane, putting her hands up, trying to calm him before he lit into her, but he was having none of it.

"What the hell do ye think ye're playing at?" he yelled at her.

Chapter Twenty

Aoife woke the next morning to a glaringly bright sunlight pouring in through the curtains and the sound of birds tweeting in the trees outside the house. It was a marked difference from the noise of the night before.

As her brain slowly came back to life, she realized she'd woken up not in her own bed as she'd expected to, but on the Queen Anne sofa she'd set up in one of the spare bedrooms. It was one of the few rooms that was still sparsely furnished. For a few moments, she just lay back with her head on the arm of the sofa, the bright glare of the sunlight suddenly seeming to be too bright for her bleary eyes.

Last night still largely seemed like a blur of alcohol and noise to her. She gingerly tried to right herself into a sitting position, but her head began to swim, and she lay back, staring up at the ceiling. After a few minutes, her head began to clear and she attempted to sit up again, breathing slowly. This time, she was successful in her endeavour to sit up without feeling like she was about to vomit. Pausing for a moment, she gripped the edge of the sofa and tested her balance.

Cautiously making her way across the room, she softly opened the door and peeked outside, almost terrified to see what state her house was in. She was surprised to find no one was the hallway. As she walked through the house, she noticed every room had occupants, most of them looking as if they'd crawled to wherever looked comfiest as they eventually passed out from their boozed stupor.

Where the upstairs hallway had been empty of revellers, the main staircase housed many of them. She carefully picked her way down the stairs, trying not to trip over anyone or fall headlong down the stairs and break her neck. She made it safely to the bottom with only a few people stirring and talking in their sleep, but none of them woke.

The ground floor was a disaster zone of half-empty glasses, pizza boxes, bowls of munchies, and paper plates of half-eaten canapés. She had no idea how or when food had been put out because she didn't remember doing it. One of the unknown guests must have brought them with them.

There were more guests sleeping on the floor of both sitting rooms on the ground floor, the dining room, and all the way through to the kitchen. She noticed Bex and Millie had chosen a chair and sofa, respectively, to sleep on in the main sitting room. She carefully picked her way through the mess to throw some blankets over them so they'd keep warm while they dozed. It had gotten quite chilly in the house now the throngs of party-goers had stopped dancing.

Millie stirred at the movement, mumbling something in her sleep about rainbows and leprechauns which made no sense to Aoife. She left her friends to their slumber and made her way towards the kitchen, feeling like she should probably make some tea or toast or something, despite her iffy stomach.

The kitchen was as much of a disaster zone than the other rooms on the ground floor: snacks, drinks, empty glasses, plates and bowls, and God knew what else strewn across its surfaces. She was grateful no one had fallen asleep in here, though, grateful for a moment alone with some peace and quiet.

Putting the kettle on to make some tea, she moved about the kitchen now with an ease she hadn't had when she first arrived in Ballyclara. She put some toast into her brand new toaster and unplugged the kettle just before it could emit a piercing cry, lest she wake any of the people sleeping in the main hallway just outside the kitchen. Realizing there wasn't a single clear space for her to sit and eat, she took her mug of tea and plate of buttered toast outside to the back porch and settled herself on her favourite wicker chair.

The view before her was predictably astounding, the village shrouded in mist from the coolness of the previous night and the rising warmth of the morning sun. Ballyclara was clothed in a slightly ethereal look. She was beginning to see why St. Kevin had decided to make his home here.

She took a long sip of her tea, enjoying the peace and quiet of the early morning Saturday. She sipped some more of her tea and put her hands in her pocket; the morning air was still chilly and nipped at her fingertips like an overexcited puppy. A curious frown crept across her face as she felt something in the pocket of the jumper she was wearing and she had the sudden realization that it was two sizes too big for her. Wondering how in hell her jumper could have grown in size overnight, she realized it was because it wasn't *her* jumper at all. Her fingers grasped something cold and metal and as she brought it out of the pocket she saw it was a set of keys. There were several keys on the key ring, none of which she recognized. One of them had a fob attached and turning it over in her palm, she saw that it had the word "pub" scrawled across it in a man's handwriting. The only person she knew who would have keys to a pub was either Michael or Brendan, and of the two, she'd only seen Michael in the last twenty-four hours

Just as she'd been trying to figure out exactly why she'd be wearing Michael's jumper, the memories of last night came flooding back to her.

"What in God's name do ye think ye're playin' at woman?" he'd yelled at her.

She hadn't been expecting to see him there in the middle of the lane at that time of night and, being quite insensibly inebriated, she didn't have time to come up with an appropriate retort.

"What did you say?" Her ears had still been ringing from the music inside the house and she hadn't been quite sure she'd heard him properly.

He'd approached her then and had taken her by the arm, marching her a little further down the lane away from the party. Not entirely sure what he was trying to do, she took his actions as a threat.

"Oi! What the hell do you think *you're* doing?!" she'd yelled at him trying to yank her arm back from his firm grip.

"I said, 'what are ye playin' at?'" He'd motioned wildly at the house behind her.

"I'm not *playing* at anything," she'd retorted, affronted with having been manhandled. "I should be the one asking *you* that question! What the hell do *you* think *you're* playing at, Michael Flanagan? Manhandling a person like that and dragging her down the lane in the dark of night. You could be a serial killer for all I know, or a rapist or God knows what else."

Michael's face had gone from serious and angry, to astonished. "I'd think ye'd know me well enough to know I'm neither a rapist nor a serial killer, Aoife."

"Well, that's exactly the sort of thing a serial killer or a rapist would say, now isn't it?" she'd spat back at him, rubbing the spot where he had gripped her upper arm. He must have mistook the action for thinking she was rubbing her arm to keep warm because she was surprised when he began to take off his jumper and handed it to her.

"Here," he'd said.

"What're you doing?" she'd asked him, wondering why he was trying to take off his clothes in the middle of the lane.

"Here, take it." He'd handed her his blue knit jumper with the pockets in the front. She'd looked at him sceptically, cautiously accepting it. "You look like you're freezing in that outfit."

"Thank you."

She'd taken the jumper from him and slipped it over her head, feeling the soft wool against her skin.

"Look, I just wanted to come here and ask that ye keep this party down a bit, alright? Ye just can't go around waking up the dead with all this noise."

She'd looked at him with a mixture of astonishment and surprise; she hadn't invited these people to come to her house to make such a mess or all this noise, but of course, Michael didn't know that. Just as he'd been affronted when she'd accused him of possibly being a serial killer, she'd been affronted by his perceptions of her as a spoiled, rich, party girl.

"Is that what you think of me, Michael? Party all night long and do drugs? Is that really what you think I'm like?"

"I didn't say that," he'd begun, but she wouldn't let him finish.

"Oh really? Then what are you trying to say?"

"Well, if you'd let me finish…"

"No, actually, I think I've changed my mind. I don't think I would like to listen to what you have to say."

She'd crossed her arms in front of her then, not caring if she looked like a petulant child right now.

"What?" she'd asked him as she noticed the beginnings of a smile tugging at the corners of his mouth.

"It's nothing," he'd said, trying to hide the smile behind a cough into his hand. "You really don't want to know."

She'd glared back at him in silent response.

"Look, I'm not saying ye need to kick your friends out, but could you at least turn it down? The rest of us in the village are just trying to get some sleep, for the love of God. That's all I'm asking for."

"Well, maybe if you say 'please' then maybe I will." Her voice had been haughty, nose stuck in the air. She'd done her best to stare down at him, despite their difference in height, trying to make him feel the way he'd made her feel when he'd tried the same thing on her.

He'd sighed, clearly tired, but she'd been surprised when he'd turned to her and said, "Please," with all the frustrated sincerity he could muster.

"Alright, your wish is my command," she'd told him, sighing heavily as if it were the most difficult thing in the world he'd asked her to do. "Now am I free to go? Or would you like to interrogate/yell at me some more?"

She wasn't sure what it was about Michael Flanagan that made her get so blustery with him all the time.

"Yes, of course," he'd said gesturing to her to return to the house.

She'd hugged his jumper closer to her, both of them forgetting she'd borrowed it and stalked back towards the house with her nose in the air, pretending to ignore the fact that Michael even existed. She got exactly two steps up the lane before she began to lose her balance and stumbled slightly. Without knowing exactly where he'd come from, she felt big, strong arms around her.

"Woah there. You alright?" he'd asked, a note of concern in his voice.

She'd put a hand up to her spinning head trying to reorient herself. "I'm fi-" she began and then promptly doubled over and threw up there on the spot.

"Jaysis, Mary and Joseph!" Michael had exclaimed trying to step out of the way and just narrowly missed being in the line of fire.

She'd felt his strong hands rubbing her back as she continued to upturn the contents of her entire stomach. Even when she stopped, his hands continued to linger, making sure she could stand on her own two feet.

"Are ye alright?" he'd asked her again when it seemed like she'd stopped dry heaving.

"I think so," she'd said thickly, her mouth acidic. She wasn't entirely sure it was true but she'd still been determined to stand on her own two feet.

"Woah there," he said to her again as she tried to stumble forward and suddenly she'd felt herself up in the air for a brief moment, two strong arms lifting her up and holding her safe.

"Let me down," she'd groaned, trying to struggle against Michael's solid grip on her but she was too weak to fight back.

"Just calm down would ye? I am trying to help you," he'd snapped back at her, narrowly dodging a rogue elbow as it passed within an inch of his nose.

"Hey now! Keep your god-damned elbows where they aren't going to take me eye out."

"Hmph!" she'd harrumphed but tucked her elbows in and had rested her head against his chest, not struggling against him anymore. She'd listened to the sound of his breathing as he carried her towards the house, the steady rhythm of his heartbeat beneath her ear.

He must've carried her inside and she'd passed out sometime soon afterwards because she didn't remember anything else that came after until she'd woken up in the spare bedroom.

Oh God, how embarrassing!

It was bad enough she'd acted exactly like the spoiled brat Michael clearly though she was, but she'd also vomited in front of him, a sight no one should see. *And* she'd walked away from the whole thing and taken his jumper with her.

She rubbed a hand over her face, as if it would wipe away the embarrassment she felt.

What's the best way to apologize to someone in this situation?

She knew her grandmother would have the answer; she always knew the perfect way to try and buy back anyone's good favour without actually saying sorry for something. It was like an art form to her. But the last thing Aoife wanted to do right now was talk to her grandmother, especially about this. It would bring up too many questions about how exactly she knew Michael, why they were fighting with one another, and why the hell she'd even moved down here in the first place.

She had it: she would bake him a cake. That's what people did when they wanted to truly show how much they were sorry or how much they cared for the other person, right? They made them something homemade, because the time and effort put into the making of whatever it was would prove their sincerity and intent. So that was it; how she'd prove how sorry she was. She would bake him a cake.

And he'll damn well like it too.

She returned to the kitchen with her tea mug and empty plate and went about cleaning up the mess that had accumulated there in order to make space for baking. After several minutes of doing some deep cleaning, she managed to wrangle the place into some sense of order, and flipped through a cookbook she'd bought at the little bookstore in the village earlier in the week, trying to find the right recipe.

"Now, which recipe says 'I'm sorry for the extremely loud and annoying party which woke up the entire town, and made you come all the way over to tell me off for it,'" she muttered to herself.

She searched through pages and pages of intricate and delectable desserts, discarding each one with a flip of a page. Michael didn't seem to be the kind of person who'd like the any number of fancy chocolate desserts leaping from the pages, so she settled on a simple red velvet cake.

"How hard can it be?" she asked herself.

Now that she had a clean space to work with, she set to work pulling down the baking ingredients for the recipe. She found the process relaxing, and she was beginning to see what others saw in doing it. It felt good to be making something, doing something with her own two hands. She was just about to add the final ingredients when she realized she didn't have any sugar.

"Shit."

She knew she'd bought some when she'd been out with Bex yesterday. There had been a brief moment where she'd left Millie and Bex alone to unpack some of the groceries; it must have been then that it got put somewhere else. She went back to the cupboards, searching each jar until she finally found the one she was looking for.

"Aha!"

Pulling the jar down from the cupboard, she added it to the batter. Pouring the batter into the cake pan, she placed it in her brand new oven and waited patiently for it to cook. Cleaning up the kitchen around her some more until it looked much the way it had before her house had been invaded by a bunch of strangers, she heard the *ding!* of the oven's timer and pulled the cake carefully out. She didn't know how, but she'd managed to make the best-looking cake she'd ever made in her entire life.

The only cake you've ever made, her subconscious reminded her.

She let it cool for a few minutes, then iced it and stood back looking at her handiwork: it looked just like something that Martha-feckin'-Stewart would make. Placing it carefully in a plastic container so it would be preserved until she made it to Michael's, she carried it carefully through the house, trying not to step on any of the people sleeping in the hallway.

The late morning air was cool around her still, but she was safely ensconced in Michael's jumper, cozy and warm. It was turning out to be a beautiful day, the kind where the sun is shining and seems to flood everything with light; not a cloud in the sky. She was thankful she'd thought to grab a pair of sunglasses – whose exactly, she wasn't sure – to protect her eyes against the glare of the sun glinting off the stones in the driveway. She tried to ignore the mess still in the front garden as she walked by; she'd deal with that later.

As she walked down the lane to Michael's cottage, she rehearsed what exactly she planned to say to him. A straight-out apology seemed like the most sensible approach, but a small part of her still selfishly didn't want to give him an inch when he might take a mile from her. It was a matter of principle, after all.

Muttering to herself, the sheep in the pasture next to her looked up from the stalks of grass they were munching on to gaze at her impassively. Deciding she wasn't a threat, they left the crazy city girl to her ramblings and went back to their meal. She was just going over the final details of what she was going to say to him, when she found herself standing at the gate to Michael's cottage. She could hear the sounds of water being sluiced through a high-pressure hose, the scent of cleaning solution and water in the air. Carefully opening the gate to let herself in, she walked down the stone path, her sandals flapping against the ground. Not immediately seeing him in the front garden, she turned the corner of the cottage.

There he was, washing an old 1950's Thames pick-up truck. He was dressed in a pair of jeans and the same work boots he'd on the day he'd come over to pull down the vines from the roof, his bare chest and the muscles on full display.

When the hell had he gotten so good-looking?

Not that she was looking, of course. No, that would be rude, or leering, or something. She was so distracted by the view in front of her she almost dropped her cake on the ground.

Get a hold of yourself, dammit!

Having successfully saved the cake from hitting the stone pathway, she checked to make sure Michael hadn't witnessed her little stumble. He had not. He was too focused on washing his truck and looking all great doing it. Collecting herself, she continued down the path with her head held high, trying to pretend she hadn't noticed his half-dressed state.

"Good morning!" She raised her voice above the sound of the hose so he could hear her. He seemed startled and confused to see her.

Clearly still just a wee bit grumpy about last night then.

However, she wouldn't let his dark stare scare her away. She plastered an even bigger smile on her face and continued to walk towards him.

"How are you today, Michael?"

He raised an eyebrow at her and gave her a "what the hell do you think?" look. He didn't answer her immediately, just continued to wash his truck for several seconds before finally turning off the house.

"Well, let's see. Considering that a crazy city girl started a really loud party up the lane from me, and she nearly puked all over me, and she nearly took me out with her flailing elbows, *and* her cad of a boyfriend got all up in my face, I'd say I'm just dandy."

Aoife did her best to look contrite as she took in his account of last night's events.

"Wait, you and Danny got into a fight?"

She didn't remember any of that, although, she could honestly say that she didn't really remember much of anything after almost vomiting on him.

Michael looked surprised he'd said it, like he'd been saying it in his mind but hadn't actually meant to say it aloud. He seemed doubly upset with himself after realizing she seemed to have no memory of whatsoever of the altercation he'd had with her boyfriend.

"Well, it wasn't so much of a fight as… a difference of opinion, ye might say." Michael looked distinctly like he didn't want to talk about it any further.

She ignored the unspoken warning and continued to press the matter. "What were you having a difference of opinion about, exactly?"

"Let's just leave it, alright? We sorted it and there's no need to go bringing it up again."

"Alright," she replied, though she found she wanted to know what it was he was trying so hard to keep from her.

She'd have to ask Danny about it later when she got back to the house.

"Look, I'm sorry if Danny gave you any trouble," she said after a moment's awkward pause. "He's just not exactly thrilled that I decided to move down here in the first place, and then his job keeps him away most of the time and it's all just kind of stressful for him right now. Whatever he said, or did, I'm sure he didn't mean any of it."

"Right," was all he muttered, not quite under his breath enough for her not to hear. She decided for both their sakes to ignore the comment and move forward with her apology, otherwise she might never get it out.

"And about last night…"

Suddenly, everything she'd rehearsed in her head on the way down here seemed woefully inadequate. Although she'd not been the one to start the party, nor invite all the guests, she did feel responsibility for letting it get out of hand. Feeling herself becoming flustered and unsure exactly what to say, she held out the cake to him.

"I've brought you a cake. You know, as a sort of peace offering."

Michael looked at her oddly.

"I feel like ever since I moved down here that you and I have gotten off on the wrong foot, and I just wanted to start over." She continued to hold out the cake tin to him, urging him to take it.

"*You* baked?" he asked her, sceptically eyeing the cake like it might be a bomb.

"Yes, I baked it. Made it from scratch in my very own kitchen this morning only an hour ago. Why does everyone think I don't know how to fend for myself?" she muttered to herself. "And you don't have to keep looking at it like it will explode in your face. I can assure you it won't."

After giving it one more look over for anything that might suggest she was lying to him, he nodded towards his cottage.

"Alright," he said, taking the cake tin from her, "Let's put that to the test, shall we? Come on inside and I'll put the kettle on."

"You're actually going to invite me in?" she asked astounded. She didn't know what outcome exactly she'd been planning for when she'd come down here but she supposed now that she hadn't thought he'd actually accept her peace offering.

Maybe he's actually willing to give me another chance?

"Why not? Or would you prefer we eat right outside?"

It was at this precise moment that Anna and Maud happened to turn the corner into the lane and walked by the edge of Michael's property. They smiled and waved from the road, the two of them looking like cats who'd just had the best cream of their lives.

Michael raised his hand to them and called out, "Good morning Mrs. McCaffrey! Mrs. Drummond!"

"Good morning, Michael!" they called back.

Anna looked like she wanted to stop and talk to them but Maud tugged gently on her arm. However, both of them looked mightily pleased to have caught Michael and Aoife out in the open like this. Talking rapidly to one another in hushed tones as they walked by, Aoife was suddenly very aware that she was still standing there in one of Michael's jumpers, probably not looking her greatest. While she'd been fully clothed when she'd left the house, she couldn't even remember if she'd bothered to brush her teeth or comb her hair. She looked back at Michael in all his half-naked glory and realized exactly how this must look to the two elderly women.

Shit.

She wanted to shout at them, "This is not what it looks like!" but she knew it would do no good. There was no stopping the rumour mill now.

"Uh, yeah. Let's go inside," she told Michael, not waiting for him to show her the way in.

"Oh, don't you worry, they'll have told the whole village by the end of the hour that you and I are carrying on an illicit affair or something," he said, following her towards the door. It seemed to amuse him; the thought of her being the headline news in the village gossip column. She was beginning to regret coming over here and trying to be nice to him.

"Come along, lover. Let's get some tea," he called out, surely loud enough for Mrs. Drummond and Mrs. McCaffrey to still hear him, chuckling to himself as he followed her inside.

The inside of Michael's cottage was laid out very similarly to that of his parents' place just up the road, although a bit smaller.

"Take a seat," he told her, gesturing to the small table near the wall that separated kitchen and sitting room.

She was surprised to find Michael's little cottage had a cozy, homey feel to it. She'd only ever been inside the homes of two men around her age: Danny's and Connor's, and both of them had very bare flats, furnished with only the most basic, necessary things. Both of those places felt like vast empty, temporary living spaces compared to Michael's cottage.

Like Dermot and Sinead's place, this cottage had a tiny kitchen space off to the right when you walked in, and the main living space filling most of the rest of the ground floor, minus a small ground floor bathroom off to the left of the sitting room. A stone fireplace was at the centre of the far left sitting room wall, a beautiful landscape painting mounted above it. Along the far wall was a small desk and bookshelf. Along the right wall, above the kitchen, was a staircase leading to the second floor.

"What do ye take in your tea?" he asked her, bringing over two mugs of Irish Breakfast tea and placing one in front of her.

"Just a little milk and sugar," she replied, clutching the warm mug around her fingers, feeling the warmth spread up through her hands and arms.

He returned with a glass jug of milk and a bowl of sugar, placing both of them in front of her before going back to the kitchen and rustling down some plates for the both of them. He'd cut the cake and placed a large slice on each plate, handing her one as he came back and sat down at the table to join her.

She took the plate from him gratefully, but didn't immediately take a bite into it; her stomach was still feeling a bit off from last night's drink fest and she wasn't entirely sure all that sugar and icing was going to make her feel well. The last thing she wanted was to throw up on Michael again and embarrass herself all over again. Instead, she dropped a dollop of milk and a teaspoon of sugar into her tea, stirring them both in and took a sip, enjoying the comforting warmth filling her from the inside out.

Unconsciously, she rubbed at her neck; it had felt like she had a crick in it ever since she'd woken up.

"I see that sleeping on the sofa last night didn't exactly agree with you." He nodded to her rubbing her neck as evidence of his statement.

"How'd you know I slept on the sofa last night?"

Had he just taken a lucky guess?

"Because I'm the one who carried you inside and put you there." His face suddenly darkened, as if the memory had left him with a sour taste in his mouth.

"You did? God, I don't remember that at all."

She hadn't really thought about how she'd ended up on the sofa. She supposed she'd thought she'd somehow stumbled up there blind drunk and passed out. That, or Danny had come out and found her, and carried her inside.

"It was just after you nearly upturned your stomach on me shoes."

"Well, I guess I owe you another thank you for making sure I got home safe."

"You're welcome." He gave her a curious look then, a mixture between sadness and pity, neither of which she understood. It made her uncomfortable.

"You going to eat any of that cake? Or just let it sit there?" she asked him, nodding to his untouched cake, trying to change the subject.

He looked down at his plate like he'd just remembered it was there. Picking up his fork he and took a bite, and that's when everything went horribly wrong for Aoife, as if her day wasn't already shaping up to be a rough one.

༺༻

Michael could see that she was waiting for him to take the first bite to see how he liked it. He had to admit to himself that the cake really did look good, like something one would see in a magazine. He'd been shocked when she'd shown up this morning with it, hoping to get his forgiveness for the party last night and to thank him for letting her borrow his jumper and for making sure she got home safe. He had to admit that he hadn't been expecting that from her. He'd been fairly certain she'd been too drunk to remember most of what happened last night, thank God, and so when she'd shown up on his doorstep, he'd been pleasantly surprised.

He was also hesitant about talking to her too much about what had happened last night. He felt sorry for her, having an eejit of a boyfriend who'd do something like that to her and, strangely enough, he didn't want to hurt her. Now Michael felt torn between telling her what he'd seen, or letting Danny fess up to it himself. He wasn't sure she'd believe him if he was the one to tell her, but it didn't sit well with him leaving it up to her boyfriend to tell her what the two of them had been arguing about when he'd carried Aoife inside. The look she was giving him now, so eager for his forgiveness for the party last night wasn't making the decision any easier on him. Giving in to her unabashed need for forgiveness and wanting to please her, he took a huge bite of the cake. It turned out to be an awful decision.

As he bit into the cake, the most indescribably acrid taste filled his moth. He could feel his face contorting as he tried with great effort to swallow the bite. To his credit, he'd managed to get it all of it down – albeit with much effort – trying to resist the urge to cough it all back up again. With his hand firmly balled into a fist over his mouth, trying to force down the tickle in his throat, he looked up into her expectant eyes, watching them change rapidly from excitement to anger, to confusion, to concern.

"The… cake… I think… you… forgot to put… in the… sugar," he managed to get out between coughs. He took a large gulp of tea, hoping it would wash down the horrid taste.

Her look of confusion deepened and she took his fork from his plate, taking a small bit of her own piece of cake he'd put before her. As she bit into it, he watched her face pucker up into a similar expression that had come over his own.

"The sugar must have been salt," she said, coughing a bit and trying to swallow down the offending cake.

"I'm *so* sorry," she said to him, "I guess Millie must have filled the jar full of salt instead of sugar. She's always pulling pranks like this on me; it's her way of having fun and messing with me. I never thought to check the batter before I put it in the pan. I feel *so* awful about this. And here I was trying to do something nice to make up for last night, and I go and ruin it with this stupid idea. This is *so* something that would happen to me."

Her face crumpled into absolute devastation and embarrassment. She was so flustered and upset, and the situation so comical he couldn't help but chuckle. Except that his laughs made him cough more, and she must've thought that he was choking again, for she rushed over to his side and knelt down beside him, one hand placed gently on his upper arm.

"Michael? Are you ok?" she asked, her face full of concern.

"I'm grand, I'm grand," he said, gently waving her off, and coughing loudly to clear his throat. "I'm sorry for laughing; it's just that it's too funny. I'd accuse you of trying to kill me if it wasn't for the look of sincerity on your face right now."

He'd meant it as a joke, but he could tell from the way her face instantly darkened that he'd made the second worst decision of the day.

"You're laughing *at* me?" she asked him, her voice dangerously quiet, like the vacuum of sound that occurs right before an explosion. It unnerved him more than any of the times she'd yelled at him. He found himself wishing the two of them were having an all-out shouting match right now, like the one they'd had in her kitchen when he'd saved her from burning down the Old Rectory.

Rising from her kneeling position by his side, she stalked out of the cottage without another word, but clearly pissed off at him as all hell. The murderous look she shot him just before she turned to walk out the door confirmed it.

"Aoife!"

He wasn't sure why he was going after her; he just knew he didn't want her to leave like this. They'd been making so much progress lately he didn't want to lose that. It always seemed to be two steps forward and one step back for them.

A woman on a mission, she was already well up the lane by the time he got to the front gate. Debating whether or not to run after her, he decided to let her go. He wasn't even sure why he was running after her in the first place. To apologize? What did he need to apologize for? *She* was the one who was trying to poison him; *she* should be apologizing to him, again.

"Women!" he muttered, exasperated. Women were confusing as hell, and Aoife had to be one of the most confusing women he'd ever met in his life.

※※※

She wasn't thinking about what she was doing, she was just trying to get out of the cottage as soon as she could. She was furious with him; no doubt about it. It was bad enough she'd had to come down here, practically on her knees to ask for forgiveness for the antics of last night, and then when she offered him a peace offering – yes, one that didn't go exactly as planned, but that was not the point – he almost literally spat it back into her face. Was it any wonder then that she stomped out of the cottage as quickly as she could?

Bleeding eejit, she thought to herself about him. *I'd like to just walk up to him right now and smack that smirk off his face as hard as I can.*

She was sorely tempted to follow up on this threat, except it would mean going back and facing him, and that was not something she wanted to do right now. No, right now she wanted to get as far away from Michael Flanagan as was possible in a small place like Ballyclara.

She stomped up the path, the sound of gravel crunching beneath her sandals giving her satisfaction, especially when she imagined that the gravel was Michael's head. She could hear him calling her name behind her, but she didn't turn around to acknowledge him, and hurried even faster along the path back to Aldridge Manor, practically jogging now.

When she'd gone a few metres up the road and realized he was not following her, she slowed her pace.

Stupid eejit can't even be bothered to follow me and apologize.

"Men!" she muttered furiously and kicked at a rock on the side of the road as hard as she could.

Her sudden outburst startled some sheep, who'd had been grazing near the fence and they bleated angrily at her and moved a few feet away, as if frightened by the crazy city girl. She gave them a furious scowl and continued on her rant about how much she hated Michael Flanagan and how she should turn right around and give him a piece of her mind, but she continued on back up the hill home instead. She needed some time to cool off before dealing with him.

Her mood hadn't improved by the time she got home; there were still all the obvious signs of the previous night's party. She sighed at all the work she was going to have to do, but then again, in the mood she was in, it might be nice to cleanse the whole place thoroughly.

It will be therapeutic, she told herself.

Heading inside to get some garbage bags to begin her clean up, she found herself warm after her little jaunt up the lane and pulled off the jumper she was wearing, hoping to cool down. It was then she realized she hadn't given Michael back his jumper at all and had worn it right back here.

"Shit."

Chapter Twenty-One

"Hey Aoife!"

Michael had been standing behind the bar, pouring a pint, as she walked in and was noticed by Brendan. His head whipped up at the mention of her name. He hadn't thought to see her so soon after their altercation earlier.

"Hi Brendan."

She smiled warmly at his friend as she stepped up to the bar, but it quickly faded from her face when she spotted him. Clearly, she hadn't expected to see him again so soon either.

Well, what the hell was she expecting, coming into the pub he owned? Where did she expect him to be?

"Hello Michael." Her voice was noticeably cooler than it had been with Brendan, her blue eyes almost turning to ice.

"Hey."

It was more of a grunt than a greeting. He was still a bit resentful of her blaming him for the "cake disaster" of earlier, as well as the fact he'd had to come in on his day off and work in the pub because all the people she'd invited to her party last night were hungover and looking for a place to eat. He knew he should probably feel grateful for the increased revenue, but right now, he just wanted to be angry with Aoife.

"What can I do for you today?"

All That Compels the Heart

Brendan gave Michael one of his small glares he'd perfected over the years, the one that told him to be more polite, more civil. As always, he ignored it.

"I just wanted to give Michael this."

At the mention of his name, he looked up from the spotlessly clean glass he'd been polishing and saw her set down his jumper on the bar, sliding it towards him. He'd forgotten that she'd walked out of his place with it still on.

"Great. I'm going to go and put these in the dishwasher."

He slid behind Brendan, careful not to bump him with the tray of glasses and walked through the swinging doors to the kitchen, completely ignoring Aoife and the returned jumper.

As he walked into the kitchen, Molly looked up from preparing a customer's meal but he must have had a stormy look on his face for she thought better of asking what he was doing back here in her domain. He'd just set the tray of glasses down on the counter when the kitchen doors swung open again.

"What was that?" Brendan's voice projected off the metallic surfaces of the kitchen.

He didn't respond, just continued to go about his intended chores, pulling the freshly cleaned glasses out of the dishwasher and replacing them with the tray of dirty ones he'd brought in. He could see Brendan approach him from the corner of his eye. He stood beside him, leaning against the counter, leaning in close so Michael wouldn't be able to ignore him.

He sighed, leaving the tray of glasses in the open dishwasher. He wasn't able to close the door without closing it on Brendan's leg. Witnessing the entire silent exchange between her husband and his best friend, Molly finally decided to intervene.

"What's going on?"

Both men continued to stare silently at each other, their eyes continuing their argument, when Brendan finally broke off his glare and turned to his wife.

"Aoife came in here to return Michael's jumper to him and he, for some unexplained reason, completely brushed her off. To say he was cold towards her would be an understatement. Downright frigid would be a more accurate description."

Molly, not being overly concerned with the fact Michael was being rude to customers – after all, she *had* known him for at least as long as Brendan had – latched onto exactly the one point Michael knew she would.

"And why did Aoife have your jumper?"

"Exactly! Thank you Mol... Wait, what?" Brendan, having latched onto what he considered to be the more important point – Michael's continued rudeness to a woman who was their employer and whom he was beginning to consider to be a friend – hadn't yet thought to ask why a woman they largely still didn't know had been wearing an article of his best friend's clothing.

"Why *did* Aoife have your jumper in the first place?" he asked, finally latching onto how odd a thing that was.

"Because I was at her place last night," Michael replied with a shrug of his shoulders like it should have been obvious to the two of them.

"You were at her house last night? As in, she invited you to her party? Or you were there for another reason?" His raised eyebrow indicated the unasked question hanging between them.

Michael chuckled to himself, fully understanding the unasked question. "You *do* know that I'm back with Eliza now, right?"

"Like we haven't been here before," Molly muttered to herself. She was a no-nonsense woman about most things, was Molly, which Michael appreciated about her. It allowed her to manage both her husband and his best friend with such efficiency. But he also didn't like it when she used that trait to interfere in his personal life.

Michael chose to ignore the comment. "No, I was not invited to Aoife's party last night."

"Then what the hell were you doing at her place? You have a fiancée; you just said so yourself."

"I didn't go over there to sleep with her. Besides, she's not my type." Michael looked at Brendan like he had two heads. "I went over there to shut down her party. Oh, you're welcome for that, by the way."

Michael's slightly smug look slipped a bit when he noticed neither Molly nor Brendan looked like they were going to thank him.

"I thought you said you were going to try to be nice to her, for your parents' sake, if for nothing else?" Brendan asked him, not looking pleased with him.

"I *was* trying to be nice," Michael practically growled. "I don't know about you, but I could hear that party down all the way at my place and it was raging well into the wee hours of the morning. I was fed up, so I decided to do something about it."

"And by 'do something about it' you mean marching up to her place and giving her a piece of your mind?"

Brendan threw his hands up in the air out of frustration. Michael didn't respond, just looked at his friend, knowing he was right.

"I don't know why I bother with ye, sometimes," Brendan said, frustrated. "You just couldn't leave her well enough alone, could you? Sure, we could hear the party down here, but it was no worse than what we used to do when we were her age. Besides, I don't get the impression that Aoife's the kind of girl to have parties like this all the time. Sure, and she said herself that she came down here exactly because she wanted to get away from that kind of lifestyle."

"Well, she's doin' a helluva job of it. Also, it's not like she's *that* much younger than us," Michael muttered.

"Five years makes a difference, Michael. Besides, it's not like we're not benefiting from her party."

Brendan swept a hand towards the kitchen door, on the other side of which was a pub currently full of hungover twenty-somethings. What with tourist season beginning to wind down, it was the busiest they'd been in weeks, and even Michael had to admit that it was a welcome profit for them.

As if the mention of the crowd outside had brought him in, Jimmy came through the doors at precisely that moment. "What's going on in here, Molly? There's people outside lookin' to eat."

Brendan had brought him and his wife, Karen, in as an extra set of hands when they'd seen how busy the place was going to get today. He'd also figured they could use the extra cash, what with the baby coming soon and all. Michael had even enlisted his sister, Mara, for some help.

"These hands can only go as fast as the Good Lord can make them, Jimmy Connolly!"

Jimmy looked terrified at the thunderous look on her face, upset at having her investigation of Michael's private life interrupted. Before another argument could erupt in his kitchen, Michael intervened.

"Jimmy, there's two dishes ready." Michael pointed to two plates Molly had just placed on the warmer. "Take them over to..." He looked to Molly for some assistance.

"Table two."

"Take them to table two. And then go take care of the bar for me. Tell Karen to take the orders and get the food out to people, and tell Mara to get in here now and help Molly prepare the food."

"Here's three more orders, Molly," Karen said, swinging open the doors and attaching them to the hanging tabs Molly had set up near her workstation. Immediately sensing she'd walked in on something she may not want to be in the middle of, Karen paused, watching everyone in the room warily. She placed a protective hand over her rounded belly, as if all this tension might somehow affect the baby.

"Here, take these out to table two." Jimmy placed the plates in her hands.

"But I thought those were your tables...?"

"Change of plans." Jimmy gently pushed her towards the door before the two of them ended up in the middle of whatever "this" was that was going on between Michael, Brendan, and Molly.

Molly, who had been quietly watching her husband and his best friend argue things out up to this point, decided to bring the conversation back to her original question.

"So how exactly *did* Aoife end up with your jumper, Michael?" Molly stood there with her arms folded across her chest, her hawk-like eyes expecting an answer.

"Molly, Jimmy said you needed help in here?" Mara chose just that moment to walk into the middle of their conversation, something she'd come to immediately regret.

All That Compels the Heart

"For the love of all that is holy!" Molly exclaimed explosively. "Can a girl not ask a simple question and expect a simple answer without a million bloody interruptions?"

Everyone in the kitchen looked at her, surprised; Molly wasn't the type to normally just have an outburst like that.

"Oh, is this about Aoife being caught wearing your jumper this morning?" Mara asked, the puzzle pieces suddenly coming together.

"You stay out of this," Michael warned his big sister.

"How do *you* know about Aoife and Michael's jumper?" Molly asked, ignoring Michael's dark stare. He knew she'd not be intimidated by him.

"Maud Drummond and Anna McCaffrey were in earlier and telling everyone how they saw Aoife and Michael at his place this morning, and she was wearing your jumper there in plain sight. Said it looked a cozy scene, so it did."

Michael sighed; they'd all jumped to exactly the conclusions he wished they hadn't jumped to. Instead of addressing the situation head on and clearing things up with them though, he chose to hide behind their current pressing duties.

"Help Molly get the food prepared. We have customers out there who need their orders."

"I'm very well aware of that, Michael." Mara's voice was on edge. "Jimmy, Karen, and I have been holding down the fort when you and Brendan should be out there helping."

"Here, take this one." Molly handed Mara an order, pointing to another workstation for her to begin preparing the meal. "And Brendan, you take this one. We can work while we listen. So, Michael, let's have it."

She wasn't about to let him get off the hook a third time.

He sighed and rubbed a hand over his face, suddenly feeling weary. "So, ye know I went up to the Old Rectory to put a stop to the party?"

"Yes, yes. We know that part." Molly waved a butter knife at him, encouraging him to get to the part she was more interested in.

"I didn't know that," Mara said, though there was no hint of surprise in her voice. She knew Michael well enough to know it was exactly the sort of thing he would do.

"Well, when I got to the Old Rectory, Aoife was outdoors, standing around in the middle of the lane in something completely inappropriate for last night's chill, so I offered her my jumper to keep her warm until she went back inside. Instead, she ended up puking her guts out all over the ground in front of me and nearly passing out. So, I carried her back inside and got her settled – no thanks to that useless, cheating boyfriend of hers, I might add – and then, I forgot until I got back to my place she still had my jumper on when I left her."

"Wait, you caught Danny cheating on Aoife?" Mara asked, astonished by this bit of gossip.

He immediately wished he'd said nothing.

"'Twas nothing. I didn't mean anything by it."

"Bullshit." Brendan looked up from the basket of chips he'd just placed in the deep fryer.

Michael grimaced as he thought back to what had happened at Aoife's housewarming party after he'd arrived.

After finally wrangling Aoife into a position where he could carry her inside without her taking one of his eyes out, he'd entered into the chaos of the house. He hadn't exactly planned on this happening, so he was wondering where to put her down exactly as he stood there in the foyer. There hadn't been a single sofa, chair, or other surface to put her down on; not that he'd felt comfortable just leaving her there, almost passed out on her own. Anything could have happened to her.

He didn't know any of these friends of hers; he'd only seen her with two friends before, and that had only been from a distance. He'd looked around for them now, but with the press of bodies around him he wasn't able to spot them in the crowd. The only other person he knew was Danny, but Michael hadn't seen him in the crowd either.

With Aoife getting heavy in his arms, he'd made the judgement call to take her upstairs, away from the main noise of the party. Dodging passed out drunks on the stairs, he'd carefully navigated his way to the upper floor. He'd take her to her bedroom and set her down there, where she was more likely to be safe. Assuming she'd have set herself up in the master bedroom, he'd gone straight for the end of the corridor with the ease of someone who knew the house as well as anyone who lived there.

He'd been half-expecting to find the room occupied with passed out drunks looking for a place to hide from the noise going on downstairs, but he hadn't been expecting to find Danny, the man he'd been looking for to take Aoife off his hands, about to have sex with some long-legged blonde he didn't recognize in Aoife's bed. He'd been so shocked by the sight that he'd stood in the doorway for a full second, unsure of what to do. Knowing this wasn't something he wanted Aoife to come around to and see – and not wanting to be witnessing it himself – Michael began to back out of the room. Unfortunately for the both of them, Danny caught the movement in his peripheral vision. Michael saw that it took him a half-second to recognize who he was and the fact he was carrying his girlfriend in his arms.

"Fuck," Danny roared, practically throwing the blonde off him and onto the bed beside him.

"I'm sorry. I didn't realize that someone would be in here." It was all Michael could think to say in the moment.

"What the fuckin' hell are you doing with my girlfriend?" Danny had growled at him as he'd hastily grabbed for his clothes.

"What - ? What am *I* doing with *your* girlfriend? What the feckin' hell are you doing with *her*," he pointed to the blonde, who was hastily putting on her bra. Michael had rounded on Danny, almost knocking Aoife's head into the doorframe in the process. Feeling instinctively protective of the city girl, he subconsciously pulled her in closer to him.

This action had not gone unnoticed by Danny. He'd jumped out of the bed, pulling on his trousers and crossed the room to stand in front of him. He was a good deal shorter than himself – probably only a couple of inches taller than Aoife – with the kind of clean-shaven good looks girls always seemed to swoon over. What he lacked in height though, he'd learned to try and make up for in assertiveness and was now trying to use this to intimidate his opponent.

It didn't work.

Somewhere in his mind, Danny must have realized he was not going to win this staring contest and had broken off his gaze to pay attention to his girlfriend.

"Aoife?"

She'd stirred in Michael's arms at the sound of her name. "Danny?"

"That's right baby." Danny had placed a hand on one side of her face.

"Hand her over."

Danny held his arms outstretched to Michael, ordering him to give Aoife over to him, like he was concerned Michael might do something to her. He seethed with disgust at the other man.

"Your *girlfriend*," Michael couldn't help but sneer at how the word clearly meant nothing to Danny, "has had too much to drink and needs to rest."

Danny scowled at the jab. "Then give her to me and I'll take care of her."

If he hadn't been so disgusted by Danny, he may have been tempted to just dump Aoife in his arms and walk away. However, Michael's protective instinct only deepened and he pulled her a fraction of an inch closer to him, standing just outside of Danny's grasp.

"I got this," Michael told him, sharply.

Abruptly, he turned on his heel and headed back down the hallway, trying to find an empty room to place Aoife in. He'd remembered passing by one of the old sitting rooms that had been empty a few minutes ago. Luckily, he found it still unoccupied. He'd gently laid her down on the sofa she'd made him and Brendan bring in here the other day, ensuring she'd be comfortable. She'd placed a blue tartan blanket over the back of the sofa, which he now laid across her to keep her warm. She'd stirred a little, pulling it tighter around her, but she soon settled again and began a soft snoring that comes with a deep, dreamless sleep.

Satisfied she'd sleep safely and soundly in here, Michael rose from the sofa and was startled to see Danny standing right behind him. He hadn't heard the smaller man follow him down the corridor. He'd tried to skirt around Danny and the blonde, who'd follow them in here as well. Danny pushed his lover aside, purposefully stepping into Michael's path and blocking his exit. Michael could tell he was looking for a confrontation.

"Where the hell do you think you're going?" Danny had growled at him.

"Home," Michael had replied simply, trying not to engage the other man's already flaring temper. If Danny hadn't been bolstered by the false confidence alcohol can give a man, he might have had the sense to take the warning and get out of the way. As it was, he'd ignored it.

"You think you can just prance in here with my girlfriend in your arms and leave without an explanation?" Danny had asked, trying to get up in Michael's face. Michael couldn't hold it in any longer and gave a small, amused snort at how comical the small man had looked in that moment. This, unfortunately, only had the effect of incensing Danny's rage.

"What the hell is so funny?"

Michael had snickered at him again, unable to control himself in the face of the buffoon before him. "Sorry," he'd managed to mumble between little laughs while he'd tried to get himself under control. He'd cleared his throat and said, "Nothing. It's nothing."

Danny had eyed him suspiciously, judging whether or not to believe him. Clearly still angling for a fight, he had once more stepped into Michael's path as he tried to leave.

"Hey! Where do you think you're going? I'm not done with you yet."

Foolishly, Danny had grabbed at the collar of Michael's shirt. Instinctively, he'd grabbed hold of Danny's hands and pushed him back against the wall, a warning not to mess with him, but not enough to actually hurt him. Nevertheless, frightened by the physical exchange between the two men, the leggy blonde had screamed like Michael intended to murder Danny.

Looking back on the situation now, he supposed that some part of him might have wanted to make the eejit pay for what he'd done, even though it wasn't technically his business. In any case, the distraction had been just enough that Danny had been able to extricate himself from Michael's grasp and make an attempt to punch him. Being infinitely more inebriated than his opponent, Danny's punch went wide and Michael was easily able to dodge the swinging fist. Rebounding, he was able to strike a blow of his own at Danny's right eye socket. He hit him just hard enough to make him stumble backwards into the arms of his lover, and just hard enough that he would have a sizeable bruise in the morning, but not enough to do any real physical damage to him.

Let's see how you explain that to your girlfriend in the morning.

Satisfied to hear the little upstart groaning from the punch, Michael had sneered down at him. The blonde had tried to pull Danny closer to her, trying to protect him from Michael in case he meant to finish him off. He'd raised his hands in a gesture of peace, showing her he didn't mean either of them any further harm.

"You're done with me now ye little shit, and if you have any heart or common decency at all, you'll be done with Aoife too after what you've done to her tonight."

Not waiting for his opponent to regain his footing or his strength, Michael had stalked out of the Old Rectory, fighting his way down the stairs and the foyer through the crowds that were still well into party mode, and had headed back home, the steady beat that had brought him up to the house in the first place following him down the lane.

"Jaysus feckin' Christ," Brendan exclaimed as Michael finished recounting the events of last night.

Everyone in the room looked at him surprised; Brendan normally wasn't one to use the Lord's name in vain unless under special circumstances.

"Ye have to tell her, Michael."

Everyone's head whipped around and saw Jimmy standing there with Karen, waiting to pick up their customer's orders. Before anyone could make a move, Michael crossed the white-tiled floor of the kitchen with the swiftness of a cat.

"Ye don't breathe a word of this to anyone, understand?" His darkened expression must have sufficiently scared the young man, for Jimmy nodded quickly, as did Karen.

"I said, do you understand?" Michael repeated his question.

All That Compels the Heart

"Yes," both Karen and Jimmy chorused immediately, and silently exited the kitchen, carrying the plates of food they'd come for, trying to get as far away from Michael as was humanly possible.

"Now don't be goin' and terrifyin' the kids, Michael. Especially when they're right. You *should* tell Aoife what happened last night; she's a right to know." Brendan looked at Michael, his face implacable.

"You of all people should understand the situation she's in right now better than anyone." Everyone in the room froze at Mara's quiet statement, waiting to see how he'd react.

It was something they'd all silently agreed never to speak about, how Michael's on/off fiancée, Eliza Kennedy, had cheated on him just before the two of them were supposed to be married the first time. After a long process of mediation, the two of them had only just become re-engaged a few months ago. Michael knew everyone in the room still wanted to ask him why, why he'd taken her back. How could he forgive her for what she'd done? How could he trust that she wouldn't do it again? They were questions he didn't want to answer because he knew they wouldn't agree with his answers.

"Exactly. I *do* know what it's like, and the way I see it, I'm sparing her the hurt of having it broadcast throughout the village, like it was for me. This is something she and Danny need to work out between themselves; they don't need the rest of us meddling in their business. So, all of ye, keep it to yourselves."

Having said his piece on the matter, he picked one of the order sheets and began helping with the preparations.

"Like hell he's going to tell her!" Mara piped up, standing beside him. "He may have had plenty of chances to do that in God knows how long. For all we know he's been cheating on her for ages. If he's gotten away with it for this long, then he's not going to give himself up just because you caught him at it."

Michael knew she was right, and he didn't disagree with her stance on it. He just couldn't bring himself to be the one who hurt Aoife.

"It's none of our concern, and I won't be the one who causes her hurt if all this turns out to be nothing."

"Well I never thought I'd see you protecting the likes of Danny Fitzgerald," she snapped at him.

"I'm not protecting Danny, I'm protecting Aoife."

"Right, because it's *so* much better to be kept in the dark about this kind of thing."

"You know what, Mara? Maybe it *is* better to be kept in the dark. Maybe, just maybe I wished *you* hadn't gone and opened your mouth about Eliza and then she and I could have been married by now and the whole mess behind us."

Mara looked hurt by this. He knew she felt bad for being the one to tell him about Eliza, for having been the one to catch his fiancée with a tourist down at one of the cottages her parents rented out to visitors. He'd been a regular during the year, coming down every few weeks for research, he'd claimed. He'd spent many times in the pub talking with both him and Brendan, acting like he hadn't been having an affair with the man he was drinking buddies with. Michael knew Mara had only done what she'd thought was best at the time, but it was hard to deny that a part of him would have been better off not knowing.

"Or maybe she'd still be cheating on you behind your back and you too stupid to realize it!"

Michael rounded on her then, his eyes full of fury.

"Alright, alright. I think that's quite enough."

Brendan stepped in between the two siblings, arms outstretched to keep the two of them as far apart as possible.

"Michael, get out of here, go home and cool off. Ye haven't had nearly enough sleep and you're not thinking about what you're saying."

Michael was about to protest this last statement; he knew exactly what it was he was saying.

"Don't. Not a word." Brendan pointed his index finger at him, a warning in his brown eyes not to challenge him right now or he'd set him on his arse, best friend or no.

Michael knew he meant it.

Running his hand angrily through his dark hair, he took off the apron he'd put on earlier to help prepare some of the orders and stalked out of the pub with a thunderous look upon his face.

Chapter Twenty-Two

After leaving the pub – being kicked out of *his* feckin' pub, more like – Michael stalked off towards home like Brendan had suggested. Even though he wouldn't have admitted it in front of his friend, he *was* tired. Not only had the music kept him up after he'd returned home last night, what he'd seen continued to bother him, keeping him awake until the sun began to rise.

With his blood up from his argument with Mara though, he was able to push aside the tiredness for now. With his long legs and the state of fury he was in, it took him no time at all to make it back to his cottage. However, not wanting to give Brendan any satisfaction – who the feckin' hell was *he* to be ordering *him* around anyways? – he didn't stop at home. He didn't know where he was planning to go, but he found himself in front of the Old Rectory a few minutes later.

The assortment of fancy vehicles had departed, minus the few people still at the pub, most of them had decamped and made their way back to the city. The front garden looked put back together, only a few pieces of crepe paper streamers floating through the air giving any hint there'd been a party here. As he approached the house, he caught some movement in one of the upper windows.

"Who's there?"

He heard the window being raised and Aoife poking out her head, her voice wary

"It's just me." He stepped out to where she could see him.

"Michael?"

Her voice still sounded wary, like she wasn't sure what his intentions were. After all, to her, it had to look strange since they'd just been in a huge argument this morning and here he was now, practically at her front door, seemingly without a reason.

"I just... I just came by to check on a few things before Jimmy and I come back on Monday to work on some of windowpanes."

"Oh." There was a strange note of disappointment in her voice.

What had she been hoping he'd come over for?

He stood there awkwardly, not sure if he should *actually* look at a few things while he was here in order to lend credence to his excuse, or if he should just go home.

"I should probably head home. This can wait until tomorrow."

"Do you want to come in for a cup of tea?"

The question caught him off-guard.

What if she's just trying to be polite and is hoping you'll refuse? Should you apologize for this morning? Be the bigger person about the whole thing?

"Sure."

His response surprised even himself.

What are you doing? You should just get out here before she thinks you've been creeping around her house, or God-knows-what else.

"Come on in. I'll put the kettle on."

"*I'll* put the kettle on."

Remembering the "stove incident" he didn't want to take any more chances.

"I *can* boil water, you know. Especially when it's in an electric kettle."

All That Compels the Heart

"I'm sure ye can. I'm just not willing to put that to the test right now." The last thing they needed was her burning the fecking place down again.

Sensing that she might try and see this as a challenge to beat him to the kitchen first, he quickly headed inside, taking the front steps two at a time.

He was right. As he came through the front door, he saw her bounding down the last of the stairs and darting past him into the kitchen. He smiled at the little victory dance she did as she made it to the kitchen before him.

"Fine, you can put the kettle on then. Just try not to burn the place down around me ears, please."

"You're never going to let me live that down, are you?"

She filled the electric kettle with water and plugged it in, the water beginning to bubble almost immediately.

"Nope." He grinned back at her as he settled himself down at the island they'd installed in the kitchen a couple of weeks ago.

He looked around at the newly outfitted kitchen, proud of the work they'd done in restoring the place. Although it now had all new electric appliances, he was pleased that Aoife had wanted to keep it largely as it had originally looked when the house was first built.

The ground floor of the house looked much better this morning than it had last night. Several bin bags were lined up against one wall in the kitchen, full of the remnants of last night. He'd spotted some paper plates and cups piled up on the coffee table in the sitting room, and there were still some half-empty bottles of alcohol in the kitchen, but she seemed to have mostly gotten it back into some semblance of order.

She began pulling down mugs from the cupboards and brought down the sugar and milk from the fridge. He stuck his finger into the sugar, tasting it in front of her. He grinned at her slightly affronted look.

"You're not going to let me live *that* one down either, are you?"

"Nope."

He was relieved when he saw her smile in return; it seemed like their earlier argument had blown over as quickly as it had arisen.

"I promise I'm not trying to kill you."

"Can't take any chances," he teased her.

She gave him a pointed look as she unplugged the boiling kettle and poured water into the mugs.

"I'll let you make your own. That way, if you end up dead, it'll be your own damn fault." She grinned at him smugly.

"You're so kind." He took his mug and poured in a bit of milk, watching her add her sugar and milk to her own.

"Want to go out on the back porch? It's such a nice day."

"Sure." He picked up his mug and followed her out, settling himself in one of the wicker chairs.

The two of them sat in a comfortable silence for a bit looking out over the village, the only sounds were that of the wind rustling in the trees around them. Michael looked around him, enjoying the view. No matter how many times he woke up to this same view every morning, it still seemed new and fresh to him. It was always different in some way, never quite the same image each time.

He caught her looking at him from the corner of her eye and he found himself uneasy. Should he apologize for the whole debacle this morning? After all, she *was* only trying to be nice; she hadn't intended to poison him. At least, it didn't seem like it. His mother would tell him that in this situation, if he was wondering if he should apologize, then it was very likely because he had something to apologize for. Also, there was the matter of the incident with Danny last night. Should he bring it up? Should he just come out and tell her what he'd seen? Was he doing her more harm than good by doing what he saw as him protecting her?

Instead, he said nothing.

The two of them continued to sit in silence for a few minutes more before he couldn't take it anymore. "Has everyone gone back to the city then?"

She sipped her tea quietly, nodding. "Yes. Millie and Bex were the last to leave. I had to practically force them out. They wanted to stay and help clean up."

"I'd have thought Danny would have stayed behind to help."

She looked a bit surprised at the comment, and maybe, a bit amused. Taking another sip from her mug and placing it on the small table beside her, she replied, "No, he and a colleague wanted to get back to the city first thing this morning. Said they wanted to work on some report they had to get done for end of day on Monday."

He noticed the way she seemed unsettled at the mention of Danny's name, and the unnamed colleague who'd spirited him away. If Michael had had three guesses as to who it was, he would have placed all his bets on it being the blonde he'd seen last night.

Maybe you're just imagining things.

Somehow, he didn't think he was.

Although he couldn't claim to know Aoife all that well, he definitely knew what she looked like when she was bothered by something, and there was something about the tense way she held her shoulders, the way her fingers idly picked at a thread on the cushion she was sitting on that told him she was agitated.

"You wouldn't happen to know why Danny had a black eye this morning, would you?"

He was taken off-guard by the question, not expecting it. Avoiding the question at first, he took a long drink from his mug, wishing there was something stronger than just tea in there.

"No," he lied. "Is there a reason I should?"

"No." She continued to idly pick at the thread. Having separated it from the cushion, she twirled it lightly between her thumb and forefinger.

"What did Danny say about it?" he asked, trying to assess how much of last night she remembered.

"That he and Jason — that's one of his closest friends — were messing around and he accidentally punched him in the eye." Her mouth pulled at the edges, somewhere between a grimace and a frown.

"Do you have any reason not to believe him?"

Subconsciously, he rubbed at the knuckles of his right hand. Although he hadn't really hit Danny hard enough for them to be bruised or battered, there were a few small scrapes from their scuffle.

Of course she does; it's not the truth. You know what happened; you should tell her.

He cleared his throat, trying to tell his doubts to go firmly to hell, the sharp sound startling her. There was a pregnant pause before she finally shook her head slightly.

"No."

She was lying, of course; he could see that. However, he didn't think that she suspected the truth either. If she did, surely she would have confronted him head on about it?

"Then I'm sure that's exactly what happened." He smiled at her as reassuringly as he could manage. The corners of her mouth relaxed a bit. It wasn't exactly a smile, but she did seem a bit more relieved.

"Of course."

"Look, I'm sorry about this morning. I didn't realize how much it meant to you to apologize for last night. Not that there's anything you really need to apologize for; I think things just got out of hand on both our sides, and for my part, I'm sorry."

He hadn't intended to say it, but she'd looked like she needed a distraction from her no-good, cheating boyfriend, so he'd grasped onto the first thing he could think of. Besides, now he could hold it over her that he was being the bigger person by being the first to apologize.

"And, to properly apologize, I want to do something nice for *you*."

"Don't tell me that you baked me a cake?" she teased, humour glinting in her sapphire eyes.

He laughed, a full, hearty laugh, the kind he hadn't had in quite some time. It made her laugh too, a pleasant sound in the quiet afternoon.

"No. I'm going to take you on an adventure."

"Where are we going?"

"Follow me." He rose from his chair, hand outstretched towards her. She looked at it warily.

"I told you; on an adventure."

"What kind of an adventure?"

"That would be spoiling the surprise."

She gave him a skeptical look.

"You coming, or not?" He raised one eyebrow at her, challenging her to trust him.

She took a second to mull over his proposition. "I don't know… I mean, you haven't given me much to go on."

"You're just going to have to trust me, aren't ye? Besides, it's not like you were planning to do anything else today."

Giving it one last debate in her mind, she placed her hand in his and let him pull her to her feet.

"How do you know I wasn't planning on doing anything today?"

"Because if ye were, you would have said 'no' right away."

He grinned cheekily at her, knowing that she knew he was right. She drew her mouth into a slight pout at the fact that she seemed be so easy to read but didn't argue with him.

"Should I change?"

She held her arms out wide, letting him examine her. Sometime after she'd gone down to the pub to return his jumper to him – *Dammit*; he'd left it back at the pub – she'd changed into a pair of jeans, black tank top and grey cardigan.

"No. But you may want to bring a pair of sensible boots."

She gave him a curious look but headed back into the house and went to find a pair of riding boots while he took their mugs inside and placed them in the brand-new dishwasher. He heard her zip up the sides of her boots and she walked back into the kitchen, hands on hips.

"Shall we head out on this adventure, then?"

He nodded and indicated they should head out the front door. On their way out, she quickly grabbed her keys and stuffed them in the pocket of her cardigan, following him outside.

"You know you don't have to lock up around here. It's not like anyone's going to steal anything. Ballyclara doesn't exactly have a crime rate."

"I know. It's just habit."

"The only thing break-in we've ever had was thirty years ago when a sheep managed to escape its pen, wandered into the Byrnes' house, and stole one of Mrs. Byrne's apple tarts right off the counter. They'd come home from church, intending to offer tea to Father Patrick, but found the apple tart strewn across the kitchen floor and the ewe standing there in the middle of the floor, bleating at them in greeting."

"That must have been quite the sight," Aoife giggled as Michael recounted the tale for her.

"Gave the poor Byrnes quite a fright. Ye should have seen Mrs. Byrne trying to coax the ewe out of the kitchen. She was a stubborn old thing."

"Who? The ewe? Or Mrs. Byrne?"

"Aye, well both, I suppose." Michael smiled at the joke and the two of them laughed as they set off towards the main road. When they reached it, he could see Aoife turning right, as if to head towards the village.

"This way," he nodded, walking in the opposite direction.

Her interest piqued, she followed him, curious to find out what this new path had in store for them.

The two of them walked in a comfortable silence, perfectly at ease with each other. About ten minutes later, a trail veered off to their left, away from the main road. He put his hand out and lightly touched Aoife's left elbow, gently steering her towards the path and into the copse of trees ahead of them.

Although it wasn't exactly a very hot day – was any day in Ireland ever considered "very" hot? – the shade from the trees provided a nice reprieve from their walk in the sun along the road. The trail – a path well-worn by both weather, animal, and human – followed a little creek, the long lost remains of a once thriving riverbed that had slowly begun to narrow and dry up since prehistoric times. The creek bubbled and gurgled as it meandered its way beside them, leading their way through the darkening woods. Petrichor hung in the air, damp and thick, despite the fact it hadn't rained much in the last few days, the moss which clung to rocks and trees holding in the moisture. The deeper they went into the woods, the more the trail became obscured by fallen logs and large rocks.

"Here, let me help you."

Michael climbed over the remains of a long dead oak tree. When he'd made it safely to the other side, he wiped his hand on his jeans to clean off the slick wetness the soft, furry moss along the tree's trunk had left and held out a hand to her, holding her steady as she climbed down. She landed with a soft thud on the ground before him, the leaf-covered earth masking their footfalls as they continued along the trail.

They'd been walking for a good twenty or thirty minutes by this point and he could hear her breath becoming thick from dehydration, sighing more with the exertion of climbing the trail.

"Why don't we stop here a moment?" he asked as the path levelled out a bit, providing easy access to the creek beside them. "If you're thirsty, you can drink from the creek; it's safe."

Bending down to the soft earth of the creek bed, she cupped her hands together.

"How much further?" she asked him.

"Not far. The trail is much easier from here. It's just through those stand of oaks there."

He pointed to a grouping of large oak trees that stood just off to their left a bit. She nodded to him and rose to her feet, wiping her hands on her jeans to dry them and indicated for him to show her the way.

The two of them resumed their silent walk. They were in the deep part of the woods now, the canopy of evergreens and hardwoods filtering the sunlight around them like a mesh covering. Although it was by no means close to sundown, the change in lighting was noticeable.

"It's just over this ridge." He pointed in front of them to a little ridge where the treeline seemed to thin out a bit. "I promise."

Only a few minutes later, they reached the edge of the clearing and could hear the sound of water rushing over the edge of a rocky outcropping, plummeting to a pool below it, louder and swifter than the water gurgling in the stream beside them. He saw Aoife's face look around curiously, trying to identify where the sound was coming from. He offered a hand to her and led her to the edge of the trees.

Right in front of them was a small clearing, the Wicklow Mountains rising around them. On their right was a road which wound its way along a high ridge line, while right in front of them was a small waterfall gushing from the rock face of the ridge. To some, it may not be the most exciting of waterfalls; after all, it was barely a hundred feet tall, but to him, this place was special.

"Here we are."

Michael held out his arms, indicating that they'd arrived at their destination. He watched her as she took in the sight before them, a smile creeping over her face. Her happy mood was slightly altered when she looked to their right, her eyes following the road as it gently wound itself up the ridgeline above the waterfall.

"We couldn't have taken the road to get here?" she asked, confronting him.

"We could have. But where's your sense of adventure?" His eyes twinkled with a hint of mischief.

Aoife shook her head at him like she wasn't sure what to make of him, but she smiled, no hint of annoyance in her face. "Alright, I'll give it to you; you were right. It was worth it to come up here."

"So you like your surprise then?" he asked, hoping that things between the two of them had been smoothed over.

"It's beautiful."

Michael found himself smiling along with her, pleased to see her happy.

"You can't get a view like this in Dublin," she said after a brief pause, the two of them just standing there, listening to the water rush past them. "Don't get me wrong; I love Dublin. I love its character, and the people, and the noise, and bustle of the city around me, but everything there is honed to perfection by man. Out here, everything has been created by Mother Nature and her alone."

"You're right about that."

Michael held out a hand to her offering to help her down the little knoll into the clearing so the two of them could get closer to the waterfall. She put her hand in his, her touch light and soft as the two of them strolled comfortably together, nearing the small pool at the bottom of the waterfall. He helped her onto a large rock, the two of them sitting there in the sun just out of range of the water's spray, the air cool and moist against their faces.

The two of them sat there in an easy silence, watching the ripples across the small pool, the sun glinting off its surface, almost masking the pebbly sand along its bottom. It wasn't deep; if he stood in the middle of it, it would only have come about mid-way between his waist and his chest. But it was deep enough to swim around in.

"It's places like this that make me stay," he said suddenly, appreciating the beauty around him.

"Have you never thought about leaving here, Michael? Ballyclara, I mean?"

"Not in a long while," he replied honestly.

He put a hand up to his eyes, shielding them from the glare of the sun on the water's surface. He glanced sideways at her, observing her reaction. She sat up straight and looked at him sideways, not sure what he meant by this.

Michael hadn't always wanted to be the dependable son who stayed close to home to help take care of his parents; not that he minded so much now. But, when he'd been younger – *God, had it been twelve years already?* – he'd envisioned a rather different sort of life for himself.

He'd been much like Jimmy Connolly when he was around the same age. He'd been top of his class; even gotten a scholarship to UCC – University College Cork – to study Engineering. But life, as usual, had found a way to intervene.

"I haven't always lived here, ye know."

She looked over at him then, curiosity piqued. "Oh?"

He nodded. "I went to Cork for a semester at UCC."

"What happened?"

He knew she didn't mean it to sound nosy or rude, even if it did slightly come across like that. She'd asked it out of simple curiosity.

"My fiancée – well, my girlfriend at the time, Eliza – got pregnant. Found out in the middle of our first term at university. And so, things changed."

She must have sensed there was something more to the story, for she only nodded, not saying a word. Michael took a deep breath of cool, fresh air, taking his time before continuing.

"Eliza waited to tell me she was pregnant when I came home for winter break."

He remembered it very clearly. His mother had told him before he'd barely gotten in the door that Eliza had been looking for him. He'd gone out back to where she'd been standing on the porch, watching a falling star shoot across the clear night sky. A good luck charm she'd said then, a good sign for their future. Her face had been pinched with worry, scared to tell him. Finally, between a few tears, he'd gotten the truth out of her. After that, it had all been a gambit of emotions: excitement, love, fear, panic. But excitement and love had won out and he'd proposed on the spot, wanting to make their little family official.

"I made the decision to drop out of university right then and there, and moved back to Ballyclara. A week later, we'd moved in together and were mapping out our future."

There was a catch in his voice at the end, betraying him. He felt around in his pocket, looking for the packet of smokes he always had with him. Pulling one out and placing it between his teeth, he held the carton out to her, offering her one. She gave a dismissive wave, declining the offer. He lit it up and took a deep breath, letting the smoke fill his lungs and exhaled through his nose.

"And then, a few months later, we lost the baby."

There was a slight pause, like she was waiting to see if he was going to say anything else. When she finally did speak, she said, "Oh, Michael. I'm so sorry."

There was no hint of pity in her voice or face; sympathy and a certain sadness, yes, but no pity. She placed a hand in his, giving it a firm, comforting squeeze. It felt small and soft in his big, rough one, worn from years of physical labour. His free hand shook slightly as he took a drag from his smoke and exhaled deeply, the cloud of smoke drifting away lazily with the light breeze.

"It's kind of a stupid thing to say, isn't it? That we 'lost' the baby, like we were some neglectful parents who just let it wander off somewhere on its own and it never came back." His voice trailed off, lost in the painful memory. "It was taken from us too soon would be a more accurate description."

She gave his hand another squeeze and he gave her a small smile in return. The two of them continued to sit in silence, just enjoying one another's company for a few minutes.

"I can't say I know what you went through as I've never had children, but I do know what it is to lose someone you care about." Her eyes looked sad and the delicate, soft skin around them looked wet, and not just from the spray of the waterfall.

"Your grandfather?" He puffed away some more on his cigarette.

He felt her stiffen beside him and she withdrew her hand, placing it in her lap. Her auburn curls fell across her cheek creating a curtain of hair and he wasn't able to see her face anymore.

"Danny told me. The first time he came down here to visit you. Back in the pub," he confessed between drags on his cigarette. "Is he the reason ye came down here?"

"Partly."

"And the other part?" he pressed, before realizing that maybe he shouldn't. After all, it wasn't any of his business why she'd come down here. He'd just been caught up in the moment.

"To be honest, I think I was ready to leave Dublin ages ago; I just didn't want to admit it. I love my friends, but they're really the only things tying me there."

He was surprised she didn't mention her family or Danny, for that matter, as reasons to stay behind in the city. "I take it you're not close to your family, then?"

"Not in the slightest." She laughed at the statement, but it was tinged with a slight bitterness, like she had an awful taste in her mouth. "Aside from Connor, whom you've already met, and my Grandad, there's no family for me back in Dublin."

He could tell there was a story behind it all, but with that curtain of hair still between them, now didn't seem to be the right time to press her on it.

"And Danny? It seems like he thought the two of you would be ready to settle down and move in together, the way he was talking that night.."

"Well, Danny doesn't know me as well as he thinks he does." She reached up to put a curl behind her ear, partially revealing her face again, letting him back in.

Michael thought it was a curious thing for her to say. She was supposed to be in love with this guy; how could they not know each other well enough to know what the other's life goals were? He'd be the first to admit that he and Eliza didn't always see eye-to-eye on their life goals all the time, but they'd managed to work through each of those phases together over the last twelve years and made sure they were both clear about what they wanted.

"I didn't know you were engaged."

It didn't fail to escape his notice the way she changed the topic on him.

"Eliza's been away since before you arrived in Ballyclara. She has an aunt over in Limerick who's ill. She and her family have been over there staying with her, helping out. She's supposed to be back today."

"So the two of you are still together, then?"

Michael looked at her curiously. "Of course. One thing I've learned from all this is that something as devastating as losing a child can either break you apart, or it can make you stronger. I'm not going to say Eliza and I haven't had our moments, but we've always come back to each other."

Kind of like a bad habit.

He put the thought from his mind and glanced down at his watch to check the time.

"Speaking of Eliza, I should head back to the pub. She should be back any minute."

He felt a profound sense of relief and peace from their conversation. He was glad he'd opened up to her, let her see that side of him, the one so few got to see.

"Come on. Let's get you back," Aoife agreed, taking his hand and letting him help her down of the rocks. "Are we taking the road this time? Or the trek through the woods again?"

He could tell that she was trying to keep her voice even, open to both options, but it was clear which option she preferred.

"Let's take the road this time. I think I've made ye do enough hiking today." He smiled down at her, teasing her lack of ambling skills.

"Thanks for taking me out here, Michael. It's a beautiful spot. I can see why you like to come out here. It kind of makes me feel like I'm beginning to belong here."

Chapter Twenty-Three

Aoife couldn't help but think that Eliza Kennedy was probably the most annoying person she'd ever had the displeasure to meet. Even knowing everything Michael had just told her not more than an hour ago about their past tragedy, she still struggled for something nice to say about the woman.

It was clear from the moment Aoife had entered the pub, from the sound of high-pitched shrieking that could only be heard by dogs, to the gaggle of girlfriends that Eliza surrounded herself with – who seemed to be the source of the ear-splitting sound – that she and Eliza were destined to dislike one another.

It was easy to spot her amongst her friends: she was the pretty red-head surrounded by similar, yet slightly less socially important friends, who were all just *fascinated* by every word she said. That, and the fact that she clung possessively to Michael the moment he and Aoife had walked through the front door, like someone might try and steal him away from her.

"Mary, Mother of God, I had no idea that such people *actually* existed outside of films." Aoife and Bex both tried not to spill their drinks as they hid their laughter over Millie's comment.

"I mean, I know there are girls like that, *obviously*. I've just never met someone so…" she struggled to find the right word but it seemed to escape her. "It's just a bit of a shock to find out they aren't fictitious."

"*Popular* is the word you're looking for, I believe," Bex supplied.

"No, I don't think that's how I would describe her…" Millie shook her head. "I think I was looking for a word more like…"

Her words were cut off by Eliza loudly recounting for the whole pub to hear of her self-sacrifice of looking after her awful aunt in Limerick who was only nursed back to health by her being there to look after her.

Right.

When Aoife and Michael had come back to the pub, Eliza had not been the only person who'd made a return to Ballyclara. Feeling guilty for leaving Aoife on her own to clean up the house, they'd turned around after getting about halfway home only to find Aoife hadn't been at home. They'd set about cleaning the rest of the house for her, returning it to exactly how it had looked before the party had started. When Aoife still hadn't returned, they'd gone down to the pub in the hopes that Brendan might know where she'd gotten to. They'd just been starting to get worried that no one seemed to know where she was when she'd shown up and been swarmed by Millie hugging her tight like she'd been gone for years instead of just a few hours.

"I'm *so* glad now that I wasn't one of the popular girls," Bex said. "Look what I could have ended up like…"

"Thankfully, we're all a bunch of non-descript characters," Millie smiled at her friends as they continued to observe Eliza and her friends, as if they were watching some very interesting documentary on social behaviour.

"I don't think anyone could call you non-descript, honey."

All That Compels the Heart

Bex looked at Millie's latest outrageous outfit: knee-high leather boots, bright pink and purple leggings, a pink leopard print empire-waist shirt, and chunky cross hanging around her neck. Her blue and purple hair was done up in pig tails, showing off all the shades of colour in her hair.

"And what's wrong with how I look?" Millie dared her to say something.

"Look at that. I'm out of booze." Bex completely ignored the question.

"I'm surprised you two can still drink after last night," Aoife told her, impressed. Her hike to the waterfall had mostly cleared her head, but even she'd been nursing her drink for awhile now.

"Hair of the dog, and all that." Bex waved a hand dismissively.

"It's your turn," Millie pointed out, downing the rest of her glass and belching daintily. Aoife glanced over her shoulder; Eliza and her circle had shifted towards the bar now where she seemed to be flirting with Michael.

"Ewww." Millie once again had been following her gaze and witnessed what Aoife saw. "I think my opinion of him just dropped."

"Not that it was very high to begin with," Bex pointed out.

"Though things *did* look pretty interesting between the two of you earlier, which kind of made me think that maybe he was turning out to be human," Millie said, addressing Aoife. "What exactly were the two of you doing earlier?"

Aoife took a sip of her beer, avoiding the question. She knew how it would look to her friends if she told them the truth, even if nothing had happened between her and Michael.

"Nothing. We just ended up walking down here together."

"I thought the two of you weren't speaking to one another? Based on your rant this morning about him, I thought for sure he was going to be a goner the next time you saw him, and here you are, strolling into the pub together."

"Well, life's too short to hold a grudge," Aoife replied, finishing off her beer and trying to avoid more questions.

"Alright, I'm going into the fray; God preserve my soul. If I'm not back within ten minutes, come and rescue me."

Aoife slid out of their booth and headed towards the bar.

"You're on your own, there mate. If you get sucked into that dark circle, there's no saving you," Millie called out unhelpfully to Aoife's retreating back.

Aoife squared her shoulders and headed towards the bar. As she approached, she noticed Michael gave her his usual look, which was somewhere between a grimace and a frown. She couldn't explain it, but the moment he'd stepped into the pub with her, his attitude towards her had changed, as if their previous sharing of thoughts and feelings hadn't happened at all. It was like he was afraid to acknowledge her presence. Seeing the way Eliza clung to him, she couldn't say she entirely blamed him now.

Ignoring Michael completely, as much as he did her, she turned her attention to Brendan.

"Three pints, please, Brendan."

"Hey Aoife. Still carrying on from last night I see."

He nodded towards Bex and Millie as they sat there, watching Michael and Eliza like they couldn't stop watching the train wreck before them.

She was prevented from answering by what she presumed was Eliza's laugh. To her ears, it sounded more like a hyena being tortured with a cattle prod.

"Well, *she* seems happy." As soon as she said it, she knew it sounded petty and condescending, but she couldn't take it back. She noticed Brendan grimace for the first time since she'd met him.

"Well, I suppose she has a lot to be happy about. I hear she just got back together with her fiancé. Not like it's the first time, though." Brendan's face darkened in a way she hadn't seen it do before. Clearly, he was none too impressed with his best friend's choice of a wife. Aoife couldn't exactly say she was against the happy couple; it just seemed that no matter how many times people told her Michael and Eliza were engaged, it still sounded odd to her. The two of them were just, well, so *unlike* one another. She couldn't fathom what they saw in the other.

Opposites really must attract.

"We *do* have a lot to be happy about, don't we, Michael?" Eliza had picked up on the last bit of their conversation and decided to insert herself in.

Brendan silently placed the pints she'd ordered in front of her and she handed him the money, trying to get out of there before she ended up being pulled further into the conversation.

"I don't believe we've met yet."

Aoife stopped in her tracks, almost dropping the pints she was carefully balancing. She was debating whether or not to pretend she hadn't heard Eliza and head straight for her table before the cold glasses in her hands became slippery with condensation, or if she should turn around and acknowledge the fact she'd been spoken to. Although she desperately wanted to run for the hills, she knew it would look extremely impolite, and if there was one thing Grainne O'Reilly had drilled into her, it was to remain polite at all times, even in awkward social situations.

She turned around and placed the pints carefully on the bar again, determined to make introductions quickly and get out of there.

"Well aren't you going to introduce us, Michael?" Eliza asked in her simpering voice. "I can tell the two of you know one another."

There was a hardness in her hazel eyes, relaying a perceptiveness Aoife wouldn't have thought she possessed. Michael, for his part, looked like he'd really rather be anywhere else than in the middle between his fiancée and… well, Aoife didn't really know what she was to him. Boss? Friend?

"Eliza, meet Aoife O'Reilly. Aoife, this is my fiancée, Eliza Kennedy."

Aoife pasted on the best polite smile she could manage; Grainne, for once, might actually have been proud of her. Eliza was a good two or three inches taller than Aoife, forcing her to look up at her, which made her feel irrationally peeved with the other woman.

Eliza extended Aoife a limp handshake and a cordial smile that didn't quite reach her eyes.

"Nice to meet you," Aoife replied with her best fake pleasant tone.

"Michael, darling, why don't you go and get us some of your best champagne? We haven't had a proper chance to celebrate our happy news yet. Michael and I just got engaged, you know. Well, technically we got engaged before I went to Limerick, but we've been keeping it quiet until I could come home and tell everyone together."

Eliza very consciously held her hand in such a way that her engagement ring caught the pub's lights and sparkled.

It was a sizeable diamond, far bigger than she'd have imagined someone with Michael's salary could afford without saving up for some time, but really rather small compared to the engagement rings Aoife was used to seeing from her circle of friends.

"So Brendan was just telling me," Aoife replied, wanting to get out of this conversation as quickly as possible but not wanting to appear rude.

"Spoil sport," Eliza chided him.

"That's me. Always ruining things for everyone."

Aoife could tell he was trying very hard not to roll his eyes. It comforted her to know that she wasn't the only one who was struggling to remain courteous.

"Where are you going?" Eliza turned her attention to Michael, who had managed to dislodge her from his lap and had stood up.

"I'm going to get that champagne you wanted," he reminded her. Eliza looked put out that he was leaving her alone with Brendan and Aoife, although Aoife wasn't exactly sure how Eliza thought he was going to get the champagne *without* actually leaving her side for a few minutes. As Michael tried to move away, Eliza kept holding on to his forearm in such a way that reeked of desperation and insecurity, making Aoife and Brendan both feel distinctly uncomfortable.

Clearly, Michael too was embarrassed. "Sweetheart, if I'm going to get the champagne, then I'm going to have to go out back to get it. Unless ye want to come with me?"

He looked down at her hand on his arm and she reluctantly let him go with a pout on her perfect, red lips that matched the shade of her silk, sleeveless shirt beneath her black cardigan.

Aoife took the opportunity the strained exchange between the couple had provided to try and slip away.

"Leaving so soon, Aoife?"

Damn.

"I was just going to go back to my friends." She nodded towards Bex and Millie who were looking over at her empathetically, but were not making a move to help her. Aoife thought of a few choice words she'd like to say to them when she finally got out of this predicament and made it back to her table.

"They're probably wondering where their drinks are."

"Why don't we join you?" Eliza said, getting up from her barstool and picking up two of the pints Aoife had been trying to carry over with her. Not taking no for an answer, she marched right past Aoife and headed straight for the table.

Good Lord.

"We need someone to celebrate with anyhow. Brendan, why don't you go and get Molly and help Michael with that champagne and come join us over here." She pointed to where Bex and Millie were sitting, both of whom looked horrified that she'd suddenly invited herself over to join them.

Oh God, how am I going to get out of this? Shit, shit!

The last thing she wanted was Eliza to meet Bex and Millie; while Aoife could keep a civil tongue in her head – most of the time – and she adored her friends, they were not the most helpful in these kinds of tension-filled social situations.

"Eliza, meet my friends: Rebecca and Camilla. Rebecca is from America and Camilla is from London." She wasn't sure why she'd chosen to use her friends' given names instead of their oft-used nicknames. She blamed it on the awkwardness of being around Eliza.

"Oh, an American!" Eliza exclaimed, as if this was the most exciting news she'd heard in the longest time. "We don't get many of you coming through our little village. How wonderful to meet you both."

Eliza extended the same limp handshake she'd given Aoife earlier, to her friends. It was clear from the look of disdain on her face as she glanced dismissively at Bex and scornfully at Millie that Eliza was not impressed with them.

"Nice to meet you," Bex replied neutrally, while Millie barely shook Eliza's hand, preferring to return her look of disdain. Bex nudged her sharply, seeing the staring contest that was happening. Sensing that the three young women were not as impressed with her as she wanted them to be, Eliza decided to further the awkward conversation.

"I was just telling Aoife here that you must all join me for a drink. I recently became engaged and we're celebrating." Once again, she expertly flashed her diamond in front of their faces in a much practiced "casual" way.

"Oh, we wouldn't dream of intruding," Bex replied to cover the small snort of surprise from Millie as she sipped the beer Eliza had placed on the table in front of her.

"Nonsense! We'd be delighted if you joined us, wouldn't we, Michael?"

At the sound of his name, Michael appeared with the champagne he'd been tasked with retrieving and looked like he was wondering what he'd just walked into the middle of.

"Come, darling. Bring some glasses over for us."

Without waiting for an invitation, she slid into the booth beside Bex, practically sitting on her lap at first until Bex moved closer to Millie, who pouted over the intrusion. Michael went to the bar and spoke to Brendan, clearly looking for some champagne flutes for them to drink out of.

"Sit, sit," she motioned to Aoife who was still standing by the booth, trying to figure out how her quiet afternoon had gone so terribly wrong.

Sliding into the booth as she was commanded, she looked over towards the bar, hoping for Brendan, Jimmy, Molly or someone to come and save them. She noticed Eliza's gaggle of girlfriends still stood around the bar, shooting daggers at Aoife, Bex, and Millie for taking away their queen bee. As the four young women settled into the booth and waited for the others to come over, Bex tried to cover the awkward silence that had descended between them.

"So, you are engaged to Michael, then?"

"Yes." Eliza fairly beamed at having the attention placed on her.

"How nice. Have you been engaged long?"

"A few weeks now. I had to go to Limerick to look after my poor, sick aunt," she looked at both Bex and Millie, hoping for some sympathy. Not finding any, she moved on. "So, anyways, Michael and I decided to keep it a secret until I could come back and we could announce it to everyone. I know he was hoping to tell his parents first, but when I walked in here and saw my friends, I just couldn't resist telling them. I thought I was going to burst with the excitement of it all. It's not like Sinead and Dermot will be surprised anyways, right? I mean, Michael and I *have* been together now for twelve years; it's not like we're rushing into anything."

Bex and Millie were spared from making any embarrassing comments by the arrival of Michael, Brendan, and Molly with the champagne and flutes.

"Let's get this party started!" Brendan said warmly, placing the flutes in front of them and opening up a bottle, the *pop!* of the cork making them all jump. His voice was just a little too enthusiastic, his hands a little too eager to pour the champagne in order to cover up the fact that he seemed far from pleased about this whole situation.

Aoife wondered what had happened in the last twelve years to make Brendan and Eliza dislike each other – for it was pretty obvious she didn't think much of him either. Earlier, Michael had alluded to there having been more trouble between him and Eliza than just losing their baby when they were teens; she wondered if this is when things had become tense between them all, or if it had always been there? It wasn't exactly like Eliza seemed to fit in with Brendan and Molly, or Michael for that matter. Aoife was still trying to work out how this had all happened in the first place.

"I'd like to start by toasting the happy couple. To Michael and Eliza."

Brendan raised his glass as the group chorused his toast, all of them noticeably less enthusiastic than he'd been.

As the new arrivals piled into the booth with the rest of them, Eliza placed a possessive hand on Michael's shoulder, a clear marking of her territory in front of the others. Clingy wouldn't even begin to describe it.

"So, Aoife. How are you settling in?" Molly asked.

"Yes, how do you like our little village?" Brendan asked, his face showing that, not only was he eager for her to like Ballyclara, but he was also eager to talk about something other than Michael and Eliza's engagement.

"It's great," Aoife replied feeling all eyes on her, especially Eliza's, who looked like she was put out that all the attention was focused on the new girl instead of herself. Aoife felt like she was back in secondary school again.

"It's nice having an injection of new blood into this place. I hope everyone is making you feel very welcome." Brendan gave Michael a stern looking, singling him out.

"Everyone's been great so far," Aoife replied, thinking that she really needed to come up with a different adjective other than "great."

"Just don't accept any baked goods from you, am I right?" Eliza piped up and laughed that annoying, tortured hyena laugh.

Aoife looked confused for a second and then felt a deep flush rush to her cheeks as she realized what Eliza meant.

Of course he would tell her. He probably tells her everything.

She was furious with Michael for revealing her earlier embarrassing encounter with him, especially after she thought the two of them had been making progress based on their hike to the waterfall earlier. She glared over at him. Thankfully, he had the good sense to look embarrassed.

"What does that mean?" Brendan asked, wondering what inside joke he'd been left out of.

"She *is* the one who baked you that cake this morning, isn't she Michael?" Eliza asked, not responding to Brendan's question.

"I don't think this is the time, nor the place," Michael replied, taking a sip of his champagne. He glanced up, trying to catch her eye, trying to let her see how apologetic he was.

"Oh come on, it's hilarious! Tell them, Michael."

Eliza's grip on his forearm tightened, her perfectly manicured nails turning white around the edges from how hard she was squeezing. To his credit, Michael stayed silent, continuing to try and catch Aoife's eye, although she was having none of it and stared pointedly at the table before her.

"Alright, then *I* will," Eliza said after it was clear she couldn't sway her fiancé to do what she wanted. Her tone made it sound like he was giving her no choice but to embarrass Aoife in front of everyone, even though she'd been given the opportunity to drop the subject.

"So, Michael rang this morning on my way home from Limerick, and tells me about this *beautiful* red velvet cake some city girl had made him – you really did a *marvellous* job on the presentation, Aoife; Michael texted me a photo – for some incident she'd started with him. Anyways, of course I'm wondering if I should be worried if some hot shot city girl is trying to make a move on my fiancé, but then he warns me when I come home not to eat any of it. I thought he was just being a wonderful boyfriend because he knows I'm a diet and he knows how seriously I'm taking it…"

"Like *she* needs to diet," Aoife heard Millie mutter not quite under her breath. It was true; Eliza had the advantage of the slim figure that came with her height.

"…but he tells me, 'No, it's because it was baked with salt, and not sugar." Eliza laughed one of her screeching laughs, making everyone around her cringe. She paused long enough to notice that no one around the booth was laughing except her. Aoife silently thanked every one of them for their support, all the while shooting murderous glances at Michael.

"Well, *I* thought it was amusing," Eliza muttered petulantly, taking a dainty sip from her champagne glass.

"Why the bloody hell would you put salt in… Oh… *oh*…" Millie's voice trailed off as she realized what had happened.

"That's because a certain *someone* thought it would be *amusing* to replace my sugar with salt," Aoife responded tersely. Millie's face immediately blushed a guilty deep pink.

"Well, in my defense, I didn't think you'd use it on someone other than yourself. I thought you'd just put some of it in your tea this morning and we could catch you making a funny face or something. I didn't anticipate you waking up before us and baking a bloody cake. I mean, you're not exactly the culinary type."

"It was clearly an accident," Michael said, his tone warning Eliza not to take the conversation any further, but it was too late for him in Aoife's opinion; the damage had been done.

"Well, I think that's enough *amusement* for one day," Bex spoke up, the derision in her voice for Eliza clear to everyone within earshot of their booth. "We should get back to the house and help with the rest of the cleaning up. We have to be on the road back to Dublin soon and we don't want to be late. It was nice to meet you all."

Brendan and Molly immediately stood up beside Aoife, letting her and her friends slide out that way so they wouldn't have to go by Michael and Eliza, sitting on the other end. Bex practically dragged Aoife out of the pub, clutching both her and Millie's hands and marching them towards the door before anyone could say anything else. As they walked silently to the cark park, Aoife heard the pub door open and Michael call her name.

"Aoife! Aoife, wait!"

She let go of Bex's hand, folding her arms across her chest and continued to walk towards where Bex had parked her car, pretending to ignore him.

"Shouldn't you be inside celebrating your engagement?" Bex rounded on him.

"I just wanted to…"

"Back off, Michael," Bex's said in her best don't-mess-with-me-or-I-will-end-you tone she'd developed from walking around New York City at night by herself. A girl couldn't be too careful, what with sickos wandering around out there. "I think you've done quite enough for one day."

Bex turned on her heel and caught up with Aoife and Millie and the three of them hurried towards the car, leaving Michael standing there feeling like an eejit.

Chapter Twenty-Four

Aoife sat in front of her computer, staring at it blankly, hoping desperately for inspiration. Try as she might, she'd been unable to write anything for the past few days, which was driving her crazy. Ever since the incident at Michael and Eliza's quasi-engagement party, she'd locked herself in her house, trying to pretend the rest of the world didn't exist.

She'd had bouts of writer's block before, but even then, she'd been able to produce *something*. She hadn't even been able to write a single word this time. It was like her mind had gone *too* quiet, like she'd gone comatose but she was actually awake.

"For fuck's sake," she muttered to herself. Getting to her feet, muscles groaning and aching from being cramped up for so long, she sighed at her failed attempt for inspiration.

"Time to do this old school."

Grabbing a pen and leather-bound notebook she often used to jot down story ideas when she was out and about, she headed downstairs, put on her boots and jacket and stepped outside, not sure where she planned to go exactly, but not particularly concerned with not having a destination in mind either. This is when her creativity worked best; when she didn't try to overthink it.

Erin Bowlen

A light mist rolled in over the hills and into the valleys like a thin, white blanket, covering the village in a chilly wetness. She zipped up the front of her brown leather jacket, tucking the lower half of her face under its collar to ward off the chill. Despite the heavy mist that was now forming around her, she was determined to continue along her journey of inspirational discovery. She wasn't too bothered by a bit of mist anyways. Still with no particular destination in mind, she set off in what she thought was the direction for the village.

The lane leading to the Old Rectory was spooky as she walked, wisps of fog floating in the air around her. She still could see enough that she felt confident navigating her way down the lane, so she decided to push on, knowing the fog would have to lift at some point. She listened out for her neighbours' sheep, but even the sheep were quieter than normal, subdued by the fog around them. So long as she kept them on what she thought was her left, she knew she was on the right path.

She continued to walk into the thick whiteness, not realizing how much and how quickly the fog thickened around her. She'd unconsciously slowed her pace to accommodate her lack of visibility and pulled her hands into the sleeves of her jacket; the temperature seeming to drop a couple of degrees the further she walked into the white wall. Despite the chill and the damp, there was something both comforting and isolating about the fog surrounding her. She felt cocooned in her own little bubble – and yet – she was also an island, set adrift in a sea of swirling whiteness. Bolstered by her own innate sense of self-confidence, she carried on.

She'd been walking a few minutes when she realized she could no longer hear the sheep in the pasture beside her. The only sound now was that of her footfalls on the ground and the occasional scrape of her boot against a loose rock. She found the silence eerie. She figured that she must be getting close to the main road by now, but the fog was so thick she couldn't see two inches in front of her face, let alone two feet, to get her bearings. She thought for sure that she should be coming up on Sinead and Dermot's place, or even yet, Michael's cottage. She knew that it would normally take her anywhere between five and ten minutes to walk to Dermot and Sinead's cottage from the Old Rectory in good weather, but she felt sure she must have been walking for at least twenty minutes; the fog not only seemed to make her lose track of where she was, but also her sense of time.

Essentially blind, Aoife closed her eyes and listened to her surroundings, trying to find anything that stood out to her to tell her where she was. All she heard at first was the sound of her heartbeat loud in her ears and the sound of her own breathing, jagged from the cool air restricting her throat. When her head and heart both finally calmed down, she could faintly make out the sound of music. She was too far away to make out the genre or the instruments, but it was definitely music – possibly whistling – as it sounded somewhat high and tinny. She couldn't hear any cars; not that she'd expected many of them to be out in this weather, but it meant that she was likely further from the main road than she'd previously thought.

With the fog getting thicker around her with every second – *how was that even possible?* – she decided to head towards the music, frightened that if she went towards the main road and there were any cars around, she may accidentally be hit. It was likely to be coming from one of the Flanagans' cottages, anyways. She prayed it would be Sinead and Dermot's or Mara's. She could stop and visit with them while she waited for the fog to pass. She sincerely hoped it wouldn't be the cottage of the one Flanagan she didn't want to see. She'd successfully avoided him for days now; she didn't want her luck to end and have to actually face him.

Listening for the music and keeping her eyes on the ground before her – what little of it she could see, anyways – she tried to find where the road veered off into the lane of one of the Flanagans' homes. Except that, as the whistling got louder – and it was indeed, whistling – the path did not veer off to her left as she expected, but to the right. She stopped for a moment, confused. She knew from walking the lane down from Aldridge Manor to the village several times since moving here that the lanes leading down to the Flanagans' cottages should each be on the left-hand side.

"So why in hell is there a road leading to the right?" she asked the fog around her. Wondering if she *had* in fact passed all of the Flanagans' cottages without realizing it and she'd caught up to the main road. The fog unpredictably answered her back.

"Hello?" a thick, West Country accent asked.

"Jesus, Mary, and Joseph!" Aoife exclaimed at the sound of a voice coming to her through the fog about ten or fifteen paces off to her right.

"Well, ye've come to the right place, m'love; you'll find all three here," the fog responded back.

Wondering just what the bloody hell was going on, the fog began to lift slightly, just enough to reveal a low, stone wall and the shadowy figure of a man on the other side of it.

"Who's there?" she called out, not recognizing a single feature about the person or the fence.

The voice on the other side of the fence chuckled amiably, picking up on her wariness. "Ye've nothing to fear from me, child. Patrick's the name; Patrick Gallagher. Or, Father Patrick, as most of the parish calls me. And *who* might *you* be, exactly? I don't remember seeing you around these parts before, and I pride meself on knowing everyone in the village. After all, it's sort o' part o' me job description."

She knew where she was now. Somehow, she'd managed to get herself turned around in all the fog and had ended up wandering in completely the opposite direction from Aldridge Manor than she'd intended. It explained how nothing seemed familiar to her; she hadn't yet come down this way. Not being particularly religious, she'd not thought to really come down by the little parish church before.

"My name is Aoife O'Reilly. I own Aldridge Manor up the road," she said, introducing herself to the old man. "I came out here to get some work done but the fog came up on me more suddenly than I was expecting and I somehow got myself turned around in completely the opposite direction."

"Miss O'Reilly, ye say? Ah yes, I know you now. I've heard many a parishioner talk about you."

Aoife couldn't tell from this statement if he thought this was a good thing or a bad thing.

"All good things, I hope," she said, for some reason needing the reassurance.

The old priest chuckled to himself as he stood there against the low, stone wall surrounding the churchyard.

"And what is it you do, child?"

"Sorry?" The change in subject, and the non-answer to her question, caught her off-guard.

"Ye said you were out here hoping to do some work. What kind of work do ye do exactly, that would take ye outside in this weather?"

She could roughly see him gesture to the fog surrounding them.

"I'm a writer. I was hoping a walk might help me to find some inspiration."

"A writer, ye say?" Father Patrick had said it with such wonderment and fascination. "And what do you write?"

This was a tricky question for she hadn't yet quite settled on a particular genre, which was probably why she was having such a difficult time writing lately. She just couldn't seem to focus on one genre or project right now. She would start one idea in a flurry of words and excitement, inspiration pouring out of her almost faster than her fingers could type, but by the time she got about twenty-five to fifty pages in, she found she'd be distracted by a new idea and then the cycle would start all over again. It was a rather frustrating and laborious experience.

"As of right now, fiction. Though to be honest, I've no idea where this story is going," she admitted, feeling more comfortable around the old man since he seemed to be so interested in her work.

"Hmmm… Having a bit of writer's block, are ye?"

"Seems to be the case." Her voice dropped and her shoulders slumped a little, defeated by her own creativity. Or lack thereof.

"Well, I think I know how to cure that."

"You do?"

She looked at him curiously. She still had a bit of trouble making him out, even though they stood barely five feet from one another. She wondered what this miracle cure could possibly be.

"Sure, I've had my fair share of writer's block in my day. Sermons just won't write themselves, ye know." His voice was kind, sympathetic to her plight.

"And what do you do to get the creative juices flowing, so to speak?

"I take a night off," he smiled at her. She couldn't actually see him smile, but the sentiment was there in his voice. "Ye just can't force some things to happen, and writing is one of them."

She knew it was true. You couldn't force creativity. It just had to happen. "You think I'm pushing myself too hard, then?"

"Well, seeing as I've only just met you, I can't say for sure, but, ye seem to me to be a determined person and I have an inkling you're determined to hammer out as much ye can in a short period of time. You young people are always in such a big rush to do everything. Sometimes sitting back and just taking the time to observe and appreciate is just what's needed."

"I've never really been very good at relaxing. I've always been the person to throw myself into the next project before the last one is finished."

It was true. She was always looking for her next great adventure. When she'd finished secondary school, it was getting into university. When she'd finished university, it was her internship. After the internship, it was getting a job. Now that she no longer had a job, it was writing. She didn't just take time off in between to really pause and relax. She wasn't hardwired that way.

"And that is your problem. How can ye write about life when you're not out there taking the time to live it? To observe it?"

Aoife pondered on this statement for a moment, thinking how right the old priest was.

"It looks like that fog is starting to lift," he said suddenly, breaking the silence.

It was true. As the two of them had been talking, the fog had slowly begun to ebb away, revealing more and more of Father Patrick's wiry figure. He was a tallish man, not quite six feet anymore, but she guessed that he'd once been over that height in his youth. He had a thinner, wiry frame than most men but still looked to be in robust health. He was dressed in the all-black frock one is used to seeing on a priest, but he didn't have a cap covering his short silver hair.

"I should probably make my way back to the house," she said, looking back towards it. "The last thing I need is to wander around in the fog and get myself lost again."

"Would ye mind terribly if I walked with you?" Father Patrick asked her. "I've a mind to go into the village."

"Sure, I'd love the company," she found herself saying, and meaning it. "Besides, it might be handy for me to have someone who knows the area well in case the fog comes back up again."

"And that I do," he said, walking around to the little wrought-iron gate that led into the churchyard.

"Shall we?" he asked her, holding his arm to her.

She tucked her arm into the crook of his elbow, finding he was much stronger than she'd given him credit for.

The two of them walked in silence up the dirt lane towards her house, the fog around them continuing to lift more, allowing them to see a few feet ahead of them. They'd been walking for a few minutes when the priest asked, "So, how are ye liking life in our little village? I'm sorry that I haven't been around yet to properly introduce myself. I had to go up to Dublin for a procedure and I've been in recovery the last little while. I've only just sent the lay priest they sent down to fill in for me away and trying to get back to normal."

"Oh, no worries! There's no need to make a fuss over me."

"It's part o' me job to get to know everyone in the parish, even if they aren't the religious sort. Don't worry; I won't try to convert you." Father Patrick's voice was full of mirth.

"Is it that obvious?" she asked, embarrassed.

"Ballyclara's a small place, love. Your absence from church was well noted the moment you moved in. No matter though; I'm not offended."

Aoife found herself sighing in relief. Even though she'd only just met the elderly man, she cared that he had a good opinion of her.

"I've been settling in fine. Thanks for asking. I hope the procedure wasn't too serious?"

"Just a spot of trouble with the old ticker," he said, waving away her concern. "Nothing to be too concerned about." From his dismissiveness of the subject, Aoife knew it was, in fact, more serious than he was letting on but she didn't press for further information.

"So, has everyone has been treating ye well?" he asked, concerned that everyone was being friendly towards her.

"As well as can be expected when a foreigner shows up in their village and decides to stay," she said. "Sinead, Dermot, and Mara Flanagan, and Brendan and Molly McCaffrey have been a great help to me. As are young Jimmy and Karen Connolly." She pointedly left out Michael from her list; she was still bitter about their last exchange.

"Ah yes. They're all great people; couldn't ask for better. Have ye met the Flanagans son, Michael, then?"

"Oh yes, and Michael too," she replied quickly, pretending like she'd just forgotten about him, not wanting to air her grievances in front of the priest after having just met the man.

"He's been... helpful with restoring the house." She strove to find something nice to say about Michael, trying not to offend anyone in case Michael and Father Patrick knew each other well.

"He and Brendan are good lads. Helped me out with me house more than once. There's none better than those two to help you in restoring the Old Rectory. They know that place inside and out. I know they must be thrilled you asked them to help you in the process. If Michael could have afforded it, I'm sure he'd have bought the place himself. The poor lad's just never been able to catch a break when it comes to money."

Aoife nodded, pretending to be interested in the priest's story, but secretly wishing to be talking about almost anything else. However, Father Patrick seemed determined to keep the conversation going.

"If he'd spent more time focusing on his own dream instead of putting everything he had into that house he and Eliza Kennedy were living in, maybe things would have been different. But who's to say? I shouldn't be talking out of turn like that."

Father Patrick's face turned down into a slight frown, as if mentally chastising himself for being harsh on one of his flock, no matter how trying Eliza Kennedy could be on the nerves.

"Well, with the two of them being back together again, maybe they'll find a new dream to focus on," she said, trying to console him.

"Oh?" Father Patrick paused a moment and glanced sideways at her, surprised to find out this bit of news.

"Yeah, they were having a celebration down in the pub not too long ago. Eliza was showing me the ring Michael got for her." Aoife tried her hardest to keep the edge out of her voice.

"Hmph," was the only response the priest gave. "The same one he gave her the first two times they were engaged, or a new one, I wonder?"

Aoife shrugged. "I'm not sure."

"I'm sorry. I shouldn't be going on about Michael's troubles. I've always tried to keep the regular gossips in check and now look at me, I'm going on about things I shouldn't. It's just, he's a good lad, that Michael. Too good to be stuck with a girl like Eliza Kennedy.

"Oh, I know. I'm supposed to care for all my parishioners the same," he said, as if sensing some judgement from her, "But I'm convinced that young Miss Kennedy would give the Lord Almighty himself pause before saying something nice about her. She's a difficult one, she is, and Michael's borne the brunt of it for the last twelve years. Shame what happened to the two of them, losing the baby the way they did. Nearly broke that poor boy. But, he's stuck by Eliza ever since, even after she was unfaithful to him."

Aoife stood still in the lane at this news, forcing Father Patrick to stop as well.

"I didn't know that," was all she could think to say.

"Oh yes. The talk of the whole village it was. Some fancy lad from over in England, so it was. Anyways, young Eliza caught his eye, or maybe it was the other way around, but the two of them ended up together. Scandalous, so it was.

"It was poor Mara that found them. She used to work for the Kennedys as a maid, cleaning up the tourist cottages they rent out. She thought the guest had departed for the day and had gone down to tidy up when she'd found the two of them. Weighed something heavy on her too, I know. Things were rough between her and her brother there for the longest time after she'd told him."

Aoife just nodded, trying to stay out of Michael's private life.

"I know I shouldn't speak ill of anyone, and I'm certain that I will thoroughly chastise myself for this later, but there's just some people in this world who are meant to be together, and Michael and Eliza are just not those people. I understand the attraction; she's a nice-looking girl and she comes from one of the wealthiest families in the village. And he's a good worker and has a good head on his shoulders, if a bit stubborn."

I can agree with that!

However, Aoife continued to keep silent, letting the priest prattle on.

"Still, I never saw the two of them settling down together and having a family. I just wouldn't have put it in the cards for them.

"He must be some grateful to you, having him in there and helping with the place," he said, changing topics once more, perhaps sensing her reluctance to say anything to the rumours and gossip. "Next best thing to actually living in it, I suppose. Did ye know his parents used to work there?"

"I did know that," she replied, both proud to show off her knowledge of local history, and trying to avoid any more talk of Michael.

"Well, here we are," she said, when the house came into view through the fog.

The priest seemed reluctant to let her go right away, perhaps because he enjoyed her company or perhaps because he felt guilty for having talked so much on their walk back to Aldridge Manor. "Here we are and I haven't even asked you about yourself. I shouldn't be such a village gossip."

She smiled at him. A bit of an old gossip he may be, but there was something so endearing about the way he cared for his parishioners that she forgave him for it. "Well, how about this: we will have tea sometime soon and I'll tell you my whole life story."

Father Patrick mulled this idea over. As if inspiration suddenly struck him, his long, thin face brightened, his green eyes twinkling. "Ye can do one better. Come with me to the céilí in the pub tonight. Some of the villagers wanted to hold one to welcome me back home. Ye need a night off from writing and I need a date for my big soiree."

Perhaps sensing she might say no, he said, "Come on, humour an old man, won't ye?"

Well, it wouldn't be the worst thing in the world, would it? You do *need a night off.*

"Father Patrick, are you asking me out to a dance? Talk about gossip! Whatever will the village say?" she teased him, gently.

"Say yes, and we'll find out." A smile crossed his thin lips.

She wasn't sure that she *should* go. Yes, she could probably use a night off, and a céilí would be a welcome distraction for her. But, on the other hand, there was the huge risk that she'd run into Michael and/or Eliza again, which she was greatly hoping to avoid. Seeing how hopeful the priest looked though, she found herself unable to turn him down.

"Alright," she agreed.

"Excellent! I will pick up you here later tonight. Around seven o'clock shall we say?"

"See you then."

She extricated herself from the crook of his arm and watched him head down the lane towards the village, whistling a tune.

ಸಾಡ

As seven o'clock neared, Aoife still wasn't sure if she wanted to go down to the pub or not. She was tired and cranky after struggling through yet another unproductive day. Even though Father Patrick had advised her not to push it, she'd tried to go back to her computer and do some writing, but still couldn't find inspiration. Eventually, she'd admitted defeat and given up, turning instead to unpacking some of the boxes of clothes she'd left on the floor of her bedroom. As she hung up each garment, she found herself assessing whether or not that particular outfit would be appropriate to wear out on a night out on the town with an elderly priest or not. Determining that each one of her outfits was too racy to be seen in with a priest of all people, she was beginning to really feel that this was a bad idea. However, a bigger part of her found herself not wanting to disappoint the old man on a night where he was the guest of honour, so at seven o'clock, she found herself dressed in a green tank top, her cleanest pair of dark jeans, and a black cardigan with lace-capped sleeves. She hoped it struck the right balance between looking dressed up for a night out – especially paired with her up-style hairdo and dangly earrings – and looking casual enough for the pub. And so, there she was, right at seven o'clock, sitting on the main staircase with her boots on, waiting for Father Patrick to come by. He was right on time.

Before he could even ring her doorbell, she stood up and crossed the little foyer in front of the door and opened it.

"Well, don't you look nice," she said to him. He'd changed out of his priest's frock and was now dressed in a brown tweed suit jacket, tan-coloured trousers, and a white shirt which was open at the collar.

"Now I feel under-dressed."

She looked down at her jeans and boots and thought about running upstairs and trying to see if she could find an appropriate LBD or something to put on.

"You look lovely," he reassured her, examining her outfit.

"It occurred to me as I was getting dressed that I wasn't sure if I should go casual or dressy and tried to find something in the middle."

"I think ye achieved it perfectly."

He gave her an approving smile and offered his arm to her. Putting aside the fact that she was tired and cranky and would rather just sit at home and feel sorry for herself, she took his arm and the two of them headed out into the night, closing the door to the house behind her.

All That Compels the Heart

It was another nice night, but clouds gathered along the horizon threatening the possibility of rain. She wished she'd thought to bring a jacket with her or at least an umbrella, but she wasn't willing to make Father Patrick wait for her while she walked back to the house to grab either right now. She would just have to hope the rain would hold off until she got back home.

The lane was dark, so she fumbled in her pocket for her mobile and turned on the torchlight app. As they drew near to Dermot and Sinead's cottage, she noticed the couple coming out their front door and she and the priest slowed their pace, allowing them to catch up.

"Hello Father Patrick. Aoife," Sinead greeted them as she and Dermot joined them on the lane.

"Hello Sinead, Dermot," Father Patrick greeted them.

"I suppose the two of you are heading down to the céilí?" she asked him.

"Yes. Miss O'Reilly here has agreed to be my date for the evening."

"And will we be hearing you sing tonight, Father?" Dermot asked. Turning to Aoife he said, "Ye may not know it yet, Aoife, but Father Patrick here has one of the best singing voices in the county."

"Well, I don't know about that now," the priest replied, suddenly shy and embarrassed. "And what about your Michael? Now there's a fine voice."

"Ah well, ye know my son, Father. You'll be hard-pressed to get Michael up there to sing tonight, even if ye begged him to." Fatherly pride shone through Dermot's words.

"What about you, Aoife? Do you like to sing?" Dermot asked her.

"No, no. I mean, I *do* like to sing; I'm just not particularly good at it."

"Well, we'll be the judge of that tonight," Sinead replied with a smile.

"Oh no. I don't sing in public," Aoife replied quickly, hoping that they didn't think she was just being modest. "I really can't hold much of a tune."

Father Patrick came to her rescue by changing the topic. "Where's Mara and Rory tonight?"

"Rory's down with the McCaffreys tonight. He and Des are having a sleepover. And Mara's down at the pub. Brendan plays bodhran you see, so he'll be playing tonight and she's lending a hand to Michael and Molly for the evening."

"I didn't know Brendan could play."

"Oh yes. And a fine bodhran player he is too. And a lovely voice on him as well," Dermot said proudly, as if Brendan were his own son. She supposed, with Brendan and Michael having been best friends for so long, Brendan was as much at home with the Flanagans as he was with his own family.

"Ballyclara is just full of surprises."

The four of them continued walking to the pub, chatting away. By the time they reached the pub, they could hear the band warming up. Opening the front door and stepping inside, Aoife was hit with a wall of sound, not just from the band, but also from the sheer number of people crammed into the small space. The entire village must have turned out, every chair and standing space along the walls occupied by people. A makeshift stage had been erected off to their left, its tiny space full from the drum kit, leaving little room for the singers and guitarists.

"Don't worry," Sinead said to her, shouting over the cacophony. "Michael said he'd save a table for us."

"Da! Mam!" Mara's voice rose above the din. She pointed to a table in the corner, the only one in the place with empty seats, which had clearly been reserved for them.

Aoife and her party weaved their way through the crowd, climbing over chairs and people, trying not to jostle anyone. Father Patrick held out her seat for her as she sat down and settled herself in. She waved and smiled to Brendan who sat on the stage waiting to begin.

"Can I get a bit of quiet in here?" he asked over the microphone, seeing that Father Patrick was settled in now. A hush descended upon the room, contrasting sharply with the noise from before.

"I'd like to welcome ye all tonight. I'd also like to welcome back our guest of honour for tonight, Father Patrick."

All That Compels the Heart

A couple of whoops and cheers, and a round of applause went up at the mention of the priest. "We're glad to have ye home safe and sound."

"Glad to be back!" Father Patrick shouted enthusiastically over the cheering.

"To welcome ye home, we've decided to throw you this little party. And, just as a reminder, half of the proceeds from tonight are going to the school for some new schoolyard equipment. So, everyone drink up; it's going to a charitable cause. And no, Mark, you don't count as a charity case."

A roar of laughter went up as poor old Mark, who by now was probably the pub's most regular customer, turned a bright shade of red.

"Alright, let's get this party started!" The band did one last check of their instruments, and with that, the band struck up a rather lively version of "Wild Rover," with everyone joining in.

Thirty minutes later and a couple of rounds in, everyone was having a grand time. They hadn't even noticed the storm breaking on the horizon, the tiny flickers of lightning and the low rumbling of thunder masked by the sound of the music coming from the stage. After another fifteen or twenty minutes, the band was in need of a break and paused their performance, much to the disappointment of their fans.

"Don't worry; we'll be back up soon. I just need a pint is all," Brendan told the crowd, who laughed and smiled along with him.

The din from before returned as everyone began talking loudly, replacing the music. Brendan, his brow sweaty and the collar and armpits of his dark grey t-shirt dark from the same, came to sit down beside Aoife and Father Patrick.

"Come sit down and take a breather," Father Patrick encouraged him, as Molly showed up and placed a pint in front of her husband. Brendan pulled her in close and sat her on his lap, planting a wet kiss on her cheek, which she tried to fend off.

"You're all sweaty!" she complained but didn't make a move to leave his side.

"I thought ye liked me all hot and bothered," he teased her, as she gave him a playful slap with the towel she held in her other hand.

"Don't be saying things like that in front of Father Patrick!" Molly exclaimed, tugging unconsciously at her red, short-sleeved cotton shirt, a pink flush rising in her cheeks at her husband's suggestive comment.

"Oh don't worry, love. I've heard far worse in my lifetime," the priest reassured her.

"So, Father, are ye having a good time?" Brendan asked, changing the subject at his wife's request.

"I'm grand. Thanks for asking, son. I couldn't have planned it better meself. It's so nice to see so many out and thank ye for donating the money to the school."

"Well, we knew you wouldn't take any of it for yourself for your hospital fees, so we decided to put it where it was needed."

"Too right," Father Patrick agreed.

"And you, Aoife? How are ye enjoying your first Ballyclara céilí?"

"I'm grand, Brendan," she echoed the priest's sentiment. "I'm glad Father Patrick invited me."

"Well, look at you, asking the second prettiest girl in the village to a dance, Father," Brendan teased the old priest. "I would say you're the prettiest, Aoife, under normal circumstances, but I'm afraid the top spot is taken by this one." He patted Molly's side.

"You're such a charmer," she teased him, wrapping the towel around his neck and planting a kiss on his mouth. "Now, I've got to get back to work or Michael will likely have my head."

A glance over at Michael, who was pulling pints over at the bar was enough to sour Aoife's previously good mood. As always, his shadow, Eliza, was planted right in front of him, sitting on the barstool directly across from him. Aoife downed the last of her pint, disgusted by the two of them.

"Can I get anything for anyone while I'm up?" Molly asked the assembled group.

"Another round, please, Molly," Dermot told her, indicating the same again for the whole table.

All That Compels the Heart

"Sure thing, Dermot. I'll have Michael bring them right over." Before anyone could say anything else, she weaved her way through the crowds and back to the bar.

"You play very well, Brendan." Aoife pointed to the stage, in case he couldn't quite hear her over the loud cheer that had gone up behind her at something a crowd of lads had seen on the television behind her.

"Thanks."

"I didn't know you played."

"Oh Brendan here has been playing since he and Michael were youngsters," Sinead reminded her. "I can remember many a time wee Brendan coming over and sitting on the back porch with Michael, the two of them singing and playing away."

Brendan smiled, remembering. "How about it, Michael?"

He'd shown up at just this moment with their drinks, placing them in the centre of the round table. "What's this?"

"How about you come up on stage with me and we do one of the songs we used to on your parents' back porch."

Michael snorted and shook his head, his long fringe falling into his eyes, reminding Aoife somewhat of a recalcitrant horse. He brushed his fringe back from his face with his fingers and said, "You're having me on, right?"

"No, I'm serious."

"Maybe another time." Michael patted his friend on the shoulder, tucked the tray he'd used to bring over their drinks and wove his way through the crowd back to the bar.

"Well, I tried," Brendan said, throwing up his hands in defeat. At just that moment, lightning struck close by, dimming the lights and a low, deep rumble reverberated through the building.

"Well, now," Sinead exclaimed, surprised by Mother Nature's display. A hush fell over the crowd, waiting to see if the electricity would hold out, or if they would be plunged into darkness.

"Well, I guess it's time to get this party going again before Mother Nature decides to shut us down," Brendan roared, an enthusiastic cheer going up around him as he downed his pint and headed towards the stage to resume the show.

The band played on in the face of the storm brewing outside, trying to mask its fury. As some latecomers arrived, a big gust of wind and rain blew through the pub, sending a shiver down Aoife's spine at the sudden drop in temperature. Although she hadn't realized it, the pub had become a cocoon of warmth and safety from the storm. She could see the rain pounding outside, soaking the pavement. She really wished she'd thought to bring a jumper or an umbrella now, knowing she'd have to walk back home in the driving rain. She took another sip of her pint, trying to put the thought out of her mind.

As the music got livelier, she noticed more and more people getting up to dance. Sinead and Dermot soon joined in the fun, leaving her alone with Father Patrick.

"Ye should go up there and have a dance. I'm sure there's plenty a young lad around here who would be happy to dance with you." Father Patrick nodded to the far wall where she noticed more than one wallflower boy trying to catch her eye.

"Oh, I wouldn't want to leave you here on your own." She tried to come up with an excuse so she wouldn't have to embarrass herself with her awful dancing. She took another drink instead, purposefully ignoring the guys across the room.

"Nonsense! Go and have some fun!"

As if to emphasize his earlier point, he tapped Jimmy – who was sitting at the table in front of them – and beckoned for him to come closer so he could shout his request over the music.

"Jimmy, get this girl up and dancing." He nodded over his shoulder at Aoife, who was trying to shake her head.

"Sure!" Jimmy rose from his chair and held a hand out to her.

"Go on Aoife! Leave me with Father Patrick," Karen reassured her, moving chairs to sit beside the priest. "Go and have a dance for me, will ye?"

"How can I resist a request from a pregnant woman and a priest?"

She put her hand in Jimmy's outstretched one and let him lead the way as they wound their way through the chairs and people sitting in front of them. The pair of them joined in with the jig, picking it up as best they could.

All That Compels the Heart

Aoife had never been a great dancer; she'd be the first to admit it. She could slow dance with Danny if asked to, but she was much more comfortable being the wallflower. She wasn't sure whether her nerves were bolstered by the alcohol or if she just simply lost her inhibitions, but she found herself enjoying the twirling and spinning around much more than usual. When the song finally finished, she found herself wishing it hadn't stopped.

"I thought ye said you couldn't dance?" Jimmy teased her, giving her a hug as they made their way back to their seats. She plopped herself down in her chair, tired by the exertion and took a large gulp of her pint.

"Normally I'm an awful dancer. I think having you as a dance partner just makes me look better."

Jimmy smiled at her as a slow song began to play. He held out a hand to Karen, bringing his heavily pregnant wife to her feet and making their way slowly to the dancefloor.

"Make way! Pregnant lady coming through!" he shouted at the crowds as they parted for the two of them.

Father Patrick smiled at her, not saying anything.

"Alright, I'll admit it; you were right. That was a lot more fun than I thought it would be," she conceded.

"Ye don't get to be my age, dear without knowing a few things," he told her, tapping the side of his nose in a conspiratorial way. "Now, ye better drink up; I think there's going to be a long queue of lads wanting a dance with you."

Sure enough, she'd only been sitting down for a minute or two before Dermot had her back on her feet, followed by pretty much every man – young and old – in Ballyclara. As she was taking a turn around the dancefloor with Mr. Dempsey, she noticed that the one man in the whole pub who did not want to dance with her – Michael – currently looked to be engaged in an argument of some sort with Eliza. She was much too far away, and the music too loud, for her to get the gist of their argument, but they *were* clearly rowing about something. In fact, Mr. Dempsey was forced to spin her out of the way lest she bump into Eliza as she stormed right through the middle of the dance floor for the front door, her face perfectly serene except for the flash of anger in her eyes. Aoife felt a shiver run down her spine again, and this time it was not because of the cool, rainy air entering the pub as Eliza made her exit. When the music finally ended, she still couldn't help but get the feeling that Eliza blamed her for something; she just wasn't sure what.

With the alcohol jostling around in her veins and the exertion from dancing, Aoife began to feel a bit dizzy. When Mr. Dempsey let her go and had moved on to the next dance partner, she found herself standing in the middle of the dance floor. She moved out of the way as Brendan and the band struck up a version of "Black Velvet Band," so as not to be in the way.

"You alright there?"

She looked up to see Michael with his arms outstretched towards her, holding onto her forearms.

"I'm fine," she began to say, trying to push him out of the way without getting in the way of the other dancers. Lightning flickered and the lights above them dimmed to the point of almost going out. Jumping at the unexpected crash of thunder above them, Aoife nearly stumbled forward, saved only by Michael's arms around her waist, holding her in place.

"It's ok, I've got ye," she heard him say, even though it was barely discernable above the noise around them.

"Do you think you can walk over to the table?" he asked her, bending his head down so his mouth was close to her ear. His breath felt warm against her cheek, smelling faintly of beer and whiskey.

"No," she replied honestly. Her head still swam a little, and the room seemed to be spinning faster than she was moving.

"It's alright. We can just stay here as long as you need."

There was something very safe, secure about the way he held her. He blocked out the rest of the world for her as she laid her head softly against his chest, feeling the wool of his shirt scratch against her cheek. Somehow, although she'd intended to stay as far away from Michael Flanagan as she could, she found herself dancing with him.

Lightning flickered around them as the storm grew in intensity, but Aoife no longer heard the music or the storm, or the other patrons chatting loudly around her. All she heard was the sound of her own breathing still coming quickly as her heart raced, and the sound of Michael's own heartbeat under her ear as she rested against his cheek. It was if the two of them were the only two people in the whole world, the only people who mattered in this very second. She let her body sway with his, feeling the rhythm of the music through him and closed her eyes, breathing in the scent of his aftershave, feeling safe like she'd never felt before.

Chapter Twenty-Five

Aoife woke suddenly, like someone who's been dreaming of running for their lives and then suddenly finds themselves wide awake just before they're about to fall off a cliff. Michael had been keeping an ear out for the steady rhythm of her breathing, watching her chest rise and fall reassuringly. It wasn't as though he'd been worried about her; of course, he wasn't. And yet, it hadn't stopped him from sleeping in the armchair across from her all night, just to be sure.

Even though he'd been listening out for her breathing since waking just before dawn, Michael had still been startled by her abrupt, sharp intake of breath when she woke. He rose from his place at the table where he'd sat to have his cup of tea and sat in the chair he'd slept in all night, across from the sofa. Her eyes roamed around his small sitting room, bewildered, trying to latch onto something familiar. When she finally looked over at him, he raised his hands, palms facing her in a calming gesture, much as one would to a frightened animal or a madman.

"It's alright. Ye're safe." He pitched his voice low, trying to sound soothing and comforting rather than alarming. He could see her brain was still trying to work through exactly where she was and latched onto his voice.

"Michael? Where…? How…?" she began to ask. He could see her mouth working hard for the words, her tongue seemingly thick in her mouth.

Well, she did *have quite a bit to drink last night.*

"Ye're safe," he repeated, seeing his calming tone was working. "Ye're at my place. I brought you here last night after the céilí down at the pub."

He could see her mind trying to recall the events of last night, trying to remember exactly how drunk she'd gotten and how exactly she'd ended up sleeping on his sofa.

"I slept on your sofa?" she asked him, still trying to clear the fog from her memories. "Why didn't you bring me home?"

"Well, I *was* actually trying to get you home to your place, but ye told me you'd be perfectly fine getting there without my help, and then you nearly tripped over your own feet and so I told you I was driving you home, even though ye did put up a good fuss over it."

"That sounds like me," she conceded, rubbing a hand over her face, slightly smearing her mascara.

He gently massaged his chest, just above his ribs where she'd managed to elbow him rather hard as he'd struggled to get her into his truck. Even drunk, Aoife was pretty good at defending herself.

He could have just let her go with Mara, his parents, and Father Patrick after Mara offered to drive them all home. In hindsight, it probably would have been the better course of action. However, knowing how Aoife had reacted the last time he'd seen her drunk, he'd thought it more prudent to take her himself, just in case she'd needed carrying inside.

"By the time we got here, ye said you were going to be sick, so I stopped the truck and brought you inside. Ye made it as far as the sofa, so I decided it was easiest just to leave you there until you could sleep it off.

"Ye know, for someone who says they're Irish, ye really can't seem to hold your liquor very well," he teased her.

"I can hold my liquor just fine," she grumbled at him, rubbing her face again, this time rubbing off the mascara she had just smeared on the tops of her cheeks, leaving behind a rosy hue where her skin peeked through her foundation. "In fact, in uni I was known to have an iron stomach when it comes to drinking. I'm just… out of practice, is all."

"Sure," he replied, not even remotely believing her. "For this morning though, let's try not to put your iron stomach to the test, alright? Just because you didn't go puking on my floor last night, doesn't mean you won't this morning. Can I get ye some tea?"

"Please."

He stood up, crossing the short distance to his small kitchen, placing the kettle on the stove. He went about bringing down some teacups from the top shelf of his cupboard, the ones that had belonged to his grandmother and which his mother insisted he have in case he ever had any company. He'd planned to give the little china teacups with their purple and yellow floral design around the rim to Eliza; they were more her style than his, and she'd be able to make more use of them at her place than he would here. But, somehow, he'd never gotten around to doing it yet. Considering how fond his mother was of the city girl, he supposed she counted as the sort of company she would approve of him using the teacups for.

Even with his back turned, he could feel her eyes on him while he moved about the kitchen, watching him as he brought down the sugar and the milk from the small fridge. He didn't mind it; he strangely felt both at ease with her in his home. Before he had too much time to think on this, the kettle whistled and he pulled it off quickly lest its piercing wail hurt her head too much. Pouring an equal amount of tea in both cups, he poured a little milk in his and little of both sugar and milk into hers. He placed both cups on their matching saucers and brought them into the sitting room, carefully setting hers down on the little coffee table in front of her. She still had a hand over her eyes, protecting them from the light around her.

"Here." He put his own teacup down and held out a hand to her, helping her to sit up carefully as she tenderly held her head, probably still feeling that it might try and fall off her shoulders at any moment. "Drink this."

He picked up the teacup and placed it in her hands, making sure that she was holding onto it. She cupped it between her hands, breathing in the scent and ventured a sip. As the warm brew settled her, she turned to him slightly and asked, "So what exactly happened last night?"

"Well, how much do you remember?"

The question seemed to bother her, the details clearly still hazy in her mind.

"I remember Father Patrick asking me to go to the céilí with him, and us walking down with your parents to the pub. I remember we got there and listened to the music for awhile, and then I got up and started dancing. After that, that's when things start to get a bit fuzzy."

"Aye, well, ye were well into the drink by that point, so that's not surprising," he chuckled. "Do ye remember anything else?"

"Um… I remember it was raining at some point, but I'm not sure when exactly that happened or why I know that."

"A storm broke out during the céilí. Eventually, the electricity went out and everyone decided it was time to pack up and go home. The rain was still pouring down by the time you were ready to leave, which is why I offered to drive ye home."

"Thank you. That was rather gentlemanly of you."

"No problem at all."

A curious look crossed her face like she was embarrassed at having to need his help again after another drunken incident, but there was also something else, a worry of some sort.

"Is there anything else I should remember? Anything embarrassing?"

"Oh well, there was the time you were dancing on the table…"

"What?!" she spluttered, little droplets of tea falling onto her chin.

"Here," he said, grabbing a handkerchief out of his pocket and dabbed delicately at her chin, wiping away the tea. She brought up her hand to his and he suddenly realized how closely the two of them were sitting next to one another. Slightly embarrassed, he placed the handkerchief in her hand and cleared his throat.

"I'm only messing with you." He decided not to torture the city girl by making up any escapades she hadn't done. "Although, you *were* up and dancing with several of the men in the village throughout the night. Ye made quite a few of the lads very happy men last night, although I can't say the same for their wives."

"Who all did I dance with? I think I remember dancing with Jimmy and your father."

"Aye, young Jimmy, Da, Brendan, Mr. Byrne, Mark, Mr. Dempsey, and meself, although I don't know that you could call it dancing so much as me holding you up to make sure ye didn't fall down drunk in the middle of the dancefloor."

The amusement left his voice at the memory of the two of them dancing, suddenly serious. He hadn't meant to step in from Mr. Dempsey when he had; he'd meant to go after Eliza after she'd stormed out of the pub, angry with him because she thought he'd been staring at Aoife. He hadn't been; merely just watching everyone dancing. It just so happened that the city girl had been at the centre of the dancefloor for most of the night, so it was difficult for him *not* to look in her direction occasionally. It wasn't like he'd been gawking at her, and besides, he'd been too busy working the bar to really notice Aoife. It had been pure coincidence that he'd been there at just the right moment to catch her and, with her still being in the mood to dance, he'd gone along with it until he could guide her to a table where she could sit down and sober up.

He could only guess what Eliza would think once she heard about the whole thing, especially after he'd told her he couldn't dance with her because he was working. And he knew Eliza would find out; he'd seen the looks the two of them got while they were dancing. There was no doubt that he and Aoife would once again be the talk of the Ballyclara gossips. Oddly enough, he wasn't ashamed or bothered by it. It wasn't like the two of them had done anything wrong. He'd been helping her, is all. However, he knew that wasn't how it would look.

"You and I?" she asked, her voice a little more incredulous than he'd been expecting.

"Yeah."

All That Compels the Heart

So what? Was it really that strange of an idea that the two of them could have an innocent dance together?

He hadn't failed to notice how Aoife had been avoiding him since Eliza had decided to announce their engagement to the whole village and had embarrassed Aoife in the process. He and Eliza had gotten into a right row over the whole thing later, which was likely why Eliza had been so upset with him last night. But even though Aoife had been avoiding him, it wasn't like he'd been purposefully avoiding her. In fact, he'd rather found he missed her over the days since she'd locked herself into the Old Rectory and kept out of sight from the rest of the village.

"Oh," was all she said, taking another sip from her teacup, not quite hiding the small smile that crossed her lips. He wondered what that was about, but before he could think it over, she said, "And Eliza was ok with that?"

He shrugged, taking another sip of his tea.

"I really hope it doesn't cause any problems for the two of you, especially where you were just trying to be nice to me."

"Nah, you're grand," he told her, protecting her. He would smooth things out with Eliza later and everything would be grand. Of course, it would.

She gave him a direct look, her blue eyes much clearer and focused now. She knew he wasn't telling her the truth, but she let them both believe the lie anyways.

"Well, I should probably head home," she said eventually, trying to get to her feet. She was still a bit shaky and he instinctively put his teacup on the coffee table in front of him, reaching up to grab her in case she fell. However, he needn't have worried; she managed to stay upright on her own.

"Are ye sure? You can rest here a bit, if ye need to."

He knew he should probably send her on her way before Eliza decided to pop by, trying to be the first one to mend things with him after last night, but he also didn't want to send Aoife on her way without first ensuring she'd be alright.

"Sure, I'll be grand," she told him, waving off his concern, smoothing some of the winkles out of her green tank top and readjusted her black cardigan about her shoulders.

He raised an eyebrow at her. "That's what ye said last night."

"I'm sure I'll be fine this time," she reassured him. Still, he wasn't taking any chances.

"Come on, I'll walk you home."

"Really, that's not necessary," she began to protest, trying unsuccessfully to cover up a slight dizzy spell.

"Well, I think it is," he told her, taking her hand, holding her steady. "Come on, let's get you home."

She huffed loudly, but didn't protest any further as he led her outside. She shivered a little in the cool, damp morning air, the ground still drenched from last night's storm. Even with his flannel shirt on he felt a bit of a chill as the wind picked up, blowing away the grey storm clouds.

"Stay right there," he commanded as he ran quickly back into the cottage, grabbed two of his jumpers off the hook beside the front door and went back outside. As he reached the bottom of the stairs, he held one out to her, indicating for her to put it on. She looked at it with trepidation.

"Go on, take it. We don't need you to freeze out here. Don't worry; I'll make sure to get it back from you this time. And no, there's no reason to give me any baked goods in thanks; getting you home safe and sound is thanks enough." He smiled broadly at her, hoping she wouldn't mind the joke.

She took the jumper from him reluctantly and put it over her head, the static from the wool making her auburn curls fly up in odd angles.

"Here," he said, coming close to her, and smoothed down a particularly stubborn strand of her hair.

"Ouch!" A snap of electricity stung his finger as he touched her hair.

"You alright?" she asked, her voice full of concern, taking his hand in hers to have a look at his finger.

"Yeah, just a bit of static is all." Her hand lingered on his for a second, before she removed it, leaving his skin cool in the absence of her warmth.

"Come on, Sparky," she teased him, heading out of the driveway. He lingered a moment longer, still feeling the spark of their connection on his fingertips, until the cool autumn air rustled around him, severing the moment.

Chapter Twenty-Six

Things with Eliza, as it turned out, were not as easy to smooth over as Michael had assured Aoife they would be.

After dropping her back at her place, he'd gone back to the cottage to clean up before intending to go over to Eliza's to talk to her. However, just as he had thought, Eliza had been the one to come around to try and talk to him first. She liked being thought of as being the reasonable one.

He smiled and waved to her as he walked down the lane to his cottage, trying to look pleased to see her. She stood at the bottom of the steps, her arms wrapped around her to ward off the chill. Her strawberry-blonde hair was pulled back in a neat ponytail she had pulled over one shoulder, the highlights looking even more fiery red against the white of her angora wool jumper. Despite his attempt at a friendly demeanor, she did not look best pleased with him.

Oh boy...

Wondering just how much hot water he was in, he approached her cautiously.

"Hello, love," he smiled at her again, leaning in to place a small kiss on her cheek. She purposely leaned back out of his reach. Respectfully, he took a step back out of her personal space, not making a big deal out of it.

"Would you like to come in?" he asked, pointing at the front door. Silently, she nodded, following him inside.

Once inside the warmth of the cottage, he removed his jumper and hung it up with the one he'd lent to Aoife. He held out a hand to Eliza, offering to take hers and hang it up too, but she sauntered by him and sat herself down at the table instead.

He sighed. He knew he was going to be in for it.

"Tea?" he asked, moving towards the kitchen to put the kettle on again.

He looked back at her when she didn't respond and noticed her eyes had landed on the two teacups sitting on the coffee table where he and Aoife had left them earlier. She turned her gaze back to him and raised an eyebrow, curious as to how he was going to explain this to her. Instead of responding right away, he went about making tea for the both of them. He brought down a pair of mugs from the cupboard – a much safer option than the teacups in case Eliza decided to try and throw one at his head.

"I hear you had a fun time last night," she finally said, her voice bristling with annoyance and jealousy.

Michael sighed. He'd known, of course, that she'd find out about Aoife; he'd just hoped to talk it over with her before her friends got to her and made it out to be something it wasn't.

"If by 'fun' you mean spending the evening with a packed pub, worked off my feet serving a bunch of drunks, having the electricity go out due to a wicked storm, and not being able to spend time with my favourite woman in the world, than yeah, it was 'fun.'"

Her perfectly manicured hand rested on the table only inches from his. He moved his so their fingertips were almost touching. She withdrew hers, folding her arms across her chest. Clearly, she was not yet ready to forgive him for whatever wrong she'd perceived he'd done.

"I see Aoife has been here." It wasn't a question.

She nodded to the two teacups sitting on the coffee table in the sitting room as her proof.

"It's not what you think."

All That Compels the Heart

"And what exactly am I thinking, Michael?" She gave him a direct look, challenging him.

"Why don't *you* tell *me*?" he asked, throwing the conversation back to her. After all, it was best to find out exactly what she thought was going on so he could come up with his best defense. It was how he'd managed to weather their previous arguments.

"Everyone saw you last night, dancing with her. Said it looked like the two of you were real 'intimate.'" She sneered at the word.

Michael remained quiet, knowing full well that she wasn't done.

"And now I come here this morning to find that not only has she been here," she waved to the offensive teacups once more, "I also find you coming back from her place. Are you trying to make a fool of me, Michael?"

Michael took a sip of his tea, wishing he'd put something much stronger than just milk in it. He could have brought up the irony in her coming to him accusing *him* of cheating on her when it had, in fact, been *her* infidelity that had been the cause of their most recent break up. That *she'd* been the one to make *him* look like the fool in front of the whole village.

He paused to clear his throat before answering. "I'm not trying to make a fool of you, Eliza."

She scoffed at the remark, clearly not believing him
. "Then what are you doing with her?" Her voice was quiet now, pained. Tears began to form at the corners of her eyes. Even though he knew he was being manipulated, Michael still couldn't help but feel his chest tighten with anxiety when he saw her on the verge of tears. He knew he'd done nothing wrong, and yet, she knew exactly how to make him feel like he had.

"I'm not doing anything," he told her, his voice soft. "I swear, I'm not."

He looked across the table at her, hoping to catch her eye, but she was staring down at her lap like she was struggling to remain angry with him.

"I don't believe you." Her voice was shaky, full of emotion.

"Eliza…"

"She was here, wasn't she?"

"I was only making sure she got home safe. She'd had too much to drink last night, and she was trying to walk off in the storm on her own. You and I both know how dangerous the main road can be in the dark, on a stormy night."

The words hung between them like a great weight, a burden they'd to share in order to carry it. They knew all too well how dangerous that road was on a stormy night, and the tragedy that could come from it. After all, it was on such a night as last night that they'd lost their baby.

They'd been arguing about the colour of the window drapes for their new cottage of all things when she'd gotten frustrated with him and had gone out into the storm by herself. As she'd been walking by the shoulder of the road, a car had come up behind her and, unable to see her in the driving rain, had almost struck her. The close encounter had been enough to scare Eliza, as it would anyone, and she'd fallen into the ditch by the road where she'd hit her head. Perhaps it had been a sixth sense telling him something was wrong, or he'd just felt it was the right thing to go after her, but he'd found her lying in the ditch twenty minutes later.

It was a night neither of them would forget, the night they'd become parents to a little girl, even though now all they had to show for it was the little grave marker in the parish cemetery. Despite rushing her to the hospital as quickly as he could, the complications from her fall and the injury to her head had caused her to miscarry. The doctors assured him over and over that he'd done the best he could, that no matter what he'd done, the situation would likely have ended up the same. But still, he blamed himself.

A silent tear slid down her cheek.

They'd tried to put that night behind them, to try again. Only a year after, Eliza had become pregnant again, and all had seemed right between them. All the hurt and resentment that had been building up between them was suddenly replaced with love again. But no matter what they did, how careful they were to get everything right this time, they'd suffered another miscarriage. After that, Michael had refused to try again. It was just too much for him to bear. Things got rocky between the two of them; they were on and off again so many times they'd begun to lost count. Then there'd been the affair. And yet, that pain of losing their children was what brought them back together. They just couldn't seem to move past it, somehow.

"It's not the same thing at all, Michael! You can't try and justify being out with another woman because of what happened that night. It's not the same situation at all."

"Eliza…"

"Save it, Michael," she said, rising from her chair.

"Eliza, don't leave. Let's talk this out."

"Goodbye, Michael." She turned her back to him and hurried out the door, letting it slam behind her.

"Eliza!" he shouted to her retreating back, but she wasn't listening to him. Michael rubbed a hand over his tired face, feeling the dark stubble chafe against his palm and sighed.

"Shit."

Chapter Twenty-Seven

While the storm the night of the céilí had been loud and blustery, it had – thankfully – caused very little physical damage to Ballyclara. With the exception of a couple of downed trees and few panes of broken glass, everything in the village was still standing, and had generally gone back to normal. That is, except between Michael and Eliza.

There was nothing Aoife could tangibly point to and use as proof of this statement, but there seemed to be a definite coolness between the couple. There was something distant about the way they acted around one another when they thought no one was watching.

She'd thought about going to Eliza and trying to clear the air with her about what happened – or, rather, what *didn't* happen the night of the storm – and said as much to Mara.

"Best to leave it be," Mara warned her. "I can tell ye from firsthand experience that it's better to keep out of whatever is going between those two."

Aoife noticed the pained look that had crossed the other woman's face at her statement.

"I just get the impression that Eliza thinks something happened between Michael and I that night, and I just wanted to reassure her that it did not."

"Look, Eliza's going to think whatever she wants to think and there's no changing her mind from it. Best just stay out of her way until she finds something else to obsess over. Whatever you say to her will only fan the flame. Besides, she's gone to Belfast for awhile now anyways, so you won't have the chance to talk to her for a few days at least."

"Belfast?"

"Yeah, her mother's side has family up there. It'll be good for her; give her something else to focus on for a bit."

Aoife shrugged, conceding defeat in the matter.

"So, have you heard from Connor lately?"

Aoife knew Mara and Connor had been keeping in touch since he'd been deployed; she'd received letters from him in the beginning until he'd gotten Mara's address from her and had begun writing directly to her. Every once in awhile Mara would get this excited smile she simply couldn't hide, like the one she'd had the day she'd met Aoife's cousin, only to be replaced by a sadness the day after talking to him, the reality of being on opposite ends of the world setting in again.

Aoife knew the feeling all too well. Even though she put it aside and got through daily life, the worry was always there with her, lodged stubbornly in the back of her mind. It helped having someone she could talk to about it, someone who understood how she felt.

At the mention of his name, the goofy, excited grin returned to Mara's face. "Yeah, we Skyped the other day."

Aoife smiled to see her friend so happy. Although she still had reservations about Mara and Connor dating, she'd begun to come around to the idea.

"How was he?"

"Good," Mara replied, not supplying much information.

Aoife nodded, taking a sip of her pint, waiting for her to say something more. Mara, clearly seeing that Aoife was expecting more details finally admitted, "We didn't do much talking."

Aoife tried not to splutter her drink. Thankfully, she was saved any need for further commenting on the subject by the phone behind the bar ringing loudly throughout the largely empty pub. Brendan, who'd been wiping down the far end of the bar, picked it up.

"*O'Leary's*," he answered.

Within seconds, his face turned sour and he took the cordless phone with him into the kitchen. A second later, Michael came out of the swinging doors, ushered by Brendan shooing him out of the kitchen. Not sure what else to do, he came over to stand beside Mara and Aoife. The three of them watched Brendan through the porthole windows of the kitchen doors, talking rapidly with arms flying about in frustration. After a few minutes of what sounded like Brendan cajoling and then nearly threatening the other person on the end of the line, he hung up the phone with force and joined them back at the bar.

He leaned over the bar, placing his elbows upon it and put his head in his hands, uttering some unintelligible noises of frustration. Finally, he lifted his head, poured himself a whiskey and downed it in one go.

"Damn," he finally exclaimed.

"What's wrong?" It wasn't like Brendan to get flustered over something. She'd always thought of him as one of the most cool-headed people in Ballyclara.

"The hotel in the Dublin just called to say that they had a fire in their kitchen last night and the place is wrecked. I don't know what I'm going to do."

Brendan emitted another low, frustrated groan.

"What's the occasion?" Aoife asked, at his despair.

"It's our wedding anniversary, and I promised Molly a relaxing weekend away, no Des, no worrying about the pub. Just the two of us out on the town, like we used to do before being responsible adults got in the way. I got us the hotel room, tickets to a show she wants to see, booked us in at a fancy restaurant; the whole works. This one was the only one with availability this weekend; I'll never find a replacement now before tomorrow night, and Molly's going to kill me."

"Well, if it's a place to stay you need, why don't you just use my flat?"

Brendan's head whipped up, his face the perfect mix of hope and confusion.

"I never did end up sub-letting my flat to anyone, so it's just sitting up there mostly empty while I'm down here. I only use it when I go up to visit Bex and Millie.

"I know it's no hotel, but it has everything you should need: on-site parking, full kitchen, bath, ensuite laundry, pool, gym; it's even got a king-sized bed. You'll be able near to all the transportation systems to get you wherever you need. I can just call Bex and Millie to let them know you're coming up and you can come by and pick up the key any time you like. Whatever works for you."

Brendan's face got progressively more hopeful. "You'd do that for us?"

"Of course! It's no problem at all. I mean, I'm not using the place; you might as well make use of it." Aoife smiled at his look of relief and was surprised when he came around from behind the bar and squeezed her in a big bear hug.

"You're a lifesaver!" he exclaimed and planted a kiss on top of her head.

Aoife giggled and said, "No problem at all," when he finally let her go, feeling the air rushing back into her lungs.

"Well there, that's settled. Crisis averted," Mara said, a smile on her face.

"Wait." Brendan's exuberant expression suddenly turned dramatically crestfallen. "Jimmy and Karen are both out sick with colds right now and Mara, you said you were taking your parents over to Waterford for the weekend, didn't you?"

"Yeah," Mara replied, not immediately understanding where he was going with this. "They want to see Da's aunt and have a visit. Why?"

"Because it means no one will be here with Michael to run the pub." Brendan's face once more was hidden behind his hands, another low groan escaping his throat, this time as if dredged from the very bottom of his soul. "As generous as your offer is, Aoife, I'm going to have to turn it down."

"No, ye won't," Michael told him firmly. "Leave me here; I'll be grand."

"Don't be an eejit. Ye can't manage the whole pub by yourself all Saturday night and Sunday, Michael," Brendan exclaimed.

"I know how to run a pub, Brendan, and I'm telling you that everything will be grand, and so it will be. Now, you are going to go home and tell Molly that there was a change in plans and you're going to be staying at Aoife's for the weekend instead of the hotel. And then you're going to pack, and then you're going to get the keys from Aoife, and tomorrow you'll be on your way to Dublin and everything will be grand."

Brendan gave him a skeptical look.

"I can see if there's anyone else who could take Ma and Da over to Waterford, and that way I can stay and help."

They all knew that the unspoken alternative of closing the pub for the weekend was something that neither Brendan nor Michael could afford.

"Or, you could let me help out."

Everyone turned to look at Aoife with surprise, like they'd forgotten she was there. She stared back, slightly offended by their looks of incredulity.

"It's not like I haven't spent my whole life in a pub. If I haven't picked up a few things by now, then I'm worse off than I thought."

Michael began to laugh when he noticed she was serious and tried to disguise it behind a cough. Aoife looked at him with one eyebrow raised.

"And what exactly qualifies you to work here? Beyond the whole 'I grew up in a pub' thing?" he asked. "Which, I might add, I find very hard to believe."

"Considering what a bind you're in, are you really all that concerned with qualifications, Michael?" she countered. "Or, is it because you think that I grew up with a silver spoon up me arse that you think I can't do the job?"

Brendan and Mara both snorted loudly at this comment. Michael responded simply by glaring at the two of them. Aoife cut him off before he could give a retort.

"I will have you know that I am the granddaughter of Paddy O'Reilly who, as it happens, created one of the largest and most successful pub chains in this country. Maybe you've heard of him?"

She paused long enough to see if the name registered with Michael. Of course, it did. You'd have to have been living under a rock for the better part of the last fifty years not to have heard of *O'Reilly's*.

"And before you get any notions of him having just been a figurehead behind the brand, my grandfather was pulling pints long before he was even allowed to drink them, and he made both my cousins and I learn to do the same so that we would learn the business inside and out, so that it would be in safe hands when we took it over.

"And, when he died," she paused a second to take a breath, the reminder of her grandfather's death still stinging, "he made me a majority shareholder in the company because clearly he thought that I was capable of running the pub he'd dreamed of and spent his whole life building. So, for your information, I *am* going to help you out this weekend, whether you like it or not because I *do* know how to run this place just as well as you do, Michael Flanagan."

If she weren't so riled up, she might have thought it comical how Mara, Michael, and Brendan all stared back her, mouths agape, unable to think of something to say.

Finally, it was Brendan who broke the silence. "She's got ye there, mate," at the same time Mara said, "You're *that* Aoife O'Reilly?"

Both Brendan and Michael looked at Mara, confused.

"What?" she asked. "I read tabloids sometimes. I mean, I thought ye looked familiar when you first came to Ballyclara, but I just didn't realize we had a *celebrity* living here."

"I'm hardly a celebrity," Aoife assured Mara.

"I mean, I've seen more of your cousin, Caitlin, in the papers, but still. You're famous. "You and I are going to have a *long* chat about every celebrity ye know." Mara began looking at Aoife as if with a new appreciation that did not entirely make Aoife feel comfortable.

"Alright, then. Be here tomorrow morning at 7 am. Ye want to help out? You can start with working the morning shift. Bright and early."

Michael stared at her, seeing if she would flinch from his challenge.

"Molly and I will still be here in the morning to help out," Brendan said, looking at Michael like he didn't know what the hell his friend was thinking. "There's no need to make her come in for then. You can come in for 3 o'clock; Molly and I will get the morning and noon rush over with for you and you can help out for the evening. That'll be plenty of help."

Aoife nodded. "Come up to the house any time to pick up the keys to the flat, Brendan. And I'll see you here tomorrow at 3 pm, sharp," she said to Michael, hopping off her bar stool and heading out of the pub.

"Wait, we have so much to talk about," Mara called out.

"Leave off, Mara," Michael scolded her. When he thought she was out of earshot, he turned to Brendan and say, "If she screws up, it's on you."

"And what exactly do ye think she's going to screw up?" Brendan asked Michael seriously. "You heard her, she has experience and, by the sounds of it, more than the two of us combined before we got this place. Besides I think it'll be good for the two of you to work together."

"Or, it could be completely disastrous and ye won't have a pub to come home to at the end of the weekend," Michael muttered.

"You can't keep up this rift with her forever, Michael. I think it's about the time the two of you buried the hatchet and learned to live in the same village. If not for your own sakes, then for the rest of us so we don't have to listen to your whining anymore."

Michael looked like he was going to say a few choice words to Brendan but Aoife was out of earshot before she could hear anything else.

Chapter Twenty-Eight

The next day, Michael whistled to himself as he walked through the main square and over towards the pub. Looking up as he crossed the street, his keys jangling in his pocket, he noticed there was someone standing there by the front door. He knew it was Aoife before he even reached the door. In order to avoid looking her in the eye, he glanced down at his watch as he approached the pub and sighed. Sure enough, she was right on time.

Of course she would be...

He would be lying to himself if he said he hadn't been hoping she would be at least a few minutes late, that way he could hold it over her and stick it to Brendan that this was an awful idea. He knew it was childish, but there was a part of him that would just like to be right about her for once, but, here she was, proving him wrong yet again.

"Hello."

"Hello." She smiled at him pleasantly. "So, where would you like me to start?"

She took off her jacket and revealing the white scoop necked top with silver chains she'd paired with her leather trousers.

"Here," he said, heading behind the bar and finding a broom and dustpan, handing them to her. "Ye can start by sweeping up, wiping down the bar, and bringing all the chairs down off the tables."

Aoife took the broom and dustpan from him without a word and began sweeping the place up, humming cheerfully to herself. Leaving her to it, he headed into the kitchen and set about bringing out everything they'd need.

When he'd finished setting up the kitchen, he came out and noticed Aoife had already finished everything he'd asked her to do.

"Right, what's next?" she asked him, hands on her hips and looking eager to begin the next task.

"The specials," he said, pointing to the chalkboard behind the bar. "We need to put them up."

"Sure thing," she replied, bringing it down and locating a piece of chalk to write with. "What's for supper tonight?"

"Fish and chips, and also put the lamb stew down there. All the beer specials stay the same. Dessert will be apple pie and chocolate cake."

She nodded and began wiping away the old specials with the damp cloth he handed her and waiting for the board to dry before writing out the new ones.

"I think it's probably for the best if I operate the kitchen tonight." It would be safest for both of them if she stayed far away from the kitchen. He was relieved to see her shrug her shoulders in acquiescence.

"Do you think you'll be able to handle out here on your own?"

She looked up from writing out the specials on the board and placed it back behind the bar where she found it. He noticed how she'd managed to make the board look neat and tidy, with fancy lettering and had even drawn some designs of clover leafs and Celtic knots around the edges of the board to smarten it up a bit. Even he had to admit it looked much nicer than his or Brendan's scrawling handwriting.

"No problem at all," was her only response.

"Alright then, let me show you behind the bar."

He lifted the pass-through for her to follow him behind the bar. "Here's what we have on tap, and here's where everything else is stored."

He pointed to a large refrigerator packed with beer, soda, juice, and other beverages below the bar. "Wines here, sodas here, juices here, bottled water here, and other lagers and whatever we don't have on tap over here.

"Clean glasses we keep here and the empties we stack here. Now, if ye get a chance, try to bring the tray of empties in as soon as ye can and load them in the dishwasher in the kitchen. Come on out back and I'll show you."

He motioned for her to follow him through to the kitchen. "Here's the dishwasher. Detergent is here. It loads pretty much how you think it does and works just how you think it does."

He looked up at her to see if she was paying attention and saw her nodding at him. He was surprised she hadn't once rolled her eyes at him or put up a fuss at making her do any of the grunt work so far.

"Any questions so far?"

"No. I think I got it. What's next?"

He noted her eagerness. She wasn't as easy to scare off as he had thought she would be.

At her question, he motioned for her to come back through the kitchen doors and into the pub. "I assume from your prior experience, you know how to pull a pint?"

Without a word, she took one of the clean glasses he'd stacked earlier in the day and pulled a pint of Guinness, handing it to him for him to judge.

"I admit, I'm a bit rusty at it, but it's like riding a horse, right? Once you get back on again, the muscle memory kicks in."

"I'm sure it will come back to you, just fine," he said, setting the pint down on the bar in front of him, trying not to look like he was impressed or enjoying the pint too much.

"In the meantime, ye'll do fine."

He noticed the flicker of a smile cross her lips but she hid it quickly, her face returning to an implacably neutral mask.

"Well, that's everything, is it?" she asked him, still trying to keep her face void of emotion.

"Just about," he replied, taking another sip of the pint. *Damn, that's good.*

"You can write orders on this here," he handed her a pad of paper and a pen. "Table numbers start there in the corner with one and work your way clockwise around the room. There's a place in the back where you can hang them so I'll know what to make."

"I saw it," she replied, acknowledging she knew how it worked.

"Alright then. Here's an apron for you. Tips go in this jar here and we split everything at the end of the night. Looks like you're all set."

"Just in time then." She nodded towards the door where his sister and parents were coming in.

"Ma, Da," Michael greeted his parents. "I thought ye were going to be in Waterford this weekend?"

"Ah, we were, but then your auntie said she wasn't feeling up to it, so we decided to stay home for the weekend and go another time. Besides, we heard it was Aoife's big debut working in the pub; we knew we couldn't miss that. Had to make sure you hadn't scared her off," Dermot teased his son.

"He's been a great teacher so far," Aoife told him, surprising Michael. "Besides, I think even he has to admit he can't afford to scare me off. He can't run this place on his own."

Yes, I bloody well could.

"So, what can I get you?" Aoife asked his family.

"Three pints to start, please," Dermot said.

"Coming right up." Aoife went straight to the bar and began pulling the pints with ease.

"How's she settling in?" his father asked him, standing aside from Sinead and Mara a bit.

"Grand," Michael admitted non-committedly.

"I should say so. She seems to be a natural."

They both looked over at Aoife who'd pulled three perfect pints and was handing Mara her change.

"We'll see how the rest of the night goes after she's rushed off her feet."

Dermot shook his head in what seemed like exasperation, confusing Michael.

"What? Why do ye have that expression?"

"You're like a little schoolboy who has a crush on a girl in the playground, so ye call her names and pull her pigtails to get her to notice you."

Michael looked at his father like he had two heads. "I do *not* have a crush on Aoife. Besides, have you forgotten? I'm engaged to Eliza!"

"This week," Dermot muttered just loud enough for Michael to hear, but just low enough to be considered polite.

Michael gave his father a pointed look in response to his comment.

"I'll believe you and Eliza will last forever when you two have been married as long as your mother and I."

"What are you two talking about?" Sinead asked, coming over to hand Dermot his pint.

"Ah, just imparting some fatherly advice, is all," Dermot said, clapping Michael on the shoulder.

"More like dithering like a doddering old fool," Michael teased back. "I think old age is affecting your brain, old man."

"Who're you calling old?" Dermot retorted, but hadn't taken offense. "I feel as if I were a man half my age."

"And what age would that be? Eighty?"

"Why you…" Michael and Dermot playfully jabbed at each other, their little tête-a-tête ending in the two of them hugging it out.

"Why don't ye be a good son and get us some supper, eh?"

"Right. Four specials coming up. Wait, where's my nephew, then, if you lot aren't going to Waterford?"

"Over with at the McCaffreys' place. He wanted to play with Des, so Jimmy and Karen said he could stay over for his tea since they're watching Des already for Molly and Brendan. It's just the three of us," Mara replied.

Michael nodded and headed back into the kitchen to begin preparing supper for his family. Some minutes later, just as he was setting out the food on the plates, Aoife swung through the kitchen doors to grab the orders.

"I'll take those out," she said, taking the plates from him and heading back out, placing the plates on the table in front of Mara, Dermot, and Sinead. Michael could see that the pub was beginning to fill up; half the tables were now occupied, everyone with a drink and seemingly well-taken care of.

"Aoife? Can I get another?" one of the punters at the bar tipped his empty glass at her.

"Sure thing. Just one sec," she replied to him, not skipping a beat.

"Orders for tables three and four," she said, handing the order slips to Michael before heading back behind the bar to take care of the customer who was looking for a refill.

He noted the easy way she talked to each of the customers, making everyone happy and ensuring they were looked after. He also had a glance at the tip jar and noticed it was twice as full as it should have been at this stage of the night.

The night went on surprisingly quickly. In only a few short hours, the place was comfortably full, and he could hear everyone talking and laughing through the kitchen doors. As more and more people came in, Aoife and Michael settled into a comfortable rhythm with him preparing the orders and occasionally stepping in to pull a pint or two if she were busy, but all in all, he had to admit that she could more than take care of herself out on the floor. Before he knew it, the night was over and he rang the bell for last call. A collective groan arose from the crowd.

"Go home ye drunks," he teased his regulars. "Some of us want to go home and sleep tonight."

They grumbled but dutifully downed their drinks and headed out of the pub. When the last customer had gone, Michael quickly went to the front and latched the door behind them so he and Aoife could clean up. He noticed she'd already begun the clean-up process without having to be asked.

He went back into the kitchen and began turning off the stoves and putting away all the food. When he'd come out, she'd stacked the chairs on the tables and swept the floor, cleaned the top of the bar, and stacked all of the empty glasses and cleaned up all of the dirty dishes.

"Here, let me get those," he said to her as she went to grab the heavy tray of dirty dishes and took them from her.

"Thanks."

"You can begin counting the tip money, if ye like." He nodded towards the overflowing jar. He hadn't seen it that full since he, Brendan, and Molly opened the place. When he came back out of the kitchen from loading the dishwasher, he noticed she'd counted all of the money and had it neatly divided up.

"That half's yours. You deserve it. Ye did well tonight."

"So, I passed the test?" she asked, an eager smile on her face.

He smiled to see her look so happy and proud of herself and smiled in spite of himself.

"Yes, ye passed the test. Now, if ye want, ye can work the lunch shift with me as well."

"Yes," she replied quickly and he was surprised by how enthusiastic she was.

"Great," he said. "Well, I have one more load of dishes to finish up with, so you go on home and I'll see ye here at eleven am sharp."

Aoife looked down at her watch and looked surprised to see the time. "I can stay with you if you want…"

"No, I'll be grand. You go on home. Just be hear at eleven. Going to church is hungry work, and the parishioners here will want their food on time."

"Yes boss," she said and headed out of the pub, pocketing her money as she headed out the door.

ഗ‌ര

The next morning, Michael heard the front door to the pub open and came through from the back to see who it was. It was just before opening, so he was a bit surprised to see anyone in so early.

"Well, the place is still standing," he heard Molly say as she and Brendan came in the pub. There was a faint hint of surprise in Molly's voice that set Michael's voice on edge.

It's not like I don't know how to run my own damn pub…

It had, in fact, been Michael's idea to purchase the pub in the first place. Three years ago, old Mr. Murphy who'd owned the pub had passed on. As all of his children had moved out of the village and had no interest in running the place, his widow had decided to sell. Michael and Brendan had been barely getting by with their contracting business and, looking for some additional income, had scraped together as much as they could in order to make an offer. Molly had gone to culinary school to become a chef, but the demands of motherhood and having fewer opportunities living in such a small place, she'd found it tough to find the right place to work at. Michael had talked it over with the both of them, pointing out that it would be perfect as it would bring in more money for all three of them, and Molly would have a chance to use her skills and still live in Ballyclara. In fact, they lived only a stone's throw away from the pub itself, just across the little creek that separated their street from the village's main square. It was ideal for all of them.

They hadn't actually thought when they'd put in their offer that it would be seriously accepted. They'd been barely able to put up half the money she was asking for, and they hadn't yet been approved by the bank for a loan for the rest of it. But, knowing that it would be in good and capable hands with the three of them, and that it would remain with locals, Mrs. Murphy had agreed to their offer.

"Look who's come back," he greeted his friends with a smile.

"I see ye haven't managed to burn the place down while we were gone."

"Ye trust me enough to make me godfather to your son in case anything, God forbid, ever happens to the two of you but you don't trust me with running me own pub?" Michael feigned annoyance.

"Ah now; he's only having you on," Molly replied, coming over to give him a quick peck on the cheek to mollify him.

"So how'd she do then?" Brendan asked. The smug look already on his friend's face made him want to tell him Aoife had done a terrible job and that he'd been right about her all along, but it wouldn't be the truth and if wouldn't be fair.

"Ah, she did alright," he replied, trying to downplay things.

"Just alright?" Brendan pressed. He tried to ask it nonchalantly, leaning on the bar while Michael set about wiping it down, but the smug smile still on Brendan's face told him that he knew Michael wasn't telling him the full truth.

"Alright," he admitted. "You were right. Is that what you'd like to hear?"

"Well, it wouldn't hurt," Brendan replied, smug smile in full force now.

"You were right." He tried not to twist his mouth into a rueful grimace but couldn't stop himself.

"It was wonderful of her to step in and help like that. I hope ye were nice to her and didn't end up scaring her off."

"I think if she's been here this long and survived a night working in here beside him, that she's not going anywhere anytime soon." Molly smirked at him.

"So how was your weekend?" Michael asked, bringing the topic of conversation back to the two of them.

"It was wonderful. We got to see a show…"

"…And Aoife set us up with a reservation at her family's pub. It was great! We could pick up a pointer or two from her on how to run this place, I bet."

"Ask for advice? Ye do know who you're talking to, don't you?" Brendan said, flabbergasted his wife would even think Michael would broach the idea of asking Aoife for help.

"I can ask for help when I need it," Michael replied defensively.

"You will be arguing with St. Peter himself about which direction heaven is in when ye get to the Pearly Gates," Brendan laughed.

Michael frowned at his friend's jibe, only slightly annoyed.

"And it was so nice of her to lend us her place for the weekend," Molly said, changing the subject. "It's funny; her place in the city is so different from here. I mean, don't get me wrong, it's a gorgeous spot and it's so close to everything, but there's something just impersonal about it. It's nothing like the Old Rectory. I reckon she's put in more effort into that place than she ever did in making her flat a home."

"Well, I'm glad it worked out for you, then," he said.

"Come on, wife. Let's pick up Des and leave Michael here to eat his humble pie before we come back for the night shift. Clearly, he's just a sore loser over our bet that Aoife would be a great fit working here." Brendan grinned at Michael who simply glared back at his friend in response.

"I'm not sure I'm glad to see the two of you back, now that you're taking that attitude."

"Oh, so you want to hire Aoife on permanently, then? Replace us with her?"

"I didn't say that..." Michael looked up as Mrs. Drummond walked in with her son.

"Sure," Brendan said, rolling his eyes in Michael's direction. "We'll see ye back here in a couple of hours."

Putting an arm around Molly's shoulders, the two of them turned and walked out of the pub, heading over to Brendan's parents' place to pick up their son.

"Humble pie," Michael muttered at their retreating backs as he wiped at the bar furiously.

Chapter Twenty-Nine

"So, like, this guy, like, just comes up to me, and like, starts, like, *talking* to me, like…"

Aoife tried to tune out the inane chatter of the young, twenty-somethings sitting next to her at the café. From their backpacks and the way they were dressed, she guessed that they were probably first years, having just come out of one of their last classes before exams began next week. She sipped her second hot chocolate of the day, watching Dubliners rushing about, doing some Christmas shopping, and wondered if she and her friends had ever seemed that annoying to others when they'd been in uni.

She'd come back to Dublin a few days ago at her grandmother's request.

Command, more like.

Grainne had left her a rather terse voicemail message pointing out that she'd not been back to the city in quite some time as she'd promised she would. Knowing she could only plausibly come up with so many excuses to avoid seeing her family without getting on her grandmother's bad side – *did the woman seriously have a good side?* – she'd made the trip up.

Besides, it wasn't like she was missing much in Ballyclara: Mara, Rory, Dermot, and Sinead had finally gone on their trip to Waterford, even dragging their son along with them.

Michael had been moping about the village ever since Eliza had decided to extend her stay in Belfast indefinitely, and they'd all agreed he needed to get away for awhile and get her off his mind. So, with the Flanagans gone for awhile, Father Patrick busy getting prepared for the upcoming holiday season, and the McCaffreys busy with running the pub in Michael's absence, she figured now was as good a time as any to come back home. Danny had even managed to get a couple of days off work – which mostly meant that he was working from home instead of at the office – so they could, theoretically, spend some more time together. She knew it was best she was here now while he had the time; who knew when they'd have another chance like this to see one another.

Aoife glanced down at her watch for the third time in ten minutes, silently tutting to herself.

Millie was late.

Another wave of students emerged like a great flood, filling the square across from the coffee shop window.

Aoife immediately spotted her friend in the crowd. It was kind of hard *not* to. She was wearing a bright patchwork poncho made in all manner of colours and hues under the sky, like a modern-day version of Joseph's technicolour raincoat. To add to the assortment of colours, her hair was a dyed a vibrant peach with lime highlights.

Only Millie…

Somehow her friend made it all work together, the hair, the poncho, the ocean blue yoga pants she was wearing as well; somehow it all pulled together to look as completely normal on Millie as Aoife's black leather trousers and red cable knit jumper did on her.

She gulped down the last of her hot chocolate and grimaced, the drink having gone mostly cold by now. Picking up her purse and slinging it over her shoulder, she deposited her empty cup in the nearest bin and headed out into the drizzle to meet her friend.

"Aoife!" Millie greeted her warmly, leaning in to give her a big hug.

"Hi Millie," she greeted pleasantly, the annoyed tirade she'd been rehearsing in her head for the last forty-five minutes forgotten in her friend's presence.

"This is Laura; she's in my Art History course."

"Nice to meet you," Aoife held out her hand to shake hands with the young brunette, who beamed back at her eagerly. Where Millie was gregarious, Laura was demure in a white, knee-length trench coat, her dark hair pulled up into a loose bun, minimal make-up on her freckled skin, allowing the naturalness of her slate blue eyes to shine through.

"Art History now, is it?"

Millie had changed her mind as to what she wanted to do with her life a good three or four times in the last year alone. She'd wanted to be a welder, then a veterinarian, then a painter, and now?

God knows…

The problem with Millie was not a lack of enthusiasm for any one subject. Rather, she had the opposite problem: she loved learning about *everything* and so it was difficult for her to settle on just one thing. She had so much interest in the world and everything that happened in it, she simply couldn't see herself settling down into just one role for the rest of her life. She rarely stuck with any project long enough to finish it.

"Yes! I met Laura on the first day of term and she had such a passion for the subject, she convinced me to sign up for the course. So, I switched out of my Psychology elective and decided on Art History instead."

"I don't think it took much convincing," Laura replied, looking shy at the compliment. "Anyways, I have to run, but I'll see you here tomorrow for study group? It was great meeting you, Aoife!"

"You betcha!" Millie replied, using one of Bex's Americanisms.

"Nice to meet you too," Aoife replied, she and Millie waving to the young girl as she walked in the opposite direction across the square.

"Shall we head out?"

"Yes," Millie replied, linking her arm in Aoife's and the two of them left the campus and headed down Grafton

Street. They'd walked for a few minutes when Aoife asked, "No Bex today?"

"No, she texted to say that she had to work on something. So, it's just you and I today."

"Well, I guess we'll have to make do," Aoife smiled at her.

They'd walked past a few of the shops when Aoife noticed Millie had been glancing over at her the last few minutes, looking like she wanted to ask her something but was too nervous to do so.

"Alright, what is it?" she asked.

"Mmm... what?" Millie asked in what Aoife supposed was her best attempt at a poker face. It failed miserably.

"You've been staring at me for the last few minutes now. What's up?"

"No I haven't." Millie's tone was defensive.

"Yes, you have and you know it." Aoife tried to keep her tone kind, not wanting to start an argument with her. "Come on. Out with it."

"What are your plans for the holidays this year?"

"I don't know... I guess I haven't given it much thought, to be honest."

"So you have nothing planned so far?"

"Nope."

"Good," Millie replied, sighing a breath of relief. "Look, Bex and I have it all planned out."

"Planned what out?" Aoife stopped in the street, the people around them muttering under their breath at the sudden stop in the flow of traffic and Aoife pulled Millie to one side, out of the way.

"Remember how the three of us have always said we'd go to Edinburgh for Hogmanay? Bex and I thought we should do that this year. In fact, we may have already bought the plane tickets and booked the hotel. Even Danny is coming along. In fact, he sort of made all the arrangements for us and got us into a great hotel and snagged us tickets to the Ceilidh."

Millie's voice was conspicuous with admiration for Aoife's boyfriend. Of all the things she'd just heard, she was most surprised that Bex and Millie had included Danny in their holiday plans and Millie seemed to be perfectly alright with this.

"You 'may' have done those things? Or you already *did* those things?"

"Ok, so we *did* book everything, but we were ninety-nine percent sure you'd be ok with it."

Aoife smiled at her friend, seeing how she was trying so hard not to look panicked right now, worried that perhaps she had overstepped with her plans.

"I think it's a great idea," Aoife declared, nudging Millie's upper arm affectionately with her own.

Millie's breath exploded in a *whoosh!* of relief.

"How long have you guys been planning this for, anyways?"

"Since last week. We knew that this was going to be a more difficult Christmas for you, what with it being the first one without your grandfather. We wanted to make sure you didn't have to spend it just with your family, or down in Ballyclara by yourself."

Aoife pulled her jumper closer around her at the mention of her grandfather, feeling a sudden chill. She wasn't quite sure what to say.

"Don't worry, I know what you're going to say: that you don't know what to say, that we're the best friends in the world, blah blah blah. Of course we are! That's why we're *your* friends."

Aoife pulled Millie into a tight hug, the patches of her poncho feeling soft against her cheek. Releasing her a few seconds later, she linked her arm with Millie's and the two once more resumed their walk down Grafton Street.

"I hadn't really thought of it like that, you know," she said a few minutes later, her voice quiet. "As the first Christmas without Granddad. It's not that I'd forgotten," she was quick to state. She didn't want Millie to think that the passing of the months had made the grief any less than it had been the day he'd died. "It's just that I guess I was putting off thinking about it until I had to."

"I know. That's why we wanted to plan this for you. We knew how much it would mean to you."

Aoife smiled at her. "How'd you convince Danny to come along with us, by the way?"

"Well, that was Bex's suggestion," she replied honestly. She looked apprehensive, like she was worried Aoife might be offended that Millie hadn't necessarily wanted to invite him, but Aoife simply nodded, unsurprised. "She thought he might have some connections that could get us in to the hotel at the last minute and into the party on Princes Street. And then, she said it wouldn't be right to ask him for the favour and *not* invite him, so we asked him. Neither of us expected him to say yes, though," Millie admitted. "We thought he'd be busy with work or away in the Caribbean with his family."

Aoife nodded again. She and Danny hadn't discussed what they were going to do over the holidays, but she was kind of surprised he wouldn't be busy with something. The last few Christmases he'd shown up on Christmas Day and done dinner with her family, but he'd never stuck around when she'd gone to hang out with Bex and Millie for the rest of the holidays. He'd always said he hadn't wanted to intrude on their time together. Usually he went out to his parents' place and spent time there or went to their holiday home in the St. Lucia. It was a strange feeling, knowing he was coming with them and it wouldn't just be a girls' trip.

You should be grateful he's taking the time away from his work and family to spend time with you. You know how difficult it is for him to get time off. You shouldn't complain when he does *find time to spend with you.*

She put the thought out of her head as she and Millie came upon one of their favourite shops. Stopping outside its doors, she turned to her friend and said, "Well, I guess I'm going to need a new wardrobe for our trip. Shall we see if we can find anything?"

Millie nodded to her excitedly; she might have a very eclectic taste for her own wardrobe, but there was no one better to shop with than Millie. She was just one of those people who knew what would look exactly right on you.

The pair spent the next couple of hours perusing the shops, coming out with several shopping bags of new clothes. They'd just stopped outside of Beweley's when Millie asked, "Want to grab a bite to eat?"

Aoife glanced down at her watch, checking the time. "Shit…"

Her heart sank in her chest remembering that hanging out with Millie hadn't been her only appointment for the day.

"I'd love to, but I have to meet Maureen and Anton. I promised I'd have dinner with them tonight at *O'Reilly's*. I wish I could." Her tone pleaded for Millie to forgive her for cutting out on their fun time.

"No worries," Millie replied, giving her a quick hug. "Try not to kill your mother."

Aoife knew Millie meant it jokingly, but they both knew that there was at least a ten percent chance where Aoife might be tempted to go through with it.

"I'll do my best, but no promises." She kissed her friend lightly on the cheek and waved farewell as best she could under the weight of her bags of new clothing and headed back the way they'd come.

Chapter Thirty

Aoife hurried along Grafton Street, weaving her way through the crowds. She was supposed to be meeting her mother and stepfather at seven-thirty and she knew that her mother wouldn't like it if she were late. Maureen O'Reilly had a terrible habit of being early to everything and expecting that everyone else in the world did the exact same thing and she was merciless to anyone who did not do the same. She walked through life with the confidence of someone who expects the entire world to revolve completely around her.

As Aoife arrived in front of the pub, she glanced at her reflection in the front window. Her unruly hair fell in curls about her shoulders under her knit hat, and she hastily took it off, trying to strategically place the curls in a way that would not offend her mother. Maureen was forever chastising Aoife for not taming her locks, as if it were fault for being born with curly hair.

Aoife dreaded walking into the restaurant with every fiber of her being, knowing this evening was going to be as tedious and painstaking as trying to walk across a bed of nails. In fact, she pretty much would rather have driven a nail into her foot than go inside. It was difficult to be enthused about spending time with her mother and step-father when she knew she would be spending the entire meal having her every move or gesture scrutinized and all of her life's decisions would come under a microscope, all the while her mother would be trying to bully her into doing something for her. Aoife was under no illusions that this was a battlefield, not a family dinner. Squaring her shoulders, she walked through the doors with more confidence than she felt.

This particular *O'Reilly's* had been the first that designed by her grandmother. It looked nothing like her grandfather's original vision for his pub, the embodiment of which happened to stand only a few blocks from here. As soon as you stepped inside, there was no doubt that this was a five star restaurant in the style of Victorian elegance, and not some local the regular folks went to every night. She doubted most people would be able to afford to eat here once a month, let alone every night.

A massive crystal chandelier hung from the ceiling above the bottom floor, drawing the eye to the centre of the room where a large staircase led to the upper floor. Each table was covered in a crisp, white cloth with silverware polished to a bright gleam. The entire place was done up in clean, classic colours: whites, greys, blacks, and some hints of green to add a pop of colour. Uniformed staff moved silently about the place, only speaking when spoken to. A dour-looking maître d' greeted her at the front door, looking her up and down. She wished now that she had worn something a little dressier – if rather more impractical given the chilly weather – than her cable knit jumper and leather trousers.

"Can I help you?" she asked crisply, her tone implying that she really didn't want to help Aoife, nor did she think she belonged here.

"Yes. I'm meeting my mother, Maureen O'Reilly. I believe she's already here?"

She saw the other woman's eyes widen slightly, clearly surprised that Maureen O'Reilly's daughter didn't look anything like she would have thought.

Pick up a tabloid, love, Aoife wanted to say. *Or, wait until tomorrow. I'm sure I'll be headline news.*

She and Millie had passed by a newsstand on their way down Grafton Street, and while neither of them had talked about it, neither of them had failed to notice the headlines and pictures of Aoife and her family splashed across the front, detailing the upcoming painful holiday as they prepared to spend the first Christmas without her grandfather. It also hadn't escaped her notice how more than one person in the shops had pulled out a mobile to take a photo of her and Millie while they were shopping, having recognized her face. If the maître d' had bothered to do any snooping on her boss, she'd be able to find out all about Aoife and her strained relationship with her family.

"Right this way."

The woman gestured for her to follow her to a table in the back room where her mother and stepfather sat in a secluded area. No other patrons were in the vicinity; her mother not wanting their inevitable family squabbles to be overheard by nosy diners.

"Ah, there you are," Maureen greeted her daughter, and held out her cheek for Aoife to kiss it dutifully. Aoife obliged her mother, conceding the first battle to her in order to avoid an immediate all-out war. Aoife knew she was just on time, maybe five minutes late, but she refrained from pointing this out.

"Hello," Anton greeted her as formally as the dark blue suit and tie he was dressed in, awkwardly shaking her hand.

Anton and Aoife never knew how to act around one another. While he was technically her stepfather, circumstances had conspired against them becoming close. She was sure in another lifetime the two of them may have been on more cordial terms, but with her virtual estrangement from her mother, the fact that he was not her first stepfather and unlikely to be her last, and that she essentially saw him as a puppet of her mother's, worked against the two of them becoming anything more than just acquaintances. Aoife knew from experience not to get too attached; the next thing she knew, her mother would probably divorce him and move on to the next husband. It was easier just to keep her distance for the time being.

Aoife settled herself in her chair.

"Can I get you anything to drink?" a waiter asked her, nearly frightening her. She hadn't noticed him pop up beside her. She looked at the table before her and noticed her mother was drinking wine, while Anton was drinking a beer. She toyed with the possibility of getting through this evening without alcohol and waved it away, almost laughing out loud at the notion. There was no way in hell she was making it out of this dinner without being drunk. Dinner with her mother was like an extreme drinking game; every time her mother said something critical of her, Aoife drank. It was amazing she'd not become an alcoholic long before now.

But, back to the question at hand.

If she had a pint like she wanted, she knew she would get the *tut tut* of disapproval from her mother and not just the look. Beer was a man's drink in her mother's opinion. However, Aoife hated wine and, if beer would garner her mother's disapproval, drinking hard liquor as Aoife *really* would have preferred, would garner outright hostility and the two of them wouldn't make it through the rest of the evening.

"Prosecco, please," she told the waiter. "Bring the bottle."

She noticed the look of disapproval at her comment about the bottle, but Aoife knew she'd need it, and likely another as well. It was a concession; it was technically wine, but at least it was something palatable.

Maureen = one win. Aoife = zero wins and one draw.

Her mother could have the early battles. So long as Aoife didn't concede the important ones, she would declare the evening a success.

"What are you thinking of having?" Maureen asked her, nodding at the menu in front of her that she hadn't even looked at yet. She picked it up.

If she thought of choosing her drink as a battle, choosing her meal was even more so. If she chose a healthy option like a salad, her mother would ask her if she'd become a vegetarian, wondering why she wasn't eating meat. If she chose something like chicken, her mother would ask her why red meat wasn't good enough for her, but if she chose the lamb or the steak, for instance, her mother would say it was too fattening and that she should be watching her weight; something her mother had been critical about since she was a child. And dessert was most certainly out of the question.

Erin Bowlen

Who the hell cares what she thinks about what you eat? If you want to eat the chicken, then eat the chicken. If you want the lamb, eat the lamb. If you want to eat an entire chocolate cake, then eat the God-damned chocolate cake. She can keep her loud-mouthed opinions to herself!

She was sorely tempted to take her own advice.

"I was thinking the coq au vin," she replied.

Maureen = one win. Aoife = one win, one draw.

She noted her mother weighing this decision. "Not going to have the lamb?"

"No, I don't feel like it today."

"You used to love the lamb."

In actual fact, Aoife had never liked the lamb. Her cousin Caitlin had, but she refrained from pointing this out to her mother because it wouldn't make any difference.

"I just don't feel like it."

"Is this how this night is going to go?" her mother asked her, her tone suddenly changing from disdain to accusatory, pinching the bridge of her nose like Aoife was one of the most exasperating people in the world.

Aoife sat up straight in her chair at the change of conversation; it was one of her mother's signature moves: find something Aoife had said or done that was perfectly harmless and turn it around to make it look like *she* was being unreasonable or mean, when it was in fact Maureen who was being unreasonable. While this little charade might seem utterly ridiculous to an outside observer, Aoife was under no illusions that she as wading into dangerous waters. Maureen was feeling the sting of losing the battle over the food to her daughter and now was looking for a way to get an easy win by riling her up. Aoife would have to be very careful if she were to win this battle round.

"Sorry?" Aoife replied, playing dumb to her mother's tricks and taking a sip of the Prosecco the silent waiter had brought before slithering into the background again, probably reporting the tension brewing between mother and daughter to his fellow colleagues. She was at least five drinks behind her mother's critiques and she needed to catch up, especially with the nastier battle brewing right in front of her.

All That Compels the Heart

"Is this how this evening is going to go? With you being difficult?" Maureen repeated her question, looking at Aoife exasperatedly.

"I'm sorry, Mother. I didn't realize I was being difficult." She tried to keep any edge from her voice, knowing it would be perceived as the very sort of attitude her mother was accusing her of.

"We barely see or hear from you since you decided to move into that place in the country, and the one time you are in town again for a visit, we are nice enough to clear our schedules in order to take you out for dinner and you give us this attitude. I had hoped that some time on your own might improve your attitude towards us, but now I see that it's only made you worse."

Breathe. Stay calm. Don't rise to the bait.

Aoife took another sip of her drink and tried to appear perfectly calm. She was distracted by Anton, who was fidgeting with the collar of his white dress shirt, clearly uncomfortable that his wife and stepdaughter were arguing, but unwilling to step in and provide any sort of help to either party. Aoife knew if he were pressed to choose between the two of them that he would choose her mother. After all, he had to live with the woman on daily basis; she didn't envy him, nor resent his allegiance.

"I apologize, Mother. I meant no offense." She tried to sound sufficiently apologetic even though there was nothing, in fact, that she needed to apologize for. She didn't even mean the words anyway; they barely held much meaning to her when used around her family, and so it didn't really cost her much to say it.

"Is everyone ready to order?"

For once, she was glad when the silent waiter slithered his way up to the table. He'd interrupted at just the right time and had turned the argument in her favour. Ending on her apology meant that she'd won this round, as Maureen wouldn't risk looking foolish in front of the help.

Maureen = one win. Aoife = two wins, one draw.

She knew she would pay for coming out ahead in the tally, but for now, she took a victorious sip of her drink. They placed their orders with the waiter who took the menus from them and scurried away like a cockroach.

Several minutes passed by in silence, no one at the table speaking to, or looking at, one another. Aoife looked calmly around the restaurant, observing the people around them. The nearest people were an elderly couple; she thought she recognized the man as a local politician, and the woman with him must be his wife. There was a party of people her mother's age on the upper floor, near the balcony railing. They looked to be celebrating a birthday or some other celebratory event. At the front of the restaurants, near the windows looking out onto the street were a few young couples, probably in their mid-thirties, probably hoping to grab a couple of hours away from their children and the demands of their jobs.

Bored with how lifeless they all looked, dressed in their fancy clothes and barely eating their overpriced meals for fear of gaining a pound, she reluctantly turned her attention back to her own table where silence still reigned supreme. She noted that her stepfather had the sense not to try to break the silence himself. One of her mother's ex-husbands had had the awful habit of feeling awkward during these long silences between mother and daughter, and had always tried to break the tension by speaking up and lightening the mood with a joke or funny anecdote. Needless to say, he hadn't lasted long. Maureen was a champion of the long, awkward silences. Anton, it seemed, while not enjoying the silence, at least knew enough not to interrupt it.

Having to concede the last argument to her daughter, Maureen's mouth was twisted petulantly. Aoife felt sorry for her mother; she knew she lived for these moments when she could tear down another person – especially if that person happened to be her own daughter – and she was upset to be losing the war. Deciding to throw her mother a bone, she decided to be the one to break the silence by asking, "So how have the two of you been?"

"Oh, very good," Anton responded, looking relieved that a ceasefire had been called. "Work is very interesting right now."

Aoife doubted that very much, or at least in her own terms of what constituted as "interesting."

"Good," she smiled at him, trying to appear conciliatory for the earlier argument.

"And you, Mother? How have you been?"

"Oh, you know. Keeping myself busy with work," Maureen patted her hair self-consciously checking to make sure it still looked perfect, somewhat mollified by having the conversation turn towards her. If there was one thing she enjoyed on the same level as tearing someone down, it was talking about herself.

"You haven't asked about your grandmother," Maureen pointed out, suddenly striking upon another way to begin an argument.

"Sorry, I was just coming to her. How is Granny?" Aoife asked, trying her best not to sound apathetic.

"Oh you know. She's not doing so well. It's the holidays. They just don't hold any joy for her now that your grandfather is gone."

Aoife nodded and took another sip of her sparkling wine. She could feel the alcohol sloshing around in her empty stomach and she knew she had to take it a bit easier or she would be drunk in no time and she wouldn't be able to win any arguments then.

And Michael isn't here to save you this time.

The thought had sprung, unwelcome, to her mind at the reminder how the last two times she'd been drunk, Michael had been there to make sure she'd gotten home safe.

I do not need Michael Flanagan to come to my rescue. I'm perfectly capable of taking care of myself. She could feel the voice in her head wanting to disagree with her, but it refrained from doing so.

"You *are* coming up to the city for Christmas, aren't you, Aoife?"

"I…" Aoife knew, of course, that she'd be expected to visit with her family over the holidays, but what with the excitement of planning their trip to Scotland fresh in her mind, she hadn't really given any thought to what she'd be doing the rest of the holidays.

The last thing she wanted was another tense Christmas with her family, especially with this being the first one without her grandfather to rely on when she needed an escape from her mother or grandmother. She would have Connor at least; he'd called yesterday to let her know that he would be home for a few days' leave over the holidays. But still, she'd rather just be with Bex and Millie for the holidays more than with anyone else.

Not even with the Flanagans? Especially, a particularly, dark, handsome one?

She took another sip of Prosecco and tried to put any thought of Michael out of her mind.

"You know it's the first Christmas without your grandfather and how difficult it's going to be on your grandmother," Maureen continued her cajoling to get Aoife home for the holidays.

"Of course... and..."

"Really, Aoife. It's the least you could do. See Anton? I told you she'd be like this."

Maureen swept a perfectly manicured hand exasperatedly, the light glinting off the diamond bracelet she was wearing. Anton, who'd previously been ignoring his wife and stepdaughter while they argued, snapped his head up at his wife's command and immediately looked like he'd rather be anywhere in the world other than where he was right now.

Aoife ground her teeth together to stop herself from saying something she'd regret. She seethed at her mother's comment that "it was the least she could do" to show up for a woman who'd done nothing in her whole life but try to make the world a more miserable place for everyone else.

It's the least you could all do to leave me the hell alone!

For once, she and the voice in her head were in agreement. It might be petty, it might be selfish, but there it was, and she didn't care what anyone else thought about it. At least this is what she told herself as she poured herself another glass of Prosecco. She took a sip to calm herself and wished the damned waiter's timing would be better and he'd arrive with their food already.

"Your grandmother isn't going to be around forever, you know. The doctor said when your grandfather died that it's often the way with older people that when one dies, the other follows shortly afterwards."

We could only be so lucky.

She immediately felt terrible for the unkind thought and mentally chastised herself for it, but it didn't prevent her from muttering under breath, "Pretty sure that's only with couples who *actually* love one another."

It earned her another disapproving glare from Maureen.

"She misses you now that you're down in the country so much. You don't come up to visit very often; she would love to see you."

"Of course, I'll be there at Christmas, Mother." She said it with a great deal more enthusiasm than she actually felt. "Bex, Millie, Danny, and I are going to Edinburgh for Hogmanay, but I'd love to spend Christmas at home this year. Connor called to say he's coming home too; it'll be wonderful to have the whole family in town again."

She wondered if her voice sounded as sickly-sweet to her mother's ears as it did to her own. If it did, Maureen showed no sign of it.

Score one for Maureen.

The waiter appeared then and placed their orders silently in front of them.

Where the hell were you earlier? she wanted to shout at him. Instead, she glared pointedly at him from across the top of her glass and noticed his apprehensive look before he slithered away again, wondering what he'd done to deserve her ire.

"Is there anything else I can get you?" he asked, retreating as quickly as was polite to do, still looking concerned at Aoife's menacing glare.

"No, that will be all." Maureen dismissed him with a lazy flick of her wrist. The young man looked relieved and practically bolted for the kitchen.

Aoife took another sip and decided to tuck into her meal.

It's true what they say: there's no such thing as a free lunch. In this case, dinner.

While her mother may have won the biggest concession from her regarding her Christmas plans, Aoife felt proud of the groundwork she'd established on the battlefield, defining her independence from her family, even if it was not recognized by them.

You can't win them all, she reminded herself, munching contentedly on her coq au vin, pleased with the choice she'd made.

※※※

After her dinner with Maureen and Anton, Aoife felt exhausted. She'd made quick goodbyes to her parents, relieved she wouldn't have to be burdened with the experience of dining with them again until Christmas, and had hailed a cab back to her flat.

Immediately, she noticed the silence, the emptiness of the place.

"Danny?" she called down the hallway, even though she knew from the silence he wasn't there. There was always some sort of noise when another person was in your flat, some awareness that you were not alone. But right now, the only thing of Danny's in her flat was the lingering scent of his aftershave.

Sure enough, pulling her mobile out of her purse, she noticed the blue light flashing, indicating that she'd missed a call. She listened to the message.

"Hey babe; just wanted to say that I got called out to the office in Spain for the next couple of weeks, and also to let you know that I won't be in Dublin for Christmas this year, and I won't be able to make it to Hogmanay. All the managers are required to go on one of those stupid team-building exercise conferences or some such bullshit. After Spain, they want us to fly down to the Caribbean to do one of those stupid managers' retreats. We're going to be stuck on a cruise boat for ten days. Anyways, Mum and Dad said they were going to just spend the holiday down in the Caribbean anyways, so I might as well spend it with them. You know what my mother's like. She's complaining how she never sees me."

Considering she'd just gotten the same diatribe from her own mother, Aoife had some idea.

All That Compels the Heart

Aoife didn't really know Danny's parents that well. She'd only ever met them the once in all the years they had been dating, and that had really only been briefly. Danny's parents owned a six-bedroom villa on the island of St. Lucia and they spent most of their time there, especially since his father retired. His parents had invited the two of them to come down and have a visit for a week and, feeling like she should meet his parents, she had agreed to go. They weren't really unlike her own family, cut from the same cloth, really, and so Aoife hadn't really been bothered to spend any time with them beyond that initial meeting.

While she was disappointed by Danny's message to let her know he wouldn't be joining them on the Hogmanay trip, she felt sorry for him rather than angry. It wasn't like he was going to have an enjoyable time in the Caribbean with his parents. Besides, she'd have been lying to herself and everyone if she'd said that she hadn't been expecting it, even just a little.

She sighed, knowing she was going to have to call Bex and Millie and let them know that Danny wasn't going to be able to make the trip. She knew they were not going to be surprised by the news either, and they'd probably be secretly relieved he couldn't go, even though they'd try to hide it from her. She supposed she shouldn't be too hard on them; they *had* planned the trip with him and invited him along in the first place, even if they'd only done it out of obligation. But still, they hadn't put up a fuss when he' originally agreed to go with them.

Exiting her voicemail, she looked up Bex's name in her Contacts section and pressed her number, listening to her phone dial her friend.

Chapter Thirty-One

After a couple of weeks back in Dublin, Aoife had finally had enough. Confident she'd dutifully put in an appropriate amount of time with her family, and with her anxiety from being around them beginning to spike to unusually high levels, she'd decided to return to Ballyclara.

Walking into the grocer's, she spied Brendan at the end of her aisle. As he went to pick a bag of flour off the shelf and put it in his basket, he noticed her standing there.

"Hello Aoife. Have a nice trip back home, did we?" he called out to her.

"Hi Brendan," she returned his friendly smile and walked down the aisle to talk to him. "Well, some of it was good, some of it, well, let's just say that I'd rather talk about you and how you've been."

"Oh, well there's nothing much new on this front. Been working hard. This one's been a slave driver ever since you left."

Michael came around from the other aisle at just that moment to join his friend, carrying an assortment of fresh vegetables, which he placed in the basket Brendan was holding. He clapped Michael on the shoulder in a vice-like grip at the mention of his name, bringing him into the conversation.

Laying eyes on Aoife, she saw his face draw slightly into a frown and she felt her own face contorting from the pleasant smile she'd given Brendan, into an implacably cool glare.

"What are you saying about me?" he asked, not acknowledging Aoife's presence or offering her a greeting.

"Oh, just that you've been your ever pleasant and wonderful self lately," Brendan replied with a smile on his face.

Michael glared back, knowing his friend was lying.

Aoife tried to politely hide her smile at Brendan's joke. Inexplicably feeling sorry that they were teasing him, she asked Michael, "How's Eliza?"

She'd barely asked the question before Brendan, who'd now moved slightly behind Michael, coughed as if he were trying to cover up her question and made a gesture for her to stop talking. Confused, Aoife stared at him until she realized that something must have happened between Michael and Eliza while she'd been away. But by then, Michael had turned around, raising an eyebrow suspiciously at his friend, who coughed politely into his hand again.

"Must be a cold coming on or something," he replied feebly.

Michael simply rolled his eyes. "Well, don't cough near the vegetables. We don't need the punters catching your cold and blaming us for it."

He snatched the basket out of Brendan's hand and turned to Aoife to say, "We broke up."

He shrugged as if to brush it off.

"Oh, I'm sorry," she replied, realizing she actually *was* sorry for him. Even though she didn't exactly like Eliza, or Michael for that matter, she didn't want to see them broken up either.

"It's grand. I'm grand," he responded, a little too quickly, like someone who was most certainly *not* fine about the situation. "Now, I'd like to go and pay for these so we can get back to the pub and get back to work. One of us needs to do some work around the place or we'll never get paid."

He stalked off towards the cashier.

"Wow, what happened?" Aoife asked. It was none of her business, but she found herself curious.

"Not sure what exactly happened this time," Brendan said watching Michael as he paid for his stuff. "But I hope this time that it's for good."

She'd heard Brendan and Father Patrick give much the same sentiment before, but still, it surprised her.

"Don't get me wrong; I want to see him as happy as the next person. After all, he *is* my best friend. But, I also don't think the life he's looking for, he's going to find with the likes of Eliza Kennedy. It'd be best for the both of them if this time they just realize that they're done and over with. It's time he moved on with someone new."

Aoife found herself not quite sure how to respond to this statement. Thankfully, she was thankfully saved by the arrival of Father Patrick.

"Oh hello, Brendan. Aoife," he said to them, nodding his head in greeting. "And what brings you all out on this cold day?"

"Needed to pick up a few things for the pub, Father. The wife's orders," Brendan replied humorously.

"Ah yes, and the husband must obey the wife's orders as quickly as he does God's, for both are just as wrathful as the other at times," he replied with a twinkle in his eye. "And what about you, Miss O'Reilly?"

"Oh, I was up to Dublin the last couple of weeks to visit with friends and family. I realized when I got back that there wasn't anything to eat in the refrigerator, so I decided to come out and get a few things."

"Ah, Dublin City. I suppose you'll be spending more time up there, what with the holidays right around the corner," he said to her as they walked to the front of the store to pay for their goods. Michael was waiting impatiently by the door for Brendan.

At the sight of Father Patrick, his face turned friendlier and he came over to the elderly man saying, "Here, Father, let me carry that. Aoife?"

All That Compels the Heart

She realized Michael was holding his hand out to her, offering to take her basket as well. She handed it to him, shrugging. It wasn't all that heavy but she didn't mind him carrying it even though she was fairly certain he was doing it more out of impatience to get him and Brendan back to work, than out of kindness.

"Yes. I'm planning on going up for Christmas Day to spend with the family. A couple of my friends and I are going over to Edinburgh for Hogmanay as well," Aoife replied to the priest's question before Michael interrupted them.

"Well now, that sounds like it will be exciting!" The old man's face lit up at the mention of her trip.

"Yeah, I hope so."

"Well, if you'll be here for Christmas Eve, please feel welcome to attend the service. It's going to be quite good, if I do say so meself," he said with a proud smile.

She wasn't sure why, but she found herself saying, "Sure, that'd be nice, Father. Thank you for inviting me."

"I'll see you there," he patted her on the hand as he turned to leave with his groceries.

"See you then," nodding at his retreating form as Brendan and Michael helped him carry his things out of the store.

Chapter Thirty-Two

Christmas Eve arrived on a clear and cold night, the moon and the stars casting a white glow over the fields and road as Aoife made her way to the little stone church. The icy air felt like the prick of a needle on the inside of her lungs as she walked through the quiet darkness.

She'd had a mind to just stay inside tonight, try and keep her mind off the impending visit with her family. However, she'd resolved that she should not just sit around on Christmas Eve, hiding away in her big house by herself, moping. Instead of lying on the couch, she decided to take up Father Patrick's invite and come down for the church service, even if she wasn't exactly sure she belonged there.

The last time Aoife had attended a Christmas Eve service had been when she and Connor had gone backpacking one winter throughout southern Europe and they'd accidentally ended up in this tiny little village in central Spain right at the time when the whole village had gone to their Christmas Mass, and they'd felt too awkward to leave the service.

She was completely alone on the path now; even the sheep from her neighbour's farm had gone into the barn for the winter. The only sound was that of the frozen ground beneath her boots and Aoife's own singing voice as she hummed to herself, the torchlight app from her mobile phone swinging in front of her with the sway of her gait. A sense of peace and calmness descended upon her. As she approached the little stone church, she heard the sound of voices and could see parishioners gathering outside the front entrance. She entered the wrought-iron front gate of the churchyard, forming into an orderly queue like the rest of the parishioners waiting to go inside out of the cold.

"Aoife! I'm so glad you made it." Father Patrick's face was beaming as he greeted her at the door.

"Father Patrick," she greeted him pleasantly. "You have a packed house tonight."

She peered around the kindly priest and could only see a tiny portion of the church, but from what she could see, she could tell that every pew in the small stone church was nearly occupied.

"I don't think I'm even going to find a place to sit." She'd meant it only half-jokingly.

"Ye can sit with us."

She didn't need to turn around to recognize Michael's voice. Looking over her shoulder she saw that Sinead, Dermot, Mara, Rory, and of course, Michael stood directly behind her. Brendan, Molly, Des, Jimmy, and Karen were huddled in a group behind them and gave her a little wave in greeting. She smiled and waved back.

"Thank you. That's very gracious of you," she replied to Michael's offer, trying not to sound as surprised as she was by it.

"Sinead, Dermot. It's always wonderful to see you and your family," Father Patrick greeted the elder Flanagans as they all walked through the entrance of the church.

"We're just up here." Michael ushered with his right hand, indicating a pew three rows from the front.

As she approached the pew, she felt Rory slide in before her and all the way down to the end closest to the wall.

"I want Grandad to sit with me!" he declared.

"Rory, we don't speak like that to other people. And especially not when we are in church," Mara admonished her son.

"Oh, let him have what he wants. It's Christmas," Dermot himself admonished his own daughter. He genuflected before sliding down the pew to sit with his grandson, his daughter following closely on his heels.

Michael indicated to Sinead that she should go next and, genuflecting himself, he slid into the pew beside his mother. Aoife smoothed the skirts of the new dress she'd bought for the holidays and sat upon the hardwood pew, feeling its cool surface on the back of her thighs. She began to take off her coat, struggling with one of the sleeves, which had managed to get caught in her bracelet. Suddenly, she felt a pair of strong hands picking up the neckline of her coat. Michael was holding it for her, trying to help her with taking it off. She managed to free one of her arms but the other wouldn't budge.

"I think I'm stuck," she told him, trying to gently tug on her other arm to see if it would come free of the lining inside of her black pea-coat. Michael pulled down her jacket, letting it rest on the pew behind her, and took her wrist in his hands. Without saying anything, he reached inside her sleeve. Finding the offending threads that had managed to get themselves tangled, she felt his deft fingers unclasp her bracelet and free the threads that had gotten stuck in the clasp. Able to free herself, she slipped the rest of her coat off her arm, re-situating it around her on the pew's hard surface. She wanted some padding under her bottom as she sat on its hard surface. When she'd gotten herself situated, Michael held out her bracelet for her.

"Thanks," she said quietly, reaching out to take it from him and return it to her wrist, but he held it there and she realized he was going to put it on for her. She held out her wrist to him, watching how he was so careful with the small clasp of the Celtic-knot-style bracelet, his fingers seeming almost too big to do the job, but he deftly secured it around her wrist once more. He didn't reply, just nodded at her, looking her up and down, a faint glow of surprise in his eyes like he'd only just really seen her for the first time that night.

It was an unsettling feeling and she immediately felt self-conscious, although she wasn't sure why. It wasn't like she hadn't received more severe glances from him in the past. But this time, it was somehow different.

She was wearing a new dress tonight; a sleeveless, high-necked, red silk one with an A-line skirt that fell mid-thigh. She was feeling like she might be slightly over-dressed when she looked around her and saw that everyone was mostly in their regular Sunday clothes she'd seen them in down at the pub on Sunday afternoons after church.

"That's a lovely dress, Aoife." Sinead leaned around Michael to compliment her.

"Thank you."

Music from the old slightly-out-of-tune piano at the front of the church resounded through the church as the altar boys and Father Patrick made their way up to the front, interrupting any chance of a conversation with Sinead.

Aoife settled in against the pew and listened to the priest's words as he conducted his service. A sense of peace descended on her with the ease of familiarity and kindness the old priest had, relaxing her and making her feel like she was sitting in his sitting room having a conversation with him rather than sitting in a church on a cold, hardwood pew during a service.

"Now, let us sing."

Father Patrick sat down as the music began to play.

"Hark the herald angel sing…" Aoife began to sing the familiar Christmas carol.

Standing beside Michael as she heard him sing, she realized Dermot had been right. Michael *was* a good singer. He had a rich baritone, a little rough around the edges from disuse, but still a fine voice. There was something about it that reminded her of her grandfather's singing voice, and a sudden awful sadness filled her, chilling her to the bone in a way that was colder and deeper than the cold outside had ever felt.

"Are ye alright?"

The sound of Michael's whispered voice beside her ear made her realize that she'd begun to cry, the tears running quietly down her cheeks. She looked up at him and saw the look of concern in his eyes, genuine concern for her.

"Sorry," she muttered.

She hurriedly placed her songbook in the holder on the pew in front of her and carefully stepped out of the pew into the aisle, hurrying down it towards the entrance of the church. She pushed the old, heavy wood and wrought-iron door open, the cold air smacking her on the face, the wind whipping strands of her loose curls into her eyes. She wrapped her bare arms around herself feeling goose pimples form under her fingertips.

She took a few steps until she was around the corner of the building and leaned against the cold, hard stone wall, feeling its rough edges against the silk fabric of her dress. She leaned heavily against its solidness, fairly certain that it was the only thing holding her up right now as her frozen, bare legs felt oddly weak beneath her. The tears on her face had cooled when they'd touched the air, leaving cold streaks on her cheeks, and she pushed the curls out of her eyes, wiping carefully at the tears, careful not to smudge her make-up.

"Aoife? Are ye alright?"

She jumped at the sound of Michael's voice as he rounded the corner of the church and stood before her.

"Jesus!" She leaned forward, clutching her heart, racing in her chest with the shock he'd given her.

"Sorry. I didn't mean to frighten ye. I was just worried."

"It's alright. I just wasn't expecting anyone to follow me out here. I'm grand."

Of course she wasn't fine. It was why he'd come out here in the first place, because she was acting like a madwoman right now.

"Clearly you're not." The tone of his voice indicated that he wasn't going to expect any argument to the contrary.

"Do you always have to turn every conversation into an argument?"

She hadn't meant it to come out quite like that, but with the weight of the crushing sadness from over the loss of her grandfather making it feel like there was an elephant sitting on her chest, and with him being so oddly *normal* with her – which was extremely *unnatural* for him – she wasn't sure how she should be feeling right now. It was enough work just trying not to have a complete meltdown right here in the churchyard.

He shrugged when she yelled at him, as if to silently say that he understood she didn't mean what she was saying. Except that she *did* mean what she was saying, and it only made her feel angrier with him that he wouldn't validate her feelings by getting angry with her in return. Arguing with Michael had somehow become commonplace between them and she needed something commonplace and familiar right now.

"I'm not arguing with you; I'm just stating a fact that happens to disagree with ye right now."

She paced before him like a caged animal prowling the confines of its cage.

"And that wasn't an argument right there?"

"No. It's another fact. Just because you don't like my facts, Aoife, doesn't mean I'm arguing with ye."

She looked up at him, trying to think of something to say in retort that wouldn't sound like she was proving him right. *Of course* she knew she was arguing with him, trying to pick a fight, but stupid, stubborn pride wouldn't let her admit it.

"Would ye stop pacing?"

The question threw her off-guard and she inadvertently acquiesced. Still feeling a well of nervous energy inside her, she tried to quell it and leaned once more against the stone wall of the church. When she'd settled herself, he cautiously approached her, coming to stand beside her.

"Here."

She saw the flash moonlight glinting off something metal in the dark of the churchyard. There must have been just enough light in the shadows of the church for him to see her sceptical look. Or, perhaps he just knew she would be wary of anything he tried to offer her.

"A peace offering."

She took the flask from him, feeling the icy metal beneath her fingers and held it there in front of her.

"Go on; it's not poison. Just whiskey," he replied before she had time to ask him. "It'll warm ye up and help calm ye down."

She took a sip of it, the amber liquid warming her throat and her insides pleasantly on this cold night. Aoife could swear it had somehow gotten colder since she'd gone into the church. Perhaps it was just the fact that she was standing out here in nothing but her sleeveless dress, having left her coat inside on the pew, but the air around her seemed chillier than before.

"Thanks," she told him, handing it back to him. As he took it back from her, his fingers brushed hers. They were still somewhat warm from being inside the church and felt comforting against her now chilled hands.

"You're freezing," he stated.

She'd selfishly thought of refuting his statement to prove him wrong, but her body betrayed her and shivered.

"Here," he said, taking off the red scarf he'd left around his neck when he'd been sitting in the church and placed it around her own, adjusting it so that it would provide the most warmth on the cold night. Both of them knew it would hardly protect her from the cold, dressed as she was, but it was the gesture that mattered, the fact that he cared enough to worry about her being cold.

She gently lifted her hair up, letting the curls fall on the outside of the scarf and pulled it in closer to her neck. The soft material was still warm from being around his own neck. It smelled of the cold air around them, wood smoke, and Michael's cologne.

She leaned back against the stone wall of the church and wrapped her arms around herself. Michael took his cues from her and leaned his back against the wall as well, the two of them just standing there in the cold night, looking up at the stars. He stood close enough to her that the fabric of his wool jumper brushed against her bare shoulder, the warmth of his body emanating towards her, through the fabric. The world around them was quiet; only a slight breeze rustling along the ground, and the shriek of an owl finding its prey. She wasn't sure if it was the emotions still welling up inside her, or the reassurance of his presence beside her, or just his silence that made her feel like she needed to talk, but she was the first to break through the quiet of the night.

"It was the song," she said finally, breaking the silence of the night. "It was my grandfather's favourite Christmas carol."

She swallowed hard, trying to keep the lump that was stubbornly trying to form in her throat at bay.

"I think it just reminded me of him and then I began thinking about how I won't be seeing him tomorrow when I go up to Dublin to visit with my family, and to be honest, he's the main reason I would even go…" Her voice trailed off, the lump refusing to stay away. She cleared her throat hard, temporarily releasing the pressure on it.

"It's silly really. I mean, it's been months now since he's passed away. I know in my head that he's not alive… I think everything just got the better of me. And now the whole village probably thinks I'm a total eejit."

She leaned her head against the wall, the cold, rough stone pricking her scalp and she closed her eyes, trying not to focus on how silly she must seem to everyone now.

She felt, more than saw, Michael nod. There was only the moon and stars to light up the night, the stained glass windows of the little stone church offering little more than an orange glow from its panes. He didn't say anything to her, just stood there with her.

He was good at that, she realized; just being there. Michael had been there for her during some of the times when she'd really needed a friend, ready to just be there for her and do whatever needed doing. She realized how dependable, reliable, he'd been with her, even when he was driving her crazy.

"Grief doesn't have a time limit." His voice was soft and gentle, soothing. "I can't say that I know what you're going through. My grandparents were all gone by the time I was a teenager. It's a rare thing to be in your twenties and still have your grandparents around you. A special thing. But, I know the other side of it is that you have time to form a deeper attachment, and so it makes it all the harder when they're gone."

She looked up at him, thinking it was the nicest and most profound thing she'd ever heard him say before.

"I think that some people come into our lives and no matter how much or how little time we have with them, they leave a lasting impression on us," she said, acknowledging that he *did* know how she was feeling, at least when it came to grief. Some wounds just never healed; you just learned to live with the pain.

A light wind came up then, its icy fingers caressing her face and hair, making her shiver with its freezing touch. Michael shifted beside her. She knew he was only staying out here because of her and she felt a pang of guilt. Even though he wasn't shivering – unlike herself, she noted, whose shivering had become more pronounced the longer they'd been out there despite the scarf Michael had loaned her – she knew that he had to have been just as cold as she was. Nevertheless, he stood there, leaning against the cold stones of the church wall, like he could have been standing there on a summer's day, the weather inconsequential to him.

"It's not difficult to see how much he meant to you. I imagine it has to be extremely difficult to go through the 'firsts' – the first Christmas, the first birthday – without him." There was a slight catch in his voice, which he disguised behind a light cough. She imagined it brought up memories of his "firsts" after he and Eliza had gone through their miscarriages and how difficult it had been.

"I just wish there was a way to stop the feelings, you know? Something to make them just go away," she suddenly blurted out, not sure how to acknowledge his grief and her own at the same time.

"No ye don't, and ye know it. The fact you're feeling anything for him even after he's gone means that you cared for him. They say that the opposite of love is indifference. I think you'd rather have loved him and lost him, than have lived indifferently towards him."

She felt him glance over at her, and she looked up, seeing the passion in his eyes on this particular subject.

It was her time to nod silently, not sure what else to say. He was right, of course. She wouldn't have given up a second of time she had gotten to spend with her grandfather, even if it meant that she had to go through this grief again. She knew he felt the same about his unborn children.

"I'm not going to say that it's going to get easier, but I think you'll find a way some day to just live with it and move forward in spite of it."

All That Compels the Heart

"You're surprisingly good at cheering a person up, even if you have the bleakest advice." The words had just sort of come out before she knew what she was saying. "I'm sorry, Michael; I didn't mean it. I appreciate you being kind enough to try and help me. It can't be easy for you, given what you've gone through."

Even though it was too dark to tell for sure, she thought she saw the glint of a smile from him.

Rather than respond right away, he leaned his head back against the wall again, cocking his head towards the window above them.

"It sounds like they're almost done," he finally said.

"I suppose that means we should go back inside…"

"Good. I was hoping you'd make that suggestion. I'm freezing me arse off out here. I'm surprised you're not a block of ice." He'd said it with a laugh, no hint of impatience or anger towards her for staying out here so long. She wholeheartedly believed he'd have stayed out here with her all night without a word of complaint if she'd asked him to. It was a comforting thought.

"Though, from the way your hands feel, ye may just turn into a block of ice soon enough." He took her hands in his, rubbing them gently, trying to coax the blood to flow through them again.

"Thank you."

He brought her fingers up to his mouth and blew lightly on her fingertips, his warm breath tickling her skin as blood began to flow back into them. As if realizing how incredibly intimate the gesture was, he paused for a second and looked at her to see if she gave her consent. She nodded and he continued to blow gently on them and rubbed them. Seemingly satisfied that her fingers wouldn't fall off from frostbite, he simply replied, "You're welcome."

He let go of her hands and wrapped his arms around himself as he half-leaned against the church wall, warming his own fingertips under his armpits. She was just trying to think of a way to avoid making this awkward and thought about just heading inside the church to break the tension building between them, when she remembered how she'd exited the church earlier. She groaned at the thought of having to go in and explain politely to everyone in the village why she'd rushed out here in such a hurry.

"Come on," Michael said to her, silently picking up on how she was feeling. He nodded to her and pushed off from the stone wall of the church.

"Where are we going?"

"On an adventure."

She saw the flash of white teeth in the white light of the moon.

"An adventure?"

"Yes, an adventure. You'll be grand. Trust me."

You survived the last one. Surely you'll be fine with whatever "adventure" he takes you on now.

Choosing to trust him, she placed her hand in his.

They rounded the side of the little church, and skirted their way carefully around the edge of the walled-in cemetery, careful not to slip on the patch of ice that had formed from some run-off rain from the roof. A cloud drifted past the moon, letting more light shine on the cemetery around them and her eye caught two small headstones, both with *Flanagan* etched across them. She didn't need to read the dates to know who they belonged to.

It was difficult to tell in the darkness of the night where exactly they were going until they crossed the path that intersected the east end of the cemetery and saw that he was taking her towards the little priest's house on the edge of the property.

"Wait. We're not breaking into Father Patrick's, are we?" Aoife asked him, placing a hand on his upper arm just before he opened the door.

"Breaking in? Don't ye trust me, yet Aoife?"

She looked at him, surprised by the question. He'd said it like he'd meant it half-jokingly, but the look in his eyes now made her believe that perhaps he questioned her ability to trust him.

"Of course I do," she replied, without hesitation.

"Good." His voice sounded more relieved than she'd have expected. She hadn't expected him to care whether or not she believed him or trusted him with anything.

"We're not breaking in," he reassured her. "Besides, can ye really call it breaking in when the man never locks the door? No, I just wanted to get you in out of the cold while I go back to the church and fetch your coat. Besides, Father Patrick invited us all back here for some holiday cheer after the service; it's not like I wouldn't be coming back here anyways."

"Oh."

She stepped inside the small house – more of a cottage, really, and a small one at that. It was tinier than Michael's place, not even having the benefit of a second storey. It was laid out all on a single floor, the front door opening up immediately into the small sitting room, with the kitchen off to her right and a door that looked like it might lead down to the small root cellar below the house. On the other side of the sitting room was the small bedroom where Father Patrick slept. The place had no bathroom; only the outhouse at the back. A little fire crackled in the fireplace, mostly just embers now, left to burn slowly while the priest was doing his service, and easily stoked again once he returned.

"You'll be warm enough in here until I get back." Michael raised an eyebrow questioningly, even though he hadn't said it as a question.

"Yes. Here," she said, removing his scarf from around her neck. "You need it more than I do."

She reached over and he ducked his head enough for her to reach around and place it around his neck. His hands came up and touched hers as she situated it around his neck, the two of them connected once more.

"I'll be right back," he told her quietly and she let her hands fall by her sides. He turned to go then, wrapping the scarf tighter around his neck as he pulled open the door and headed into the night air again, quickly running across the churchyard.

Aoife looked around the empty sitting room, suddenly unsure of what to do with herself now that she was alone. She decided that she would, at the very least, stoke the fire and try to get warm again. The embers glowed red and let off a plume of embers as she used the poker to stir them up a bit. A puff of smoke rose, making its way out the little, soot-stained chimney. She stood close to the fireplace, feeling the warmth of the little fire as it slowly came back to life and observed the small sitting room before her. There was a small settee opposite the fireplace, a pair of wooden rocking chairs with little knit cushions providing some comfort for those bottoms sitting on their hard surfaces, and an old armchair with a very dated and faded floral pattern on it. A faded rug, whose pattern was now undetermined due to years of peoples' feet treading upon it, lay under her own feet in front of the stone fireplace.

The mantle of the fireplace was decorated with various things: a couple of black and white photographs of smiling people that Aoife assumed were either family members or friends of Father Patrick's. One of them looked to be of a man in uniform circa World War II and had a faint look of the elderly priest. She wondered if it was, in fact, a younger version of the priest, or perhaps a brother or cousin of his?

She realized then that she knew very little about the priest whom she'd come to think of as a friend. Father Patrick rarely spoke about himself in the times they'd talked since she'd gotten lost in the fog. Granted, they'd spoken a great many times to one another since that day, but as much as they had, he'd managed to deflect any questions about himself and his past with the expertise of a therapist, always deflecting questions back onto his patient. She knew from his accent that he was not from here; he sounded more like he was from the west coast, possibly Galway. He never talked about where he grew up or who his family was, he was always more interested in her and what was going on in her life, or sometimes providing her with some tidbit of gossip from the village.

Other things on the mantle included a hand-stitched Irish blessing:

May the road rise up to meet you.
May the wind be always at your back.
May the sun shine warm upon your face;
the rains fall soft upon your fields and until we meet again,
may God hold you in the palm of His hand.

All That Compels the Heart

As with everything in the small cottage, it was old and faded, the white background having once been crisply white had become off-white with age and the blue letters once a brilliant cerulean were now pale. Little flowers formed the border of the design, lovingly made, and she wondered who had made it for him.

She didn't have time to ponder for she noticed movement beyond the lace curtains of the sitting room window and heard voices outside the house. The wooden door creaked loudly as Father Patrick pushed it open, admitting entrance to himself and the Flanagans.

"Aoife! We were worried about you," Mara said, coming over to her and giving her a quick hug. She pulled back a bit to have a look at her, a questioning look in her eye but didn't have time to ask her how she was before Michael stepped in and said, "Here you go."

He held out her coat, scarf, and hat to her.

"Thanks, Michael." She gave him a small, grateful smile in return.

He just nodded, going quiet once again. She took her things from his hands and began putting them on.

"You're not leaving so soon, are you, love? I thought ye might stay awhile with us." Sinead looked at her expectantly.

"I… uh…" struggling to find the polite words to turn her down. It was more difficult than she'd expected. Dermot and Sinead were always so kind to her, she felt rude not spending time with them. However, she also desperately wanted to get out of here before any questions were asked about her abrupter departure in the middle of the service.

"Oh come on, Ma. Don't guilt her into staying if she wants to go home," Michael cajoled his mother.

Aoife gave him a grateful look at his show of support.

"I'm not guilting her," Sinead replied stubbornly, even though it was exactly what she'd been intending to do.

"Sinead is right; you don't need to rush off so soon," Father Patrick piped up, taking Sinead's side. "Stay with us and have a drink. Ye look half-frozen to death. I can't just let you head out into the cold again without letting ye warm up a bit. Besides, I have the best mulled wine brewing in the kitchen right now. It's a family recipe. Ye won't want to miss out on it. Dermot, you'll agree with me on that, won't you?"

"It's true," Dermot agreed. "It's the best mulled wine in at least the entire county, if not the whole country."

Even though she wanted to turn him down, there was something so eager in his kind, elderly face – like a kid on Christmas Day – that wouldn't let her say no to him.

"Alright. But just one cup. I need to be sober enough to drive to Dublin in the morning," she warned him, caving into the guilt.

"Of course! How much trouble do ye think you'll get up to in a priest's house, anyways?" He smiled at her with a twinkle in his eyes as he took her coat, hat, and scarf from her and hung it up on a hook by the door with the others.

"Please, everyone have a seat. I'll be right back with some cups."

"Would ye like some help?" Sinead offered, more used to being the one serving others than being served herself.

"No, no. I wouldn't dream of it. You all take a breather and I'll be right back."

And with that, Father Patrick disappeared into the little kitchen. They could hear the sound of cupboards being opened and the clink of cups being placed on the wooden countertops.

"Ye should've made a run for it," Michael whispered in her ear, and moving to take one of the chairs at the priest's request. He'd settled himself in one of the rocking chairs, removing the knit cushion from its spot resting against the back of the chair, and placed it on his lap, clearly unsure of whether or not it would be appropriate to place it on the floor. Taking her son's cue, Sinead sat in the chair opposite Michael, and Mara and Aoife sat themselves on the settee. Dermot was the only one not sitting, standing by the window.

"I dare say that ye might not make it to Dublin in the morning, Aoife," Dermot told her, standing by the window and looking out at the night sky. "It feels like there's snow in the air."

"Snow?" his daughter asked, incredulous. "We haven't had snow at Christmas for years, Da. I hardly doubt Mother

Nature is about to start now. I mean, the last time we had snow must have been when Michael and I were kids."

"You were seventeen," Sinead reminded her. "I remember we had a very cold, clear night on Christmas Eve, just like tonight, and the next morning we woke up, there was snow everywhere. A good inch of it too. I remember we had to call over to Dermot's father – Michael lives in his cottage now – to let him know that his supper was going to have to be delayed because we had to shovel our way out, and then Michael and Dermot had to go over to his place and help shovel him out so we could carry the pots and pans of food over to his place.

"He was mostly homebound by that time," she said to Aoife, giving her some context.

"I remember that," Father Patrick said coming into the room carrying a tray with cups of varying shapes and sizes, each one steaming with warm mulled wine inside. "Old Liam Flanagan called down to me that morning and said, "Pat, do ye think ye could convince the Good Lord to melt the snow a bit faster? I'm hungry and missing out on me Christmas dinner because of this weather. If I'd the choice between a white Christmas and Sinead's Christmas dinner; I'll take the dinner."

They all chuckled.

"Liam never did like anything to get between him and his dinner. I remember he once told me after a service that I'd done a good job, but if I could be a little less long-winded the next time, that'd be excellent, because he was ten minutes late for his dinner that day."

Aoife took the mug Father Patrick offered her as he finished his story. It was warm in her hands, the aroma wafting up to her nose filled with the scent of oranges, cinnamon, nutmeg, and red wine. The heady mixture tickled her nostrils.

"Here, Da," Michael said, rising from the rocking chair and returning the cushion to it, seeing his father looking around the room for a place to sit, but not wanting to bother any of the people already seated around the fire. Dermot looked like he was going to protest, but Michael had already crossed the tiny sitting room and sat down on the floor next to where Aoife sat on the settee, his shoulder resting gently against her knee. Even though it might have been the proper thing to do, she didn't move her leg away from him, maintaining the physical connection between them. Dermot obliged his son, settling himself into the low rocking chair with a bit of a groan, as if his joints had given him a spot of trouble. He too looked perplexed as to what to do with the knit cushion behind his back, and finally settled on leaving it in its place, squirming his lower back around to try and find a comfortable spot.

A pleasant silence descended on the assembled group as they sipped their mulled wine. She was nearing the end of her mug, the wine sloshing around in her insides and warming her from the inside out. The silence seemed odd with all of the Flanagans assembled, and Aoife realized why: Rory wasn't there.

"Where's Rory at?" she asked Mara.

"Oh, he went with Brendan and Molly. We let him open one of his presents before church and he wanted to show off his new toy to Desmond, so I let him go with them for a bit. Speaking of which, I should probably go down and get him…" she said, taking a huge gulp of her mulled wine.

"I'll go and get him." Michael stirred at Aoife's feet, setting his mug on the floor and rose to his feet, carefully bending down to pick up the cup without spilling any dregs of wine on the floor. He'd rested his hand gently on Aoife's knee to steady himself as he'd leaned down and as he straightened, their eyes met. Suddenly self-conscious, he cleared his throat and removed his hand, straightening up.

"I should go too," Aoife found herself saying. She wasn't just saying it because she wanted to spend more time with Michael. In fact, she wanted to just get back to the safety of her home and forget that most of tonight had ever happened. She'd made enough of a fool of herself in front of the whole village, and Michael. She knew when the wine wore off in the morning she'd be mulling over every foolish thing she'd done and regretting all of them.

"So soon?" Father Patrick and Sinead both asked.

"Yeah, I'm feeling a bit tired, and I have to get up early to go to Dublin in the morning. I should probably get some rest," she told them, setting her cup down beside Michael's and walking over to where Father Patrick had hung her coat.

"I'll walk you home." Michael came over to join her, putting on his boots.

"You don't need to. Brendan and Molly's is in the opposite direction..."

"I can take the long way into the village. It will give me time to clear my head. I swear this mulled wine gets stronger every year you make it, Father." He patted the priest kindly on the shoulder in jest.

"It's the same recipe every time. You're just getting less able to hold your liquor the older you get, Michael," Father Patrick teased him.

"Thank you for inviting me tonight, Father. I had a great time," Aoife told him, hoping he wouldn't take offense to her leaving so soon.

"You're welcome any time, child. And not just on Sundays or holidays either. Don't be a stranger." He smiled up at her hopefully.

"I won't, I promise."

Aoife smiled at him and made a move to put on her coat when she noticed it wasn't on the hook by the door. When she looked up, she saw Michael standing there holding it out to her. He held her jacket open while she slipped it on and did it up, putting on her knit hat and wrapping her scarf tightly around her neck. As Michael opened the front door to the priest's house, a blast of icy wind greeted them.

"Good night!" Aoife waved to the rest of the Flanagans and the priest as she exited the house, careful to pull the door shut tightly behind her. She stuck her bare hands in her pockets and debated taking the time to put her gloves on, feeling them in the bottom of her pockets. As Michael had already gone a considerable ways across the churchyard, she decided against it and hurried to catch up with him.

The two walked silently side-by-side up the road a bit before she turned to him and said, "What did you tell them?"

"Hmmm?"

It had been a question on her mind since Father Patrick and the Flanagans had come back to the priest's house. None of them had spoken to her about why she had left the church in tears, so she knew Michael must have said something to them.

"Father Patrick, and your family. What did you tell them about me running out of the church like a madwoman? They didn't ask me any questions about it after they showed up at Father Patrick's house, so you must have told them something to explain it to them."

"I told them that you're a crazy girl from the city and it's not possible to know exactly why ye do the things you do."

There was mirth in his chuckle. She could see him smile at her in the moonlight. She wasn't sure if it was the wine or the fact that he'd actually laughed and smiled in her presence, but she laughed along with him too.

"Seriously, what did you say to them."

"I told them that Father Patrick's sermon had bored you to tears and that ye needed to go out into the cold air to wake up. He just wouldn't stop prattling on, would he?" He chuckled again.

"Michael, I'm being serious," she said, trying to contain her laughter and make her face look as serious as she could.

"Does it really matter? I mean, it could be that they're just not as interested in you as ye think they are." His voice was a bit more serious this time, and she could tell if he was wondering if it really *was* that important to her.

She supposed it wasn't. Whatever he'd said, it had done the trick and none of them had bothered her about it.

Just take the win.

She nodded to her subconscious, agreeing with herself.

They walked on again in silence, that comfortable, pleasant silence the two of them had with one another when they weren't arguing over something. It was an oddly reassuring thing for her; she didn't think she'd ever felt so comfortable around someone to be completely silent with them.

She tried not to dwell too much on this thought and what it all meant. Instead, she focused on the clouds above them, moving in swiftly and quietly, obscuring the moonlight that was lighting their way home. As one of said clouds passed over them, she reached out and grabbed Michael's arm, suddenly unable to see the path ahead of her clearly. Worried about ice and the amount of wine she'd had to drink, she wasn't entirely sure she was going to make it down the road without a little help. Sensing her worry, he reached out to her, tucking her hand in the crook of his elbow, letting her lean on him for support.

"Do you think your father is right? That there's snow coming?" she asked him, breaking the silence.

He looked up at the sky above them. "Perhaps."

She didn't have time to think of some other talking point, as she saw the roof of Aldridge Manor rising on the ridge above them. All too soon, they were standing outside her front door.

"Well, this is me," she said, pointing to the house.

Of course this is you, you eejit. It's not like he doesn't know where you live. He's only completely restored the place for you and been in here several times.

"Well... goodnight," he said to her, clearly unsure what else he should say.

"Goodnight."

He nodded and began to step away, letting her hand fall beside her, the connection between them broken. For some unknown reason, she felt the need to prolong their time together.

"Michael?"

"Hmm?" he asked, turning around like he'd been hoping she'd say something to him.

"Thank you. For tonight," was all she could think to come up with. It didn't nearly cover all of what she wanted to say to him, but it would suffice.

"You're welcome," he told her and turned once more to head back into the village to pick up Rory. He'd gotten two steps when he turned around and said, "Be careful on the roads tomorrow. With the snow."

He looked up at the sky, indicating the gathering clouds.

"I will," she promised. He nodded to her once again and disappeared into the fading moonlight, heading back into the village.

Chapter Thirty-Three

Aoife woke to a chilly room, the embers in the fireplace having gone cold some hours before. She snuggled deeper under the covers and tried to fall back to sleep. It was no use. She knew she'd have to get up sooner or later, and it should be *sooner* rather than later. Admitting defeat, she grudgingly threw the duvet off her and sat upright in bed, feeling the chilly wooden floorboards beneath her feet. Through the curtains of her window she could see snow lightly falling. Intrigued, she crossed the floor to the window and brushed the curtain aside to find that the world she'd become accustomed to had been transformed into a magical, snow-covered place. It was a rare sight; Ireland was not known for getting much snow, even in the dead of winter. So, to wake up and suddenly find ten centimetres of it on the ground was quite the shock.

There was a quiet hush over the house and the world beyond it, so quiet that she could hear the snow falling to the ground, the little ice particles tapping at the window. A layer of freezing rain lay on top of the snow, making it sparkle in the early morning light. She sat down on the little window seat, enthralled as she watched the storm blanket the countryside. She hadn't seen this much snow in Dublin since she was seven years old when a freak snow squall had shut down the entire city. It had all melted by the next day, of course, but for that one Christmas morning, the world outside her window had been a winter wonderland and she'd stayed there for hours, just watching the snow fall.

She crossed the room to her closet and began throwing on some warm clothes – a respectable black jumper with little sequins around the neckline for some added festiveness, a small pearl necklace her grandmother had given her years ago with a matching set of earrings, and a pair of black trousers – and headed downstairs to put on her boots and coat and prepared herself to go out in the cold.

The snow was pristine, but not in a clinical or impersonal way; more in a picture perfect way. The only problem was that with all this snow, and not having snow tires on her car – because who needed them in Ireland anyways? – she wasn't entirely sure she was going to make it to Dublin today. Nevertheless, her grandmother's nagging voice in her ear propelled her forward, right into a shallow snowdrift.

"Ah jaysis!" she exclaimed. Her body twisted around like a skater pirouetting on ice and she landed squarely on her back, a little puff of fluffy snow settling around her.

"Owwwww," she groaned, feeling a dull pain in her side where she'd bumped her hip. She'd forgotten that her riding boots did not have the proper treads for walking on ice-covered snow.

She lay there a few seconds, looking up at the great grey sky above her, until the falling flakes of snow in her eyes began to annoy her. Sighing, she pulled herself to her feet, thankful no one was around to see her flail and almost fall again. Her once magical wonderland was starting to become a right – almost literal – pain in the arse.

Or in the hip, rather.

She delicately rubbed at her sore hip. None of this was not boding well for her journey, for she began to realize one thing as she stood there looking at her car, buried beneath the snow: she didn't have a way to clean it off. She supposed she could use her mittened hands, but if she was having trouble even getting to her car, if she *could* clean it off, how was she supposed to get it out of the drive? She pondered this predicament a moment.

"If I can clear enough snow from around the car, it should give me enough momentum to get out the drive and down to the main road," she said to the car before her.

There was just one problem with this plan: she didn't have a shovel. She looked around her to see if there was anything she could use in lieu of a shovel, but failed to come up with something. She traipsed back into the house to see what she might have in there, but she didn't even seem to have a bucket lying around in her storage closet in the kitchen to use as a temporary measure. It appeared that Michael had cleared all of them away after he'd made the restorations to the house.

"Bloody man always seems to be doing something just to piss me off," Aoife muttered under her breath, then felt guilty for he'd been really sweet to her last night.

She looked around frantically again but found she had nothing. She was just toying with the idea of calling down to Dermot and Sinead's to see if they might have a shovel – they did, after all, mention last night about how they once had had to shovel out Dermot's father's place when last it snowed like this – when her power cut out and she was plunged into a grey darkness.

"God dammit all to hell!" she yelled into the gloom of the kitchen. "Well, what am I going to do now?"

The smart thing to do would have been to start a fire, stay indoors until the storm passed and go up to Dublin tomorrow. She could probably scrounge up some food from what was left in the pantry and make it through the day. However, Aoife's stubborn pride wasn't going to just let her sit around and do nothing all day when she could still put in more effort to get to Dublin. Besides, there was no excuse in the world good enough to get Grainne to forgive her for missing Christmas dinner, not even a bloody blizzard.

Sighing to herself, she once more headed out into the cold. She remembered this time to gingerly put one foot in front of the other, the dull throbbing in her hip a reminder of what would happen if she fell again. Determined to make it at least as far as Dermot and Sinead's to borrow a shovel, she

All That Compels the Heart

carefully set out along the icy lane, walking much like one of those people in the circus who walked around on stilts. Except that she wasn't feigning that she was going to fall when she started to flail her arms around.

The icy snow crunched under her boots, the only sound on the empty lane before her. As far as they eye could see, everything was white. If she'd paused to take a proper look, she undoubtedly would have thought it quite pretty. However, as the icy path was, there was no stopping to admire the beauty of the countryside.

Deciding that the safest way to make it to the Flanagans' cottage was by using the fence to keep her upright, she carefully navigated her way to the pasture that bordered her property. She heaved a sigh of relief when her hands gripped the reassuring solidarity of the stone fence. She made her slow, laborious way down the lane, one hand on the fence at all times for support. At first, she looked around furtively, making sure no one could see how utterly silly she looked right now, but her innate sense of self-preservation eventually won over and she stopped caring what others would think of the situation. The goal right now was just to make it to Sinead and Dermot's place, and that's what she needed to focus on. Besides, it wasn't like there was anyone in all of Ireland, except for herself, who was crazy enough to be out on this cold and unfriendly day. She breathed a laborious sigh of relief when she noticed smoke rising from the chimney of the Flanagans' cottage, and hoped it meant they were at home.

Not much further now.

She urged herself forward. As she got closer to the cottage, she realized she was going to eventually run out of fence. The Flanagans' lane sloped into their property, and the fence would only take her as far as the entrance to the lane. After that, she would be on her own.

Steeling herself to the task, she gingerly put one foot out into the undisturbed snow and let go of the fence. She managed quite well, for a few steps, even making it to the entrance of the lane without so much as one slippery step. Gaining a bit of confidence, she took one bold step into the lane, and ended up straight on her back in the snow, staring once more up at the grey sky above her.

She just lay there on her back for a few seconds, assessing the damage. Her bruised hip did not throb any more than it previously had, so at least she hadn't further injured it. No, most of the damage seemed to be to her pride, which was shivering in the snowbank with her.

She was just lifting herself into a sitting position to begin finding a way to get to her feet when she heard the front door of the Flanagans' cottage open. Not wanting to know who she was going to be humiliated in front of, she continued to lay in the snow, wishing she'd just melt into it. Footsteps crunched through the snow towards her, coming to a stop right beside where she laid. Even before she opened her eyes, she knew from the distinctive chuckle that it was Michael who'd come to her rescue. She groaned internally.

"Do ye need a bit of help, then?" he asked, looking down on her, his black peacoat open, offering up a glimpse of a green knit jumper with a reindeer on it. Seeing her glancing up at the jumper, he pulled his coat around him a little tighter, trying to hide his embarrassment over his Christmas attire. "Looks like ye've taken a wee bit of a tumble there."

"Nah, I'm grand," she waved a hand nonchalantly, like it was perfectly normal to be lying in a pile of snow. "I happen to enjoy falling on me arse, in the snow, making, well, an arse of meself in front of my neighbours. I happen to love laying in the cold snow and ice."

"Oh well then, here was me thinking I should come out and be a knight in shining armour and save ye. But, if ye like it out here in the cold and the snow, then I'll just leave ye to it."

She felt – for she still had her eyes closed, not willing to see Michael making fun of her – him shrug and heard him turn on his heel to head back inside.

She finally opened her eyes and yelled, "Wait!"

He promptly stopped and turned around, standing over her with a huge grin on his face.

"Help me up." She flung an arm out at him, indicating for him to grab it and help her get to her feet.

"What's the magic word?" he asked her, prolonging her humiliation and clearly enjoying it, not taking the proffered hand.

All That Compels the Heart

"Seriously? You're going to choose right *now* to be a jerk to me when I'm lying here in the snow, cold and wet?"

"According to you, I'm a jerk all of the time," he replied smugly, as if to let her know that he knew exactly what she thought of him, last night being an exception to the rule.

"True, but I don't think you'd leave a poor, helpless woman lying all by herself out in the snow. So, come on. Help me up," she demanded flinging her arm at him once more.

"I think you are the farthest thing from helpless, Aoife," he said, and she was surprised by how happy the comment made her.

"I'm still not hearing the all-important word," Michael said, still not taking her hand.

Aoife sighed dramatically, her contentedness at his compliment fading.

"Please," she muttered.

"I'm sorry. I didn't quite catch that," he taunted her.

"Please," she replied, a bit louder, just enough for him to hear her clearly.

"Nope. I still didn't quite catch that," he continued to tease her.

"Please!" she yelled at him sharply.

"Jaysis; you don't have to yell so the whole village can hear ye. You don't want them to know you've landed on your arse in a snowbank now, do ye? Now come on up off that cold ground before ye freeze to death," he said, coming over to her and leaning down to extend his hand to her.

She looked at him suspiciously, like he might try to play some trick on her, but seeing that he seemed to be sincere, she grabbed his hand and let him pull her up to her feet. The ground below her was still icy and she nearly fell back down again. She instinctively grabbed his shoulders to keep herself from falling.

"Woah there klutzy," he said to her, gripping her firmly.

"Ever the gentleman," she muttered under her breath at him and saw him smile. She tried not to giggle as she looked down and caught another glimpse of the reindeer jumper.

"A present from me mam," he replied to her unasked question, trying to pull his coat around him again to hide the jumper. "Shall we give this a go?" he indicated the lane ahead of them, his breath forming a little cloud around them.

"I'm grand. I can do it on my own," she said, removing her hands from his shoulders and took a step forward. She must have found another ice patch, for she pitched forward, saved only from hitting the ground again by Michael's hands around her waist.

"Sure ye can," he told her, ensuring she was standing upright again. "Ye know, it's a good thing I came out here when I did, as you don't seem to be able to go anywhere without me to help you out."

It grated on her nerves how smug his voice sounded.

"I made it the whole way here all by myself without your help," she retorted, tempted to shrug off his arms but knowing that she'd likely fall down again without the assistance.

"And where exactly were ye planning to go all by yourself on a day like today?" he asked.

"To come here to your parents' place. To borrow a shovel." She admitted it reluctantly, knowing what he was going to say about her plan even before he said it.

"And what the hell were ye planning to do with a shovel?"

"Well, if you haven't noticed, there's a fair amount of snow down and I wasn't going to be able to get my car out without one." She gestured at the snow still falling from the sky – *Good Lord, how much were they going to get?* – as if it should have been fairly obvious what she was planning to do.

"Well, I hate to be the one to tell ye, but you're not goin' to Dublin today," Michael replied, as if it should have been equally obvious to her that her plan was silly.

"Great, well, I suppose that spending Christmas on my own down here is much the same as spending it with my family," Aoife replied, gesturing in a frustrated manner, about to abandon all hope of succeeding in her plan. "I'd just be spending the holiday drunk and finding an empty niche to escape from my crazy family, anyways, so I guess this really isn't the worst thing to happen. At least now, I can just get drunk on my own and not have to deal with the rest of them."

"Well don't the holidays sound grand at you're place, then?" Michael said sarcastically, and she could tell he was trying to elicit a smile from her, trying to cheer her up.

"Look, if you're not too busy keeping all that company with yourself this Christmas, why don't ye come 'round to ours for Christmas and spend it with us? The parents won't mind another mouth to feed, and no one should be on their own at Christmas. Besides, you're already practically standing outside the doorstep." There was a note of sympathy in his voice for her plight, but also something resembling hope. Hope that she would take him up on the offer, perhaps?

Aoife looked at Michael with slight suspicion, not entirely sure that he was being serious. She wasn't sure what to make of the offer. Was he only asking her out of pity or some weird sense of obligation? Or was it because he wanted her to be there?

Does it really matter?

She supposed the voice in her head was right; it didn't really matter.

"Well if ye don't want to come over for Christmas, then you can just spend it all alone in that big old house, then," he replied snarkily to her unvoiced suspicion.

"No, no. I didn't mean any offense," she replied hastily, more because he seemed to be moving away from her and she was certain she wouldn't make it back to the fence to walk back to Aldridge Manor by herself. "I'd love to come over, so long as you're sure your family won't mind."

"Of course they won't mind. We'll find room for ye, don't you worry."

She looked down the lane at the cottage. It *did* look cozy and inviting; much more inviting than sitting back up at her place by herself all day.

"C'mon," he said, tucking her hand in the crook of his arm like he'd done last night. "Let's get ye inside where it's warm."

Chapter Thirty-Four

"Mam, Da; we've got another guest for Christmas dinner," Michael announced as he led Aoife through the main door of the cottage. He needn't have shouted; his parents, nephew, and sister were all gathered either in the small kitchen off to the right, or in the little sitting room right in front of them. The scent of pine needles from the Christmas tree, oranges and cloves, turkey, and homemade sweets lingered in the air around them.

Sinead came through from the kitchen, wiping her hands on a towel, brushing back wisps of greying hair that had come out of her bun and smoothing the skirt of her red dress.

"Aoife! What a pleasant surprise! Come in, come in." She motioned with the towel for Aoife to come inside and give her a hug.

"Let me take your coats. Mara, be a dear and put these in the closet," she said, handing the coats and scarves over to her daughter.

"Hello, Aoife," Mara greeted her, kissing her on the cheek, and taking her coat and scarf from her, carried them off to the closet. Like her mother, she too had chosen to dress in red, but had opted for a deep burgundy top and black skirt instead of the cherry red of her mother's dress.

All That Compels the Heart

"I'm so sorry for intruding. I wasn't expecting this storm to come in and ruin my chances of getting to Dublin for Christmas. I really hope I won't be a nuisance," Aoife apologised.

"No, of course not. We're delighted to have ye. Now come in, come in, and take those boots off," Sinead once more motioned for her to come inside.

"Well no wonder you fell so much on the way here. These boots have no treads on them," he scolded as she placed her boots next to his by the door.

She was tempted to correct him and let him know that she'd only fallen twice on the way down here, but she was interrupted by Sinead.

"Who would like some tea?"

"I'll make it, Ma," Michael told her, heading into the kitchen without argument. "Aoife, you take milk and sugar in yours, right?"

"Yes, please. That'd be lovely." She rubbed her hands together, feeling how damp and chilled they were.

As the kettle boiled on the wood stove, she heard him rummaging through the small refrigerator. A few seconds later, he came through to the dining room carrying the two pale yellow mugs and handed her one of them. It felt comforting and warm against her still warming fingertips, the scent of Irish Breakfast tea wafting up towards her nostrils. Taking a sip of the still-too-hot tea, she gazed around the Flanagans' home, admiring how cozy it felt. Every nook and cranny in the small kitchen was being put to use in some way, either with a homemade crafts made by Rory or from a craft fair, or being used as a home for some dishware or utensils or a cupboard. It had a lived-in and welcome feel, especially with the power being out and the woodstove being lit, keeping the place warm, and candles lit throughout the place to dispel the gloom.

"Aoife, why don't you come in here and sit with Dermot and Rory a bit?" Sinead asked, motioning from the sitting room for her to join them.

"Are you sure you don't need any help in the kitchen, Sinead? I feel bad, what with you being so nice to take me in like this. I should help in some way."

She set her mug down on the table beside her, and rose from her chair, trying not to look like she was on a tea break. She was more than capable of helping out.

"No, no. I wouldn't dream of it, love. You just come over here and sit down now next to Dermot and leave supper to us. Everything will be ready in a jiffy."

"Yes, love," Dermot said, leaning over the arm of his wooden rocking chair and lowered his voice. "You're much better off in here out of the way. You're likely to get recruited into slave labour under the general's orders standing around in that kitchen. Much safer in here with me."

He winked at her.

"I heard that," Sinead called out as she returned to the kitchen and began barking out orders to Michael and Mara. Aoife and Dermot sat there in silence a moment, listening to the dry logs crackling in the fireplace.

"Helluva storm what's come up, eh?" Dermot asked her, looking across the cozy sitting room to the front window. "Sure and the phones are down still too, which means ye probably haven't been able to talk to your family yet to let them know you won't be coming. They'll be worried about you," Dermot said, his brow furrowing in worry.

"Nah, I'm sure they haven't even noticed that I'm not there yet. Don't worry; they won't miss me," Aoife reassured the elder gentleman, though feeling a certain hollowness at the realization that her words were true. Her family really *wouldn't* miss her, let alone even notice that she wasn't there. Often enough, they didn't even know she was there when she *was* present at a family function unless it was to pick on her about something. She was much better off here, imposing on the Flanagans as she was, who at least acted like a proper family. Aoife's gloomy thoughts were interrupted by young Rory.

"Uncle Michael?"

"Mmmhmm?"

"Eliza's not joining us for Christmas dinner, is she?"

"No, she's spending it away with her own family this year."

Aoife noticed how Michael's face looked slightly pained at the mention of Eliza.

"Oh good," Rory sighed a sigh of relief. "Mammy says she's an annoying and highly-strung cow, and I'd much rather we have Aoife with us this Christmas." They boy beamed innocently at her.

"Rory Dermot Flanagan!" his mother shouted loudly in exasperation from across the kitchen, clearly embarrassed to have her true feelings about Eliza revealed.

"What?" the little boy asked innocently. "I've heard Grandmammy say the same thing about her too."

Dermot chuckled quietly beside her. Before all hell could break loose, he rose from his rocking chair and came into the kitchen to save the little boy and restore peace.

"Come on wee lad, the kitchen's no place for us menfolk. We're woefully under-qualified to work alongside the excellent skills of your mammy and grandmammy. Someone's more than likely to get foot-in-mouth disease if we stand around here too much longer. Let's you and me and your Uncle Michael take a walk outside and get some fresh air. There's some wood in the shed that needs bringing in. Let's leave your mammy, grandmammy, and Aoife alone so they can work their magic in getting us some Christmas dinner, eh?

"Aoife, ye don't mind taking over for Michael in the kitchen, do you?"

"No, of course not," she assured him, placing her mug of tea on the coffee table and crossing the room to where he was standing. "I'd love to help."

Dermot nodded gratefully at her and corralled his son and grandson over to the door to put on their things, and quickly ushered them outside.

ೞ☙

Michael, Dermot, and Rory stepped out into the cold, crisp air, trudging through the ankle-deep snow across the small meadow to the woodshed. The scent of wood smoke from the cottage's chimney drifted lazily through the air.

Michael had many a fond memory of the woods near the shed; they'd always seemed a magical place to him since childhood. He remembered how when he and Mara were children, they'd go into the woods to play and, being ever the annoying brother, he would sneak off behind some trees and make scary noises to frighten his sister, or jump out at her when she was least expecting it. It had been great craic.

As teens, Michael and Mara had used the woodshed as a place to sneak their teenage crushes to when they wanted a quick make-out session without their parents finding them. He was fairly certain it was the place his daughter had been conceived, not to mention wee Rory, before his no-good-for-anything father, Alistair Byrne, had shagged off to God-knows-where and left Mara to raise Rory on her own.

A sour taste still lingered in Michael's mouth at the thought of Alistair. No one in the village had seen hide nor tail of him since he'd run off, not even his own family. Though Michael supposed it was a good thing no one had; Alistair's keen sense of self-preservation meant Michael didn't have to go to jail for attempted murder, for if he ever stepped foot in Ballyclara again, Michael had no doubt he *would*, in fact, try to kill the bastard.

Michael leaned against the low, stone fence which divided the Flanagan property from the O'Bradys' farm next door, and lit a cigarette while his father unlocked the woodshed and began taking out some logs and stacking them up. Rory leaned up against the wall in perfect imitation of his uncle and blew out his breath slowly into the cold air creating clouds of steam. He gave the boy a small smile and reached down to ruffle his hair affectionately. The one good thing Alistair Byrne had done for this world was to leave them Rory, and no matter how much Michael might want to beat the shit out of Alistair for being an eejit and breaking his sister's heart, he'd never want to be without his nephew.

"So if Aoife isn't your lady friend, Uncle Michael, then who is she?" Rory asked his uncle, resuming his conversation from before.

"She's just a friend," Michael replied, thinking that it was a stretch to call her even that. In truth, Michael wasn't quite sure what Aoife was to him.

A riddle, wrapped in a mystery inside an enigma. Churchill's famous quote came to mind.

While he was pondering this thought, he saw his father give him a look, which he plainly ignored. He knew what his father thought Aoife was to him, or what she could be, rather.

"But that's not what Mrs. Maguire was telling Mrs. Walsh the other day," Rory told him. "They said you two were more than just friends."

Michael cursed the old gossips. He was keenly aware of what they were all saying about him and Aoife; he hadn't been able to avoid it any time he walked into his own pub, especially since Eliza had gone to Belfast. He knew they were all saying that it was Aoife driving a wedge between the two of them.

"Never you mind what those old biddies are saying. It's all just gossip," Michael told his nephew sternly, hoping to put an end to any further awkward questions about his relations with the city girl.

"But it's not just the old ladies who are gossiping about it," Rory pressed on, like a dog with a bone. "Jack Murphy was telling me at school just the other day that his mam was telling his da about you and Aoife, and that she's the reason you called off your engagement. But I thought you and Eliza had broken up before Aoife had come to town?"

"We did," Michael confirmed for the boy.

And then got back together, and then broke up again. His life was becoming as dramatic as a soap opera on the telly.

"Then why would Mrs. Murphy say that it was Aoife who'd broken you two up?" Rory asked him.

Because Mrs. Murphy is another old gossip who doesn't know when to keep her gob shut, was what Michael wanted to say, but instead decided to plead ignorance.

"Who knows why people say the things they say, Rory? That's between Mrs. Murphy and herself. And what happens between Eliza and myself is none of anyone's business, either. Now don't you go worrying about it anymore," he said, ruffling his nephew's hair playfully, trying to end the conversation. Rory made a sound of protest and annoyance at having his hair mussed up. He frantically began putting it back the way it had been.

"But -," Rory was about to press on with more questions until Dermot stepped in again.

"Are you two going to just stand around watching an old man haul out these heavy logs from the woodshed? Or is one of you going to come over and help me?"

"Go over there and help your old granddad, Rory," Michael said, with a playful emphasis on the word "old."

Dermot scoffed at this but smiled at his son to show he'd taken no offense. Rory reluctantly walked over to his grandfather to lend a hand, unhappy to have his questions go unanswered. Michael put out his cigarette and walked over to grab several logs and put them under his arms, feeling their rough edges rub against his coat.

"Your uncle's right," Dermot told his grandson as they gathered up the rest of the logs to take inside. "Don't worry about what people in the village are saying. Most of what they say isn't true, and anyways, they'll soon find another person to gossip about and they'll forget all about your Uncle Michael and Miss O'Reilly."

Michael sincerely hoped that his father was right and that some poor sod would soon take his place as the topic of conversation on everyone's lips, uncharitable a thought though it may be.

Chapter Thirty-Five

When Michael, Dermot, and Rory went back into the cottage, they found the women engaged in a cheerful banter. Aoife, elbow-deep in pie crust and flour, looked up as she heard them come through the front door. A cool breeze swept lightly through the house as they opened the door to come inside, and a stray lock of hair fell in front of her face. Aoife, with her hands covered in flour, blew at it ineffectually. Michael crossed the room to her and tucked the lock of hair behind her ear.

"Here, let me help." He practically dropped the logs he was carrying on the floor and came over to rescue her.

"Thanks," she murmured, not exactly sure how else to respond. No matter how many times the two of them were in the same space together, she still felt this odd mixture of being slightly uncomfortable around him and yet, totally at ease at the same time.

"Sorry, I should have asked."

"It's alright."

He smiled at her and she looked at him warily. "What?"

"You, ah, you have something just here." He pointed to her nose where a cloud of flour had billowed up and left a residue on her skin. Self-consciously, she wiped at the spot on her nose and looked to him for to confirm it was gone.

He smiled and chuckled at her.

"What now?"

"You just made it a million times worse. Here," he reached over and grabbed a red-and-white checkered dish towel from the counter beside her.

"May I?"

She nodded.

He wrapped the dish towel around his index finger and gently wiped at the flour stains on her nose and cheek until he was satisfied it had all been removed. His eyes were intent on the task at hand, his touch gentle on her skin.

"There, all better." His eyes bashfully lifted and met hers. For the first time, she noticed the tiny flecks of almost indigo-violet near the irises of his eyes, something she'd not been close enough to notice in him before.

"Michael Flanagan, don't you leave those logs on my kitchen floor," Sinead chastised her son, breaking the moment. "And make sure to clean up that mess."

He returned the dish towel to the counter where he'd found it and did as he was told, picking up the logs and placing them near the fireplace. Before he could return to the kitchen, Sinead had already swept up the stray splinters of bark that had fallen onto the laminate surface.

Aoife returned to her pie crust, focusing on trying to mould it into the pie tin but not before she caught Mara's eye, the same observant blue eyes of her brother who hadn't missed the tender moment that had passed between them a moment ago. As she finished the pie and popped it into the oven to bake, Sinead said, "Rory, help your Grandad and Aoife to set up the table, will you? And Michael, can ye go and bring down the candles from the top shelf, please?"

Removing the patterned apron from around her neck, Aoife tidied up the rest of the counter from her pie-making and went over to the table to help Rory and Dermot to set up the dinner table. She unfolded the beautiful white lace tablecloth, pristinely clean, having only ever been brought out a few times a year for extremely special occasions. Michael came along behind her with the candles, placing them around the centre of the table and lighting them while Rory placed the utensils on the table. Mara, bringing over the special china plates used for special days such as these, placed each one carefully in between the knives and forks her son had just laid out. Aoife went back to the kitchen and began helping Sinead to put the various cooked dishes on the table.

"Alright, you all have a seat," she motioned to take their seats at the table as she went back into the kitchen for the turkey. Rory claimed his seat to the left of his grandfather – who was sitting at the head of the table – and put his hand on the seat of the chair to his right.

"Mam, you sit here," he commanded, patting the seat next to him.

"Yes, alright," Mara replied, wrapping her arm around her son as she sat down. Rory snuggled into the crook of her arm, perfectly content.

"Here, you can have a seat next to me," Dermot said to Aoife, indicating the empty chair to his right. She obliged the request as Michael sat down beside her.

"And here we are." Sinead placed the roast turkey near to Dermot, its succulent juices making their mouths water, and handed him a carving knife.

They passed the meal in an amiable silence, the kind that comes with good food. Aoife felt a sense of relaxation and contentment wash over her. She wasn't sure if it was the food, the soft candlelight, or the company of the Flanagans, but she felt that this was perhaps the best Christmas she'd ever had. They never once made her feel unwelcome or like she didn't belong; they treated her as if they'd known her for a lifetime.

As they finished their meal and dessert with some light banter and a general catching up with what was going on in the town, Aoife tried to stifle her third yawn in as many minutes. Her attempt to be polite and hide her half-sleepy state did not go unnoticed by Michael.

"I think we're boring our guest," he announced, his tone teasing but it still made her feel slightly self-conscious.

"Sorry," she mumbled, trying to stifle yet another yawn. "I swear it's the good food, candlelight, and the warmth from the fire and not the company that's making me sleepy."

"Oh, don't you worry, love," Sinead replied, getting up from her chair with a bit of a groan and began to clear up some of the dishes. "We understand. I think it's going to be early bed-times all 'round tonight."

"Yeah, I should get this one back home to bed," Mara said, looking at Rory who'd fallen asleep in his chair a good ten minutes earlier and was snoring softly as he leaned against his mother's shoulder.

"He looks so peaceful," Aoife said, watching Rory as he dozed comfortably, blissfully unaware of the world around him.

"He may be cute and peaceful now, but you should have seen him tearing around the place this morning, all hyped up on sugar and excitement as he opened his presents," Mara said, but she smiled down at her son, showing that it was all worth it.

"Do you want children, Aoife?" Sinead asked out of the blue, startling her awake. She hadn't been expecting the question and nearly choked on the last piece of dinner roll she'd just popped into her mouth. She noticed everyone around her looked up at her expectantly, waiting for her to answer the question. She took a moment to make another attempt to swallow the partially chewed up piece of dinner roll before she proceeded to answer.

"Ah no. At least, I haven't given it much thought. Danny doesn't want children," she replied hastily giving her usual response when asked when the two of them were planning to start a family. While he might have talked about buying a house together and settling down, this did not necessarily mean having children. The two of them had both agreed that their own childhoods had been unhappy enough and they didn't want to subject a child to that kind of environment.

"Just because your boyfriend doesn't want to have kids doesn't mean you can't have them." Rory's matter-of-fact statement surprised them all. They hadn't realized he'd woken up and had been listening into the conversation. "My mam had me on her own."

"Well aren't you a clever little one. I could do it on my own, but I guess I'm just not there yet. Maybe I'd re-think it if they turned out to be as handsome and clever as you."

All That Compels the Heart

She expected that to be the end of the conversation and began to help clearing up the plates near her when Rory piped up, "Well, if you want your kids to look like me, you should marry Uncle Michael."

Aoife nearly dropped the china plate she was stacking on top of Dermot's, and murmured exclamations went around the table. Michael cleared his throat, clearly embarrassed by his nephew's comment.

"Mam and Granny always say I'm a lot like he was when he was my age. Which was a *million* years ago," Rory continued, much to the embarrassment of everyone around the table. But he wasn't content just to end it there.

"He's single now that he's not dating Eliza anymore."

"Alright you," Michael said trying to get off the subject of his love life and shooting his nephew a pointed look. "I think it's time to help with the washing up, eh?"

"What?" Rory asked innocently, not comprehending why everyone seemed to want to get him to stop talking. "I'm just saying. Aoife doesn't need her boyfriend in order to have a baby. I mean, Mam had me without a husband or a boyfriend."

"Well I think things are a bit different for Aoife," Sinead began to say, and before Rory could say anything further, Mara cut in and said, "I think it's time we help Granny with the cleaning up and then we'll head home."

Her tone was firm and brooked no argument from her son. Silently, but with a little pout on his face, Rory hopped down from his chair and began to help his mother, grandmother, and Aoife to take the dirty dishes into the kitchen. The four of them worked in amiable silence once more, clearing away everything while Dermot and Michael sat together at the table having a quiet conversation.

Once the dishes were air-drying in the rack and the leftovers placed in the still-cool refrigerator, Aoife felt the tiredness from earlier returning.

"C'mon sleeping beauty, let's get you back to your palace," Michael gently teased her, bringing her coat over to her as she put a hand up to her mouth to stifle yet another yawn. "Do ye think ye can make it on your own two feet? Or will I have to sling you over my shoulder and carry you again?"

"I am *not* a sack of potatoes," she retorted. "I'm sure I can manage on my own."

"Good, because he'll be heavy enough to sling over my shoulder and carry home," Michael said, pointing to Rory who'd gone over to the table to sit with his grandfather about half-way through the clearing up. Once more, sleep had set in and he was fast asleep in his chair.

"It seems a shame to move him when he's so tired. He looks so cute when he's asleep."

"He's not so cute when he's a deadweight on your shoulder," Michael said ruefully, likely thinking about having to carry the boy home.

"Well ye know you're always welcome to stay the night if you don't want to walk back tonight," Sinead said, stifling a yawn herself this time. "And that goes for you too, Aoife."

"That's very thoughtful of you, but I feel I've imposed enough on you," she replied as Dermot waved his hand dismissively and made a "pshaw!" sound.

"You've been no trouble at all, and it was lovely having you over. I hope this isn't the last we'll see of you over the holidays. In fact, we'll be having a dinner of leftovers tomorrow and you're more than welcome to come."

"Thank you," Aoife replied, her tone sincere. She wasn't used to this level of kindness over the holidays. Usually the plan was to get to her grandmother's as late as she possibly could to avoid as much pre-dinner chatter, survive dinner, and then make a hasty exit.

"I'd like that. This has been the best Christmas I've had in years. Thank you for everything."

"Excellent! Michael will go and get ye tomorrow when we're ready."

"I'll do what now?" Michael asked, helping Mara to put on Rory's boots and then slinging a bag of Christmas gifts over one shoulder.

"You'll go and get Aoife tomorrow for dinner," Dermot told his son, his tone firm.

All That Compels the Heart

"Sure." Michael shrugged, trying to appear aloof about the subject. "Alright, I think we have him all set. You two ready?"

"Yes, I think we're good here," Mara told her brother, and Aoife nodded to him that she was ready, too tired now for words. She just wanted to curl up in bed and sleep for a month, she was that tired.

"Right then, up ye get little man," Michael told his nephew as he picked him up, securing his arms around his neck and shoulders and keeping a firm hold of his legs, with the utmost care. Rory only stirred slightly at the movement, then snuggled himself in against his uncle's shoulder. Aoife was touched to see the usually gruff Michael showing his gentle, more caring side when interacting with the rest of his family. It was a side he so rarely let the rest of the world see. It was these rare moments when he let her see the side he didn't show to anyone else, that somehow endeared him to her.

"What are you smiling at?" Michael asked, curious.

Aoife was surprised to find her guard had slipped and she hadn't realized she'd been smiling while watching Michael with wee Rory.

"Nothing. Just content," she replied, smiling at him.

With the expression of curiosity still on his face, he said, "Ok, well let's head out. Time to get you all home." And with that, he turned to the door and walked out, the women following him as they waved their final goodbyes to Dermot and Sinead.

The night air was still chilly after the snowfall, preserving the snow which had fallen on the ground. The sky was clear, and a harvest moon shone in the sky, illuminating everything around them. It looked to Aoife like a beautiful painting.

The problem with the snow not having melted straight away is that the roads still hadn't been cleared, so it made walking back every bit as treacherous as it had been earlier in the day. Mara and Aoife walked arm in arm to keep each other upright as best they could, following the trail that Michael made in the snow, while he walked ahead of them with Rory, occasionally turning around to make sure that they hadn't fallen behind. The air around them was quiet in the cold night, the only sound was their boots crunching through the snow and their giggles as they nearly slipped. Surprisingly, despite a couple of near slips, they all managed to stay upright the whole way down the road to Mara's cottage.

"Oh bed, how I look forward to thee," Mara exclaimed as they came closer to the cottage and she pulled out her keys from her jacket pocket to open the front door. She fumbled around in the darkness looking for a flashlight. Having found what she was looking for, she switched it on and beckoned to Aoife and Michael to come inside. They walked in and closed the door to keep out the cold. Aoife made to take off her boots, but Mara waved at her.

"Don't bother. It's too late right now for me to care, and it'll dry up by morning. I'll deal with it then," Mara told her.

"I'll just wait here then while Michael puts Rory to bed," she told her, not wanting to drag more snow and dirt through the cottage than necessary.

"Ok," Mara told her as she pulled off her own boots and tossed them on the floor and took off her jacket and flung it over the back of the chair she was sitting on.

"I'll just run him upstairs and tuck him in, and then I'll be right back down," Michael told Aoife.

"Take your time. I'm in no rush," Aoife reassured him, even though she wanted nothing more than to just curl up on the couch in the little sitting room, which she could see through the kitchen archway. Michael nodded to her and walked upstairs with Mara and Rory. She leaned against the doorframe to prop herself up and keep her awake.

A few minutes later, he returned.

"Well, he's still sound asleep. I don't think an earthquake would wake him," Michael told her as he came down the stairs. "You ready to go?"

"Uh huh," she yawned again, trying to hide it behind the back of her hand.

"I have a free shoulder again if you want to be carried home," he offered her in jest.

"I'm still not a sack of potatoes, nor a child," she told him, proving that even in her sleepy stupor she still had some fire in her.

"Alright then. I'm just trying to be helpful. Ye look like you could fall over at any moment."

"I'll be grand once we get back out into the cold air. It'll wake me up again."

They headed outside and began the walk back to the Old Rectory. A bit of a wind had begun blowing since they'd last been out, and Aoife crossed her arms above her stomach to keep warm in the chilly breeze. They walked along in silence for most of the way, lost in their own thoughts. All too soon, they reached her front door.

"Well, here we are," he said, suddenly reluctant to see her go home.

"Yeah." She lingered on the front steps with him, like she didn't want to leave just yet either.

"Well, I should leave you to it and get back home." Still, he didn't move.

"Yeah."

She was just thinking about how she should really go inside now, but there was something about him that just kept bringing her closer to him until suddenly, the power came back on. They both blinked at the sudden glare from the porchlight outside the front door, and she realized how close she'd been standing to him.

"I… uh… Goodnight," he finally managed, and made as hasty an exit. The lights from the village below twinkled like stars on the horizon as she watched him head down the lane.

"Goodnight," she said softly, feeling suddenly alone without him.

Chapter Thirty-Six

After a restless night's sleep, Aoife woke to an entirely different scene than the one from the day before. The snow from the previous day had almost all but melted, gone as suddenly as it had arrived. Around six o'clock in the morning, she'd finally determined that there was no hope of her falling back asleep and so she crossed her bedroom to the far window, looking down on the front yard below. The lane looked clear and safe enough that she should be able to drive back to Dublin today, but as Sinead and Dermot had so graciously invited her to dinner again, she felt like she should delay the trip to the city for another day. Dublin wasn't going anywhere; it wasn't like she'd need to rush up there. But then again, there was the near kiss with Michael last night, or at least that's where she'd felt things were going before the power had come back on and the moment had been broken.

She'd stayed up for most of the night, tossing and turning, the events of the day playing over and over in her mind like film in a projector. She'd over-analyzed every second the two of them had spent together, from him helping her on the ice, to inviting her to have dinner with his family, to walking home last night and leaning in so close to her like that… Maybe it had been all the talk from Rory about how she should marry Michael that had kicked her brain into overdrive, but she didn't think she was being crazy. There was something there; she just couldn't put her finger on it.

This was a *huge* problem because Aoife didn't know how she felt about this. After all, Michael had a fiancée – well, ex-fiancée technically, but how long would those two be split up for? – so did this make this just an attempt at a rebound for him? And in any case, *she* had boyfriend herself to think about, so what was she doing thinking about another man?

"Shit!" she exclaimed, remembering Danny. Frustrated with herself for forgetting about him, she crossed her room to the bedside table where she'd left her mobile to charge the night before. She'd completely forgotten her phone here yesterday, so she hadn't yet checked her messages. Even though Danny was in the Caribbean, he would probably have tried to call to talk and escape from his parents for as long as he could in order to avoid an awkward dinner with them.

And you weren't there for him. Instead, you were with another man.

She made a guttural sound deep in her throat in response to her own chastisement. It wasn't like she'd *meant* to forget about Danny; it had just happened. And it wasn't like she'd done anything wrong with Michael…

And yet you still feel guilty.

She mentally told herself to shut the hell up and turned her phone on.

There were no messages from Danny, but there were plenty from Bex and Millie. She'd forgotten to let them know she was safe and sound in Ballyclara and wouldn't be coming up, as they' been expecting. As predicted, when she didn't show, they'd panicked and had tried to reach out to her.

When are you coming up today?
- Millie

Hope the weather is cooperating for you. Looks like there's a bit of snow on the ground. Be careful.
- Bex xox

Where are you? :S
- Millie

Are you ok?
- Bex

Alright, Bex is starting to get worried. And by Bex, I mean the both of us. Where the bloody hell are you?
- Millie

LET ME KNOW YOU ARE OK
- Bex

"Shit!" she exclaimed again, seeing the thirty-four messages they'd left for her. She quickly dialled Bex's number, hoping her friends weren't going to be too mad at her. It barely rang twice before Millie answered.

"Aoife!" Millie's tone went from relief to annoyance in less than a second. "Where the bloody hell have you been? We've been trying to reach you since yesterday! When you didn't answer our texts, we began to worry something might be wrong, so we called your grandmother's place and spoke to your mother – let me just tell you, every time I have to speak to *that* woman, it makes me want to strangle her just that little bit more – and then she said you didn't show up there. To tell you the truth, she didn't even seem to notice until we pointed it out. I tell you, if I ever get my hands on her... And then we talked to Danny and he didn't know where you were either..."

Millie's words came out in a flood at her, like a big *whoosh!* of air through a wind tunnel.

"What Millie is *trying* to say," Aoife could hear Bex's voice over the speakerphone, "is that we missed you, but we're glad to hear from you because it means you're safe."

Bex's tone was somewhat calmer and more rational than Millie's but there was a sufficient amount of relief that Aoife was safe that showed how concerned she'd been.

"I'm *so* sorry. The power went out some time the night before, and then the roads were really bad and even though I tried to go out, I ended up falling down several times. Michael ended up coming to my rescue and then he invited me to spend the day with him and his family and I didn't really want to be rude, and seeing as there was no way I was going to make it to Dublin I didn't think it would be a big deal, and then I forgot my mobile at home…"

"Wait, you spent the day with Michael?" Millie's voice suddenly switched from concern/annoyance/relief to curiosity. "Well that sounds interesting, considering I'm fairly certain the last time you talked about him you were firmly all about hating the bloke."

"Of course that would be the one thing in all that, that you'd focus on," Aoife muttered.

"Well, it's a pretty big fucking deal that you spent Christmas with a man you say you can barely stand instead of being here with your friends, family, and boyfriend," Millie exclaimed.

"Wait, what do you mean about my boyfriend? Danny's in the Caribbean for the holidays."

There was a long enough silence on the other end of the phone that Aoife checked to make sure the call hadn't dropped.

"Um, well, he's actually here in Dublin." Bex was finally the one to speak up. "Apparently he wanted it to be a surprise for you and come home early or something. He showed up at your grandmother's place for dinner. We spoke to him when we called over there looking for you, after talking to your mother."

A sinking feeling settled into the pit of Aoife's stomach, a harbinger of the enormous guilt she felt. All day yesterday she'd barely given any thought to Danny, except when Rory had questioned her about wanting children, and then she and Michael had had that moment of almost kissing on her doorstep last night when he'd dropped her off. How foolish could she be, losing sight of the people she cared about like that, and for what? A brief moment of attraction to a man she normally couldn't stand? How much of an eejit was she that she was willing to put everything she and Danny had in jeopardy like that? Aoife had a sudden need to talk to him and clear things up.

"What exactly did you tell him about me not showing up yesterday?" she asked, panic beginning to set in.

"Just that you were supposed to be here by eleven in the morning and that you hadn't showed up yet. I think that was around noon or one o'clock. We asked him if maybe you'd been running behind and had gone straight to your grandmother's place instead, and then were planning to join up with us later." Bex's voice was calm and soothing.

"And he didn't seem angry or upset that I wasn't there?"

"Well, it wasn't the first time we called. When we called back later in the day and still no one had heard from you, then we all became a little panicked. If the roads hadn't been so bad, I think Connor would have driven down there to find you himself. You should probably call him too to let him know you're safe."

Aoife felt terrible. If she'd not been so stubborn and hadn't gone out into the lane, determined to shovel her way out, she would've been near her phone and she'd have been able to get her missed calls. She would have been able to talk to Danny, and then he wouldn't be upset with her.

"I need to call him." But it wasn't Connor she was concerned about right in that moment. She knew he would forgive her for anything, including leaving him on his own for the first Christmas since their grandfather had passed. No, right now, she was more concerned about the fact that Danny would be furious with her for not being there. She needed to call him, explain what had happened.

"I'm sure everything will be fine," Bex told her reassuringly, even though they both knew that once the anxiety set in, there was very little one could do to reassure her.

"Look, I should probably go. Michael will be here soon and I want to make sure I call Danny before I go down to the Flanagans again."

"You're going to spend more time with him? I thought you were coming home today?" Millie asked.

"Sinead and Dermot invited me to come over last night before I left and I thought..."

"You thought it would be rude to refuse, yadda yadda." Millie's sounded annoyed yet again. "Meanwhile, the people you're supposed to be spending the holidays with are up here in the city, patiently waiting for you and you're fixated on spending more time with a man who is not your boyfriend and who, by the way, is supposed to be engaged to another woman."

"I'm very well aware of the fact I have a boyfriend, Millie, thank you very much," Aoife retorted sharply, becoming extremely annoyed.

She's just upset you didn't spend the holiday with her like you had planned. Once you see her again, she'll be fine.

She hoped the voice in her head was right.

"Alright, you two," Bex replied sharply, getting in between the two of them. "Aoife, I presume you'll be up here for tomorrow?"

"Yes, that was the plan." She heard Millie mumble something on the other end of the line before Bex cut in.

"Great. We'll see you then. Millie say goodbye to Aoife." There was more mumbling on the other end of the line before Millie finally replied, "Fine. Goodbye."

"Goodbye," Aoife replied more harshly than she'd intended.

She hung up the phone, feeling frustrated by the conversation. She knew Millie didn't really mean anything by her comments about her and Michael, but her friend's words struck a chord with her. She could see now how people were beginning to get the wrong impression about her friendship with him. Maybe it was Rory's comment from yesterday about how she should marry Michael, but she couldn't help but feel how this all spoke to the deeper issue at hand: that she and Michael hanging out together was sending out the wrong message. She also knew that if she didn't put a stop to it, things would only spiral from here. She wished now that she could turn down the invitation to his parents' place.

Well, there's no getting out of going to Sinead and Dermot's today, but some time apart from one another is probably best.

Sighing, she got up from the bed and headed for the shower. She would call Danny right after. She just needed some time to clear her head and figure out what she was going to say to him.

ೞ☙

Emerging from her shower feeling slightly less on edge than she did after her conversation with Bex and Millie, Aoife grabbed her mobile off the bedside table again and dialled Danny's number. It went straight to voicemail. Hanging up, she dialled the number again. Straight to voicemail again. Still feeling the nerves creeping around in her stomach, she left him a brief message asking him to call her back.

"Just because he didn't answer doesn't mean he's ignoring your calls. He could be somewhere without a signal, or he could be busy," she said to herself.

Or he could be ignoring you on purpose, the little voice in her head nagged her. She did her best to put it out of her mind. Instead, she turned her mind to the task of calling her mother, who also did not pick up.

"Hello Maureen, it's Aoife. Just wanted to say that I'm sorry I missed Christmas dinner. The roads were too icy and I couldn't make it out of the drive. I'm hoping everything will be clear by tomorrow and I will stop by Granny's. Hope to see you then." Her mother's voicemail machine beeped loudly to let her know her time had run out and she hung up the phone.

She was tempted to try and give Danny another call to see if she would be able to reach him this time, but she resisted. Something inside her told her it was better to try and let him reach out to her now. The ball was in his court.

Instead, she turned to the texts Connor had left her when he'd begun to worry about where she'd gotten to yesterday.

Hiya! Sorry about yesterday. Icy roads. You still in the city?
- Aoife

She was just finishing her text when she heard her front doorbell ring. Knowing it was Michael, she sighed, grabbed the first shirt she could find – a white turtleneck – and a pair of trousers, put them on as she headed down the stairs. Sure enough, when she opened the door he was standing there smiling at her like seeing her standing there had just made his day a little brighter.

"Hi." He leaned against the doorframe, angling his body so he was closer to her without actually coming inside uninvited.

Aoife's stomach did a bit of a flip-flop at seeing him. It had begun snowing again, a few light flurries falling softly to the ground and falling about his dark hair and onto his shoulders and he looked even more handsome than last night. At the same time, the sinking feeling in the pit of her stomach at knowing she shouldn't be thinking of him in that way returned.

"Hi."

"Aren't you going to invite me in? It's freezing out here."

He was right; it *had* gotten considerably colder outside than yesterday. Subconsciously, she tugged at the sleeves of her turtleneck, drawing her hands up inside the comfort of the woolen sleeves to ward off the chill.

"Sure, come in," she said, remembering herself and stood back a bit to let him in. Michael gave her a quick look over, noticing she didn't have her coat or boots on yet.

"You ready to go? Everyone's gathering down at Ma and Da's place. We should head over soon or there won't be any food left. You've never seen how Father Patrick can tuck away his food. He may be a skinny old man, but I swear he has the appetite of a man twice his size and age."

He smiled at her again, his hands in the pockets of his peacoat and his shoulders hunched up about his bare ears as he tried to warm up again. When his banter didn't elicit a response from her, he asked, "Are you alright?"

His smile faded into a perplexed look, uncomprehending the change in her mood from last night.

"I'm grand," she replied, her tone clipped.

He gave her another perplexed look and she felt bad for being cranky with him, but the way the morning had transpired so far had left her feeling on edge around him. She turned to put on her boots and pulled on her coat, purposely stepping just out of reach when he tried to help her into it.

"Ready," she said, buttoning her coat. Looking more serious now, he simply nodded.

"After you," he said motioning for her to head out the door. "Just be careful on the step there. They're still a bit icy."

Boldly, she went ahead of him, acting more confident on the still-slippery lane than she actually felt. Thankfully, most of the lane had begun to thaw and there were enough clear patches that she was able to navigate the path by herself.

Michael stayed close but hung back at a distance respectful of her earlier coldness toward him.

Let's just get this day done with, she told herself, skirting around an icy patch in the middle of the lane. *You only need to stay as long as to be considered proper and polite, and then you can make your excuses to leave. Putting some distance between you and Ballyclara is for the best right now.*

She just wished she could make both her head and her heart agree with one another.

She and Michael passed the short walk to his parents' place in silence, the friction between them palpable. She could feel the confusion and hurt emanating from him even though he'd not said anything to her since leaving her house. She was fairly certain that her own confused feelings were radiating from her and that they were a contributing factor in dampening his mood. Just before they drew up in front of his parents' front door, Michael turned to her and asked, "Have I done something?"

The question both surprised her, and yet didn't at the same time. She knew how it must seem from his perspective: they were getting along great yesterday and now it was like a bucket of ice water had been thrown over the both of them. What made it worse for her was knowing that the two of them were finally becoming friends again, and now here they were drifting apart again, but this time it was because she was the one holding back.

"Michael, look…" she began to say, trying to find the words to explain everything.

"What are you two doing standing out here? You'll freeze to death. Come inside."

The front door opened and Sinead's friendly face beamed up at the both of them, interrupting Aoife before she could finish her sentence. She heard Michael sigh in frustration at the intrusion into their conversation.

"Hello Sinead," she said, turning towards his mother. "Lovely to see you again. Thank you for inviting me over." She gave the woman the best smile she could muster, trying to hide the awkwardness between her and Michael.

"No problem at all," Sinead replied, her voice indicating she'd noticed the change between Aoife and her son, but being too polite to mention it, she refrained from pointing it out. She exchanged looks with Michael, who only shrugged in response to the unanswered question and pushed his way past them both to enter the cottage, leaving them there standing in the doorway.

"Is that Aoife? Tell her to hurry up and come inside! You're letting all the warm air out," she could hear Dermot call to them both from where he sat at the head of the dining room table.

As she stepped inside the cottage, she could see that he was joined by Father Patrick, Jimmy, Karen, Brendan, and Molly. She had to take a step back in order to avoid a collision as Rory and Desmond raced past her.

"Rory Flanagan! How many times have I told you about running around in the house?" Mara roared at her son.

The two boys paused mid-step for half a second but quickly resumed their play, ignoring the orders from the adults to settle down while Mara resumed helping her mother to get the leftovers ready to put on the table. Seeing that Michael had settled himself around the now crowded table and wanting to avoid him a little longer, Aoife turned to Sinead and Mara as she hung up her coat and asked, "Can I help with anything?"

Sinead looked like she was going to tell Aoife that everything was under control and she could just go and have a seat at the table, but perhaps it was something in the way Aoife looked at her that made her say, "Why don't you set the table?"

At just that moment, the boys came running into the kitchen again. "Boys!"

Both Des and Rory stopped and turned towards Sinead, this time paying attention.

"You've already been warned about running around in this house. Now, go and help Aoife set the table."

She opened one of the kitchen drawers, pulled out a handful of utensils and handed them to the boys as they both groaned about having to help with chores.

"Go!" Sinead ordered, pointing in the direction of the dining room table. As the boys sauntered over reluctantly to the table, Sinead handed Aoife a stack of plates, mouthing, "Thank you."

Like the boys, Aoife too was reluctant to approach the table. She did her best to put on a smile and took a breath, trying to pretend that Michael wasn't there. She could get through this dinner; she could.

Just one step at a time.

"Hey Aoife," Brendan greeted her as she approached and began laying the plates on the table.

"Hey," Aoife replied, smiling at Brendan. She tried to look as happy as possible. After all, she *was* excited to see him, Molly, Father Patrick, Jimmy, and Karen. It wasn't their fault she didn't want to be around Michael right now. "Happy Christmas."

"Happy Christmas to you as well. I thought ye were supposed to be going to Dublin?"

"I was, but with the roads being so icy, I didn't make it out of the driveway."

"That's too bad; I'm sure ye missed being with your family, having to spend Christmas alone," Father Patrick replied.

"Mmhmm."

"Too bad the roads haven't cleared today either. We had a difficult enough time trying to come here from the other side of the village today," Molly told her. "It must have been hard spending the day by yourself."

"She didn't spend Christmas alone." Everyone was surprised by Michael's interruption. "We invited her down here to spend Christmas with us."

His tone was sharp, like he was bothered by the idea that his friends would think he'd let Aoife spend the holiday by herself.

"Oh well. That was very kind of you Michael," Father Patrick replied in an apologetic tone.

"Yes, very nice," Brendan echoed the priest's sentiment while at the same time shooting Michael a rather pointed look for his interruption.

"We love having Aoife here," Rory interrupted the conversation, much like his uncle had just done, and smiled at her. She returned the kind smile with one of her own, grateful for his enthusiasm.

"Yes, we do," Michael replied, agreeing with his nephew and giving her a rather pointed look of his own. Aoife began to feel herself blush and become uncomfortable under his gaze.

Brendan cleared his throat politely, trying to break through the palpable awkwardness of the situation. "We had a great time at my parents' place yesterday. There definitely wasn't enough food, and they spoiled Des too much…"

Molly snorted derisively at her husband's comment. "Between you and our son, I still think your parents got *you* more presents. And if there wasn't enough food, it's because you ate it all! You should've seen this one, Aoife; he can tuck away more than anyone else sitting at this table, and that includes Karen who is eating for two."

"Well, I'm not actually eating that much these days," Karen piped up, shifting on the hardwood kitchen chair, trying to find a more comfortable spot for her and her huge baby bump. Aoife could've sworn that she didn't think the poor young girl's stomach could have grown any more than when she'd first met her, but it had somehow seemed to double in size.

"That's perfectly normal," Mara told her, bringing over a dish of freshly cooked carrots in butter and placing it on the table in front of Karen. In her other hand, she carried a bowl of herbed stuffing, the scent of oregano and onions wafting up from the warm dish. "The closer you get to your time, the less you'll eat because there's simply no more room for anything in there now that the baby is taking up most of the space."

"I've gotten to the point where I'm just so ready for this to be all done and have the baby out now. You hear that?" she asked, poking gently at her baby bump and adjusting her Christmas jumper over her stomach yet again, even though there was no hope of it covering the entire expanse of flesh. "It's time to come out now. Mama wants her body back."

"You look beautiful," Jimmy reassured her, placing one arm around her shoulder and his other hand on her stomach.

Aoife was grateful for the distraction and return in normality to the conversation. Just as she was about to turn towards the kitchen to look for something else to do, something to just get her away from Michael, Mara came over with the rest of the dishes and Sinead brought over the tray of leftover turkey.

"Go, have a seat," the older woman gestured to her as she placed the tray on the table. Aoife turned back to the table and noticed that Mara had settled herself next to Father Patrick, and Sinead was clearly going to take her place at the opposite end of the table from her husband, which only left the one place for her to sit at, which also happened to be right beside Michael.

Of course.

Doing her best not to look completely flustered, she settled herself in the empty chair, wishing desperately that there was room for a third person at the little card table that had been set up for Rory and Des in the living room.

After a quick blessing from Father Patrick over the dinner, Sinead turned to her guests and said, "Well, eat up before it gets cold."

While everyone seemed ravenous for their food, Aoife felt like each bite was a chunk of ice in the pit of her stomach and she suddenly didn't feel all that hungry. However, not wanting to appear rude, she dutifully ate when everyone else did and smiled at all the right places when Father Patrick or Dermot made a joke, nodded in agreement at some of the things Karen or Molly said, but she wasn't really paying attention. Everything felt very mechanical to her.

Smile. Take a bite. Chew. Swallow. Repeat.

After what seemed like hours to her, the meal was done and everyone pushed their chairs back, ready to relax. Mara and Sinead both rose from their places to pick up the plates and Aoife breathed a sigh of relief. She'd gotten through it without arousing suspicion.

Now get out of here before you miss the opportunity!

"Well, I should be getting back to the house," she said, pushing her chair back from the table and getting up from her seat.

"Oh, won't you stay a little longer?" Sinead asked, coming back to the table with leftover pies in her hands and placing them on the table for everyone to begin eating dessert. The faint crow's feet around her eyes deepened and her mouth – a pretty shade of light pink for the special dinner – drew down into a disappointed frown. "You've only just gotten here…"

"Well… I…" Aoife found herself having difficulty in disappointing the older woman, especially given how kind she'd been to her and opened her house to Aoife for the holidays.

"I… um… I really should be making some calls to family since I didn't make it up yesterday…"

"Oh go on, Mam; leave her alone. We can't monopolize all of her time," Mara chastised her mother, coming to Aoife's defense.

"By the way," Mara whispered in Aoife's ear, "If ye happen to be talking to Connor, let him know I'm thinking of him, will you?" Her face was so earnest in her affection for her new crush that Aoife smiled back and nodded.

"I'll be sure to let him know." Mara gave her a quick hug before taking her seat at the table again and reaching for a piece of pie.

As Aoife tried to sidle away from the table, Sinead cornered her again. "Ye know, if you'd like to stay and have some dessert, I'm sure your family wouldn't mind if you were a little late in calling them back…"

"Let the poor girl go, Sinead. She needs to spend some time with her own family too." Dermot's voice carried across the table and his wife reluctantly gave up her guilt trip, but not without one last point to make.

"Well, it was wonderful to have ye with us, and don't be a stranger!"

"I won't, I promise," Aoife assured her, giving her a quick hug. "And thank you for taking me in over the holidays. I had a great time."

Aoife walked quickly to where she'd hung up her coat and was putting her boots on when she noticed that Michael had gotten up from the table and followed her over.

"Listen, before you go," he said, leaning against the wall, just a fraction of an inch closer to her than made her completely comfortable. "I don't know what your plans are for New Year's but Brendan and I always have a big céilí down at the pub. You'd be welcome to join, if ye want."

She looked up at him as she put on her coat and his smile was so sincere that the icy feeling in the pit of her stomach from before seemed to get colder and sharper. She could see that he obviously was hoping she'd say yes and she hated turning him down.

"Thanks, but I've actually already got plans for New Year's."

She saw his smile falter slightly, but he composed himself so quickly that it was hard to tell it had even happened.

"Right."

"Bex, and Millie and I planned a trip to Edinburgh..." she began, trying to explain that it wasn't anything to do with him.

"Yeah, of course. Just thought I'd put it out there."

He shrugged like it meant nothing to him, like he couldn't care less if she came or not, but it was a little too forced for her to believe it.

"We've been planning it for a really long time..." she tried once more to let him down gently, feeling awful.

"No problem at all." Michael crossed his arms over his blue knit jumper, the one he'd loaned to her the night of her housewarming party.

"I really appreciate it though. It means a lot to me, you inviting me to spend time with your family over Christmas."

"Sure."

"Maybe next year, yeah?" She tried to give him a smile, trying to soften the disappointment but she wasn't able to get more than monosyllabic answers from him.

"Yeah."

An awkward silence fell between them and Aoife stared down at her riding boots.

"Well, I should probably head home," she said, not knowing what else to say.

"Yeah, you said that already."

"Right. Well, thank you for everything. Goodbye everyone!" she called out, giving those assembled at the table a quick wave before finally opening the door to the chilly air.

"Bye." Michael's voice was soft but she could still hear the disappointment nonetheless. Doing her best to tell herself that this was all for the best for the both of them, she set off back towards the Old Rectory, wishing she'd thought of some excuse to miss the party in the first place.

ଛଡ଼

"Aoife didn't seem to be herself today," Sinead noted as Michael closed the door and returned to his seat at the table. "I hope nothing is wrong."

He'd just been thinking the same thing. "She was like that earlier when I went to go and get her."

"Well, ye *do* have that effect on women," Mara teased him, but he wasn't in the mood. His stomach felt like it was twisted up in knots and he wasn't sure why. Or, rather, he *did* know why; he just didn't know if he was ready to admit it to himself or not.

After the moment the two of them had shared last night, he'd been expecting a rather different response from Aoife today than the ambivalence she'd displayed toward him. It wasn't like he was expecting her to fall down at his feet in love with him, but he'd been fairly certain that the two of them had been heading towards a kiss before the electricity had come back on last night.

She's with Danny...

The thought pushed itself to the forefront of his mind, making him grimace ruefully. Brendan happened to look over at just that moment and, seeing the look on his, raised a questioning eyebrow. He waved a hand in silent response, trying to allay any curiosities or fears.

Maybe it was that jerk Danny who'd put her in this mood. It was clear as day to him that Danny was no good for her, that he was more interested in having Aoife as some kind of trophy than as a partner. It also wasn't natural the way the two of them spent so much time apart. He knew that she'd said Danny had to travel for work, but still, the man hardly seemed to make an effort to see her except the one time for her party, and he'd definitely not been interested in seeing Aoife that night. Michael's blood still boiled at the memory.

You could have told her.

And then where would they be? He'd been with Eliza at the time, and Aoife would only have ended up hurt. Worse, she might have blamed him for being the one to tell her.

"I should go and check on her."

Michael got up from the table and was making a move to find his coat and boots when he was stopped by Father Patrick.

"Ye should leave her alone for a bit. Sometimes women just need some time to think things over when something is bothering them, and it's a difficult time of year for her and all."

"Right. Because you know so much about women," he retorted.

"Michael!" Dermot exclaimed, shocked, but he wasn't listening anymore. Slipping on his boots, laces still undone, and throwing on his coat, he headed outside.

Of course, by this time, Aoife had gone up the lane and around the bend, pretty much back to the Old Rectory. Torn now between wanting to follow her, but fearing that the priest might be right after all and she just needed some time to herself, he stood in the lane, the cool air nipping at his nose. He was cold, but he didn't want to go back inside to face his family and friends just now – not after his little outburst – but also not wanting to push Aoife further from him, he knelt down to tie his laces and hurried back to his cottage, cold air floating in puffs around him. He'd have to remember to apologize to Father Patrick tomorrow, when he'd calmed down. Hurrying down the lane towards his place, he heard Brendan and Jimmy calling after him; they must've followed him outside hoping to catch him before he did something he'd regret.

No worries there lads. He ignored them and continued on home, his mood darkening with each step.

Chapter Thirty-Seven

The sky had been overcast and grey as she drove to the city, but thankfully the snow seemed to be keeping at bay.

"You made it!" Millie exclaimed when she arrived throwing her arms around Aoife in a bear hug.

Well, this is a good sign.

It wasn't like Millie to hold a grudge for long; maybe things between them would clear up easier than she'd been expecting.

"Oh come now; only one of Mother Nature's freak snowstorms could keep me from being home over the holidays," she said, returning Millie's hug and reiterating that it was only down to Mother Nature she'd not come home sooner, and not a desire to stay with Michael Flanagan.

"She's just being dramatic," Bex said, coming over to give Aoife a quick hug and took her suitcase from her, wheeling it into the living room. "Come on in and have a seat. Do you want a drink?"

"I probably shouldn't. I should probably make a stop at Grainne's place soon."

"You literally just arrived!" Millie looked disappointed that she was leaving already.

"Yeah, I probably should. Get it over and done with, so to speak. Besides, Connor texted to say he's leaving soon, so I want to make sure to catch him before he goes."

"Fiiiiiiiine," Millie replied dramatically, rolling her eyes. "But we're holding your suitcase hostage just to make sure you come back."

She pouted and folded her arms across her chest. She looked the perfect image of the bratty teenager from her spiky lavender hair, blood red lips, to her Metallica t-shirt and leather leggings.

"I'll be back," Aoife promised.

"You better!" Millie shouted as Aoife closed the door and headed down to her car. She felt a sense of relief that their normal dynamic seemed to have returned, the easy friendship back to the way it should be. Feeling a little more relaxed, she took a deep breath and turned the car back on again, heading towards Malahide and to face her grandmother.

ഗ‍ര

As Aoife pulled her Jaguar into her grandmother's drive, she checked her mobile again. There was a text from Connor saying that he hoped to see her soon and to drive safe on the way up from Ballyclara, but still nothing from Danny. She desperately wished he was with her right now; her grandmother seemed to adore him and it would certainly help to have him there as a buffer between the two women.

He'll call back. He will *call back.* She kept telling herself that, hoping to believe it was true.

Taking a deep breath to calm herself, she got out of the car and headed towards the front door of the house. She had barely finished ringing the doorbell when Moore opened the door.

"Miss Aoife," he intoned in his usual bored drawl. His eyes perked up, however, when he saw her. No doubt he was relishing listening through the door when Grainne would chastise her for not being home during the holidays.

"Hello Moore." She narrowed her eyes at the butler.

"Your grandmother is in her sitting room," he answered her unasked question. He didn't even flinch or waver under her stern gaze, not worried or intimidated by her.

Not wanting to get into a staring contest that she more than likely wouldn't win, Aoife simply nodded and walked briskly through the house to the sitting room, denying him the opportunity of announcing her to her grandmother.

"Oh hello, Aoife," Grainne greeted her. "I see you finally decided to come up from the country."

Grainne's tone was both clipped and yet somehow indifferent and Aoife knew she was really annoyed with her. It wouldn't have mattered to Grainne O'Reilly if there'd been a blizzard or not; Aoife hadn't shown up for Christmas and so she must be punished for her insolence.

"Hello grandmother," Aoife greeted her formally, showing her own annoyance at being chastised for something beyond her control.

"You've missed your mother."

Grainne seemed to be casually examining her perfectly manicured nails before placing her hands in her lap. She was dressed all in black, still in her mourning attire even though Paddy O'Reilly had been dead for several months now, and who even dressed in mourning these days?

Grainne feckin' O'Reilly, that's who.

"She and Anton have gone now to Odessa and won't be back for another couple of weeks."

What a shame, that. Aoife tried not to let her subconscious' thoughts show on her face.

"And John and Sinead have gone over to London with Caitlin and Nathaniel."

What a pity I couldn't see them either.

"However, Connor said he'd stay behind as he wanted to see you."

It was clear from Grainne's voice that she couldn't understand why he'd want to stay and see Aoife rather than go to London with the rest of his family before he shipped out again for God knew how long.

"At least Daniel came by the house and had dinner with us; at least one of you could be here."

I'm the one who made all the effort to try and come up here to be with them, and yet, it's Danny – who only came back to Dublin at the very last second – who gets all the credit for showing up.

She sighed, but quickly straightened up as Grainne's eagle eyes took in her slightly slouched shoulders. She knew she should be grateful Danny showed up; at least her grandmother liked him and it had likely softened the blow of Aoife not being there as well. If neither of them had shown up at all, she knew she'd be receiving a much worse lecture than she was right now. She also knew she shouldn't let Grainne get under her skin like this, but no matter how accustomed she'd become to her grandmother's verbal assaults, one of her barbs were bound to jab below the surface of calmness Aoife had worked so hard to create for herself.

"A friend dropped him off; Alice, I think she said her name was." Grainne pursed her lips in that way she did when she didn't approve of something or someone. It was a near constant look on her face, from Aoife's experience.

"Alice?" Aoife's head snapped up at the mention of Danny's co-worker. She wondered what on earth Alice would be doing with Danny for the holidays, especially showing up to her grandmother's place.

"Yes. Alice. A co-worker of his, I believe he said?" Grainne asked, like it was a question, but it was obvious that she already knew the answer she was looking for and she did not approve. Before Aoife could respond, her grandmother cut in.

"You should pay more attention to Daniel, Aoife. He's a good catch; don't you think it's time the two of you were settled down now?"

"She's a co-worker, that's all," Aoife snapped, a little too defensively. She didn't like the implications her grandmother was making. "They were on some team-building thing, so she must have travelled back with him on her way back home. He was planning on staying in the Caribbean over the holidays, but he must've decided to come home early, and I suppose Alice was traveling with him. I didn't even know he was in town until Bex and Millie rang yesterday to tell me they'd spoken to him."

She knew that she and Danny were a bit unconventional in their relationship and, sure, Alice was certainly more beautiful than herself but she and Danny were happy with things the way they were.

Are you?

She pushed the thought from her mind. She was interrupted from making any sort of further comment on the subject by the arrival of her cousin.

Connor knocked lightly on the doorframe to announce his arrival before leaning his tall frame casually against it. Moore stood a step behind him, huffing and puffing at the insolence of having his duty to announce the arrival of guests taken from him by both grandchildren.

"Hello Granny. Aoife," he greeted them both.

"Connor!"

She practically sprang from her perch on the arm of the chaise she'd sat on when she'd come into the sitting room and flung herself at her cousin. Connor caught her in a big hug, chuckling at her enthusiasm. Behind them, Grainne clucked her tongue in disapproval at Aoife's un-ladylike display of affection. They ignored her.

"I'm glad I caught you both," he said, but turned towards Aoife, indicating he was here more to see her than he was to see their grandmother. "I wanted to make sure to say goodbye before I head back."

"Well, goodbye then," Grainne replied quickly, dismissing him with a wave of her hand as if it didn't matter that she wouldn't be seeing her grandson again for months on end. Connor and Aoife exchanged looks; they both knew she'd not-so-secretly be pining for him for days. Connor held a special place in Grainne's heart that neither Aoife nor Connor's sister Caitlin could hold, and they all knew it.

Aoife and Connor decided to move their conversation into the corridor and left her grandmother to it. He glanced over her shoulder, giving Moore a pointed look. The butler, who'd obviously been standing near the doorframe to listen in on their conversation, cleared his throat and made his way downstairs. They both knew he'd likely be standing at the bottom, hoping to catch as much of their conversation.

The two of them suddenly not knowing what to say to one another. She hated it every time he was deployed somewhere, hated saying goodbye to him, hated seeing him leave, hated the worry every time the news reported on a skirmish or when they announced a soldier had been killed and she imagined it was him, but she knew she couldn't make him stay.

"It was nice of the Flanagans to let you spend Christmas with them. Mara said they loved having you."

"I didn't realize you and Mara were talking so much," she replied, turning the conversation on him and trying to get away from the inevitable mention of Michael. "You don't mention her much in your emails."

"Ah… well, you know… we talk every now and again."

A light flush spread over his cheeks and crept upwards towards his hairline. He coughed nervously and tugged at the collar of his uniform, as if it had been done up too tightly. She hadn't seen him this bashful since his first serious crush.

"You really like her, don't you?" she asked him.

"I can't stop thinking about her," he replied, a big grin on his face. "Even when I'm out there in the field, she's always on my mind," he admitted. "Does she ask about me?"

"Yes," she admitted. A rush of air left him, relieved at the news.

"Will you give this to her for me?" he asked. He removed a folded-up piece of paper from his pocket and placed it in her hand. She realized it was actually a few pages all folded up in neat lines and corners with military precision.

"Of course," she told him. She didn't ask him what was in the letter. If he'd wanted her to know, he would have told her. Knowing he trusted her to deliver the letter was worth more to her in any case than knowing what he'd written.

"Speaking of the Flanagans, I didn't realize you'd become so close to Michael, of late. *You* don't mention him in your emails," he said, turning the conversation back to her.

It was her turn to feel uncomfortable, shifting her stance in her high heels, her blue eyes looking down at the floor beneath her.

"Ah… well, you know…" she began, repeating his very words. "He was just being nice, that was all. And you know what it's like for us, having been raised by Grainne. It would've been rude if I'd turned him down."

"Right." He stared back her, knowing she wasn't telling him the whole truth.

"When do you ship out?" she asked, quickly changing the subject. He looked down at his watch and she noticed that a sad look came over his face.

"I should head out now in order to make it back in time," he said, a faint tinge of reluctance in his voice.

"Look at you all handsome in your uniform," Aoife said, smoothing out imaginary wrinkles on the breast of his jacket, trying to cover up her own reluctance about watching him leave. She held back the sudden tears that threatened to form at the corners of her eyes.

"I'll miss you," he said, taking her hand in his, forcing her to be still.

"I'll miss you more."

He nodded and kissed her forehead gently. "Goodbye, Aoife."

"Don't say goodbye!" she scolded him as a tear slipped down her cheek. They never said goodbye when he shipped out, neither of them wanting to say something so final lest it jinx his return.

"Sorry," he replied quickly brushing the tear aside. "See you soon."

"See you soon."

All too quickly, he'd left her standing there in the hallway, descending the staircase and headed out of the house, ignoring Moore who *tsked* at the poor manners of Grainne's grandchildren as he left the house.

"Aoife!" Grainne called out from her sitting room. "Are you still there? What are you and Connor talking about that is taking so long?"

Her grandmother's voice grated on her nerves and she sighed, heading back into the sitting room. She pasted on her best fake smile, just like she'd been taught to do, and tried her best not to think about smothering the old bat with one of the throw pillows on the settee.

Chapter Thirty-Eight

As Aoife's plane left Dublin for Edinburgh on New Year's Eve, the rift with Danny played heavily on her mind. She felt guilty for leaving and having a good time when she knew she should be at home, trying to make amends with him. Although she'd tried reaching out to him numerous times, he still hadn't returned her calls.

As the plane landed in Edinburgh, she tried to put him from her mind. Bex and Millie had spent every day since she'd arrived in Dublin talking about the trip and planning what they were going to do. They only had a few days in the city before they had to go back to work and university, and they wanted to make every moment count.

Try to have a good time. Do it for Millie and Bex. They're so looking forward to this.

The cold Scottish air whipped around them as they walked up to a taxi and began placing their suitcases in the boot of the car. It was the same kind of cold that had gone through her when Michael had come for her the day before she'd left Ballyclara. It reminded her of how disappointed he'd looked when she'd said she was coming her instead of spending the holidays in Ballyclara, and she wouldn't be able to make his New Year's Eve party.

"You alright?" Millie asked her, noticing the look on her face.

"Just cold," she replied, quickly trying to cover up any signs of disappointment with a big grin.

"C'mon, let's get you to the hotel so we can get changed and go down to the party!" Millie grabbed her by the arm and practically forced her into the backseat of the taxi.

※

Hogmanay was unlike anything Aoife had ever experienced before in her life. She'd rung in New Year's Eve in many different places around the world, but nothing compared to the sheer energy and spectacle that came with ringing in the new year in Edinburgh.

They'd begun in the Old Town with the ceilidh and then had moved outside to the Street Party. Fireworks had been going off every hour on the hour for the last four hours and there was an electric energy about the place that was infectious. Even Aoife, consumed with anxious worry from earlier, couldn't help feeling more uplifted than before. At least in the beginning.

Everything had started out with good intentions. They'd enjoyed the music at the ceilidh and she'd gotten enough alcohol in her to sufficiently begin to relax and forget her earlier woes. But, as the night wore on and the alcohol began to wear off, the music sounded too loud to her ears, the shouting and noise from those around her became more startling than amusing. Time seemed suspended in this odd place where it felt like time was racing towards midnight for everyone around her, but for her, it seemed to drag on eternally. Every time she looked down at her watch, it seemed that the minute hand had barely moved at all. The press of people around her tightened and she began to feel almost claustrophobic.

Just as quickly as the claustrophobia set in, so too did a sense of complete isolation, almost as if she were on an island set adrift in the sea of people surrounding her. She had a sudden sense of desperation, like she wasn't supposed to be here, that she needed to be somewhere else; *with* someone else. Beginning to feel like she couldn't breathe, she pushed her way outside to the Street Party.

"Aoife?" she heard Bex shout above the din, but she didn't stop. She needed to get outside where there was some air, where she could breathe.

The crowds in the Street Party were not any better than at the ceilidh. In fact, they seemed thicker here, pressing against her more closely. She was acutely aware that she'd forgotten her coat back with her friends and she only had her scarf wrapped around her neck to keep her warm.

She didn't mind at first; the crowds were piled so closely around her that she didn't really notice the lack of body heat. She was so focused on trying to get away from the problems that had been creeping up on her for months now – ever since her grandfather had died, really – that she wasn't focused on something so trivial as her own comfort. She'd been too focused on running away from her problems the last few months: when he grandfather had died, she'd run away to Ballyclara; when she and Danny were having problems, she'd run straight to Michael; when she and Michael were getting close, she'd run here to Edinburgh. All this time, she'd thought she'd been trying to deal with her problems but she'd only been doing exactly what she'd always done: run away until her problems finally began to catch up with her.

Suddenly tired from all this running, she stopped moving and found herself smack dab in the middle of Princes Street, feeling more alone than she'd ever been in her whole life. Her cheeks felt cold and as she brought her fingers up to touch them she realized she was crying. She was distracted, however, by the crowd beginning to count down the seconds until midnight.

"Ten... Nine... Eight... Seven... Six... Five... Four... Three... Two... ONE! Happy New Year!"

Fireworks exploded above Aoife's head, the night sky lit into an array of blues, reds, whites, and purples, a booming exaltation to ring in the new year. A chanting could be heard around her under the noise of the fireworks, the words of Auld Lang Syne being sung collectively by thousands of voices. As the music ended, she was jostled forward by some drunken reveller, breaking her out of her reverie of isolation and loneliness. She was about to turn around and give the person a piece of her mind when she saw that the person who had bumped into her was Millie.

"Aoife!" she exclaimed and reached over to hug her friend.

She could smell the booze coming off her friend as she leaned heavily on her, off-balance in her inebriation and tottering on her too-high heels. Aoife pursed her lips and blew a white feather from Millie's coat away from her face, lest it begin to tickle her nose.

"You alright?"

She saw the look of concern on Bex's face as she handed Aoife her coat. Grateful, slipped it on, wrapping it around her and blowing on her fingertips. She searched the pockets, hoping to find her gloves.

"Yeah, I'm grand. I just think I'm at that point where I either need to drink more alcohol, or sober up."

"Then drink!" Millie exclaimed, laughing loudly, clearly still consumed by alcohol herself.

She took the cup that Millie held out to her and stared at the questionable blue liquid. Ever since her first year of university when she'd an unfortunate mishap with a blue drink, she'd vowed never to drink anything blue again. However, not wanting to disappoint her friends and wanting to feel something other than completely alone right now, she downed the entire contents. She giggled as the blue alcohol took over her body.

Bex and Millie gave off a little cheer at seeing her happy again, and Aoife sank into the oblivion the alcohol provided for her, beginning to dance with the crowd around her, running from her problems once more.

※

ꖛꕤ

It was a dark, cloudy night, the air as cold as it had ever been in quite some time. Rubbing his hands together and blowing on them to warm them, he silently wished the whole walk down to the village that he'd thought to bring his gloves.

He could, of course, turn back and get them, but that would mean turning around and walking back to the cottage. He was already well down the road and could see the lights of the village ahead of him; he might as well push on.

Arriving at the pub, his cold fingers whinged as they gripped the cold metal of the key and let himself inside. Brendan had not shown up yet; the lights in the place were still dark. As he turned on the lights, they cast a glittering glow over the decorations Molly, Mara, and Karen had put up earlier in the day.

The pub looked quite transformed; everything seemed to glitter and sparkle in some way, from banners hanging from the ceiling, to balloons placed in bunches in the corners of the room. He noticed they'd set out the bags of hats, noise makers, and Christmas crackers for them to sell tonight to get everyone in the festive mood. He made his way across the pub and turned up the thermostat behind the bar. The electric heater clanged and groaned, protesting against the cold.

He went through the swinging door leading to the kitchen and turned on the bright fluorescent lights, their brightness hurting his eyes momentarily. He began hauling out trays of glasses, stocking up for the night. It was going to be a busy night, he hoped. The pub needed the business badly; now that the tourist and contracting seasons had long since dried up, they'd fallen behind on several bills.

"Michael?"

"In here!" he called out from the kitchen, hearing Brendan's voice from the front of the pub.

"Mighty cold out there tonight. Think anyone's going to show up?" Brendan asked, rubbing his hand together to warm them.

"The amount of money we've spent on this night, I sure as hell hope so."

"Me too."

Brendan wiped a cold hand over his face; the poor man looked like he hadn't slept in a couple of days. Michael knew he'd been worrying over their finances too.

"Don't worry," he told his friend, patting him on the back, "Everything is going to work out just grand."

"Of course it will," Brendan replied with a certainty Michael knew he didn't feel.

"Hello? Brendan? Michael?"

The two friends poked their heads out of the kitchen door at the sound of Molly's voice. A rush of cold air swept through the pub as Jimmy held the door open for Molly and Karen to walk through and the heater clanged and groaned. Molly set down the large number of bags she'd been carrying and placed them on the bar, a big rush of air expelled from her lungs in the process.

"Oh good. You're both here. Help me carry these into the kitchen, won't you?"

"Ye bought enough food for an army!" Brendan exclaimed, and Michael could see him mentally tallying the cost.

"Yes, well. We have to serve food, love. The whole village is coming out tonight. Don't worry so much; everything will be fine." Molly gave him a quick kiss on the cheek before carrying some of the bags into the kitchen.

"Here Karen, have a seat." Michael pulled out one of the chairs, helping her to settle herself.

"Thanks," she said, her voice a little winded from the short walk from the car park to the pub. And it was no wonder; she looked like she was ready to give birth any second. Michael wondered if she should even be here tonight, but he wasn't about to question her.

"Can I get you anything? Something to eat or drink?" he asked, as Jimmy and Brendan carried the rest of Molly's bags into the kitchen.

"No, we're grand, Michael. Thanks." She rubbed her huge belly.

"Well, if you need something, just let me know." Michael moved to the bar, setting everything up just as members of Brendan's band began to come in the front door.

"Hello lads," he greeted them. They made their greetings and began setting up on the little stage he and Brendan had placed in the corner for when they did special events.

Half an hour later, the band was set up and warmed up, and patrons began to arrive. Brendan emerged from the kitchen, leaving Jimmy to help Molly with the food prep and greeted people as they arrived.

The pub filled up quickly. Michael found himself looking up every time the door opened, though he wasn't exactly sure what he was looking for. Or, rather, *whom* he was looking for.

"I don't think she's coming, mate," Brendan told him, clapping him on the shoulder in sympathy.

Then the person he least expected to be here walked in.

"Michael? Are you listening to me?" Brendan waved a hand in front of his face, trying to catch his attention. Following his gaze, he realized who it was Michael had been staring at, the person who'd made him freeze right to the floor.

"Ah jaysis," Brendan exclaimed as his eyes latched onto Eliza. She stood there in the doorway, her eyes searching out and finding Michael.

"What?" Michael finally asked, as if just now realizing that Brendan had been talking to him.

"Nothing."

There was no point in competing for Michael's attention, not with Eliza here. At least, not until he'd gotten her out of his system again.

"Michael! Brendan? Where are those drinks?" Mara's voice cut through the din of the pub, finally reaching the both of them.

"Huh?"

"Drinks?" she asked again, giving them both an exasperated look.

"Right."

Michael took the glass he held in his hands and began pulling pints, placing them on a tray for his sister. Brendan, seeing that Eliza had sat herself down at a table, felt sufficiently safe to leave Michael and Mara to handle the running of the pub and went to the stage.

"Alright, who's ready to get this party started?" Brendan asked the crowd, taking over the microphone. A cheer went up from the crowd and the band began to play.

After a couple of hours of roof-raising music and fun, Brendan once more took over the microphone, getting the crowd's attention, motioning them with his hands to get them to quiet down.

"Alright lads, here we go:

"Ten… Nine… Eight… Seven… Six… Five… Four… Three… Two… ONE! Happy New Year!"

A cheer went among the crowd as everyone began to link hands and sing Auld Lang Syne. As the song came to an end and everyone was settling themselves back in their chairs to enjoy some more music, Jimmy turned to his wife and, noticing that her complexion was paler than normal even under the dim pub lights, he asked,

"Karen? Is something the matter?"

His slightly panicked tone caught the attention of everyone in the pub, who turned to observe the young couple, ensuring they were alright.

"I think my water's broke," Karen said, clutching her stomach with one hand and gripping the back of the nearest chair to her for support, a puddle of clear liquid on the hardwood floor of the pub pooling beneath her.

"Ah jaysis! I'll call the ambulance," Brendan said, hopping down from the stage and rushing over to the phone behind the bar and dialling the number for the emergency services.

"Just come over here and have a seat, love," Sinead, appearing suddenly by Karen's side, said to her in a soothing tone.

"I don't think I'm ready for this," Karen said, her voice rising as a small contraction hit her.

"Everything's going to be just grand," Molly told her soothingly, rubbing her shoulders while furiously motioning for Jimmy to come over and hold his wife's hand. The poor lad's had gone as white as a bed sheet, a look of terror etched onto his face as the prospect of impending fatherhood finally hit him.

"Jimmy get over here and sit with your wife!" she hissed at him as he stood there frozen before them.

Suddenly, as if shocked to life by a jolt of electricity, Jimmy bolted to his wife's side and tried to hold her hand as a contraction hit her. He tried to make comforting noises, but Karen wasn't going to have any of it.

"Get away from me!" she yelled at him, the pain taking over. "This is all your fault!"

Looking up at Molly with a bewildered look like he wasn't sure what to do, Molly sighed and motioned for him to keep holding his wife's hand anyways, despite the murderous glare she was giving him.

"Don't worry lad; she'll say much worse things to you before the day's done," Dermot chimed in with a tone that said he thought he was being extremely helpful. Both his wife and daughter turned to glare at him. A snicker went through the crowd in the pub, particularly from those who were fathers and had been yelled at by their wives in the throes of labour pains and knew very well what young Jimmy was about to go through.

"Alright, everyone, let's give her some space," Mara yelled out at them. "In fact, why don't you all head home? There's nothing here for you to see."

There were a few grumbles as some patrons began to pull on their coats, annoyed they were being forced out on their big night out.

"OUT! The lot of ye!" Mara roared at them, making everyone in the place jump. Anyone who'd had any thoughts of lingering to see if they could add any tidbits to the gossip they would undoubtedly be spreading as soon as they left the pub, jumped off their stools or chairs, everyone hurrying out of the pub doors lest Mara come after them. When she'd finally shooed out the last of them, she heard Karen giving a slightly strangled groan as another contraction hit her.

"Where the feckin' hell is that feckin' ambulance?" she practically screamed at her husband, making poor Jimmy go paler than any of them thought possible.

"Now, now, let's not use that kind of language..." Father Patrick began to say before he was cut off.

"Sorry, Father Patrick, but the day you push a human the size of a football out of your fanny is the day you can lecture me on what kind of feckin' language to use when I'm next in labour!" Karen told him sharply and clamped her jaw down, emitting a low keening as she tried to breathe through another contraction.

All That Compels the Heart

The normally genial priest looked slightly put out at this rather abrasive treatment, but thankfully knew better than to reply any further.

"It should be here any minute now," Molly told her reassuringly, still rubbing her shoulders and trying to keep her calm.

"Oh look! I think they're here now."

The lights from the ambulance glinted off the stained glass windows of the pub. They all looked up as the paramedics burst through the front door, letting in a rush of cold January air.

"Get me to the feckin' hospital. NOW!" Karen roared at them.

"You go on with her in the ambulance, love," Molly told Jimmy as he helped Karen to her feet, helping to lie her down on the stretcher the paramedics had brought in to carry her to the ambulance with. "We'll follow along behind you and meet you at the hospital.

Poor Jimmy looked terrified out of his mind, but obeyed.

"You lot get into the car. I'll drive," Sinead ordered the rest of them as she was the only fully sober one amongst them and ushered them out of the pub.

Chapter Thirty-Nine

Weeks had passed and January was already halfway through when Aoife finally decided to return to Ballyclara. After Edinburgh, she'd returned with Bex and Millie to Dublin, spending some time in her flat. She'd told them she'd wanted to stay so she could spend some more quality time with them, but it was rather apparent to all that she was waiting around in the city to see if Danny would come back. After two weeks of waiting for him to come home, she knew it was fruitless. If he was going to come back to make things right between the two of them, he would have done it by now. She just had to make peace with the fact that he'd come to her when he was ready.

As Aoife drove back into Ballyclara, she noticed a crowd of cars at Brendan and Molly's place. Wondering if there might be a party going on, or if something had happened, she pulled to the side of the road and put the Jaguar in park. Turning off the ignition, she stepped out into the cold, clear air and looked both ways before crossing the street. As she approached the house, she saw Sinead and Dermot coming out the front door.

"Aoife! Welcome back."

She felt slightly on edge at seeing them, guilt sinking in from the way she'd behaved the last time she'd seen them, but she noted they were both smiling, looking genuinely pleased to see her.

"Thanks!" she replied, trying to give them one of her best smiles, hoping that all was well between them.

"You missed the big excitement on New Year's Eve. Well, New Year's Day, I guess it was by that point."

"Oh? What excitement was that?"

She looked over their shoulders to the house. She could see through the front windows that there seemed to be a bit of a crowd inside, which would explain the number of cars parked outside.

"Karen Connelly only went into labour right after the clock struck midnight and the baby came a bit early."

"Oh my gosh! How is she? Are she and the baby alright?"

"Everyone's grand," Sinead was quick to reassure her. "A little baby girl for the two of them."

"Oh that's so wonderful." Aoife beamed from ear to ear to hear that her friend and her young family were well.

"You should go inside," Dermot said to her, pointing over his shoulder at the house. "I'm sure everyone would love to see you."

"I think I'll do just that."

"Well, love, we should head out." Dermot pointed to their car, indicating he and Sinead should be on their way. "It was nice to see you again. Hopefully you'll stop in and have tea some time?"

"Sure," Aoife replied, not able to find a good reason why she shouldn't accept the offer. After all, it wasn't Dermot and Sinead's fault that she was avoiding Michael. Sinead smiled and nodded to her, she and Dermot walking back to their car, leaving Aoife standing in the drive. Heading up to the house, Aoife noticed the front door was open, a small crowd gathered in the front sitting room.

"Aoife! Welcome back!" Karen's voice cut through the din in the house, everyone stopping what they were doing to look at her as she walked through the front door.

"It's so good to see you," Molly said to her, crossing the room to give her a hug. "Come in, come in and make yourself comfortable."

She ushered her towards a spot on the sofa beside Karen, Jimmy and the baby that Mara had just vacated.

"Thanks." She settled herself and gazed down at the tiny baby girl Karen held in her arms. "Oh she's gorgeous," Aoife crowed. "What's her name?"

"Molly Aoife Mara Connelly."

"That's gorgeous!" she exclaimed. "Wait; you gave her my name?"

"Well, Jimmy and I were trying to come up with the right name for her, and we wanted her to have a strong name. One that reflected the strong, influential women in our lives. It was rather easy to come up with Molly, because of everything Brendan and Molly have done for us, giving us a place to live and taking care of us like they have. And Mara, well, she's been there for me and helped to train me, and she and the rest of the Flanagans have been so supportive and kind towards us. And then we thought of you, where you've been so helpful and generous towards us, and we thought, well, if even just a little of that generous soul of yours rubbed off on her, then Miss Molly here would be all the better for it."

"I'm *so* flattered!" Aoife replied, feeling moved by the gesture. "Thank you both so much! I don't know what to say!"

"Here, why don't you hold her?" Karen said, handing the baby carefully to her.

Aoife held her arms out carefully towards her, gently cradling the little infant in her arms. She was a tiny little thing, but solid. Her eyes were closed, resting comfortably and her little rosebud mouth pursed in a little moue, small bubbles of saliva forming at the corners. Her skin was soft and smooth, little rolls of fat around her elbows and knees. She hadn't protested at being shifted from her mother to Aoife, only brought a little balled fist to her brow and scrunched up her face before yawning and settling again. Aoife stroked her little cheek, feeling the softness of her skin which smelled like baby powder and that special scent that all newborns had.

"Well, I never thought to see you holding a baby."

All That Compels the Heart

Michael's voice cut through Aoife's special bonding moment like a knife. Little Molly must have sensed the consternation Aoife was feeling for she began to fuss and kick at the blanket her feet were wrapped in.

"Shhh…" Aoife cooed to the little girl, trying to soothe her, sorry for having disturbed her sleep. It only seemed to make her more upset.

"Here, may I?" Michael asked, holding out his arms to her. Acknowledging her limited capabilities with children, she conceded the child to him.

He was a complete natural, of course. He'd barely held little Molly for a second before she'd settled back down again in his arms, sleeping peacefully. She found it both infuriating and yet somehow completely adorable the way he held the little girl in his arms, able to bond with her instantly, as if he'd done it a thousand times. He was a natural parent, and it pained her a little to remember that he had lost both of his own children so young and had never been able to experience this moment with them. There was something so tragic about it all. He must have felt her staring at him for he looked up from the little sleeping angel and gave her a little smile.

"Ah, there you are."

The look between Michael and Aoife was broken by the appearance of Eliza by his side. She rose on her tiptoes to give him a quick kiss on the lips, turning her head slightly to make sure that Aoife was watching, letting her know that she had staked her claim on Michael once more.

Aoife was surprised that she wasn't surprised to see the two of them back together again. A part of her had always assumed that it would only be a matter of time before Eliza returned to Ballyclara, and it was only inevitable that she'd worm her way back into Michael's heart again. After all, wasn't this their pattern? Wasn't this what Brendan had warned her had happened countless times before?

Speaking of Brendan, he was sitting in the corner of the room, observing the little show Eliza was putting on for them all, looking less amused than Aoife did, if it were possible. She couldn't say she blamed him; more than a little part of her was not only disappointed by this reunion, but slightly heartbroken.

Little Molly didn't appear to like Eliza's intrusion, once more beginning to fuss in Michael's arms, her little fists curling in anger and her face pinched and red. She gave a whimper of annoyance and tried kicking her little foot out of her blanket once more. Michael tried to shush her, but she was having none of it.

"I think someone wants to go back to her mammy."

"There, there now," Karen said, coming back over and sitting down on the sofa, taking her daughter from Michael. Molly continued to fuss for a few seconds but eventually was soothed into calming down once more. As the little girl settled and everyone was focused on her, Aoife found herself in the awkward position of being left alone to talk with Michael and Eliza. Clearly, they too felt the awkwardness of the situation.

"I see you've come back to Ballyclara, Eliza. Did you have a good time in Belfast?"

Aoife didn't really care one way or another, but she didn't want to seem impolite.

"Yes." Eliza smiled blandly at her and linked her arm with Michael's making sure the two of them were never more than an inch apart.

What does she think I'm going to do? Steal him from right under her nose right here in front of everyone?

Of course, it was *exactly* what Eliza feared she'd do, which was why she was putting on this show for Aoife's benefit. Michael, for his part, looked slightly uncomfortable about the overt display of affection from Eliza in front of her, but didn't object. Another long pause hung between them.

"And yourself, Aoife?" Michael finally asked. "I trust your visit to Edinburgh was a nice one? I didn't think you were planning to stay there long. I would've thought we'd have seen you back in Ballyclara sooner."

Aoife noticed Eliza's eyes narrow at the comment.

"It was nice, thanks," she replied quickly, trying to get off the topic. She didn't want to talk about the failure that was her trip to Edinburgh, where she'd tried to run away from her feelings for him and all she'd ended up doing was thinking of him. "And I decided to stay on for a bit in Dublin after we got back."

Michael nodded. The dark look on his face indicated he was troubled, but by what, she did not know.

"Well, I should head back to the house. It's been a long day of travelling…"

The awkwardness had settled between them again and she didn't much want to stick around for more glares and petulance from Eliza.

"Oh, so soon?" Karen asked, disappointed. Now that her daughter had settled back into her nap, she'd been following the tail end of their conversation.

"Why not stay for just a little longer?" Michael surprised her with the question and she wasn't sure how to respond.

"I really shouldn't. I should get back home and unpack and make sure the place is still standing."

She'd meant it as a joke, but Michael quickly replied, "Don't worry about the Old Rectory. I've been keeping an eye on it while you've been gone."

She nodded to him.

"Thank you. Well, I'll be back to visit this little one," she turned to Karen and gazed down at little Molly, "very soon. I promise."

"We'll hold ye to it," Jimmy told her, as she rose from the sofa.

She waved to the both of them and headed towards the still-crowded front entrance of the house. In order to pass through the tiny doorframe to leave the room, she had to squeeze by Michael, her body lightly brushing up against his as she passed.

"Sorry," she mumbled and quickly headed outside. She was crossing the street to where she'd parked her car when she heard footsteps behind her. She turned and looked over her shoulder and saw that it was Michael who'd followed her out.

"What do you want, Michael?" she asked him tersely, opening the car door.

"You forgot this inside," he replied, holding up her scarf.

"Oh, thanks."

She took the blue and yellow plaid scarf from him and was about to sit in the driver's seat when she was surprised by Michael putting his hand on the door, firmly closing it.

"Have I don't something wrong?"

He stared down at her, his eyes intent and she felt herself withering under that intensity.

"No," she lied, even though she could tell that he knew she was lying.

"Really? Because ye barely said two words to me after Christmas Day and as soon as I show up here, you're suddenly tired and need to head straight home? Not to mention no one's heard from you the whole two weeks you've been gone," he replied.

"I don't need to give you a full itinerary of when I come and go, Michael," she replied, her tone angry and defensive. "Now, I'm tired and I would like to go home."

She put her hand on the door handle of the car, but Michael made sure the car door remained firmly shut.

"Well, if you're really that tired, Aoife, perhaps I should be driving you home."

"I'll be grand," she said, trying to open the door again and glaring at him to move out of her way. "Get out of my way, Michael."

"Not until you tell me what's wrong." A determination burned in his eyes.

"Won't Eliza come looking for you soon if you don't go back to the party?"

The mention of his former fiancée made him straighten up and a grimace came over his face. Reluctantly, he removed his hand from the door. Not waiting for him to change his mind, Aoife quickly hopped into the car, roaring the engine to life and sped off, not even bothering to buckle her seatbelt in her haste to get away from him. She tried not to look back in the mirror at him standing there on the side of the road, left wondering what he'd done.

૭૦૦૨

Aoife spent the rest of January holed up in Aldridge Manor. It had been unseasonably cold since she'd come back, an excuse she often used as to why no one had seen her in the village and, when that didn't suffice, she told them she'd been busy with her writing.

She hadn't seen Michael since their argument outside of Brendan and Molly's place. Karen and Jimmy had stopped by with little Molly to visit a couple of times, as did Mara with Rory. She'd even had Brendan and Molly over for dinner one night, and she'd been down to visit with Sinead and Dermot, but in all of those times, she'd neither seen hide nor hair of Michael or Eliza. No one had even brought up their names around her, like it might offend her to do so. She wanted to remind them all that nothing had happened between her and Michael, so there was no need to treat her with kid gloves. She was happy for the both of them, if they were happy. And the rumours floating around the village certainly seemed to confirm this.

Indeed, according to the gossips – Maud and Anna, primarily – it seemed that while Michael and Eliza's engagement was not back on yet, they expected an announcement rather imminently. Maud had patted her hand delicately as she'd relayed this news to Aoife, giving her a rather sympathetic look like she was expecting her to collapse in a puddle of tears at any second.

Really, why does everyone think I should care whether or not Michael and Eliza are back together?

Everything would have been easier to deal with if she and Danny were talking again. She could remind everyone that she already had a boyfriend and the last person in the world she was thinking about was Michael Flanagan. Except that she wasn't sure where she and Danny stood right now and that nagged at her.

Distracting her from her current train of thought, the phone rang loudly beside her. Looking at the caller ID, she could see that it was Simon, her former boss. Wondering what in God's name he could want, she decided to pick up, despite the voice inside her head screaming and telling her not to.

"Hello?"

"Aoife? It's so good to hear your voice!" His tone was sickly sweet, like toffee-covered chocolate. She immediately recognized it as his I-want-something-from-you voice.

"Hello Simon."

Aoife kept her own tone measured. After all, what the hell could he possibly want after all this time? It had been six months or more since she'd last worked for him; surely any statute of limitations on what he could ask her to do for him had run out by now?

"I hope I haven't caught you at a bad time, have I?" he asked, probably noting the edge in her voice.

She'd quickly thought about telling him that she was actually just about to head out the door to some super important appointment, but her curiosity had sunk in enough to want to know what he wanted from her that she decided against it.

"No, it's fine. What can I do for you?"

"Well, I was actually hoping to talk to you about what *I* can do for *you*."

You can get off the bloody phone and stop bothering me, that's what you can do for me. However, she tempered her inner voice, telling it to shut up.

"What you can do for me?" she repeated, a little stunned by the proposition.

"Yes. You see, we've done some re-evaluations here at the office, and we'd like for you to come back and work at Arbour Hill. We think you're the right fit for a fiction editor position that has come up, and we'd like to offer you the job."

Aoife would have been lying if she'd said that she wasn't floored by the job offer. Never in a million years would she have thought about returning to Arbour Hill, let alone that they'd have come to her with a job offer.

A job offer that has better pay and a better position than you were in the last time you worked there, no less.

"I... ummm..." she stammered, suddenly wishing she'd thought of something more eloquent to say.

"Yes, well, I'm sure you'll want some time to think it over."

"Yes."

Why? Why did she just say that? These were the people who'd treated her like crap while she was working for them last, and then let her go, and now here she was, saying that she'd give consideration to a job offer from them? Sure, it would be better pay, but was that enough to make her come back?

"Great, well why don't you take some time to think about it and I will check in with you in, say, a week or so? It's so exciting to have you back on the team! I mean, if you take the job of course."

"Of course." She was beginning to regain some of her mental faculties, the shock beginning to wear off a tiny bit.

"Great! Talk to you soon. Bye!"

"Bye."

The dial tone rang in her ear as she began to process everything that had just happened in that two-minute conversation. Was she really considering going back to Arbour Hill? It was crazy, wasn't it? What would this mean for her writing if she went back to work as an editor? It would certainly mean less time for her own writing. It would also mean moving back to Dublin and being based out of the city again. Thankfully, she'd kept her flat, so she'd have a place to say. Was that why she'd kept the place? Because a part of her had always known something like this may have been a possibility?

There were so many things to consider now. She took a deep breath, but still feeling too on edge to settle down and continue writing, she got up and began pacing. She knew what she needed to do, whom she needed to talk to about this. Grabbing her keys and her purse, she headed out to her car and headed for Dublin.

ℬ)ℭ

Aoife, Millie, and Bex sat around the little island in the middle of Aoife's kitchen back in her flat in Dublin. She'd sent them an SOS text, telling them to meet her immediately.

"What? What's wrong?" Millie had practically burst through the front door when she'd arrived, her eyes frantic and worried.

"Have a seat," Aoife had told her, waving towards one of the stools.

"What the bloody hell is going on?" Millie had demanded once more. Aoife took a deep breath before recounting to them the phone call she'd received from Simon. After she'd finished, she saw Millie take a big sip of wine while Bex just looked shocked, not sure what to say.

"Well?" she asked nervously, wondering what they were thinking. A short silence fell between them until Millie finally made her stance clear.

"Do NOT go back to them, Aoife. They didn't appreciate you when they had you, and they won't appreciate you now. Sure, it's going to be more money, but it's not worth it."

Aoife saw Bex nod.

"Millie's right. They were complete cads about how they let you go in the first place, and now they suddenly want to have you back just because you're about to publish an amazing novel? Don't do it; they're just looking for the media attention it would give them if you were to publish the novel while working for them. You're better than them, and they know it."

She hadn't even thought of the implications of publishing while working for Arbour Hill. She knew they were right though; she had sent around some query letters while she'd been here in Dublin for the last few weeks and Arbour Hill had probably gotten wind of her novel. She also knew that there was a part of her that was afraid the novel wouldn't live up to the hype and she'd end up a failure, which was why she'd been considering the editor position. At least she'd have something to fall back on.

"And what about if I need a so-called 'real' job? Don't you think I should at least consider it? I mean, there's plenty of perks that comes with being an editor."

"If you really want to go back to Arbour Hill, of course we'll support you," Bex said, elbowing Millie in the ribs when she began to protest. "We just think you'd be happier somewhere else is all."

"Thanks. You two are the best friends a person could have," she said, coming around to the other side of the island to give them both a big hug.

"So, you're going to turn them down, right?"

"I just want to think it over some more. Just make sure that I'm completely sure, but I think so."

"Well, if you need a reminder as to why you left there in the first place, you just call us and we'll be there to save you from saying yes to them."

Aoife smiled at her friends, grateful to have them.

༄༅༅

One good thing to come out of the days that followed her job offer from Arbour Hill Publishing was that it had been the catalyst to bring her and Danny back together again. Well, not in person – he was at a conference in Dubai and she was back in Ballyclara – but he *had* called to let her know that he was sorry for not getting in touch with her sooner and that he'd heard from her grandmother, who'd found out that Arbour Hill wanted her back.

"I think it's a great opportunity for you, babe. I think you should seriously consider it. Besides, think of all the fun we could have together once you're back in the city."

"But *you're* never in the city," she reminded him. Their time apart had been a reminder for her that the things between them were still complicated by him always being away for work.

"Well, I've been thinking about that… How would you like it if I could spend some more time at home instead of traveling all the time?"

Aoife was floored by the question. There'd never been a time in their relationship where she'd questioned the amount of time he needed to spend traveling. It had just been an established rule in their relationship that Danny would be traveling for work a lot of the time, and if she wasn't ok with that, well, she could leave at any time. But now that he was talking about being in Dublin more, it made her begin to wonder if their previous discussion about settling down in Malahide might have been driven by more than just him being upset with her for buying Aldridge Manor.

"Are you saying that you'd do that?"

"Well, I've been giving it some thought and there's a VP position coming up in the next few months, and if I get it, it'd mean being based in the Dublin office more. Which means that we could see each other more often. Would you like that?"

She knew she should be thrilled with the prospect of seeing Danny more often. After all, hadn't she just spent the better part of the last month trying to communicate with him more? And how much easier would have it been if he'd just been based in Dublin the whole time? She *should* want this. Anyone else in her position would want this.

"Of course."

"Great. Well, listen babe, I have to get going back to this meeting but seriously consider the offer from Arbour Hill, alright? They clearly want you back and it would be good money."

"I will."

After hanging up the phone, Aoife felt more confused about her decision than she had before. Bex and Millie had both made good points against going back to work, but Danny had also touched upon all the considerations she'd thought about in terms of returning to the publishing house.

"Gahhh!" she exclaimed, frustrated with herself. She needed a third opinion. Seeking enlightenment, she threw on her winter jacket and headed outside into the cold. Perhaps a walk would help clear her mind and give her an idea as to what she should do.

Without any real destination in mind, she'd found herself walking towards the little parish church. Believing Father Patrick might be able to help her, she headed inside to get out of the chilly winter breeze. She hadn't seen any smoke coming from the chimney of his little cottage, so she'd gone into the church itself in the hopes of finding the elderly priest.

While the old stone church provided shelter from the breeze, it was still freezing inside. Aoife rubbed her bare hands together, trying to warm them. She spotted the priest at the front of the altar, looking like he was trying to practice his sermon for Sunday's service. The old door creaked behind her as she let herself in and closed it behind her. He looked up at the noise and smiled when he saw her.

"Ah, Aoife! Come in, come in. Come for a visit, have ye?"

"Yes, Father." She blew on her fingertips once more and proceeded up the main aisle to the front of the church.

"Well, come in and sit down," he said to her, indicating the front pew. "It's a cold one out there, isn't it?"

"Yes, Father."

Something about the look she had on her face must have indicated the conflicted feelings she was having, for he asked, "Is something on your mind, child?"

"You could say that…"

She wasn't exactly sure how to begin, so she decided to start from the beginning. "I don't know if I've told you before, Father, but I used to work for a publishing house in Dublin."

"Ah yes. I seem to recall hearing that." He nodded, encouraging her to go on.

"Well, I didn't just come down here to the country to work on my writing. I got let go from the publishing house back awhile ago, which is how I came to have the time to live down here and work on my novel."

"I see." He pondered over the information.

"They were in a bad way back in the spring. The economy and all."

Again, a small nod from the priest, indicating he understood and was patiently waiting for her to make her point so he could help her.

"Well, I got a call from them, and they'd like me to come back and work for them again."

"I see. And are you thinking of going back?" he asked her, one eyebrow raised.

"I don't know, Father."

"Would it be a better position than what you had before?"

"Yes. They want me to be a fiction editor. It would be better pay and better work than what I was doing before."

"Ah. Well, that doesn't sound so bad," he said to her with a little smile.

"No, it doesn't. But…"

"But?" he asked, the quizzical brow raised once more. Light shining through the stained glass windows cast light shades of green and red across his face.

"Well, there's my life here to think about."

"Ah, yes." He nodded again, understanding her meaning. He clutched the Bible that contained his notes for his sermon in his lap. "Well, it sounds like you have a lot to consider."

"Mmmhmm. And, on top of it, Danny – that's my boyfriend – he's going for a VP position within his company, which would mean he'd be in Dublin more."

"Right, he does a lot of traveling, doesn't he?"

"Yes."

"So, having him based in Dublin would be important for you both in your relationship."

"Yes."

"And I take it that this, Danny, would prefer ye to take the job in order to be in Dublin more?"

"Yes."

"Well, that is a lot to consider." His tone was measured, thinking over her dilemma.

"This is why I need your help Father." She looked down at her hands in her lap. The fingertips had gone white from the cold and she shoved them into her pockets, hoping to warm them. "What do you think I should do?"

The elderly priest mulled over what he was going to say for a minute before speaking. "Well, I think it's entirely your own decision and that it's up to you to determine what's best for you."

"What kind of priest are you, if you can't direct your flock in the right direction?" There was mirth in her tone to let him know she was saying it in jest. "Aren't you supposed to tell your flock what to do all the time?"

He smiled at her.

"I know that it seems a cruel piece of advice, telling ye that ye should do what is best for you, but you're the only one who can determine what that is. You're of perfectly sound mind, and I have faith you'll come to the right decision for you."

He patted her lightly on the knee in a fatherly gesture, which she supposed was meant to be reassuring. She wasn't entirely sure that she was reassured by it. Coming here had only left her with more questions than answers.

She sighed. She was just going to have to make this decision on her own.

Chapter Forty

Before she knew it, February had arrived, and Aoife had made her decision. But, before she was able to relay this news to Danny, he'd called to tell her that he'd received the promotion he'd told her about.

"That's great! So, when will you start?"

She held the receiver close to her ear, listening intently.

"Well, officially not for a few months," he replied on the other end of the line. His voice sounded excited.

"But still, that's amazing!"

"Exactly. Which is why I want to celebrate."

"Of course. I was planning to come up to Dublin in a few days…"

"No. We're celebrating tonight. Look outside your window."

Aoife's face looked puzzled, wondering what he could mean.

"Go on. Have a look."

Aoife crossed her bedroom to the front window and pulled the curtain aside. In front of the house was a limo, a driver, and Danny standing under her window, waving up to her.

"Wait, what?" she asked, still holding the phone to her ear. She waved back down at him.

"You don't have anything going on, do you?"

Something about his tone indicated that he didn't think there could possibly be anything she was doing down in Ballyclara that was *that* important, irked her.

"No, no," she replied quickly, not wanting to offend him or sour the occasion, even though she was slightly annoyed at the implication that he didn't view what she did as being all that important.

"Then put on your best dress and get down here; we're going out on the town!" he shouted up at her, holding his mobile away from his mouth so as not to shout in her ear.

Aoife extracted herself from the windowsill, nearly bumping her head on the open window. She sighed, glancing at herself in the mirror.

Well, we'll have to make do with what little time we have…

She knew Danny wouldn't wait for her forever, so she ran over to her closet, pulling out a blue and silver peplum dress, hastily removing her pyjamas and throwing the dress over her head, trying to locate a decent pair of high heels as she reached behind her to zip up her dress. Finding what she was looking for, she sprinted to the bathroom, slapping on some blue eye shadow the same shade as her eyes, and some foundation and mascara.

Sighing at the sight of her hair, she pulled her auburn curls back from her face in a hasty up-do, teasing some curls to hang around her face. She looked a mess – or so she felt – but it was the best she could do with the time she had. Grabbing her shoes off the chair where she'd laid them and running down the main staircase, she hastily slipped them on along with her coat and headed outside, careful on the steps in case they were slippery.

"You'll do," Danny told her, looking her up and down as she walked towards the limo. He tucked a stray curl behind her ear before giving her a quick kiss on the cheek.

"Well, if you'd given me more than ten minutes to put myself together, I would've been able to do much more," she replied a little tersely. "Well, you at least look dashing."

He smiled at her, appreciating the compliment.

"So, where are we going?"

"First," he said, holding up a finger with one hand and revealing a bouquet of red roses he'd been hiding behind his back with the other, "Happy Valentine's Day."

"Danny! They're beautiful!"

She took the roses from him, holding them up to her nose, breathing in their heady scent. She instantly felt bad; she'd forgotten it was Valentine's Day and had not gotten him anything.

"Don't worry; I know we don't normally celebrate these kinds of things, but I felt this time we should put a bit of extra effort in now that our fortunes have changed."

He smiled at her, reading her face.

"So, are you ready for your Valentine's surprise?"

"Where are we going?" she asked again, wondering if they were heading back to Dublin. He held out his hand to her.

"It just told you; it's surprise," he whispered, a devilish grin on his face.

Intrigued, she took his hand and let him help her into the back of the limo. Aoife watched the lights from the village pass by and was expecting to cross over the little bridge and head out of town towards Dublin when it turned right, heading straight to the pub.

"What?" she asked, rolling down the window to see that they had, in fact, stopped outside of *O'Leary's*. "I don't understand?"

"I know you think I hate this place, but you love it here, and while I'd much rather whisk you away to Dublin, I thought I'd give this place another chance."

He smiled at her, looking like he hoped she wasn't disappointed in the surprise.

"It's perfect," she replied, smiling at him.

Danny helped her out of the car and the two of them carefully walked towards the front entrance of the pub. As predicted, the place was pretty busy for a Wednesday night considering the holiday and this being the only pub for miles. As they walked inside, she noticed one table had a tent card with Brendan's scrawl on it, reading "Reserved."

All That Compels the Heart

"Here we go, Aoife," the very man himself said, greeting them both at the door and indicating the empty table. She saw that it had been carefully set for two, with silver candlesticks placed in the centre.

Brendan held out her chair to her as she took off her coat and settled in. Instead of asking what they wanted to drink, he began to pour some champagne into two flutes that had been sitting on the table, waiting for them.

"Molly will be right out with your meals," he said, a smile on his face. "Is there anything else I can get for ye in the meantime?"

"Everything's lovely, Brendan. Thank you."

"If ye need me, I'll be just over there at the bar."

He pointed over to where Michael was standing, glowering at her and Danny. Shrugging off Michael's gloomy presence, she focused herself instead on the man in front of her.

"Happy Valentine's Day, baby," Danny said to her, raising his glass in a toast. The champagne tasted sweet on her tongue as she took a sip.

Just as promised, Molly arrived with their meals only a moment later, placing the dishes in front of them. She was curious to see what Danny had chosen for them: chicken cordon bleu, his favourite.

"Looks fantastic! Thanks Molly."

The chef smiled smugly, looking pleased with herself at her accomplishment. She tucked into her meal, a peaceful quiet descending between her and Danny as they ate away.

As their meal came to a close, she looked up at him and said, "Thank you for all of this."

"Well, we have a lot to celebrate this Valentine's Day with me getting the VP position and you taking up the editor position at Arbour Hill, and…"

Aoife's stomach felt like it was going to fall to the floor, her meal suddenly turning a sour taste in her mouth. She hadn't yet told him about turning down the editor position and now she wasn't sure whether to bring it up or to let it slide. She would, of course, tell him; she *would*. She was just afraid of ruining this lovely meal he'd planned out for her and everything he'd done to make the night special. After all, this was his big day too, what with celebrating his new position. She was loathe to ruin it for him, but she also felt like she should lead him on.

"Listen, Danny. There's something I…"

He held up a hand to stop her and pushed back his chair, standing up. She looked up at him, mouth agape, wondering what he could be doing.

Was he upset with her over something? Had he found out she'd turned down the position with Arbour Hill and was about to confront her about it?

"Before you say anything, I have something to say to you." She looked at him, even more confused than she was before.

"Hey, can I get a bit of quiet here," Danny called out to everyone in the pub. Everyone in the room looked at him curiously, but obliged. Aoife too gave him a curious look, wondering what he had to say to her that would involve half of the village.

Oh. Oh…

Before bending down on one knee, she saw Danny glance towards the bar where Michael was standing, like he wanted to make sure that he saw this. Aoife heard a gasp from somewhere in the crowd as Danny pulled out a little, black velvet box, opening it for her to see. Inside was one of the largest engagement rings she'd ever seen. A square-cut diamond set on a white-gold band, it and the twenty other diamonds surrounding it glittered off the pub's lights, sparkling like white caps on rough waters on a sunny day.

"Well, what do you say to it then, eh?" he asked, nodding towards the ring.

It wasn't the most romantic of proposals, but nevertheless, a rush of emotions washed over Aoife and a million thoughts raced through her mind in the matter of a few seconds. Once shock and surprise had presented themselves, doubt and indecision crept up behind them. Was Danny the one? Did she want to spend the rest of her life with him? Of course, they'd talked briefly about moving in together, but that was a whole other conversation compared to getting *married*. And if she didn't want to be married to

Danny, how could she say "no" in front of all these watching and waiting people?

She suddenly realized everyone around her was waiting for her to answer and that the longer she hesitated, the more awkward the silence was going to become. Instinctively, she glanced towards the bar to see Michael's reaction to all of this, but he had on his best unreadable poker face.

Come on Aoife, pull yourself together.

Even though she was sure only two seconds had passed by, it felt a whole lot longer, and she knew that things were about to get really awkward really fast if she didn't at least say something.

When she thought of it all, she and Danny had been together for what seemed forever, and how could she really do better than him, anyways? He came from a good family, he wasn't scared off by her family, they'd love for her to be married to him, and he could maintain the lifestyle she was used to from when she was growing up. Not that that really mattered to her, but it *would* matter to her family. Like Grainne had said to her at Christmas, Danny was a good catch and she'd be a fool to lose him.

"Yes," she said, smiling down at Danny.

He rose up off his knee to kiss her on the lips and a big cheer went up throughout the pub. Smiling to the cheering crowd, Danny slipped the ring on her finger.

"Oh. It's too big."

"It's alright," she said to him, seeing he was annoyed that it didn't fit and not wanting to ruin the moment. "We can take it in to be re-sized."

She adjusted the ring to her middle finger, afraid of losing it, right before an influx of well-wishers descended upon them to give their congratulations.

ଛେଉ

"I'm taking a break," Michael told Brendan, tossing his towel onto the bar and heading out to the back via the kitchen door.

Brendan sighed, worried for his friend. Going over to the bar, he pulled two pints and nodded to Jimmy to indicate he was following Michael outside. He found his friend leaning up against the back wall of the pub, tendrils of smoke from his cigarette curling around his head along with the wisps of cold air as he breathed out. February had come in cold and dark, and tonight was no exception. The backdoor light cast shadows on Michael's face and frame, but Brendan didn't need the light to show him that his friend was tense.

"Well that was a bit of shocker now wasn't it?" he asked handing one of the pints to Michael.

"Hmmm…" Michael took a long swallow.

"I wasn't sure if she was going to say yes or not there for a minute," Brendan prodded, trying to gauge where his friend's head was at. Michael didn't say anything, only smoked his cigarette in silence.

"I mean, how embarrassing would that have been?" he pushed, still receiving no reply from his friend.

Knowing Michael too well to know that he'd gone past the point of being able to push him into answering, he just stood there with him in the cold, feeling the stucco wall behind him and drinking his beer. He knew Michael would open up to him when he was ready.

"I was kind of surprised she *did* say yes," he finally said, a few minutes later.

Brendan nodded cautiously, waiting for Michael to elaborate.

"Ah well, good luck to 'em both. At least there's a few good things to come out of it."

This response shocked Brendan more than his first one had, and he made some indistinct noise to relay his confusion.

"Well I mean, he *is* the biggest eejit I've ever met in me whole life. I would've thought Aoife could see through him, but I guess she's not as bright as I thought she was."

This last statement was made with a rueful twist of his mouth, like he was disappointed in Aoife somehow.

"Ah well. Now she'll move back to the city and buy some big fancy house with him in Malahide somewhere, and we won't have to put up with either of them anymore.

"I warned you when she came here that she'd be the type to buy up the Old Rectory and flip it a few months later."

He wagged a finger at Brendan, looking like he expected him to confirm his superior skills in the art of deduction. Except that Brendan wasn't so sure his friend was right this time.

"Ye really think she'll move back to the city?"

His tone was serious. He liked Aoife – despite the little game she and Michael seemed to be playing with their feelings for one another – he hated the thought of seeing her go, not least of all because he wondered what it would mean for Michael if she did.

"Ye don't think Danny, the man who has only deigned to come down here to Ballyclara twice in all the months Aoife has lived here, is going to let her keep this place, do ye?"

Brendan thought over his friends words.

"No, probably not, though I'd like to think he'd respect the fact that she seems to really like it down here. She's put a lot of work into the Old Rectory; it'd be a shame for her to leave it all now."

"Ye mean all the work *we've* put into the place," Michael corrected him.

"Ye know what I mean," Brendan conceded. "But, you'd think after all that work that the last thing she'd want to do is just up and leave the place."

"Well, good riddance to her."

"Ye don't mean that, Michael."

"Sure, I do."

Michael took a long drag from the butt of his cigarette and threw it onto the ground, stamping it out.

"And here I thought you'd rather a different opinion of her, of late."

Brendan saw Michael raise a quizzical brow at him.

"What do ye mean?"

"Ye know very well what I mean. Just what are ye doin' with Aoife, anyways Michael?"

Brendan turned to face his friend and gestured towards the window where they could see Danny and Aoife sitting at their table, holding hands and kissing. His tone was serious this time. It was time for Michael to face some truths before someone ended up hurt.

"Nothing."

"Don't tell me that because I know it's not true. Ye take her out to the falls, ye make a fine spectacle of the two of you at the céilí, and then there was Christmas where you yourself admitted that the two of you almost kissed."

Great puffs of air billowed around Brendan's head as he talked excitedly.

"How do ye know about that?"

"About what?"

Brendan was confused, wondering which point he'd made that had finally seemed to sink in.

"About us going up to the falls?"

Of the three things he mentioned – which were only the tip of the iceberg, he might add – he did not expect Michael to question him on that one. "Walter and Mary Collins were driving up that way and saw the two of ye. They were telling everyone in the pub about it."

"Yeah, well they can keep it to themselves."

"It was merely an observation, but from that tone, it sounds like something more happened. I know that's your special place, Michael, the one you don't take anyone else to, not even your best friend. Aoife must be someone real special to ye for you to bring her up there."

Michael's face disappeared behind a cloud of smoke as he lit another cigarette, giving him a second to compose himself.

"You're off your head, ye are. There's nothing going on between me and Aoife."

"Oh really?"

"What the hell makes ye think there's something going on between us?"

Brendan looked at Michael incredulous, but he was met with friend's stony gaze, asking him to provide good evidence of Michael's feelings for Aoife.

"Well, I don't know… there's everything I mentioned earlier."

Michael made a guttural noise in his throat, a distinct note of derision in it.

"Maybe it's the way you're always going on about her, how stupid her boyfriend – excuse me, *fiancé* is – or how ye broke off your engagement to Eliza and not two seconds later, you're after chasing Aoife."

Michael made another derisive noise and muttered something to himself. Brendan could distinctly hear the word "crazy" in the jumble of words.

"Am I though?" Brendan asked. He knew he was playing with fire, being direct with Michael like this. He was likely to shut down and not talk about it further if Brendan continued to push him too much.

"What's it to you? I'm back with Eliza, Aoife is with Danny; everyone's happy. I know you don't like Eliza much, but you know what? It's too feckin' bad."

"I never said I don't like her, Michael," he defended himself.

It was true; he wasn't much fond of Eliza, but in all the years she and Michael had been dating – or what he supposed was their version of it – he'd tried to be as supportive as possible.

"Ye don't have to; it's written all over your face. And Molly's too, for that matter. Neither of ye have ever liked Eliza, even since we were kids."

He wasn't wrong, and Michael knew it.

"Look, I'm not saying that I'm overly fond of Eliza or that I'll ever be, but if you love her, then Molly and I accept her as part of your life, just as we've done for the last ten years. We just want you to be happy, Michael, and if that means being with Eliza, then so be it."

Michael puffed away on another cigarette for a second, the two of them listening to the faint strains of music and laughter coming from the pub. Brendan was fully riled up by this point and couldn't stop himself from going on, no matter what his friend thought of it.

"I mean, you've been engaged to Eliza now for years and yet you two haven't managed to make it to the altar. Doesn't that tell ye something? How long do ye really expect her to wait around for you to make up your mind?"

"There's no rule which says you have to get married right away after becoming engaged," Michael replied defensively and Brendan could see the line of tension in his shoulders as he continued to lean against the wall. "Eliza and I just haven't found the right time to get married."

"The right time? Jesus, Mary and Joseph, surely if the right time was coming for you two, it would have come sometime in the last ten years, Michael, don't ye think? In my opinion…"

"Which no one asked ye for."

Brendan ignored the interruption. "I think ye settled for Eliza because you felt you had to, because of the baby."

Michael straightened up and cleared his throat sharply, a warning sign to Brendan that if he hadn't crossed the line yet, he was dangerously close to it. Brendan knew better than anyone how much the pain of losing his children had affected Michael; Christ, he'd been the one to pick him up off the floor more times than he could count. He knew he had to be delicate about this, but he knew he also wanted Michael to see his relationship with Eliza for what it was: one of duty and obligation, of familiarity, but not one of love.

"I think you were always waiting for something, some*one*, better to come along. And now that she has, you're standing here, pretending you could care less. Ye need a reality check, mate. Either you're going to take a chance on a life with Aoife, or you have to settle for Eliza and be fine with it."

Done with his speech, Brendan exhaled deeply.

"So ye think ye're my life coach now, do ye? Think you can just come out here and tell me what I should be doing with meself?"

"Well, someone's got to. Someone has to knock you on your stubborn ass sometimes in order to save you from doing something stupid that you'll regret." He tried to say with humour, even though he meant it entirely.

Michael took a long swallow of his beer, finishing it off and setting the glass down on the bench below the window. He turned and gave Brendan a pat on the shoulder and smiled at him.

"Thanks mate."
"For what?"
"For the advice."

Brendan looked at him suspiciously. He wasn't used to Michael agreeing with him. His confused look just made Michael's smile even wider. With another pat on the back, he began to walk off.

"And where the hell do ye think you're going?" Brendan called out to him. They still had a full pub inside and half a shift to finish.

"I'm taking your advice," he shouted back to him and stalked off into the night.

"Christ," Brendan muttered, gathering up the glasses and headed back inside. If his best friend was going to make the worst decision of his life, he planned to make sure that at least he'd have a job to come back to when everything was said and done.

※

"Let's get out of here."

Danny draped a heavy arm around her shoulders and whispered in her ear as she showed off her engagement ring to Molly and Mara. Aoife could tell from the way he leaned against her where he thought the end of this night was going. She'd sent him to settle the bill with Jimmy and make sure the limo was out front waiting for them.

"Congratulations, Aoife," Mara said, squeezing her hand and giving her a smile, but there was a certain disappointment behind it that made Aoife think she wasn't entirely thrilled for her. "Well, Molly, we should get back to work and let these two enjoy the rest of their night."

"Thanks," she replied, squeezing Mara's hand in return before she and Molly returned to their work. She couldn't explain why, but Aoife found herself suddenly reluctant to leave her friends.

"Should we go?" Danny asked her, giving her a deep kiss and not waiting for her response. He ushered her towards the door, the two of them nearly bumping into Brendan as he walked back into the pub.

"Sorry," he mumbled to them as he brushed past.

There was something about the way his face was drawn down that made her think something was wrong. Brendan was usually the one they could all count on to be amiable, to always be ever the optimist. She wanted to stop and talk to him, but Danny was moving her along swiftly to the limo.

Getting inside, the car sped along Ballyclara's narrow streets back to Aldridge Manor. They'd barely pulled up in front of the house and the front door closed behind the two of them when Danny started pulling off his clothes. Caught up in the whirlwind of emotions the night had presented, she followed his lead, removing her outer garments, tossing them on the floor around her. As she ascended the staircase, heading towards the bedroom, she dropped her dress, and then her under-garments along the way, enticing him to follow her. It didn't take much. Aroused as he was, Danny followed behind her closely.

Sex with Danny was always fast, quick as lightning and just as fleeting. She was always left breathless when everything was said and done – like she'd been on a carnival ride – but just like on one of those rides, she was always left with this dissatisfaction, this feeling that what she'd gotten wasn't nearly as satisfying as she'd thought it would be. She was always left with this longing to try again until she achieved that perfect high.

When he finished, Danny groaned and rolled off her, fast asleep and snoring within seconds. Aoife lay there on her back, staring up at the ceiling above her. She knew she was too wound up with pent up energy to sleep now, so she got up carefully from the bed – not that she needed to; Danny was sound asleep and only a natural disaster could wake him – and went to the shower, washing the day away.

Emerging from the steamy bathroom twenty minutes later, she found Danny still in the same position she'd left him in. Grabbing an afghan from one of the chairs by her dressing table, she tossed it over his naked form so he wouldn't get cold. Her mind still too busy for her to settle down just yet, she went into her study and began to write.

೫つ౧೩

Michael knocked on the door. Every light in the house was off, but he pounded even harder. Brendan was right: he had to make a decision, and that decision was that he was going to get back with Eliza. He needed to prove to Brendan and everyone that he wasn't interested in Aoife. She'd made her choice to marry that eejit even though it was clear to everyone in the world that he would break her heart, and it was time for him to move on. It wasn't like anything had happened between the two of them so far, anyways. That near kiss at Christmas was the furthest either of them had gone.

And yet…

No, he needed to be done with this. He belonged with Eliza, no matter how sick he felt at the thought of Danny and Aoife together as she'd shown off that ridiculously big diamond. Did he not know her at all? She wasn't interested in flashy jewelry so much as having the person she loved with her.

Oh well, if she's too stupid to see what an eejit he is, then she deserves him, Michael thought unkindly. But somewhere deep down, he knew he didn't really mean it.

No, enough.

He needed to be done with her and with thinking about her. Brendan had been right: Eliza had waited on him long enough; the two of them would make it work this time, he was sure of it. He just needed to commit more to the relationship. He could do that. Aoife been just a silly little flirtation while he and Eliza worked through things. Now that he was committed to doing that, everything would be fine. Or so he kept telling himself all the way to Eliza's place.

It took quite a bit of knocking before he finally saw a light turned on in the bedroom window upstairs and the sound of someone coming down the main stairs. He heard the bolt on the door sliding across and the door opened to show a still-sleepy Eliza.

"Michael?" she asked, surprised to find him standing at her door at this time of night. "What are ye doin' here?"

Michael didn't respond right away, but instead pushed his way inside despite the annoyed sound Eliza made. He would make his case to her and if she wanted him to leave, he would.

"I wanted to talk to you," he finally told her when he entered the small sitting room off the main hall. It was arranged perfectly, like a show room in a furniture store, everything in just the right place. He felt slightly guilty standing there in his boots and made sure to stand only on the hardwood portions of the floor, lest he drag any dirt into the cottage Eliza had taken so much care to design for herself.

For *them*, he reminded himself.

While she may now live in it and it may be designed the way she'd wanted, it had technically been given to the both of them by her parents. It was just that it hadn't exactly felt like *his* place or *their* place, even when they were both living together. Well, that would change now.

"At this hour of the night?" she asked him, clearly annoyed by his intrusion and the late hour. She pulled her white silk dressing gown around her, folding her arms across her chest. "It couldn't wait until a more normal time of the day?"

"No," he replied simply.

"Alright, then," she sighed loudly, following him into the sitting room and sat down on the sofa and crossed her legs. "What do you want to talk about?"

"Us," he replied, again in monosyllables.

"Us?" she asked, clearly surprised by his answer. Then her posture became defensive, her mind grappling onto the source of the problem between them. "Don't tell me you're calling things off for her again, are ye Michael? Because if you are, so help me God..."

"No, there's nothing between me and Aoife, Eliza, ye know that. There never was."

There never was, he told himself firmly, willing himself to believe it.

Eliza looked at him skeptically, but he held his ground.

"No, what I want to talk about is not about us breaking up, but rather, about us getting back together again. For good this time."

Michael saw her shoulders relax a little at this, curious about what he was getting at.

"You and I have been together since we were kids, Eliza, and I don't want to give up on that. After all we've been through, I think we owe it to ourselves to see this through. I know I'm not the easiest person to love, but somehow, ye get me. And over the last couple of months while you've been gone, I've had some time to think. And I realized during that

I want to give us another chance and I'm hoping that you do too."

Eliza looked at him suspiciously. "And you're completely sure that there's nothing between you and Aoife? Nothing to hold you back this time?"

"I'm all in. I always have been."

Eliza's expression darkened a bit at the reminder of her affair, at the implication that *she* was the one who hadn't been completely invested in this relationship from the beginning.

"Besides, Aoife's just got engaged to that boyfriend of hers down in the pub only twenty minutes ago. It's not like she's going to be around much longer to be a problem."

Eliza took in this information, mulling it over carefully. "Alright."

"Alright?" he asked, looking for clarification to where her train of thought was going. It wasn't like she was Aoife, who had a face he could read in any situation.

"Let's do it. Let's get married."

"Ye mean it?"

"Yes, Michael." She smiled up at him and he rushed over to the sofa, sweeping her up in an embrace. This was a good thing, it was. It was all working out exactly like it should.

"Michael! Your boots!" Eliza chastised him as he stepped onto the immaculately white carpet.

"Feckin' hell, woman you drive me mad."

He swept her up in his arms, ignoring her protests about him dragging dirt throughout the house and carried her upstairs.

Chapter Forty-One

Winter departed in a flurry of activity for Aoife. After their spur-of-the-moment engagement, Aoife and Danny returned to Dublin, with Danny taking up his new position at work and the two of them moved into her flat. It was an odd sensation for her and Danny to spend so much time together; they'd never been in the same city for more than a month before, but now, with Danny home more often, the two of them attempted to settle into a routine. It had taken quite a lot of adjusting, not helped at all by the blatant hostility coming from her friends. To say that Bex and Millie had not exactly been thrilled to hear about the news of their engagement would be an understatement.

"You're doing what?" Millie had spluttered into her wine glass when Danny and Aoife had announced their engagement at a party they'd hosted for their friends.

"We're engaged," Aoife had replied tersely, hoping to avoid making a scene in front of Danny's friends and colleagues. She knew how he got when he thought someone was trying to make him look bad in front of them. Thankfully, Bex had stepped in before Millie could say anything else.

All That Compels the Heart

"Come on, you," she'd told Millie in a tone that brooked no argument, linking her arm through hers and forcefully removing her from the room.

"Don't tell me that you're alright with this?" Millie had demanded when Bex had pulled her into the spare bedroom of Aoife's flat.

"Of course I don't like this any more than you do, but I believe we should support Aoife if this makes her happy."

"Happy? Can't you see she looks miserable out there with all of *his* friends?"

"They're not all Danny's friends, some of them are our friends too," Bex had tried to point out.

"Yeah, like a handful of them. The rest of them are as pompous and idiotic as he is!"

"If you don't want to be here, Millie, then you know where the door is."

Aoife's voice had cut through her friends' argument like a knife, and they'd both stared at her, mouths agape.

"You heard me. Leave."

"Aoife…" Bex had started but was cut off by an angry gesture from Aoife.

"If you'd like to follow her out the door as well, you're more than welcome to," she'd responded sharply. "In fact, let me get your coats for you."

She'd stepped in between them and had rummaged through the pile of coats on the spare bed.

"Here," she'd said, handing them both their jackets and holding out her arm, gesturing for them both to leave.

"Aoife…" Bex had tried again to reason with her.

"Just GO!"

It was the last she'd seen of her friends for weeks.

She'd meant to talk to them again once she'd cooled off, tell them that she'd understood that they had misgivings about Danny but that he wasn't as bad as they thought, and she really *was* happy with him, but she'd let the wound between her and her friends fester, and the silence had lingered on.

To make matters worse, when she and Danny had told her family about their engagement, they'd been over the feckin' moon. It had been decided by Grainne that they would have a June wedding.

"There's something so romantic about a June wedding, isn't there?" she had asked with glee – *actual* glee – that Aoife had hardly seen in her grandmother since Caitlin had been married. It was a good thing Aoife wasn't too fussy as a bride about how her wedding should look or be, for her grandmother had completely taken over the planning of the whole thing from the caterer to the flowers. The only thing she'd been left with was her dress, though Grainne – of course – had had her opinions on what her granddaughter should wear on her big day. Aoife, still in the throes of depression and anger over the argument with Millie and Bex, was more than happy to just leave it all to her grandmother to plan in any case.

By April, Aoife had had enough of the claustrophobia of the city and – being ever increasingly more miserable without her friends – had decided to retreat to Ballyclara. She found herself missing her life there, missed being able to write – which she hadn't been doing much of lately – and missed her friends from there. With Danny away on a business trip, she'd been alone in her flat for the first time in awhile and just couldn't take it anymore. Grabbing the keys to her car and packing a light suitcase, she rushed down to the car park and headed down to Ballyclara.

As she made her way along the rolling hills of County Wicklow, she felt a sense of calm and ease returning to her mind and soul. The combination of being around Maureen, Grainne, Caitlin, and Siobhan as they planned her wedding for her, the isolation from her best friends, the strain of adjusting to living with Danny full-time, had all begun to take its toll on her, making her feel anxious. It was nice to return to a place where she could feel calm and at peace again.

Driving through the centre of the village, she smiled and waved to the friendly faces she recognized, happy even to see Maud and Anna, despite knowing that her arrival in Ballyclara would give them some great new gossip to spread around town.

In her absence, Mara and Karen had been looking after Aldridge Manor for her, and the place looked in incredible shape. The plants they'd put in last year were now fully in bloom. The heady scent of roses and lilacs filled her nostrils, and the sun shone off the bright yellows of the daises and sunflowers along the front. It looked breathtaking, like a perfect precious gem sitting on a velvet cushion, and she realized she'd never seen the place in all its glory before. She felt a twinge of sadness that she hadn't been here to see the first blossoms make their appearance in the early spring days.

Heading inside, she saw that Sinead had kept the place clean and tidy for her, everything spotlessly clean. She made a mental note to do something nice for her as a thank you. She was just settling herself in when she heard the doorbell ring.

"Karen! It's great to see you," she greeted her friend with genuine delight. "And look at you, Miss Molly! You've grown so much!"

The baby gurgled happily in her pram, smiling toothlessly up at her.

"It's great to see ye back in Ballyclara. We've missed you; haven't we, Molly?"

She smiled again, soothed by the sound of her mother's voice.

"It's great to be back," Aoife admitted, calmed by their presence. Realizing that she was keeping them standing there on the doorstep, her good manners kicked in. "Come in, come in. I shouldn't keep you standing here outside."

She ushered to Karen to bring the pram inside.

"Actually, I was rather hoping to go into the garden? I haven't checked on it in a few days, and I want to make sure everything is looking good."

Aoife nodded to her and joined her outside, closing the door behind her. "That'd be lovely. I haven't had a chance to see it all yet, but everything I've seen so far is just grand. It looks so beautiful."

Karen smiled broadly, pleased at the compliment for her handiwork. "Well, Mara did most of the work…"

"I remember you having quite a lot of input into the design of the whole thing," Aoife reminded her. "You may have had to rely on Mara to do some of the heavy lifting, but you put as much into reviving this garden as she did. And would you look at that…"

Aoife's voice trailed off in wonderment as she lifted the little latch to the door in the stone wall, revealing the secret garden inside. Bees hummed lazily in the afternoon sunshine, floating from flower to flower, spreading the pollination. Every flower under the sun could be found here: hyacinths, roses, daisies, lilacs, petunias, the list went on. It was a riot of colours and scents, but a perfectly organized chaos, a beautiful kaleidoscope of colours and shapes.

"It's gorgeous."

"I'm glad you like it," Karen replied, smiling at her.

"Like it? I *love* it!"

She wandered around the garden, taking the time to smell each of the flowers, marveling at the arrangements Karen and Mara had created. Karen pushed Molly's pram over towards the patio, adjusting it to make sure she was kept in the shade while she went and checked over the flowers, ensuring everything was growing to her satisfaction. When they'd both completed their inspections, they settled themselves on the wrought iron patio furniture that someone had found in storage and set up for her while she'd been away. Aoife relaxed in her chair, sinking back against the cushions, letting the late afternoon sun gently warm her skin. She sighed in perfect contentment.

After a few minutes of silence, her and Karen just listening to the hum of the bees floating lazily around them and Molly gurgling to herself in her pram, making little contented noises as she watched the clouds above her drifting by, Karen brought up the reason she'd come by.

"I'm glad you came back to Ballyclara in time."

"In time for what?" Aoife asked, her eyes still closed as she sat there peacefully.

"Molly's christening is tomorrow and Jimmy and I – and Miss Molly, of course – would love it if you could come."

She rummaged around in her purse and, when she'd found what she'd been looking for, handed Aoife a folded piece of paper, thick and embossed with gold lettering.

"I know it's last minute…"

"No, I'd love to be there," Aoife said, smiling at her reassuringly.

"We were going to mail you an invitation, but we didn't know your address in Dublin and then we knew you'd be busy with planning your wedding and we figured you probably wouldn't have time."

Aoife felt a slight panic at being reminded of her wedding and everything that still needed doing, but she pushed it down. Right now, her focus was on relaxing and enjoying the company of her friends.

"Of course I'd love to be there. It doesn't matter how busy things are; I'll always make time for you and this little one."

Molly had finally begun to fall asleep, her eye lids becoming heavy and she gave a little yawn.

"In fact, since it doesn't say here that you're having a reception afterwards, why doesn't everyone come here after the christening for a little party?" she suggested, trying to prove that she really did want to make time for her friends here.

Karen looked at her, surprised. "Ye don't mind?"

"Of course not!" She reached over and gave Karen's hand a reassuring squeeze. "I'd love to host the reception for you. We could have it right here in the garden you've worked so hard, how fitting would that be? And, if it happens to rain, we can just move inside to the sitting room."

"That's *so* generous of you!" Karen exclaimed, reaching over and pulling Aoife into a hug. She patted her shoulder, pleased to see her so happy.

"No problem at all. Now, how about you and I go and ask Mara and Molly for some help and we'll throw something together?"

Karen nodded her approval and checked on her daughter. "I think she's finally gone to sleep. Let's walk down to Mara's before she wakes up again."

ೞಞ

The sun was out in full force the next day as Aoife left the house to walk down to the little church at the other end of the lane. She could hear the sound of laughter and Molly's pram bumping along the lane as she stepped outside to join the McCaffreys, Flanagans, and Connellys as they made their way to the church.

"Aoife! Welcome back!" Sinead called to her and waved.

Aoife waved back, waiting for the group to catch up to her and fell in step with them. One would think she'd been gone for a year or more instead of just a few weeks, the way everyone welcomed her back. She noticed that everyone seemed thrilled to see her again, everyone that was, except for Michael and Eliza.

Eliza threw her nose in the air and sniffed loudly at the sight of Aoife; she couldn't say she was any more thrilled to see Michael's fiancée than she was to see her. Michael, for his part, looked at her, his expression dark and stormy as per usual. She did her best to ignore them both and focus instead on Jimmy and Karen.

"Well, don't you look handsome," she said to Jimmy who looked quite smart in his best suit and navy-blue tie, his hair slicked back. The young man blushed instantly at the compliment, suddenly bashful. "Fatherhood suits you."

"Thank you," he mumbled, unsure of how to take the compliment. "You look quite lovely yourself today."

He nodded to the blue and white floral dress she'd chosen for the occasion. She smiled back at him. She couldn't believe how grown up the two of them looked, years older than when she'd first met them. Where had the time gone?

She suddenly felt much older than her age, compared to the young couple who'd married and had a child when Aoife felt like she was still trying to sort out her life and figure out how to grow into the person she wanted to be.

When they arrived at the church, Father Patrick greeted them all pleasantly, welcoming them inside. The inside of the little church was cast in shades of red, blue, yellow, and green from the stained glass windows. The stone baptismal font had been set up at the altar, ready to welcome the newest little member into the Church.

As the service came to a close, Aoife and Mara discreetly slipped out of their pews and headed back to her place, trying to get ahead of the small crowd to set up the garden for the reception. As they set out the punch bowl and began pouring

All That Compels the Heart

in the mixture they'd made earlier that morning, Mara broke the comfortable silence between them.

"So how is the wedding planning coming along? It's coming up quite soon, right?"

"Oh. Yeah, it is," she replied, realizing how close the end of June was now compared to when Grainne had set the date for her back in February. "I guess it's coming along."

Mara raised a quizzical brow, curious at this statement.

"It's just that my grandmother is doing most of the planning, she replied hastily, trying not to sound like she wasn't interested in planning her own wedding. Of course she was. It was just easier to let someone else do it for her.

"Are you and Rory planning to come with Connor? I noticed that we still haven't received your RSVP."

She was thrilled that Connor had asked Mara to come to the wedding. Despite her earlier misgivings about the two of them dating, she saw how happy the two of them were with one another and she couldn't stand in the way of that.

"Oh, I don't know. I don't think a big society wedding is exactly the right place to meet your family. I mean, Connor and I haven't even gone on a proper date yet, with him still being overseas."

Mara looked suddenly shy, focused a little too intently on setting out the little paper napkins they'd purchased yesterday, with their little pink soothers on them.

"I'd love to have you there," Aoife told her honestly. Without Bex and Millie, she was longing for some familiar, friendly faces to be there for when she got married. Her heart sank a little at the thought of Bex and Millie not being there for her big day.

"Then I'll be there," Mara replied, her voice sounding slightly concerned at the downcast look on Aoife's face. "Besides, Eliza's family has her wedding planning all under control; it's not like I'll be needed here for that."

"Oh, Michael and Eliza are planning to get married soon too, are they?"

Mara looked like she wished she hadn't said anything.

"In August," she finally replied, looking worried at revealing this news.

Aoife nodded. She'd heard through Connor, who'd heard it from Mara, that Michael and Eliza had gotten back together and were planning to marry, this time determined to make it work. She focused on laying out the silverware as Mara placed the plates on the buffet table they'd set up. She was pleased for them, truly. They deserved to finally be happy.

"I'm sorry you had to find out that way," Mara said, surprising her. It wasn't like anyone had to be concerned with her feelings on the matter; no, she was fine with it.

"Oh it's alright. I wouldn't expect Michael to ring me to tell me he was getting married. It's not like we're close friends or anything," she replied quickly, wanting to reassure her friend that she had taken no offense. "I'm happy for the both of them."

"Mmhmm," was all Mara said with a certain look on her face. She didn't have time to elaborate though, for they heard voices coming towards the garden as the little party arrived.

They'd managed to get everything in order just in time. The garden – as beautiful as it was – looked even more resplendent in the spring sunshine, the pink and white decorations they'd set up providing a nice added touch. The peace of the garden was disrupted by Rory and Des chasing each other around in a game of tag, Molly and Mara both calling out to them to mind their nice suits and not to get them dirty. Little Molly could be heard laughing, a shrill delighted little thing, watching the boys as they played. She kicked at the long, white baptismal gown she was dressed in, looking like she'd much rather be playing with the boys than being held in her father's arms.

Everyone eventually gravitated towards the buffet table where Molly had made a whole host of squares, cookies, cupcakes, and sandwiches for the occasion. Aoife noted that Karen's parents had come and were holding themselves to one side a bit from the main group, looking like outsiders. She saw Karen go over to them, trying to make an effort to include them, but the way they looked at Jimmy as he held their granddaughter, it looked as if they were not willing yet to accept their son-in-law or their granddaughter completely. And if they were less than thrilled with seeing their granddaughter, they completely ignored, Rory who was, in fact, their grandson through their son, Alistair. This seemed to suit the Flanagans just fine; they ignored the Byrnes as well.

Aoife sighed, thinking about the rifts that could happen between people. It reminded her of her own rift with Bex and Mille. She also knew she should call them, try to mend fences.

I will. I just need a bit more time.

But time before the wedding arrived was beginning to become a precious commodity. She pushed the thought from her mind and went back to tending to her guests, trying not to think of Dublin and the complications it currently held for her.

Chapter Forty-Two

Unfortunately for Aoife, she couldn't avoid Dublin, or her family, forever. A few days after little Molly's christening, Aoife knew she needed to go back. Not only would her grandmother be looking for her to make sure she was still searching for the right wedding dress, there was a poetry reading she'd wanted to attend at Trinity College. She'd been planning to attend the event with Millie, but now that the two of them were not speaking, she was just going to have to go by herself and, if she ran into Millie there, she was just going to have to put her pride behind her and try to make things right.

Packing up her suitcase and getting into her car, Aoife turned the key in the ignition. Her Jaguar made an awful screeching noise that grated on her teeth. Turning the car off and wondering what the hell she could have done to the poor thing to make it sound like that, she counted to ten and tried again. It produced the same result.

"What the feckin' hell?" she exclaimed, wondering what the hell was wrong with the car. Turning the car off, she got out and went around to the front, lifting the hood. It was hopeless; she only had a rudimentary understanding of a car engine, and this amounted to how to change the oil. She knew little else, as the rest could usually be easily solved by a mechanic.

She made a noise of frustration deep in her throat; this meant she was going to miss her poetry reading. Walking around to the other end of the car, she hauled out her suitcase, and muttered something very unkind to her car.

"Do ye need some help there?"

Michael. She'd recognize that voice anywhere.

She thought about telling him "no" and that everything was "just grand" but a part of her knew that he might also be able to help.

What was that you were just saying about putting your pride behind you?

"Actually, I could use a bit of help. Do you know anything about cars?"

He smirked, and headed for the open hood of her Jaguar, giving it a look. She abandoned her suitcase by the side of the car and came over to his side. "Well, can you fix it?"

"Probably, but probably not in time for ye to get back to Dublin. It'd be quicker if I just drove you there meself."

She looked at him, a little taken aback by his offer, wondering if he was being serious. This must have been written all over her face, for he said, "Well, if you've a better idea, you're welcome to give it a try, but it will cost ye a fortune and it'll waste your time to call a taxi, and this car is not going anywhere today. So, unless ye don't have to be back in the city today and can wait until I can look it over for ye, I think you should take the offer on the table."

"Surely you have better things to do today other than driving me back to Dublin."

She didn't want it to come across as rude, but neither did she want to be considered presumptuous. Also, she wasn't exactly sure she wanted to be stuck in a car for over an hour with Michael, the two of them trapped in the tiny, enclosed space with nowhere to escape.

"Actually, I don't." He looked at her, slightly amused, like he was trying to challenge her to find another reason not to take him up on his offer.

"What about just now? You were clearly going to do something."

"I was coming back from Father Patrick's. I was helping him with one of the pipes under his sink. It's done now and I've got the whole day free."

He leaned against the car, his arms folded across his chest, defying her to continue this game.

"And Eliza? She doesn't need you for anything? Wedding plans or something?"

"She's with her mother the whole day, scouting locations for the wedding photos. They're making a whole day of it and they most certainly do *not* want my opinion."

Aoife sighed, resigned. She knew that if she was going to make her poetry reading, she was going to have to take him up on his offer. She'd look completely ridiculous if she tried to go and ask Brendan or Mara for a drive now when she had a perfectly good offer in front of her. She just wished it hadn't been Michael who'd offered.

"Alright. I guess you can drive me to Dublin."

He raised one eyebrow, looking like he was going to give some biting remark about how she was *letting* him drive her Dublin when it was him who'd offered in the first place, but he wisely held his tongue.

"Alright, I'll go and get my truck. I'll be right back."

He unfolded his arms and then sauntered off back to his place to get his truck, leaving her there in the drive. She wheeled her suitcase around to the end of the drive where it met the lane. A few minutes later, Michael pulled up and hopped out of the driver's seat, silently lifting her suitcase into the back. Just as silently, she climbed into the passenger seat beside him. The truck roared to life as Michael threw it into drive and the two of them began their journey.

They'd gone the entire journey through Ballyclara in silence, listening only to the hum of the engine. Aoife kept her hands folded in her lap, feeling the denim of her jeans beneath her fingertips, watching the pub, and the rest of the village racing by the window.

Finally, just as the silence seemed to become completely uncomfortable for the both of them, Michael asked, "So what's the novel about, anyways?"

The question completely threw her off. She must have had the most perplexed look on her face for her clarified, "I realized in all the time you've been here, I've never asked you about it before."

He shrugged, like he could really care less what it was about, but something in his manner made it seem like an affectation, like he was only pretending not to be interested in her work.

"It's about a young woman who ups and leaves her boring, mundane life and decides to go and live somewhere new and exciting. While she's there, she falls madly in love with one of the locals, and they live happily ever after. Or, well, I actually don't know that for sure because I haven't written the ending yet, but I assume there'll be some trouble they have to overcome and then they'll live out the rest of their lives together."

Silence descended upon the truck again, once more the hum of the engine the only noise they could hear. Aoife was torn between glancing over to see what Michael thought of this premise and not wanting to know. There were just some people whose opinions she valued and, strangely, his was one of them. A sense of panic began to fill her stomach, making her feel uncomfortable and slightly terrified that he wasn't saying anything.

"So, it's a bit of an autobiography, then," he finally said.

"No, not at all. It's nothing like my life."

She saw him glance over at her, one eyebrow raised like he was trying to see if she was joking or not.

"You're telling me you don't see the parallels?" he asked her. "I mean, you up and left your life in Dublin to come and live down in Ballyclara."

"Except that my life in Dublin was far from boring and mundane," she pointed out.

"Right. Ye just needed something different to give you perspective."

"Right. I mean no; I didn't need perspective. My life in Dublin was perfect, *is* perfect."

"Of course."

Michael looked straight out of the windshield, never taking his eyes off the road. Even though he wasn't looking at her, she thought she detected more than a hint of disbelief in his tone. It irked her that he doubted her.

"It *is*," she insisted, folding her arms across her chest in a slightly petulant move. She didn't know why he was questioning her life decisions like this, but she didn't like it one bit.

"I believe ye," he said, but once again it was in that tone that made her question if he actually did.

"Then why doesn't it sound like you do?"

"I don't know... perhaps you're just imagining things."

"Hmph."

Aoife re-crossed her arms, this time more pointedly, showing how annoyed with him she was. A tense silence fell between them once more.

"So the whole part about your main character falling in love with one of the locals down in the little village she moves to, and the two of them living happily ever after, that part is totally not like anything in your life either?"

"Of course not," she retorted, still annoyed with him. "I'm happily engaged to Danny, if you remember, and if this were in any way autobiographical it would mean that my character would end up with..."

You. Someone like you.

She stopped herself before she said it out loud, embarrassed by the parallel.

"Right. Of course."

She knew he'd drawn exactly the same conclusion.

"Let's just not talk about my book, ok? It's not done yet, anyways. I might end up changing everything about it, who knows?"

"Ok."

He glanced over at her, looking like he was worried he might have offended her. He paused for a second before he asked, "So what's this thing you're going to in Dublin? Am I dropping you off at your flat? Or your grandmother's place? Or Danny's?"

"It's a poetry reading at Trinity College. I was supposed to go with Millie but..."

"But?" he asked, curious.

"I don't want to talk about it." She'd responded more sharply than she'd intended to.

"Did something happen between you two?" he pressed, his voice sounding concerned.

She didn't like it; it didn't feel normal coming from him. Why would he care if she and Millie had fallen out? It wasn't like the two of them were friends. It wasn't any of his business.

"I *said*, I don't want to talk about it."

"*Alright*." He made a noise of frustration deep in his throat like *she* was being the annoying one instead of him with all of his questions.

"I'm sorry." His voice sounded sufficiently contrite and, finally, she nodded to him, letting him know she forgave him for overstepping. "It's just that you and Bex and Millie seem so close, so I find it odd that you three wouldn't be talking."

"I didn't say we weren't talking."

"Well, you indicated that something was off between you. But," he held up a hand, warding off her lecture, "I get that you don't want to talk about it. However, if you ever *do* want to talk about it, you can let me know. Alright?"

She looked at him curiously, but he seemed to be genuine in his offer. It confused her, but she nodded, accepting his gesture.

"So, what's this poetry reading all about? Is it the work of someone I know?" he asked, changing topics.

"I should hope so; it's a reading of Shakespeare's sonnets."

"Ah." He nodded, sounding like he was trying to sound appropriately interested when he didn't think it was very interesting at all.

"Don't worry; I don't expect you to come with me. The ride will be fine."

"And what makes you think I wouldn't enjoy a bit o' Shakespeare?" His tone sounded slightly offended.

"I don't know... just the way you sounded there a second ago when I brought it up. It just doesn't seem your kind of thing, is all."

She hoped her tone sounded appropriately apologetic; she hadn't expected him to be vehemently interested in anything remotely related to Shakespeare.

"Well, you can't judge a book by its cover," he responded, sounding like he was putting her in her place.

"Do you want to join me?" she asked, wondering if she should have asked him earlier. It probably would have been the polite thing to do considering he was driving her all this way; she just hadn't thought he would be interested.

"Sure."

Great. Now what am I going to do?

~ ⁂ ~

Michael glanced at Aoife as she looked up at the speaker, enthralled by Shakespeare's Sonnet 18. She'd been partially right; he wasn't exactly interested in Shakespeare or his sonnets. He had a general interest in the Bard's work, but it certainly didn't extend to going to a reading. No, he'd come here today to be with her, which was a feckin' stupid thing for him to do.

He'd started out with the best intentions. He'd been coming back from Father Patrick's after helping him with some pipes which weren't working properly in his kitchen, and he'd heard – rather than seen – Aoife yelling at her car. Knowing something was wrong, he couldn't help himself from stopping to see what the matter was. He'd told himself that he should just keep on walking, but he'd stopped and had a look at the car, the whole time telling himself that if he just fixed the car, she could be on her way back to Dublin as soon as possible and out of Ballyclara, and everything would go back to being fine again.

Except that it *hadn't* been fine since she'd left and gone back to Dublin after her engagement. Michael had thrown himself into his work and trying to pay attention to what Eliza was telling him about her plans for the wedding, but his mind had always drifted back to *her*. It was as if – even though she wasn't with him – that she was always there.

He probably *could* have fixed her car in time enough for her to return to the city, but somehow, the offer to drive her up here had just slipped out of his mouth before he could take the words back. It was as if once he'd seen her again, he

All That Compels the Heart

couldn't help himself but try to find a way for the two of them to prolong their time together. It was foolish he knew, but it still didn't stop him from feeling the way he did.

And that was how they ended up here, at the poetry reading together. He'd told himself the whole time he'd been driving in the car that he was just going to drop her off where she needed and go back home, that it would put her out of his mind for good, but there'd been something in the way she'd talked about Millie and how they were supposed to go to this together that made him realize she didn't want to come here by herself. He'd also known that it was highly unusual for her and her friends to be having an argument over something. In the short time he'd known Aoife and her friends, he could see that the three of them were exceptionally close. He knew he couldn't just leave her here by herself.

In truth, it hadn't been so bad. He'd been more fascinated with watching Aoife and the way that Shakespeare's words spoke to her, bringing out that rare smile of pure happiness he'd only seen on a few occasions. He even had to admit that he'd been slightly disappointed when the presentation was over and he knew he'd have to return her to her flat, and then who knew when he'd see her again?

"Shall we go?" she asked, pulling on her jacket, lifting the collar up so her auburn curls wouldn't be trapped beneath it.

"Yeah. Sure."

With more reluctance than he'd been expecting, he'd risen from his seat and walked towards the door with her. As they approached the doorway, he could see that the clouds that had been in the sky as they'd driven up earlier had unburdened themselves.

"Shite. It's pouring out."

He hadn't thought to bring an umbrella with him on the journey, and neither of them were wearing the appropriate jackets. They'd be soaked within seconds if they attempted to make a run for the truck.

Rain beat down on the pavement and grass, petrichor hanging heavy in the damp air. Michael looked up at the grey sky above them, the dark clouds hanging low in the sky and full of more rain. People jostled around them, either trying to brave the weather and make a run for it to their next destination, or wisely they'd brought umbrellas and were unfolding them.

"It doesn't look like it's going to stop any time soon," Aoife said, taking a look at the sky. "Shall we make a run for it?"

He didn't exactly have a desire to head out in the rain, but who knew how long it would take for it to lighten up? Knowing she wanted to be on her way, he reluctantly turned up the collar of his jacket, affording him as much shelter as he could and held out his hand to her.

"Let's make a run for it."

She seemed hesitant to take his hand, but took it anyways, and the two of them set off at a run, dodging raindrops. They managed to make it across the square to an archway where they paused a moment to catch their breaths. They'd been soaked through within seconds of being out in the rain and Aoife's hair was plastered to the sides of her face. He ran his fingers through his own hair, lifting the damp strands from his forehead.

Thunder rolled over their heads, loud and rumbling. The sound momentarily frightened her, and she instinctively moved closer to him. As the thunder dissipated with an angry growl, they both looked at one another, their eyes locking. He'd put his hands on her upper arms when she'd come closer to him, wanting to reassure her, and now he was very aware of her body, so close to his own. Perhaps it was their proximity or the way this reminded him of Christmas Day when they'd nearly kissed on her front doorstep, or the way she looked so beautiful despite being drenched by the rain, but Michael leaned down to kiss her. Just before their lips met, a crack of lightning broke over their heads, making them both jump again – this time apart from one another – from the shock.

After the thunder abated, Aoife said, "I think we should make a run for it again. I don't think it's going to get any better out."

Distracted as he was by the enormity of his feelings for Aoife, it took him a second to process what she'd said to him. She was still standing close enough for him that it would take nothing to just simply reach out and touch her, to close the distance between them. And it was in that moment that he knew that Brendan was right and things were never going to work out between him and Eliza. He'd finally found a reason to move on from that life, found *someone* to help him move on from the pain of his past and all the loss he'd experienced.

Aoife was about to move towards the carp park, intending to head to the truck. Without thinking, he took her by the hand and pulled her back towards him, pulling her into an embrace. Searching her eyes for half a second to make sure this was something she wanted too, he saw a look of surprise but also one of desire for him. Encouraged, he tilted his head towards her and kissed her passionately.

The world seemed to stop for that moment, everything around them completely irrelevant for one blissful moment. It was a perfect kiss, like the kind you would see at the end of one of those sappy romantic films where everyone ends up living happily ever after.

As their lips parted, the two of them finally emerging for some air, they both let the kiss linger between them, not anxious for the moment to end. When Michael finally took a reluctant step back, creating some distance between them, it felt like a big gust of cold air had come between them and all the warmth had been sucked out from around them.

"Well," Michael said, clearing his throat.

"Well," Aoife said, her voice breathy.

"I'm sorry. About that," Michael said, at a loss for words. "I shouldn't have done it."

In fact, he wasn't sorry one bit for kissing her. Even if she rejected him now, as painful as it would be, he didn't regret kissing her.

"Oh. Right. Of course."

His heart was thrilled to hear more than a little disappointment in her voice at his apology. Did this mean there was even a tiny part of her that felt the same way as he did about her?

She looked down at her shoes, the both of them not sure how to proceed from here. While he would have loved nothing more than for her to declare her love for him right there on the spot and kiss him back, it didn't seem like that was going to happen.

Trying not to feel devastated, he turned to her and said, "Right. Shall we?"

He offered her his hand once more, craving just one more small connection between them. She looked down at his hand, giving it a long pause before she finally shook her head, refusing the offer and he felt a small sadness at the rejection. He couldn't blame her; he'd just spontaneously upended her world in one swift motion, but it didn't mean it hurt him any less that she seemed to have doubts now about their kiss. Mentally brushing it off, he took off and headed for the truck, hearing Aoife's boots on the pavement behind him. Water sluiced off them both as they got into the truck, small puddles forming on the leather seats.

"Where to now?" he asked, hoping she might want to go somewhere to eat or something; anything to prolong their time together.

"Home, please. If you don't mind?"

She looked at him apologetically, like she was sorry for imposing on him. Small worry lines formed where the bridge of her nose met her forehead.

"No problem at all," he replied, giving her a small smile, turning the key in the ignition and driving towards her flat.

They were silent throughout the entire drive, the two of them both thinking about the kiss. The rain continued to drum a steady beat on the windshield before them, the world around them obscured by the rivulets running down from the roof of the truck. As Michael pulled into the visitor parking and put the truck into park, he looked over at her, not sure what to say.

Aoife too looked like she was unsure what to do and finally said, "Would you like to come upstairs? I don't think this rain is going away for now, and I would hate the thought of you driving all the way down to Ballyclara in it."

His heart raced at the thought of staying with her just a little longer and he nodded.

"Sure."

He turned off the truck and the two of them got out, making a run for the front door of her building. As they stepped into the front lobby, he could tell that this was a vastly different sort of place for Aoife to live than Aldridge.

All That Compels the Heart

The lobby smelled faintly of chlorine, as if there was a pool nearby, and everything had a sort of faux antique look to it. As they climbed the stairs to her flat, he was struck by how impersonal the place looked compared to her place in Ballyclara. Everything was white, black, or stainless-steel, completely clean and pristine. It was not readily obvious that anyone actually *lived* here, except for the laptop on the kitchen table, and the boots by the front door.

"So, this is your second home, is it then?" he asked, still impressed at how impersonal it looked. She'd done so much with her house in Ballyclara, re-painting the walls, choosing all the furniture, putting up paintings and photographs so that it looked like a proper home. This place looked like it was being photographed for a magazine. Her two homes could not be more different if they tried.

He supposed it was sort of an unconscious testament to the fact that she was caught between two worlds: her perfect, ordered life in Dublin, and her infinitely more complicated one down in Ballyclara. While Aldridge Manor had supposedly been her escape from the chaos of the city, it would seem that perhaps Dublin was her escape from the turmoil within her that allowed her to be open and honest with herself when she was in Ballyclara.

"Here, let me hang that up for you," she said, offering to take his jacket from him. At the Old Rectory, she was the kind of person to not care about whether a person left their shoes on or not, or if they just threw their coat on the coat rack by the door.

"Thanks," he replied, bending down to take off his boots, afraid of getting the spotlessly clean linoleum floors dirty.

"Is there anything I can get you to drink?" she asked as she hung up his coat.

He could see that even the closet had everything in just the right place, everything neat and organized. He hated it. This was not real life; real life was messy and disorganized. This was not the Aoife he knew, and he wasn't sure he liked her trying to contort herself into this person.

"Uh, no thanks," he replied, putting his hands in the pockets of his jeans and standing there awkwardly in her kitchen. He was afraid to sit down anywhere or touch anything lest he spoil it. If they were back in Ballyclara, he would have no problem sitting down at her kitchen table, making himself at home but here, this was different.

He could tell that she was also feeling just as awkward as he was, the two of them still not sure whether to bring up the kiss or not. He was afraid that if they spoke of it, it might ruin the magic of the moment. It had been perfect just as it was and there was no need to over-analyze it. But if they *didn't* talk about it, they risked there always being this awkward distance between them. He wasn't sure which was worse.

"Michael, look…" she began but was interrupted by the front door opening and Danny standing in the front doorway.

"Aoife? I'm home," he called out, his voice trailing off as he saw Aoife and Michael standing there in the kitchen before him. Water from his plain black umbrella dripped a steady pitter-patter onto the linoleum floor beneath him.

"Danny? I wasn't expecting you." Aoife's tone was full of surprise. Michael – and Danny, for that matter – didn't fail to notice the hints of worry and panic in her voice. Instinctively, Michael took a step closer to her, as if to protect her from some threat.

"Clearly," he responded to Aoife's remark, but his eyes only saw Michael. He looked him up and down, taking in his wet, dishevelled appearance. It was apparent from the way his eyes narrowed that he was not thrilled he was here.

"I thought you weren't supposed to be back in town until the end of the week?"

"The conference wasn't really all that helpful so I left Alice and a few others there to take over for me so I could come home and surprise you."

"Well, mission accomplished."

Michael noticed the way she looked uncertain as to whether or not this was a good surprise or not.

"Um, Michael took me to the Shakespeare poetry reading I told you about a few weeks ago. The one Millie and I were supposed to go to?" she asked, sounding like she hoped this wouldn't be one of those times where he hadn't been listening to her when she'd told him about her upcoming plans.

"Something was wrong with the Jag and it wouldn't start, so Michael offered to drive me up to Dublin. We got caught in the rainstorm, and so I suggested we come back here until we got dried off and the storm passes."

She pointed to the window where the rain was still beating furiously against the panes, as if presenting evidence of why they'd come back to her flat.

Michael tensed to hear her working so hard to try and defend herself to Danny. Yes, he knew he'd been too forward with her with the kiss, throwing her off-guard, but there should not have been a need to work so hard to explain how he'd just been kind enough to drive her up here to Dublin and how she'd told him he could stay at her flat until the storm passed.

If I were her boyfriend, she wouldn't have to defend the situation to me.

He knew it was a lie; if the situation were reversed and he'd come home to find her and Danny in his kitchen, he *would* be suspicious, just as he would of any straight male friend of hers. However, male pride aside, he would have believed her if she'd told him what she'd just said to Danny.

But you're not her boyfriend.

"I had no idea you were such a lover of Shakespeare's work," Danny said to him. Although his words were perfectly innocent, his tone clearly accused him of having ulterior motives.

"You never know what you're going to find out about a person," he responded, trying to sound amiable.

Danny hadn't exactly been wrong about the situation; he *had* had ulterior motives in coming here with Aoife, and to deny that would be to lie. However, the last thing he needed was to get into a fight with Danny right in front of Aoife, no matter how much he might want to punch the guy in the face.

"I should go," he said to Aoife, touching her elbow lightly. He knew it could start a pissing match with Danny, but he wanted him to know he wasn't the only man in Aoife's life. Danny might be able to force him out of the flat, but he wouldn't force him out of her life.

"I'll take a look at the Jag for you and let you know what I find out."

"Thanks."

Aoife gave him an apologetic look. She knew how territorial Danny could be and she clearly was feeling more than a little ashamed at how he was acting in front of Michael now.

"No problem at all," he reassured her, lightly rubbing her forearm before brushing past Danny – who was still standing in the doorway – and hurriedly put on his boots and coat and showed himself out. He hated the idea of walking away like this, leaving her alone with him, but he didn't exactly have a choice right now. It was her decision whether or not to tell Danny about the kiss and he had to respect that.

Just like you have to talk to Eliza.

He hadn't forgotten the consequences of kissing Aoife and how they affected her; he'd been thinking about how they affected him and his own relationship too. Could he just go back to her now and pretend that everything was fine? Could he just pretend that nothing happened? He wasn't so sure.

As he reached the front lobby, he paused and looked out at the rain. It had abated somewhat, not coming down as furiously as it had been before but it was still coming down considerably harder than he would have liked for driving in. Knowing he would have to go outside eventually, he opened the door and made a run for it, faced with the fact that he would have the entire trip back to Ballyclara to figure out what the fecking hell he was going to do about his life.

ೞගೞ

"He *kissed* you?" Millie practically shouted through the phone and Aoife had to hold her mobile away from her ear.

After the kiss between her and Michael, Aoife knew there were only two people in the world she wanted to talk to about it, and neither of those people were Michael or Danny. No, the only people in the world she wanted to talk this whole dilemma over with were her two best friends. Putting aside her stubborn pride, she'd told Danny she'd needed to take a walk after the rain had cleared and had called Bex and Millie's place.

It had been surprisingly easier than she'd expected, and hearing Millie's voice now, talking to her like the two of them hadn't been avoiding each other for months, it had somehow calmed the riot of emotions going on within her.

"Yes."

It still felt weird admitting that Michael had kissed her, unsure as to how she felt about the whole thing. She knew on some level that there'd always been some sort of tension running just under the surface between them but neither of them had ever acted on it.

Until now.

She got up from the park bench she'd been sitting on, pacing around. She'd so much pent up energy that she couldn't just sit down right now. Besides, the bench was still slightly damp from the deluge of rain from earlier.

"What was it like?"

She stopped to think about the question, honestly trying to put everything she was feeling into words.

"Aoife? Are you still there?"

"I'm here," she replied quickly, reassuring them. "I just don't know how to describe it."

In fact, she *did* know how to describe it. It had been amazing, and wonderful, and everything she could have ever hoped for. She was just afraid of putting it into words. Talking about it made it real, made it a thing.

"I don't know; I suppose it was grand."

"You 'suppose it was grand?' What kind of response is that?!"

"Let her breathe a bit, Millie, jeez. Let the poor girl think things through. It's a lot to take in."

She was calmed by Bex's sensible voice, reassured by her understanding of the situation.

"So, does this mean that the engagement is off?" Millie's voice sounded a little too enthusiastic at the prospect.

"What?" Aoife asked, thrown off by the question as she'd been thinking back to the kiss. "No, of course not."

"So, you haven't talked to Danny about this?" Bex's voice was a mixture of concern and astonishment. Clearly, they hadn't expected her to keep this from him, but how could she talk this over with him in a rational way so he would understand it, when she didn't even understand what she was feeling?

"Millie," Bex's voice was low, a warning to not go any further lest it cause any problems.

"What?" Millie asked, clearly sounding like there was something she wanted to get off her shoulders. "Aoife knows all of this; we just haven't said it out loud before."

Somehow, when she was mulling things over in her mind, she'd lost track of the conversation and had missed something.

"Some things are better left unsaid," Bex replied.

"And sometimes it's better to get things off one's chest," Millie retorted.

"What's going on?" Aoife interrupted the two of them.

"Come on, Aoife," Millie started, "don't play dumb. You know that Danny isn't the right person for you. If he was, you wouldn't have kissed Michael, and you would have told him about the kiss before you told us."

"Oh I know this, do I?" she asked, incredulous that Millie was going to risk going down this road again so soon after they had just reconciled.

Millie hesitated for just half a second but was determined to press on and damn the consequences. "Yes, you do. We've been skirting around this issue for months now, but I think now is the time that we address this.

"Have you not noticed the way Danny always talks you into doing things for him, but he never does anything you want to do? You're always following him along to those stupid dinner parties and soirees for his company, to further along *his* career, even though he knows you hate going to them, but how many book readings or launchings or signings has he been to with you? None. That's how many. And where has he been the whole time you've been down in Ballyclara writing your novel? He's been here, or somewhere else in the world. He's barely been to visit you since you moved in.

"And let's not even talk about the fact he's never been there for you at any of your important family occasions. He couldn't even be bothered to come home and be there for you after your grandfather died, the one person who meant the whole world to you. I'm sorry, but I was raised to believe that relationships were about give as well as take. But it seems like Danny is all about the take with you and not the give."

She could hear Millie exhale heavily, exhausting her breath with her spiel.

She was upset at hearing her friend's opinion of her fiancé. Even if she was being honest with herself and the fact that she knew Bex and Millie were never going to like Danny – and vice versa – it still stung.

"It's not Danny's fault that work takes him away all the time. It's the nature of his job. I knew that when we first started dating and I accepted it as something that was going to be a part of our lives. He was straight with me from the beginning; he told me that he'd be away on long business trips, and that it would mean long hours at the office, as well as attending all those social events. I knew he'd be away for most of those launches and readings and whatever else I was taking part in, and really, it wasn't that big of a deal that he didn't show up to them. He would have been bored at them anyways. Besides, I knew I could always count on you two to share those kinds of things with."

She tried to shrug off Millie's conclusions with her own defense of Danny, but even she had to admit that her words still niggled at her mind, drilling little bores of doubt into her. Even though she didn't want to admit it, her mind was now flipping through everything Danny had missed over the course of their relationship, everything she'd done on her own without him. There was always some sort of excuse on his part to not be there for her when she needed/wanted him to be there, and no matter how she might try to ignore it, she couldn't quite ignore how familiar these excuses were starting to sound.

"That's my point!" Millie said, clearly happy Aoife had voiced a point she could expand upon. "It has always been Bex and I who've filled in for him when he should have been there for you, supporting you."

"But you're forgetting that he has done things to make it so we are closer together. I'm moving back to Dublin full-time and selling Aldridge Manor, and Danny has taken his new position in his company so that he'll be around more often. He even flew back early from his conference because it wasn't relevant to him and he wanted to come home to see me."

She tried to push down all of the doubts Millie had brought to the surface. Danny cared about her, *loved* her. He'd told her so. He'd noticed the distance between them since she'd moved to Ballyclara and he wanted to do something about it. He wanted to make things work between them, which is why he'd suggested she move back to the city, to give the two of them their best chance of making this work. And, now they were looking that place in Malahide he'd wanted last year that was still on the market.

She had to be willing to make this work between them, even if it meant giving up Aldridge Manor, right? This was the price she would have to pay for having everything she had wanted.

But is *it everything you ever wanted?*

"You're doing *what*?!" Bex and Millie both exclaimed.

She hadn't realized she was going to sell Aldridge Manor until she'd just said it to them. She and Danny had obviously been talking about it the last few months, figuring out the logistics of where they'd live once they moved in together. No matter how many scenarios she ran in her mind, she knew he'd never end up moving down to Ballyclara with her.

And, as amazing, wonderful, *perfect* that kiss between her and Michael was, he wasn't her future. Danny was her future, and Michael was just a temporary distraction. He'd always been just a distraction from her real life while she'd sorted herself out. And now that she had, she no longer needed Michael or Ballyclara. It was time to let them both go in order to move forward. She just wished it didn't feel so much like her heart was breaking by making this decision.

"It's for the best. Danny and I are getting a place in Malahide…"

"The one he was looking at months ago?" Bex's voice was sharp, annoyed.

"That's one of the ones we are looking at," she conceded. "It's still on the market."

It was a sign, or that's what Danny had said in any case. The fact that the house was still on the market, just waiting for them to buy it, was a sign that they should get the place.

"But you love your house and you love Ballyclara, and all your friends there," Bex tried to reason with her.

"What exactly do you two want me to say? That I'll miss Ballyclara? Of course, I will! But that doesn't mean I won't have an exciting life in Malahide with Danny."

Aoife was saddened and frustrated by the turn of the conversation and how they'd ended up fighting over the one topic they'd been trying to avoid fighting about.

"We just care what happens to you, Aoife. That's all," Millie replied, her voice soft, trying to be soothing.

"And you don't think Danny cares about me or about what makes me happy?" she asked, annoyed.

"No, Aoife, that's not what I'm saying, but you can't look at this situation and tell me that you haven't noticed that it's me, and Millie and Michael who've been around for you in the last few months a hell of a lot more than Danny has."

"Enough, Bex, enough," Aoife said, putting her hands up in a gesture of surrender. "I don't want to argue with you about this anymore. Clearly, we're not going to agree on this topic, so let's just leave it alone."

Bex sighed, but she didn't push the topic any further.

"I have to go. Danny will be wondering where I've gone to," Aoife told them.

"Alright. Well, if you need anything, you know we're here for you."

Aoife let the line go silent for a moment, not sure how to respond, before hanging up and tried to put the conversation behind her. She hated fighting with her friends, and she hated the way Michael was making her feel, and…

Frustrated with herself, Aoife stomped back towards her flat, feeling more confused than before.

Chapter Forty-Three

It had been a week since Aoife had returned to Dublin and had made the decision to sell Aldridge Manor. Even after a week, it still pained her to make the decision, but she was determined to move forward and not look back. The only problem now was that she was faced with having to go down to Ballyclara in order to pack her things. Danny had started making inquiries into the place in Malahide, reopening the conversation with the realtor about purchasing it. In order to put a proper bid on the place, it would mean having to sell Aldridge Manor as soon as she could. While she could've asked her mother or grandmother for a loan, or Danny could have asked for one from his parents, neither of them wanted to be indebted to their families when trying to start their new life together.

As her Jaguar was still in the shop – Michael's message on her phone had been a confusing jumble of words relating to car parts, only some of which she'd heard of before – she had gotten a lift from Danny's realtor, Saoirse, down to Ballyclara so she could have a look at the place and properly assess it.

"It's a gorgeous place," the woman said, admiring the work Mara and Karen had done in the rose garden. "Are you sure you want to sell it?"

"I'm sure."

There was only a small catch in her throat as she looked around at the place that had been her home for the better part of the last year. She was going to miss it.

It's not the only thing you're going to miss about this place...

She firmly told her subconscious to shut the hell up and leave her alone.

"Well, I've got some great photos of the place to put up on the website, and I'll get back to you about what we can expect for a listing price, but I expect you'll be quite pleased with the offer you could get for this place."

"Thank you."

"I need to head back to the city; did you want a drive back?"

"Ah no, you're alright," Aoife told Saoirse, with a wave of her hand. "I want to get a start on packing some things up."

"Alright. Well, I'll give you a call in a day or two."

Aoife stood in the front door, watching Saoirse speeding down the lane. She turned back to the house and sighed as she thought of the monumental effort it was going to be pack everything up. Knowing that the later she put it off the more hectic it would be, she got to work.

After a few hours of boxing up her possessions, she began to feel hungry. Knowing she had no food in her fridge, she walked down to the pub. She had to pick up her car and car keys from Michael in any case.

For a sunny, spring day, there were a surprising number of people inside the pub. She nodded to the regular patrons who welcomed her back into the village. Her heart rose in her throat a bit at the prospect of seeing Michael again; the two of them hadn't really talked since the kiss happened. Sure, he'd called to let her know about her car, but they'd not *properly* spoken to one another since the kiss. She was nervous and excited all rolled into one.

She was surprised, therefore, when she saw that Michael wasn't behind the bar. She tried not to seem too disappointed when Brendan came over to her to take her order.

"Hey Aoife. Welcome back."

"Hi Brendan. Thanks."

"Anything I can get for ye?" he asked, pen hovering above his little notepad he used for taking orders.

"Um... I'll just take whatever the special is today, thanks."

She handed him back the menu he'd placed in front of her when she sat down.

"Sure thing. Coming right up." He smiled broadly at her and headed off to place her order with Molly.

When he came back a few minutes later with her lamb stew, he tried to ask casually, "So, I heard ye came down with someone new today. A friend of yours from Dublin, I take it?"

"That was Saiorse, Danny's realtor."

"His realtor? Oh, is he looking for a property down here in Ballyclara as well?"

Brendan looked confused, wondering why she and Danny would be purchasing separate houses in Ballyclara.

"Um..." she wasn't exactly sure how to break the news to him gently. This was going to be one of the difficult parts of selling her house and moving to Dublin: how much she was going to end up disappointing everyone that she'd become friends with over the last year. In the end, she decided it was best just to rip the plaster off.

"Actually, Danny isn't moving down here. I'm moving back to Dublin. Permanently. I'm selling the Aldridge."

It was at just this moment that Michael happened to come out of the kitchen and walk by her table. Hearing her comment, she noticed his face transform from disappointment to downright melancholy, to anger before he was able to put up his mask of invulnerability.

She knew it would hurt him to hear she was going back to Dublin and she hadn't wanted him to find out about it like this, but she couldn't take it back now.

All That Compels the Heart

As Brendan searched for the right words to say to her, Michael went behind the bar and retrieved her car keys, placing them on the table in front of her.

"Well, I guess you'll be needing these back, then."

His eyes were unreadable, except for the slight twitch beside his left eye, a sign of the barely contained emotion he was trying to hide from her.

"Michael..." Her tone was pleading, hoping he'd give her a chance to explain.

"I'm taking a break."

He'd said it to Brendan, his tone sharp and curt. He removed the dark green apron he'd tied over his dark t-shirt and jeans and handed it to Brendan. Turning on his heel before either of them could stop him, he stormed off through the back.

"Aoife? It's good to see you back!"

She was distracted for a second by the arrival of Karen and little Molly. The baby slept peacefully in her pram, blissfully unaware of the turmoil going on around her.

"Have I interrupted something?" Karen looked from Brendan to Aoife, to Michael's quickly retreating form, assessing the situation.

"Aoife here was just telling us how she is moving back to Dublin. For good," Brendan finally spoke, his voice rueful and sad. "I should go and check on him."

Without waiting for a response from either Aoife or Karen, he went through the kitchen after Michael.

Aoife stared down at her bowl of lamb stew, suddenly not feeling very hungry at all. She looked up as Karen sat down across from her, seeing the look of disappointment in the younger woman's eyes.

"Wow," she said simply, her eyes searching Aoife's for some sort of explanation as to why she was leaving them, *abandoning* them. At least, this was how it felt.

"Yeah," Aoife replied quietly, pushing the bowl of stew further from her. Its rich, meaty scent was making her stomach gurgle, but not in a good way.

"Well, we're sure going to miss you," Karen said to her. "And little Molly here is going to miss you so much."

Perhaps finally picking up on the mood of the conversation, Molly chose that time to begin squirming, and she whimpered for her mother.

"Shh, shh." Aoife tried to soothe the little girl as she woke from her bad dream, but she only cried louder.

I'm making a total mess of this. I didn't want everyone to find out like this.

She wasn't sure how exactly she'd planned to tell them, but it hadn't been like this.

"I'm going to miss her terribly too," Aoife replied, her voice sad as she watched Karen take little Molly out of her pram and put her over her shoulder, trying to stop her from crying. While the noise garnered them some irritated looks from the other patrons, Aoife couldn't blame the little girl. Right now, she felt like all she wanted to do was just cry too.

○○○

"Well, that could've gone better."

Brendan found Michael outside the back door in his usual spot, smoking on a cigarette. Even though he'd said he was going to try to quit – Eliza didn't like him carrying on the habit – Brendan had noticed he seemed to be doing a lot more of it lately, particularly when he was frustrated by a particular auburn-haired girl with blue eyes.

"I'm not in the mood, Brendan."

"Since when are you ever in the mood to talk about your feelings, Michael?"

Brendan loved his friend dearly, but he wasn't the most open and honest when it came to expressing his feelings. You'd have better luck getting a closed clamshell to talk than Michael when he was being particularly stubborn about something.

"Well, I'm definitely not in the mood to talk now."

"Fine, ye don't have to talk about how you feel about Aoife. *I'll* do the talking."

Michael made a derisive snort. "There's a surprise. You never shut up for anything. Even when you're dead and buried, I'll bet you'll *still* be talking in your grave."

All That Compels the Heart

"Well, you're more than welcome to contribute to the conversation at any time."

Michael folded his arms across his chest, taking a drag of his cigarette, his face stony and unreadable. Brendan knew Michael wasn't going to like this conversation, but he pressed onwards anyways.

"You're in love with Aoife, Michael."

He felt his friend tense beside him, pausing in the middle of bringing his cigarette to his lips, frozen in fear by the revelation that Brendan knew exactly how he felt about the city girl. He noticed that he didn't deny it.

"You've been in love with her for some time now too. And something happened between the two of you when you took her up to Dublin the other week. Ye haven't been the same since you've come back. You've been…"

Michael raised a questioning eyebrow, daring his friend to tell him how he felt.

"I don't know," Brendan admitted. "*Cantankerous*, is the word that comes to mind."

"You don't even know what 'cantankerous' means," Michael retorted.

"I *do* and you've been the very definition of it." Brendan looked at his friend, agitated by his moody demeanor.

"Why don't you just ask me, Brendan?" Michael finally asked, feeling his friend's eyes on him.

"Ask ye what?" he feigned incomprehension.

"What happened between Aoife and I. I know ye want to."

Brendan looked over at Michael, gauging to see how serious he was about giving him a straight answer if he chose to ask him. Deciding it was worth the risk, he asked, "So what happened between you and Aoife?"

"I kissed her."

It was a simple enough answer, but it nearly bowled Brendan over. He'd thought that maybe they'd had an argument, that Michael had said something unforgivably rude to her, but he wasn't expecting *this*. And why the hell…

"Why the feckin' hell didn't you *tell* me!?" he exclaimed, both astonished and annoyed.

"Because I knew you'd react like that," Michael replied simply with a shrug of his shoulders. "And, because I don't want it getting around to the rest of the village."

"But this is big news! Ye can't just keep something like this to yourself!"

"I can, and so will you." Michael turned to Brendan and gave him a pointed look. "I mean it, Brendan; I don't want you telling anyone about it. It'd be a feckin' disaster if this got out."

"Well, at least tell me how it was then." He knew very well how much of a disaster this news would be to both Michael and Aoife if it got out, and although he was sorely tempted to want to know all the details, he also would never betray his best friend by telling anyone other than Molly about it.

"Perfect."

Brendan was surprised to hear more than a hint of contentment and sadness in his friend's voice. He was happy for him, but sad to see the torment he was going through over the prospect of Aoife moving back to Dublin.

"I take it ye haven't brought this kiss up with Eliza then, have ye?"

"Do ye think if I had, that you'd be hearing it from me instead of the little old gossips?"

Brendan nodded, accepting the truth of it. If he'd told Eliza, the entire village would know about it within a matter of hours.

"Besides, I can't."

"Why not? I mean, ye can't still be thinking to go through with the wedding?"

"I can, and I am."

"But Michael, you're clearly in love with Aoife!"

"Yeah, and she's not in love with *me*." Michael sighed, his face turning grim at admitting the truth of the situation. "If she were, she wouldn't be moving back to Dublin in order to marry that eejit, now would she?"

"Well, did ye tell her how you feel about her, Michael?"

He gave Brendan an exasperated look.

"Kissing her is not the same thing as actually *telling* her how you feel, Michael," he replied to the unanswered question. "Kissing her just tells her that you're interested, sure, but ye want to let her know that you're interested in more than just a good shag. You want someone who's going to be a wife, someone who's going to be a mam to your children, someone ye want to wake up beside for the rest of your life, someone who you can talk to about everything. And in order to get that, ye have to actually say the words to her."

Brendan gave him a pointed look.

"I *have* dated before, Brendan McCaffrey, so it's not like I need advice from you," Michael retorted.

He sighed, his voice taking a less defensive tone. "Relationships are hard work, Brendan; you know that. And yes, Eliza and I have a lot of history together and I don't necessarily think that's a bad thing. I mean, what if I throw all of that away again for Aoife only to find out six months, or a year down the line that it was Eliza all along? It's happened to us before."

Brendan knew Michael was thinking back to Eliza's affair, which had fizzled out the minute Michael had found out about it. Eliza had been head over heels for the guy but, when it came to the prospect of losing Michael over him, the affair had ended.

"Relationships *are* hard work, and we can't know how they'll all turn out, but I think Aoife's worth taking a risk on, Michael. I've seen ye love-struck, but never like this before. She's different for you, somehow, and I think it'd be wrong to give her up. Especially to the likes of Danny."

"I don't know." Michael rubbed a hand over his face and ran his hands through his dark hair, brushing it back from his face. "We should get back."

Brendan nodded.

"And Brendan?"

Brendan turned to look at his friend, hand on the door to the kitchen. "Yeah?"

"Thanks. For the chat."

"You're welcome." Brendan nodded to him, grateful Michael had opened up to him about this. "Now, let's head inside shall we?"

Chapter Forty-Four

After the mess of things she'd made down at the pub, Aoife had gone to the car park and picked up her car. She'd intended to head back to Aldridge Manor and stay for the night; after all, Danny wasn't expecting her back until sometime tomorrow. However, all the feelings she was having about leaving Ballyclara left her feeling too anxious to stay the night in the big house by herself and she unconsciously steered the car in the other direction, heading north back to Dublin.

In the fog of thoughts that clouded her mind, she drove herself to Danny's flat, where she knew he'd be staying the night. Although the two of them had mostly been living out of her flat since the engagement, he'd kept his own flat in town.

"Just in case I get stuck on a late night at the office," he'd told her. "My place is closer to the office than yours, so it's just easier to keep it until we get the house in Malahide."

She hadn't minded; they'd have plenty of time together when they officially moved in together.

After what had transpired earlier in the day, she felt she just needed to see him, have him reassure her that she was making the right decision in selling Aldridge Manor.

All That Compels the Heart

Aoife parked in the visitor parking section and headed inside the front lobby of his building. Like her own building, the place was effortlessly clean, everything shiny and brand new; it smelled faintly of the solution the cleaners used to dust the place. She went to the lift and pressed the button, hearing the lift chime as it made its way down to the main floor. Each *beep* seemed to take forever, as if the lift was moving in slow motion. Aoife pressed the button again, impatient, even though she knew logically that it wouldn't make it any faster. It was just a way to relieve some of the tension she was feeling.

The ride up in the lift to the seventh floor where Danny lived seemed to take an interminable amount of time. As it finally drew even with Danny's condominium, she hurried out, anxious to see him. She needed to feel better about all of this, needed to know she was doing the right thing.

She used the key Danny had given her and let herself in. The front corridor was dark, but the faint glow of a lamp from the living room suggested that someone had been home recently. She quickly peeked inside the living room, but no one was there, only the lamp that had been left on. She crossed the room to turn it off and she caught the whiff of a sweet scent in the air – coconut or something, she thought. It seemed odd to Aoife as she'd never known Danny to use any coconut-scented products before.

Weird.

She shrugged to herself, and walked towards the kitchen, passing by the two dirty wine glasses sitting on the counter as she went towards the master bedroom. All the other lights were off in the rest of the flat, all save the one in the master bedroom; she could see the glow of it under the closed door. Figuring that Danny must still be up doing some reading or work, she went to the bedroom and turned the doorknob.

If she'd stopped to think about it when she'd gone into the flat and reviewed the evidence right in front of her – the perfume, the wine glasses, the sounds coming from the bedroom – she wouldn't have been so shocked at finding Danny and Alice in bed together when she'd opened the door. However, in her need to see him, to be comforted by him, she'd willingly ignored what was right in front of her.

In truth, this was a testament to their whole relationship. When Aoife had met Danny in uni, she'd been been lacking in self-confidence from years of being put down by her mother, her grandmother, her cousin. Sure, in front of others she seemed like a confident young woman, but underneath, she was just someone looking to love and *be* loved, to have someone refute the negative self-talk her family had instilled in her. Danny had been seemingly happy to fill that role for her. He propped up her self-confidence just enough to make her think she was loved, just enough that she'd blissfully ignore what was really going on in front of her. She hadn't realized she'd been so naïve until right that moment.

"Aoife?"

Danny was laying on his back on the bed, Alice's back to her, straddling him, completely naked. His face was frozen in fear at having been caught. They stared at one another for only the briefest of seconds before Aoife turned around and fled the flat.

She could hear Alice and Danny arguing behind her as she went for the lift, could hear Danny calling her name. She felt like all the air in the room had been sucked out and she couldn't breathe. Aoife furiously attacked the button for the lift, trying to get the doors to open so she could leave. When they finally opened, she just as furiously pounded on the button for the main lobby, watching Danny racing towards her, dressed only in his boxers. Thankfully, the doors closed just in time that he couldn't follow her. Aoife choked back tears, trying to keep herself together long enough to reach her car. She just needed to reach the car, just needed to get out of there.

Racing through the lobby to the front door, she clicked the automatic starter on her keychain. She didn't know where she was going to go, she only knew that she just had to get far, far away from here.

ಸಿಂಜ

Michael was idly wiping down the bar, trying to keep thoughts of Aoife at bay and humming to Ed Sheeran's

"Drunk" playing on the radio, when the door to the pub opened up and in came the very woman he was trying *not* to think about. He immediately noticed her tear-streaked face and he felt his chest tighten.

So help me God, whatever he's done to her, I'll make him pay for it.

He had no proof that Danny had done anything to her, but he was willing to stake his life on it that he was the reason she'd been crying.

"Shot of whiskey, straight up," she told Brendan, sitting down heavily on a bar stool, but it was Michael who pulled out the shot glass and filled it with the best whiskey the bar had. Without any hesitation, Aoife picked it up and downed its entire contents in one gulp. With an audible *clink* she plunked the shot glass back on the countertop.

"Another, please."

He didn't miss a beat and refilled it to the top. Aoife knocked it back as if it was water. Setting the glass back down on the countertop, she requested another. This pattern repeated itself for another three shots, by which time he was becoming increasingly more worried for her. They'd proven on more than one occasion that she was not able to hold her liquor nearly as well as she thought she could, and he was concerned about how she was going to feel in the morning if she continued on like this.

He could see by this time that the whiskey was starting to kick in, and Aoife's shoulders began to look a little less tense. Without a word or prompting from her, Michael filled the shot glass again.

"I'm not sure that's a good idea," Brendan whispered to him.

He shot him a look that told him he knew what he was doing and the two of them watched as Aoife picked it up and drained it again in one fluid movement.

"I don't want to talk about it," Aoife answered his unasked question.

"Fair enough," he replied. "Another?"

"Absolutely."

He held the bottle over the glass for a second before pulling it back, not pouring anything. "You've just got to do one thing for me before I pour it."

"What's that?"

"Hand over your car keys."

"I'm not dri--- oh, right." She looked down at the car keys she'd pulled from her coat pocket, and she smiled a big, foolish grin at him and giggled as she handed them over.

Brendan and Michael glanced at each other, wondering if she'd gone off her rocker.

"It grabbed the wrong keys," she finally said between giggles, which had now turned to hiccups. "They're *his*."

Her face suddenly darkened and she looked like she might cry. Just as suddenly as it had come, the dark expression turned blank.

"Keep the damned thing for all I care," she snapped and downed the drink he'd poured for her. "Key it, sell it, drive it into the ocean; whatever you want. I really couldn't care less."

And there it was. He *knew* her current behaviour had something to do with that eejit, and she'd gone and taken his car out of revenge. Well, good on her.

"I told ye, I don't want to talk about it," she repeated.

She put her chin in her hand and swayed a little on her stool. He put out a hand protectively towards her, but she managed to stay upright.

"I didn't say anything," he told her, reassured she wouldn't fall off for the moment.

"You didn't have to. I could see it in your eyes."

She waved a finger a little too close to his face and he gently redirected her hand to the bar, placing it where she couldn't accidently poke his eye out.

"You know, you have these little flecks of almost violet in your eyes," she said, leaning forward and staring straight at him, getting close enough to him to smell the whiskey emanating from her breath. "They're really quite pretty, your eyes."

Michael leaned back from her a bit.

"Umm...thanks."

"Though I don't suppose I'm supposed to say 'pretty' to a man, now am I? You want to hear something about how…how manly ye are. That's what men want to hear, right? Bloody eejits, the lot of ye."

"Maybe it would help to get whatever it is I didn't ask ye about off your chest. Isn't that what works in therapy?" he asked her, trying to get her off her diatribe on men.

"Oh, and you're my therapist now are you, Michael?"

"Well, I'd say that being a bartender is near enough to being a therapist. Ye have to stand here all night listening to people tell ye their whole life story. Only the pay isn't near as good," he said with a wink at her.

This finally seemed to elicit a response from her, as he caught the faintest upturn at the corners of her mouth.

"I had a therapist back in Dublin," she revealed nonchalantly, "and I can tell you that after all my family has paid him over the years, all he's told me is that 'I'm not quite right in the head.' I think he should charge less, and *you* should charge more, as I'm sure you're *much* more helpful. And you give out booze, which is always a bonus. If all therapists were more like you, I'd sign up to be your first client straight away."

This time she gave him a big smile and held out her glass to him.

"I think you'd be a hellish client," he told her honestly. "But, seeing as you've already given me a sizeable downpayment in the form of Danny's car, and as I've no other customers right now, I suppose I can't be too fussy. And as I'm now your therapist and I need to give ye a professional assessment, I'd say that right now you're drunk, and I'm cutting you off."

He pushed the glass she was holding out to him away gently, directing her to place it back on the bar.

"I take back everything I just said. You'd make a terrible therapist," she replied grumpily. "Can't I just have one more before I go home?"

"If you can walk from here to the bathroom and back in a straight line without stumbling once, then ye can have another drink."

"Ye can't be serious, man," Brendan whispered to him frantically. "What if she does it? You just going to let her drink herself to death?"

"No chance she makes it," Michael told him confidently. "She won't even make it off the barstool."

"I accept your challenge," Aoife said getting up quickly from her stool. Despite a little wobble, she somehow managed to stay upright.

Brendan shot him a concerned look, but Michael held out a hand, silently urging him to wait.

Confidently, she headed for the bathroom, managing to deftly avoid all the chairs and tables in her path, and walked the same line back to her bar stool and plonked herself down. When she'd settled herself, she beamed up at him, looking triumphant.

"I'll take that drink now."

Michael would have been lying if he'd said she hadn't impressed the hell out of him. Brendan glared at him, but Michael was nonplussed. He'd agreed to give her one more drink; he'd said nothing about giving her more after that.

"'Tis a good thing I didn't make a bet on you," he muttered as he filled up her shot glass again. "Now, this one for sure is your last."

"Oh come on, I passed your silly little test. I'm perfectly fine and can take care of myself. Shall I prove it to you by walking to the door and back?" she asked, downing the whiskey in one gulp. The distance was twice as far as between the bar and the bathroom.

"You'll never make it. I'll actually put good money on that."

"Fine, twenty euros," she said, slamming her hand down on the bar.

Michael looked at her a moment. "Fine. Twenty euros says you won't make it to the door and back."

"Prepare to lose your money and your whiskey. If I can get to the door and back, I can have all the whiskey I want for the rest of the night."

Without waiting for his response, she got up from the barstool, raised her head and threw her shoulders back defiantly, and began walking towards the door.

She started out well, walking with complete confidence and in a completely straight line. However, after about ten steps she began to wobble a bit, and within the next five steps she was completely on the floor. There were outbursts of incredulity from some of the patrons, applause from others.

"Shite," he muttered as he rushed over to her side. "Aoife? Aoife? Are you still with us, love?" he asked, pushing back the hair from her face to check that she was still breathing.

Her head lolled from side to side, but she eventually opened her eyes and smiled up at him. His heart, pounding in his chest with worry, slowed a little.

"I'm still here, though I don't know quite where 'here' is," she responded slightly slurring her words.

"'Here' would be the floor of the pub, my love. Now let's get ye up and back on your feet."

He slowly brought her into a sitting position and then firmly gripped her arm and pulled her to her feet. She managed, albeit shakily. He let go of her arm to try to get her to stand on her own two feet, however, as soon as he let go of her, she began to wobble and lose her balance again. Seeing her falter, he expertly scooped her up into his arms.

"Alright, up we go," he told her.

He shifted her into position so that her head was resting on his shoulder and her legs were swung over his left forearm. Before leaving he turned back towards the bar.

"Brendan, I better get this one back to her place safe and sound. Ye'll be alright to close up?"

He didn't wait to his response. He didn't need him lecturing him out enabling Aoife to the point of drunkenness. With a nod of thanks, Michael turned towards the door of the pub and someone held it open for him, ensuring the two of them got through safely.

He thought to take Danny's car at first, but that would mean awkwardly fishing out the keys from his pocket while trying not to drop her. It was just easier to take her in his truck.

"Alright, love, mind your head," he said to her as he opened the door and placed her inside. She snored softly as he buckled her up.

Coming around to the driver's seat, he found the keys in the ignition where he'd left them. There was never a need to worry about leaving your keys in your car in a place like

Ballyclara. The sudden noise of the engine coming to life made Aoife shift and stir a bit in her seat, but she didn't fully wake up. Rest assured that she wasn't disturbed, he put the truck in gear and started off for the Old Rectory.

The roads were cleared of traffic, nearly the whole village being in their homes watching the telly, or in the pub having a pint. Michael enjoyed the empty night, the sky lit only by the full moon and the stars, looking like a million tiny diamonds on dark blue velvet.

A few minutes later, he arrived at the Old Rectory, parking right out front. He turned the key in the ignition and the drive went dark as his lights dimmed. Jogging around to the passenger side, he opened the door, careful to rest her head against the back of the seat while he unbuckled her and picked her back up in his arms again. He carried her up the front path and up the steps and turned the knob. Except the knob didn't turn.

Shite, he thought to himself, *She has to be the only person in the whole village who'd think to lock her doors before leaving.*

Cursing under his breath, he looked around for the geranium flowerpot where the spare key had always been kept ever since he'd been a child, in case his father or mother ever locked themselves out and didn't want to walk back to their place to get their own keys. He looked around, but in the dark, all the flowerpots looked the same.

He decided to put Aoife down on the wooden bench near the front door while he felt around under all the flowerpots to find the key.

Damn, Mara and Karen must have moved it when they were doing some gardening out front.

With any luck, they hadn't moved it far. After a few more minutes of searching underneath all the flowerpots around the front door, he managed to find the one he was looking for and grabbed the spare key. Heading back to the front, he turned the key in the lock and opened the door. He went back to the bench, scooped Aoife back up into his arms, and carried her inside.

Deftly moving through the house in the dark, Michael expertly carried her up the stairs, making sure not to bump her head or her feet against any of the walls or stair railings.

Finally making it to the master bedroom, he made his way over to the bed and laid her gently on it. He glanced down at her to make sure she was still breathing and let go the breath he hadn't realized he'd been holding when he saw the gentle rise and fall of her chest.

Suddenly, not sure whether he should go, but not quite ready to leave her here on her own, he hovered near the bed, watching her sleep. Feeling like he should at least get her boots off for her – it was never comfortable to wake up hungover in your clothes from the day before – he knelt before the bed and began unzipping her boots. He'd do that much for her; the rest she'd have to do on her own when she woke up. As he was placing them on the floor by the foot of the bed, she began to stir.

"Wha--? How did I get here? And where is here?" she asked, slightly slurring her words.

"You're at home. I brought ye here after you got so drunk that you gave me your fancy car," he teased, sitting down on the bed beside her.

"Ssss not my car," Aoife mumbled, wiping at her eyes with the back of her hand like a small child. Michael couldn't help but give a small smile at how adorable the gesture was, and at how ridiculous it made her look, smearing her make-up like that.

"You're right, it's my car now," he told her jokingly.

Aoife thought about this for a second, her bleary eyes clearing and she hiccupped, laughing at the joke.

"Alright. I think we should get ye out of those clothes and get you to bed," he told her as she continued to laugh.

"Michael Flanagan!" she exclaimed, looking at him, shocked. "I'm scandalized! Is this why you brought me back here? To get me into bed?"

Suddenly her face was quite serious and her eyes clearer than they had been all night. He was suddenly quite aware that his face was only mere inches from hers, her lips looking inviting.

No, she's too drunk right now. Wait until the morning when you can sort all this out and then see how she feels.

But, before he knew what was happening, Aoife had closed the distance between them, placing her hands on either side of his face kissed him.

Her mouth tasted warm and soft and a *lot* like whiskey. He'd been so surprised by her kiss that he found himself feeling like he was thirteen again kissing Maggie Cochrane behind the gardening shed at his parents' house. He hadn't known where to put his hands or his tongue on that night, and he felt found himself in the present situation with much the same problem. He finally settled on placing one of them on her waist with the other one behind her head at the base of her skull, twining his fingers through her wavy, auburn hair.

Removing her hands from his face, she reached down and brought her shirt over her head, temporarily breaking off their kiss. Michael tried his best not to look down at her cleavage, right there in front of him.

"Aoife…I don't think…"

"Don't think. Just kiss me," she demanded, and pulled him into another long kiss.

Good Lord; it's going to be an interesting night.

Chapter Forty-Five

Aoife woke sometime just before dawn. Her room was filled with a grey light, the kind you see just before the sun rises. The world around her was still and quiet. The only sound she heard was that of Michael snoring softly beside her, his breath gently disturbing the hairs at the back of her neck. She knew it was him without having to see him; she could smell his cologne mixed with a hint of booze and cigarettes, and earthiness. It was something that was distinctly *him*. She could feel that he had one arm under her head, nestled in the crook between his neck and shoulder, while the other lightly rested on top of her own.

Her mouth felt like it was stuffed with cotton balls and she had the sudden sense of desperately needing to use the bathroom. Her head swam as she tried to remember the events of last night. She wasn't sure how she had ended up here in her bed, much less with Michael in it.

Oh God...

She heaved a sigh of relief as her mind panicked for a second, wondering if the two of them had slept together. However, beneath the covers, she could feel she was still in her clothes from yesterday, minus her shirt. Careful not to disturb him, she gently rolled onto her back. Michael was laying on top of her duvet, fully clothed, his face restful in slumber. Although she'd tried not to wake him, he'd sensed that she'd woken before him, attuned as he was to her in every way.

"Good morning." His voice thick with sleep, his eyes bleary but pleased to see her. She noticed that he made no attempt to remove the arm that lay across her stomach.

"Good morning," she replied, trying to clear her own throat.

"How'd you sleep?"

"Like a log, apparently. I don't remember a thing from last night."

He smiled in a way that made her curious as to what exactly the two of them had done last night.

"That might be for the best."

She was sorely tempted to ask him what exactly that meant, but her full bladder demanded her attention.

"Um, Michael?"

"Hmmm?" His eyes had closed again.

"Could you...?" She nodded to his right arm, which was still laying across her.

He opened his eyes to see what she was nodding at.

"Oh." Suddenly self-conscious and removed his arm from the top of the duvet.

"Thanks," she replied, lifting the duvet off her and sidling out of bed. "I'll be right back."

He sleepily rolled over to the other side of the bed as she crossed the room to the master bathroom and closed the door behind her. Her head had gone from swimming to pounding as she sat there on the toilet. Fragments of the night's events came back to her as she tried to steady herself, memories of being in the pub, being upset, Michael taking her back here... but why had she been so upset? And why was she here in Ballyclara? She was supposed to be in Dublin with Danny...

Danny.

That's when it came back to her. Danny, Alice, the whole thing. The emotions she'd been holding in since last night hit her like a punch to the stomach. She stifled a cry, not wanting Michael to hear her. She took a shaky breath as the tears rolled down her cheeks.

All That Compels the Heart

Finally, feeling like she could pull herself together, she rose from the toilet and put herself back together and walked over to the sink, letting the warm water run over fingers. She caught a glance at herself in the mirror and was startled. Her mascara had run down her cheeks, forming long, dark streaks and circles under her eyes. Her auburn curls were matted and tangled, and her clothes were wrinkled and dishevelled.

God, I look dreadful.

Cupping her hands together, she splashed some water on her face, feeling the warm water cleansing away her dried tears and the make-up that had caked to her skin. As she used the towel to dry her face, a rosy hue rose in her pale skin. She didn't bother to re-apply her make-up; if Michael had seen her with her make-up all messed up like that and not run for the hills at the sight of her, he could survive seeing her without any make-up on. Running a brush quickly through the tangled mess of her hair, she took one of her hair elastics and pulled it into a ponytail. Remembering that she was standing there in just her bra and trousers, she grabbed a shirt out of the laundry bin, sniffed it, and determined that it would suffice until she could find something cleaner to wear.

When she opened the door and went back into the bedroom, she saw that her bed was empty. No trace of Michael in her room, no sign of him anywhere. Just when she was about to head downstairs to see if he was there, he reappeared just outside of her door, knocking softly to get her attention.

"Sorry; I didn't mean to startle you. I just wanted to see if you'd you like me to put the kettle on for some tea? I was just about to make us some toast."

"That would be great." Her stomach, although still a bit unsure of itself, grumbled lightly, reminding her that she hadn't eaten in some time.

He smiled at her and headed back downstairs. As she followed him into the kitchen, she sat down on one of the stools by the island in the middle of the kitchen. He moved around the kitchen with a familiarity of someone who'd been there for years, taking down two teacups from the cupboard, the sugar, and milk and placed them on the island in front of her. As the kettle boiled, he reached for the toast which had just popped out of the toaster.

"Here," he said, putting it on her plate and placing a block of butter beside it. "Eat this; it'll make you feel better."

"Listen, about last night..." she began, but he held up a hand to her.

"Ye don't have to explain, if ye don't want to."

She looked up into his face and saw that while he *did* look like he wanted to ask her what had possessed her to come into the pub and get so drunk last night, but he didn't want to make her uncomfortable and wouldn't press the issue if she didn't want him to.

"Thanks," she replied, taking a bite of the toast. Her stomach grumbled, but it was more of a hungry grumble than an "I'm-going-to-be-sick" grumble.

"I caught Danny cheating on me," she said, completely out of the blue, surprising even herself. It wasn't that he needed an explanation; he'd already proven that he was more than willing to wait for her to make the decision when – or if – she was going to tell him anything. No, it was more that she *needed* to tell someone, and she wanted him to know. She needed someone to be there for her right now to help her through this.

Michael's breathed whistled through his clenched teeth as he slowly exhaled. His knuckles were white as he gripped the edge of the counter, his whole body tense with anger. She could see that he was barely containing his rage, holding it in only for her. She reached across the island and held his hand, letting him know she was grateful for the support.

"I was in such a rush after I... I saw them in bed," her voice broke a little, wavering as tears threatened to obscure her vision. The piece of toast she'd eaten before caught in her throat and she coughed, trying to clear it. Michael moved his hand so that he was now holding hers, stroking it gently with his thumb.

"I took his car."

"I know." His voice was rough, full of emotion. She could tell that he hated seeing her like this. "Oh, that reminds me; here are the keys."

He fished her car keys out of his pocket and placed them on the counter in front of her. "It's down at the pub. Ye can leave it down there for as long as you need to."

She nodded to him. "Look, I'd like to make it up to you. For having to look after me last night."

"Really, ye don't have to. There's nothing to make up for."

"No, I want to. Let me make it up to you. This is three times now that you've had to carry me home because I was drunk. I want to do something nice for you to thank you for being there for me."

Perhaps it was the sincerity in her eyes, but he nodded, allowing her to do something nice for him.

"Alright then," he gave in. "But on one condition."

"And what's that?"

"That ye don't try to cook for me."

She smiled at him and he looked relieved to see her happy, even if it was just for a moment.

"Probably for the best."

"I think so. I want ye to do something nice for me; not end up having to rescue you again."

She rolled her eyes at him, like he was being dramatic, but conceded the point to him. "Ok, great! Meet me back here at five o'clock. Oh, and wear something nice."

"Something nice?"

"Yeah, you know: a suit jacket and button up shirt or something. Just not…"

"What I currently have on?" he asked looking down at his scruffy jeans and t-shirt.

"Right."

He shrugged in acquiescence.

"Great."

༺༻

"Hello Michael," Aoife greeted him, later that evening when he showed up on her doorstep.

He smiled at her. She was dressed in a beautiful white satin peplum dress with a black lace overlay, her auburn hair pulled up into a sleek bun. She looked just as beautiful now as she did when he'd taken her home last night, messed-up make-up and all.

"Ye look beautiful."

She blushed at the compliment, a faint rosy hue rising in her cheeks. "And you, Michael, look very handsome. I don't think I've ever seen you in anything other than one of your jumpers or t-shirts and jeans."

He'd done as she'd asked and made an effort to dress up for her. He'd chosen a navy blue, button-up shirt, a pair of dark trousers and a matching tie. He'd even run some gel through his hair in an attempt to make it look somewhat less all-over-the-place like it usually was. He was pleased she appreciated the effort.

"So, where is it you're taking me?" he asked, curious as to what she had planned.

"Well, technically, *you're* taking me there because I haven't got a car."

"Right," he said, smiling at her. "So, where to?"

"I thought it'd be nice for us to do something a little bit different than normal, and take a drive out to Greystones."

"Greystones?" he asked. He hadn't been to the little coastal Wicklow town in years.

"I hope that's alright?" She sounded concerned, worried he might not like it.

"It sounds lovely," he replied, smiling at her.

"Great. Well, shall we?" she pointed towards his truck.

"Right." Michael followed her outside, shutting the door behind them and walked her to the truck.

The two of them drove in a comfortable silence the whole way to Greystones, the two of them simply enjoying each being in each other's company, both still a little nervous and shy around one another. When they'd arrived at their destination, she'd taken him to a nice restaurant on the main street, a classier sort of place than he'd normally have gone to – unless he was trying to impress a date – but still low-key enough that he didn't feel too out of place.

"Ye know, if you'd wanted to go out to eat, we could have just gone to the pub," he had teased her.

"I thought that – considering you spend so much of your time there – that you might like to go somewhere different," she'd said but seemed like she might be slightly unsure of herself now.

"It's grand," he'd told her, his tone serious as he reached across the table to take her hand, giving it a little squeeze. "Besides, if we'd gone to the pub, we'd probably have given all of Ballyclara plenty to talk about."

Her face paled a bit and she took a sip of the beer she'd ordered. Seeing she was a bit nervous at the thought of what people back in Ballyclara would think of the two of them hanging out right now, he said to her,

"Come on. Let's get out of here for a bit."

"Where are we going?"

"On an adventure," he said, smiling at her as she took his hand.

As they reached the beach, they both slipped out of their shoes and walked along the pebbled ground, just talking for a bit as they ambled aimlessly. As the sun began to set on the horizon, Michael – still holding Aoife's hand and carrying her high heels for her in the other – directed her back to towards the truck, ready to begin the journey home.

They arrived back in Ballyclara all too soon for Michael's liking. As he turned the key in the ignition, the night seemed very quiet and the interior of the car seemed much smaller and more intimate than it had before. He looked over at her silhouette outlined by the moonlight.

"Well," he said, suddenly at a loss for words. He wanted to just stay here in the car with her for a little while longer, but he had no plausible reason to extend the night any further. Not unless she invited him in.

"Well," Aoife repeated. A part of him was thrilled when she sounded like she too didn't want to end the night just yet either.

"Thank you for today," she finally told him. "And for last night. And just being there for me in general."

"I had a wonderful time."

He smiled at her, unable to stop thinking about how beautiful she looked right now. Without realizing it, they both leaned in closer to one another, their shoulders touching, their lips only inches from one another. She closed the gap before he could, locking lips with him.

"Do you want to come inside?" she asked when they came up for air.

"Are ye sure?" he asked, gazing into her eyes, wanting to make sure that this was not just going to be a rebound for her, that it wasn't going to be something she was going to regret in the morning.

"I'm sure."

He smiled at her and kissed her quickly before opening the truck door and the two of them went inside. They began taking off their clothes the moment the door closed behind them.

"Race you upstairs?" A mischievous smile came over her face right before she bolted up the stairs towards the bedroom.

"Dammit," he exclaimed, still hopping on one foot as he tried to pull off his boots. He managed to pull the damned thing off and bounded up the stairs behind her, taking them two at a time to catch up to her.

They raced through the house, both trying to be the first to reach the bedroom. Aoife slid down the polished wooden floors of the hallway in her bare feet and stumbled into the bedroom. By the time that Michael caught up to her a couple of steps later, she'd already crossed the room to the four-poster bed, waiting for him, a trail of clothes behind her. He caught the door so as not to crash into it, and stood there for a second, breathless, just admiring her. Before either of them could catch their breath, he crossed the room and pulled her into a swift kiss.

As their lips parted, she asked, "Are you going to take me on another adventure?"

He looked down into her blue eyes, noticing for the first time the flecks of light and dark blue mixed together near the irises. His nostrils were filled with the scent of her, a mixture of vanilla and something floral, a heady mixture that was making his head swim from all the hormones racing through his body.

"Ye could say that, yes." His voice was breathy, anxious to kiss her again.

All That Compels the Heart

He kissed her then, gently but deeply. Her hands roamed down to his trousers and she undid his belt, untucking his shirt. Swiftly, he turned her around to face the bed, leaving a trail of kisses from the back of her neck to the small of her back. As he kissed his way back up to her shoulders, she turned around in his arms to face him. Helping each other out of their underwear, flinging them around the room so they fell helter-skelter, Michael pulled her close to him.

Michael kissed the top of her forehead, her closed eyelids, and the tip of her nose until eventually reaching her lips.

"Do ye trust me?"

"Yes"

He put his index finger under her chin, forcing her to lift her mouth towards him and kissed her deeply. Sliding his hands down her sides and under her buttocks, Michael picked her up and carried her to the bed.

Chapter Forty-Six

Aoife woke the next morning to light filtering through the light purple drapes, shining through her closed eyes, dragging her unhappily into consciousness. She just had the most amazing dream about her and Michael, that the two of them had gone on the most amazing date and had come to have – well, she certainly didn't want to wake from *that* particular part of her dream. But wait: it *hadn't* been a dream!

She stretched out her arm and tried to burrow her face in the crook between his neck and shoulder, but all she felt below her cheek was her pillowcase. Confused, she opened her eyes and raised her head slightly to look around, but there was no Michael in her bed.

She sat up in bed and saw the trail of her and Michael's clothes lying all over the floor, the only sign that last night had indeed happened. Wondering where on earth Michael could be, Aoife got up to go in search of him. She picked up his shirt from the floor and put it around her, sniffing it as she buttoned it up. It smelled faintly of his cigarettes, his cologne, fresh country air and a more subtle scent underneath, which was the man himself. It anchored last night in reality for her and made her smile at the thought of him here in her house.

All That Compels the Heart

When she reached the top of the stairs, the aroma of something cooking wafted from the kitchen, and she followed the scent down the staircase. As she reached the bottom, she could hear the sounds of Daft Punk's "Get Lucky" playing over the radio, and she walked down the hallway towards the kitchen.

She stood in the doorway, watching Michael move around the kitchen with an ease like he'd always belonged there, singing to the music on the radio as he managed all the various frying pans and other kitchen utensils simmering away with various foods. Aoife couldn't help but wonder at how handsome he looked standing there, half-naked dressed only in his boxers, stirring the batter for pancakes and tipping some expertly into the frying pan and then turning his attention to the bacon frying in another pan, and the eggs in another.

She started laughing from the sheer enjoyment of watching him. He hadn't seen her standing there before and when he heard her laugh, he turned to her and gave her a big grin. It thrilled her to see him so happy.

"So, someone finally decided to get out of bed, did they?" he teased her.

Still smiling, she walked over to him, circling her arms around his waist and kissed him.

"It was lonely in there all by myself," she complained, kissing his shoulder as he flipped the pancakes.

"Well, I was hungry after our work out last night. And this morning," he smiled mischievously at her over his shoulder. "And you looked so beautiful and peaceful laying there that I hated to wake you. Besides, I knew you'd eventually find me."

"So, what's for breakfast?" she asked him, snuggling his shoulder.

"Well, because you apparently don't keep any food in this great kitchen of yours," he admonished her, "except for various bags of junk food and packets of instant noodles, I went down to the store to pick you up a few things. Eggs, bacon, fruit, pancakes, toast. Nothing fancy."

"Nothing fancy?! This is more food than I've ever made in this kitchen."

"I can tell. It's a shame that ye have such a wonderful kitchen, and ye hardly seem to use it."

"What can I say? When I get writing, I get so absorbed that the last thing I remember is food," she replied sheepishly, feeling judged for her poor eating habits.

"Ye need to take better care of yourself and introduce a few more fruits and vegetables into your diet," he teased her. "We can't have you dying of scurvy, ye wee pirate lass."

He quickly stole a kiss.

"Guess it's a good thing I have you around to look after me then," she told him smugly.

"Oh, what's this now? Finally admitting that I might be right about something? I never thought I'd hear the like from your lips," he said with mock surprise, kissing said lips.

"Oh, shut your mouth," she muttered, playfully punching him in the shoulder.

"Ouch! Hey! Don't abuse the chef," he responded. "Otherwise ye just might have to starve."

"Oh, you'd let me die of starvation and scurvy, now would you?" she asked him, looking up at him with her best impression of big, sad eyes.

"I suppose ye can still eat with me," he responded, looking back at her with a loving expression in his eyes. "I'd hate to see you dying of anything."

Aoife could tell by the look in his eyes that he meant it.

"Now go and sit down at the table," he commanded.

"Yes, sir," she replied with mock seriousness and sat at the kitchen table.

Michael came over carrying two plates, both stacked high with more good food than she'd eaten in awhile. Perfectly content, the two of them ate in a companionable silence, perfectly happy and content with one another. When they'd finished, Michael handed her a cup of tea.

"Go and have a seat outside and don't worry about the washing up; I'll do that in a bit."

She did as he bid her, taking her mug and curling up on the sofa outside on the back porch. A few seconds later her joined her, bringing out his own mug of coffee and curled up beside her, the two of them watching the sun rise above the early morning fog which had settled on the fields before them. The sun's rays landed on her skin, warming her.

She looked over at him as he sat down next to her, crawling under the blanket she'd placed over her bare legs to ward off the last of the morning's chill. She smiled at him over her mug of tea and snuggled closer to him under the plaid blanket, the warmth of his body and the sun's rays making her feel safe. Resting her head on his shoulder, she breathed in the heady scent of the dewy morning air and closed her eyes, completely at peace with the world and everything in it.

"So how long are we going to go on like this before we tell everyone?"

The question was like a crash back to reality.

"Do we have to?" she asked seriously.

"I'm not saying I'm in any rush, but this is a small town and people are going to find out pretty quick." His voice rumbled in his chest under her ear.

"You mean Eliza, don't you?" She felt a stab of jealousy as she thought of his fiancée – or was it now ex-fiancée? She couldn't keep up.

"She deserves to hear it from me and not from one of the old biddies in the village."

She nodded in agreement. Michael and Eliza had been together for years, after all; the two of them had had children and had been about to get married several times. There was a lot of history there that needed to be respected.

"When you tell her, you know we're going to have to tell your parents and your sister right away. She won't keep it a secret for long."

If at all.

It wasn't just the little old ladies in the village who were the only gossips; Eliza was the ringleader of the new generation of village gossips.

"I was thinking that there's no time like the present."

"What, you mean today?"

"And why not?"

She settled her head against his shoulder again, not sure how she felt about it. It was one thing to know she had to tell everyone soon; it was quite the other to know that the deadline had been moved up drastically. They'd only just been together last night. Sure, they'd been dancing around things for months now, but they'd only just gotten together hours ago. This was all moving just a bit too fast.

"I suppose," she relented, against her better judgement.

"Aoife, if you're unsure about this, then I won't do it."

He shifted in his seat, forcing her to lift her head and look up at him.

"I mean it; what we have together is important to me, and I don't want to ruin it by rushing into things. If you're not ready to tell anyone, then we won't."

She searched his face and saw he was being sincere, and she adored him for it. She knew though, that if the secret broke before he had a chance to try and put things right with Eliza that he'd blame himself for it. And then he'd come to resent her for it too, and that was something she didn't think she could live with.

"I'm ok with it," she told him, pushing down any qualms from her subconscious..

He smiled and kissed her lightly. Carefully extricating himself from the sofa, he grabbed the coffee cup he'd placed on the little table beside the chair and drank it down in one gulp.

"Well, I better go and get this over and done with."

"I'll be here when you get back," she reassured him.

He leaned down to kiss her one last time, his tongue tasting strongly of the coffee he'd just had, and headed back into the house to change, leaving Aoife sitting there on the back porch watching the sun as it made its ascent in the sky.

※※※

Michael inhaled deeply; the morning air still a bit cool and it pricked the hairs inside his nose. It smelled of the cool, damp dew that had fallen overnight, intensifying the fragrance of the lilacs and the pink roses Eliza had planted outside of the house. It felt strange to him to find himself standing outside of the house he'd shared with her for years, wondering whether or not to use his key to just let himself in or whether to knock on the door. Taking a deep breath to gather his strength about him before he chickened out, he decided to reach for the brass door knocker shaped like a shamrock, hanging from the bright red door.

It's now or never.

He rapped the door knocker quickly – once, twice, three times – and then took a step back, fighting the strong urge to just walk away right then and there before she opened the door. It would only be worse the longer he put it off, which is why he'd made the decision when he'd woken up this morning that he had to get it done today, even though he knew it meant rushing things with Aoife a bit.

There was no immediate answer at the door, so he reached out and knocked firmly once more, a not-so-insignificant part of him hoping that she wouldn't be at home. He was more than a little disappointed when he heard a sound from inside the house and the door opened, Eliza standing in its frame and looking at him curiously.

"Michael; come in. I wasn't expecting you."

Despite the early hour, Eliza looked like she'd been awake for some time, her hair and makeup perfectly done up as always and she was wearing that nice pink floral dress she liked so much.

"Sorry for the early hour. Am I interrupting ye?" he asked, still hoping to delay the inevitable, but afraid to lose his nerve at the same time.

"No, no. Come on in. I was just getting some things together for the church bazaar. Can I offer you some tea? I was just putting the kettle on."

He could hear the kettle whistling from the kitchen.

"No thanks," he replied, still standing at the doorway, closing it behind him.

Stepping inside, Michael felt even more a stranger in this place than he had standing outside. Despite having lived in this house with Eliza for years, it felt no more of a home to him now than it had when the two of them had first moved in.

The house had been a gift from her parents when the two of them had gotten engaged the first time. It was meant to be the place where they would settle down together, a place to raise their family. They'd both set about renovating the three-bedroom, two bathroom house as soon as they moved in; Eliza was very particular in the kind of place she wanted to have and Michael had gone along with whatever she'd wanted. He supposed that it should have felt odd to him the whole time he'd lived here that it had always felt more like her place than theirs, like he was just a temporary guest. Even looking around the house right now, it was difficult to find anything of his here. The furniture, the paint colours, the decorations; all of it had been chosen carefully by Eliza. The whole place had been designed for her and no one else, much like their relationship had been mostly all on her terms, until Aoife had walked into his life.

"So, what can I do for you then?" She returned from the kitchen with her mug of tea, taking one of the neatly stacked coasters from the dish in the centre of the coffee table and setting the hot mug on top of it.

"Please, take off your shoes and sit down." She motioned for him to sit in one of the overstuffed chairs instead of standing in the doorway like the eejit he felt he was.

"Nah, I'm not staying long," he replied.

She raised an eyebrow but didn't say anything. Instead, more concerned about what was happening in her own life, she'd begun yammering away about the church bazaar and other inanities. As he heard her talk about herself, he wondered: had their relationship always been like this? When Aoife said something to him, he listened. Even if it was the most mundane thing, or something he didn't understand, he listened to her. When Eliza spoke, his mind drifted somewhere else, no matter the topic she was discussing. With her, he spent most of his time pretending to hear what she said and less time on *actually* listening to her. The realization gave him an inexplicable sense of regret – not because he wanted to go back to what he'd had with her – but because the two of them had wasted so many years on something that was never going to work out.

"Well, enough about me, tell me: how are things with you? You've barely had any time for me in the past few weeks."

The hurt in her tone instantly made him feel guilty. Ever since the kiss with Aoife last week, he'd been coming up with excuses to be in the pub, or helping out Father Patrick with something, or looking after Rory or his parents, anything to avoid talk of the wedding or seeing Eliza. He felt guilty for all the times he'd been telling her he'd been working on something else when, really, he'd just been avoiding her, and this conversation. He began to wonder now if he'd slept with Aoife last night so that he'd be forced to finally have this conversation and get it over with, so that there'd be no going back.

"Yeah, it's um… No, ye know what, I just need to get this out."

All of the emotions he was feeling were coming to a head and he felt like he might burst if he didn't tell her soon.

"Get what out?" she asked him, a look of confusion on her face.

Sighing out of frustration, he crossed the sitting room floor - still in his boots - and sat down beside her, taking her hands in his, shushing her when she tried to lecture him about getting the floor dirty.

"What's wrong, Michael?"

"I wanted to talk to ye about us," he replied carefully.

He looked at her cautiously, afraid of what he might see. She didn't look surprised at the turn in the conversation and he realized how the last couple of weeks must have looked from her perspective. He was doing the same thing he'd done back when they'd broken up the first time they'd gotten engaged, after they'd lost the first baby. He'd thrown himself into his work, stopped coming home to her at night, withdrew into himself while he mulled over whether or not he was really ready to make a commitment to her. Except this time, the decision he was mulling over was when he would tell her that they were done for good. Without really thinking about it, he pulled out the house key from his pocket. Taking her hand in his, he pressed it into her palm and closed her fingers around it.

"I think you should have this back."

She looked confused for a moment as he wrapped her fingers around the metal, warm from his pocket. Her face took on a distinct sadness as she realized what it meant.

"Would ye just say something, please?" he begged her after the two of them had sat in silence for several seconds.

"And what would you like me to say?" she finally asked him, so quietly that he wasn't sure that he'd heard her and hadn't just imagined it.

"I don't know," he told her truthfully. "Something. Anything."

"Is this because of Aoife?" Her face was pinched and pale, her shoulders tense. "It was quite clear from the moment she paraded herself into Ballyclara that she wanted you."

"We didn't act on it until just last night, Eliza. I swear. I mean, there was a kiss the other week…"

"Do you think it matters to me when you first slept with her, Michael? You've been thinking about her ever since she came here and that's as bad as having slept with her all these months. You've let her come between us, let her push me out of your life since the moment she arrived. So, do you really think it makes it better that you only slept with her last night?"

She rose from her position on the sofa and folded her arms across her chest, as if protecting herself from him.

"No." He sighed, running his fingers through his hair. "I'm sorry, Eliza. I truly am. I didn't expect for any of this to happen."

He rested his elbows on his knees and put his face in his hands, not sure what else to say to her.

"You're sorry." Her voice was acrid, dripping with pain and hurt. "And what do you expect me to do with an apology, Michael?"

He didn't know what to say. There was nothing more left *to* say. "I don't know."

He rubbed his face lightly, long fingers trailing down his cheekbones.

"I hope she breaks your heart," Eliza said sadly, unkindly.

Michael knew he deserved it. He nodded, taking her words as his penance for the poor way he'd treated her over the years. After everything the two of them had been through, she deserved better than this, better than *him*.

"I know it's a lot to ask of you," he began, not sure how this was going to go given her earlier reaction, "but could you please not tell anyone? About me and Aoife, I mean."

He looked up at her to gauge her reaction. Her look of incredulity told him all he needed to know. "It's just… we haven't told anyone else yet, and I'd like very much to tell my family before the whole village knows."

She didn't say anything for a moment while she thought over what he was asking of her. "So, you want me to pretend that everything is just peachy while you and your tart figure out what to tell your parents?"

Michael sighed. He knew it wasn't a fair request, but it was there on the table before them, nonetheless.

She made a frustrated – and slightly disgusted – sound in her throat. "Fine, Michael. What's one more day of us lying to everyone anyways, right?"

"Thank you." He sighed, slightly relieved.

"Don't," she replied, her voice bitter with anger. "I'm not doing it for you. I know how people in this place love you, and how much they don't like me. Even though you're the one who's cheated, I'll be the one they'll blame, while you and Aoife will come up smelling like roses. Call it self-preservation, if you will, but I'd rather put off the whole of Ballyclara making me out to be the wicked with in your fairy tale.

"I do have just one thing to ask you, though."

"What's that?" He asked, apprehensively.

"Did you ever love me, Michael?"

He looked up at her, astounded she felt she had to ask the question.

"Yes, Eliza. Of course, I did." He meant it. It hadn't only been duty or whatever keeping him with her all these years. There had been love there, once.

He saw tears form at the corners of her eyes and her bottom lip began to tremble.

"I think I should go now."

He rose slowly from the sofa, unsure what else to do. He wanted to offer her some sort of comfort to make this easier for her, but he wasn't sure how to make that happen. The last thing he'd wanted was for them to end up here, like this.

Her eyes were wet as she held back her tears, waiting for him to leave before she began to sob, and Michael involuntarily reached out a hand to wipe away her tears.

"Just go!" she yelled at him, flinching off the gesture.

He dropped his hand mid-air, letting it fall back to his side again. He turned then and walked out the door, careful to close it gently behind him. The sound of the door closing resonated loudly within him, as if he were shutting the door to a part of himself forever.

Chapter Forty-Seven

Aoife couldn't remember the walk to Dermot and Sinead's from the Old Rectory ever being this long before. It should only have been a five or ten minute walk on a normal day, but today it felt like they'd been walking for both an hour and five seconds at the same time. It didn't help that with every step she took, the pit of her stomach churned a little more with nerves.

"Are you sure this is a good idea?"

She looked up at Michael in the fading daylight. His face was slightly pinched; she could tell he was thinking about his earlier episode with Eliza. He'd come back to the house after his talk with her and she could tell immediately without him saying a word that it had not gone well.

Well, it was never going to go well.

They'd both known that, even if Michael had not exactly been ready to face it just then. His shoulders had been slumped, his body looking defeated as he'd walked slowly up the steps. She'd watched as he'd changed his face, forcing a smile when he'd seen her, not wanting her to see what it had cost him to go and end things with Eliza for the final time.

"I mean, once we tell them, the whole village will know, and there's no taking it back."

She was still looking up at him, waiting for his reassuring smile to calm her fears. She saw his Adam's apple move as he swallowed hard before responding. "Yeah, of course it is. Everything'll be grand."

He placed an arm around her, falling heavily on her shoulders. His words came out a little more forced than she'd have liked; maybe it was the brisk way they were walking, making him winded or maybe it was the fact that as they got closer and closer to his parents' place, the reality of what it would mean to share their relationship with people – God could they call it a relationship when they'd never really been on a proper date? – was making him nervous now too. The pit in Aoife's stomach sank a little further.

It wasn't that she wasn't confident in what she and Michael had. Even though they'd never been on an official date and they'd only slept together just the once, she'd never felt more safe and secure when it was just the two of them. But that was the problem; it was easy to feel that way when the two of them were at home in the Old Rectory. They didn't have to listen to everyone else's opinions and ideas about what the two of them should and shouldn't do, or should and shouldn't be. But that bubble was about to burst. Finally – and yet, all too soon – they found themselves standing outside of Dermot and Sinead's place.

"Everything will be just grand," Aoife whispered to herself and she felt Michael's arm tighten around her at her words. Before he had a chance to lift his hand and knock on the door, it swung open wide, Dermot standing in the doorframe.

"Son," he said, reaching over to Michael and giving him a firm hug.

"Aoife!" he said, turning towards her and giving her the same familial greeting. "Come in the both of ye."

Aoife looked up at Michael one last time for encouragement before the two of them stepped inside the Flanagans' home. As per usual, the place was busy with movement. She could see Sinead and Mara in the kitchen getting dinner ready, with Molly standing in the archway to the kitchen, offering to help in any way she could.

All That Compels the Heart

"No love, you go and have a seat at the table. And you as well, Aoife; go and have a seat," Sinead said balancing a mixing bowl on one hip and waving in the general direction of the dining table where Rory and Des were putting out the knives and forks. "We have everything almost done here, so there's nothing to worry about."

"Michael. Good to see you, man." Brendan pulled his best friend into a hug. "So, your mam tells us that you had some news you wanted to share."

"Yeah," he replied, distracted by Rory who'd been talking with his hands while putting out the butter knives. Deftly, he took the knife from his nephew and placed it firmly on the table where it couldn't be used to poke out someone's eye.

"It'll have to wait. Dinner will be on the table soon," Sinead admonished them, indicating for them all to take their seats.

"It sure smells great in here."

The aroma of roast chicken and veggies and baked rolls wafted through to the table. As the chicken was pulled from the oven, it looked perfectly crisped to a golden hue, the juices simmering in its pan and making Aoife's mouth water. She couldn't help but notice that the good china – normally reserved for special occasions in the Flanagan household – had been laid out on the lace tablecloth.

What exactly did Michael tell his parents when he set up this dinner? she wondered.

Michael had called over to Dermot and Sinead's when he'd returned from Eliza's, saying that he thought it would be great to get together for dinner tonight as he wanted to tell them about some news he had. Somehow, out of that, Sinead must have inferred what it was that he'd planned to tell them.

She settled herself near the end of the table near Dermot and looked across the table to where Michael was sitting with Brendan laughing at some joke that Dermot – who sat in his place at the head of the table – had just made. His smile broadened when he saw her. She didn't have time to interrogate him about what exactly he'd said to his parents before Sinead and Mara arrived with the food.

"Rory sit down; and watch out for that plate because it's hot."

Mara nodded to her son, who was leaning over Desmond's chair pointing something out to him on the game console he had in his hands. She placed the roast chicken in the middle of the table, forcing Rory to swerve out of the way in order to avoid having the plate come down on his head. Clearly wanting to play the game he and Des had been looking at earlier, he sighed and flopped resignedly down beside his grandmother with Desmond on his right and his mother and Molly sitting across from them.

As Sinead placed the last of the hot dishes on the table, she settled herself in her chair on the opposite end of the table from her husband, rounding out their little group.

"Alright, everyone eat!"

It took less time for Sinead to give the command than it did for both Michael and Brendan to reach over and grab a hold of the dishes in front of them and begin piling their plates with food. A comfortable silence descended on the small room as everyone tucked into their meal; only the sounds of cutlery on plates could be heard.

"Sinead, you've done it again! This is fantastic!" Brendan exclaimed, his booming voice cutting through the silence.

"Thank you, Brendan; you're very kind."

Sinead's face looked pleased at the compliment to her cooking, her cheeks rosy from the warmth and from the wine, her eyes sparkling.

"It's really very good, Sinead. You'll need to teach me the recipe some time," Molly seconded her husband's sentiment, as she looked up from her plate. Everyone around the table murmured their own agreements. The rest of the meal passed with familial conversation; asking about each other's days, telling the latest gossip heard down in the village. When the last of the plates had been cleaned and everyone began to sit back a bit from the table, their stomachs fit to bursting, Dermot turned to his son.

"So, what's this news you have for us then, Michael?"

Just like that, all the time her stomach had spent undoing the knots that had formed earlier in the evening, somehow re-tied themselves. She looked across the table at him as he wiped his mouth with his napkin and cleared his throat before talking.

"Well, it's more something that both Aoife and I have to share," he began.

"Oh, praise the Lord. You and Aoife are together and she's pregnant!"

Aoife – who at that very moment had been in the middle of taking a sip of water – nearly spit it out right then and there.

"What!?"

Everyone around the table fell silent, completely in shock for a second, before a chorus of "Congratulations!" erupted around the table.

"No, Mam, you've got it wrong," Michael began, completely thrown off by his mother's assumption.

"But all the signs are there!" Sinead exclaimed, confused. "Ye told us you had some big news to tell us, and Aoife's only been drinking water this whole time."

Aoife realized just then how her choice to drink only water instead of wine could be misconstrued by the others. She'd made the choice because she'd been afraid it would – combined with the nervousness – make her light-headed and giggly. And that was *not* the image she'd wanted to stick with Dermot and Sinead when she told them that she was dating their son. She wished right now that she'd opted for the wine.

"Hold on! Let's let the boy speak!" Dermot's voice rose above the din and everyone settled into their seats once more. "Go on, son."

Dermot gestured to Michael, sure now that everyone around them would be quiet and let him talk.

"What we just wanted to tell everyone was that Aoife and I are together now. And *no* it's not because she's pregnant."

He looked to the end of the table where his mother's face was a mixture of disappointment at not having another grandchild – not just yet, anyways – and pleased for her son.

"We're dating; that's all. We just wanted to let you all know so that you wouldn't have to hear about it from everyone in the village."

"I thought the two of you were already dating?" young Rory piped up, a confused look on his face.

"Exactly what we've been saying all along," his mother agreed with him.

"No, contrary to popular belief, we were *not* dating before; it's only been a very recent thing."

He took a gulp of wine after his announcement.

"Well, congratulations, son. Aoife's a fine girl and we're thrilled to see you two together." Dermot placed a hand over hers and gave a squeeze, smiling at her then clapped his son on the shoulder in congratulations.

"Finally," Brendan said, his tone stating that this was old news to him. "It's about time the two of ye made things official."

"Agreed," Mara and Molly agreed with him.

"Well, I think this calls for some celebration. Mara, Molly; will the two of you help me get the dessert out from the kitchen? And boys, you and Brendan clear those plates and put them in the sink carefully for me, aye?"

Aoife began to rise from her chair, eager to help with something, *anything*, to keep herself busy right now. Her nerves were starting to calm down a bit since telling everyone the news, but the nervous energy was still pent up inside her.

"No, no, Aoife. You and Michael stay right there. You two are the guests of honour for tonight." Sinead motioned for her to sit down, which she reluctantly did.

There was a bit of hustle and bustle in the kitchen with the dirty plates being put in the sink for cleaning and dessert – a double-layered chocolate cake with ice cream – being brought out to be served. Aoife sat there at the table awkwardly. She didn't know what to say now to Dermot or to Michael now that everything was out in the open. Thankfully, she was spared by Molly who came out and placed a big piece of chocolate cake in front of her with a smile. When everyone had been served and had sat down to begin their dessert, Sinead raised her glass.

"Before we eat dessert, I would just like to toast my son *and* his new girlfriend."

She smiled at Aoife as she said it. The word still felt foreign to Aoife's ears.

"To Michael and Aoife," the whole group chorused. Aoife took a sip of her water, suddenly shy at all the attention being placed on her.

All That Compels the Heart

"Now they're finally dating, it will be no time at all before they're engaged, and then married, and then we can have some more grandchildren around this table."

Aoife nearly choked on her sip of water – again – at Sinead's words, as Michael exclaimed, "Mam!"

He looked across the table at her then and smiled, rolling his eyes in his mother's direction.

"If ye want out now, I'll understand," he whispered to her.

She smiled back at him. She found herself realizing that was the last thing she wanted.

Chapter Forty-Eight

It turned out that once everyone in the village knew they were dating, their lives became a lot easier. She hadn't been expecting that. Of course, not everything had been easy for them; Eliza had given them a hell of a time, spreading a few untrue rumours around the village, but mostly everyone seemed to ignore her. As it would turn out, they'd have much bigger news to gossip about.

She was down at the pub and, although not packed yet, it was certainly busy. When she walked in, Michael smiled at her from the bar. She felt butterflies as she smiled back at him.

"I've got this one," Michael said to Brendan, coming over to welcome her.

"Since when do you greet people at the door?" Brendan asked. "Oh, I see," he replied, seeing her standing in the doorway. "You're only doing this because your girlfriend came in."

"Just give me one of those," Michael replied testily and snatched a menu from his hand.

"Shall I show you to a table?"

"Can you show me to a - ?" she began to repeat his question. "I say, what have you done with Michael Flanagan?"

"What do you mean?"

"Over the last couple of weeks that we've been dating, you're an entirely different person: a pleasant one to be around, a *courteous* one, even. What have you done with the real Michael Flanagan?" She grinned up at him, her eyes teasing.

"What are you talking about? I've always been a gentleman," he feigned insult to his character.

"*Right*." Her voice was dripping with sarcasm. "Well, I don't know about a perfect gentleman. Let's just say you're a pretty decent bloke."

"Come on you." He ushered her to one of the tables nearest the bar. "Let's sit you down over here."

She smiled up at him, but her smile quickly faded when she heard Brendan utter, "Oh, hell no."

She and Michael both stared in the direction he was looking, their smiles fading. Michael's face took on a distinctly thunderous look. The whole pub had gone eerily quiet, like everyone knew a storm was about to break out.

I should've known.

Standing there in the entrance to the pub was Danny. A wave of emotions washed over her at the sight of him: she was still furious over his affair with Alice, but there was also a surprising tinge of regret that all the years they'd put into their relationship would never come to anything.

His eyes searched the room for her, looking determined. As soon as he spotted her, he stalked across the room and stood behind her, completely ignoring Michael's presence. Placing a hand on the back of her chair and leaning down close to her ear in a very familiar manner she was no longer comfortable with, he whispered: "Can I speak with you outside?"

She looked at him, surprised. The last thing she wanted was to talk to him about anything, but the last thing she wanted was to make a big scene in front of everyone. Knowing that she'd do as he asked, he left without waiting to see if she was following him. She hated him for it.

Knowing all eyes were still focused on her, Aoife rose from the table. She refused to meet anyone's eyes, especially Michael's; his eyes before had pretty much made everything clear about how he felt right now.

She stepped out into the brilliant sunshine. It hurt her eyes to see the bright daylight after being in the dim interior of the pub. She stood still for a second, letting her eyes adjust and looked around for Danny. She spotted him a couple of metres away, leaning against a lamppost, smoking a cigarette.

"Well, I'm here. What do you want?" she asked, wanting to get straight to the point and get this over and done with.

Danny didn't say anything at first, just leaned there on the lamppost and puffed away on his cigarette, smug in the knowledge that she still did his bidding. She stood there with her arms crossed and wished she'd thought to bring out her jacket; it had gotten cooler than she'd expected.

"Well if you're not going to talk, then I'm going back inside," she told him impatiently, annoyed at having been interrupted from her lunch.

"Wait," Danny called to her. "I came back here to try to talk to you. To make some sense of things."

Aoife stopped in her tracks when she heard him speak. There had been a vulnerability in his voice she'd never heard from him before. She turned on her heel and looked back at him; the way he stood there reminded her of a small boy afraid of being left alone. In spite of herself, she felt sorry for him. Sighing with frustration she walked back over towards him, maintaining an arm's length between them.

"And what things do you need to make sense of?" she asked him, even though she already knew the answer.

"Us," he replied earnestly.

He seemed relieved that she was willing to talk to him.

"I don't like the way we left things the last time we saw each other, and I wanted to make things right. I know that I made a mess of things, but I wanted to come back and prove to you that I'm sorry for how things ended between us. I'm still in love with you, Aoife, and I know that might be hard for you to believe right now, but I want to show you how much I love you. I want to make another go of things, and I sincerely hope you do too."

He reached over then and took her hand in his. She considered very strongly snatching it back from him, a stubborn and petty punishment for everything he'd done to her, but she realized that it was just that: a petty move. She stared at him now, seeing him for what he was: a liar, a cheat, a manipulator, and she wondered how she'd ever ended up with him.

"And what about Alice?" she asked him coldly. "What does *she* think about you saying that you're still in love with me?"

"She and I are through. It was a silly mistake and it's over now. I told her that she and I are over and that I just want to be with you," Danny said, giving her one of those dashing smiles she would have fallen for in an instant before she found out that he was cheating on her. And in that moment she was suddenly glad he'd shown up today. She'd been dreading it since she'd caught him and Alice in bed together, but now she realized it was better this way. Danny hadn't changed in the slightest since she'd walked out that night; it was all an act, an act she'd previously been too naïve to see. But now, she was no longer blinded by whatever it was she'd thought she'd felt for him. Attraction, lust maybe; it certainly hadn't been love. She wasn't sure now that in the whole time she and Danny had been together that either of them had really loved the other, and that thought suddenly made her feel sort of sad. Not because things were over between the two of them – that she wasn't sorry for at all – but that the two of them had wasted years on a relationship that neither of them had been happy in.

"And what would this life together look like, Danny? If I were to say that I was going to give you another chance and we would get back together, what would that life look like? Would it go back to you going away on business trips every couple of weeks, to the two of us going to an endless string of parties making perfectly boring conversations with perfectly boring people? Would the two of us go back to telling everyone that we're 'just grand' when everything between us isn't? Because let me tell you right now, that's not enough for me, Danny. If that's what you're offering, it's just not enough."

She looked him square in the eye and she could see that he was surprised by her reaction. Clearly, he'd thought she'd be gullible enough to take him back with no questions asked, and she wasn't sure if that made her more disgusted with him, or herself.

"I thought you liked our life together? Was it all so terrible for you?"

"It wasn't all bad, Danny," she conceded. "But it wasn't all that great either, at times, and you know that. I know that some part of you realizes that even if you don't want to admit it right now. There's no trust between us anymore, Danny; even you have to see that."

He shied away from her gaze because he knew she was right; Danny knew he was the one who'd benefitted the most from the way their life used to be.

"Look, Danny, I know this is not what you were hoping for when you came down here today. I know you were hoping that you could just flash that charming smile of yours and everything would go back to the way it was, but the truth is – things can't go back to the way they were. I won't go back to that. So, I'm sorry if this hurts you, but my answer is no. And I'd like you to leave now."

She tried to extricate her hand from his, but he held on tighter, not ready to let go of her just yet. Aoife sighed and was ready to make it clear – again – how she wasn't going to go back to him when they were interrupted by the sudden arrival of Michael bursting out of the pub's front doors. He strode determinedly towards them and before either of them knew what was happening, Michael landed a blow on Danny's chin, throwing him off-guard and off-balance. Danny let go of Aoife's hand as he staggered backwards, gripping the side of his face.

"Michael!" she exclaimed, shocked by this sudden outburst of violence. But Michael – consumed with rage as he was – did not pay her any attention. He was focused solely on his target and nothing was going to come between him and giving Danny a good thrashing.

"What the hell do you think you're doing?" Danny roared at Michael.

He'd regained his balance but still gingerly held the side of his face where Michael had punched him. Michael didn't respond to the question but instead started marching towards him. Knowing the other man was coming to attack him again,

All That Compels the Heart

Danny waited until Michael got close to him and punched him in the gut. Michael doubled over at the blow and grunted in pain but only for a brief moment before launching himself at Danny and the two fell to the ground.

"Ah jaysis," Brendan muttered, appearing beside her. "Here you two, feck off! That's enough now!" he roared at Michael and Danny but neither of them listened.

"You bastard!" Michael yelled at Danny.

The two of them had managed to disentangle themselves from one another – not before landing a few strategically placed blows to the arms and abdomen of their opponent. When they parted, Michael wiped his lip – which Aoife noticed was now swollen and bloodied – with the side of his hand. In addition to the angry bruise that was forming along Danny's jawline, he also had a small trail of blood coming down his nose but neither of them seemed to be suffering any broken bones.

At this point.

"She told ye to leave her the hell alone and what do you do? Ye come down here and harass her. Probably begged her to take you back, didn't you?" Michael accused him. Danny dabbed a finger at the spot of blood under his nose, looking almost surprised to find it there.

"Did you think you could just swan back into her life and she'd take you back?"

"What the hell do you care?" Danny shouted back at Michael. "Who do you think you are? Her boyfriend? Sorry, mate; that position is already taken."

Aoife could see Michael's eyes cloud over with rage and the fighting started all over again as Michael – unable to control his temper – launched himself at Danny, knocking them both to the ground again.

"Stop it!" she screamed at them. "Stop it the both of you!"

But neither Michael nor Danny could hear her anymore, the two of them focused intently on trying to strangle one another. Brendan, clearly fearing the worst, threw himself into the fray.

"Alright that's enough now! Get a hold of yerself, man!" he shouted as he pulled Michael off Danny just before he was able to punch him in the nose. Even though his arm was still raised and his fist balled, ready to land another punch on whatever part of Danny's body he could find, he looked up at Aoife and the look of horror on her face must have been enough to make him stand down.

"Stop it Michael! Just stop!" Her voice wavered slightly with emotion.

Brendan – using the distraction she'd provided – gripped his friend's raised arm tightly and hauled him off Danny. Still gripped with the blood frenzy of the fight, Michael resisted, but Brendan refused to let go.

"Michael! Snap out of it, man!"

Danny lay on the ground groaning. Seeing that Brendan had Michael under control now and was checking him over for any grievous bodily harm, she rushed to assess the damage Michael had done to Danny.

"Danny?"

He grunted in response but didn't say anything. He appeared to be cut and bruised all over his hands and face as he lay there on the gravel path. He was short of breath, his breathing slow and laboured, possibly from bruised ribs, but Aoife didn't think he'd hurt anything major.

"Are you alright?" she asked him.

Stupid question, Aoife! Clearly the man is not *alright.*

"I feel like I've just been attacked by a madman, but yeah, I think I'm alright. I don't think anything's broken," he said confirming her earlier diagnosis.

"Come on; let's get you to your feet."

She held out a hand to him and he groaned as she helped him stand on his own two feet again. When she was sure he could stand there without collapsing, she let go of his hand and he dabbed at the little bit of blood coming from his nose.

"Oh, I am *so* pressing charges against you," Danny said, glaring at Michael.

Michael, who was still being restrained by Brendan as he checked over his injuries, muttered, "Get off me!" but Brendan – knowing his best friend too well – kept him restrained.

All That Compels the Heart

Seeing that Danny was not going to back down, she stepped between them and said, "Stop it! The both of you! Please!"

Her voice was quieter now, pleading with them both. Seeing her distress, they both backed down.

"Brendan; let go!" Michael muttered, giving him a murderous look.

"And if I do that, do ye promise not to do anything stupid like clobber this wee eejit?" Brendan glared back at him to let him know it was a serious question.

The two of them glared at each other for a second before Michael nodded reluctantly, and Brendan let him go, still standing close by in case he needed to restrain him again. Michael shook his friend's arms off him angrily and paced around a bit but made no move to further assault Danny.

"Alright everyone, you've had your show for the day," Brendan said, addressing the crowd that had emerged from the pub to watch the fight. "Either head home or go back into the pub. Please."

It was the first time since the fracas had started that Aoife realized that anyone other than her, Michael, Danny, and Brendan were there. Everyone around them stood stock still, mouths open and flabbergasted while some of the younger kids had their mobiles out and were taking videos.

"Come on," Molly said, her tone becoming sharp. "You heard the man. Get back into the pub, the lot of you."

She turned to the crowd then and waved her hands at them as one might to encourage a flock of sheep to move off the road.

"Give me that," she said, annoyed, to one of the young kids who'd been filming the whole fight with his mobile and snatched it out of his hand.

"Hey!" the kid yelled in protest.

"You can get it back when you get inside," she told him, her tone indicating not to argue with her just then. She stood there with her hands on her hips glaring at the kid and his circle of friends until they finally stood down – albeit reluctantly – and headed back into the pub. She looked over her shoulder at her husband before heading in.

"Everything'll be grand, Moll. Go back inside," Michael said to her.

She nodded and followed everyone else back inside, closing the door firmly behind her. Aoife could see movement around the stained glass windows at the front of the pub and she suspected that most of the people who'd been watching the fight were now gathered around what clear pieces of glass they could find, trying to see what would happen now.

"Now would someone like to tell me what the feckin' hell is going on here?" Brendan asked the three of them.

Neither she, Michael, nor Danny responded right away. She imagined the three of them must look like sullen children who'd been caught doing something naughty and were now getting a lecture for it from their father.

"Ok," Brendan said. "Play it that way."

Turning first to Michael, he rounded on his friend to launch into his lecture.

"My guess, Michael, is that ye went after Danny here first because you got your blood all up the moment he walked in those doors and asked Aoife to come outside with him."

Michael, who'd been holding onto his undoubtedly bruised ribs, stood up as straight as he could before wincing in pain and folded his arms across his chest looking straight ahead, pretending to ignore his friend but not contradicting the accusation.

"What did ye expect me to do, Brendan?" he asked. "He comes down here after the way he treated Aoife and expects her to take him back. No! Not going to happen."

Michael's voice was hoarse, and he coughed a bit to clear his throat, his cheeks flushed red with both emotion and with the effort of trying to breathe after having Danny try to choke the life out of him.

"That's right," Danny piped up petulantly, focused now on gingerly touching his eye. He was going to have a right shiner in the morning.

"Shut up, you," Brendan snapped at him. "And you, Danny. What the hell were you thinking? Or, I suppose you weren't thinking at all, were you? Did ye really think that

Aoife was down here pining away for you after what you did to her?"

"What did you do? Go and tell the whole bloody village?" Danny asked, rounding on her, sounding both angry and betrayed.

"Excuse me; *I'm* the one talking here," Brendan interrupted him before launching back into his tirade. "I suppose ye thought you could just come down here and sweep Aoife off her feet and win her back, did you? Well let me tell you something, mate."

Brendan jabbed his finger at Danny's chest to drive home his point, making him yelp in pain as yet another part of his bruised body was assaulted.

"Aoife here wants nothing to do with the likes of you. So why don't ye piss on off back to Dublin or wherever and leave her the hell alone."

"Thank you!" Michael piped up, glad someone was driving home the point he'd tried to make with his fists only moments earlier.

"Shut up you; I'm still not done," Brendan snapped once again.

"And you Aoife," Brendan said, rounding on her.

She looked up at him, confused, wondering how she was being dragged into this. "Why are you angry with *me*?"

"What were you thinking, coming out here with Danny? I mean, it was pretty obvious what he wanted from the second he walked into the pub and I would hope that it would be pretty obvious to you what a jerk he is. So, what the hell were you thinking coming out here and talking to him when you knew it would set Michael off and cause a scene? Did ye want the two of them to fight for your honour like in some sort of messed up medieval drama?"

"I am *not* to blame for this!" she retorted, her voice haughty and imperious in the face of Brendan's accusation. He had no right to talk to her like that. *She* wasn't the cause of all this.

Well...

"I didn't ask Danny to come down here, and I certainly didn't ask Michael to go and try to kill him. If I *had* known Danny was going to come down here, I would have told him to piss off and leave me alone. *I* was handling the situation like a grown adult by talking things out with him and making it clear that he and I are over when Michael came charging out here like a madman and started attacking him. I can't help it if these two eejits here decided to go all caveman and fight things out rather than sort them out like calm, rational human beings!"

She stifled a scream of frustration at being told that *she* was the one to blame for the fight, even though she knew Brendan wasn't entirely incorrect. Of course she'd known it was likely that Michael would try to start a fight with Danny, which was why she'd come out here in the first place to talk to Danny on her own, rather than letting them get physically violent about it.

"Now," she said pointedly at Brendan taking over his tirade. "I think we've had enough for one day, don't you? I think the whole bloody village has had their fun in watching this stupid display of male posturing and I, for one, am not going to stick around here and give them anymore of a show. Danny, where's your car?"

"What?" he asked her, confused.

"Your ca-ar," she drawled out, like she was talking to a small child. "Where is it?"

"It's parked over there," he replied, pointing to the BMW parked a few metres away.

"Keys," she demanded of him.

"What? Why do you want my keys?" he asked her. She couldn't entirely blame him; the last time she'd taken his car, it had taken days before she'd had a driver take it back to him.

"Keys!" she yelled, her hand outstretched before him. "I'm taking you back to the house to get you cleaned up and I am not having you bleed all over the interior of my car."

"Aoife!" Michael's voice rang across the car park as she and Danny began walking towards his car. She could hear the hurt in his voice, but right now she was too angry at him and Danny and – more importantly – herself for causing this mess. Right now, she just didn't want to deal with him. He was safe with Brendan; she'd get Danny looked after to make sure he was fit enough to drive himself back to Dublin, and then he'd be out of her life for good. Then she would deal with Michael.

Ignoring his plea for her to stay, she got in the car with Danny, barely waiting for him to sit down and close the door before throwing the car into drive and speeding out of the cark park. Danny winced and groaned in pain at being jolted around.

"You deserved that," she told him unsympathetically. He wisely didn't respond.

When they finally reached the house, she switched off the car and – without waiting for him to catch up to her – headed straight to the kitchen where she knew she had a first aid kit. Danny dutifully followed behind her like a puppy who's been naughty. By the time she'd located the first aid kit, he'd caught up with her and sat down on one of the kitchen chairs with a groan, still lightly touching his bruised face.

"C'mon. Let's get you fixed up."

She took his chin firmly between her thumb and index finger, assessing the damage.

"Well, I think you'll have a nice bruise on your eye and your chin in the morning," she told him, slightly squeezing just below the bruise on his chin and making him wince again, the air sucking through his teeth sharply. "But you'll survive. The rest just seems to be cuts and bruises. How are your ribs?"

"They're fine, unless you start going and poking at them," he complained.

Aoife nodded at him and sat down on the chair next to him. She opened the first aid kit and began pulling things out of it: plasters, rubbing alcohol, gauze. She took the rubbing alcohol and tipped the bottle lightly with some gauze covering it and lightly dabbed at some of the cuts on Danny's face.

"Ouch!" he yelped at her.

"Stop being such a baby," she retorted. "You don't want any of these to get infected, do you?"

He grimaced at her but settled down in the chair and let her dab at him again with the stinging liquid.

"Why are you helping me?"

It was the question of the hour.

"Your new boyfriend made it abundantly clear that I'm no longer your concern, so why are you helping me?"

She put down the cotton swab and placed a plaster over one of his cuts.

"There. All done."

After finishing up with the cuts, Aoife rose from the table and went to the freezer looking for an ice pack.

"Here," she told him, wrapping it in a piece of paper towel and handing it to him. "Put this on your eye; it should keep the swelling down. Last thing you want is to have to go into the office on Monday morning with a great big bruise on your face. That would look really great to your clients, wouldn't it?" she asked him, a wry smirk on her face.

"Thank you," he told her, taking the ice pack from her and gingerly putting it on his eye.

"No problem at all. And you can keep that," she told him, pointing to the ice pack.

"Not just for this," he said, indicating his cuts and bruises. "For everything. Thank you for helping me out and not just leaving me there in the car park to bleed all over the pavement."

She was silent, aware that she still hadn't answered his question from earlier, a question he still wanted an answer to.

"So why are you helping me? You could have just left me there, but you didn't."

"Well, I was hardly going to leave you there on your own. God knows; Michael might have tried to beat you up again."

"Why did you choose me, Aoife? After everything I did to you? Why not go after Michael instead? Clearly you two are more than just neighbours."

Danny took the ice pack off his eye once more and leaned forward, elbows cautiously perched on his knees. He looked up at her as best he could with one eye beginning to swell shut.

"Do you still love me, Aoife?" he asked her, sincerely. "Because if you do, then why are we doing this? Why are we dancing around this? Why not just give it another go? We could make it work this time."

Aoife made a slight noise of incredulity and disgust in her throat. Now that she's had a moment to think about it, the

All That Compels the Heart

reason she'd helped him was because she still like she had to believe there was a hope that he was still a good person under the bad thing he'd done. But, seeing his true self come out once more, that glimmer of the person she thought he might have been once was gone, replaced with this selfish, arrogant, conceited person he'd become. This has always been his true self; the person she'd thought she'd known had been the act.

"No, Danny. I do not love you. You went and slept with someone else, for Christ's sake!"

She rose from the chair and began clearing away the items from the first aid kit.

"And I've apologized for that," Danny replied in a tone that was unreasonably accusing towards her, as if it were *her* fault that she wouldn't just accept his apology and move past it all. He rose from the chair and came over to stand opposite her, leaning against one of the counters. "Can't we just have a conversation about this and talk it over? You haven't spoken to me since it happened; you haven't even given me a chance to explain anything."

"Oh, I'm sorry. I didn't realize there was a need to explain anything," she said in a tone which indicated she was not sorry at all. "I felt you explained your position perfectly when you were screwing another woman; I don't think things can get any clearer than that."

"You're right," he told her, his voice rising and matching hers in annoyance. "You're right about it all. You're always goddamn right about everything, Aoife."

"Fine, Danny. Have it your way. You wanted to explain how the affair happened; go ahead and explain it to me. How long have the two of you been sleeping together? Were the two of you just laughing behind my back the whole time, pretending to be away at your stupid business conferences?"

She wasn't entirely sure she wanted to know the answers to her questions, but they just kept pouring out of her before she could stop them. It wouldn't make her feel any better to know they'd been having an affair for only a few weeks before she walked in on them together than it would if they'd been having an affair since she moved down here to Ballyclara.

Or even longer.

"I wasn't pretending to be away at conferences and business meetings. I actually *was* at them, Aoife. You can check with the company about it. It's far less sordid and complicated than you think it is. But you know what? I think you were right. I think it was a mistake to think that we could talk about this like rational human beings."

Aoife made a noise of shocked incredulity at Danny's accusation.

"Don't make this about me," she finally retorted. "*You're* the one who had the affair, Danny; *you're* the one who screwed this up."

"Oh really? And what happened to relationships being a two-way street? Because I know that I'm not the only one in this relationship who's messed up."

He raked his fingers through his hair then, clearly agitated by where this conversation was headed.

"Relationships are about two people, Aoife. We didn't get here just on my actions alone. Have you thought about why I went and had the affair in the first place?"

"Because you're an asshole who wasn't content with what was in front of him!" Aoife screamed at him. It all seemed perfectly obvious to her.

"It's a little hard to be content when your girlfriend is never there, Aoife," he said quietly.

"So, what? You're blaming *me* for the affair now?" she rounded on him.

"Well, it's a little hard to not go looking for something else when your fiancée is down here shagging the farmhand! If you'd have spent more time in Dublin with me…"

"More time with you? And when do you figure exactly that would have happened? You're always away on business, Danny! Even when I *was* in Dublin, you were never around!"

"You have to admit a part of you must have been pleased to not have to come home to me, though. I mean, you *are* dating the guy now," Danny deflected, his tone disgusted.

"So, what if I have? At least I never slept with Michael until *after* we'd broken up." She was not going to let him guilt her.

"Fine," Danny said petulantly. "I was jealous of what I thought was going on down here and so yes, I slept with Alice a few times while we were away at some conferences. But after awhile, I realized that I was still in love with you and so I broke things off with her, and that's when I proposed. And I meant every word of what I said the night I proposed to you. I do love you, Aoife. I don't work without you."

"And I suppose she just happened to flaunt her naked self in your face the night I caught you two together?"

"She came on to me. She couldn't let me go; she was jealous of you and what we have together. She kept flirting with me and then yes, I gave into her and we had sex, but it didn't mean anything to me. And it's the last time it'll ever happen again, I swear."

Aoife looked at him. She had no doubt he thought he was being sincere about his promises, but did she believe him?

"We had something together. Something special. We've lasted together for longer than any other relationship I've had before. That means something to me, Aoife."

"Just because our relationship went on for a long time doesn't mean it was good or right for either of us, Danny."

She looked up at him, the tears that had been forming in the corners of her eyes threatening to fall. "You hurt me bad, Danny. I think it's time for you to go."

Her voice was quiet but determined.

"You've had your say and I think it's clear that I'm not going to change my mind. I think you should just go back to Dublin and leave me the hell alone."

Danny looked at her as if to see if she was completely serious. When it became obvious to him that she was, he replied tersely, "Fine."

Throwing down the ice pack onto the counter, he turned to leave, but not without turning back to say one final thing to her.

"You won't be happy here with him, you know. You're not built for this kind of life, Aoife. Do you really think Michael is going to be the kind of person who'd move halfway around the world to let you pursue your career? Is he going to love you when you force him to choose between you and this village he's never left? Whatever you may think of me, at least I'd do that for you."

Aoife didn't reply to Danny's questions; they were designed to hurt her and she knew it. She set her jaw firmly. "Don't let the door hit you on the way out."

Chapter Forty-Nine

"Did ye see that?" Michael asked, flabbergasted. "She just took off with *him*." He couldn't even bear to bring himself to say Danny's name right now he was so pissed off. "What the hell is she thinking?"

"Maybe she's thinking about what a big eejit her new boyfriend is and how much she'd very much like to get away from him right now," Molly retorted, coming out of the pub now that she'd managed to get everyone back inside and back to some semblance of order. A great many of the punters were still hovering around the windows to see if they could see any more of the action but, for the most part, they'd gone back to their pints. There was no doubt now, though, that he'd be the most talked about person in Ballyclara around the dinner table tonight.

"And what did I do that was so wrong?" he asked, honestly confused. It was Danny they should all be angry with for starting this whole thing.

"We should get ye looked at," Brendan muttered, not answering the question. "Make sure ye didn't break anything in that fool head of yours."

"Leave him," Mara commanded, coming into the pub. "I'll take him home and get him fixed up, and then I might just box him 'round the ears myself."

With the look she was giving him right now, Michael didn't doubt she would make good on her threat.

Michael and Brendan looked over at her in surprise.

"Molly called me and told me what happened," she said, giving them an explanation to their unasked question.

"Make sure he's fit and ready for tomorrow, eh Mara? He's got the early shift from now until the end of the week."

And with that, Brendan stalked back into the pub, ready to face the horde of curious punters who'd witnessed the brawl with Danny.

"Alright all of ye, pipe down," he could hear Brendan shout to everyone in the pub.

"Come on, you," Mara growled at him and he – slowly but steadily – rose to his feet and followed her out to the car park. As they jolted up the road towards Mara's little cottage, Michael wondered if he might've been better off walking all the way back to his place. It was like she was purposefully trying to hit every bump in the road in order to make him hurt. A few minutes later – thankfully – they swerved down the lane to Mara's place and she stopped very suddenly in front of the house, sending Michael flying back into his seat.

"Jaysis, Mary, and Joseph, Mara!"

His sister glared at him like she wanted to say something but decided the better of it. Instead, she got out of the car and headed towards the house, slamming the car door behind her.

"Well, if ye don't like my driving, Michael, you can just walk yourself back over to your place when we get ye cleaned up. I sure as hell won't be doing you any more favours today!"

Slowly and with great care, he extricated himself from the car and followed his sister inside. The place was in quite the state: toys everywhere, dishes piling up in the sink, boots and hats and coats piled up by the door. Michael opted to lean against one of the kitchen counters rather than clean off one of the dining room chairs, its reassuringly solid presence helping him to stay upright as he held onto his bruised ribs.

All That Compels the Heart

The world was still slightly spinning around him and he closed his eyes, trying to ground himself again.

A few seconds later, he heard Mara coming down the stairs, a bottle of iodine and some gauze in one hand, a box of bandages and a bottle of Paracetamol in the other. Without talking to him, she poured a bit of iodine onto a piece of gauze and dabbed at his face.

"Ow! Would ye be careful with that?!"

"Stop being such a big baby, Michael," Mara scolded him.

"Hold still, will ye!" she yelled at him as he instinctively tried to lean back from the offending piece of gauze she held in her hand. "We'll never get ye cleaned up at this rate if you won't stay put!"

Michael sighed heavily but didn't flinch away from her.

"What the bloody hell were you thinking!" she asked him for what seemed like the millionth time that day.

"I don't know," he muttered. "But I can tell you, I remember the last fight I got into in front of that pub, I felt a lot less injured than I do now."

"That's because the last fight you got into in front of that pub, Rory was still an infant," Mara replied idly, then paused for a second, remembering that very fight. It was right after Rory had been born and Alistair Byrne had come into the pub to tell Mara he would be shagging off to God knew where and had no interest in taking care of her or their son. Michael, defending his sister's honour, had gone out to beat the pulp out of him.

"Ah jaysis!" he exclaimed, a deep stinging pain above his eyebrow bringing him out of his reverie.

"Hold still!" Mara yelled at him again. "It's a nasty cut, but I don't think it will scar. No trophy for you," she muttered at him, examining the deep cut above his right eyebrow. One of the flashy rings Danny liked to wear must have caught him in the face when he'd managed to land a punch.

Though he didn't get many opportunities, Michael smirked, remembering the fight.

"Don't touch it!" Mara slapped his hand away from the cut. "You'll get it dirty again. Here," she said, placing a plaster over it, "this should keep it covered."

"What's wrong with Uncle Michael?"

Both Michael and Mara turned around at the sound of Rory's voice from the entrance to the kitchen. In all of the hubbub surrounding him and the fight, Michael hadn't realized that it was time for school to get out already. From the look of surprise on Mara's face, clearly she'd forgotten too.

"Your Uncle Michael," she began, and he could tell that she was trying to think on her feet exactly what to tell her young son, "got into a fight at the pub. You see, Rory?"

She pointed to Michael's current damaged state. "This is what happens when you get into a fight with someone. You come home bruised and bloodied and possibly with broken ribs, and then you have to have your sister drive ye home to patch you up because you were being a real eejit."

She shot Michael a glare at the end of her speech and he tried to look as contrite as possible. Rory stood there with a mixture of concern and puzzlement on his face as he mulled over his mother's life lesson. Suddenly his face brightened with excitement.

"Did you win?" he asked.

"Well -" Michael began, pretending not to brag too much.

"No, he did not," Mara replied firmly to her son. "No one wins when you brawl like that. Now I think that's plenty enough questions for your Uncle Michael. Run along upstairs now and do your homework."

Rory looked disappointed at his mother's command and looked like he was about to protest.

Michael crouched down to his level and crooked a finger at his nephew, indicating he should come closer.

"I'll tell you all about it later, eh?" he whispered.

A big smile came across his face and he nodded before skipping off upstairs to do his homework.

"What did you tell him?" Mara demanded.

"Oh, just how he should pay attention to what his mother tells him," Michael lied.

Mara looked up at him, arms folded across her chest and with a look that said she didn't believe him.

"Uh huh."

"Look, thank you for patching me up. I appreciate it, I really do," he said coming over to her and pulling her lightly into a hug despite her stubborn struggles. He planted a kiss on top of her head before she struggled out of his arms.

"And what about those ribs?" she asked him, pulling up his shirt to reveal the dark purple bruise beginning to form there.

"Oh, they're grand," he told her, trying to take the hem of his shirt from her grasp and pull it back down again.

"And what if you've broken one of them?" she asked him. "I think ye should go to the hospital and check them out, just to be sure."

"And what's the doctor going to tell me, eh? Go home, take a few paracetamol and stay out of fights?"

He raised one of his eyebrows at her, asking her to contradict him as he took the bottle of paracetamol from the counter, popped the lid, and swallowed a couple.

"Fine, but if you end up puncturing a lung and bleed to death internally for hours, don't come crying to me about it," she muttered angrily.

"Thanks, sis," he said, planting another kiss on top of her head.

"Do ye want me to drive you over to your place? Last thing we need is you falling down and breaking your neck between here and home."

"I thought you didn't care and that you were going to force me to walk home anyways?" he asked her, reminding her of her earlier statement.

Mara glared at him again but didn't say anything in retort.

"Don't look so serious, Mara, or your face'll freeze that way," he teased her. "I'll be grand, I promise," he said to her more seriously.

She nodded at him then and he gave her a half-smile before heading outside. Every bone in his body ached with every step, but he forced himself to walk as normally as possible all the way home, knowing his sister was watching him from the window.

ഗ്രര

"Michael? Are you there?"

Aoife knocked on the front door of the cottage. His truck was not in the drive, but she suspected that, given the state he was in when she left him, neither Mara nor Brendan would let him drive himself back home. After sending Danny on his way, she'd walked down here, determined to make things right with him. She knew she'd hurt him by seeming to choose Danny over him, but she'd needed to talk to Danny alone, to put the final nail in the coffin of their relationship so they could both move on.

She stood there for about twenty seconds, listening for any movement inside the small house. She was just wondering if he might be over at Mara's place and was just about to head over there when she heard the door open behind her. She turned around and saw him standing there, cut and bruised around his face and arms, gently holding his left side with his right arm.

"Michael."

Her voice was soft, almost a whisper as she took in the full extent of the damage done to him during the fight: the plaster above his left eye; the small bruise forming beneath the other one; the way he was holding his side, indicating that he probably had a couple of bruised ribs. Though his injuries might look bad, they seemed to be mostly superficial; he seemed to have come out of the fight better off than Danny had. The thought gave her a little sense of satisfaction. She had an instinctual need then, to make sure her wounded warrior – her gallant knight – was safe from harm.

She took a step forward, one hand outstretched towards him, but Michael took a step backwards in response, putting some distance between them. She wasn't surprised by his reaction; after all, his body language since he'd opened the door all spoke to how angry he was with her, but she couldn't help the crestfallen look that came across her face as she let her hand fall back to her side again.

"Are you alright, then?" she asked him instead, trying to cover up the awkwardness between them.

"About as well as can be expected." His tone was polite but curt. His whole body was still tense as he leaned against the wooden frame of the doorway, pointedly not inviting her in but not exactly turning her away either. At least there was

All That Compels the Heart

that one small thing, which he didn't want her to leave just yet, even if he wasn't quite ready yet to forgive her.

Not knowing what to say, she just nodded at him.

What could *she say?*

She was mad as hell at him for starting the fight in the first place, but a part of her was hugely grateful to him for defending her, even if it was a barbaric way of handling the situation. She just wasn't sure which part of her – the mad as hell, or the hugely grateful part – was going to take over in this situation.

"What do ye want then, Aoife?" he asked her, trying not to wince as he shifted his stance against the doorframe, moving his sore ribs.

Ok, mad as hell it is, then.

"What do you think?" she asked him. "I was worried that you might be hurt, so I wanted to come here and see for myself if you're ok."

Michael gave her a look like he was assessing whether or not she was telling the truth, incensing her further.

"Well, it's a bit late for that, don't you think?" There was an edge to his tone, a dark look on his face.

"It's not like I left you there on your own, you know," she retorted. "Molly and Brendan were there."

He looked at her, eyes hard and untrusting. "But *you* weren't."

"I'm sorry."

His eyes searched her face and she could tell he was judging whether or not to believe her.

After a few seconds he said, "If that's the truth, then why the hell did you run off with him?"

There was an edge to his tone, a jealousy and a hurt she hadn't heard from him before.

"I don't know," she replied quietly, honestly. "I don't know if it was because of the fact that we were once friends…"

"Do you still love him?" Michael asked, interrupting her.

"No! God no!"

She was surprised by the question but completely sure in her response. She didn't love Danny – not like that – not anymore.

"Danny and I are done, Michael. If there's one thing in this whole mess that I'm sure of, it's that."

He stepped forward towards her then and, not sure what else to do, she stood stock still. He leaned down gently and kissed her deeply. She was completely surprised by his reaction – one minute they were fighting and now they'd seemed to skip straight through to the making up part.

"That's all I needed to hear," he whispered in her ear.

She threw her arms around his neck then and kissed him back just as deeply. She wasn't foolish enough to believe that Michael had let everything about Danny go – that would take more time – but right now, she wanted to be here in this moment with him.

He staggered back a bit as she launched herself at him, mumbling, "Ow. Ow. Ow."

"Shit! Sorry!"

She'd been so wrapped up in the moment, she'd forgotten about his injuries.

"It's alright. I'm alright." He was breathless and holding onto his side once more, and she thought he was probably saying it more for his sake than for hers.

"We should get you upstairs so you can lie down. Here, lean on me."

She took his free arm and positioned it around her shoulders, reaching around to steady him by the waist with her other arm, allowing him to lean some of his weight against her. The two of them navigated their way – very slowly – through his cottage.

"Ok, this part you may have to do on your own."

She looked up from the bottom of his narrow staircase, wondering how the two of them were possibly going to manage to go up them side-by-side.

"I've got this. You go on ahead."

He winced as she extricated herself very slowly from underneath him, letting him put the full weight of his body against the wall of the stairs. He nodded at her when she stood there, watching him, making sure he was alright. Still concerned, she nonetheless did as he asked and began going up the stairs slowly. She heard his laboured breathing behind her slowly – but steadily – following her. She waited

All That Compels the Heart

patiently at the top for him, giving him a hand to grasp as he reached the top step and helped guide him to the bedroom.

"Here; let's get you out of those clothes and into bed."

Michael smirked as she began to help him with unbuttoning his shirt.

"I can do it." He gently clutched her fingers mid-way through unbuttoning his shirt.

She withdrew her hands slowly, watching him as he winced a bit, but he managed to unbutton it and slip it off his shoulders. He then carefully lifted his undershirt over his head and heard a small gasp from her.

"Oh Michael," she said seeing the angry purplish-red bruise forming over the ribs on the left side of his body. She reached out gingerly to touch them, feeling his skin contract slightly under her touch, the body protecting itself from any further injury to the area. She looked up at him, her eyes full of remorse and worry for him.

"Hey," he said softly, placing his right index finger under her chin, forcing her to take her eyes away from his bruises and look into his eyes. "I'm grand, I promise."

He leaned down to kiss her, his arms around her, strong and reassuring. He guided her carefully towards the bed, laying her gently down on it. He hovered there above her, using his arms to support his weight as he leaned down to kiss her. Despite his injuries, it was clear what was on his mind.

"Are you sure you're up to doing this?" She placed a hand on his bare chest, just beneath his collarbone. Her eyes searched his, looking for any traces that he was in too much pain to have sex right now.

"Oh, I'm more than ready for this," he said, a devilish smile forming on his lips and he kissed her gently but he winced and gave a little sigh of pain as he shifted to be closer to her. She immediately pulled back from the kiss, looking down the lengths of their entwined bodies, searching for other injuries. She felt his muscles slowly relax a bit, and his breathing even out again, as the pain subsided.

"But I think you'll need to be on top this time," he groaned as he rolled over on to his back. He pulled her on top of him, giggling with laughter.

☙❧

"How do you feel?"

She ran her fingers lightly over the bruises along his chest and stomach. He reached down with his left hand, clasping hers gently in his and bringing it up to rest on his chest.

"Exhausted, but then again, you've just about worn me out," he replied.

She could hear the low rumbling of his laughter beneath her ear. She smiled and snuggled in closer to his chest, smelling his cologne mixed in with sweat and the faintest traces of blood and iodine.

"Well, I aim to please."

"That you do," Michael replied, resting his chin on top of her head, his stubble scratching lightly against her hair.

"Seriously though, are you alright? I'm not sure you should be participating in any physical activity at the moment… I really don't like the way those bruises look. Are you sure we shouldn't take you to the A&E to get you checked out, just to be sure?" She raised her a head a bit to look into his face, needing to make sure he was indeed as fine as he said he was.

"Well, I don't think that could be counted much as 'physical activity' on my part," he replied, that adorably devilish grin returning to his face. "As I recall, you did most of the work."

The two of them burst out laughing.

"I'm grand Aoife. It's nothing more than a few bruised ribs and a small cut above my eyebrow. Sure, it looks worse than it feels, alright? Now stop worrying about me. You're killing the mood."

She lay her head down on his chest again, feeling the reassuring rise and fall of it beneath her cheek.

"Maybe I should go and get you some painkillers or something?" she asked, thinking of something she could do to help him.

"No." He pulled her in closer to him with his right arm, encircling her shoulders, holding her as close to him as he could without wincing. "I have all the medicine I need right here with me."

Michael kissed her on top of her head again and lay his chin against the top of her head again. She closed her eyes, feeling herself beginning to drift into post-coital sleep when she felt him shift beneath her, reaching for something and heard the squeak of the bedside drawer opening beside her.

"What are you doing?" She raised her head to look at him, wondering what he was up to.

He winced and gave a small gasp as he moved a bruised rib but managed to find what it was he was looking for: a small, wrapped box. He poked at the drawer with his index finger, closing it again. Once he'd settled himself back on the bed into a more comfortable position, he held the box out in front of her.

"I was going to wait a bit to give you this, but what the hell?"

It felt light in her hand as she took it from him.

"What is it?"

It was *much* too early in their relationship for a ring, wasn't it?

Look at you, already thinking ahead to marriage when you've only just gone and ended it with your previous fiancé.

Aoife couldn't disagree with her subconscious; it was far too early for her to be thinking of such things.

"Go on. Open it."

He nodded towards the box he'd painstakingly wrapped for her the night before. Curious, she held the box up to her ear and gently shook it, listening to the rattle of a small object inside.

"I suppose I should have asked if it was breakable before I did that," she said, sheepishly.

"Too late now. Now you've got a broken present."

A serious look crossed her face for a second until she realized he was joking.

"I'm only teasing," he reassured her. "Now hurry up and open it."

"Sheesh. You're worse than a small child."

He smiled at the jibe and watched her carefully unwrap the cellotaped present. She carefully opened the lid of the small box, overturning it in her hand to reveal a key. It felt smooth and metallic in her hand, newly made. She looked at it for a moment unsure what it meant until realization dawned on her a second later, and her mouth drew into a perfect "o" shape.

"Is this your way of asking me to move in with you?"

"I'm not saying that ye need to give up living at the Old Rectory," he was quick to reassure her. "But where you've been spending so much time here lately, I figured it was time ye had your own key to the place. You're welcome to stay here as long as ye like and as often as ye like."

Not knowing what to say, she kissed him quickly. "Yes! I'm thrilled to move in here with you."

She felt him smile and sigh, his whole body relaxing.

"So, am I forgiven?" he whispered against her ear.

She looked up at him curiously, wondering what he was talking about.

"For going all 'caveman and defending your honour in some antiquated attempt at dominance or something' as you so eloquently put it?"

"I'd like to say no, but actually, I *did* find it kind of hot. Does that make me a terrible feminist?"

She laid her head down on his chest once more.

"Thank you. For defending my honour. You didn't have to."

"I know," he replied. "But any time ye need me to, I will."

Chapter Fifty

After Danny's swift departure from Ballyclara, Aoife and Michael settled into an easy rhythm of blissful co-habitation. She'd been avoiding her life in Dublin during the time since she'd moved back down to the country. Of course, Bex and Millie knew about her and Michael, and the three of them talked every day, but she'd been avoiding her family. She just couldn't bring herself to have to deal with the inevitable lecture that would come with telling Grainne about her break-up with Danny.

As if the thought of her summoned the woman herself, Aoife heard her phone ring, the word *Grainne* popping up on her caller ID. A sense of dread settled in. Debating whether or not to answer the phone or let it go to voicemail, she sighed and muted the music on her laptop, and answered the phone on the fourth ring.

"Hello, Granny."

She did her best to keep her tone even and pleasant. Steeling herself for the inevitable lecture she was about to receive – for there could be no other reason her grandmother would be calling her – Aoife sat up straight in her chair, feet planted on the ground, her shoulders back, just how she'd been lectured to sit by her grandmother her whole life. There were just some things that had been drilled into her for so long that they'd become second nature.

"Hello Aoife. I wasn't sure if you were at home or not."

"You caught me in the middle of writing," Aoife replied, trying – not entirely successfully – to keep any edge out of her voice.

"Oh really?" Grainne's voice was a mixture of surprise that Aoife was still doing this writing "thing," and boredom because it was uninteresting to her.

"How can I help you, Granny?"

Aoife refused to let her grandmother get under her skin today. Things had been going so well between her and Michael of late – which had been excellent for her creativity – and she would not let her grandmother dampen it like the rain beating against the panes of her study's windows.

She heard her grandmother sniff disdainfully on the other end of the line at Aoife's brusqueness.

"Well, I hadn't heard from you in quite some time and it's been quite lonely up here in Dublin as of late, and I thought it might be nice of you to come and visit for awhile. You haven't been back to the city in quite some time, you know."

Aoife was very well aware of the last time she'd been in Dublin. It had been seared into her memory.

"Besides, I heard about how you and Daniel broke off your engagement."

Aoife froze at the mention of Danny. She hadn't told anyone in her family that she and Danny were no longer together, not even Connor. The only people in Dublin who knew were Bex and Millie, and neither of them would have told Grainne.

"Oh?"

It was all she could manage to say. Her mind raced, frantically trying to come up with a good enough excuse as to why she hadn't told her grandmother the wedding was off – the fact that she would be receiving this very lecture from her grandmother would not be considered an acceptable excuse – and also wondering exactly how much her grandmother knew about the break-up.

All That Compels the Heart

"Yes. I had to hear about it from Caitlin, who heard it from Nathaniel, who heard it from one of Daniel's business partners."

Her grandmother's voice was as hard as steel. Clearly, she was not best pleased at not being the first to be told the news. Grainne would find it embarrassing not that Aoife and Danny had broken up – not that she would be pleased about that either, considering all the wedding planning she'd been doing – but that she'd had no control over how the news got around to her circle of friends.

"Apparently, this business partner heard it from that woman Daniel brought to Christmas dinner – Alice, I think her name was. Anyways, apparently she is telling everyone how your engagement has been broken off and that *she* is now engaged to Daniel."

Danny is engaged to Alice?

The news came as a shock to her. This was very quick, especially for Danny.

"In any case, it appears there are a great many things for the two of us to discuss, including this Michael Flanagan that you are now dating."

How the hell does she know about Michael?

Grainne didn't give her a chance to say anything before continuing.

"Nathaniel will be returning from a business trip in Asia this week, and your mother and Anton will be returning from Las Vegas in a few days; oh, and Connor will be home by the end of the week as well. So, we will be having dinner on Saturday at six-thirty. And bring this Michael with you."

Grainne's brusque tone made it clear that dinner was not a request for either her or Michael. She briefly entertained the idea of defying her grandmother, but thought the better of it; there were going to be enough battles with her to come over the cancellation of the wedding; she could concede this argument for now.

"Brilliant, Granny."

Internally her stomach began to sink, already beginning to dread the weekend and wondering how she would convince Michael to come with her.

Oh God, Michael. They'll tear him to shreds.

If there was one thing her family was good at, it was interrogations.

"See you then."

Aoife heard the click of the phone as her grandmother hung up on her. Placing her mobile on the desk beside her, she tried to put her grandmother and her dinner plans out of her mind and get back to her writing but it was no use; her creativity had been thwarted and her writer's block returned.

"Arrrrggh!" she exclaimed, frustrated, banging her fingers against the keyboard angrily.

"I'd ask how the writing is going, but I think I just got my answer."

Aoife's head snapped up as she heard Michael's voice from the doorway of the study. She hadn't heard him come in the house. He stood before her, his head and shoulders slightly damp from the heavy drizzle going on outside, holding out a cloth bag towards her. She raised an eyebrow, curious.

"Chicken pot pie," he replied, following her gaze. "Some mashed potatoes, rolls, and even some apple crumble. I thought you might be caught up in your writing and forget to eat, so I thought I'd try to entice you to take a break by having an indoor picnic with me."

Aoife's stomach grumbled at the mention of the food and the faint aroma of the chicken pot pie wafted towards her from the doorway. She *was* known to skip a meal – or two, or three – when she was caught up in writing, oblivious to the passing of night or day. She smiled at him gratefully, thankful to be reminded that she had someone in her life who was so thoughtful.

"I'd love to have an indoor picnic with you."

Michael smiled at her and crossed the room to place the bag on her desk. "Good, because I was not going to take no for an answer."

He leaned down and kissed her quickly on the lips before turning towards the tan-coloured leather sofa and snatched the tartan quilt from it, spreading it out on the carpet of the study. He went about unpacking the bag full of plastic containers, setting everything up. Aoife's stomach growled louder as the scent of food wafted up to her. Glancing down at her document, she deleted the random characters her frustrated outburst had typed, saved her document, and closed her laptop.

"This looks amazing," she said, joining him on the blanket.

"I can't take the credit," he confessed. "Molly did most of the work. I just tried to sneak out without getting caught taking the food with me."

He winked at her then, a boyish grin on his face and she couldn't help but smile along with him.

"Here, eat up."

He handed her a plate loaded with the best-looking chicken pot pie, potatoes, and veggies she'd ever seen. Molly had outdone herself this time. Hunger fully setting in now, she took the plate from him and hungrily tucked into her food. They ate in silence, only the sound of the rain pattering against the windows reminding them that there was a world outside of the little bubble they'd created here on the floor of her study. When they were halfway through their plates, Michael suddenly spoke up.

"So, what had you so frustrated when I walked in? I thought the writing was going well lately?"

Suddenly, the bite of mashed potato she'd taken seemed heavy in her throat and she swallowed hard to get it down. Feeling slightly put off her food, she put her plate down on the blanket and cleared her throat.

"My grandmother called."

She looked up at Michael who paused in the middle of chewing before resuming and placing his plate on the blanket beside hers. He took a sip from his can of soda before nodding. She could tell that he was trying to be supportive of her; she hadn't told him much about her family, but most of what she *had* told him had painted a pretty clear picture for him that she wasn't close to them and she didn't like to talk about it.

"What did she want?" He looked at her, his gaze full of concern.

"She wants me to come up to Dublin to see her." She decided to leave out the bit that the reason Grainne wanted to see her was to rake her over the coals about breaking off her engagement; that could wait for now. "Actually, she wants *us* to come up to see her."

She watched him digest this news, wondering how he was going to take it. Discussions about her family was virtually uncharted territory for them so far in their relationship, and she wasn't sure how he was going to feel about meeting them.

"And are we going to? See her, I mean?" He looked to her for direction, letting her be the one to steer the ship on whichever course she thought best for them.

Aoife sighed. She didn't want to pretend everything was rainbows and sunshine with her family – she didn't think he'd believe her in any case – but she didn't want her jaded view of them to cloud his own judgement either. He should get to know them for himself without too much influence from her.

"I don't really want to, but I feel like we probably should."

He nodded again, at peace with her decision. "Look, I know ye don't have a great relationship with your family, Aoife; that much has been pretty clear to me since we met, given that ye hardly ever speak about them. I mean, apart from Connor, I've never even *met* anyone in your family; none of them have ever come down here to visit you, as far as I know."

He looked to her to see if she would contradict him. She couldn't. Not even her mother could be bothered to see her daughter's new home.

"If ye don't want to go and see them, I'm not going to force you. But, I feel like, since you've spent so much time getting to know my family, that I should put in the effort to get to know yours, but I'm going to support you no matter what you choose."

There were *so* many reasons for him not to want to be bothered to get to know her family, but she knew he wouldn't understand any of them until he actually met them for himself. After all, how could he understand what it was like to be distant from your family when he had one which was so warm, open, and loving? The best way to explain to him what her family was like was to just show him, but she felt a sense of great trepidation at the prospect of him meeting them. What if he met them and he didn't like side of her? She knew he was interested in her – possibly, even, that he loved her – but the world she'd grown up in was so different from his. Would he be able to cope with what it meant to be one of the O'Reillys? She wasn't so sure.

"I suppose," she conceded, dreading the thought of the weekend even more than she had before, something she hadn't thought possible.

"Great." Michael picked up the plates from the blanket. "I'm going to go and put these in the fridge for later. You don't look like you're very hungry anymore."

She nodded at him only half-listening, her mind focused on how she was going to get through the weekend with both her and Michael still intact by the end of it.

Chapter Fifty-One

All too soon, the dreaded weekend had arrived. It had preyed on Aoife's mind all week. She'd hoped something would come up that would prevent them from having to go up to Dublin. She'd even tried to enlist Brendan's help by trying to get him to schedule Michael to work on the weekend, even though he'd already enlisted Mara and Jimmy's help.

"Aren't you and Michael going to meet your family this weekend?" he'd asked her.

"Well, I mean…"

"In fact, I think things are coming back to me now," he cut her off. "I'm pretty sure Michael's own words to me were: 'If Aoife asks you to come up with a reason for why I shouldn't go to Dublin this weekend, just tell her you have everything sorted.'"

Brendan had arched an eyebrow at her. She'd wisely chosen not to say anything.

"In fact, I scheduled Jimmy and Mara in specially to fill in for him, and both of them are delighted to have the extra cash."

"That's great," she'd replied, unenthusiastically. "Don't you think you might still be a bit understaffed, though? I mean, tourism *is* picking up at Glendalough, and I'm sure the pub will be packed this weekend."

"I'm sure between Jimmy, Molly, Mara, and meself, we have it covered, Aoife."

Brendan had smiled kindly at her as he gently placed a tray of clean glasses down on the bar, the glasses clinking against each other.

"Look, I'm sure you're nervous about him meeting the family and all, but it'll all work out. You've nothing to worry about."

"It's not so much that I'm worried about what they'll think of him. I'm worried about what he'll think of *them*."

And me, by proxy.

Michael had never seen where she'd come from, the kind of people who'd influenced how she'd been raised. Once he met them, she was afraid that he wasn't going to like what he saw, and that he wouldn't like the person she was anymore.

"I think you're worrying too much about it, Aoife. I'm sure it'll all be grand." Brendan had begun to walk towards the swinging door between the bar and kitchen, thinking their conversation was done when she'd called out, "Whatever Michael's paying you to turn me down, I'll double it."

Brendan had paused with his hand on the door and looked at her.

"I'm serious, Brendan. I'll even triple it."

He'd shook his head and laughed a little, making her heart sink in her chest. "Not a chance, Aoife."

"Please Brendan." She'd done her best to sound as pathetic as possible. He'd looked up at her tone and she'd done her best to try to put on the saddest face she could.

"Look, it's not that I couldn't use the money," Brendan conceded. "But he's not paying me anything. I happen to think he's right and that he should meet your folks. I mean, the two of you practically live together now and you two spend loads of time up at his parents' place; don't ye think it's only fair that he at least meet your family once? They can't be all that bad."

"You greatly underestimate my family," she'd muttered.

༺☙༻

Later that evening, she and Michael had gone to his parents' place for dinner, much like they'd done every night in the last couple of weeks.

"So, you two are all set to go up to Dublin tomorrow?" Sinead had asked and Aoife shot a look at Michael.

Her mouth pinched into a moue of dissatisfaction; had he told the whole bloody village about meeting her family?

"Just about," she replied, trying to keep her voice calm and even.

"Your parents must be so excited to see you."

Highly unlikely, she thought but didn't say.

"You should bring them down here sometime soon so we can meet them too. I don't think they've been down to visit you since you've moved to Ballyclara, have they?"

"No."

She didn't even try to offer up an excuse as to why her own family wouldn't come to see her new home, despite the fact that she'd lived here for nearly a year now. She knew the polite thing would have been to say something along the lines of "They're just really busy with their work" or "They're away a lot of the time" but she just couldn't be bothered to make excuses for them anymore.

Perhaps sensing how uncomfortable this conversation was making her, Mara cleared her throat and said, "Shall we eat?"

Aoife smiled gratefully across the table at her. The brief reprieve from worry did not last long, however. Just as the food had been served, Dermot paused, his face gone a scary white pallor.

"Da? What's wrong?"

Everyone looked up at Mara's concerned and alarmed tone, for Dermot sat there, hand on his chest, his breathing laboured.

"I'm calling for Doctor Kelly." Michael got up quickly from his chair and reached for the phone on the stand between the kitchen and the dining area.

"No… don't… I'm… grand," Dermot said, clearly struggling to breathe.

"You are not grand, Dermot Michael Flanagan." Sinead's voice was very-matter-of-fact, but it belied a great deal of concern underneath it.

Ignoring his father, Michael punched in the number for the doctor's house and waited for it to ring.

"What's wrong, Grandad?" Rory asked, his voice pitched higher than normal, worry written all over his young face.

"Nothing… son." Dermot's face was pinched as he tried to give his grandson a smile that was intended to be reassuring but turned out to frighten the child more.

"Thank you." The phone clicked in its cradle as Michael set it down. "Doctor Kelly will be right over."

"There's no… need… to fuss."

Dermot's face had become a little less white than it was a moment before, but he was still struggling to breathe.

"Here, let's get your collar open." Michael came over to his father and unbuttoned the first couple of buttons on his shirt. Concentrating as he was to breathe, Dermot didn't have the strength to fend off his much stronger son.

"Just take slow, deep breaths. In… and out."

Aoife, who'd been shocked enough that she'd been unsure what to do, finally came to her sense and reached across the table to hold of Dermot's hand, giving it a bit of squeeze to let him know that she was there. He nodded and breathed with her. In… and out.

After what felt like hours but was, in reality only a few minutes, there was the sound of footsteps outside the house. Sinead rose from the table, her face lined with worry and concern as she let in the doctor. Mara motioned for Rory to come out of the way as Sinead and Doctor Kelly – a tall, thin, man in his mid-forties who looked permanently gaunt in the face – swiftly went to Dermot's side.

"And how are we today, Mr. Flanagan?" the doctor asked, bringing out his stethoscope and other tools from his medical bag.

"A little… out of… breath," Dermot replied, his breathing coming back to him slightly better than it was, but still clearly restricted.

"Alright, well let's have a listen then, eh?" the doctor asked, putting the stethoscope to his ears and placed the other end on Dermot's chest. After a few seconds, he turned to Michael and said, "Could we have everyone just give us a bit of space for a moment?"

Michael nodded to the doctor and gestured for everyone to exit the dining area into the small adjoining sitting room.

Doing their best not to look worried, the small group sat down, all of them silent in case something important could be overheard in the other room, each of them pretending like they were not listening in. After a few minutes of quietly talking to Dermot – just quietly enough that no one in the sitting room could hear them – Doctor Kelly appeared in the entranceway. Everyone looked up at him, concern in their eyes, anxious to hear the news, praying it wouldn't be what they'd feared.

"I'd like to take Dermot down to hospital and admit him for the night for observation."

Sinead could be heard drawing in a shaky breath, fearing the worst.

Doctor Kelly held up a hand to delay the onslaught of questions he was clearly expecting.

"It's just a precaution to make sure all is well. I believe he's had an acute attack of angina, which is not serious in and of itself at the moment, but it could be sign of something bigger happening with his heart. I'd like to bring him in for some tests to rule anything out."

"Of course," Sinead said, breathing a little easier herself after hearing from the doctor that it wasn't as bad as they had all feared.

"I've rung for an ambulance to transport him. You can go in and see him now, if ye like."

As soon as the words were out of his mouth, Mara, Michael, and Sinead practically ran to the dining room to check on Dermot. Aoife hung back a bit with young Rory who still looked positively frightened, but a little more reassured now his grandfather wasn't going to drop dead in front of him. She placed a hand on his thin shoulder and tried to smile down as reassuringly as she could at him.

"I'm sorry wee man. I didn't mean to scare you. I promise I'm alright."

Rory looked up at Aoife, unsure what to do.

"Go on. It's ok."

She nodded in Dermot's direction, indicating he didn't have anything to be frightened of. Something in her words or actions must have reassured him for the young boy ran through to the dining room and gave his grandfather a big hug.

"Whoah there," Dermot said with a little chuckle.

"Ok be careful there now, Rory. We need to treat Grandad a little gently until we get him all checked out at the hospital."

At his mother's words, the little boy withdrew a bit, his look of concern returning to his face, worried he had hurt his grandfather. Dermot smiled down at him and gave him a small wink, letting him know he was alright.

"The ambulance is here," Doctor Kelly announced from the front door, breaking up the little family moment.

"Ok." Dermot tried to push back his chair, displacing Rory who ran over to his mother's arms.

"Where do you think you're going?" Michael looked sternly at his father.

"I can walk out there. I'll be grand."

Dermot pushed away Michael's hand as he got up. He'd just about stood on his feet but had to stop as he winced in pain, touching his chest lightly.

"You stay right there, Mr. Flanagan."

A male emergency first responder stepped through the front door, carrying one end of a stretcher. His female colleague carried the other end. Mara and Sinead automatically reached over to pull the table out of the way, giving them more space to set up the stretcher. Still not one to take orders easily, Dermot carefully and slowly walked his way over to the stretcher, only accepting help at the end from the emergency first responders to get onto it. His breath came out in a *whoosh!* of air as he lay back on the stretcher; even the short walk had completely tired him out and his face had gone pale again.

"Alright Mr. Flanagan, you just lay back there and relax for me, ok? We'll get you on your way here soon." The first responder nodded to his partner and the two of them navigated their way through the house, careful not to jostle their patient too much. The family followed them out into the cool night air.

"Would I be able to ride with him?" Sinead asked the male first responder.

"Of course," the dark-haired, middle-aged man replied, offering her a hand to step up into the ambulance where his colleague was checking Dermot's vitals. Closing the doors carefully behind them, he turned to the doctor and said, "You can ride with us, if you like doctor."

"Yes, that sounds good. I will meet you at the hospital," he said, turning to Michael before heading around to the front of the ambulance and getting inside. As Michael, Mara, Aoife, and Rory watched the ambulance's blue lights pull out of the driveway, Aoife turned to Michael and said, "I'll go and get my car. It's got more room for all of us."

His face was drawn into a look of concern. Worried he hadn't heard her, she placed a hand gently on his upper arm. Interrupted from whatever dark thoughts were occupying his mind, he nodded down at her.

"We'll lock up here and meet you in a couple of minutes."

Mara nodded at her and headed back into the house with Rory to clean up the dinner and lock up the house. Aoife lingered a half a second longer, worried for him.

"Go," he reassured her. "I'm grand. See you in a few minutes."

He turned back towards the house to help his sister and Aoife headed out into the dark towards the Old Rectory. She walked briskly through the cool night, so focused was she on getting back to Michael as soon as she could, she barely noticed her surroundings. Trying to hurry, she pitched forward in the dark as she accidently stepped into a pothole in the road, nearly sending her flying.

"Jesus, Mary, and Joseph!" she exclaimed. She paused for a moment, taking a deep breath to steady herself.

Steady on there, Aoife. The last thing we need is for you to end up in the hospital along with Dermot.

She took another breath and then began her brisk walk back to her place, paying more attention in the moonlight to where she was walking. As she pulled into their driveway a few minutes later, Michael, Mara, and Rory were standing there on the front porch, waiting for her. She pulled up beside them, waiting for them all to get in and get buckled before driving off into the night to follow where the ambulance had gone.

All That Compels the Heart

It was a silent ride to the hospital, no one in the car able to say anything that would make them feel less anxious than they were. As they arrived at the hospital, Aoife pulled up to the front entrance.

"You all go on inside. I'll find you in there."

As Mara, Michael, and Rory exited the car, Aoife sped off towards the visitor parking area and paid to park her car. Making sure her ticket was tucked safely into her purse, she hurried towards the A&E where she found the four Flanagans sitting there, looking anxious and forlorn.

"Any news?" she asked, her heart in her throat, worried something might have happened while she was parking the car.

"No," Michael replied, taking her hand as she sat beside him. "They're just getting him admitted now and they're going to do some tests. Doctor Kelly told us to wait down here and he would come and get us when they were done."

Aoife nodded to him, settling herself into an available uncomfortable hospital chair.

The minutes seemed to drag on as they waited there, watching as people got slowly admitted through triage and into the actual emergency room itself. The scent of latex and disinfectant permeated everything.

None of them spoke to one another, consumed with worry as they were for Dermot. Every now and again, Aoife would glance up at the television screens hanging from the ceiling, showing Coronation Street or Hollyoaks or some other soap opera. The sound had been muted in order for the hospital staff to get on with their work and a hush descended upon those who waited to either be admitted for their injuries or were waiting to see their loved ones. Only the occasional cough or groan from a patient interrupted the quiet.

Just when she didn't think she'd be able to sit on the hard plastic chair any longer, she caught the sight of Doctor Kelly out of the corner of her eye. Seeing him too, Michael rose from his chair to catch the doctor's attention.

"There you are," the doctor said to them, smiling. "He's all checked in upstairs now and you can go up to see him. Visiting hours are almost over, but I talked the nurses into giving you a few extra minutes with him. If ye follow me, I'll take ye up to him."

The five of them rose from their seats, stiff and aching. Following the doctor through the maze of corridors, they eventually came upon the ward for cardiac patients. Going through the heavy metal double doors that separated the ward from the corridor, there was a hush to the area. A nurse greeted them outside of Dermot's room.

"Are you the Flanagan family?" she asked.

"Yes," Sinead replied, taking a step toward her. "I'm his wife. Would it be alright if I went in to see him?"

"Of course. But we don't want to overwhelm him. You can all have a few minutes, but then I'm going to have to ask you to leave and return in the morning."

"Thank you," Sinead said to the nurse.

She took a deep breath before walking through the entrance to her husband's hospital room and smiled at him. Mara and Rory followed closely after her, with Michael and Aoife bringing up the rear of the group.

Maybe it was the smell of the hospital – that distinct mixture of disinfectant and death – or the fact that Dermot looked much frailer than his normal self, lying there in his hospital bed hooked up to a multitude of tubes, or the stress of the whole situation that night, but something about the whole situation made her flashback to when her grandfather was lying in a hospital room much like this only a year ago. Trying to fight against the panic rising within her, Aoife's heart caught in her throat, preventing her from breathing properly.

While the others were occupied with checking on Dermot, she slowly backed out of the room, feeling too much like the room was closing in around her. While she wanted to be there for Michael – to support him and his family – before she realized it, she was out of the ward and standing in the corridor. She took a deep breath to steady herself and sat down on a nearby bench.

Trying to distract herself so she wouldn't cry, she scrolled through her texts, checking to see if she'd missed any messages. She saw that she had a text from Connor, who was complaining about the upcoming dinner with their grandmother and warning her that she'd better not back out this time and leave him there on his own.

Oh God, the dinner!

Although the dread of tomorrow had never gone away, it just had taken a place in the back of her mind when Dermot's angina had flared up. She felt selfish for having made a big deal about the dinner. After all, what if all this worry over a stupid dinner had caused this?

Don't be foolish, Aoife, she chastised herself. *The world does not revolve around you, and you do not have the power to cause heart attacks just because you didn't want to go to dinner with your grandmother.*

Still, it was difficult to not feel some sort of guilt over Dermot's sudden illness.

Trying to push the thought out of her mind, she figured that she should call her grandmother and let her know that they wouldn't be able to come up tomorrow. Michael would want to be here with Dermot, after all, and Aoife wouldn't feel right making him go with her when she knew how worried he'd be about his father. Also, she wouldn't want to just leave him down here to go through all of this on his own. Grainne would be furious, but Aoife was used to it. Grainne would just have to deal with it.

Searching through her phone's directory for her grandmother's number, she hit the green phone button to call her grandmother.

"Who are you calling?"

Michael's voice behind her surprised her and she hung up the phone before finishing dialling. She hadn't heard him come out of the ward.

"I was going to call my grandmother and cancel for tomorrow."

"Why?"

Aoife looked up at him, confused. It should've been obvious to him, after all.

"Because your father just almost had a heart attack and had to be admitted to the hospital."

"Sure, and he's going to be grand, though. Doc says he'll be discharged tomorrow morning. The tests have come back and Da's going to have to take some new medication and go on a bit of a diet, which he will not be thrilled with, but otherwise he's grand. There's nothing to worry about. We can still go up to Dublin."

Aoife breathed a sigh of relief. It was great news that Dermot was going to be fine. A little bit of the guilt and selfishness she'd been feeling earlier lifted from her.

"Still though, you'll want to be there tomorrow when he gets discharged, and we should stick around to keep an eye on him, don't you think?" She looked up at him, expecting him to agree with her.

"I will stop by first thing tomorrow morning to drive him and Mam back home, but she and Mara will be around to look after him. Don't worry, Aoife; you're not getting out of this weekend, come hell or high water."

He kissed her on the top of her head.

"Now, I'm going to go and say goodbye to Ma and Da, and then we can go home, alright?"

She nodded at him, not really listening to him. The sudden relief she'd had at finding out Dermot was going to be fine was replaced by the dread she'd been feeling all week.

"I'll go and bring the car around to the front," she said to him, her stomach twisting in knots again.

Chapter Fifty-Two

"How much farther?" Michael looked up at Aoife's back as she walked down the steep street towards the River Liffey, weaving her way through the late afternoon crowds.

They'd just come from Bex and Millie's flat, where he'd spent most of the time trying to apologize for being such a gobshite to them in the beginning. Thankfully, Bex and Millie had been very understanding.

After they'd put him through his paces – he was more than certain that Millie's direct threat that if he hurt Aoife that Millie would end him was entirely true – they'd all been able to relax a bit more, get to know one another properly. He'd been pleased to see that Aoife had such great friends in her life that wanted to look out for her. He liked Bex's kind, mothering attitude she had towards both Aoife and Millie – who, he was sure, was more than a handful most of the time – and he appreciated Millie's directness, her way of being able to say exactly what was on her mind without fear of consequence. It wasn't until he and Aoife had left their flat and he felt the sense of relief washing over him that he'd noticed that he'd been so nervous to meet them. He shouldn't have been too surprised; after all, every time that Aoife mentioned them, she always brought up how they were practically as close as sisters.

"Don't worry," she'd told him, linking her arm through his and rubbing his forearm lightly, "they liked you. I told you there was nothing to be nervous about. You've passed the friend test."

"Is that really a thing?"

"Uh, yeah," she'd replied, surprised he was even asking. "Of course it is. While we may not say that it's important to us, it's incredibly important for us that you like our friends and, more importantly, that they like you."

He only hoped his meeting with her family would go this well.

After leaving Bex and Millie's place, Aoife had taken him on a quick walking tour of Dublin, making their way through St. Stephen's Green and Trinity College to wind up here in the famous Temple Bar district. Michael had, of course, been to Dublin before – but this was the first time he'd been to the city with someone from here. As they made their way through the streets of the city – avoiding the main streets clogged with tourists – she spouted off historical facts and pointed out things to him he'd never had noticed before. It was all well and good, spending time with Aoife and going on this little tour, but now that his stomach had been grumbling for the last fifteen minutes or so and a light mist had begun to fall, he was beginning to get tired, hungry, and a bit cranky.

It had been late when the two of them had gone back to the Old Rectory from the hospital last night, and it had been early when he'd gone back to the hospital to pick up his father after being discharged, leaving Aoife with most of the packing for this weekend. She'd thought to pack him some breakfast rolls his mother had made the day before and some coffee, but breakfast seemed a long time ago and he was starting to run low on energy. He knew he would have to snap out of it before he went to her grandmother's tonight; it hadn't been just Aoife who'd been nervous all week about this dinner, and the nerves, combined with the hunger, was making him feel on edge.

He knew Aoife hated the idea of him meeting her family, but why was still a bit of mystery to him. He knew who she was – she was one of the O'Reillys, one of the wealthiest families in the country – but because he was the sort to avoid most celebrity gossip, he didn't really have an idea of where Aoife came from. His sister had warned him off doing any internet research, which probably would have been for the best, had he listened to that advice.

He'd wanted some advanced warning about the people he was going to meet tonight, and Aoife had made it clear she wasn't going to be giving him much info on them. What he'd found out was more than he could have imagined. Michael had stayed in the same small village his whole life, had a mountain of debt from the pub he was barely able to keep afloat, and had one good suit which was worn at every wedding, funeral, and special occasion until it was worn thin. He'd never even finished university. He knew he had nothing in common with her family, could never hope to give her a life that looked anything like the one she'd grown up in. Trepidation about tonight's dinner with them began to sink in.

"Just a few more steps." Aoife's voice broke through his dark reverie. "Et voilà!"

At first he just saw yet another street in Temple Bar, nothing outstanding about the brown brick buildings before him. His eyes scanned the names of the pubs in front of him and that's when he saw it: the word *"O'Reilly's"* scrawled in gold lettering across a brilliant blue background with black trim.

"This isn't?"

"It is. The one and only – original – *O'Reilly's Irish Pub*." She looked at him proudly, her smile beaming. "Come on, let's go inside."

O'Reilly's being such an internationally famous pub chain – and the original being housed in one of the most popular tourist areas – Michael supposed he'd been worried the place might have fallen into an Americanized version what an Irish pub should look like, devoid of actual Irish character. However, what lay before him was none other than a typical local pub you'd find anywhere in the country; it could even have been his own pub back in Ballyclara rather than a fancy, five-star Michelin-rated, polished-to-perfection restaurant.

That was, of course, why she'd brought him to this one specifically. It was the only one in the whole chain that was like this. It embraced its older, dingier, more local, more natural atmosphere. Booths lined the walls of the place with tables filling up the middle of the floor. A small stage for live music stood off to one side, a couple of local boys up there providing some background music above the din of the patrons. The patrons themselves – rather than being tourists with their cameras out, mouth open agog at everything around them, like the kind he was used to seeing in his own pub – seemed to be mostly locals.

The interior of the pub lacked natural light, every window in the place being covered in stained glass. Small brass lamps hanging from the ceiling cut through the gloom, like little lighthouses on a foggy night. Even though no smoking had been allowed in the pub for years, the smell of cigarettes and cigars hung in the air, vestiges of a time long past. What the place lacked in lighting though, it more than made up for in comfort and providing its patrons with a sense of open friendliness and charm.

"Aoife!"

Both Michael and Aoife looked up at the sound of her name being called across the pub.

"Gerry!"

Aoife quickly weaved her way through the crowd of people towards the bar, catching the older man in a big hug. Gerry was a stout man, a good head shorter than Michael and at least twice as wide. His once dark brown hair was greyer on the sides now and thinning considerably on top. His face was lined and marked by years of worry and hard labour.

"It's great to see you."

"You've been away too long," he admonished her. "So, who's yer man?" he asked, eyeing Michael.

"Gerry, I'd like you to meet my boyfriend, Michael."

"Boyfriend, eh? You've never brought a boyfriend back to this place before. I was beginning to think you'd up and joined a convent down there in Glendalough." Gerry's voice was teasing.

He turned to Michael, holding out his hand to him. "Pleasure to meet you, Michael."

All That Compels the Heart

Gerry's grip on his hand was firm but friendly. The strong – almost fatherly – grip belied the man's age. "Nice to meet you too."

"C'mon, let's get you two to your booth."

Gerry guided them to a booth nearby where two young lads were sitting, having a drink. Both of them looked hardly old enough to be in the pub, let alone having a pint.

"Sean, Ronan; get yer arses outta there. The boss' granddaughter is here."

Sean and Ronan looked up at Gerry mid-sip, sheepish looks on their faces.

"Sorry, Aoife," the two of them quickly replied, slipping out of the booth, still clutching their pints.

"Thanks boys," she said to them. "How's your mother doing, by the way, Ronan?"

"Ah she's grand; thanks for asking."

"And you, Sean; how's your grandfather getting on? You're staying out of trouble for him, right?"

Sean looked up at her sheepishly. "Best I can."

"We keep their noses out of trouble, for the most part." Gerry said, putting an arm around the two lads. "Now you two; get lost. There's plenty of better things you could be doing than sitting in here. Go and do something that'll contribute to the world, or something."

The boys downed the last of their pints and handed their glasses to Gerry, then headed out of the pub.

"Ye didn't need to kick them out," Michael said, feeling bad that they'd interrupted the lads in the middle of their pints, though he had to admit he wasn't sure else where they were going to sit; the pub was quite full for the middle of the afternoon.

"Ah well, they'll be grand," Gerry reassured him. "This here is the O'Reilly family booth. It was her grandfather's favourite booth in the whole place, and it's been an unwritten rule that whenever a member of the O'Reilly family is here, they get the booth."

He shrugged, as if this made perfect sense.

"I guess there's perks to being the boss' granddaughter," Michael smiled at her as they slid into the booth Sean and

Ronan had recently vacated, the leather seats still a bit warm from where they had been sitting.

"Stick with me, kid," she said in her best American accent, referencing Humphrey Bogart.

"Right, pints for the both of you and anything to eat?" Gerry asked.

"Packet of crisps for me, please Gerry," he said, his stomach still grumbling. It was getting close to dinner time, but he knew he wouldn't make it until then without something on his stomach.

"Coming right up."

"Thanks Gerry," Aoife called to him as he weaved his way through the crowd back to the bar to get their pints.

"So…" he said, not sure how to fill the lull which had fallen upon their conversation. "This is the first O'Reilly's."

"Yea. It's not what you were expecting, is it?" she asked, the hint of a smirk on her face.

"Not exactly, no," he admitted. "To be honest, I was expecting something more along the lines of what you'd find in the magazines."

"I'm surprised you read those things," she replied with mock sarcasm.

"Well, Mara and Molly like to think they're helping by showing me all these magazines of fancy restaurants so they can have excuses to spend money we don't have on upgrading the pub. Sometimes, something is bound to stick."

She nodded.

"Is it difficult? Being back here now you're grandfather has… passed on?"

He didn't know how to ask the question without seeming to pry, but ever since they'd arrived, she'd had a slightly forlorn look in her eye, the hint of a deep pain that couldn't quite be masked.

She took a sip of her pint – which Gerry had just delivered to them – her eyes downcast, avoiding the question.

"Is he the reason you ran out of Da's hospital room last night?"

Aoife seemed surprised that he'd noticed the way she'd hurried out of Dermot's hospital room the night before, which – of course – he had. He just hadn't had the right

All That Compels the Heart

opportunity to ask her about it. He could tell from her slumped shoulders, her downcast eyes trying to avoid his own, that she was still as devastated by the loss as she'd been back at Christmas.

"Oh Aoife." His voice was full of sympathy for her.

Reaching across the table, he placed his hand gently over hers, stilling it. "I'm sorry. I shouldn't have made you come with me to the hospital last night."

It had been a great comfort to him, having her with him last night. Just her being there next to him had made the whole frightening ordeal with his father more bearable, but he'd never had asked her to go with him if he'd known it would cause her any harm.

"You didn't make me. I wanted to go. I wanted to help."

She finally looked up at him and he could see the sincerity in her watery eyes.

"It was just; I hadn't been back in a hospital since he… passed on… and it just became a bit much after awhile. I promise I'm alright though."

He rubbed her hand gently with his thumb, reassuring her that he was there for her, and leaned over to kiss her on the forehead.

"C'mon; we'd better get back to my place, or we'll be late to my grandmother's," she said, looking at her watch. He knew they had more time than they needed, but he could also tell that she seemed to be anxious to get out of there. He knew it had been an extraordinarily special thing for her to bring him here, to the place which was so dear to both her and her grandfather. In the absence of being able to introduce him to the man himself, this had been the next best thing. Considering the trying evening ahead of them both, he didn't want to push her beyond her limits.

"And that is one thing we do *not* want."

Rising from the table and grabbing his bag of crisps – he'd still not had a chance to open them up to eat them – he took her hand and the two of them headed back out into the late afternoon drizzle, ready to face the bigger test yet to come.

Chapter Fifty-Three

"Arrrrghh!" Michael made a noise of frustration as he tried to tie his tie, which happened to be acting as stubborn as a mule right at that moment.

"Here let me."

He felt Aoife's hands on his shoulders turning him around and took the tie in her hands, deftly tying it within seconds. Even though he felt slightly like an invalid for not being able to get the tie to cooperate with him, he did appreciate that it gave him a few minutes to appreciate how beautiful Aoife looked tonight.

She'd donned a navy-blue lace and chiffon halter dress, the hem of which fell just above her knees, cinched at the waist with a silver braided belt. She'd pinned her hair into a half-up, half-down look, the ends of her wavy curls falling perfectly on her shoulders. She'd kept her make-up light and natural, highlighting her dress and the pearl necklace and earrings she'd worn as accessories.

"There. All done. You look very handsome."

She patted his tie after tightening it to the appropriate length. He took her hand in his, holding it there on his chest for a second. He leaned down and kissed her lightly on her nose, lest he mess up her make-up.

"Everything is going to be grand," he repeated, not for the last time that night for both their sakes.

Aoife didn't respond, just smoothed out an imaginary wrinkle from his suit jacket and tried to give him her best smile, given the situation. Silently, she walked towards the bed where she'd laid out her heels, black pumps that went perfectly with her dress.

"We should probably get going. We don't want to be late."

She glanced down at the gold and mother of pearl watch she'd put on her wrist when she'd been getting ready. Michael nodded at her, adjusting his tie slightly once more.

The drive out to Malahide was a smooth one; traffic was lighter this time of evening, and the two of them made good time as they headed to the northern part of the city.

"Don't get your hopes up tonight, you know? Don't go in there with the expectation that they're going to like you and that we're all going to be friends, and hang out on weekends. They're not like your family." Aoife's voice broke through the quiet of the car's interior.

"You make them sound *so* friendly and welcoming," Michael told her sarcastically.

Aoife didn't respond, only looked straight ahead into the darkening night.

"Let's just see how things go, eh? Ye never know; they might find me extremely charming. *You* did, after all."

He glanced over at her, a rakish grin on his face. She didn't smile back.

"Why exactly is it that you're working *so* hard to get me to not meet your family? Are ye ashamed of me, Aoife?"

"What?" Clearly he'd thrown her off with his question. "God no! That's not it at all."

Michael's heart soared a little to hear her reassuring words. In their little world in Ballyclara, he'd never really had to worry about what Aoife thought of him. She was the outsider, and – despite all her wealth and influence – that fact alone put them on a more equal footing when they were in his hometown. There was just something about being in Dublin that put him on edge that made him feel like maybe he wasn't enough for her world.

"So, what is it then?" he asked her.

"You need to take this turn," she responded instead, pointing to a sign up ahead and Michael guided her car towards the turn in the road.

They entered an up-scale neighbourhood, the houses and yards growing in size the longer they drove. Michael noticed she hadn't answered his question, but he didn't press her. This night was stressful enough for the both of them; the last thing they needed was to end up in a fight just before they got to her grandmother's, so Michael made the decision to drop the subject until after the dinner.

Maybe she'll feel differently once she sees how things go.

Their conversation was interrupted by their arrival outside the front gate of the property, leading up the crushed gravel drive to Grainne O'Reilly's house. The pale-red brick, neo-classical house loomed in front of him, seeming ominous and almost sinister in the dark of night, despite every room in the house being lit up, casting a bright glow around the property.

"Just park somewhere over there."

Aoife pointed to where a number of expensive-looking cars – Jaguars, Lamborghinis, and Mercedes – were parked by what looked to have once possibly been a stable, now converted into a multi-car garage. Michael carefully guided Aoife's car to where the others were parked. Turning off the ignition and taking a breath to steady himself, he turned to Aoife and asked, "Shall we go in?"

She sat there for half a second and Michael half-thought she might panic and tell him to drive back out of there, but she nodded and opened the door to get out of the car. Following her outside, he once more fidgeted with his suit and tie, desperately trying to make it feel more comfortable against his skin. Just as they reached the top step of the front stairs, the door opened without them having to knock, held open by Grainne's butler.

"Miss Aoife," he droned in a bored, but polite, greeting.

"Moore," she replied, giving him a quick nod to acknowledge his presence but then proceeded to ignore him.

"Sir," Moore greeted Michael in a rather more surprised tone than he'd given to Aoife. The older man's eyes widened slightly as he watched Michael follow Aoife into the foyer. Michael raised an eyebrow at the butler's curious expression but was distracted when he noticed around the house before him.

The largest house he'd ever been inside had been the Old Rectory; until now. Grainne O'Reilly's house was considerably larger than even the Old Rectory; his entire cottage could fit into the foyer and front drawing room alone. Off to his left, he could hear voices coming from the drawing room and he followed Aoife towards it, always keeping one step behind her, both as a reassurance to her and so that he wouldn't get lost in the place.

It seemed that Aoife's entire family were already gathered in the drawing room; he recognized them from their online profiles. There was Aoife's aunt, uncle, and cousin, Caitlin, along with her husband, sitting on one of the plush white chairs near the fireplace. He noticed the way in which their cold eyes looked him up and down, instantly dismissing him as somebody of less importance than they'd been expecting.

He was relieved to see that Caitlin's twin, Connor, stood near them; at least he would recognize one other friendly face in the group. Out of all the men in the room, Connor was the only one who'd dared break the suit-and-tie rule for dinner, instead choosing to wear trousers and a stylish white wool jumper.

Aoife's mother, Maureen – looking every bit as regal as her twin sister in a light purple dress, was sitting on the plush white, overstuffed sofa immediately to the right of the archway leading into the room with her husband, Anton, sitting next to her. And sitting in the largest of the chairs in the room, situated between her two daughters, was Grainne O'Reilly herself – the matriarch of the clan. Dressed in a cool shade of blue with matching diamond accessories, she looked every bit as intimidating as Aoife had warned him about.

The room went silent as the two of them stood in the archway.

"Aoife."

Grainne's voice cut across the room, like an arrow finding its target.

"Hello, Granny."

Aoife carefully stepped down into the drawing room, crossing the room to plant a dutiful kiss on her grandmother's cheek.

"And I see you have brought a guest with you."

Michael suddenly realized how a specimen of a virus in a petri dish must feel when being examined under a microscope. From the way every member of the O'Reilly clan – with the exception of Connor, of course – was looking at him, it was quite obvious that *he* was the virus.

Placing his hand in his pocket to stop it from fidgeting with his tie, he followed Aoife into the drawing room, trying not to seem either too bold or too cautious to meet Grainne and extended a hand to Aoife's grandmother.

"Michael Flanagan, Mrs. O'Reilly. It's a pleasure to meet you."

Grainne looked up at him from the edge of her chair. He could see in her cold eyes that she was both impressed with his height and annoyed at being forced to strain her neck back to see all of him from her perch. Both of her hands rested delicately in her lap and firmly remained there. She sniffed at his proffered hand and didn't say anything. Realizing that he'd been snubbed, he withdrew his hand and put it back in his pocket, trying not to seem awkward.

Aoife did say not to get my hopes up.

"Granny, Michael is my boyfriend."

Before he had too much time to dwell – or have the situation become even more awkward, if such a thing was possible – he felt a hand on his shoulder.

"Michael." Connor smiled and extended a hand to him, pulling him into a brief hug and pat on the shoulder in friendly greeting. "How is your family? And your sister?"

Michael tried to hide his relief at the distraction behind a broad smile at seeing his sister's boyfriend or, whatever Mara was calling him these days. Normally, he'd be wary of his sister dating someone she'd barely spent more than five minutes with, but seeing how happy he made her, seeing how much Rory liked him, he was reluctant to give Connor too much trouble for dating his sister. Besides, his was going to be the only friendly face he was going to see tonight, other than Aoife's.

All That Compels the Heart

"Da gave us a bit of a scare last night," he began. Seeing the look of worry flash through Connor's eyes, he quickly reassured him. "Just an angina attack. He's doing much better today. Mara and Rory are looking after him."

Connor's face looked relieved at the news about Dermot.

"She says to say 'hi' by the way. And Rory wanted me to tell you that he loves that model airplane you sent him at Christmas; it's one of his favourite toys. Mara can hardly get him to stop playing with it."

Connor's previously serious look brightened considerably at the mention of Mara and Rory.

"It was nothing," he replied with a slight wave of his hand at the mention of the gift for Rory. "I remember how much he said he loved planes when I was down to visit last, and when I saw it a shop window, I thought he might like it."

"Well, it was very generous of you, and he does love it. You should come back down to Ballyclara when ye get a chance; I know both Mara and Rory would love to see you again."

Mara would probably be furious with Michael for telling Connor all of this – he'd never understand why women felt the need to get so worked up about these things – but he also knew she wouldn't ask Connor to come down herself, and so he felt it his duty as her brother to try to get the two of them together again so they could figure out where this relationship was going.

"Let's get you a drink." Connor stopped by the mini bar that had been set up by one of the staff, pulling out a crystal glass and taking off the top of a matching crystal decanter. "Whiskey?"

Connor raised an eyebrow in question.

"Please," he replied, relieved to have something to take the edge off.

Connor filled the glass generously with the amber liquid and held out the expensive-looking glass to him. "So, you and Aoife? When did *that* happen?"

Michael smiled and ran the hand that was not holding his glass, nervously through his dark hair. He looked over at Aoife; her shoulders were held straight back, a clear line of tension running through them. She was talking with her hands – in her usual manner – but her movements were more clipped than normal. It was obvious that the rest of the family was grilling her about something – their tones were hushed and he couldn't hear the conversation, but he presumed it had to do with either himself or Danny or the both of them – and he felt like he should go over and try to rescue her.

"I wouldn't, if I were you." Connor, ever the perceptive one, seemed to pick up on his thoughts. "That is one minefield you do *not* want to wade into the middle of. Best leave it to the pros, for now. There'll be plenty of time for you to engage in battle over dinner, believe me."

"She tried to warn me something like this might happen."

Michael looked ruefully over at Aoife, whose face looked positively thunderous as she spoke to her mother. He was sorry now that he'd doubted her.

"You should have listened to her." Connor patted him on the shoulder in comfortable familiarity. "Now you're going to be the most interesting thing about this little dinner party."

Michael raised an eyebrow in a quizzical look.

"You see," Connor explained as he took a measured sip from his glass, "Instead of us turning on one another and picking at old, scabbed over wounds, now they're going to try and tear you apart. And boy are they going to *love* devouring you."

Connor's face looked a cross between outright sympathy and what Michael supposed a Roman's face might have looked like as he watched a gladiatorial fight between man and exotic beast: pure enjoyment of a blood sport. Michael took a gulp of his whiskey, looking for courage anywhere he could find it.

"Ye don't think I should try to go and rescue her?"

"This is just the opening skirmish; there's an entire war ahead to face over dinner. Save your energy for that," Connor advised him. He took another sip from his glass before asking, "So, shall I point out who's who to you?"

"Just tell me which ones bite, and which ones have claws so I can avoid them," Michael said, only half-joking.

"You'd better run for the hills now then," Connor replied in the same half-joking tone.

All That Compels the Heart

"Let's start with the less scary ones, eh? So, you've got 'the husbands.' That's how my father, John – he's the one over there in the dark suit – and my uncle, Anton – he's the one over there sitting on the sofa – are classified here. Neither one of them will probably pay you much attention. My father might try to break the ice with you by talking about business, sports, the weather; something easy to try to put you at ease. Though, if you don't know anything on any of those topics, I don't know how much it will put you at ease," Connor said, clearly figuring that Michael probably didn't know care much about any of those topics; he was right.

"And Anton probably won't say much; he rarely contributes to the conversation here unless he's called upon. He's made an art of trying to fade into the background during family gatherings. I used to think it was because his English isn't all that great, but now I think he just pretends not to understand us because it makes it easier."

Michael couldn't say that he blamed Aoife's stepfather. He was kind of wishing he had a good excuse like a language barrier to avoid talking to Aoife's family right now.

"They've both been through this process before, so they know how you feel right now. However, don't think that makes you allies with them," Connor continued. "If Granny forces their hands, they'll always side with her and their wives. They won't bite the hand that feeds them."

Michael looked over at the two older men. If they couldn't be counted on as allies, at least they might not be his enemies.

"Your father works in the British embassy, right? And Anton is a financier of some sort?"

"So, Aoife *has* told you about us."

"Not exactly. I looked all of you up online before we came here," Michael confessed.

"Ah. Well, don't believe everything you read in the tabloids; we're actually much worse than they portray us to be."

Michael looked at him and his face must have looked more concerned than he'd realized, for Connor laughed and replied, "Don't look so serious! I'm only joking. Mostly."

Michael managed a little nervous laugh in response.

"Well, you're correct," Connor replied, returning to their previous conversation. "Father is an attaché to some foreign dignitary who works for some other stick-up-his-arse important person. A professional brownnoser, essentially. And Anton, well, when he *does* talk, it's usually about his work, which quite frankly, is boring as hell, so I try not to pay attention. Nate could probably tell you more about what he does; they both work in a bank."

Michael nodded, taking the information in.

"Speaking of 'the husbands,'" Connor said, returning to their conversation, "You've got the new generation, starting with my brother-in-law, Nate, over there."

Connor pointed to a young man about Connor's age standing next to Connor's twin, Caitlin.

"His family are all bankers. He's fairly alright, once you get to know him. A little bit of a self-important, selfish arsehole at times, but he *hates* coming to these dinners, so he can sympathize with your position right now. It wasn't too long ago he had to go through his own initiation rite to get into the family."

The only difference being that he – along with John and Anton – all came from a position of wealth and privilege, just like the O'Reillys.

It wasn't hard for Michael to see that things were going to be more than a little different for him, than it had been for the other men in the room.

"Next, you've got 'the girls,'" Connor continued pointing out family members. "That would be my mother, Siobhan – she's the one over there with the blonde hair, wearing the grey dress – and my aunt, Maureen – she's the one who's over there talking to Aoife right now."

Connor pointed to the middle-aged woman in a purple satin dress whom Aoife had been talking to earlier. It looked like the two of them were still engaged in what looked like a rather tense conversation.

"You want to watch out for those two. While the men will mostly ignore you, it's the O'Reilly women who are the most likely to drive a knife into your back without thinking twice. They're also the ones who are the most likely to grill you with the questions over dinner. They'll come across all interested and caring about who you are, your background, what you do, but don't think for a second they really care; they're just trying to draw you in for my sister and my grandmother to go for the kill."

Michael took a moment to observe the two sisters from across the room. Connor was right: they appeared harmless enough, but he was willing to bet that he was also right about them being more dangerous than they first appeared. After all, there had to be a good reason Aoife barely spoke to them.

"Your mother is the one who works in the HR department for *O'Reilly's*, correct?"

Connor nodded. "And Aunt Maureen is on the Board of Directors. She's more the brains behind the business than any of us, except Granny.

"And that brings us to the most dangerous of the bunch."

Connor nodded in the direction of his twin sister who was standing next to their grandmother. "Caitlin, as you know, is my twin sister. I love her dearly, but even I have a difficult time getting along with her at times."

Connor's mouth twisted ruefully like this revelation didn't sit well with him.

"You're going to want to watch out for her; I don't know what it is about her and Aoife, but she's had it out for her ever since we were children. Whatever she tries to tell you, or how nice she seems to you; don't trust her. It's always a safe bet that if Cait's being nice to anyone but myself or our grandmother, she's most likely just building you up so it will make it all the more fun for her when she tears you down. It's something she's learned – and perfected – from our grandmother."

As if she knew she was being talked about behind her back, Grainne once again turned her icy stare towards the two of them and Connor coughed politely into his hand, clearly nervous she might try to draw attention to the two of them but she was distracted by something Nathaniel said to her.

"And Caitlin's the one who works in marketing, right?" Michael asked him, staring at the young woman from across the room. She looked to be a couple of years older than Aoife, and while there was some family resemblance between the cousins, Caitlin appeared to take more after her grandmother than any other person in her family.

"You really *have* done your homework." Connor's voice was full of appreciation for Michael's research. "But, to say she *works* is a bit of an overstatement; my sister would rather be arranging the latest social function than *actually* doing her job, which she mostly leaves to her assistant. She's a good delegator, my sister, I'll give her that.

"And, of course, you've met Granny."

Something I'm kind of regretting now, Michael thought to himself and resisted the urge, once more, to fiddle with his tie.

"I'd like to say she's not as scary as she comes across, but then I would be lying." Connor leaned an elbow against the edge of the bar, his glass balanced perfectly in the palm of his hand. "Truth is, I'm more scared of my own grandmother than I am when I'm out there fighting. Grainne O'Reilly could give any military opponent a run for their money.

"And that's the O'Reilly clan for you."

He downed the last of his drink in one swift gulp and poured himself another, gesturing with the decanter to see if Michael wanted a top-off.

"No, I'm grand, thanks."

Last thing I need to do is to get drunk.

"So where does this put you and Aoife then?"

"Well, I guess you could call Aoife and I the black sheep of the family." He smiled at Michael. "We're not quite like the others; we like to think we're more like our grandfather."

"Paddy O'Reilly."

"Right."

"I'm sorry for your loss," Michael said, seeing how the same look of loss had come into Connor's eyes that he'd seen in Aoife's earlier. "Aoife told me how you lost him last year. She showed me the original *O'Reilly's* earlier today."

"You must be someone quite special indeed." Connor seemed impressed. "She's never taken a boyfriend there before, not even Danny. It's a special place for us both. The others, they see it as a bit of a blight on the family business as it hasn't been turned into the circus they've made of the others in the chain, but for Aoife and I, it's kind of like a second home."

"Have you ever taken any of your girlfriends there before?" Michael asked, suddenly curious about the man whom his sister seemed to be falling for.

Connor shook his head. "I suppose I've just never found someone special enough to bring there, yet. Now our grandfather is gone, it's kind of like the only place where we can go to feel close to him, so we'd only take someone who was very close to us to see the place.

"Anyways, you were asking about where she and I fit into the dynamics of our family. We're definitely the outsiders, though if I quit the military and joined in the family business, I know I'd be pushed into the inner circle with my sister and grandmother. Granny's been trying to get me into the business ever since I graduated school.

"And as for Aoife, well, she's always been the heart and soul of this family. Unlike me, the only person she feels any loyalty to in this family now is me. I've got my sister, mother, and her to be loyal to, but Aoife's only ever felt loyal to me and our grandfather. If I didn't practically force her into coming here most of the time, I don't think she would. Aoife would rather be anywhere in the world than with this family. I can't say I blame her, really, but like my grandfather, I can't seem to escape this damned need to be loyal to these people even though they'd probably turn on me in a heartbeat if they chose to."

Before Michael had a chance to as Connor how he could balance being loyal to his sister and his grandmother, while at the same time being loyal to Aoife, a ripple ran through the atmosphere of the room and everyone looked towards the archway.

"Sorry, I'm late."

Danny.

Michael would recognize that smug bastard's voice anywhere. His first reaction was to look across the room towards Aoife, who stared at Danny uncomprehendingly for a second, before darting her eyes towards Michael. Silently, they pleaded with him not to do anything foolish.

Keep your cool, man. Keep your cool.

"Ah, Daniel. There you are." Grainne rose gracefully from her chair, walking over to greet Danny with a smile. Dutifully, he kissed her on the cheek.

"Hello, Grainne. Sorry I'm late. The flight from Bangkok was delayed, so I arrived back later than expected."

"No problem at all, Daniel," Grainne reassured him. "We were just waiting on you to serve dinner."

Michael couldn't help but feel a swell of anger rising within him at how she patted Danny's hand endearingly, this man who'd caused her granddaughter so much pain - not just in the last few weeks but over the entire course of their relationship - and yet, she couldn't even be bothered to shake *his* hand, the man who loved Aoife so much, who wanted only to look after her and care for her.

"Aoife. Won't you come along and say hello to Daniel?" Grainne's voice was stern, indicating that - whether Aoife liked it or not - she was not being given a choice. Michael felt more than a little relieved at seeing how Aoife struggled over the decision, debating the pros and cons of making a scene, but in the end, she thought better of it.

"Hello Danny." Her voice was cool, collected, making it clear that Danny was nothing more to her than someone she was being forced to be polite to. Everyone in the room stood frozen, waiting to see how the scene would unfold.

"Hello, Aoife." Danny's voice was considerably warmer towards her than she had been to him. He flashed her a dazzlingly smile intended to try and charm her.

The smug bastard is enjoying this!

"Can I talk to you over here for a moment?" She gestured slightly with a nod of her head towards where Michael and Connor were standing.

"Excuse us, Grainne." Danny placed a hand on Grainne's elbow in apology, with the kind of tone which said "you know what she's like when she doesn't get her own way" and a nod in Aoife's direction. Aoife merely rolled her eyes and placed her own hand on Danny's elbow, practically shoving him towards Michael and Connor. Michael felt Connor's hand on his arm, holding him back as Danny and Aoife approached.

"What the hell are you doing here?" Aoife hissed at him quietly.

Danny looked at her quizzically, like it should be obvious. "I was invited."

"And you didn't think to say no?" Aoife hissed at him again.

"You know what Grainne's like better than anyone. Even *you* couldn't turn her down tonight."

"You never had a problem leaving me to make excuses for you in the past," Aoife muttered at him. Before Danny had a chance to defend himself, their little tête-a-tête was interrupted by the Nate clapping Danny on the shoulder in friendly greeting.

"Danny. How are you?"

"Hey," Danny replied, pasting a smile on his face to cover up the recent tension with his arrival. "How's it going?"

"Oh you know; have to follow the old ball and chain around to *these* things, but you know how that goes right? Or… well… *did…*" Nate suddenly realized who he was speaking to as Aoife raised an eyebrow at him.

Nate coughed nervously to try to cover his faux pas. Thankfully, he was saved by Moore appearing in the archway to let them know in that droning voice of his that dinner was served. As everyone began making their way towards the dining room, Connor grabbed Nate's arm and said, "Just remember that that 'old ball and chain' is my sister."

Nate tried to jerk his arm out of Connor's strong grip, but Connor held on for a second longer, ensuring his point got across. When he finally let Nate go, he looked like he might say something to Connor but quickly thought the better of it. Caitlin walked past them all at just that moment. He smiled and joined her with the other family members walking to the dining table, leaving the incident behind him.

Aoife waved to Danny and Connor to follow the others, bringing up the rear of the group with Michael.

"I didn't know he would be invited tonight, I swear," she said to him apologetically.

"I know." He tried to sound reassuring for her but, still distrustful of Danny, kept his eyes peeled to the other man, making sure he wouldn't pull anything to try and flirt with Aoife.

Just as they were about to enter the dining room, Michael felt Connor's hand on his shoulder.

"Right. Well, it's time for the real battle to begin. Just remember: in there, it's every man for himself. I've done what I can to prepare you, but at the end of the day, I'm one of them."

Connor looked over at Michael only half-apologetically. He had his loyalties, after all.

"Good luck, and oh, welcome to the O'Reilly clan."

Michael wasn't sure the greeting came across as warmly as Connor had intended it to be.

Trying to dissolve the block of ice that was forming in his stomach, he gulped down the rest of his whiskey and followed Connor into the dining room.

Chapter Fifty-Four

Grainne O'Reilly's dining room was elegantly dressed for the evening. A pristine white satin tablecloth covered the long, cherry-wood table. Eleven Delft pottery table settings had been laid out for them, each with their own tent card, their names written in gold ink and placed on top of each salad plate. Light from the two glittering antique chandeliers above the table cast light around the pale cornflower blue walls creating both an elegant feel to the place.

Michael scanned the room and noticed that mostly everyone had taken their seats: Grainne was naturally at the head of the table, the big marble fireplace behind her, with Connor seated opposite her in his grandfather's old place near the kitchen doors. John, Siobhan, Caitlin, and Nate were seated on the far side of the table with the big bay windows behind them, leaving Danny, Aoife, Maureen, Anton, and himself opposite them. Michael noticed how Grainne had given Danny pride of place on her left, Aoife to his right, and Maureen and Anton at the other end, close to Connor. Michael had been squeezed between Aoife and her mother, right in the middle of the table.

"Well this is not going to be in the least bit awkward," he heard Aoife mutter as they settled themselves at the table, her smile grim and forced.

He noticed the way in which she squared her shoulders when she sat in her chair, her spine straight as a rod. He heard her take a breath and a swig of wine from her glass on the table before her, like a soldier about to throw themselves into the melee with a reckless determination.

The battle analogy was not unwarranted; he saw Caitlin across the table fiddling with a bobby pin in her hair, much like a soldier idly plays with a weapon, reminding themselves that it was still there. He had a sudden feeling of being trapped, completely unable to leave the table without being noticed, even though it was very much what he wanted to do right now.

The meal began in silence, everyone quietly passing around the various serving dishes with only the barest of murmurs to one another in hushed tones. Everyone was waiting, watching, to see where the first blow would land and, more importantly, who would deliver it. Thankfully, for the spectators, they did not have to wait long.

"So, Michael, what do you do for a living?" Maureen was finally the one to ask.

"I own a pub in Ballyclara," he responded, his tone measured. He was trying not to be embarrassed by his modest income compared to that of Aoife's family.

"It's more of a B&B, really," Aoife interjected. "The pub's on the main floor, and there are rooms on the upper floor, which Michael and Brendan let out to guests and tourists visiting the village."

When we have tourists...

Michael glanced sideways at Aoife. He knew she was feeling the same pressure as he was, to try and overcompensate in front of her family, to try and make him seem grander than he was. He'd made a promise to himself before coming here that he would resist that temptation; either Aoife's family would accept him as he was, or not at all. She ignored him, instead focusing her gaze on her mother, daring her to make a snide remark or comment.

All That Compels the Heart

"He also owns his own contracting business," Aoife continued. "In fact, it was Michael who did most of the work on Aldridge Manor, the house I bought down in Ballyclara," she clarified, after the confused looks her family gave her.

"Owning two businesses. How very… entrepreneurial of you," Maureen replied. Michael noticed there was even a little hint of admiration in her voice. Clearly, she hadn't been expecting him to amount to anything.

"Not that you'd ever know what it was like to start or own your own business," Aoife muttered under her breath, but just loud enough for her mother to hear. Maureen's fork paused halfway to her mouth, and Michael could see that in that particular action she took offense at her daughter's comment but chose to ignore it.

"Do you own only the one pub then?" Grainne Reilly finally deigned to speak to him.

"Yes, just the one."

Grainne sniffed, like she smelled something unpleasant, much as she'd done since he'd arrived.

"And what a pub it is," Danny spoke up, surprising everyone, including Michael. "It's no O'Reilly's, that's for sure, but it's pretty decent as far as pubs go."

While Danny was trying to sound like he was coming to Michael's defense, it was clear from his tone that he was mocking him.

"What the hell are you doing here, Danny?" Aoife asked, suddenly. Everyone in the room went quiet. "And this time, I want you to answer me honestly?"

"I told you earlier; I was invited by Grainne," Danny replied, a small smirk on his face, like it should already be obvious. He smiled at Grainne, the two of them looking at each other conspiratorially.

"Yes, but why are you here?" Aoife repeated her question. "As I said earlier, you've never had a problem in sending your excuses for not coming to these dinners in the past. So why bother to start coming to them now?"

"Aoife, you are being rude." Grainne's low tone cut through the conversation, a warning shot to her granddaughter to quit while she was ahead. Aoife ignored her.

"Tell me, Danny; why are you here?"

"Because he is my guest," Grainne answered for Danny. "I asked him here to dinner, and so he is here. Now, let us get on with our meal." She indicated with her knife for everyone to resume eating. However, Aoife wasn't finished.

"And why did you invite him here, Grainne?" she asked, knowing she was being rude but not caring either way. "Do you know why Danny and I called off the engagement, or rather, why *I* called off the engagement? Did Nate and Caitlin not tell you?"

Grainne took a sip of her wine, not saying anything, while Caitlin and Nate both looked sufficiently guilty as they sat across the table. She could see they'd guessed why the engagement had been called off, if they didn't exactly know for sure.

"No, I suppose not. After all, Danny wouldn't have wanted to have everyone here know that it's because he cheated on me. With Alice.

"Oh, you remember Alice, don't you, Grainne? She's the one you warned me about at Christmastime, the one you said that I should be wary of because if I didn't pay more attention to Danny, he'd leave me for her. So, are you happy now? Are you happy that you were right?"

Grainne's mouth twisted, grimacing. It was obvious that she hadn't been informed of this little bit of information just yet, and she was none too pleased by it. While Grainne may have always backed Danny in any argument against Aoife, this was not something she would tolerate. She turned her hard gaze on Danny.

He swallowed, hard. Looking like he'd much rather be anywhere than right here at this moment, he opened his mouth as if to speak, to come up with some silly excuse to explain himself, but Grainne held up a hand to silence him.

"You bastard," Connor hissed at Danny from the other end of the table, looking like he would love nothing more in that moment than to bash Danny's skull in.

"That is a topic for another conversation," Grainne said, continuing to stare hard at Danny and then at Connor to silence them both. Michael thought that if was possible for a person to wither and shrink, that Danny would very much like to have done so in that moment. He was very glad that

All That Compels the Heart

Aoife had decided to take charge of this dinner so that he would not be subjected to Grainne's withering glare himself.

"Well, I'd very much like to get this conversation over and done with right now," Aoife said, challenging Grainne. "Go on, Danny; tell everyone here about your little affair."

"Aoife, you are being unforgivably rude."

Grainne's tone cut deep, trying to regain control of the situation. After all, this had not been what she'd intended for this dinner at all and they were straying far from the situation at hand, which was to try and intimidate Michael into giving up on his relationship with Aoife.

"Maybe I'll leave Michael to explain the affair to you," Danny replied snidely to Aoife. She looked at him sharply then, confused as to his meaning. Seeing that his words had hit their mark, he continued.

"After all, he's known ever since the house-warming party about it. I gather he didn't tell you, otherwise we'd have been having this conversation a long time ago. Isn't that right, Michael?"

Michael, who'd been in the process of taking a sip of wine, nearly spluttered it all over the white tablecloth at this revelation. He'd known, of course, that Brendan, Mara, and Molly had been right, that not telling Aoife what he'd seen that night between Alice and Danny would come back to haunt him. He'd just never expected that moment to be right now.

"He saw Alice and I together that night, didn't you, Michael? He was bringing you up to your room when he saw the two of us together."

Danny sneered down at Michael, knowing exactly what he'd done by telling Aoife this, here and now in front of her family. He had nothing left to lose now that Aoife had left him, so he wanted to make sure that Michael suffered for it.

Aoife looked to him then, for the first time since they'd sat down to the table. Her eyes searched his, looking for the truth. As she found what she'd been looking for, he watched her own eyes sadden, then darken and harden over. It pained him deeply, like a knife through his chest, to see her look at him that way.

"I think I've quite had enough," Aoife said, setting her linen napkin down on her plate, covering her half-eaten meal. Rising quickly, she pushed her chair back and left the table, marching for the front door, much to the shock of everyone seated around the table.

※

"Aoife! Hold up!"

He rushed down the path towards her then, forgetting he hadn't closed the door, he rushed back to close it and then jogged to catch up with her. Yes, he could have left it for the butler to do, but he'd not been raised with a butler and some part of him somewhere felt that he should still be polite when he wasn't in his own home. She ignored his plea, determined to get away from her grandmother's house as quickly as possible.

"Aoife! Stop!"

He reached out to her, lightly grabbed her arm, only trying to get her to stop, to turn around and look at him so they could discuss this, but she shook off his hand like it was annoying gnat, buzzing around her.

She did as he asked, turning around to look at him. Out of respect for her, he kept an arm's length of space between them. And also in case she decided to lash out at him – rightfully so – in a violent manner.

"Did you see what they were like in there?" she asked him, gesturing emphatically at the house.

"Sorry, what?"

He was confused by this turn of events. He'd really been expecting her to be furious with him over the whole incident with Danny, and not revealing his affair with Alice to her sooner.

"It's not good enough for them that I'm happy with you and that I love you. To them, you have to be rich, and successful and be every stupid thing that they think you should be in order to check off all the right boxes so that you can fit into their stupidly narrow vision of the world! You're amazing and wonderful and you're far too good for them.

All That Compels the Heart

That's why I didn't want you to meet them. I was worried that you'd think less of me because of who they are. I mean, they're not exactly the kind of people I'm proud to be related to. They can be really cruel."

When she'd finished, she looked at him perplexed, searching his face for a response, and he realized he had a beaming smile on his face.

"What?" she asked him.

"Just back up for a moment, and repeat what you last said," he told her.

"About how my family thinks narrowly?"

"No, before that," he tried to encourage her.

"About how I... love you," she responded, it finally dawning on her.

"I love you," she said, with more confidence and a smile.

"I love you too," he said, still beaming at her. He closed the distance between them, pulling her into a kiss. When their lips parted, she said to him, "Don't think this means that I'm not furious with you for not telling me about Danny and Alice."

"Aoife, I'm sorry. I should've told you about Danny and Alice back when I first saw the two of them together. I know I should've said something. I didn't because... I don't know why. I wasn't your boyfriend then and I didn't think it was my place...And mostly, I just didn't want to see you hurt."

She turned around to look at him, her arms folded across her chest, staring up at him. "Yes, you *should've* told me. But, right now, I just want to get the hell away from this place before I blow up at you over it."

"So, I should get the car?"

"Yes, just get the damn car, Michael!"

Chapter Fifty-Five

For weeks after the dinner party from hell, Aoife refused to speak to him. After he'd taken her back to her flat, she'd really battled it out with him, letting him know all the million douche-bag reasons why it had been wrong for him to keep the information from her this whole time. She'd like to think that she'd have handled the situation in a more mature manner, but instead, she'd forced him to sleep on the sofa all night, sulked the entire way back to Ballyclara the next day in the car, and then refused to talk to him.

"Of course you're completely justified in feeling like this!" Bex said on the other end of the phone when Aoife had called to talk to her and Millie about it. "He shouldn't have lied to you about seeing Alice and Danny together. He should've told you straight away."

"I just wish I hadn't told him I loved him," Aoife said, rubbing a hand over tired face. She'd been unable to sleep well since they'd argued, the anger and resentment setting in and bothering her. "I mean, I don't regret it, but I do at the same time, you know?"

"Wait? You told him you love him?" Millie's voice rang out over the speakerphone. "Isn't it way too early to be saying that kind of thing? The two of you've only been dating for a few weeks."

"I know…" Aoife had known it seemed like she was rushing things: sleeping with him, having him meet her family, telling him she loved him… it had all just felt so right in the moment when she'd done those things. She felt like she and Michael had known each other forever and so it wasn't weird for them to take things to this level. But then the dinner party had happened and what had been said had been said, and now here she was, in the middle of their first big fight as a couple.

"It just felt right at the time."

"And how do you feel right now?" Bex asked her, her voice concerned but also a little curious.

"I don't know…" Aoife groaned. "Angry, upset, I suppose, but also, sort of like I'm still in love with him."

"Well, we will support whatever decision you make," Bex replied. "Won't we Millie?"

Millie made a guttural noise like she didn't exactly agree with what Bex had said, but eventually replied, "We support you. But, that doesn't mean that when I next see Michael that I won't be giving him a piece of my mind over how he lied to you all this time."

Aoife smiled, grateful for the love and support from her friends.

"Now, let's focus on something else! How is the novel coming along? You must be done by now?" Bex asked, trying to turn the conversation around.

"I just finished yesterday," Aoife replied.

It felt like a weight had been lifted from her shoulders. Not that writing had been a chore; quite the opposite, in fact. She'd really enjoyed the process and felt that she had produced something she could be proud of. But, it sure did feel good to have things completed.

"Well, when are you going to send it out to publishers?" Millie asked excitedly.

The question held more terror in it than it probably should have. There was something very satisfactory about completing her novel, but there was something absolutely terrifying about the thought of other people reading it.

"I don't know…" She responded sincerely.

"Come on, Aoife. You *have* to send it out to publishers! Talent like yours shouldn't be hidden away."

She smiled at her friend's confidence in her. She knew Millie was right; this was what she'd been working towards all along. She just needed to take that next step.

"I know…"

"Do it! Do it right now. Before you lose your nerve." Bex's tone cut through the line, crisp and sure.

"Alright," she agreed after a slight pause.

"You're not going to back out of it, are you?"

"No. I'm ready."

"Want us to stay on the line for you?"

"Nah, I'll be alright," she assured them. Hanging up the phone, she set about the difficult task of sending out her query letters.

ഗ്രൂ

Perhaps it was the relief in knowing she'd finished her manuscript, and that she'd gotten the task of sending out her query letters out of the way, but Aoife felt her mind was clearer somehow, less bogged down in what had been bothering her before. She began to see the fight with Michael from his perspective, how he was trying to protect her and, although she still didn't agree with it, she felt ready to try and work things out with him. After all, besides this one incident – which, she admitted was a pretty big one – he hadn't given her reason not to trust him. Was what they had worth throwing away over one argument?

To celebrate their reconciliation, Sinead and Dermot had invited Michael and Aoife over for Sunday lunch, in the hopes that everyone could put the past behind them. Arriving at the Flanagans' home after Sunday service, the men had gone to work on their latest project: fixing Michael's truck, which had recently broken down, not for the first time.

"Now Rory, come on over here and you and I are going to show your Uncle Michael how to fix this carburettor."

All That Compels the Heart

Dermot waved to his grandson, motioning for him to come closer to the hood of the truck. At the sound of his name, Rory – who'd been idly kicking some loose stones in the dirt driveway – whipped his head up and came skipping over to his grandfather's side. His face lit up in wonderment as he stood on his tiptoes to peer inside the hood at the truck's innards. Michael smiled at the two them looking like a bunch of doctors around a patient on the operating table. He was about to lean into the truck and begin showing his father and his nephew what needed fixing when he heard his mother's voice in the backyard.

"Michael Dermot Flanagan! Don't you dare get that shirt dirty. Give it here to Aoife so she can look after it for you." Sinead called over to her son as she and Mara were clearing away the dishes from their al fresco Sunday lunch.

Carefully extracting himself from underneath the hood of the car so as not to smear grease on himself, Michael took a quick glance down at his hands to ensure no grease was on his fingertips and began unbuttoning the white shirt. As he slipped it off the curve of his muscled shoulders and stripped down to his white undershirt, he heard a wolf whistle from the backyard and heard Aoife's laugh as she watched him from over a bedsheet she was hanging on the clothesline.

"Lookin' great there," she called out to him.

Playfully, Michael wrapped the shirt around his index finger and gave it a slight twirl as if he were in a strip show. She laughed robustly along with him.

"Give it here," Aoife said to him, cupping her hands before her to catch it from him. "Preferably before you fling it into the dirt like that."

She stretched out her hands to catch it but instead he surprised her by jogging quickly over to her and planting a big kiss on her lips. He felt her smile against his lips as he kissed her generously.

"Alright you two; get a room!" Mara told them teasingly as she carried in the last of the dirty dishes for washing.

Michael ignored his sister and held the kiss a second longer, releasing Aoife as suddenly as he'd kissed her in the first place, and jogged back over to the truck to help Dermot and Rory. As Michael leaned on the hood of the truck - his head ducked slightly to avoid hitting it on the propped up cover - an inescapable grin formed on his face as he watched her go about the chores, thinking of how he'd like nothing more right now than to tell his family to feck off for awhile and leave him and Aoife alone in his cottage. His thoughts were interrupted by the sound of his nephew's voice close to his ear.

"Grandad…"

"Yes, Rory?" Dermot asked, looking down at his grandson.

"What's a carburettor?"

"Well, the carburettor is this part here," Dermot said pointing it out to Rory and explained how it worked in relation to the truck..

"Ohhh," Rory said in that tone children use when they want to appear like they understood what another person has told them, but they don't actually understand. "So, what's the problem with it?"

"That's what we need to find out," Michael said, finally pitching in. "I think it might be one of the valves, but your grandad here thinks it might be something else. So, we need to go in and have a look."

"Ohhhh," Rory said again in the same tone as before, though this time with a little more wonderment.

"And you get to help us with it," Michael told him, tousling his hair playfully until the little boy giggled and then tried to smooth down his unruly dark curls.

"What do I get to do?" Rory asked.

"Well, first of all, you can start with fetching Uncle Michael's toolbox down for us. You know where he keeps it right?" Dermot asked him.

"In the press under the sink," Rory said, proudly displaying his observational skills.

"That's right," Michael told him. "Now, you go along and get your mam to help fetch it here, and then you and I, and Grandad will get the truck fixed."

"Here Rory, I'll help you bring it out," Aoife said as the young boy skipped his way into the backyard and ducked under one of the bedsheets blowing in the light summer breeze. "I have to bring this basket back in the house anyways."

"Ok," Rory replied, continuing to skip along contentedly as he reached the back door. Like the polite young boy he'd been raised to be, he opened the door for Aoife and held it open until she passed through.

"Why thank you," she told him and smiled at him as he followed along on her heels.

While she went and put the wicker laundry basket back into one of the built-in cupboards under the staircase, Rory went and crawled between his mother's and his grandmother's legs to open the cupboard door under the sink.

"Oi, what are ye doin' down there?" Mara exclaimed as the wooden door banged against her leg.

"Uncle Michael wants me to fetch him his toolbox," Rory replied, pulling out the red metal toolbox. It made a heavy thud as it hit the linoleum floor and its contents rattled against their metallic cage.

"Don't you scrape that across the floor young man," Sinead warned her grandson, "Or it'll be comin' out of your allowance to replace it."

Rory looked up sheepishly and put all the effort his little arms could into lifting the toolbox off the floor, but it only budged an inch before he had to put it down again.

"Here, let me help you with that," Aoife said, a smile on her face. She reached down and picked up the heavy toolbox with a bit of a grunt, not expecting the weight of it. She tucked it awkwardly under her arm and turned to Rory.

"Come on; let's get this out to your Grandad and Uncle Michael."

Rory went ahead of her and once more held the door for her. The two of them walked along the little stone path through the back garden and over to where Dermot and Michael were both still hunched over the front of the truck when they arrived.

"Here you go," Aoife said, handing the toolbox over to Michael. He turned around at the sound of her voice and took the toolbox from her, planting a firm and quick kiss on her lips in thanks.

"Do you boys need anything else before I head inside and help with the cleaning up?"

"No, love; that's grand," Michael told her, giving her another quick kiss.

"Alright then. You boys have fun."

Aoife turned to go back into the house, leaving them to the truck. Michael watched her retreating form, enjoying the sight of her backside as she walked into the house until Dermot gave him a little tap on his forearm.

"Here you; pay attention and hand me that wrench. There'll be plenty of time for looking at your girlfriend later."

Dermot's voice was gruff, but he knew his father was only putting on a show. Reluctantly pushing thoughts of Aoife out of his mind, he turned around and went back to helping Dermot with the truck, Rory standing on a chair he'd dragged over from the back garden, looking over their shoulders.

As he went through the repetitive and calming motions of working on his truck, the summer sun making one of its rare appearances today, it reminded Michael of when he'd been Rory's age, doing the exact same thing his nephew was doing now, watching and learning as his father and grandfather worked on this very same old truck. There was something very comforting and familiar about the process, something almost ritualistic, like the handing down of a torch through the generations.

They'd isolated the problem and had it nearly fixed when Dermot, who'd been reaching down to tighten a screw suddenly went still and slowly withdrew his arm. Michael – who'd been leaning down to put some of the tools they'd been using back in their box – looked up and saw his father's face go an unusual ashen colour, and then go extremely pale.

"Are you alright, Da?" Michael asked, concern creeping into his voice as a block of cold fear settled into the pit of his stomach. His father did not look well at all and Michael was beginning to panic, all the while trying to remain outwardly calm for his father and nephew, who'd noticed his grandfather's change in colour and had a frightened look on his face.

All That Compels the Heart

Dermot nodded and half-heartedly waved Michael off, but suddenly, he clutched his chest, and slumped forward. Instinctively, Michael reached out and grabbed his father, breaking his fall. As the two of them slumped to the ground and he felt his own heart jump into his throat.

"Rory! Go and get your mam and tell her to ring for an ambulance!" Michael roared at his nephew, breaking the little boy's paralytic state. Without hesitation, Rory ran as fast as he could into the house yelling,

"Mam! Grandad's having a heart attack! Call an ambulance!"

Seconds later – which felt more like hours to Michael – Aoife and Sinead burst out the front door of the cottage, rushing to his side. He heard a wail escape his mother's throat at the sight of Dermot on the ground there and he felt like one might escape his own soon enough. His father's face had gone from ash to white to an angry purple-red that scared Michael. Dermot's lungs made small gasping noises as he tried to draw breath and a fear he'd rarely seen in his father before crept into his eyes. He tried to raise a hand towards Michael's face, and it was only then he realized tears were rolling down his cheeks.

Crouched on her knees beside him, his mother was sobbing, Aoife holding her around her shoulders, trying to comfort her. Only a moment later, Mara – with Rory following her closely, like a lost puppy – rushed over to where they were gathered and fell to her knees before them, worry and fear for her father's life clear on her face.

"The ambulance said they'd be here as soon as they could," she whispered, not able to say anything else.

"Do ye hear that, Da?" Michael asked his father, whose lungs sounded more and more like they were tightening on him. "An ambulance is going to come soon. We're going to get you to the hospital and everything's going to be grand. You're going to be just grand. You're going to be just grand…"

Michael kept repeating it to himself over and over, trying to keep calm while they waited for the ambulance.

He wasn't sure how long they'd waited there for the ambulance to come. Everything from the time his father collapsed in front of him seemed to happen through blurred vision goggles; everything out of focus and disorientating. He could have been waiting there days and he wouldn't have known it. He only knew that an ambulance eventually *did* arrive. He could hear his father's laboured breathing in his ears, still gasping for air as if all the air around them had been sucked away in a vacuum. He felt strong hands holding his shoulders and someone telling him that he could let go now but he was afraid to. What if he let go and something happened to his father?

Aoife's face appeared then through the fog, like a beacon from a lighthouse on a foggy night.

"It's alright, Michael. You can let go now."

Reluctantly, he did as she asked.

The only thing he remembered from the drive to the hospital, the only thing that stayed sharply in the in his mind, was the image of his father's face as he'd collapsed, his mind replaying the scene over and over like some cruel joke.

When they arrived at the A&E, they found it virtually empty, except for an elderly woman with an awful cough sitting at the far end of the room from them, attended by her equally elderly husband, and a young family with a crying baby and a whiny toddler sitting across from them. Not built for large-scale emergencies, the waiting room couldn't hold more than ten people at a time, meaning they were one chair short with all of them crammed inside. Not being family, Aoife immediately ushered for Mara and Rory to take the last of the seats as Michael sat down beside his mother, trying to console her.

"Are ye sure ye wouldn't like to sit, Aoife?" Mara asked her kindly.

"No, no. I'm happy standing," she reassured her.

"Is Grandad going to die?" Rory asked suddenly. The question seemed to startle all of them; no one had been expecting the question that had been on all of their minds to be voiced aloud.

"No sweetheart; of course Grandad is not going to die."

Mara's voice was firm and confident for her son, but they all knew it was a bluff. Nonetheless, her words gave them hope.

All That Compels the Heart

As they waited, time seemed both to drag on, and to go all too quickly. Each of them sat there in silence, each of them worried intensely for Dermot's well-being right now. Would he survive the night if it *had* been a heart attack? When they'd arrived, Dr. Kelly had stood aside and reassured them it might not necessarily have been a heart attack, that it might have been some lesser ailment. None of them had been sure what exactly qualified as a "lesser ailment;" all of the options presented to them had seemed to sound equally terrifying.

Just when they all felt that they couldn't take it any longer, Dr. Kelly finally walked through the doors into the waiting room.

"He's going to be alright," he told them immediately, seeing all of their panicked faces looking up at him. Audible sounds of relief rushed out of their lungs.

"Oh, thank God," they all chorused.

"Do ye know what caused it?" Mara asked now that the relief had set in.

"It was another attack of angina. He has an artery that has a small blockage, which is causing his heart to not get enough blood and oxygen, so his heart is having to work harder than it should at the moment. We will need to discuss some methods of treatment and some dietary and lifestyle changes, which is going to mean a lot of bed rest and taking it a lot easier than he has lately, but I wanted you to know for now that he's going to be fine and this is treatable."

"He won't like that," Michael smiled ruefully at the thought of how Dermot was going to react to the lifestyle changes, given how he'd largely ignored them after the last attack of angina.

"Well, he won't have a feckin' choice this time."

Everyone looked over at Sinead, surprised to hear her use a curse word.

"Mammy, Granny said a swear word," Rory said with a newfound respect for his grandmother.

"Yes, well. I think Granny is entitled to a few curse words right now," Sinead replied tartly to the young boy.

"How would you all like to come and see Dermot?" Dr. Kelly asked before any further swear words could be uttered. "I'm sure you'd all like to see that he's alright for yourselves."

Rising stiffly from the hard plastic seats, they followed him through the hospital up to the cardiac unit where they'd been before. Michael was worried that they were going to become a little too used to this route and prayed it wouldn't be so.

"Oh dear," Sinead exclaimed, making a little strangled noise in her throat at the sight of Dermot's still-ashen face. He suddenly appeared much older, much frailer, than he usually looked, worn out as he was from his attack. It nearly broke Michael's own heart to see his father like this.

Dermot had been moved into a room with three other beds, but the others were currently unoccupied. Moving the chairs around from the other beds, they settled themselves by Dermot's bedside, each of them watching the steady fall and rise of his father's breathing, reassuring themselves he was still alive, though currently asleep.

Some time later – he wasn't sure exactly how long he'd been entranced by keeping an eye on his father – he was startled by the feeling of a warm styrofoam cup being pressed into his hands and he looked up to see Aoife as she sat down beside him. As he drifted away from the thoughts tormenting his mind, he was suddenly aware of the hard plastic chair beneath him, only a thin layer of fabric providing some sort of cushioning for his bottom. His muscles ached from being hunched forward, elbows on knees. He wasn't sure how long he'd been sitting in that position, but it felt like a good long while.

He could see that the corners of Aoife's eyes were wet, as if she'd been holding back her tears but couldn't quite prevent some of them escaping. She pulled the light jumper she'd had on earlier for church around her shoulders and he felt the coolness of the room from the air conditioner, and he began to shiver. The warmth from the cup in his hands reminded him that it was there, feeling returning to his numb digits, and he took a sip. Tea with a bit of milk and sugar, just the way he liked it.

"Thank you," he told her, his voice hoarse from not speaking for God-knew-how-long, and he coughed once to try and clear it. She was startled when he spoke; clearly he'd been non-responsive for longer than he'd thought.

All That Compels the Heart

"No problem at all," she told him and slipped her hand into his, giving it a little squeeze and giving him a half-hearted smile.

He brought her hand up to his lips, brushing the knuckle of her index finger lightly with his lips. He continued to clasp her hand in his, the feeling of warmth and comfort emanating from her body into his with even only this slight connection, but giving him a steady feeling of reassurance that everything would be alright if he could just stay here in this bubble with her.

"You go on home, son. You look exhausted. I'll stay here with your father tonight, and we can take it in turns to stay with him after that. You go and let Aoife take you home."

"Are you sure, Mam?"

Every bone and muscle in his body was screaming at him to take his mother's offer and go home and get some sleep. After hours of adrenaline coursing through his body, he was exhausted, and he wasn't sure how long the adrenaline was going to keep him awake.

"I'm sure, son. I'll sleep better tonight here in this chair, knowing I'm beside your father than I will at home by myself tonight. The two of us have barely spent a night apart in our years together. I just can't sleep without him there beside me. Now, you go and rest and come back in the morning."

His mother patted his hand lightly and nodded in Aoife's direction, indicating he should go with her and go home.

"Alright," he said, reluctant to leave his father, even if he knew there was no better place for him right now than in the hospital with Sinead by his side.

"Come on, little man," he said to Rory, setting aside his cup of tea and picking his sleeping nephew off the chair he'd been sprawled out on. "Let's get you home."

"Ye don't have to carry him," Mara told him, though she looked just as exhausted as he felt right now.

"Oh, he's alright," Michael reassured her.

"We'll be back first thing in the morning, Mam," Mara stood up from her chair and leaned down to kiss her mother on the top of her graying hair. "Call us if there's any change at all."

"I will, love; don't you worry. You all go home and get some rest now and I'll see ye in the morning."

With Rory getting heavy in his arms – despite the little boy's size, he was rather solid in weight – Michael followed Aoife into the corridor, Mara following closely behind. He tried not to look back one more time at his father lying pale-faced and frail-looking in the hospital bed, afraid it would be the last image of his father imprinted on his mind for all time.

The hospital was quiet this time of night; Michael hadn't even realized it *was* night until he looked up and saw the darkness of the night sky in front of him. He let Aoife guide him through the maze of corridors, he, Mara, and Rory looking like lost sheep following their shepherd back to their flock. As they emerged from the hospital, Rory gave a little shiver; it was a cool night and he hadn't realized how warm it had been in the hospital – even with the air conditioning – compared to the cool summer night air.

"If you want to wait here, I'll just go and get the car," Aoife said to them and hurried off into the dimly lit car park to where she had parked her car earlier.

He found it difficult to keep himself awake as the car wound through the countryside back to Ballyclara. Darkness surrounded them, the trees and fields and hills of the countryside an inky blur on the other side of the window. The interior of the car was quiet; only the sound of Rory's soft, steady breathing as he slept and the quiet hum of the engine disrupting the silence. Mara shifted in the leather seat behind him, poking the back of his seat lightly as she moved into a more comfortable position. Although he desperately wanted to close his eyes and sleep there in the car, his body was still on high alert, subconsciously afraid to go to sleep until he was back home in his own bed.

A faint glow began to appear before them and the darkness on the other side of the car window was punctuated at more and more regular intervals with white thatched cottages and farmhouses.

"You can all stay at my place, if ye like," Aoife said as they began to approach the village. The sound of her voice punctuating the silence seemed unnaturally loud to his ears.

"That way we can all leave together first thing in the morning."

"I appreciate it," Mara said, "but I think this one would sleep better in his own bed, and I think I would too. But it's so kind of ye to offer, and you've been marvelous for coming with us and staying at the hospital the whole time, hasn't she Michael? I don't know what we would have done without you there."

Too tired to respond, Michael mumbled his consent, hoping he sounded suitably grateful. He looked over at her, giving her the best smile he could muster, hoping she could see it in the dark. He took the free hand she was keeping on the armrest between them and gave it a small squeeze. She glanced over briefly from watching the road and smiled at him.

"No problem at all," she told them, and he knew she meant it. He knew she wouldn't have thought it was anything special to be there with him this whole time, it had meant the world to each member of his family, and most of all to himself. He didn't know what he'd have done without her.

As they pulled into Mara's drive, Michael went around to the backseat, carefully extracting his nephew. Rory, still slumbering away peacefully, snored softly as he was once again exposed to the cold night air but didn't wake.

"I'll be right back," Michael assured her, following Mara inside the house.

A few minutes later, both he and Aoife were walking up the steps to the house, both he and Aoife – too tired to care – dropped their jackets and boots by the front door and headed upstairs to her bedroom. Stripping down to his boxers, he crawled under the covers and sidled up to her naked form, her back pressing against his chest. Exhausted as he was, he still had a need for her, a desperate need to lose himself in the comfort of her presence, to forget about the last few hours. He pulled her in tighter and drifted into a deep and dreamless sleep.

Chapter Fifty-Six

It's true that you don't know how much something is missed until it's no longer there. Although life for Aoife, the Flanagans, and the rest of the village had returned somewhat to its normal rhythm since Dermot had been admitted to the hospital, his absence in the fabric of daily life in Ballyclara was noted. Dermot Flanagan had managed over his lifetime to integrate himself unknowingly into all aspects of Ballyclara and none of the family could go anywhere without someone stopping to ask them how he was doing. Sinead had had a steady round of visitors calling at the house to express their sympathies for her husband, asking if there was anything they could do to help. As it happens in small towns, there was suddenly enough food in the Flanagans' home to feed the whole village; several of the casseroles were currently sitting in Aoife's large freezer because there was no more room at Sinead's and she couldn't bear to see them go to waste.

While things were certainly not easy for Michael and his family, he and Aoife had settled into a new routine, commuting to the hospital every day so they could visit his father. Every third night, Michael would spend over at the hospital, taking it in turns with Mara and Sinead to sit with his father through the night. Dermot hadn't stirred much since he'd gone into the hospital, and even when he did wake, he was rarely lucid. He'd taken a couple of turns for the worse since being admitted to the hospital, needing heart surgery to repair the blocked artery, which had become worse than the doctors had originally predicted. It was an awful feeling, this feeling of being helpless in the wake of watching someone you loved die in front of your eyes. She wouldn't wish this on her worst enemy, let alone the people who were dearest to her.

She'd risen early this morning, the late summer sun beaming through her curtains and waking her. Groaning because she was still tired, but not enough to sleep anymore, she rose from her bed and headed into the kitchen to make a cup of tea. Aoife stood there as the kettle boiled, looking out over the village, the sun's rays lighting up the dewy grass, making it look like a prism of colours. It was exactly the type of morning Dermot would have loved seeing. She couldn't help but think about unfair of this was, and she felt an irrational anger towards the gods who could do this to Dermot, and towards Mother Nature for not being more considerate of the pain they were all going through.

She tried to push the gloomy thoughts from her mind, trying to find some sort of inner calm and optimism. After all, she needed to be the pillar of strength for Michael when she saw him in a couple of hours. Her tea boiled, and steeping in its cup, she headed out to the front porch carrying her mobile with her – she'd become accustomed to having it with her at all times now in case there was any change in Dermot's condition – and sat down on one of the large wicker chairs, her body sinking into the overstuffed cushions. She'd sat there sipping her tea for no more than a few seconds when the phone rang, startling her. She pushed down the block of ice that had settled into the pit of her stomach, hoping beyond hope that it would not be the call she'd been dreading since Dermot had been hospitalized.

"Hello?" she asked with more than a little trepidation in her voice.

"Hello." The voice on the other end was foreign, a man's voice with a distinctly American accent she didn't recognize.

"May I speak with," Aoife heard the man on the other end of the line rattle some papers around, "an Aaaaooohhhhiiifeee O'Reilly, please?" he asked, stumbling over her name.

"This is Aoife O'Reilly," she answered pleasantly, pronouncing her name correctly and trying not to wince as he butchered its pronunciation.

"Oh Eeee-faaa," the man repeated her name, sounding pleased to find that her name was much easier to pronounce than he'd been expecting. "Please hold for Jack Henderson, fiction editor for Broadstone Publishing."

A thrill of excitement bubbled inside of her at talking to her former supervisor. She'd kept in touch with Jack via the occasional email every few months since moving back to Dublin, just to let him know how things were going over at Arbour Hill and then, eventually, how the novel was coming along. As soon as he'd heard about her losing her job at Arbour Hill, Jack had promptly told her that there was always a place for her back at Broadstone and they'd love to have her back any time.

"Aoife!" Jack's voice boomed over the other end of the phone.

"Hi Jack! What can I do for you?" She was happy to hear from him again.

"Is now a good time to talk?"

"Sure, it is on my end, but it's a bit early for you, isn't it?" She glanced down at her watch and mentally calculated the time difference. It was at least an hour before the office would officially open but, then again, Jack always had a hard time keeping to "normal" hours.

"Well, when I got your manuscript, I was so excited I couldn't put it down until just now. And then I knew I had to talk to you about it. I mean, I knew you had talent from when you were working here, and I knew you said you were working on your own material now, but… Wow. This is some seriously great stuff."

"Oh, ha ha," Aoife laughed nervously, not sure if he was having her on or if he was being serious.

"No, I'm being serious, Aoife. I loved it. And, I want to talk to you about publishing it through Broadstone. You're exactly the kind of author we want here."

Jack's voice was sincere.

"Oh my God!" was all Aoife could think to exclaim, the realization that someone else appreciated her work finally beginning to sink in. And not just anyone: Jack Henderson! Someone she'd looked up to as a mentor when she'd been working in New York.

"Feckin' hell."

She heard his mirthful laughter on the other end of the line.

"I'm sorry," she apologized for her language.

"I'd forgotten, and missed, your colourful language," Jack laughed. "Look, I know we're not one of the bigger publishing houses over here, but you know us, and we know you. I think we would work well together on this."

He launched then into his pitch, telling her of all the wonderful things Broadstone would like to do to help her with the finishing touches of her novel, all of the things they would do to help her with marketing the book, etc. The whole time, she listened in awe at the enthusiasm he had for her novel, at the sincere dedication he seemed to have in wanting to get it published.

"As you know, we also have our mentorship programs here, and I think… if you were up for it, that is… coming to work here at the office again and taking part in the program. I know, we don't pay as well as some other places would, but I'm hoping that my charm and the fact that you seemed to love working here before will win you over." Jack's tone was hopeful, praying she would say yes.

Aoife was silent for a long second as she took all of this in.

"Are you still there, Aoife?" he asked.

"Yes, I'm still here. Sorry, this is all just a bit much to take in at the moment," she replied quickly. "I wasn't expecting anyone to love my novel, let alone want to publish it."

"I'm sure it's a bit of a shock, but this is the real deal. Now, I'm sure you want some time to think this all over and

I won't rush you to a decision, but I hope we'll be hearing from you very soon."

"Thanks Jack. I will give it some thought, and I will try to let you know by the end of the week."

"I'll look forward to it. You have a great day. It was so great talking to you."

"You too."

As soon as she hung up the phone, she immediately picked it back up again and began to dial Michael's number. There was no one else in the world she wanted to tell about this opportunity more than Michael – with Bex and Millie coming in a very close second – but before she had even completed the call, she knew she couldn't tell him.

Her heart sank in her chest. What with worrying over his father, this was the last thing Michael would want to hear about right now. It wasn't the publishing deal that would upset him – she knew he'd be completely supportive and thrilled for her, even; it was the moving to New York part that would cause a problem.

A big problem.

As if Mother Nature finally decided to listen to her and mirror her feelings, the bright glare of the sun was hidden behind a large cloudbank, forewarning rain in the near future. Her joy was tempered with the knowledge that when she told Michael that she was thinking of moving to New York to take part in this mentorship program, to take up the offer to work alongside some of the best in the field, that he would hate the idea.

Not wanting to worry about that just now, wanting to revel in the joy instead, she decided instead to call Bex and Millie to let them know the good news. After all, she wanted to celebrate with someone, even if that someone couldn't be Michael. Dialing the number to Bex and Millie's flat, the phone rang precisely three times before she finally heard a familiar American voice.

"Hello?" Bex answered.

"Bex! It's Aoife. I've got some news for you."

Before Bex could get in another word, Aoife blurted out, "I got an offer on a publishing deal!"

All That Compels the Heart

"What?! That's amazing! Congrats, Aoife! I'm so happy for you! Hold on for just a second, ok?"

Aoife heard the sound of Bex putting her phone down on a counter and then a click and the echoing sound of having been put on speakerphone.

"Can you hear me?" Bex asked her, her voice sounding like it was floating somewhere nearby.

"Yes, I can still hear you," Aoife replied.

"Millie!"

Aoife heard Bex yell out to her roommate and best friend.

"Come in here. Aoife has something she wants to tell you."

Aoife held the phone away from her ear after hearing Bex begin to shout. There was a pause on the other end and some muffled mumbling she couldn't quite understand and then Millie's voice.

"Aoife?"

"I'm here, Millie, and I have some great news. Are you sitting down?"

"Do I need to sit down?" Millie asked, though Aoife heard her friend sitting down on one of their kitchen stools anyways.

"I got an offer from a publishing house for my novel!"

The sound of exciting squeals and Millie clapping her hands together could be heard over the phone.

"This is so wonderful, Aoife! Which publishing house is it with? Is it a good deal? Are they going to give you millions for it? If they aren't, you should hold out for more money. You're worth it."

Millie's voice was full of confidence in her friend's talent, which made Aoife smile in appreciation.

"It's with Broadstone Publishing, and I won't bore you with the details, but suffice to say that I will not be going hungry for awhile if the book does well," Aoife replied. "They've also thrown in some other perks as well."

"Broadstone Publishing?" Millie asked. "I don't recognize that one."

"That's one of the smaller ones based in New York, right?" Bex asked.

"Right," Aoife confirmed, pleased that at least someone had heard of them. "They sound really interesting. I know that they're a smaller publishing house so they don't have the access to all the markets like the bigger publishing houses do, but I think it will work itself out. Also, they have this great writing program for new authors. They bring in experienced authors and do workshops and training sessions with them. They also have this great lecture series with new authors and give them the opportunity to talk to prospective new authors to help give them advice on how they got their start. They've asked me if I would like to be a part of it."

"Wow," Bex replied, the only word that seemed fitting at the moment.

"So, wait a minute," Millie said, and Aoife took a deep breath, knowing what was coming. "Does this mean you would have to go to New York to participate in this program?"

She hesitated a second before answering, bracing herself for the onslaught of questions to follow. "Yes."

"And how long will you have to be in New York for?"

"Well, the program runs for a year, so I'd be expected to be there until it's done."

Aoife let this information sink in. It was difficult not seeing her friends' faces right now, gauging how they would react. She imagined that Bex would have a look of shock – initially – but then she would accept whatever decision Aoife made and take it in her stride. Millie, on the other hand, would be crossing her arms across her chest in defiance, unwilling to accept change to her world and her friends, annoyed and upset that Aoife was planning to leave her again.

As if sensing the argument that was about to explode between Aoife and Mille, Bex asked, "And how does Michael feel about all of this? Have you told him yet?"

Aoife sighed. Right now she was thinking that she might have preferred the argument with Millie to being asked about Michael and thinking about how he would react to all of this.

"I haven't told him yet," Aoife replied honestly. "What with Dermot in the hospital –"

She heard both Bex and Millie making sympathetic noises on the other end, understanding her reasons for not wanting to tell him just yet.

"How are things with Dermot? Are Michael and his family doing alright?"

Aoife gratefully noted the concern in Bex's voice when asking about him. Even though her friends barely knew the Flanagans, they'd invited them into their little circle because Aoife cared about them, which meant Millie and Bex would care about them too.

"There's been no change in his condition for the last couple of days, but the doctor says this isn't necessarily a bad thing."

"Well, I guess that at least it means he's not getting worse," Bex replied. "That's something, right?"

"Right," Aoife replied. Trying to steer the conversation away from Michael – even though there were not necessarily any safe options to talk about right now – she decided to address Millie.

"You're being awfully quiet, Millie."

"I'm just letting it all sink in," Millie said truthfully. "I'm thrilled that you're being given this opportunity, but I'd be lying if I said that I wasn't upset you have to move to New York in order to take it. I hate the idea of you moving away again. I thought it was bad enough when you moved to Ballyclara, let alone New York. I just don't want to be a terrible friend is all."

"You're not a terrible friend, Millie; you could never be that. You've always had my best interests at heart, even when I disagree with you on what exactly that is."

Aoife's voice almost caught in her throat. The thought of moving away from the two dearest friends she had in the world filled her with all kinds of emotions she wasn't prepared to feel just yet. "You and Bex are both amazing friends and I would be lost without the both of you."

"Don't say that! You're going to start making me cry," Millie responded, a catch in her voice.

"Right, well before we all begin to cry, let's just say that we're extremely proud of you, and no matter what, we're behind you all the way. Whatever you decide."

"Thanks you two," she said, her voice catching again.

"Right, now you go to the hospital and look after Michael and Dermot.

As Aoife hung up the phone, she desperately hoped Michael would be as understanding.

Chapter Fifty-Seven

Aoife had meant to tell Michael about the publishing deal; really, she had, but there had just never seemed to be a "right time." Dermot's condition had remained relatively stable over the last week, but recovery was gradual and she knew it weighed heavily on Michael; he wanted nothing more than to see his father bounce back to the person he was before his heart problems. However, reality was slowly beginning to sink in that that was not going to happen. Michael, Mara, and Sinead had been in meetings all week with Dr. Kelly to discuss all of the care Dermot was going to need, and every time Michael emerged from one of those meetings with his shoulders slumped and a sadness to his eyes, Aoife couldn't find it in her to add to his burden.

And so, she kept the publishing deal to herself, but it preyed on her at night. She'd listen to Michael's even breathing after he finally fell asleep and her mind would go over it again and again, the tick of the grandfather clock downstairs a reminder that her time to tell him before her deadline was running out.

The day night before her deadline, she and Michael had driven back from another long day at the hospital, arriving at his cottage late in the evening. The long drive back through the dark, the stress of the past week and a half, and the quiet lull of the car's engine had pulled her into a trance-like state somewhere between wakefulness and sleep.

"Do you mind if I leave the car parked down here tonight? I don't think I'm awake enough to drive it up to the Old Rectory."

They'd been using her car to drive back and forth all week. Michael's truck still wasn't fixed; he hadn't had the heart to even look at it since his father had collapsed. Aoife didn't mind at all; after all, it was something she was able to do for him, even if it was only a small gesture. Besides, she had reasoned with herself, she would rather drive him back and forth than worry that he might end up in an accident himself trying to drive in the state he was currently in.

"Of course, ye can."

He opened the car door and a rush of cool, damp air filled the car, breaking the bubble of warmth and silence that had once filled it. It roused her from her stupor a bit and she had a childish desire to just curl up right there in the car and sleep where she sat, her body protesting the idea of walking back home.

"You look exhausted. You should stay here tonight. I don't like the idea of ye walking home by yourself in the dark."

He reached over and brushed back a strand of hair that had fallen out of the ponytail she'd hastily put her hair into this morning and tucked it behind her ear. He rested his hand gently on the side of her face, his thumb stroking her cheek. The leather chair creaked beneath him as he leaned over and kissed her gently.

"Come on; let's get you to bed," he told her and stepped out of the car.

She knew he was right. If she did try to walk back home by herself tonight, she was more likely to end up asleep face down in the bushes along the side of the road. Despite her protesting limbs, Aoife climbed out of the car and followed Michael into the house and up to the bedroom.

Too tired to be bothered with changing out of their clothes, the two of them lay down on the old mattress, Aoife laying with her head on Michael's chest. She lay there a second or two, trying to slip into the sleep her body so craved but she could hear the grandfather clock ticking downstairs and it reminded her once again of her impending deadline. She had to let Jack know tomorrow what she was doing.

It was a great offer; truly it was. And no other offers had come in, in the meantime. If she passed on this opportunity now, would another one come along? And should she pass this one up now because it wasn't great timing? Was that really fair to herself? Nothing in life ever came along at just the perfect moment; she knew that. If she kept waiting for the right time to come along, she might be waiting for the rest of her life, because who was to say that something else wouldn't just keep coming up and distracting her from getting her novel published?

Aoife sighed. She knew she was not going to go to sleep tonight until she dealt with this once and for all.

"Michael?"

"Mmmhmmm?" He asked non-verbally. Even though she couldn't see his face, she could tell he was balancing on the thin edge between sleep and wakefulness.

"There's something I need to talk to you about."

Something about the tone of her voice must have brought him around, for he shifted on the bed and she sat up beside him, shaking off the arm he tried to put around her. Michael's face was haggard with stress and lack of sleep, but his eyes were alert. She could see a flash of hurt and confusion when she shrugged him off, but he didn't say anything. Even though they weren't touching, she could feel his body tense, unconsciously preparing for fight or flight mode, bracing himself for whatever was about to come at him. She felt her stomach drop, wondering if this was really the right time to be doing this.

There's never going to be a right time.

She took a breath to calm herself and then began to speak. "I got a call earlier this week, a call from New York."

She could see his brow was furrowed, still confused.

"It was from a publishing house, a place called Broadstone Publishing and they want to publish my book."

She paused for a moment, a bit of relief setting in that she'd finally told him and the words were out now. She looked up from the thread of the duvet she'd been idly picking at and saw that Michael's face had gone from confusion to happiness.

"Aoife this is great!" he told her, a big smile on his face and her heart sank further down.

He doesn't get it.

Of course he didn't get it, because she hadn't told him the hard part yet. She'd told him the safe part of the news first, trying to soften the blow to come.

"Why do ye look so worried? This is amazing news! You should be thrilled. Why didn't you tell me sooner?"

Aoife sheepishly cast her eyes downward and began playing with the thread again. There was something comforting about the feel of its softness between her fingers despite the fact that it meant the duvet was unraveling slowly, much the same way her life was about to.

"Well, you know, what with your father being in the hospital and all… I just didn't want to add to all of that."

"But this is great news, Aoife! It's not adding any stress on me; in fact, it's just about the best news I've heard since Da was admitted to hospital. I'm so proud of you."

He placed a hand on her knee but she leaned back just out of reach and hopped off the bed, putting some more distance between them. She couldn't bear to have him touch her right now, to have her try and comfort her – reassure her – when she knew their world was about to come undone.

"What's wrong, Aoife? I'd have thought you'd be a lot more pleased about this but you don't seem excited at all. I thought this was what you wanted."

She folded her arms across her chest and leaned against the windowsill opposite the bed, looking down at the floor so she wouldn't have to look at him.

"Nothing's wrong." She felt horrible lying to his face like that, especially after they'd only just weathered through him lying to her over knowing about Danny and Alice.

"Don't lie to me, Aoife."

His voice was quiet and low but there was a warning tone in it that commanded she look up at him and tell him the truth. She threw her hands up in exasperation, knowing she couldn't hold off on it any longer.

All That Compels the Heart

"It would mean moving to New York."

Michael was silent, absorbing the news.

"It's a great opportunity," she said, her voice quiet and wavering, tears forming behind her eyes.

Michael sat there on the bed, not saying anything. She wasn't sure what was worse: his silent, brooding quietness or the yelling and shouting she'd been expecting when she'd played out this scenario in her mind.

"How long would you have to be in New York?" he finally asked.

"A year. Maybe longer." She felt a pang in her heart as she watched his eyes widen in surprise and the realization of what this all meant for the two of them.

"And when do you leave?"

"Three weeks."

Three weeks. That's how long she had in order to get everything together to move to New York. It suddenly seemed like a daunting task on top of everything else that was going on right now.

It suddenly occurred to her that she had just confirmed that she was, in fact, taking the position. It hadn't even occurred to Michael to ask *if* she were taking the deal; he'd asked *when* she'd be leaving to take it up, knowing before she did that she would take it.

Well, of course you were going to take it. You'd have been an eejit not to.

"It's a great opportunity..."

"Yes, you've said that," Michael snapped, sucking his breath between his teeth in frustration. His face was dark, clouded over with an array of emotions.

"I'd be part of a community in New York, connected to other young writers like myself. And, I'll be mentored by some of the best authors out there..."

"You're already a part of a community, Aoife; right here in Ballyclara. We invited you into our homes, made ye a part of the village. Or is that no longer enough for you? Because I don't really know what more we could do to make you feel like you belong here."

His words hurt her, just as they were designed to do. She'd come to love living in Ballyclara; the people here had shown her a kindness and gave her a sense of belonging she'd never had anywhere else before.

"I *do* feel like I belong here…"

"And yet you want to leave us." The implied *"you want to leave me"* hung between them, unspoken. The argument she had been expecting was about to break loose like a thunderstorm upon an unsuspecting countryside.

"I don't want to leave… I love it here but…" She didn't want to leave the life she had carefully built for herself here in Ballyclara but neither did she want to give up on the opportunity that New York could provide for her. "It's just… there's more opportunities for me in New York than there are here. I just feel this is the next logical step for me."

Michael once again went silent, but she could tell he was annoyed by her response. His arms were folded across his chest, his jaw set. He was done with shouting now, his voice gone quiet and scarily calm, though it took only one look at him to know that he was barely reigning in his emotions.

"The next logical step for you," he said quietly. "And what about *us*, Aoife? What's the next logical step for us?"

"I don't know –"

She honestly didn't. The two of them hadn't been together long enough for her to really know where this relationship was going. It was obvious where everyone in the village expected it to go: down the aisle of the church and into a happy marriage. But, was that what she truly wanted? She'd just gotten out of one engagement; did she really want to jump into another one? Or should she spend some time on her own, trying to find herself? Hadn't that been the purpose of her coming down here in the first place? And yet, she'd only just gone and made life more complicated for herself by jumping from one relationship and straight into another without really any pause to think.

"There seems to be a lot you don't know right now, Aoife," Michael said, cutting through her thoughts.

"Well, it's not like I've exactly had much time to think about all of the details over the last week. There's been a few other things on my mind."

Aoife's voice rose, sounding loud in the small space of Michael's bedroom.

All That Compels the Heart

"Can ye really blame me for reacting like this when you're trying to uproot my whole my life to New York, Aoife?"

"I'm not asking you to move to New York with me, Michael."

In fact, the thought of him going with her to New York had never crossed her mind before. She'd always assumed he would want to stay here, with his family, where he'd always been. And then there was his father's health to consider… He wouldn't want to leave with Dermot so ill.

"I know you want to stay here with your father, and I completely understand and respect that. I would never ask you to move away from him, especially not in his current condition," she replied quickly.

"You never had any intentions of me moving to New York with you, did you? When you were planning out this whole year, you never once saw me there with you, did you?"

"I didn't want to presume…"

"You didn't want to presume what?" he asked her defensively.

"I didn't want to put you in the position where you would have to choose between me and your life here. I know how much you love your father and how much his heart problems have scared you. The last thing I wanted was to add to that."

Michael sighed in frustration and threw his hands up in the air. "But you *are* making me choose, Aoife, whether you wanted to or not. By deciding to run off to New York, you've put me in the position where I have to choose between you and my father."

"You don't have to choose, Michael –"

"Apparently not," he snapped back at her. "You've already decided how I feel, and you've made the decision for me." His words were choked, full of emotion.

"What are you saying, Michael? That you would have come to New York with me?"

"Well, we'll never know now, will we?" he replied snarkily.

"You know what? I don't want to argue about this anymore. I think I should go," Aoife said and headed for the open door of the bedroom.

"There you go making all of the decisions for us again."

His voice went quiet again and it made her pause in the doorway.

"So, if you are done with this conversation, Aoife, does this mean we're done as well?"

One of the tears that had been threatening to fall during their argument slipped down her cheek, leaving a wet, slimey trail down the side of her face. She wiped hastily at it lest any more tears decided they should fall too.

"I don't know," she replied again. She hated that she had so much uncertainty over all of this. "I guess."

Michael didn't say anything further, just nodded his head resignedly. She turned on her heel and headed quickly down the stairs, her feet thudding loudly on the wooden steps beneath them. She hastily located her purse that she had flung on the sofa when they'd walked in, slipped on her shoes that she'd left by the door and went back out into the cool, dark night. In her haste to get out of the cottage, she hadn't heard Michael follow her down the stairs and out into the night.

"Aoife! Look, you're exhausted, you shouldn't be driving."

"I'll be grand!" she snapped back and opened the driver's side door, hopping into the dimly lit interior. Even though her body was beyond the point of exhaustion, her fight with Michael had woken her up, in more ways than one. She started the engine and, not even putting on her seatbelt, she hastily pulled out of the drive.

"Aoife! You really shouldn't be driving!"

Despite everything they'd just said to one another, Michael's concern for her safety could be heard in his voice over the purr of the car engine. It just made her feel worse about everything. Pretending she hadn't heard him, she left him standing there in the glow of her rear-view lights and the small cloud of dust her tires had kicked up.

※

Aoife wasn't sure exactly how she'd made it up to the Old Rectory without swerving into the bushes or going through a fence – she didn't remember the drive up from Michael's –

All That Compels the Heart

but somehow she'd made it home alive. Opening the door of the car, she listened to the steady *ping!* from the car. Annoyed by the sound, she took the keys out of the ignition and just listened to the silence of the night around her. She was fairly certain Michael wouldn't follow her up here but just in case, she dragged herself out of the car and went inside as quickly as her aching limbs would take her, slamming the front door shut and locking it behind her. Knowing that if she sank her to the floor she would never get back up again, she walked through to the sitting room and flopped down on the sofa and began to cry.

And not just a few tears running down the sides of her face; *really* sobbing uncontrollably for minutes on end until she didn't think there were any tears left in her. She tried to take a couple of deep breaths to calm herself, to stem the flow of tears. As she began to settle a bit, she had the sudden urge to call Bex and Millie. Not caring how late it was, she reached over blindly towards the coffee table and took her mobile out of her purse and began dialing the number for Bex and Millie's flat.

"Hello?" Bex's voice sounded tired, dazed, and confused as she answered the phone.

"Bex?" Aoife asked as a little sob caught in her throat.

"Aoife? Aoife, what's wrong?"

Where do I begin?

"Everything," she replied truthfully.

"Sweetie, what's the matter, eh? Everything's going to be ok, I'm sure of it."

"No, it's not."

"Oh God, did something happen to Dermot? Has he had another heart attack or something?"

Aoife swiped at some of the tears that had fallen onto her cheeks. She felt around feebly for the box of Kleenex she kept on the coffee table.

"I have to blow my nose," she said thickly to Bex and put down the phone beside her, blowing her nose until she felt she could breathe a bit better again. When she picked up the phone again she could hear Bex on the line with Millie in the background.

"Aoife? Are you still there?" Millie asked.

"I'm here. God, I'm sorry. I didn't mean to wake you both. I should just hang up."

Guilt over not thinking about her friends and the fact that it was really early in the morning and they would have to go to uni in a couple of hours began to set in.

"No! No, don't do that," Bex replied quickly. "What's wrong, sweetie? Why are you so upset? Has something happened to Dermot?" she asked again.

"No, he's grand."

At least I think he is. How will I ever know now that Michael will probably never speak to me again?

The thought of losing not just Michael but also his entire family made the tears start to fall again.

"Then what is it, sweetie? What's wrong?"

Aoife took in a ragged breath, trying to calm herself so she could speak to her friends and try not to worry them anymore than she'd already done. "I told Michael about the publishing deal tonight."

There was a silence on the other end of the phone as both of her friends took in this information and processed it.

"The bastard!" Millie finally exclaimed. "Did he break up with you because of it?"

"Well, I don't know who broke up with whom, really," Aoife confessed. "But suffice to say that it's done now."

"I'm so sorry, love," Millie replied.

"It doesn't matter," Aoife mumbled pathetically, more to convince herself than her friends.

"Yes, it does," Bex contradicted her. "Otherwise you wouldn't be crying about it."

She was right, and this made Aoife begin to tear up again.

"I know you and Michael haven't been together for very long, but the two of you have found something together that really means something to you, Aoife. I can see that, Millie can see that; everyone can see it. There's nothing wrong with shedding a few tears over losing that. I mean, I've never seen you happier with anyone else, the way you've been happy with Michael. And that includes he-who-shall-not-be-named."

The mention of Danny made Aoife wince.

"Oh God," she laughed wryly. "Danny will love hearing about this. You know, he warned me this would happen before I kicked him out of here when he had that big fight with Michael last month. He told me that I would never be happy down here and that if I ever had to leave here for my writing that Michael would break up with me."

Aoife ran a hand over her face. She felt exhausted again. She was just about completely spent.

"Well what does that jerk know?" Bex retorted angrily.

"Apparently everything," Aoife heard Millie mumble after not so effectively trying to stifle this bit of enlightenment with her hand over the phone. Aoife then heard a muffled "Ouch!" as Bex punched her in the arm for bringing it up.

"My point is: Danny doesn't know you half as well as he thinks he does. He thought you would take him back for Christ's sake! He's an asshole and he doesn't know you at all."

"Thanks," Aoife whispered, finding reassurance in her friends. "Ugh, I need to go to bed. I feel like I could sleep for days."

She ran a hand over her face again, wiping away the tears and snot and make-up.

God I must look a fright right now.

"You've had a long hard week," Bex agreed. "You should go to bed and get some sleep. Millie and I will check on you tomorrow and we can talk more then."

Aoife nodded even though she knew neither of her friends could see her. "Ok."

"Get some rest, sweetie. We'll call you in the morning."

Aoife heard the phone click as Bex hung up and then the sound of the phone's dial tone ringing in her ears. She lay there for a few seconds listening to its endless drone until it suddenly beeped at her, reminding her that she hadn't hung up. She hit the "End" button and then settled back into the sofa again. She was so exhausted that her body refused to move from this spot, but her mind was racing, going over everything she and Michael had said to one another again and again. Somewhere in the repetition of the night's events she managed to drift into an uneasy sleep.

Chapter Fifty-Eight

"Brendan? It's Michael."

He hadn't even wait for his friend to say anything to him before he'd cut him off. After the events of last night, he just didn't want to deal with pleasantries right now.

"Hello Michael." He sounded confused as to why he was calling him at such an early hour of the morning. "Oh God, is there any news of your father? Is he alright?"

"What? Oh, yeah. No, it's nothing like that. I'm calling because I have to ask a favour of you."

"No problem at all; what do ye need?" Brendan asked, his tone curious.

"I need a drive from you to the hospital to see Da today. I'm supposed to go up and relieve Ma."

"Aoife sick of being your chauffeur already?" Brendan chuckled, oblivious to everything that had transpired between Michael and Aoife the night before. "Sure, it's no problem at all. What time do you want to go up at?"

"Can ye pick me up in half an hour?"

"I can do that. Let me just tell Molly and I will be on my way."

Michael could hear Molly and Desmond in the background, the sounds of bacon crackling in a frying pan and the *ding!* as toast popped out of the toaster on the other end of the line.

"Thank you," he replied sincerely.

He knew how hard Brendan worked every day in the pub and he knew how much these days off with his family meant to him. He felt a sudden pang of guilt at taking his best friend away from his one day off. He was also surprised at the anger he felt towards Aoife for being the reason he had to tear his best friend away from his family.

If only she'd just turned down the publishing deal in the first place.

He knew it wasn't fair of him to expect her to turn down the deal, but her decision irked him, nonetheless.

"Sure thing." Brendan's tone sounded a tad confused, picking up on the change in Michael's voice. "I'll be there soon."

Michael hung up the phone without saying anything further. Picking himself up off the sofa, he went to the front door and put on his shoes; grabbed his duffel bag with a change of spare clothes, his jacket, and a toothbrush for his overnight stay; his wallet, and headed outside. He sat down heavily on the front step, waiting for Brendan. He just couldn't stand the feeling of being cooped up in the cottage anymore.

He wiped a hand over his tired face, trying to keep himself awake for the long day ahead. After his fight with Aoife, he'd been unable to sleep all night, going over and over what had been said. He was furious with her, of course, for making the decision to move to New York without him. While he couldn't leave Ballyclara right now because of his father, he *would* have eventually followed her to New York if she'd asked him. He was willing to uproot his whole world in order to be with her, but she'd gone ahead and made the decision for him, choosing to be alone rather than share this experience with him.

And it wasn't only that – though, of course, that had been the major issue at hand; he'd also been furious with her for going and driving herself back to the Old Rectory in the dark like that, when she was too exhausted to be driving. He knew, of course, that it was silly to worry about her; after all, she'd made the short journey several times since living here and she was more than capable of looking after herself, but that still hadn't stopped him from following her out into the night and up to her house, checking that she'd arrived safely. He'd heaved a sigh of relief at the sight of her car in her drive, safe and sound with not a scratch on it. A part of him wanted to go up to the house, knock on the front door, and tell her that everything was going to be alright and the two of them would make it work somehow, but something had held him back. He wasn't sure if it was sheer stubbornness or pride – or both – but there was something inside of him that told him now was not the right time to talk to her about it. He'd leave it for the morning, hash it out with her then.

Of course, come the morning light, he'd talked himself out of it. No, by then, it seemed pointless to try and talk her out of going. Her mind was set, and so was his. He would just have to find a way to move on from her.

It wasn't like the two of you were together for very long anyways.

He tried to ignore the fact that he and his subconscious both knew that he'd been in love with her ever since she'd first stepped foot in his pub over a year ago. From that very first moment he'd met her, he'd known she was going to be trouble for him, would challenge him in ways he couldn't even have imagined at the time, and would ultimately end up teaching him what it meant to really love someone. He knew now that what he'd had with Eliza had been young love, a selfish love on both their parts, that had turned into a long-running obligation. With Aoife, it has been real love, the kind that now made his heart break to lose it.

He pushed aside the tears that threatened to fall down his cheeks as he saw Brendan pull into the drive. Not wanting to be pestered with a million personal questions right now about the breakup, he tried to look his best, to put on his best face.

"Jaysis, you look wrecked." Brendan clucked his tongue at him in disapproval. Michael merely ignored him as he got into the car and buckled himself in. "You sure everything is alright? With your father, I mean?"

"Everything is grand," he retorted, trying to shut down the conversation. He just didn't want to make small talk right now.

All That Compels the Heart

"And what about Aoife?" Brendan persisted. "Is she the reason you look like hell? Keeping you up all night?"

He winked at Michael in a familiar, suggestive way, and Michael knew exactly what he was implying.

"Everything is grand," he repeated, but with a little less enthusiasm this time.

"Well, that sounded convincing," Brendan replied sarcastically. "Would ye like to give that a second try?"

"Oh feck off," Michael snapped at him, turning towards the passenger window, watching the countryside zoom past them. Brendan gave him a whole two seconds of peace before he continued his interrogation.

"What did ye do?"

Michael was offended by the question and made a noise in his throat to indicate so. "I did nothing to her, and why would you assume that if there was something wrong between us that it would be *my* fault? And what makes you think something is wrong between us anyways?"

"Because you're all moody and annoyed, like your normal, usual self before you began to date Aoife. Since you've been dating her, you've been actually pleasant to be around. And now, you're back to being the same irascible person you were before you began dating her. So, I can tell that something obviously happened between you two.

"And of course, if the two of you were arguing over something, it would be your fault; Aoife is too good for you, so ye must have done something to her in order to scare her off. Oh, please tell me the two of you haven't broken up?"

Michael didn't reply, only continued to look out the window. Taking his silence as confirmation, Brendan said, "Oh God, ye *did* break up with her? Why the hell...?"

"*I* didn't break up with her; she broke up with *me*."

"What're ye talking about? Why would she break up with you?"

"She got a publishing deal. In New York."

Michael could see the same look of confusion on Brendan's face that he must have had on his own when Aoife had told him the news last night.

"But this is a great thing, isn't it? She's getting the recognition she deserves."

"It means she has to move to New York. For a year, maybe more."

Understanding dawned on Brendan. "And she decided to take the deal."

He nodded, seeing wherein the problem lay.

"Ye know, she didn't even discuss it with me at all. She simply made the decision on her own, without asking me what I wanted or if I would move with her."

"Would you have? Moved with her to New York?" Brendan asked, seeming surprised that Michael had been entertaining the idea.

"I might've done," Michael snapped, disliking his friend's doubting tone. "Once I knew Da was going to be fine. I might've gone to stay with her for a time or moved over. I mean, it's only a year, right?"

They both knew that once Aoife went to New York, it was unlikely that it would be easy to get her to leave. And with good reason: it was the perfect place for her to be right now, career-wise.

"So, what happens now?" Brendan asked after a few seconds of silence.

"I don't know," Michael responded truthfully, feeling some of what Aoife must have felt last night. He'd been so angry and hurt with her for not knowing more answers to his questions, for not thinking the whole process through, but now that he was faced with some of those same questions, he didn't know anymore how he felt than she had.

"I really don't know. The one thing I *do* know right now is that I just want to get to the hospital and see my Da. And no mentioning this to him either. The last thing I want is to give the man another heart attack."

"My lips are sealed," Brendan assured him, the two of them continuing their drive in silence.

༄༅

The three weeks that passed since she and Michael had broken up had gone all too quickly for Aoife. She'd placed her flat in Dublin on the market; she no longer had any reason

All That Compels the Heart

to hold onto it. It reminded her too much of her time with Danny, even though the two of them had barely spent any time there together. Still, it was something she didn't want to be reminded of.

More difficult for her had been listing Aldridge Manor. She held a much deeper affection and attachment to the house. Leaving Ballyclara behind her would be much harder than leaving Dublin behind her.

On her last day before she needed to fly out to New York, she was packing up the last of the boxes into her car, Brendan, Molly, Jimmy, Karen, Mara, and Sinead all lending a hand.

"Here we go," Brendan said, placing the final box in the boot of the car.

He'd been kind enough to go down to Michael's place to retrieve some of the items she'd left there from her overnight stays. She'd offered to go down and retrieve them herself – despite the fact that seeing Michael was the last thing she wanted right now – but she wasn't sure how Michael would have reacted to seeing her. He'd been pointedly avoiding her since their last conversation, the two of them managing to stay out of each other's way.

"Thanks Brendan," she said, reaching over to hug him.

"No problem at all," he reassured her. "Ye know, he's just as torn up about you leaving as you are. I mean, I know the two of ye aren't speaking right now, but I think that if ye wanted to talk to him, I think he'd be up for that."

"I appreciate it, Brendan," she replied, smiling weakly at him. Even if she had felt up to talking to Michael, she wasn't sure Brendan was right and that he'd want to see her.

"My brother is just being an eejit," Mara said, pulling Aoife into a hug of her own. "But I hope this doesn't mean that you and I can't talk. I get custody of you in the break-up after all."

"And here I was afraid you would take Michael's side," Aoife lightly teased her.

"Not a chance. I like you more."

"Even though things may not have worked out between you and my son," Sinead began, placing a hand on Aoife's arm, gaining her attention, "doesn't mean that you aren't welcome back here any time. And don't you worry; we'll look after this place for ye until you're able to sell it."

"Thank you," Aoife replied, surprised by all the generosity from Michael's friends and family.

Even though she'd come to think of them all as her own friends since she'd lived here, they had no reason to be kind to her now; they could easily have just written her off once she and Michael broke up with one another and took his side. Instead, they'd tried to remain impartial, trying to be supportive of the both of them. She wiped away a tear that was threatening to fall.

"Here, now. Don't you go crying; you'll get all of us started." Sinead hugged her tightly. When she finally let her go a few seconds later, she held her out at arm's length, so Aoife was forced to look at her.

"And even though Dermot couldn't be here today, he wanted me to tell you that he wishes you all the best and that you are to call the both of us as soon as you land in New York to let us know you arrived safe."

"I will," she promised. She felt bad for not having gone to see Dermot in the last few weeks. She'd known that Michael had been spending an increasing amount of time by his father's bedside since the two of them had broken up. She'd not wanted to take the chance of running into him there and causing a scene in front of his father. Dermot had had a few more setbacks and was only just beginning to stabilize and begin his recuperation; she hadn't wanted to do anything to jeopardize that.

"Well, I suppose I should get going. Bex and Millie are expecting me later tonight."

"You better go before you find something else to take with you; I don't think you could fit another thing into your poor car," Brendan teased her.

"There's plenty of room," she scoffed at him, waving a hand and dismissing his doubts. She hopped into the front seat, started the car, and rolled down the window.

"Have a safe flight, and let us know when you land," Karen said to her, approaching the car. She and Jimmy both leaned down to give Aoife a kiss on her cheek, and she waved at little Molly who smiled back at her.

"Take care, little one."

"Wave bye bye to Auntie Aoife," Karen said to her daughter, balancing her on her hip. The little girl feebly waved a hand in Aoife's direction, more interested in a bumblebee that was floating around her head.

"Safe journey," Molly told her, leaning down to give her a kiss on the cheek as well. "And we want to hear everything about New York. No details spared."

"I promise," Aoife replied, smiling at her friends. Reluctantly rolling up the window, she waved to everyone and sped down the lane to the main road, the view of Ballyclara in her rear-view mirror misting over from the tears in her eyes.

Chapter Fifty-Nine

Michael's head slipped forward on his hand, jolting him into consciousness. The steady *beep!* of his father's heart monitor and lingering scent of disinfectant in the air reminded him that he'd fallen asleep by his father's hospital bedside. Michael groaned as he stretched his long legs, pausing to check on his father to make sure he was still sleeping. Watching his father's chest rise and fall evenly for a second or two, he was reassured.

Every bone and muscle in his body ached from being hunched up in the stiff, wooden hospital chair all night, the thin foam padding offering little comfort. The only time he managed any kind of sleep was when he was sitting here in this chair, lulled to sleep by the reassuring sound of his father's heart monitor beeping steadily along.

Most of the time when he was home, he simply changed into some new clothes, and laid down in bed and found himself staring up at the ceiling, praying for sleep to come but it always eluded him. When his mind was still, Michael found himself thinking over things he really would rather not think about. Things like his father's health, all the things that needed taking care of at the pub; things like Aoife and their break-up. By the time his mind got there, he knew there would be no point in sleeping and so he would get up out of bed and head down to the pub, clean the glasses, prepare everything for the day. He wouldn't even notice the hours passing by until Brendan would come into the pub to open up and find him already in there working.

"Have ye been here all night, then?" Brendan had asked him the first time he'd found him there. While Michael would end up telling Brendan that he was coming in because he wanted to get a start on the day, truth be told, the menial work kept his hands busy, which helped still his unquiet mind.

While stretching out his left arm, Michael looked over his shoulder at the window behind him. The sky was still dark, but a smudge of indigo smeared the horizon, indicating dawn was not far off. Despite the early hour, he knew Mara and his mother would be back in soon to relieve him. Sinead couldn't stay away for more than twelve hours from the hospital; just enough time to go home and get some sleep and come back to the hospital until she was too tired to stand. She hated being away from her husband; the two of them had never spent this much time apart since before they were married.

Rubbing a calloused hand over his face, a day's growth of stubble chafed against his skin. He desperately needed a shave and a shower.

Perhaps stirred by Michael's wakefulness, Dermot snorted in his sleep and woke up, looking bleary-eyed.

"Well good mornin' to ye," Michael told him, keeping his voice soft so as not to scare him. Dermot glanced around the room as if he was still getting his bearings but was alert enough to respond.

"Michael?" he asked, his voice thick with sleep.

"Yeah, Da. It's me," Michael said, giving his father's hand a squeeze as he leaned forward and poured a small glass of water, bringing up the cup and straw to his father's mouth so he could drink.

"Ye didn't stay here all night, did ye?" Dermot asked him, concern in his voice.

"Yeah, Da. I did."

"Ach, ye shouldn't have," Dermot admonished between small sips of water. "Ye don't need to be staying here all night looking after me. That's what the nurses are for. Ye can't have gotten much sleep in that chair."

"I got plenty of sleep. You don't need to worry about me. That's what I'm here for; to worry about *you*."

"I don't need you and your sister and your mother worrying about me. I'm perfectly fine," Dermot grumbled, attempting to cross his arms across his chest but the IV line in his arm kept getting in the way.

"Here let me help you with that." Michael reached over and readjusted the IV line for his father, making sure he wouldn't accidentally tear it out.

"You don't need to worry about me," Dermot told him, letting Michael help him. "I'm not a child and I'm not an invalid. I've just had a minor setback is all."

"A minor setback?" he asked, arching his brow at his father.

"And who is the parent in this relationship?" Dermot asked Michael, giving him a direct look.

"I'm just trying to look out for you," Michael replied, making his tone less sharp than it had been previously. "I want to make sure you are here for a good long while yet."

"So, I can see you marry Aoife? Where is she, anyways? I haven't seen her here for the last few weeks, or maybe these drugs are making me more confused than I realized?"

Michael wasn't sure how to explain to his father that he and Aoife had broken up. He hadn't even been sure that Dermot would notice she hadn't been here since the two of them broke up; Dermot had been in and out of consciousness for days now and had only started to become lucid in the last day. He knew Dermot would be disappointed; he really liked Aoife and was excited that the two of them had finally gotten together. He'd be upset that they had broken up and the last thing he wanted to do right now was to upset his father in his current condition.

"She's uh… She's back home, I'm sure," Michael told her father.

"You're sure?" Dermot asked him, his tone curious. "You don't sound sure."

"Well, we haven't exactly talked for the last few days…" Michael's voice trailed off under his father's direct glance.

All That Compels the Heart

"Why don't I try and find a nurse to see when breakfast will be coming around, eh? I'm starving."

As if to confirm this statement, Michael's stomach rumbled faintly. He couldn't remember the last time he'd eaten something. When his mother and sister arrived, he really should try to go down to the cafeteria and get something to eat.

"Don't change the subject," Dermot growled. Michael settled himself into his chair again at his father's tone. "Now, what did you do?"

"What did *I* do? Why does everyone think it's something *I* did? Why do people always think it's me who's the problem?" Michael's voice rose in pitch with incredulity.

"Because usually ye are when it comes to your love life," Dermot replied evenly. "Son, I love you more than life itself, but it's no secret that you have terrible luck with your love life. As your mother and I gave you an excellent example of what a loving and lasting relationship can be like, I don't understand how you've failed to find one of your own."

"Thanks, Da," Michael whispered sarcastically but just loud enough for Dermot to hear him.

"So, what did ye do?" Dermot repeated his question.

"I didn't do anything!" Michael replied defensively, crossing his arms across his chest. As soon as he said it, he realized how childish it sounded.

Dermot said nothing to him, just continued to look at him in that annoying knowing way that parents become so good at over time.

"She wants to move to New York," Michael finally confessed under pressure. "She *is* moving to New York."

He looked over at his father and saw Dermot's raised eyebrows, but he didn't say anything at first.

"She got a publishing offer for her book, and she's going to go for it."

Dermot continued to say nothing for a few seconds and then drew in a breath. "And she asked ye to go with her, didn't she?"

Michael sighed and looked at his father. "No, actually; she didn't."

"Because she knew if it came down to a choice between her or me, you'd choose to stay here."

Dermot knew his son well; he knew Michael wouldn't leave Ireland and go to New York, even if it were for someone he loved.

"Are ye staying here for me, then, Michael? Because ye know that I will get better. Ye don't need to stay here on account of me, ye know."

"That's kind of ye to say, but you and I both know that I *do* need to stay here. This is more than just a minor setback, Da. You're going to need 'round the clock care until you're able to get back on your feet again, and even then, you're not going to be able to go back to life the way it was before. Whether you like it or not, you and Ma are going to need more help around the house now."

"Sure, and we have your sister to help, and it's not like we're without friends. There's plenty of people we can rely on in the village to help," Dermot said to Michael, clearly not seeing the point. "Ye don't need to stay here and look after me, Michael. You can go on to New York, if you want to, and you know that. But you don't want to go to New York, do ye? You're just using my heart attack as an excuse to stay here."

Michael had been leaning forward, elbows on knees as he listened to his father talk. At the mention of the real reason he was not going to New York with Aoife, Michael sat up and groaned, leaning back against the back of the hospital chair he was sitting in. Feeling uncomfortable from more than just the stiff hospital chair, he got up and went to stand by the window, looking out the view towards the car park. Knowing his father was waiting for him to respond to his question, Michael sighed and turned around, crossing his arms across his chest again, still feeling uncomfortable under his father's gaze.

"It's not just your heart attack that's keeping me here," Michael admitted, falling short of admitting to what was actually keeping him here in Ireland.

"I know," Dermot replied.

"You're staying here because you're scared."

"What?" Michael asked, his voice confused but knowing that his father was correct.

"Don't play dumb with me," Dermot told him sternly. "You're afraid, just like you have been you're whole life. You're afraid to give yourself over to another person. To find happiness with another person. You're afraid that if you give yourself to Aoife and make your happiness contingent upon her and your relationship with her, then you'll never have control again.

"Listen to me, son," Dermot said, his tone sharp as he squirmed to sit up in the bed.

Michael reached over to help him, but Dermot waved him away as he settled himself on a level to speak to his son.

"All that stuff in the books and the songs and the films are wrong. There's no music playing or fireworks going off when you find the right one. There's just this feeling, deep down in your gut. In your heart."

To emphasize his point, Dermot reached over and pointed his index finger at Michael's chest right where his heart was.

"Ye can't wait around for all that romantic stuff you hear about. You have to go with your gut on this one.

"When I met your mother, there was no music or thunderbolts of lightning come crashing down around me telling me that I was in love with her. There was just this feeling in my gut that if I didn't spend the rest of my life with her, that my life would be a whole lot sadder for it. I just knew that I needed her in my life and that I would do anything to make it happen.

"Now, I know you love Aoife; that much has been clear since the two of you met, but I think you have to ask yourself now if you'd do anything to keep her in your life, or are you willing to take the chance that she will walk away and you may never see her again?"

Michael sighed and ran his hand roughly over his face, the roughness of his whiskers scratching against his palm again. He'd been holding back his feelings towards Aoife and her departure in the wake of Dermot's heart attack but now that his father was making him face his feelings, they came rushing at him and he wasn't sure that he wanted to keep running from them.

"So, what should I do?" he asked his father looking at him deploringly, asking for advice.

"I can't tell you what to do, son," Dermot told him honestly. "But if I were in your position, and the girl of my dreams was about to go and move to another city across the ocean, I'd like to think I'd at least go to her and put up a fight to make her stay."

Dermot looked Michael directly in the eye then and he knew what he had to do. If he stayed here and did nothing, he would always regret never putting up a fight and letting Aoife walk out of his life for good. And right now, that felt worse to him than putting himself out there and trying to convince her to stay, even if she did still choose to go to New York. At least this way, he'd know he had put everything he could into making it known how he felt about her.

Michael straightened up in the chair and drew himself up to his full height.

"Da, will you be alright here by yourself for a few minutes? Ma and Mara should be here soon to relieve me."

Dermot smiled up at his son, knowing he had come to the right decision. "Go get her son. I'll be plenty fine here on my own. Go and get your girl."

"Thanks, Da," Michael said, kissing his father on the top of his head. "I don't know what I would do without ye."

"Make sure you say that to Aoife," Dermot told him. "That'll make her feel special."

"Thanks Da!" Michael said, grabbing his coat and hurrying out into the hospital corridor, nearly knocking over a nurse who was coming into his father's room to check on his father.

"Sorry," he muttered hastily as he ran down the corridor to his get out of the hospital and get to his car.

As he jogged quickly through the hospital and the car park all sense of tiredness faded from his body. He had a purpose now, a reason to get through the monotony that taken over his days. His body was on autopilot now, his mind focused on achieving one goal: getting to Aoife before she left for Dublin. If he could just get to her before she left, then maybe he could convince her how much he loved her and just how much he wanted her to stay.

ঙ৩লে

"Michael!" Brendan exclaimed as he burst through the front door of the pub.

He was so surprised by his best friend's sudden entrance that he almost dropped the glass he'd been cleaning. Safely placing the glass on the top of the bar and slinging the towel over his right shoulder, he turned to Michael and said, "I wasn't expecting to see you in here today. Has something happened with your da?"

Sudden concern filled Brendan's face, fear that something may have happened to Dermot.

"What?" Michael asked, confused by the question. "No, he's perfectly fine. No need to worry. I'm here because I need to know if you've seen Aoife today. I went up to the Old Rectory and noticed the place was boarded up again and her car wasn't there. I was hoping maybe she'd come down here to see you before taking off to Dublin."

"Aoife?" Brendan asked, his face confused, then sad, making Michael's stomach drop. "Aoife's gone up to Dublin already. Packed up the last of her things and headed out yesterday. Molly and I went up to see her off. You've missed her, mate."

Brendan's face grimaced in sympathy.

"Shite! Feck-it-all-to-hell!" A litany of other profanities slipped off his tongue as realization began to sink in that he'd missed his chance to stop her from leaving.

"Well, you've picked a fine time to realize you're in love with her," Brendan said sarcastically, his words harsh but his tone far less so.

"I've always been in love with her."

Michael sat down on one of the stools by the bar. His shoulders slumped forward as he rested his elbows on the bar and put his head in his hands, a feeling of defeatism taking over his whole body. He groaned and let his head fall forward until it rested on the top of the bar.

Brendan sighed, synpathizing with his best friend. "Ye know, if you hurry, ye just might make it in time." He glanced at his watch to check the timing of it all.

Michael raised his head a little from the bar to check the time. It was eight-thirty in the morning. "Do you think?"

"She said her flight was taking off at eleven-thirty this morning."

"It'll be awfully tight," Michael began, glancing at his own watch.

"Listen to me, Michael Flanagan," Brendan told his friend sternly. "I've been your best friend since we were four years old and I can say with all certainty that you are probably the most stubborn sonofabitch I've ever met. When ye put your mind up to doing something, there's nothing in this world that can stop you from doing it. Now, get up off that barstool, let's get out of this pub, and let's go and get the woman of your dreams and beg her to take you back. And I'm talking full on, bended knee kind of begging too. Aoife is an amazing girl, but she isn't going to just take you back because you ask her to. Ye have to make her want to stay here with you."

"Even if it means that she has to give up her dream? And what's this 'us' in 'let us go and get the woman of my dreams'?" Michael asked suddenly suspicious.

"Mate, you look like you're about to fall off that barstool from exhaustion and it looks like you haven't shaved or eaten in days. I have no idea how you made it up here from the hospital, and I'm seriously in doubt that you can drive yourself to Dublin and not manage to get yourself killed before you see Aoife. And what kind of best friend would I be if I sent you off to your death while trying to find your girlfriend? Besides, we both know my car can go much faster than that that antique you call a truck."

Brendan put down the glass he'd been holding and flung the towel he'd been using to clean it on the bar, fishing out the keys to his car from his pocket.

"Don't insult the truck," Michael grumbled, more out of habit than out of actual insult. "Aoife loves my truck."

"Pffft." Brendan let his breath whistle through his teeth as he exhaled in mirth. "I'm sure that's what she wanted ye to think. Now come on; let's get moving. We have a lot of miles to make up."

He picked himself up off the bar and followed his friend out of the pub and to his car. Although he didn't want to admit it, he knew Brendan was likely right and that they'd get there much faster if they took his car than if they took Michael's truck. As they got into the car, Michael turned to Brendan.

"Thank ye for this."

"Don't mention it," Brendan said with a bit of a smile as he started up the ignition. "Besides, what kind of a friend would I be if I didn't help ye try and get back the woman you love? I'm just happy you finally came to your senses. I thought she'd be long gone to New York before you'd finally admit to yourself that you were in love with her."

"Well, that almost happened," Michael admitted. "If it hadn't been for Da…"

"Good ol' Dermot," Brendan said with a smile, turning out of the pub's car park and onto the main road. "You can always rely on him to say the right thing at just the right time."

Michael gave a low grunt in agreement, acknowledging his father's superiority in this situation.

Michael and Brendan rode along in comfortable silence for a time, watching the scenery pass them by. He loved this part of Ireland so much; no matter how many times he'd drive by Glendalough or anywhere in Wicklow, it was always like he was seeing this magical place for the first time. He truly couldn't imagine living anywhere else in the world when you already had the most beautiful view right there on your doorstep.

He knew it would be the major thing that would always be in contention between him and Aoife; she'd led a gypsy life up until now, never settling in one place for too long. She liked the freedom of being able to pick up and go anywhere in the world for as long as she wanted to, and not have to worry about anyone and anything. Her wild unpredictability had been what had made him fall in love with her in the first place; the last thing he wanted to do was take that out of her. But he'd always known that eventually it would come down to this: that she'd get some opportunity to leave Ballyclara, and, and if he didn't go with her, then she'd feel she had to stay with him. He knew it would make her feel trapped and she'd come to resent him for it. It was why he'd let her go in the first place: that fear that if he asked her to stay here for him that she actually *would*, and then she'd come to resent him.

Brendan, picking up on his friend's brooding, he decided to break the silence. "Everything is going to be fine."

"Just drive, will ye?" Michael asked, anxious to be in Dublin already.

Chapter Sixty

"So, you're really going for this, are you?" Bex asked her as they drove up to the drop off point for travelers in front of the Dublin airport.

"Yes," Aoife replied, a small pit of anxiety in her stomach. She knew this was the right decision for her, even if it didn't feel like it. She knew she'd look back on this later in her life and regret it if she didn't go for it.

It hurt that Michael hadn't understood that she needed to do this. She'd known when she'd told him about New York that he'd be disappointed, angry even, but she'd hoped somewhere in the last three weeks that he'd have come around by now, realize that this could make them stronger and that they could survive this together. She knew he worried about his father; she was worried for Dermot too. But she knew Dermot would want her to go and do this. He'd want her to chase this book deal and try to get published because he knew it was what would make her happy. She'd just hoped his son could have seen that too.

Dublin Airport was busy this time of the morning, people hurrying to and fro as she, Bex, and Millie walked through the front entrance. The cool air from the air-conditioning hit her in the face and made her shiver a little. Unconsciously, she pulled her jumper around her a little tighter to ward off the chill. Maybe it was the change in temperature, or some subconscious nerves about moving to New York, but a cold feeling, like a block of ice, settled into the pit of her stomach.

Just breathe. Everything will be grand. This is an exciting opportunity and you will love it in New York.

Pushing any doubts that may still be lingering, Aoife walked determinedly through the throngs of people to the front desk for airline.

"Welcome! My name is Julie. Are you checking in today, miss?" the young woman at the front desk asked her in an mid-west American accent, pearly-white teeth flashing from behind a beautiful, but somewhat pasted on smile, that comes from working in customer service for too long.

"Yes," Aoife replied, pleasantly.

"Alright, can I see your passport and your ticket please?"

Aoife handed over her documents to Julie who quickly typed in the appropriate info into her computer to bring up Aoife's information.

"And just this one bag to check in, Miss O'Reilly?"

"Yes. Just the suitcase and my hand luggage," Aoife indicated the leather computer bag, which hung from a single strap across her chest and rested on her hip.

"Alright then. If you'd like to just place your suitcase on the scale here," Julie indicated for Aoife to lift her suitcase onto the scale beside her terminal.

"Here, I'll get that," Bex said, reaching over and deftly placed the suitcase on the machine to be weighed. While Julie went about weighing the suitcase and printing out the appropriate tags for her bag, Aoife gave a half-hearted smile to her friends, but was distracted by looking around the front lobby. Her eyes scanned the room, not sure what they were looking for and not sure where to settle. She knew what – or rather *whom* she was looking for – but she wasn't quite ready to admit that to herself just now.

He won't show up anyways. He made his feelings quite clear, so stop looking for him.

It did no use to tell herself this, though. A part of her still looked for Michael, hoping he'd burst through the door and say he'd changed his mind and that he wanted to be with her, even if she knew it wouldn't happen.

"And you're all set to go," Julie told her, pressing a button on her terminal, the rumble of the conveyor belt shuffling her suitcase to the loading area audible above the din of the airport. Aoife smiled at her as she took her boarding pass and watched her suitcase disappear behind the black plastic flaps that hid the internal system of conveyor belts that transported thousands of suitcases to their planes on a daily basis.

"Thanks. Have a great day," Aoife told her and received an appreciative smile in return before Julie turned to the next person in line behind Aoife and began her whole spiel again.

"Shall we?" Aoife asked Bex and Millie and the three of them walked through the airport towards her gate. They took off at a leisurely pace, arriving in plenty of time at the security checkpoint and so she had no reason to hurry. Aoife had always planned ahead when she was traveling; it came with a lifetime of boarding planes to and from many destinations, but this time she had gotten here even earlier than normal.

Don't read anything into it. You're just being thorough and prepared. It has absolutely nothing to do with Michael and giving him time to come and find you.

"I'm sorry he didn't come to say goodbye," Millie said, rubbing her arm gently.

"Hmm?" she asked distracted from her thoughts.

"Michael. I'm sorry he didn't show up. I would have thought he'd have come at least to say goodbye."

"Oh, I hadn't even noticed," she lied.

"Yes, you did," Millie said, calling her out. "You were looking for him just now."

"No, I wasn't," she replied defensively, even though that was, in fact, exactly what she'd been doing. Millie looked like she was about to argue with her but Bex intervened before an argument could break out and spoil Aoife's send off.

"No one would blame you if you were looking for him," she said, reassuringly. "But I say good riddance to him. If he can't support you in this decision, then good riddance to him."

"Thanks. You're the best," she said, hugging her tightly. "Well, I guess this is where I have to leave you."

A sense of the gravity that she was really going to New York began to sink into the pit of her stomach.

"Right. You have everything you need?" Bex asked her a note of motherly concern in her voice.

"Yes, mom," she replied in the manner of a teenager, complete with rolling her eyes, but she followed it with a big smile to let her know she cared. "I've got my passport and my wallet with a credit card. As long as I have those two things, I can buy all the rest, right?" she asked. It had been her long-standing motto when traveling. "Besides, you'll be coming over next week and you can bring anything I might need, right?"

"Right," Bex said. She'd agreed to come to America next week, both to spend some time with her parents – who had guilted her for not coming over the Christmas holidays – and to help bring Aoife anything she might need that she may have forgotten.

"I can't believe you're both leaving me!" Millie pouted, annoyed that she was going be left alone in Dublin for a few weeks until Bex returned.

"Oh, stop being such a baby. I'll be back in a month. Besides, you could've come over and visited with us too if you'd gotten your assignments done ahead of time," Bex chastised her. Millie muttered something unintelligible under breath but just loud enough for them to catch the gist of her teenage-like response.

"Oh, come here," Aoife said, pulling them into a final hug. "I love you both, you know."

"We know."

She nodded to them, taking a deep breath to steady herself. With one final look around her and not seeing Michael, she turned on her heel and went up to the security guard, handing over her boarding pass to her.

Chapter Sixty-One

"Go and get her!" Brendan yelled from the car, a big grin on his face. Michael turned back and smiled, then dashed off towards the front entrance of the airport, leaving Brendan to park the car and find him later.

The lobby of Dublin Airport was packed with people. Michael weaved his way through the throngs of newly arrived tourists to the city and locals heading out to foreign destinations, careful not to trip over suitcases and other luggage. He pulled up in front of the main arrivals and departures sign and found Aoife's flight on the electronic sign above him. A flashing sign beside the flight number showed that it was now boarding. Scanning around him in all directions, Michael looked for any tell-tale signs that Aoife had only just arrived and would be heading for her gate, even though he knew she would have been here long before him. She liked to be prepared when it came to traveling; she'd told him often enough before.

Knowing he had very little time before she would begin to board her plane, Michael took off at a run through the front lobby, forcing everyone around him to move out of his way out of fear of being bowled over by him. Faces, colours, and flashing signs passed by him in a blur, adrenaline pumping in his veins. A cold breeze from the air-conditioned building rushed passed him as he picked up speed, encouraging his aching and tired limbs to go on despite their protests. He tried to look carefully at the signs hanging above him, pointing him in the right direction to her gate, nearly tripping over himself as the floor below him turned to a moving sidewalk, forcing him to change his pace at the new texture underneath his feet. Righting himself just before he almost knocked into a woman in a brightly patterned sundress and straw sun hat who looked to be in her mid-fifties, Michael got his bearings and took off at a sprint down the moving sidewalk, dodging travellers as he tried to get ahead of them, much to their disgruntled complaints. Sounds of "Oi!" "Watch it!" and "What do you think you're doing?" followed in his wake.

Trying not to trip over himself as he stepped off the moving sidewalk, Michael took off at a sprint again, trying to gain as much distance between himself and Aoife's gate as he could. Once more on solid ground, he was able to run much faster, the way in front of him clearing a bit as he took off down one of the airport's long windowed corridors. He was soon forced to slow down again as the corridor opened up to a commercial centre, the scent of fast food, perfumes, and chocolate lingering in the air from the quick eateries and shops around him. The crowds thickened as people took time before their flights to relax and get a bite to eat or pick up some reading materials for their journeys, impeding his progress. Dodging his way through crowds of people stopping to gawk at what the stores were selling, Michael tried to find the quickest route across and finally came to another long, windowed corridor on the other side. The signs above him indicated he was getting much closer to the gate. Dredging up as much energy as he could muster, he pushed on forward.

The crowds here moved a little faster; those who had lingered a bit too long at the shops were now regretting that decision and were hurrying to make their flights. Just when he thought the warren of carpeted corridors would go on forever, he could see ahead that there was an opening. Pushing through the last group of disgruntled travelers, Michael found himself in front of a security checkpoint. It was just then he realized he was not going to get any further as he didn't have a boarding pass. Looking around frantically, he moved slightly to the side of the people he had just jostled out of his way and searched

All That Compels the Heart

for Aoife. He went up to the glass separating the entrance of the security point from the boarding area just outside her gate, but he couldn't see her anywhere. Through the glass, he could see her gate closing down, the flight staff heading down the tunnel towards the aircraft.

"Sir, can I help you?"

One of the security guards approached him, looking at him suspiciously and he supposed that, given the number of security issues over the years, a man hanging around outside of the security checkpoint without a boarding pass would seem like suspicious behaviour.

"My girlfriend; she's getting on a plane and I need to talk to her, but I don't have a boarding pass and… she's the love of my life and I just need to tell her that before she goes off to New York for a year and I don't see her again."

He tried to look as pathetic as possible, trying to play on any feelings the man might have of sympathy, or whatever. The security guard was not impressed.

"I'm sorry, sir. If you don't have a boarding pass, I'm going to have to ask you to leave the area."

Michael noticed that one of the security guards' colleagues came over to join him, the two, burly men, looking like they had no issue with throwing Michael out of the airport, if necessary.

"It's just…" Michael tried to begin again.

"Sir, I'm going to have to ask you to leave," the second security guard said to Michael, his tone firm. His arms folded across his chest brooked no argument from Michael.

Michael turned around to the glass, glancing through at the gate, watching Aoife's plane taxi out onto the runway.

"Sir!"

"Yes, I heard you," Michael responded sharply to the security guard. He was sorry for snapping at the man – after all, he was only doing his job – but he couldn't help the monumental feelings boiling up inside of him as he watched Aoife's plane leave the runway, taking off for her new life in New York.

He stood there as the plane lifted gently into the air and took flight, feeling as alone as it was possible to feel, watching as she floated up into the clouds and was lost to view.

Did you like *All That Compels the Heart?* Leave a review!

All That Compels the Heart can be found on the review site of your choice.

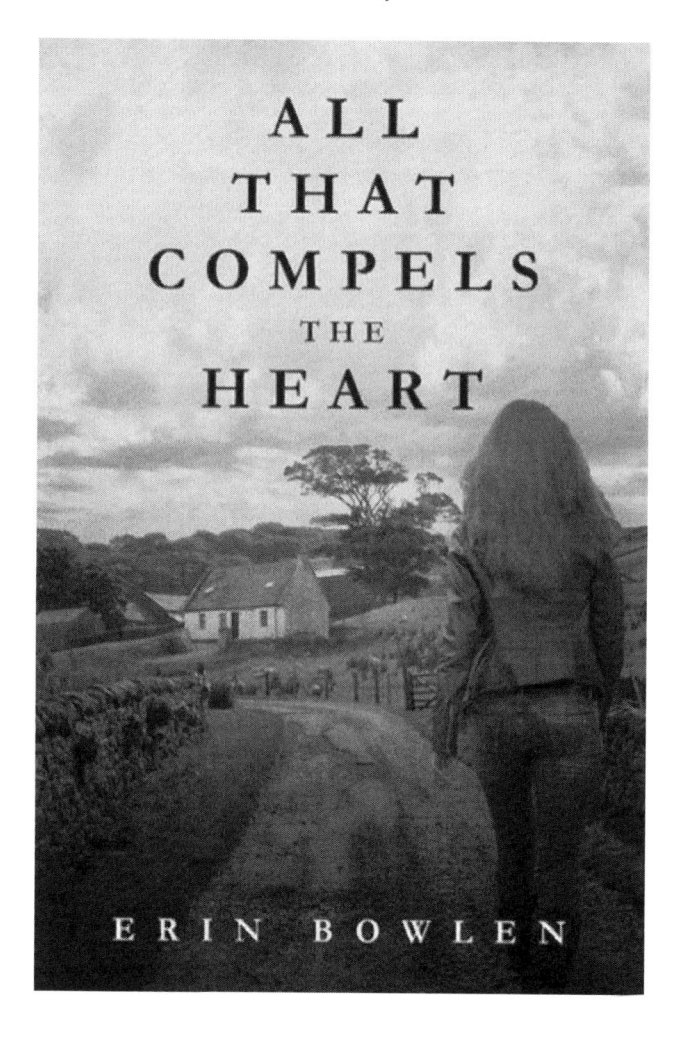

Want to read more in the Aoife O'Reilly series? Make sure to pick up a copy of the second book: *Where I'm Home*.

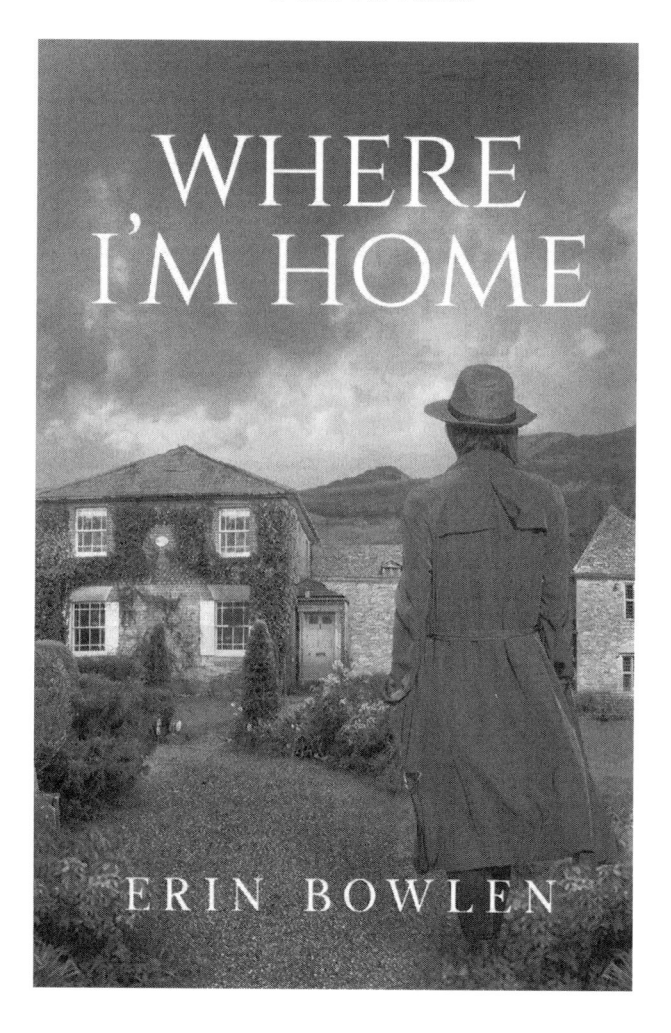

About the Author

Erin Bowlen was born and raised in New Brunswick, Canada. Growing up, she was influenced by her family's artistic roots in the art of storytelling, which fostered a deep love for literature at a young age.

Erin began her writing career during her postgraduate studies at the University of New Brunswick. Finding herself at the crossroads between being too much of a storyteller to be a "proper" academic (and afraid she might be too much of an academic to be a storyteller), she took the advice of a friend to participate in a 30-day writing competition. At the end of the month she was surprised that she not only met her word count goal, but had several novel ideas to explore.

In 2018, she published her first novel, *All That Compels the Heart*, the first book in the Aoife O'Reilly series.

Where I'm Home is her second novel.

Erin currently lives in New Brunswick.

Printed in Great Britain
by Amazon